READER'S DIGEST

BEST LOVED
BOOKS

FOR YOUNG
READERS

READER'S DIGEST

BEST LOVED
BOOKS

FOR YOUNG
READERS

selected and condensed by
the Editors of The Reader's Digest

VOLUME ELEVEN

THE READER'S DIGEST ASSOCIATION
PLEASANTVILLE, NEW YORK

For permission to reprint material in this book, grateful acknowledgment is made to the following:

Brandt & Brandt: For "Nancy Hanks" from *A Book of Americans* by Rosemary and Stephen Vincent Benét; Holt, Rinehart and Winston, Inc.; copyright 1933 by Rosemary and Stephen Vincent Benét, copyright renewed 1961 by Rosemary Carr Benét.

Doubleday & Company, Inc.: For "The Bat," copyright 1938 by Theodore Roethke; "Child on Top of a Greenhouse," copyright 1946 by Editorial Publications, Inc.; both from *The Collected Poems of Theodore Roethke*. "The Would-Be Hungarian," copyright 1955 by Delmore Schwartz, from *Summer Knowledge* by Delmore Schwartz.

Mrs. Norma Millay Ellis: For the poems "Recuerdo," "God's World," "The Buck in the Snow," all from *Collected Poems of Edna St. Vincent Millay*, published by Harper & Row; copyright 1913, 1922, 1928, 1940, 1950, 1955 by Edna St. Vincent Millay and Norma Millay Ellis.

Faber and Faber Ltd.: For Canadian distribution rights to "Preludes: I" and "New Hampshire" from *Collected Poems 1909–1962* by T. S. Eliot; "The Rum Tum Tugger" from *Old Possum's Book of Practical Cats* by T. S. Eliot.

Harcourt, Brace & World, Inc.: For "in Just-" by E. E. Cummings, copyright 1923, 1951 by E. E. Cummings, from his *Poems 1923–1954;* "i am a little church," "maggie and milly and molly and may," both from *95 Poems*, © 1958 by E. E. Cummings. "Preludes: I" and "New Hampshire" from *Collected Poems 1909–1962* by T. S. Eliot, copyright 1936 by Harcourt, Brace & World, Inc., © 1963, 1964 by T. S. Eliot. "The Rum Tum Tugger" from *Old Possum's Book of Practical Cats*, copyright 1939 by T. S. Eliot, © 1967 by Esme Valerie Eliot. "Losers" from *Smoke and Steel* by Carl Sandburg, copyright 1920 by Harcourt, Brace & World, Inc., copyright 1948 by Carl Sandburg. "Primer Lesson" from *Slabs of the Sunburnt West* by Carl Sandburg, copyright 1922 by Harcourt, Brace & World, Inc., copyright 1950 by Carl Sandburg. "Arithmetic" by Carl Sandburg, copyright 1950 by Carl Sandburg, from his *Complete Poems*. "A

Father Sees a Son Nearing Manhood" from *The People, Yes* by Carl Sandburg, copyright 1936 by Harcourt, Brace & World, Inc., © 1964 by Carl Sandburg. "Boy at the Window," copyright 1952 by The New Yorker Magazine, from *Things of This World* by Richard Wilbur; first published in *The New Yorker.*

Harper & Row, Publishers: For "Incident," copyright 1925 by Harper & Brothers, renewed 1953 by Ida M. Cullen. "A Negro Mother's Lullaby," copyright 1947 by Harper & Brothers, from *On These I Stand* by Countee Cullen. "Youth's Progress" from *The Carpentered Hen and Other Tame Creatures* by John Updike, © 1955 by John Updike, originally appeared in *The New Yorker.*

Holt, Rinehart and Winston, Inc.: For "The Ballad of William Sycamore" from *Ballads and Poems: 1915–1930* by Stephen Vincent Benét, copyright 1931 by Stephen Vincent Benét, © 1959 by Rosemary Carr Benét. "The Runaway," "Dust of Snow," "Birches," all from *Complete Poems of Robert Frost*, copyright 1916, 1923 by Holt, Rinehart and Winston, Inc., copyright 1944, 1951 by Robert Frost.

Houghton Mifflin Company: For "The Pike," "A Lady," "Misericordia," all from *The Complete Poetical Works of Amy Lowell*, Cambridge Edition, The Riverside Press. "Eleven," "Crossing," "Where the Hayfields Were," all from *The Collected Poems of Archibald MacLeish.*

J. B. Lippincott Company: For "I Wouldn't" from *You Read to Me, I'll Read to You* by John Ciardi, © 1962 by John Ciardi.

Little, Brown and Company: For "Much Madness Is Divinest Sense," "Hope Is the Thing with Feathers," "There Is No Frigate Like a Book," "I Never Saw a Moor," all from *Poems* by Emily Dickinson, First, Second and Third Series—1890, 1891, 1896. "The Octopus," copyright 1942 by Ogden Nash; "The Termite," copyright 1942, "Celery," copyright 1941, "The Parsnip," copyright 1941, "The Purist," copyright 1935, by The Curtis Publishing Company, all from *Verses From 1929 On* by Ogden Nash.

Liveright Publishing Corporation: For

Contents

BOB, SON OF BATTLE

A CONDENSATION OF THE BOOK BY ALFRED OLLIVANT

ILLUSTRATED BY THOMAS BEECHAM

In the rugged Daleland country of northern England there was no more coveted prize than the silver trophy for which the sheep dogs competed each fall. And no criminal was more feared, more hated, more ruthlessly tracked down than a good dog turned sheep-killer.

There came a year when two extraordinary dogs were to vie for the Shepherd's Trophy. One of these was Owd Bob, last of a long line of champions, whose gentleness and patience seemed as inbred as his power and skill. The other was Red Wull, a snarling, ugly dog of unknown antecedents, but a splendid worker for all his evil temper. One of them seemed sure to win the trophy. And it seemed equally certain that one of them was the elusive killer who roamed free on dark nights attacking helpless sheep. But even their masters, men as dramatically unlike as the dogs themselves, could not be certain about this, and before the truth was known terror and suspicion came to rule the countryside.

Bob, Son of Battle has been called the best dog story ever written, and although Alfred Ollivant (1874-1927) wrote many other novels, it is the only one for which he is remembered. Son of a colonel in the Royal Horse Artillery, Ollivant received a military education, graduating with honors and becoming, like his father, an officer in the Royal Artillery. He seemed slated for a brilliant career in the service, but before he was twenty he fell from a horse and so severely injured his spine that he had to resign his commission. It was during his long convalescence that he began to write the story of Owd Bob.

The book was published simultaneously in England and the United States, but—ironically—only in this country was it an immediate success, and years were to pass before Ollivant's countrymen also acclaimed him. The rest of his life was devoted to writing, but never again did he match *Bob, Son of Battle.*

CHAPTER I

The sun stared brazenly down on a gray farmhouse, lying long and low in the shadow of the Muir Pike; on ranges of whitewashed outbuildings it looked; on a goodly array of dark-thatched ricks. In the stackyard, behind the lengthy range of stables, two men were thatching. One lay sprawling on the crest of the rick, the other stood perched on a ladder at a lower level.

The latter, small, old, with shrewd nut-brown countenance, was Tammas Thornton, who had served the Moores of Kenmuir for more than half a century. The other was Sam'l Todd. A solid Dalesman he, with huge hands and hairy arms; about his face an uncomely aureole of stiff, red hair, and on his features, deep-seated, an expression of resolute melancholy.

"Ay, the Gray Dogs o' Kenmuir, bless 'em!" Tammas was saying. "Yo' canna beat 'em nohow. Known 'em this sixty year, and niver knew a bad un yet. Not as any on 'em cooms up to Rex son o' Rally. Ah, he was a one! We's never won Cup since his day."

"Nor niver shall agin, yo' may depend," said the other gloomily.

Tammas clucked irritably. "G'long, Sam'l Todd!" he cried. "Yo' niver happy onless yo' makin' yo'self miser'ble. Niver win agin? Why, oor young Bob he'll mak' a right un, I tell yo'. Not as what he'll touch Rex son o' Rally! I could tell yo' a tale or two o' Rex. I mind me hoo—" The old man broke off suddenly, and buckled to his work with suspicious vigor. "Mak' a show yo' bin workin', lad," he whispered. "Here's Master and oor Bob."

As he spoke, a tall gaitered man with weatherbeaten face, strong, lean, austere, and the blue-gray eyes of the hill country, came striding into the yard. And trotting soberly at his heels, with the gravest, saddest eyes ever you saw, a sheep-dog puppy.

A rare dark gray he was, his long coat dashed here and there with lighter touches. Upon his chest an escutcheon of purest white, and the dome of his head showered, as it were, with a sprinkling of snow. Perfectly compact, utterly lithe, inimitably graceful, a gentleman every inch—Owd Bob o' Kenmuir.

At the foot of the ladder the two stopped. And the young dog, placing his forepaws on a lower rung, looked up, slowly waving his silvery brush.

"A proper Gray Dog!" mused Tammas, gazing down into the dark face beneath him. "Amaist he minds me o' Rex son o' Rally." Then, "Did 'Enry Farewether tell yo' hoo he acted this mornin', Master?" he inquired, addressing the man at the foot of the ladder.

"Nay," said the other, his stern eyes lighting.

"Why, 'twas this way, it seems," Tammas continued. "Young bull gets 'isself loose and marches oot into yard, o'erturns milk pail, and prods owd pigs i' ribs. As he stands lookin' about un, thinkin' what he shall be up to next, oor Bob sees un. 'An' what yo' doin' here, Mr. Bull?' he seems to say, cockin' his ears and trottin' up gaylike. Wi' that, bull lashes wi' 's tail, waggles his head, and gets agate o' chargin' 'im. But Bob leaps oot o' way, quick as lightnin', and when he's done his foolin' drives un back agin. So they goes on, bull chargin' and Bob drivin' un back and back. At last Mr. Bull turns and tries to jump wall. Young dog nips him by tail. Wi' that, bull tumbles down in a hurry, turns wi' a kind o' groan, and marches back into stall, Bob after un. And then, dang me! if he doesna sit 'isself i' door like a sentrynel till 'Enry Farewether coom up. Hoo's that for a tyke not yet a year?"

"Good, lad!" said the Master, laying a hand on the dark head.

"Yo' may well say that," cried Tammas in a kind of ecstasy.

The patter of feet rang out on the plank bridge over the stream below them. Tammas glanced round. "Here's David," he said.

A fair-haired boy came spurring up the slope, his face all aglow with the speed of his running. Straightway the young dog dashed off to meet him. The two raced back together into the yard.

"G'mornin', Mister Moore! Morn'n, Tammas! Morn'n, Sam'l!" the boy panted as he passed; and ran on through the hay-carpeted yard, round the stable, and into the house.

In the kitchen, a long room with red-tiled floor and latticed windows, a woman, white-aproned and frail-faced, was bustling about her morning business. To her skirts clung a sturdy, bare-legged boy; while at the oak table in the center of the room a brown-eyed girl was seated before a basin of bread and milk.

"So yo've coom at last, David!" the woman cried as the boy entered, and, bending, greeted him with a tender, motherly salutation, which he returned as affectionately. "I thowt yo'd forgot us this mornin'. Noo sit yo' doon beside oor Maggie." And soon he, too, was engaged in a task twin to the girl's.

"Did yo' feyther beat yo' last night?" Maggie inquired in a low voice; and there was a shade of anxiety in the soft brown eyes.

"Nay," the boy answered, "he was a-goin' to, but he never did. Drunk," he added in explanation.

"What was he goin' to beat yo' for, David?" asked Mrs. Moore.

"What for? Why, for the fun o't—to see me squiggle."

"Yo' shouldna speak so o' your dad, David," reproved the other as severely as was in her nature.

"Dad! A fine dad!" the boy muttered beneath his breath. Then, to turn the conversation, "Us should be startin', Maggie," he said, and going to the door, "Bob! Owd Bob, lad! Ar't coomin' along?"

Mrs. Moore stood in the doorway and watched the departing trio. "'Tis a fine lad, Master, surely," she said softly to her husband, who came up at the moment.

"Ay," the tall man answered.

"'Tis a shame Mr. M'Adam should lead him such a life," the

woman continued indignantly. She laid a hand on her husband's arm, and looked up at him coaxingly. "Could yo' not say summat to un? Happen he'd 'tend to you." For Mrs. Moore imagined that there could be no one but would gladly heed what James Moore, Master of Kenmuir, might say to him. "He's not a bad un at bottom, I do believe," she continued. "He never took on so till his missus died."

"Nay, mother," said her husband, "'twould but mak' it worse for t' lad. M'Adam'd listen to no one, let alone me." And, indeed, he was right; for the tenant of the Grange made no secret of his animosity for his straight-going, straight-speaking neighbor.

Owd Bob, meanwhile, had escorted the children to the lane which leads to the village. Now he crept stealthily back to the yard, and established himself behind the water butt. How he teased the gray gander; how he ran the roan bull calf, and aroused the wrath of a portly sow, mother of many, is of no account. At last, in the midst of his merry mischief-making, a stern voice arrested him.

"Bob, lad, I see 'tis time we larned you yo' letters."

So the business of life began for that dog of whom the simple farmer folk of the Daleland still love to talk—Bob, son of Battle, last of the Gray Dogs of Kenmuir.

IT IS A LONELY COUNTRY, that about the Wastrel-dale. Of fells and ghylls it consists, of becks and lakes; with here a scattered hamlet and there a solitary hill sheep farm. It is a country in which sheep are paramount, and every other Dalesman is engaged in that profession which is as old as Abel.

Of all the Daleland, the country from the Black Water to Grammoch Pike is the wildest. Above the tiny stone-built village of Wastrel-dale the Muir Pike nods its massive head. Westward, the desolate Mere Marches reach away in mile on mile of windswept moorland. On the far side of the Marches, in the paddocks behind the Dalesman's Daughter, the famous sheep dog Trials of the North are held, and the battle for the Dale Cup, the world-known Shepherds' Trophy, is fought out.

Past the inn leads the turnpike road to the market center—
Grammoch-town. At the bottom of the paddocks winds the gentle
Silver Lea. Just there a plank bridge crosses the stream, and,
beyond, the Murk Muir Pass crawls up the sheer side of the Scaur
onto the Mere Marches. At the head of the Pass is that hollow
called the Devil's Bowl. In its center the Lone Tarn lifts its still
face to the sky. It was beside that black water, across whose frozen
surface snow wraiths were swirling, that many years ago old Andrew Moore came upon the mother of the Gray Dogs of Kenmuir.

In the North, everyone has heard of the Shepherds' Trophy;
everyone knows the fame of the Gray Dogs. In that country of
good dogs and jealous masters they have long held pride of place
unchallenged. And there is a saying in the land, "Faithfu' as the
Moores and their tykes."

On the dresser to the right of the fireplace in the kitchen of Kenmuir lies the family Bible. At the end you will find a loose sheet—
the pedigree of the Gray Dogs. Running your eye down the loose
leaf, once, twice, and again, it will be caught by a small red cross
beneath a name, and under the cross the one word "Cup." Lastly,
beneath the name of Rex son of Rally, are two of those proud
marks. The cup referred to is the renowned Champion Challenge
Dale Cup, open to the world. Had Rex won it but once again the
Shepherds' Trophy, which men have died striving after, would
have come to rest forever in the little gray house below the Pike.

It was not to be, however. So past Grip and Rex and Rally, and
a hundred others, until at the foot of the page you come to that
last name—Bob, son of Battle.

FROM THE VERY FIRST the young dog mastered the essentials of
sheep tactics in a manner to amaze even James Moore. Silent he
worked, and resolute; and even in those days had that famous
trick of coaxing the sheep to do his wishes. Rarely had such fiery
élan been seen on the sides of the Pike; and with it the young dog
combined a strange sobriety, a patience, that justified, indeed, the
epithet "Old." And from then on he was known as "Owd Bob."

Parson Leggy Hornbut, reckoned the best judge of a sheep dog

'twixt Tyne and Tweed, summed him up in one word, "Genius."
James Moore, himself a cautious man, was more than pleased.

In the village, the Dalesmen, who took a personal pride in the
Gray Dogs of Kenmuir, began to nod sage heads when "oor"
Bob was mentioned. Jim Mason, the postman, whose word went
as far with the villagers as Parson Leggy's with the gentry, reckoned he'd never seen a young 'un as so took his fancy. That winter
the men gathered of a night round the fire in the Sylvester Arms
and told yarns of Owd Bob.

One man only never joined in the chorus of admiration. Sitting
always alone in the background, Adam M'Adam would listen with
an incredulous grin on his sallow face. "Oh, ma certes! The devil's
in the dog! It's no clever at all!" he would exclaim.

The little Scotsman with the sardonic face had been the tenant
of the Grange these many years, yet he had never grown acclima-
tized to the land south of the border. With his shriveled body and
weakly legs he looked among the sturdy, straight-limbed sons of
the hills like a brown, wrinkled leaf holding its place amidst a
galaxy of green. And as he differed from them physically, so he
did morally. He neither understood them nor attempted to. "One
half o' what ye say they doot, and they let ye see it; t'ither half they
disbelieve, and they tell ye so," he once said. And that explained
his attitude toward them, and consequently theirs toward him. He
stood alone; a son of Hagar, mocking. His tongue was rarely still,
and always bitter. There was hardly a man in the land but had at
one time known its sting, endured it in silence—for they are slow
of speech, these men of the fells and meres—and was nursing his
resentment till a day should bring that chance which always comes.
It was Tammas who summed it up, "When he's drunk he's wi'lent,
and when he bain't he's wicious."

Yet it had not been till his wife's death that the little man had
allowed loose rein to his ill nature. With her firmly gentle hand
no longer on the tiller of his life, it burst into fresh being, and the
whole vicious temperament was directed against the boy David.
It was as though he saw in his fair-haired son the unconscious
cause of his ever-living sorrow. All the more strange this, seeing

that, during her life, the boy had been to poor Flora M'Adam as her heart's core. And the lad was growing up the very antithesis of his father. Big and hearty, with never an ache or ill in his sturdy young body; of frank, open countenance; while even his speech was slow and burring like any Dale-bred boy's. And the fact of it all, and that the lad was palpably more Englishman than Scot— ay, and gloried in it—exasperated the little man, a patriot before everything, to blows. While, on top of it, David evinced an amazing pertness fit to have tried a better man than Adam M'Adam.

On the death of his wife, kindly Elizabeth Moore had, more than once, offered such help to the lonely little man as a woman only can give in a house that knows no mistress. On the last of these occasions she had met M'Adam in the door.

"Yo' maun let me put yo' bit things straight for yo', mister," she had said shyly; for she feared the little man.

"Thank ye, Mrs. Moore," he had answered, "but ye maun think I'm a cripple." And there he had stood, grinning sardonically.

Mrs. Moore had turned down the hill, abashed and hurt at the reception of her offer; and her husband, proud to a fault, had forbidden her to repeat it. Nevertheless her motherly heart went out in a great tenderness for the little orphan David.

It became an institution for the boy to call every morning at Kenmuir, and trot off to the village school with Maggie Moore. And soon the lad came to look on Kenmuir as his true home, and James and Elizabeth Moore as his real parents. His greatest happiness was to be away from the Grange. And the ferret-eyed little man there noted the fact and bitterly resented it. It was this which was the chief cause of his animosity against James Moore.

M'Adam's treatment of David became at length such a scandal to the Dale that Parson Leggy determined to speak to him.

Now M'Adam was the parson's pet antipathy. The bluff old minister, with his brusque manner and big heart, would have no truck with the man who never went to church, was perpetually in liquor, and never spoke good of his neighbors. Yet he entered upon the interview fully resolved to appeal to the little man's better nature.

The conversation had not been in progress two minutes, however, before he knew that, where he had meant to be calmly persuasive, he was fast become hotly abusive.

"You, Mr. Hornbut, wi' James Moore to help ye, look after the lad's soul. I'll see to his body," M'Adam was saying.

The parson's thick gray eyebrows lowered threateningly. "You ought to be ashamed of yourself to talk like that. Which d'you think the more important, soul or body? Oughtn't you, his father, to be the very first to care for the boy's soul?"

The little man stood smirking and sucking a twig, entirely unmoved by the other's heat. "Ye're right, Mr. Hornbut, as ye aye are. But my argiment is this: that I get at his soul best through his leetle carcass."

The honest parson brought down his stick with an angry thud. "M'Adam, you're a brute—a brute!" he shouted. At which outburst the little man was seized with a spasm of silent merriment.

"A fond dad first, a brute afterward, perhaps—he! he! Ah, Mr. Hornbut! Ye 'ford me vast diversion, ye do indeed, *my loved, my honored, much-respected friend.*"

"If you paid as much heed to your boy's welfare as you do to the bad poetry of that profligate ploughman, Robert Burns."

An angry gleam shot into the other's eyes. "D'ye ken what blasphemy is, Mr. Hornbut?" M'Adam asked.

For the first time in the dispute the parson thought he was about to score a point, and was calm accordingly. "I should do; I fancy I've a specimen of the breed before me now. And d'you know what impertinence is?"

"I should do; I fancy I've—I wad say it's what gentlemen aften are unless their mammies whipped 'em as lads."

The parson looked as if about to seize his opponent and shake him. "M'Adam," he roared, "I'll not stand your insolences!"

The little man turned, scuttled indoors, and came running back with a chair. "Permit me!" he said blandly, holding it before him like a haircutter for a customer.

The parson turned away. Striding down the hill, he was uneasily conscious that with him was not the victory.

CHAPTER II

THE WINTER CAME AND WENT; the lambing season was over, and spring already shyly kissing the land when M'Adam's old collie, Cuttie Sark, lay down one evening and passed quietly away.

The little black-and-tan lady had been the only thing on earth M'Adam cared for, and he felt his loss acutely. A shepherd without his dog is like a ship without a rudder, and especially did he experience this on a day when he had to take a batch of draft ewes over to Grammoch-town. He would never have won over the sheep-infested marches alone with his convoy had it not been for the help of old Rob Saunderson and Shep, who caught him on the way and aided him.

It was in a very wrathful mood that on his way home he turned into the Dalesman's Daughter in Silverdale. Among the occupants of the taproom, as he entered, were Teddy Bolstock, the publican, Jim Mason, postman by profession, poacher by predilection, with the faithful Betsy beneath his chair and the postbags flung into the corner, and one long-limbed, droverlike man—a stranger.

"And he coom up to Mr. Moore," Teddy was saying, "and says he, 'I'll gie ye twel' pun for yon gray dog.' 'Ah,' says Moore, 'yo' may give me twel' hunner'd and you'll not get ma Bob.'"

"James Moore and his dog agin!" snapped M'Adam. "There's ithers in the warld besides them twa."

"Ay, but none like 'em," quoth loyal Jim.

"Na, thanks be. If there were there'd be no room for Adam M'Adam in this 'melancholy vale.'"

There was silence a moment, and then— "You're wantin' a tyke, bain't you, Mr. M'Adam?" Jim asked.

The little man hopped round all in a hurry. "What!" he cried in well-affected eagerness. "Betsy for sale! Guid life! Where's ma checkbook?" Whereat Jim, most easily snubbed of men, collapsed.

M'Adam took off his coat and crossed the room to hang it on a chairback. He reached out a hand for the chair; and as he did so, a tawny bomb leapt out from beneath it, and, growling horribly, attacked his ankles. "Curse ye!" cried M'Adam, starting back. Then turning fiercely on the drover, "Yours, mister?" he asked. The man nodded. "Then call him aff, can't ye?" At which Teddy withdrew, sniggering; and Jim Mason slung the postbags onto his shoulder and left, the faithful Betsy following.

The cause of the squall had withdrawn again beneath its chair. M'Adam stooped down, still cursing, his coat on his arm, and beheld a tiny red puppy, crouching defiant in the dark, and glaring out with fiery light eyes. Seeing M'Adam, it bared its little teeth, raised its little bristles, and growled a hideous menace.

Delighted at such a display of vice in so tender a plant, M'Adam chuckled. "He! he! ye leetle devil!" And he flipped together finger and thumb in vain endeavor to coax the puppy to him.

But it growled, and glared more terribly.

"Stop it, ye little snake, or I'll flatten you!" cried the big drover, and shuffled his feet threateningly. Whereat the puppy, gurgling like hot water in a kettle, made a feint as though to advance and wipe them out, these two bad men.

M'Adam laughed again, and smote his leg. "Though he is but as big as a man's thumb, a dog's a dog for a' that—he! he!"

"Ye're maybe wantin' a dog?" inquired the stranger. "I'm willin' to part wi' him."

The little man yawned. "Weel, I'll tak' him to oblige ye."

The drover rose to his feet. "It's givin' 'im ye, fair givin' 'im ye, mind! But I'll do it!" He smacked a great fist into a hollow palm. "Ye may have the dog for a poun'—I'll only ask *you* a poun'."

M'Adam eyed the stranger with a drolly sarcastic air. "A poun'— for yon noble dorg! Man, ma conscience wadna permit me. 'Twad be fair robbin' ye. Ah, ye Englishmen!" He spoke sadly; "It's yer grand generosity that grips a puir Scotsman by the throat."

"Take him or leave him," ordered the drover truculently.

"Wi' yer permission I'll leave him," M'Adam answered meekly.

"I'm short o' the ready," the big man pursued, "or I wouldna part with him. Could I bide me time there's many'd be glad to give me a tenner for that one."

"Yet ye offer him me for a poun'! Noble indeed!" Nevertheless the little man again approached the puppy, dangling his coat before him to protect his ankles. And again that wee wild beast sprang out, seized the coat in its jaw, and worried it savagely. M'Adam stooped quickly and picked up his tiny assailant; and the puppy, suspended by its neck, gurgled and slobbered. Then he set to examining it minutely. Apparently some six weeks old; a tawny coat, fiery eyes, a square head, with small, cropped ears, and a comparatively immense jaw; the whole giving promise of great strength, if little beauty. This effect was enhanced by the manner of its docking. For the miserable relic of a tail, yet raw, looked little more than a red button adhering to its wearer's stern.

"Ye've cut him short," he said, swinging round on the drover.

"Ay; strengthens their backs." The big man averted his gaze.

M'Adam eyed his informant. "Oh, ay," he said, and set the puppy on the floor. "Ye said ye found him?"

"Found 'im? Nay; I was give 'im by a friend. But there's nowt amiss wi' his breedin', ye may believe me." The great fellow advanced to the chair under which the puppy again lay. It leapt out like a lion, and fastened on his huge boot. "A rare bred un, look 'ee! A rare game un, mark the pluck of him!" He shook his booted foot fiercely, but the little creature held on with incomparable doggedness, till its jaw was all bloody, and its muzzle wrinkled with the effort.

"Ay, ay, that'll do," M'Adam interposed irritably.

The drover ceased his efforts. "Now, I'll mak' ye a last offer. Ye may have him for fifteen shillin'. Why, ye ask? Why, 'cos I think ye'll be kind to him," as the puppy retreated to its chair, leaving a spotted track of red along its route.

"Ay, ye wadna be happy if ye thocht he'd no a comfortable hame, conseederate man?" M'Adam answered.

It was long after dark when the bargain was finally struck. Red Wull became Adam M'Adam's property for the following realizable assets: ninepence in cash—three coppers and a doubtful sixpence; a plug of tobacco in a well-worn pouch, and an old watch.

"It's clean givin' 'im ye," said the stranger bitterly, at the end of the deal. Then he plunged out into the darkness and was gone.

CHAPTER III

AFTER THAT FIRST ENCOUNTER in the Dalesman's Daughter, Red Wull, for so M'Adam called him, resigned himself complacently to his lot; recognizing, perhaps, his destiny.

Thenceforward the sour little man and the vicious puppy grew, as it were, together. Where M'Adam was, there was sure to be his tiny attendant, bristling defiance as he kept ludicrous guard over his master. M'Adam never left him even at the Grange.

"I couldna trust ma Wullie at hame alone wi' the dear lad," was his explanation. "I ken weel I'd come back to find a wee corpse on the floor, and David singin':

> *"My heart is sair, I daur na tell,*
> *My heart is sair for somebody."*

The sneer was as characteristic as it was unjust. For though the puppy and the boy were already sworn enemies, yet the lad would have scorned to harm so small a foe. And many a tale did David tell at Kenmuir of Red Wull's viciousness toward him.

Of late the relations between M'Adam and James Moore had been unusually strained, and communications between them rare. It was for the first time for many a day that, on an afternoon shortly after Red Wull had come into his possession, M'Adam entered the yard of Kenmuir, bent on girding at the master for an alleged trespass at the Stony Bottom, which divides the two farms.

"Wi' yer permission, Mr. Moore," he said, "I'll wheestle ma dog," and he whistled a shrill, peculiar note like the cry of a disturbed peewit. Straightway there came scurrying up, ears back, head down, tongue out, as if the world depended on his speed, a little tawny beetle of a thing, who placed his forepaws against his master's ankles and looked up into his face; then, catching sight of James Moore and Tammas, hurriedly he took up his position between them and M'Adam. Such a laughable spectacle that martial mite made, standing at bay with bristles up and teeth bared, that James Moore smiled.

"Ma word! Ha' yo' brought his muzzle, man?" cried old Tammas, the humorist; and, turning, climbed all in a heat onto an upturned bucket that stood by. Whereat the puppy, emboldened by his foe's retreat, advanced savagely to the attack.

"'Elp! Oh, 'elp!" bawled Tammas, hitching his trousers and looking down on his assailant, the picture of mortal fear. "For lawk-a-mussy's sake call him off, man!" Even Sam'l Todd, watching from the cart shed, burst into a loud guffaw.

At that moment Mrs. Moore put her head out of the kitchen window. "Coom thy ways in, Mister M'Adam, and tak' a soop o' tea," she called hospitably.

"Thank ye kindly, Mrs. Moore, I will," he answered, politely for him. And this must be allowed of Adam M'Adam. Flouts and jeers he had for every man, but a woman was sacred to him. As he turned into the house he looked back at Red Wull.

"Ay, we may leave him," he said. "That is, if ye're no afraid, Mr. Thornton?"

INDOORS, THE MATTER between M'Adam and James Moore was concluded peacefully, mainly owing to the pacifying influence of Mrs. Moore. Together the three went out into the yard, Mrs. Moore seizing the opportunity to shyly speak on David's behalf.

"He's such a good little lad, I do think," she was saying.

"Ye should ken, Mrs. Moore," the little man answered, a thought bitterly; "ye see enough of him."

"Yo' mun be main proud of un, mester," the woman continued, heedless of the sneer, "an' 'im growin' such a gradely lad."

M'Adam shrugged. "I barely ken the lad," he said. "By sight I know him, of course, but barely to speak to. He's but seldom at hame."

"An' hoo proud his mother'd be o' him," the woman continued, well aware of his one tender place. "Eh, but she was fond o' him."

An angry flush stole over the little man's face. Well he understood the implied rebuke, and it hurt him like a knife. "Ay, ay, Mrs. Moore," he began. Then breaking off, and looking about him— "Where's ma Wullie?" he cried excitedly.

Elizabeth Moore turned away indignantly. "I do declar' he tak's more fash after yon little yaller beastie than iver he does after his own flesh," she muttered.

"Wullie, ma wee doggie! Wullie, where are ye?" screamed the little man, running about the yard, searching everywhere.

"Cannot 'a' gotten far," said the Master, reassuringly.

"It's robbed I am," M'Adam cried recklessly. "Ma wee Wull's bin stolen while I was ben your hoose, James Moore!"

"Yo' munna say that, ma mon," the Master answered sternly.

"Then where is he? It's for you to say."

"I've ma own idee, I 'ave," Sam'l announced, appearing on the scene, pig bucket in hand.

M'Adam turned on him. "What, man? What is it?"

"I misdoot yo'll iver see your dog agin, mister," Sam'l said, as if he was supplying the key to the mystery.

"Noo, Sam'l, if yo' know owt tell it," ordered his master.

The big man looked mournfully at M'Adam. "'Twas 'appen 'alf an hour agone, when I sees oor Bob goin' oot o' yard wi' little yaller tyke in his mouth. In a minnit I looks agin—and theer! Little yaller 'un was gone, and oor Bob a-sittin' a-lickin' his chops."

M'Adam turned on the Master. "It's yer gray dog has murdered ma wee Wull!" he said piteously. "Ye have it from yer ain man."

"Nonsense," said the Master. "'Tis but yon great idiot."

Sam'l tossed his head and snorted. "Coom, then, and I'll show yo'," he said, and led the way out of the yard. And there below them, sitting quietly on the slope to the stream, was Owd Bob.

M'Adam burst into a storm of invective, and would have rushed on the dog had not James Moore forcibly restrained him.

"Bob, lad," called the Master, "coom here!"

But even as he spoke, the gray dog cocked his ears, listened, then shot down the slope. At the same moment a little angry, smutty-faced figure was crawling out of a rabbit burrow.

"Ye murderin' devil, wad ye daur touch ma Wullie?" yelled M'Adam, and, breaking away, pursued hotly down the hill; for the gray dog had picked up the puppy and was sweeping on, his captive in his mouth, toward the stream.

Behind hurried James Moore and Sam'l, wondering what the issue of the comedy would be. After them toddled old Tammas, chuckling. Straight onto the plank bridge galloped Owd Bob. In the middle he halted, leaned over, and dropped his prisoner, who fell with a cool plop into the running water beneath.

Another moment and M'Adam had reached the stream. In he plunged, splashing and cursing, and seized the struggling puppy; then waded back, his eyes blazing, and Red Wull, limp as a wet rag, in his hand. He sprang onto the bank, and rushed at Owd Bob. "Curse ye for a—"

"Stan' back, or yo'll have him at your throat!" shouted the Master, thundering up. And, as the little man still came madly on, he reached forth his hand and hurled him back; at the same moment, bending, he buried the other hand deep in Owd Bob's shaggy neck. It was just in time; for if ever the desire of battle gleamed in gray eyes, it did in the young dog's.

The little man tottered, and fell heavily; while Red Wull, jerked from his grasp, was thrown afar and lay motionless.

"Curse ye!" M'Adam screamed. "Curse ye for a cowardly Englishman!" And, struggling to his feet, he made at the Master.

But Sam'l interposed his great bulk between the two.

James Moore stood, breathing deep, his hand still buried in Owd Bob's coat. "If yo'd touched him," he explained, "I couldna ha' stopped him. He'd ha' mauled yo' afore iver I could ha' had him off. They're bad to hold, the Gray Dogs, when they're roused."

"Ye're all agin me," the little man said, and a pitiful figure he made, standing there with the water dripping from him.

James Moore eyed him with some pity and some contempt.

M'Adam bent over Red Wull, who still lay like a dead thing. As his master handled him, the button-tail quivered feebly; he opened his eyes, looked about him, snarled faintly, and glared with devilish hate at the gray dog and the group with him.

The little man picked him up, stroking him tenderly. Then he turned away and onto the bridge. Halfway across he stopped.

"Man, Moore!" he called, striving to quell the agitation in his voice. "I wad shoot yon dog. Ye'll not forget this day."

CHAPTER IV

THE STORM, LONG THREATENED, having burst, M'Adam allowed loose rein to his animosity against James Moore. He frequently returned home from the village by the footpath across Kenmuir, just to annoy his enemy and keep a watch upon his doings.

David was the only link between the two farms. Despite his father's angry commands, the boy clung to his intimacy with the Moores with a doggedness that no thrashing could overcome. Not a minute of the day when out of school but was passed at Kenmuir. It was not till late at night that he would sneak back to the Grange and creep quietly up to his tiny bare room in the roof—not supperless, indeed, motherly Mrs. Moore had seen to that. And in the morning he would slip out of the house while his father still slept; only Red Wull would thrust out his savage head as the lad passed, and snarl hungrily. Sometimes father and son would go thus for weeks without sight of one another. And that was David's aim—to escape attention.

M'Adam lavished all the fondness of which his nature appeared capable on the Tailless Tyke, for so the Dalesmen called Red Wull, now a great grown puppy. He and his dog were much alike. Each had a grudge against the world and was determined to pay it. The two were never separated except when M'Adam came home by the path across Kenmuir. After that first misadventure he never allowed his friend to accompany him through the enemy's country; for well he knew that sheep dogs have long memories.

To the stile in the lane, then, Red Wull would follow him. There he would stand, his great head poked through the bars, watching his master out of sight; and then would turn and trot, self-reliant and defiant, down the very center of the road through the village, past the Sylvester Arms, over the Wastrel by the Haughs, to await his master at the edge of the Stony Bottom.

The little man, when thus crossing Kenmuir, often met Owd Bob, who had the free run of the farm. On these occasions he passed discreetly by; for, though he was no coward, yet it is bad,

27

single-handed, to attack a Gray Dog of Kenmuir; while the dog trotted soberly on his way, only a steely glint in the gray eyes betraying his knowledge of the presence of his foe. As surely, however, as M'Adam, in his desire to spy out the nakedness of the land, strayed off the public path, so surely a gray figure, seeming to spring from out the blue, would come driving down on him; and he would turn and run for his life, amid the uproarious jeers of any farmhands who were witness to the encounter.

On these occasions David vied with Tammas in facetiousness at his father's expense. "Good on yo', little un!" he roared from behind a wall, on one such occurrence. Luckily, M'Adam had not distinguished his son's voice among the others. But David feared he had; for on the following morning the little man said to him, "David, ye'll come hame immediately after school today."

"Why?" said David pertly.

"Because I tell ye to, ma lad"; and that was all the reason he would give. Had he told the simple fact that he wanted help to drench a coughing ewe, things might have gone differently. As it was, David turned away defiantly down the hill.

The afternoon wore on. Schooltime was long over; still there was no David. The little man waited at the door of the Grange, fuming. At length he could restrain himself no longer, and started running down the hill.

At the edge of the Stony Bottom he, as always, left Red Wull. Crossing it himself, and rounding Langholm How, he espied James Moore, David, and Owd Bob walking away from him and in the direction of Kenmuir. The gray dog and David were playing together. The boy had never a thought for his father.

M'Adam ran up behind them, unseen and unheard. "Did I bid ye come hame after school, David?" he asked, concealing his heat beneath a suspicious suavity.

"Maybe. Did I say I would come?"

David's pertness fanned his father's resentment into a blaze. He lunged at the boy with his stick. But as he smote, a gray whirlwind struck him on the chest, and he fell like a snapped stake and lay, half stunned, with a dark muzzle an inch from his throat.

"Git back, Bob!" shouted James Moore, hurrying up. "Git back, I tell yo'!" He bent anxiously over the prostrate figure. David, too, bent over his father with a scared face. "Are yo' hurt, feyther?" he asked, his voice trembling.

The little man rose unsteadily to his feet and stood, all dust-begrimed, looking at his son. "Ye're content, perhaps, noo ye've seen yer father's gray head bowed in the dust," he said.

"'Twas an accident," pleaded James Moore. "But I *am* sorry. He thought yo' were goin' to beat the lad."

"So I was—so I will. David! Will ye come hame wi' me and have it noo, or stop wi' him and wait till ye get it?"

"Yo'd best go wi' your feyther, lad," said the Master, thickly. The boy hesitated, then walked slowly over to his father.

The little man smiled bitterly as he marked this new test of the boy's obedience to the other. "To obey his frien' he foregoes the pleasure o' disobeyin' his father," he muttered. "Noble!"

Then he turned homeward, and the boy followed. There was no word said between them. Across the Stony Bottom, Red Wull, scowling with bared teeth at David, joined them. Together the three went up the hill to the Grange.

In the kitchen M'Adam turned. "Noo, I'm gaein' to gie ye the gran'est thrashin' ye iver dreamed of. Tak' aff yer coat!"

The boy obeyed, and stood up in his thin shirt, his face white and set. The little man suppled the great ashplant in his hands and raised it. But the expression on the boy's face arrested his arm.

"Say ye're sorry and I'll let yer aff easy."

"I'll not."

"One mair chance—yer last! Say yer 'shamed o' yersel'!"

"I'm not. Git on wi' it."

The little man raised the stick again and—threw it into the farthest corner of the room. Then he turned away.

"Ye're the pitifulest son iver a man had," he cried brokenly. "If a man's son dinna haud to him, wha can he expect to? No one. Ye're ondootiful, ye're disrespectfu', ye're everything ye shouldna be; there's but ae thing I thocht ye were not—a coward. And as to that, ye've no the pluck to say ye're sorry when, God

29

knows, ye might be. I canna thrash ye this day. But ye shall gae nae mair to school. I send ye there to learn—ye've learnt naethin' except disobedience to me—ye shall stop at hame and work."

His father's rare emotion, his broken voice and working face, moved David as all the stripes and jeers had failed to do. His conscience smote him. For the first time in his life it dimly dawned on him that perhaps he was not a good son.

He half turned. "Feyther—"

"Git oot o' ma sight!" M'Adam cried.

And the boy turned and went.

THENCEFORWARD DAVID buckled down to work at home, and in one point only father and son resembled each other—industry. A drunkard M'Adam was, but a drone, no.

The boy worked at the Grange with tireless energy; yet he could never satisfy his father. The little man would flout the lad's brave labors. "Is he no a gran' worker, Wullie? 'Tis a pleasure to watch him, his hands in his pockets, his eyes turned heavenward!" as the boy snatched a hard-earned moment's rest. "You and I, Wullie, we'll brak' oorsel's slavin' for him while he looks on."

And so on, week in, week out. Sometimes David thought to run away, but he was miserably alone in the world. The very fact that he was the son of his father isolated him in the Daleland. Naturally reserved, he had no friend outside Kenmuir. And it was only the thought of his friends there that withheld him. He could not bring himself to part from them; they were all he had.

So he worked on at the Grange, miserably, doggedly, taking blows and abuse alike in burning silence. But every evening, and Sundays and holidays, he would pass at Kenmuir. In this one matter the boy was invincibly stubborn. Nothing his father could say or do sufficed to break him of the habit.

Once past the Stony Bottom, he threw his troubles behind him with a courage that did him honor. Of all the people at Kenmuir two only ever dreamed the whole depth of his unhappiness, and that not through David. James Moore suspected something of it all, for he knew more of M'Adam than did the others. While

Owd Bob could tell it from the touch of the boy's hand on his head. And he would follow the lad about with a compassion in his sad gray eyes greater than words. David might well compare his gray friend at Kenmuir with that other at the Grange.

The Tailless Tyke had grown into an immense dog, heavy of muscle and huge of bone. A bull head; undershot jaw, square and lengthy and terrible; vicious, yellow-gleaming eyes; cropped ears; and an expression incomparably savage. His coat was tawny and lionlike—short, harsh, and dense; and his back, running up from shoulder to loins, ended abruptly in the knoblike tail. He never attacked another dog unprovoked; but a challenge was never ignored. Nor, in the matter of war, did he confine himself to his own kind. Long Kirby, the smith, once threatened him with a broomstick; the smith never did it again.

More than once had he and Owd Bob essayed to wipe out mutual memories, Red Wull, in such case only, the aggressor. As they fenced for that deadly throat grip, the value of which each knew so well, James Moore had always intervened.

It seemed as if there were to be other points of rivalry between the two than memories. For, in the matter of handling sheep, Red Wull bid fair to be second only to the Gray Dog of Kenmuir. M'Adam was patient and painstaking in the training of his Wullie. And after a promising display he would stand, rubbing his palms together, as near content as ever he was. "Weel done, Wullie! Weel done. Bide a wee and we'll show 'em a thing or two."

And the dog would trot up to him, place his forepaws on his shoulders, and stand thus with his great head overtopping his master's, his ears back, and stump tail vibrating.

From the very first David and Red Wull had been enemies: under the circumstances, indeed, nothing else was possible. Sometimes the great dog would follow on the lad's heels with surly eyes, from sunrise to sundown, till David could hardly hold his hands. So matters went on for a year. Then there came a climax.

One evening, David, his work finished, went to pick up his coat, which he had left hard by. On it lay Red Wull. "Git off ma coat!" the boy ordered angrily. But the dog never stirred.

"Yo' won't, won't yo', great brute!" David shouted, and, bending, snatched a corner of the coat and attempted to jerk it away. At that, Red Wull rose, shivering, to his feet, and with a low gurgle sprang at the boy.

David quick as a flash dodged, bent, and picked up an ugly stake lying at his feet. Swinging round he dealt his antagonist a buffet on the side of the head. Dazed, the dog fell; then, recovering himself, with a terrible, deep roar he sprang again. It must have gone hard with the boy, muscular young giant though he was, had M'Adam not come hurrying out of the house, shrieking commands and curses. In an imperative voice he ordered the dog to heel. Then he turned on David, seized the stake from his hand, and began belaboring the boy.

"I'll teach ye to strike—a puir—dumb—harmless—creetur, ye cruel lad!" he cried. He was panting from exertion, and his eyes blazed. "I pit up wi' all manner o' disrespect to masel'; but when it comes to 'tackin' ma Wullie, I canna bear it. Ha' ye no heart?" he asked, unconscious of the irony of the question.

"As much as some, I reck'n," David answered bitterly. "Ye may thrash me till ye're blind, and it's nob' but yer duty; but if ony one daurs so much as to look at yer Wullie ye're mad." And he turned away defiantly and openly in the direction of Kenmuir.

At Kenmuir that night the kindness of Elizabeth Moore was too much for the overstrung lad. Overcome by her sweet motherliness, he burst into a storm of invective against his father, his home, his life—everything.

"Don't 'ee, Davie, don't 'ee, dearie!" cried Mrs. Moore, much distressed. And seeing the white, wan countenance of his dear comforter, he was struck with remorse that he had given way and pained her. He mastered himself with an effort, and for the rest of the evening was his usual cheery self, teasing Maggie to tears.

Yet it was with reluctance that, later, he left for home.

James Moore and Parson Leggy accompanied him to the bridge over the Wastrel, and stood watching as he disappeared into the summer night.

"Yon's a good lad," said the Master half to himself.

"Yes," the parson replied. "And look how Owd Bob follows him. There's not another soul outside Kenmuir he'd do that for."

"Ay, sir. Bob knows a mon when he sees one."

"He does," acquiesced the parson. "And by the by, James, there's talk that you're not running him for the Cup. Is that so?"

The Master nodded. "It is, sir. They're all mad I should, but I mun cross 'em. They say he's reached his prime—and so he has o' his body, but not o' his brain. And a sheep dog is not at his best till his brain is at its best; and that takes a while developin'."

"Well, well," said the parson, pulling out a favorite phrase, "waiting's winning—waiting's winning."

DAVID SLIPPED UP INTO HIS ROOM and into bed unseen, he hoped. Alone with the darkness, he allowed himself the rare relief of tears, and at length fell asleep. He awoke to find his father standing at his bedside, a feeble dip candle in his hand. In the doorway, dimly outlined, was the great figure of Red Wull.

"Whaur ha' ye been the day?" the little man asked. Then, looking down on the white, stained face beneath him, he added hurriedly, "If ye like to lie, I'll believe ye."

David was out of bed and standing up in his nightshirt. "I ha' bin at Kenmuir. I'll not lie for your likes," he said proudly.

M'Adam shrugged his shoulders. "'Tell a lie and stick to it,' is my rule, and a good one, too, in honest England. I for one'll no think ony worse o' ye if yer memory plays yer false."

"D'yo' think I care what yo' think o' me?" the boy asked brutally.

The candle trembled and was still again.

"A lickin' or a lie—tak' yer choice!"

The boy looked scornfully down on his father. Standing on his naked feet, he already towered half a head above the other.

"D'yo' think I'm fear'd o' a thrashin' fra yo'?" he sneered.

"Ye maun be cauld, standin' there so. Rin ye doon and fetch oor little frien'"—a reference to a certain strap hanging in the kitchen. "I'll see if I can warm ye."

33

David stumbled down the unlit, narrow stairs. At his heels followed Red Wull, his hot breath fanning the boy's legs. So into the kitchen and back up the stairs, and Red Wull always following.

"I'll no despair yet o' teachin' ye the fifth commandment!" cried the little man, seizing the strap from the boy's numb grasp.

When it was over, M'Adam turned, breathless, away. At the threshold of the room he stopped and, glancing back, caught such an expression on David's face that for once he was fairly afraid. He banged the door and hobbled actively down the stairs.

CHAPTER V

M'ADAM—IN HIS SOBER MOMENTS, at least—never touched David again; instead, he devoted himself to the whiplash of his tongue. And he was wise; for David could have taken his father in the hollow of his hand and crumpled him like a dry leaf.

Meanwhile, another summer was passing away, and every day brought fresh proofs of the prowess of Owd Bob. In the Dalesman's Daughter in Silverdale and in the Border Ram at Grammoch-town, each succeeding market day brought some fresh tale. Men told how the gray dog had cut out a Kenmuir sheep from the very center of Londesley's pack—and a thousand like stories.

The confidence of the Dalesmen in Owd Bob was now invincible, and already the name was becoming known. It came, therefore, as a keen disappointment to every Dalesman when the Master persisted in his decision not to run the dog for the Cup in the approaching Dale Trials. It was nigh fifty years since Rex son o' Rally had won the Trophy for the land that gave it birth; it was time, they thought, for a Daleland dog to bring it home again. And Tammas, that polished phrasemaker, was only expressing the feelings of every Dalesman when, one night at the Arms, he declared of Owd Bob that "to ha' run was to ha' won." At which M'Adam sniggered and winked at Red Wull. "To ha' run was to ha' one lickin'; to rin next year'll be to—"

"Win next year," Tammas interposed dogmatically. "Onless"—

with shivering sarcasm—"you and yer Wullie are thinkin' o' winnin'."

M'Adam rose from his solitary seat at the back of the room and pattered across. "Wullie and I are thinkin' o't," he whispered loudly in the old man's ear. "And mair: what Adam M'Adam and his Red Wull think o' doin', that, Mr. Thornton, they do. Next year we rin, and next year we win. Come, Wullie, we'll leave 'em to chew that"; and he marched out of the room.

THE SUMMER ENDED ABRUPTLY. Hard on the heels of a sweltering autumn the winter came down, and the Daleland assumed very early its white cloak. It was the season still remembered in the North as the White Winter. On the Mere Marches the snow massed deep and impassable in thick, billowy drifts. And sheep, seeking shelter in protected spots, were buried and lost in their hundreds.

That is the time to test the hearts of shepherds and sheep dogs, when the wind runs ice-cold across the waste of white, and sheep must be found and folded or lost: a trial of head as well as heart, of resource as well as resolution. In that winter more than one man and many a dog lost his life in the quiet performance of his duty, gliding to death over the slippery snow shelves, or over-whelmed beneath an avalanche of the warm, suffocating white.

They found old Wrottesley, the squire's head shepherd, lying one morning at Gill's foot, like a statue in its white bed. And stretched upon his bosom, his old dog Jess. She had huddled there, as a last hope, to keep the dear, dead master warm.

Cyril Gilbraith, a young man not overburdened with emotions, told with a sob in his voice how, at the terrible Rowan Rock, Jim Mason had stood, impotent, dumb, big-eyed, watching Betsy—Betsy, the friend and partner of the last ten years—slipping over the ice-cold surface, silently appealing to the hand that had never failed her before—sliding to Eternity.

In the Daleland that winter the endurance of many a shepherd and his dog was strained past breaking point. Two men only, each always with his shaggy adjutant, never owned defeat; never failed in a thing attempted. In the following spring, Mr. Tinkerton, the

squire's agent, declared that James Moore and Adam M'Adam—
Owd Bob, rather, and Red Wull—had lost between them fewer
sheep than any single farmer on the whole March Mere Estate—
a proud record.

Of the two, many a tale was told that winter. They were invincible, incomparable; worthy antagonists.

The gray dog it was who found Cyril Gilbraith by the White
Stones, with a sprained ankle, on the night the whole village was
out with lanterns searching for that well-loved young scapegrace.
It was the Tailless Tyke and his master who one bitter evening
came upon little Mrs. Burton, lying in a huddle beneath the lea of
the fast-whitening Druid's Pillar with her latest baby on her breast.
It was M'Adam who took off his coat and wrapped the child in it;
M'Adam who unwound his plaid, threw it like a breastband across
the dog's great chest, and tied the ends round the weary woman's
waist. Red Wull it was who dragged her back to the Sylvester
Arms and life, straining like a giant through the snow, while his
master staggered behind with the babe in his arms. When they
reached the inn it was M'Adam who, with a smile on his face, told
Jem Burton, the landlord, what he thought of him for sending his
wife across the Marches on such a day and on *his* errand. To which,
"I'd a cauld," pleaded honest Jem.

For days together David could not cross the Stony Bottom to
Kenmuir. Then at last, one afternoon, a fallen thorn tree gave
him a bridge over the soft snow. He stayed but a little while at
Kenmuir, yet when he started for home it was snowing again.

By the time he had crossed the ice-draped bridge over the
Wastrel, a blizzard was raging. The wind roared past him, smiting
him so that he could barely stand; and the snow leaped at him so
that he could not see. But he held on. Blindly on, into the white
darkness, sobbing, stumbling, dazed. At length, nigh dead, he
reached the brink of the Stony Bottom, but nowhere could he see
the fallen thorn tree. He took a step forward into the white morass,
and sank up to his thigh. He struggled to free himself, and sank
deeper. The snow wreathed round him, and he collapsed. "I
canna—I canna!" he moaned.

Little Mrs. Moore, her face whiter and frailer than ever, stood at the window, looking out into the storm.

"I canna rest for thinkin' o' th' lad," she said. Then, turning, she saw her husband, his fur cap down over his ears, buttoning his pilot coat about his throat, while Owd Bob stood at his feet, waiting. "Ye're no goin', James?" she asked, anxiously.

"I am, lass," he answered; and she knew him too well to say more.

So those two went quietly out into a whirlwind chaos of snow, to save life or lose it, nor counted the cost. In front, Owd Bob, his hair cutting like lashes of steel across his eyes, his head lowered; and close behind, James Moore, his back stern against the storm, stalwart still, yet swaying like a tree before the wind.

So they battled through to the brink of the Stony Bottom—only to arrive too late. For, just as the Master, peering about him, had caught sight of a shapeless lump lying motionless in front, there loomed across the snow-choked gulf through the riotous storm a gigantic figure, forging doggedly forward. And close behind, buffeted and bruised, stiff and staggering, a little dauntless figure holding stubbornly on; and a shrill voice, whirled away on the wind, crying, "Noo, Wullie, wi' me! Here he is, Wullie!"

The brave little voice died away. The quest was over; the lost sheep found. And the last James Moore saw of them was the same small, gallant form, half carrying, half dragging the rescued boy out of the Valley of the Shadow and away.

David was none the worse for his adventure, for on reaching home M'Adam produced a familiar bottle. "Here's something to warm yer inside, and"—making a feint at the strap on the wall—"here's something to do the same by yer— But, Wullie, oot again!"

And out they went—unreckoned heroes.

It was but a week later that there came a day when, from gray dawn to grayer eve, neither James Moore nor Owd Bob stirred out of the house. And the Master's face was hard and set as it always was in time of trouble. Outside, the wind screamed down the Dale, while the snow fell relentlessly. Inside, there was no sound save for hushed voices, and upstairs the shuffling of muffled feet.

Below, all day long, Owd Bob patrolled the passage like some silent, gray specter. Once there came a low knocking at the door; and David, his face and cap smothered in the all-pervading white, came in with an eddy of snow. He patted Owd Bob, and moved on tiptoe into the kitchen. To him came Maggie softly, shoes in hand, with white, frightened face. The two whispered anxiously awhile; then the boy crept quietly away.

Toward evening the wind died down, but the mourning flakes still fell. With the darkening of night Owd Bob retreated to the porch and lay down on his blanket. The light from the lamp at the head of the stairs shone through the crack of open door on his dark head and the eyes that never slept. The hours passed, and the gray knight still kept his vigil. Alone in the darkness—alone, it almost seemed, in the house—he watched. His head lay motionless along his paws, but the steady gray eyes never flinched or drooped.

At length it grew past bearing; the hollow stillness of the house overcame him. He rose, pushed open the door, and softly pattered across the passage. At the foot of the stairs he halted, his forepaws on the first step, his grave face and pleading eyes uplifted, as though he were praying.

Of a sudden, the deathly stillness of the house was broken. Upstairs, feet were running hurriedly. There was a cry, and again silence. The minutes passed; hours passed; and all through that night of agony the gray figure stood, still as a statue, at the foot of the stairs. Only when, with the first chill breath of the morning, a dry, quick-quenched sob of a strong man sorrowing for the helpmeet of a score of years, and a tiny cry of a newborn child wailing because its mother was not, came down to his ears, the Gray Watchman dropped his head upon his bosom, and, with a little whimper, crept back to his blanket.

Later the door above opened, and James Moore tramped down the stairs. Owd Bob stole out to meet him. At his master's feet he stopped and whined pitifully. For one short moment, James Moore's whole face quivered.

"Well, lad," he said, quite low, and his voice broke; "she's awa'!"

That was all; for they were an undemonstrative couple.

Then they went out together into the bleak morning.

To DAVID M'ADAM THE LOSS of gentle Elizabeth Moore was as real a grief as to her children. Yet he manfully smothered his own aching heart and devoted himself to comforting the mourners at Kenmuir. In these days he recklessly neglected his duties at the Grange; but M'Adam forbore to rebuke him. At times, indeed, he essayed to be passively kind. David, however, was too deeply sunk in sorrow to note the change.

The day of the funeral came. The earth was throwing off its ice fetters, and the Dale was lost in a mourning mist. In the afternoon M'Adam was standing at the window of the kitchen, when the door of the house opened and shut noiselessly. Red Wull raised himself onto the sill and growled, and David hurried past the window making for Kenmuir. M'Adam watched the passing figure indifferently; then with an angry oath tapped fiercely on the pane.

"Bring me back that coat, ye thief!" he cried. "Tak' it aff at onst, ye muckle fool, or I'll comé and tear it aff ye." He threw the window up with a bang and leaned out. "Ye're too big for yer ain boots, let alane ma coat. Fetch it here!"

David paid no heed except to begin running heavily down the hill. The coat was stretched in wrinkled agony across his back.

"Did ye ever see the like o' that, Wullie?" M'Adam muttered. But then, tickled at the amazing impudence of the thing, he chuckled. "Ma puir wee coatie! It makes me weep to see her in her pain."

As he stood watching the disappearing figure the bell in the little Dale church began to toll. Outside, a drizzling rain was falling; snow dribbled down the hill in muddy tricklets; trees and roofs and windows dripped. M'Adam listened, almost reverently, as the bell tolled on, calling up sad memories of the long ago.

It was on just such a dreary December day that the light had gone forever out of his life. That insistent bell brought the whole picture surging back to him as if it had been yesterday: the drizzle; the few mourners; little David decked out in black, his fair hair contrasting with his gloomy clothes, his face swollen with weeping; the Dale hushed, it seemed, in death, save for the tolling of the bell; and his love had left him and gone to the happy land the hymnbooks talk of.

Red Wull, who had been watching him uneasily, now came up and shoved his muzzle into his master's hand. The cold touch brought the little man back to earth. He shook himself, turned wearily away from the window, and with a choking gasp ran up the stairs into his room. He dropped on his knees beside the chest in the corner, and unlocked the bottom drawer. He searched with feverish fingers, and produced at length a paper packet wrapped about with a stained yellow ribbon. It was the ribbon she had used to weave on Sundays into her soft hair. Inside the packet was a cheap, heart-shaped frame, and in it a photograph.

Up there it was too dark to see. M'Adam ran down the stairs, Red Wull jostling him as he went, and hurried to the kitchen window. It was a sweet, laughing face that looked up at him—a face to look at and to love. A wintry smile, wholly tender, half tearful, stole over his face. "Lassie," he whispered, and his voice was soft, "it's lang sin' I've daured look at ye. But it's no that ye're forgotten, dearie."

Then he covered his eyes with his hand as though he were blinded. Memories swarmed back on him. It was more than a decade ago now that she had lain so white and still in the little room above. "Pit the bairn on the bed, Adam man," she had said in low tones. "I'll be gaein' in a wee while noo. It's the lang good-by to you—and him."

He had done her bidding and lifted David up and laid him upon his mother's pillows, and the boy wreathed his soft arms about her neck and sobbed tempestuously. And the two lay thus together.

Just before she died, Flora turned her head and whispered, "Adam, ma man, ye'll ha' to be mither and father baith to the lad noo"; and she looked at him with tender confidence in her eyes.

"I wull! afore God I wull!" he declared passionately. Then she died, and there was a look of ineffable peace upon her face.

The little man rose and flung the photograph from him. Red Wull pounced upon it; but M'Adam leapt at him as he mouthed it.

"Git awa', ye devil!" he screamed; and, picking it up, stroked it lovingly with trembling fingers.

"Mither and father baith!"

How had he fulfilled his love's last wish? How!

"O God!"—he fell to his knees by the table, hugging the picture, sobbing and praying. "Gie me grace, O God! I ha'na done it. But 'tis no too late—say it's no, lass, and say ye forgie me. I'll mak' it up to him—and mair. I'll humble masel' afore him, and that'll be bitter enough. I'll be father and mither baith to him. But there's bin none to help me—and it's bin sair wi'oot ye, lassie!"

IT WAS A DREARY LITTLE PROCESSION that wound in the drizzle from Kenmuir to the Dale church. At the head stalked James Moore, and, close behind, David in his meager coat. While last of all, as if to guide the stragglers in the weary road, came Owd Bob.

There was a full congregation in the tiny church. For nearly every soul in Wastrel-dale had come to show sympathy for the living and reverence for the dead. When the end came in the wet dreariness of the little churchyard, the mourners slowly departed, until at length were left only the parson and the Master.

The parson was speaking in rough, short accents, digging nervously at the wet ground. The other, tall and gaunt, his face drawn and half averted, stood listening.

Of a sudden, James Moore, his face still turned away, stretched out a hand. The parson broke off abruptly and grasped it. Then the two men strode away in opposite directions.

DAVID'S STEPS SOUNDED OUTSIDE. M'Adam rose from his knees. The door of the house opened, and the boy's feet shuffled in the passage. The little man stood in the half-light, one hand on the table, the other clasping the picture. His eyes were bleared, his thin hair all tossed, and he was shaking. "David!" he called tremulously, "I've somethin' I wush to say to ye!"

The boy burst into the room. His face was stained with tears and rain; the coat was wet and slimy, and on the elbows were green-brown, muddy blots. For, on his way home, he had flung himself down in the Stony Bottom and, thinking of that second mother lost to him, had wept his heart out. Now he stood defiantly, his hand upon the door. "What d'yo' want?"

The little man looked from him to the picture in his hand. "Help me, Flora—he'll no," he prayed. Then, raising his eyes, he began, "I'd like to say—I've bin thinkin'—it's no an easy thing for a man to say—" He broke off short. The self-imposed task was almost more than he could accomplish.

He looked appealingly at David. But there was no glimmer of understanding in that white, set countenance. The perspiration stood upon the little man's forehead. Again he began, "David, after I saw ye this afternoon steppin' doon the hill—"

Again he paused. His glance rested unconsciously upon the coat. David mistook the look; mistook the tremor in his father's voice.

"Here 'tis! Tak' yo' coat!" he cried; and, tearing it off, flung it down at his father's feet. "Tak' it—and—and—curse yo'."

He banged out of the room and ran upstairs; and, locking himself in, threw himself onto his bed and sobbed.

M'Adam looked at the wet coat lying in a bundle at his feet. "Curse ye," he repeated softly. "Curse ye—ye heard him, Wullie?"

He looked at the picture now lying crushed in his hand. "Ye canna say I didna try; ye canna ask me to agin," he muttered, and slipped it into his pocket.

Then he went out alone into the gloom and drizzle.

M'ADAM NEVER FORGAVE HIS SON. He had attempted to humble himself, and been rejected; and the bitterness of defeat, when he had deserved victory, rankled like a poisoned barb in his bosom. There could be no alternative but war for all time.

Yet the heat of his indignation was directed not against David, but against the Master of Kenmuir. To the influence of James Moore he attributed his discomfiture, and he never wearied of abusing his enemy.

When the two met, as they often must, it was always M'Adam's endeavor to betray his enemy into an unworthy expression of feeling. But James Moore, sorely tried as he often was, never gave way. He met the little man's sneers with a quelling silence, looking down on his asp-tongued antagonist with such a contempt flashing from his blue-gray eyes as hurt his adversary more than words.

CHAPTER VI

OWD BOB HAD NOW ATTAINED well-nigh the perfection of his art. Parson Leggy declared roundly that his like had not been seen since the days of Rex son of Rally. Among the Dalesmen he was a heroic favorite, his prowess and gentle ways winning him friends on every hand. But the point that told most heavily for him was that in all things he was the very antithesis of Red Wull.

Barely a man in the countryside but owed that ferocious savage a grudge; not a man of them all who dared pay it. The Dalesmen had learned to swallow insults rather than to risk their lives; and their impotence fanned their hatred to white heat.

The working methods of the antagonists were as contrasted as their natures. The one compelled where the other coaxed. What determination could effect, that could Red Wull; but achievement by inaction—supreme strategy—was not for him. In matters of the subtlest handling, where to act anything but indifference was to lose, with sheep restless, fearful forebodings hymned to them by the wind, panic hovering unseen above them, when an ill-considered movement spelt catastrophe—then was Owd Bob incomparable.

Spring passed into summer; and excitement mounted as to the event of the approaching Trials, when at length the rivals would be pitted against one another. Down in the Sylvester Arms there was almost nightly a conflict between M'Adam and Tammas Thornton, spokesman of the Dalesmen, about the respective merits of red and gray. In these duels Tammas was usually worsted, for his temper would get the better of his discretion.

Tammas was easy for M'Adam to draw, but David was easier. Insults directed at himself the boy bore with stolidity. But a poisonous dart shot against his friends at Kenmuir never failed to rouse his anger. David had now a new interest at Kenmuir. On the death of her mother, Maggie had gallantly taken up the reins of government. She did her duty, young though she was, with a surprising, old-fashioned womanliness that won many a smile of approval from her father, and caused David's eyes to open with astonishment. He soon discovered that Maggie, mistress of Kenmuir, was another person from his erstwhile playfellow.

The happy days when might ruled right were gone. Then squabbles between them were unknown. He had never permitted them; any attempt at independent thought or action was sternly quelled. Now she was mistress; and they were perpetually at war. Yet he would sit for hours in the kitchen and watch her, as she went about her business, with solemn, interested eyes, half of admiration, half of amusement. In the end Maggie always turned on him with a little laugh touched with irritation.

"Han't yo' got nothin' better'n that to do, nor lookin' at me?" she asked one Saturday about a month before Cup Day. "It mak's me fair jumpety yo' watchin' me so like ony cat a mouse."

"Niver yo' fash yo'sel', ma wench," he answered calmly.

"Yo' wench, indeed!" she cried, tossing her head.

"Ay, or will be," he muttered.

The girl resumed her baking, half angry, half suspicious. "I dunno' what yo' mean, Mr. M'Adam," she said.

"Don't yo', Mrs. M'A—"

The rest was lost in the crash of a falling plate; whereat David laughed quietly, and asked if he should help pick up the bits.

On the same evening at the Sylvester Arms an announcement was made that knocked the breath out of its hearers.

In the debate that night on the relative abilities of red and gray, the little man again and again was hooted into silence.

"It's easy laffin'," he cried at last, "but ye'll laff t'ither side o' yer ugly faces on Cup Day. We'll whip ye till ye're deaf, dumb, and blind, Wullie and I."

"Yo'll not, and for good reason too," declared Tammas loudly.

"Gie us yer reason, ye muckle liar," cried the little man.

"Becos—" Tammas paused. "Becos—Owd Bob'll not rin."

"What!" screamed the little man, thrusting forward.

"What's that!" yelled Long Kirby, leaping to his feet.

They jostled round the old man's chair, M'Adam in front, Jem

Burton and Long Kirby leaning over his shoulder; while the rest peered and elbowed in the rear.

"Ay, yo' may well 'earken, all on yo'," said Tammas. Pride at the sensation caused by his news struggled in his countenance with genuine sorrow for the matter of it. "'Tis enough to mak' the deadies listen. I says agin: We'll no rin oor Bob for t' Cup. And yo' may guess why. Bain't every mon, Mr. M'Adam, as'd pit aside his chanst o' the Cup, and it a certainty, oot o' respect for his wife's memory."

The news was received in utter silence. Surprise and disappointment froze the tongues of his listeners.

Only one small voice broke the stillness. "Oh, the feelin' man! He should git a reduction o' rent for sic a display o' proper speerit. I'll mind Mr. Hornbut to let auld Sylvester ken o't."

Tammas had but told the melancholy truth. Owd Bob was not to run for the cup. And this self-denying ordinance speaks more for James Moore's love of his lost wife than many a lordly cenotaph.

To the people of the Daleland, the news came with the shock of a sudden blow. They had set their hearts on the Gray Dog's success; but now the Tailless Tyke might well win.

M'Adam, on the other hand, was plunged into a fervor of delight. To have Red Wull's name handed down to posterity, gallantly holding its place among those of the most famous sheep dogs of all time, was his heart's desire. As Cup Day drew near, the nervous little man was tossed on a sea of apprehension. His moods were as uncertain as the winds in March.

Careless as David affected to be of his father's vagaries, he was tried by them now almost to madness, and fled away at every opportunity to Kenmuir; for, as he told Maggie, "I'd sooner put up wi' your h'airs and h'imperences, miss, than wi' his!"

At length the great day came. Cup Day is always a general holiday in the Daleland, and every soul crowds over to Silverdale. Shops were shut; special trains ran into Grammoch-town; and the road from the little town was dazed with char-à-bancs, wagonettes, carriages, carts, foot passengers, wending toward the Dalesman's

Daughter. Soon the paddock below that little inn was humming with the crowd of sportsmen and spectators come to see the battle for the Shepherds' Trophy.

There, very noticeable with its red body and yellow wheels, was the great Kenmuir wagon. Many an eye was directed on the handsome young pair who stood in it, conspicuous and unconscious, above the crowd: Maggie, looking in her simple print frock as sweet and fresh as any mountain flower; while David's fair face was gloomy and his brows knit.

In front of the wagon was a cluster of Dalesmen, discussing M'Adam's chances. Teddy Bolstock dodged in and out among the crowd with tray and glasses, for Cup Day was a great day for him. All around were bobbing heads—Scots, Northerners, Yorkshiremen, Welshmen; to right and left a long array of carriages and carts. Beyond the Silver Lea the gaunt Scaur raised its craggy peak, and the Pass, trending along its side, shone white in the sunshine. Behind the carriages were booths, coconut shies, shows, bookmakers' stools, and all the panoply of such a meeting.

The Juvenile Stakes had been run and won; Londesley's Lassie had carried off the Locals; and the fight for the Shepherds' Trophy was about to begin.

"Yo're not lookin' at me noo," whispered Maggie to the silent boy by her side.

"Nay; nor niver wush to agin," David answered roughly. His gaze was directed over the heads in front to where, beyond the Silver Lea, a group of shepherds and their dogs was clustered. Standing apart from the rest, in characteristic isolation, was the bent figure of his father, and beside him the Tailless Tyke.

"Doest'o not want yo' feyther to win?" asked Maggie softly, following his gaze.

"I'm prayin' he'll be beat," the boy answered moodily.

"Eh, Davie, hoo can ye?" cried the girl, shocked.

"It's easy to say, 'Eh, David,'" he snapped. "But if yo' lived along o' them two, 'appen yo'd understand a bit."

"I know it, lad," she said tenderly; and he was appeased.

When at length Red Wull came out to run his course, he worked

46

with the savage dash that always characterized him. His method was his own, but the work was admirably done.

"Keeps right on the back of his sheep," said the parson, watching intently. "Strange thing they don't break!" But they didn't. Wullie brought his sheep along at a terrific rate, never missing a turn, never faltering, never running out. And the crowd applauded, for the crowd loves a dashing display. While little M'Adam, hopping agilely about, his face ablaze with excitement, handled dog and sheep with a masterly precision that compelled the admiration even of his enemies.

"M'Adam wins!" roared a bookmaker. "Twelve to one agin the field!"

"He wins, dang him!" said David, low.

The win had but a chilling reception. There was faint cheering; but it sounded like the echo of an echo. M'Adam pushed up through the throng toward the committee tent. No single voice hailed him victor; no friendly hand smote its congratulations. Broad backs were turned; contemptuous glances leveled.

But what cared he? His Wullie was acknowledged champion, the best sheep dog of the year, and the little man was happy. They could turn their backs on him, but they could not alter that. "They dinna like it, Wullie—he! he! But ye've won it—won it fair."

He elbowed through the press, making for the rope-guarded enclosure in front of the committee tent. In the door of the tent stood the secretary, various stewards, and members of the committee. Alone in the roped-off space was Lady Eleanour Sylvester, waiting with a smile upon her face to receive the winner. And on a table beside her, the Shepherds' Trophy.

There it stood, kingly and impressive, its fair white sides inscribed with many names; cradled in three shepherds' crooks; and on the top an exquisitely carved collie's head. The Shepherds' Trophy, the goal of his life's race, and many another man's.

He climbed over the rope, followed by Red Wull, took off his hat with almost courtly deference to the fair lady before him, and walked up to the table. There he stood, with his face still wet from his exertions, the Tailless Tyke at his side.

Lady Eleanour looked uneasy. Usually the lucky winner was unable to hear her little speech, as she gave the Cup away, so deafening was the applause. Now there was utter silence. She glanced up at the crowd, but there was no response to her unspoken appeal in that forest of hostile faces. And her gentle heart bled for the forlorn little man before her. To make it up she smiled on him so sweetly as to more than compensate him.

"You and Red Wull there worked splendidly, Mr. M'Adam," she said. "Everybody says so."

"I've heard naethin' o't," the little man answered dryly. At which someone in the crowd sniggered.

"Why, last winter the country was full of Red Wull's doings and yours," said the good lady. "It was always M'Adam and his Red Wull have done this and that and the other."

The little man, cap in hand, smiled and blushed.

"And when it wasn't you it was Mr. Moore and Owd Bob."

"Three cheers for oor Bob!" called a stentorian voice.

"'Ip! 'Ip! 'Ooray!" It was taken up; and strangers, though they did not understand, caught the contagion and cheered too. When the uproar ended Lady Eleanour was standing up, her cheeks flushed and her eyes flashing dangerously. "Yes," she cried. "And now three cheers for Mr. M'Adam and Red Wull! Hip! Hip!—"

"Hooray!" A little knot of stalwarts at the back—James Moore, Parson Leggy, Jim Mason, and you may be sure in heart, at least, Owd Bob—responded to the call right lustily. The crowd joined in; and, once off, cheered and cheered again.

But the little man waved to them. "Dinna be bigger heepocrites than ye can help," he said. "Ye've done enough for one day."

Then Lady Eleanour handed him the Cup. "Mr. M'Adam, I present you with the Champion Challenge Dale Cup, open to all comers. Keep it, guard it, love it as your own, and win it again if you can. Twice more and it's yours, you know, and it will stop forever beneath the shadow of the Pike."

The little man took the Cup tenderly. "It shall no leave the Estate or ma hoose, yer Leddyship, if Wullie and I can help it."

Lady Eleanour retreated into the tent, and the crowd swarmed

48

over the ropes and round M'Adam, who held the Cup beneath his arm. Among the last, James Moore was borne past the little man. At sight of him, M'Adam's face assumed an expression of intense concern. "Man, Moore!" he cried, peering forward as though in alarm; "ye're green—positeevely verdant. Are ye in pain?" Then, in bantering tones, "Ah, but ye shouldna covet—"

"He'll ha' no need to covet it long," interposed Tammas's shrill accents, "becos next year he'll win it fra yo'."

The retort was greeted with a yell of applause from the sprinkling of Dalesmen in the crowd. But M'Adam swaggered away into the tent, his head up, the Cup beneath his arm, and Red Wull guarding his rear.

"First of a' ye'll ha' to beat Adam M'Adam and his Red Wull!" he cried back proudly.

CHAPTER VII

M'ADAM'S PRIDE IN THE GREAT CUP that now graced his kitchen was supreme. It stood alone in the very center of the mantelpiece, just below the old bell-mouthed blunderbuss that hung upon the wall—the only ornament in the bare room. And the little man was a changed being. He forgot to curse James Moore; he forgot to sneer at Owd Bob; he rarely visited the Sylvester Arms; and he was never drunk.

"Soaks 'isself at home, instead," suggested Tammas, the prejudiced. But the accusation was untrue.

"I reck'n the Cup is kind o' company to him," said Jim Mason. "Happen it's lonesomeness as drove him here so much." And happen you were right, charitable Jim.

Even Parson Leggy allowed—rather reluctantly, for he was but human—that M'Adam was changed wonderfully for the better. "But I am afraid it may not last," he said. "We shall see what happens when Owd Bob beats him for the Cup, as he certainly will."

As things were, the little man spent all his spare moments with the Cup between his knees, burnishing it and talking to Wullie.

"There, Wullie! Look at her! She shines like a twinkle—twinkle in the sky." And he would hold it out at arm's length, his head cocked sideways the better to scan its bright beauties. David might not touch the little man's treasure; if he approached too closely he was ordered abruptly away.

So it was that M'Adam, on coming quietly into the kitchen one day, was consumed with anger to find David actually handling the object of his reverence. The boy was lolling indolently against the mantelpiece, his breath dimming the Cup's luster, and his two hands, big and dirty, slowly revolving it before his eyes. He was reading through the long list of winners.

"Ah, theer's 'im Tammas tells on! 'Rex, 183–,' and 'Rex, 183–.' If he'd only won but onst agin! Ah, theer's none like the Gray Dogs o' Kenmuir, bless 'em!" He broke off short at the last name on the list. "'M'Adam's Wull'!" he read with unspeakable contempt, and he made a motion as though to spit upon the ground.

But suddenly two small fists were beating at his chest, and a shrill voice was yelling: "Devil! Devil! Stan' awa'!" and he was tumbled away from the mantel and brought up abruptly against the sidewall. The precious Cup swayed on its ebony stand, but the little man's first impulse, cursing and screaming though he was, was to steady it. "'M'Adam's Wull'! I wish he was here to teach ye, ye snodfaced, ox-limbed profleegit!" he cried.

"I didn't know yo' was theer," said David, a thought sheepishly.

"Na; or ye'd not ha' said it." M'Adam lifted the Cup down, and began reverently to polish the dimmed sides with his handkerchief. "Ye're thinkin', nae doot, that Wullie's no gude enough to ha' his name alangside o' they cursed Gray Dogs. Are ye no?"

"Reck'n he's good enough if there's none better."

"And wha should there be better? Tell me that, ye muckle fool."

David smiled. "Nay; I was but thinkin' that Mr. Moore's Bob'll look gradely writ under yon." He pointed to the vacant space below Red Wull's name.

The little man put the Cup back on its pedestal with hurried hands. The handkerchief dropped unconsidered to the floor; he turned and sprang furiously at the boy; and, seizing him by the collar of his coat, shook him to and fro with fiery energy. "So ye're hopin', prayin', nae doot, that next time James Moore will win ma Cup awa' from me, yer ain dad. I wonder ye're no 'shamed to cross ma door! Wullie and me brak' oorsel's to keep ye in hoose and hame—and what's yer gratitude?" He dropped the boy's coat and stood back. "If I win is it no ma right as muckle as ony Englishman's?"

Red Wull, who had heard the rising voices, came trotting in, scowled at David, and took his stand beside his master.

"Ay, *if* yo' win it," said David. But he did not like the look of things, and edged toward the door.

"Ye chicken-hearted brock!" screamed the little man, darting forward. "At him, Wullie! At him!"

But Red Wull needed no encouragement. With a harsh roar he sprang through the air, only to crash against the closing door.

The outer door banged, and David ran down the hill toward Kenmuir.

FROM THAT HOUR THE FIRE of M'Adam's jealousy blazed into a mighty flame. The winning of the Dale Cup had become a mania with him. He had won it once, and would again despite all the Moores, all the Gray Dogs, all the undutiful sons in existence: on that he was resolved. He could never be happy till the Cup was his own to keep.

When now he visited the Sylvester Arms, he maintained a sullen silence. Crouched away in a corner, with Red Wull beside him, the little man would sit watching and listening as the Dalesmen talked of Owd Bob and his master. Sometimes he could restrain himself no longer. Then he would spring to his feet and denounce them passionately in almost pathetic eloquence.

"Ye're all agin us!" the little man would cry in quivering voice. "I wonder ye dinna poison Wullie—a little arsenic, and the way's clear for your Bob."

"The way is clear enough wi'oot that," from Tammas caustically.

Then a lengthy silence, broken only by that exceeding bitter cry: "Eh, Wullie, Wullie, they're all agin us!"

CURSE AS M'ADAM MIGHT, when the time came Owd Bob won. The issue was never in doubt. It may have been that the temper of the Tailless Tyke gave in the time of trial; it may have been that his sheep were wild; certainly not, as M'Adam alleged, that they had been purposely chosen to ruin his chance. Certain it is that Wullie's tactics scared them hopelessly, and he never had them in hand.

As for Owd Bob, his driving of the sheep, his penning, aroused the loud-tongued admiration of crowd and competitors alike. He was patient yet persistent, quiet yet firm, and seemed to coax his charges in the right way in his inimitable manner. When the verdict was given, and it was known that, after an interval of half a century, the Shepherds' Trophy was won again by a Gray Dog of Kenmuir, great fists were slapped on mighty backs and great feet were stamped on the sun-dried banks of the Silver Lea. Roars of "Moore!" "Owd Bob o' Kenmuir!" "The Gray Dogs!" thundered up the hillside, and were flung, thundering, back.

James Moore was visibly moved as he worked his way through the cheering mob; and Owd Bob, trotting alongside him in quiet dignity, seemed to wave his silvery brush in acknowledgment. But none was so uproarious in his enthusiasm as David M'Adam. He stood in the Kenmuir wagon beside Maggie and cried, "Weel done, oor Bob! Weel done, Mr. Moore! Yo've knocked him! Hip! Hip!" until the noisy young giant attracted such attention that Maggie had to lay a hand upon his arm to restrain him.

Alone, on the far bank of the stream, stood the vanquished pair. As the little man listened to the ovation accorded to his conqueror, there was a piteous set grin upon his face. In front of him stood the defeated dog, his hackles rising, as he, too, saw and heard and understood.

"It's a gran' thing to ha' a dutiful son, Wullie," the little man whispered, watching David's waving figure. "He's happy—and so are they a'—not sae much that James Moore has won, as that you and I are beat. Eh, Wullie, Wullie! it's you and I alane, lad."

He stood there, alone with his dog, watching the crowd on the far slope as it surged in the direction of the enclosure, in which, just

53

a year ago, he had stood in very different circumstances. He laughed a mirthless laugh. "Bide a wee, Wullie—he! he! Bide a wee.

> *"The best-laid schemes of mice and men*
> *Gang aft agley."*

As he spoke, there came down to him, above the tumult, a faint cry of mingled surprise and anger. The cheering ceased abruptly; the crowd turned. Every eye was directed across the stream at the solitary figure there. There were yells of "Yon's him! What's he done wi' it? Thief!" Then the mob came lumbering wrathfully down the slope, though Parson Leggy, the squire, James Moore, and the local constables strove frantically to stem its advance.

M'Adam, motionless, awaited them with a grin upon his face. And the Tailless Tyke rumbled a vast challenge.

"Come on, gentlemen!" the little man cried. "Come on! I'll bide for ye, never fear. Ye're a thousand to one and a dog. It's the odds ye like, Englishmen a'."

And the mob, with murder in its throat, came on.

Then from the slope above, a great voice bellowed: "Way! Way! Way for Mr. Trotter!" The advancing host checked and opened out, and the secretary of the meeting bundled through.

He was a small, fat man, and his face was crimson with rage and running; vague words bubbled forth, as his short legs twinkled down the slope. He bounced over the plank bridge, and as he came closer, M'Adam saw that in each hand he held a brick.

"Hoots, man! Dinna throw!" he cried, making a feint as though to turn in sudden terror.

"What's this? What's this?" gasped Mr. Trotter, waving his arms.

"Bricks, 'twad seem," the other answered.

"Where's the Cup? Champion, Challenge, etc.," the secretary jerked out. "Mind, sir, you're responsible! Dents, damages, delays! What's it all mean, sir? *These*—" he brandished the bricks, and M'Adam started back—"wrapped, as I live, in straw, sir, in the Cup case, sir! No Cup! Infamous! Disgraceful! Insult me—meeting—committee—every one! What's it mean, sir?"

M'Adam approached him with one eye on the crowd, which was

sullen and silent. "I pit 'em there," he whispered; and drew back to watch the effect of his disclosure. "I had ma reasons."

The secretary gasped. "Reasons, sir! No reasons can justify such an extraordinary breach of all the—the decencies."

The mob with Tammas and Long Kirby at their head had now well-nigh reached the plank bridge. They looked dangerous, and there were isolated cries of "Chuck him in!" "An' the dog!" "Wi' one o' they bricks about their necks!"

"There are my reasons!" said M'Adam, pointing to the forest of menacing faces. "Ye see I'm no beloved amang yonder gentlemen, and"—in a stage whisper in the secretary's ear—"I thocht maybe I'd be 'tacked on the road."

Tammas had now his foot upon the first plank of the bridge. "Ye robber! Ye thief! Wait till we set hands on ye!" he called.

"Wullie," M'Adam said quietly, "keep the bridge."

At the order the Tailless Tyke shot gladly forward, and the leaders on the bridge as hastily back. The dog galloped onto the rattling plank and stood facing the hostile crew, like Cerberus guarding the gates of hell; his bull head was thrust forward, hackles up, teeth glinting, and a distant rumbling in his throat, as though daring them to come on.

"Yo' first, ole lad!" said Tammas, hopping behind Long Kirby.

"Nay, the old uns lead!" cried the big smith, his face gray-white.

"Jim Mason'll show us," Tammas suggested.

"Nay," said honest Jim; "I'm fear'd."

Then Jem Burton'd go first?

Nay, Jem had a lovin' wife and dear little kids at 'ome.

A tall figure came forcing through the crowd, his face pale, and a formidable knobkerry in his hand. "I'm goin'!" said David.

"But yo're not," answered burly Sam'l, gripping the boy from behind with arms like the roots of an oak. "Your time'll coom soon enough by the look on yo' wi' never no hurry." And the sense of the Dalesmen was with the big man.

By this time there was a little naked space of green round the bridgehead. Round this the mob hedged, the Dalesmen in front, bawling to those behind to leggo that shovin'.

And as they wedged and jostled, there stole out from their midst a gallant champion. He trotted into the ring and paused to gaze at the gaunt figure on the bridge. The sun lit the sprinkling of snow on the dome of his head; one forepaw was off the ground; and he stood there, royally alert, scanning his antagonist.

"Th' Owd Un!" went up a roar. "Oor Bob'll fetch him!"

The gray champion trotted up onto the bridge and paused again, the long hair about his neck rising like a ruff, and a strange glint in his eyes, and the holder of the bridge never moved. Red and Gray stood thus, face to face: the one gay yet resolute, the other motionless, his great head slowly sinking between his forelegs, seemingly petrified. There was no shouting now; it was time for deeds.

"Wullie," came a lone voice from the far side, "keep the bridge!"

One ear went back, and the glowing eyes rolled upward so that the watchers could see the murderous white.

Forward the gray dog stepped. Then a voice, stern and hard, came ringing down from the slope. "Bob, lad, coom back!"

"He, he! I thocht that was comin'," sneered the small voice over the stream.

The gray dog heard, and checked.

"Bob, lad, coom in, I say!"

At that he swung round and marched slowly back, gallant as he had come, dignified still in his mortification.

And Red Wull threw back his head and bellowed a paean of victory in which was blended challenge, triumph, and scorn.

M'ADAM AND THE SECRETARY now concluded their business. It was settled that the Cup be delivered to James Moore the next Saturday.

"Saturday, at the latest!" the secretary cried as he started off.

"Mr. Trotter," M'Adam called after him, "I'm sorry, but ye maun bide this side the Lea till I've reached the foot o' the Pass. If they gentlemen"—nodding toward the crowd—"should set hands on me, why—" and he shrugged his shoulders significantly. "Besides, Wullie's keepin' the bridge."

With that the little man strolled off leisurely to the foot of the

Murk Muir Pass. There he turned and whistled. "Wullie, Wullie, to me!" he called.

Then, with one last threat thrown at the thousand souls he had held at bay for thirty minutes, the Tailless Tyke swung about and galloped after his lord.

CHAPTER VIII

ALL FRIDAY M'ADAM NEVER LEFT the kitchen. He sat opposite the Cup, in a coma, as it were; and Red Wull lay at his feet. Saturday came, and still the two never budged. Toward the evening the little man rose, all in a tremble, and took the Cup down from the mantelpiece; then he sat down again and hugged it to him.

"A few hours, Wullie," he wailed, "and she'll be gane. We won her, you and I, won her fair: she's lit the hoose for us. And noo they're takin' her awa', and 'twill be night agin." He stood up, and his voice heightened to a scream. "Did they win her fair, Wullie? Na, they conspired to beat us. Ay, and noo they're robbin' us! But they shallna ha' her. We'll finish her sooner nor that."

He banged the Cup down on the table and rushed out of the room. In a moment he came back, brandishing an axe about his head. On the table, serene and beautiful, stood the target of his madness. M'Adam ran at it, swinging his weapon like a flail.

"Oor's or naebody's, Wullie! Come on! 'Lay the proud usurpers low!'" He aimed a mighty buffet; and the Shepherds' Trophy—the Cup which had won through the hardships of a hundred years—seemed to quiver as the blow fell. But the axe head missed, and sank into the wood, clean and deep, like a spade in snow.

Red Wull leapt onto the table, and in his cavernous voice was grumbling a chorus to his master's yells. M'Adam danced up and down, tugging and straining at the axe handle. The shaft snapped, and he tottered back. Red Wull jumped down from the table, and, in doing so, brushed against the Cup. It toppled onto the floor, and rolled tinkling away in the dust. And the little man fled madly out of the house.

When, late that night, M'Adam returned home, the Cup was gone. Down on his hands and knees he traced out its path, plain to see, where it had rolled along the dusty floor. Beyond that there was no sign. Exhausted, the little man sat down and cried.

"It's David, Wullie, ye may depend; David that's robbed his father's hoose. Oh, it's a grand thing to ha' a dutiful son!"—and he bowed his gray head in his hands.

WHEN DAVID REACHED HOME that night he marched, contrary to his wont, straight into the kitchen. There sat his father facing the door, awaiting him. For once the little man was alone; and David, brave though he was, thanked heaven devoutly that Red Wull was elsewhere.

For a while father and son kept silence, watching one another like two fencers. "'Twas you as took ma Cup?" asked the little man at last, leaning forward in his chair.

"'Twas me as took Mr. Moore's Cup," the boy replied. "I thowt yo' mun ha' done wi' it—I found it all bashed upon the floor."

"James Moore dursena come hissel' so he sent the son to rob the father." His whole frame shook with passion. "The coward's fear'd o' me, sic as I am, five foot twa in ma stockin's."

"Mr. Moore had nowt to do wi' it," David persisted.

"Ye're lyin'. Hooiver, I'll settle wi' James Moore anither time. I'll settle wi' you noo. Ye're a thief, David M'Adam!"

"I'm no thief!" the boy returned hotly. "I did but give to a mon what ma feyther—shame on him!—wrongfully kept from him. Ay, if ony one's the thief, it's you, I say, holdin' back his rights from a man!"

"I'm the thief, am I?" cried the other, rising. "Though ye're three times ma size, I'll teach ma son to speak so to me."

The old strap, now long disused, hung in the chimney corner. As he spoke the little man sprang back, ripped it from the wall, and brought it down savagely across his son's shoulders. As he smote he whistled a shrill, imperative note: "Wullie, Wullie, to me!"

David felt the blow through his coat like a bar of hot iron laid across his back. His passion seethed within him. In a minute he would wipe out, once and for all, the score of years; now, however, there was urgent business on hand. For outside he could hear the scurry of a huge creature racing madly to a call.

With a bound he sprang at the open door; again the strap came down, and a wild voice: "Quick, Wullie! For God's sake!"

David slammed the door to. At the same moment a great body from without thundered against it with terrific violence.

"Too late!" said David, breathing hard, and shot the bolt home with a clang. Then he turned on his father.

"Noo," said he, "man to man!"

"Ay," cried the other, "father to son!"

M'Adam half turned and leapt at the old blunderbuss hanging on the wall. He missed it, turned again, and struck with the strap full at the other's face. David caught the falling arm at the wrist, hitting it aside with such tremendous force that the bone all but snapped. Then he smote his father a terrible blow on the chest, and the little man staggered back, gasping, into the corner; while the strap dropped from his numbed fingers.

Outside Red Wull whined and scratched; but the two men paid no heed. David strode forward; there was murder in his face. The little man saw it; his time was come, but his bitterest foe never impugned Adam M'Adam's courage.

He stood huddled in the corner, all disheveled, nursing one arm with the other, entirely unafraid. "Mind, David," he said, quite calm, "murder 'twill be, not manslaughter."

"Murder 'twill be," the boy answered, in thick, low voice, and was across the room.

The little man suddenly slipped his hand in his pocket, pulled out something, and flung it. The missile pattered on his son's face like a raindrop on a charging bull, and David smiled as he came on. It dropped softly on the table at his side; he looked down and—it was the face of his mother which gazed up at him!

"Mither!" he cried, stopping short, utterly unhinged. "Mither! Ma God, ye saved him—and me!"

It was some minutes before he pulled himself together; then he walked to the wall, took down a pair of shears, and seated himself

60

at the table. He picked up the strap and began cutting it into little pieces. "There! And there! And there!" he said with each snip. "An' ye hit me agin there may be no mither to save ye."

M'Adam shook like an aspen leaf; his eyes blazed in his white face; and he still nursed one arm with the other.

"Honor yer father," he quoted in small, low voice.

TAMMAS IS ON HIS FEET in the taproom of the Arms, brandishing a pewter mug. "Gen'lemen!" he cries, his old face flushed; "I gie you a toast. Stan' oop!"

The knot of Dalesmen round the fire rise like one. The old man waves his mug before him. "The best sheep dog i' th' North—Owd Bob o' Kenmuir!" he cries. In an instant there is the clinking of pewters, the stamping of feet, the rattle of sticks.

Rob Saunderson jumps onto a chair. "Wi' the best sheep dog i' th' North I gie yo' the Shepherds' Trophy!—won outreet as will be!" he cries. Instantly the clamor redoubles. Some minutes pass before it subsides and the enthusiasts resume their seats.

"Gentlemen a'!"

A little unconsidered man is standing up at the back of the room, his face aflame; and in front of him, with hackles up and eyes gleaming, is a huge, bull-like dog.

"Noo," cries the little man, "I daur ye to repeat that lie!" As he looks at the range of broad, impassive backs turned on him, waiting for his challenge to be taken up, he cries bitterly. "They dursen't, Wullie! They're one—two—three—eleven to one, and yet they dursen't. Weel, we should ha' kent Englishmen by noo. They tell lies—and they ha' na the courage to stan' by 'em."

The little man seizes a tankard. "Englishmen!" he cries, waving it before him. "Here's a health! The best sheep dog as iver penned a flock—Adam M'Adams' Red Wull!"

There is no response from his audience.

He raises the tankard and drains it. Then he addresses his audience once more: "An' noo I'll warn ye, and ye may tell James Moore I said it. He may plot agin us, Wullie and me; he may win the Cup outright for his muckle favorite; but there was niver a man or dog yet as did Adam M'Adam and his Red Wull a hurt but in the end he wush't his mither hadna borne him."

Then he walks out of the inn, the Tailless Tyke at his heels.

After he is gone it is Rob Saunderson who says, "The little mon's mad; he'll stop at nothin'," and Tammas who answers:

"Nay; not even murder."

IN THE YEAR THAT FOLLOWED M'Adam aged much. His hair was quite white now, his eyes unnaturally bright, and his hands were never still. After Owd Bob's second victory he became morose and untalkative. At home he often sat silent for hours together, drinking and glaring at the place where the Cup had been.

It was the same at the Sylvester Arms. The little man sat alone with Red Wull, drinking steadily, brooding over his wrongs, only now and again galvanized into sudden action. Other people than Rob Saunderson came to the conclusion that he was mad and would stop at nothing to undo James Moore or the gray dog.

Most of them all, David was fearful of the little man's intentions. The boy even went so far as to warn his friend against his father. But the Master only smiled grimly, "Thank ye, lad," he said. "But I reck'n we can 'fend for oorsel's, Bob and I."

Still, David was not above taking advantage of this state of strained apprehension to work on Maggie's anxiety. One evening he was escorting her home from church, when, just before they reached the larch copse, "Goo' sakes! What's that?" he ejaculated in horror-laden accents, starting back.

"What, Davie?" cried the girl, shrinking up to him.

"Couldna say for sure. It mought be owt, or agin it mought be nowt. But yo' grip my arm, I'll grip yo' waist."

She demurred. "Canst see onythin'?" she asked, all in a flutter. "I canna see nowt."

"Why, theer, lass, be'ind the 'edge," pointing vaguely. "Can yo' not see? Then yo' pit your head along o' mine—so—closer—closer." Then, in aggrieved tones, "Whativer is the matter wi' yo', wench? I might be a leprosy."

But Maggie was walking away with her head high as the snow-

62

capped Pike. "So long as I live, David M'Adam," she cried, "I'll niver go to church wi' you agin!"

"Iss, but you will though—onst," he answered low.

Maggie whisked round in a flash. "What d'yo' mean, sir-r-r?"

"Yo' know what I mean, lass," he replied, sheepish and shuffling before her queenly anger.

"I'll niver speak to you agin, Mr. M'Adam," she cried; "not if it was ever so— Nay, I'll walk home by myself, thank you."

So the two must return to Kenmuir, one behind the other, like a lady and her footman.

The suspicions that M'Adam nourished dark designs against James Moore were somewhat confirmed in that, on several occasions in the bitter January dusk, an insidious figure was reported to have been seen lurking among the farm buildings of Kenmuir. Once Sam'l Todd caught the little man fairly, skulking in the woodshed. Sam'l took him up bodily and carried him down the slope to the Wastrel, shaking him and threatening him to such effect that for a time he appeared there no more.

But soon there followed an attempt to poison Th' Owd Un. At least there was no other accounting for the affair.

In the dead of a long-remembered night James Moore was waked by a low moaning beneath his room. He ran to the window to see Owd Bob dragging about the moonlit yard, the dark head down, the proud tail for once lowered, the lithe limbs wooden, heavy, unnatural—altogether pitiful.

In a moment he was downstairs and out to his friend's assistance. "Whativer is't, Owd Un?" he cried in anguish.

At the sound of that dear voice the old dog tried to struggle to him, could not, and fell, whimpering.

In a second the Master was with him, examining him tenderly, and crying for Sam'l Todd, who slept above the stables.

There was every symptom of foul play. The tongue was swollen and almost black, the breathing labored, the body twitched horribly, and the soft gray eyes all bloodshot and straining in agony.

With the aid of Sam'l and Maggie, drenching first and stimulants after, the Master saved the victim—but only just. For a time the best sheep dog in the North was pawing at the Gate of Death.

There were no traces of the culprit, so cunningly had the criminal done his work. But the attempt aroused indignation in the countryside. As to the perpetrator there were no doubts.

Ten days elapsed, and the gray dog still had attacks of shivering; his vitality seemed sapped. At length James Moore, leaving the old dog behind him, went over to Grammoch-town to consult Dingley, the vet. On his way home he met Jim Mason with Gyp, the faithful Betsy's unworthy successor, at the Dalesman's Daughter. Together they started for the long tramp home over the Marches. And that journey is marked with a red stone in this story.

All day the hills had been bathed in fog. To the darkness of the day was added the somberness of falling night as they began the ascent of the Murk Muir Pass. By the time they emerged into the Devil's Bowl it was altogether black. But when the last steep rise onto the Marches had been topped, a breath of soft air smote them lightly, and the fog began drifting away. The two men swung steadily through the heather. They talked but little, for such was their nature: a word or two on the approaching lambing time; thence to the coming Trials; and the attempt on Owd Bob.

"D'yo' reck'n M'Adam had a hand in't?" the postman asked.

"Nay, there's no proof."

"'Ceptin' he's mad to get shut o' Th' Owd Un afore Cup Day."

"Of 'im or me—it mak's no differ." For a dog is disqualified from competing for the Trophy who has changed hands during the six months prior to the meeting.

Jim looked up inquiringly at his companion. "D'yo' think it'll coom to murder?" he asked.

"Not if I can help it," the other answered grimly.

The fog was gone now, and the moon was up. To their right, on the crest of a rise some two hundred yards away, a low wood stood outlined against the sky. From it, a blackbird rose screaming, and a brace of wood pigeons winged noisily away.

"Hullo! hark to the yammerin'!" muttered Jim, stopping. "And at this time o' night too!"

Some rabbits, playing on the outskirts of the wood, sat up, listened, and hopped back into security. A big hill fox slunk out of the covert. He stole a pace forward and halted, listening with one ear back and one pad raised; then cantered silently away.

"What's up, I wonder?" mused the postman.

"The fox set 'em clackerin', I reck'n," said the Master.

"Not he; he was scared 'maist oot o' his skin," the other answered. Then in tones of suppressed excitement, "And, look 'ee, theer's ma Gyp a-beckonin' on us!"

There, indeed, on the crest of the rise beside the wood, was the little lurcher, now looking back at his master, now creeping stealthily forward.

"Ma word! theer's summat wrong yonder!" cried Jim. "Coom on, Master!" And he set off toward the dog, while James Moore, excited now, followed with an agility that belied his years.

Some score yards from the lower edge of the spinney, upon the farther side of the ridge, a tiny beck babbled through its bed of peat. The two men, as they topped the rise, noticed a flock of black-faced mountain sheep clustered in the dip 'twixt wood and stream. They stood marshaled in close array, heads up, eyes glaring, handsome as sheep only look when scared.

On the crest the two men halted beside Gyp. Jim listened intently. Then he dropped in the heather, pulling the other with him. "Doon, mon!" he whispered, clutching at Gyp with his spare hand. "Summat's movin' i' th' wood."

They lay motionless for a while; but there came no sound from the copse. "'Appen 'twas nowt," the postman at length allowed, peering cautiously about. "Yet I thowt—I dunno reetly what I thowt." Then, starting up in terror: "Save us! What's yon theer?"

The Master raised his head and noticed, lying in the gloom between them and the sheep, a still, white heap. He sprang forward, his heart in his mouth. "Ah, thanks be!" he cried, dropping beside the motionless body; "it's nob' but a sheep." As he spoke his hands wandered deftly over the carcass. "But what's this? Look at her fleece—crisp, close, strong; feel the flesh—firm as a rock. Ne'er a bone broke. As healthy as a mon—yet dead as mutton!"

Jim came up and knelt beside his friend. "Ah, but there's bin devilry in this!" he said; "I reck'ned they sheep had bin badly skeared, and not so long agone."

"Sheep murder!" the other answered. "No fox's doin'."

Jim's hands traveled from the body to the dead creature's throat. He screamed. "By gob, Master! Look 'ee theer!" He held his hand up in the moonlight, and it dripped red. "And warm yet! Warm!"

"Tear some bracken, Jim!" ordered the other, "and set it alight. We mun see to this."

The postman did as bid. For a moment the fern smoldered and smoked, then the flame shot up in the darkness. The victim was subjected to a critical examination. The throat, and that only, had been hideously mauled; on the ground all about were dabs of wool, wrenched off apparently in a struggle; and, among the fern roots, a snakelike track of red led down to the stream.

"A dog's doin' and no mistakin' thot," said Jim at length.

"Ay," declared the Master with slow emphasis, "and a sheep dog's too, and an old un's, or I'm no shepherd."

The postman looked up. "Why that?" he asked, puzzled.

"Because," the Master answered, "'im as did this killed for blood—and for blood only. If had bin ony other dog—or even a young sheep dog—d'yo' think he'd ha' stopped wi' the one? Not he; he'd ha' gone through 'em, and be runnin' 'em as like as not yet, till he'd maybe killed the half. But 'im as did this killed for blood. He got it—killed the one, and nary touched the others."

The postman whistled, long and low.

James Moore added, "I've never seen the like afore myself, but I've heard ma granddad speak o't mony's the time. An owd dog'll git the cravin' for sheep's blood on him, just the same as a mon does for the drink; he creeps oot o' nights, gallops afar, hunts his sheep, downs 'er, and satisfies the cravin'. And he nary kills but the one. Then he's for home, maybe a score mile away, and no one the wiser i' th' mornin'. And so on, till he cooms to a bloody death."

"If he does!" said Jim.

"He does, they say, nigh always. For he gets bolder wi' not bein' caught, until one fine night a bullet lets light into him. And some

66

mon gets knocked nigh endways when they bring his best tyke home, dead, wi' the sheep's wool yet stickin' in his mouth."

The postman whistled again. "Ma word," he said, "I wish Th' Owd Un was here. He'd 'appen show us summat!"

"I nob' but wish he was, pore owd lad!" said the Master.

As he spoke there was a crash in the wood above them, as of some big body bursting through brushwood. They rushed to the top of the rise. In the dark they could see nothing; they could hear only the faint sound of some creature splashing over the wet moors.

"Yon's him! And a main big un, too, hark to him!" cried Jim.

Then to Gyp, who had rushed off in hot pursuit, "Coom back, chunk-'ead. What's use o' you agin a gallopin' 'potamus?"

Gradually the sounds died away and away, and were no more.

"Thot's 'im, the devil!" said the Master at length.

"Nay; the devil has a tail, they do say," replied Jim thoughtfully. For already the light of suspicion was focusing its red glare.

"Noo I reck'n we're in for bloody times amang the sheep for a while," said the Master, as Jim picked up his bags.

"Better a sheep nor a mon," answered the postman.

CHAPTER IX

THAT, AS JAMES MOORE HAD PREDICTED, was only the first of a long succession of such solitary crimes.

It was always black nights, nights of wind and weather, when no man would be abroad, that the murderer chose for his bloody work; and that was how he became known from the Red Screes to the Muir Pike as the Black Killer. There was hardly a farm in the countryside but was marked with the seal of blood. Kenmuir escaped, and the Grange; Rob Saunderson at the Holt, and Tupper at Swinsthwaite; and they were about the only lucky ones.

As for Kenmuir, Tammas declared, "He knows better'n to coom wheer Th' Owd Un be." And as for the luck of the Grange—well, there was a reason for that too, so the Dalesmen said.

Though the area of crime stretched from the Black Water to

Grammoch-town, twenty-odd miles, there was never a sign of the perpetrator. The Killer did his bloody work with a devilish cunning that defied detection. Yet it was plain that each murder might be set down to the same agency. Always one sheep was killed, its throat torn into red ribands, and the others were untouched.

The squire imported a bloodhound to track down the Killer. Set on at a fresh-killed carcass at the One Tree Knowe, he carried the line a distance in the direction of the Muir Pike; then was thrown out by a little bustling beck, and never acknowledged the scent again. Afterward he became unmanageable, and could be no further utilized. The Master of the Border Hunt lent a couple of foxhounds, who effected nothing; and there were a hundred other attempts and as many failures. Meanwhile, the Dalesmen raged and swore vengeance, their impotence and their losses feeding their wrath. And the bitterest sting of all lay in this: that though they could not detect him, they were nigh positive as to the culprit.

There was scarcely a man in the countryside who doubted the guilt of the Tailless Tyke; but where was the proof? They could but point to his evil notoriety; say that, magnificent sheep dog as he was, he was known even in his work as a rough handler of stock; and remark significantly that the Grange was one of the few farms that had so far escaped unscathed. For with the belief that the Black Killer was a sheep dog they held it as an article of faith that he would in honor spare his master's flock.

OVER M'ADAM, SEEMINGLY unaware of all this, a change had come, and he became his old self again. His tongue wagged gaily and bitterly, and hardly a night passed but he infuriated Tammas almost to blows with his innuendos and sarcasms.

Old Sam'l Todd, one evening at the Sylvester Arms, inquired of him what his notion was as to the identity of the Black Killer.

"Why *black?*" the little man asked earnestly; "why *black* mair than white—or *gray*, we'll say?" Luckily for him, however, the Dalesmen are slow of wit as of speech.

David, too, marked the difference in his father, who nagged at him now with all the old spirit. At first he rejoiced in the change, preferring this open warfare to that aforetime stealthy enmity. And he believed that, for the nonce at least, his father had abandoned those sneaking night visits to Kenmuir.

Yet Maggie Moore could have undeceived him. For one night, alone in the kitchen, she had seen to her horror a dim, moonlike face glued against the windowpane. It was M'Adam, she recognized that: the pale face, the hair lying dankly on his forehead, and the white eyelids blinking. She thought of his sworn vengeance on her father, and her heart stood still, though she never moved. At length with a gasp of relief she discerned that the eyes were not directed on her. They rested on the Shepherds' Trophy.

An hour, it seemed to Maggie, elapsed before the face withdrew into the night. She told no one what she had seen. Knowing how terrible her father was in anger, she deemed it wiser to keep silence. As for David, she'd never speak to him again!

And not for a moment did that young man surmise whence his father came when, on the night in question, M'Adam returned to the Grange, chuckling. And when his father sat down and began muttering to Red Wull, at first David paid no heed.

"He! he! Wullie. Perhaps we'll beat him yet. There's many a slip twixt Cup and lip—eh, Wullie, he! he!" And he made allusion to the flourishing of the wicked and their fall.

In this strain he continued until David, his patience exhausted, asked roughly, "What is't yo' mumblin' aboot? Wha is it yo'll beat, you and yer Wullie?"

M'Adam turned on his son, leering at him. "Wha should it be but the Black Killer? Wha else is there I'd be wushin' to hurt?"

David was almost the only man in Wastrel-dale who denied Red Wull's identity with the Killer. "Nay," he said once, "he'd kill me, given half a chance, but a sheep—no." Yet he knew what the talk was, and was astonished at his father's remark. "The Black Killer, is it? What d'you know o' the Killer?" he inquired.

"Why *black*, I wad ken? Why *black*?" M'Adam asked, leaning forward in his chair.

Now David, though repudiating in the village Red Wull's complicity with the crimes, at home was never so happy as when casting innuendos to that effect. "What would you have him then?" he asked. "Red, yaller, dirt color?"—and he stared significantly at the dog, who was lying at his master's feet.

The little man giggled, and his two thin hands rubbed his knees. "Perhaps his puir auld stupid fool of a dad kens mair than the dear lad thinks for, ay, or wushes—eh, Wullie, he! he!"

"Then what do you know?" David asked irritably.

"Naethin', laddie, naethin' worth the mention. Only perhaps the Killer'll be caught afore sae lang."

David smiled incredulously, wagging his head in offensive skepticism. "Yo'll catch him yo'self, I s'pose, you and yer Wullie? Tak' a chair onto the Marches, whistle awhile, and when the Killer comes, why, pit a pinch o' salt upon his tail—if he has one."

At the last words, heavily punctuated by the speaker, the little man started. "What wad ye mean by that?" he asked softly.

"What wad I?" the boy replied.

"I dinna ken for sure," the little man answered; "and it's perhaps just as well for you, dear lad, that I dinna."

CHAPTER X

DAVID AND MAGGIE were now drifting further and further apart. He thought the girl took too much upon herself; that this assumption of the woman and the mother was overdone. Consequently he was seldom at Kenmuir, and more often at home, quarreling with his father.

Since that day, two years before, when the boy had been an instrument in the taking of the Cup from him, father and son had been like two vessels charged with electricity, contact between which might result at any moment in a shock and a flash.

Meanwhile the Black Killer pursued his bloody trade. The terror had reigned already two months when, with the advent of the lambing time, matters took a yet more serious aspect.

It was bad enough to lose one sheep; but the hunting of a flock at a critical moment, the scaring of these woolly mothers-about-to-be almost out of their fleeces, spelt for the small farmers something akin to ruin, for the bigger ones a loss hardly bearable. Loud were the curses, deep the vows of revenge.

Many a shepherd at that time patrolled all night through with his dogs, only to find in the morning that the Killer had slipped him and havocked in some secluded portion of his beat. It was heartrending work; and all the more so in that, though his incrimination seemed as far off as ever, there was still the same positiveness as to the culprit's identity.

IT WAS ABOUT THE MIDDLE of the lambing time, when the Killer was working his worst, that the Dalesmen had a glimpse of Adam M'Adam as he might be were he wounded through his Wullie.

Thus it came about: It was market day in Grammoch-town, and in the Border Ram old Rob Saunderson was the center of interest. For on the previous night Rob, who till then had escaped unscathed, had lost a sheep to the Killer; and—far worse—his flock of Herdwicks, heavy in lamb, had been galloped with disastrous consequences. The old man, with tears in his eyes, told how in the dawn he came upon a mangled sheep and the pitiful relic of his flock. All about were cold wee lambkins and their mothers, dead and dying of exhaustion and their unripe travail.

The Dalesmen were clustered round the old shepherd, listening with lowering countenances, when a dark gray head peered in at the door and two wistful eyes dwelt for a moment on the speaker.

"Talk o' the devil!" muttered M'Adam, but no man heard him. For Red Wull, too, had seen that sad face, and, rising from his master's feet, had leapt with a roar at his enemy.

Long Kirby was standing at the door with a cup of hot coffee in his hand. Barely had he greeted the gray dog with—"'Ullo, Owd Un!" when hoarse yells of " 'Ware, lad! The Terror!" mingled with Red Wull's roar.

Half turning, Long Kirby saw the great dog bounding to the attack. Straightway he flung the boiling contents of his cup full in that rage-wracked countenance. With a howl of agony, Red Wull checked in his charge. From without the door was banged to; and

71

again the duel was postponed; while within the room a huddle of men and dogs were left alone with a mad man and a madder brute.

Blind, demented, agonized, the Tailless Tyke thundered about the little room banging his tortured head against the wall. And all the while M'Adam pattered after him, laying hands upon him, crying in supplicating tones, "Wullie, Wullie, let me to ye! Let yer man ease ye!" and then, with a murderous glance, "By——, Kirby, I'll deal wi' you later!"

The uproar was like hell let loose, as the men fought for the door. Long Kirby was the first one out; and after him the others toppled one by one in a frenzy of fear. Then the door was shut with a clang, and the little man and mad dog were left alone.

In the street a crowd gathered, attracted by the noise; while at the door was James Moore, seeking entrance. "Happen I could lend the little mon a hand," said he; but they withheld him forcibly.

Inside was pandemonium: banging and bellowing; and always that shrill, beseeching prayer, "Wullie, Wullie, let me to ye!" And, in a scream, "By ——, Kirby, I'll be wi' ye soon!"

Jim Mason it was who turned, at length, to the smith and whispered, "Kirby, lad, yo'd best skip it."

The big man obeyed and ran, and panic seized the crowd. In two minutes the street was naked of men. One only scorned to run. Alone, James Moore stalked down the center of the road, slow and calm, Owd Bob trotting at his heels.

A COINCIDENCE IT MAY HAVE BEEN, but for the fortnight succeeding Kirby's exploit there was a lull in the crimes. There followed, as though to make amends, the seven days still remembered in the Daleland as the Bloody Week.

On Sunday the Squire lost a Cheviot ewe. On Monday a farm on the Black Water was marked with the red cross. On Tuesday Tupper at Swinsthwaite came upon the murderer at his work; he fired into the darkness without effect, and the Killer escaped. On the following night Viscount Birdsaye lost a shearling ram. Thursday was the one blank night of the week. On Friday Tupper was again visited and punished heavily, as though for that shot.

On Saturday afternoon a big meeting was held at the Manor to discuss measures. The Squire presided; gentlemen and magistrates were there, and every farmer in the countryside. To start the proceedings Viscount Birdsaye rose and proposed that a reward larger than the paltry £5 of the Police should be offered. He backed his proposal with a £25 cheque. Several others spoke, and, last of all, Parson Leggy rose. He reiterated his belief that a sheep dog was the criminal and suggested that every man who owned a sheep dog tie him up at night.

The farmers clustered in knots to talk over the proposal.

"Weel, Mr. Saunderson," M'Adam said, "shall ye tie Shep?"

"What d'yo' think?" asked Rob, eyeing the man at whom the measure was aimed.

"Why, if ye haud Shep's the guilty one I *wad*, by all manner o' means—or shootin'd be perhaps better. If not, why—" The little man shrugged significantly, and left the meeting.

James Moore stayed to see the Parson's resolution negatived by a large majority, and then he too quitted the hall.

At the lodge gate was M'Adam, playing with the lodge-keeper's child; for the little man loved all children but his own, and was beloved of them. As the Master approached he looked up. "Weel, Moore," he called, "and are you gaein' to tie yer dog?"

"I will if you will yours," the Master answered grimly.

"Na," the little man replied, "it's Wullie as frichts the Killer aff the Grange. That's why I've left him there noo."

"It's the same wi' me," the Master said. "He'll not come to Kenmuir so long as Th' Owd Un's loose, I reck'n."

"Which road are ye gaein' hame?" M'Adam called as he started on. "Because," with a polite smile, "I'll tak' t'ither."

"I'm off by the Windy Brae," the Master answered; and he headed away to the left, by the route along the Silver Mere.

It is a long sweep of almost unbroken moorland, the well-called Windy Brae; sloping gently down in mile on mile of heather from the Mere Marches on the top to the fringe of the Silver Mere below. In all that waste of moor the only break is the quaint-shaped Giant's Chair, puzzle of geologists, looking as though plumped down by accident in the heathery wild. The ground rises suddenly from the Brae until at length it runs abruptly into a sheer curtain of rock—the Fall—on the top of which rests that tiny grassy bowl—not twenty yards across—they call the Scoop.

The Scoop forms the seat of the Chair; in front is the forty-foot Fall; behind, rising sheer again, the wall of rock which makes the back of the Chair. Inaccessible from above, the only means of entrance to that little dell are two narrow sheep tracks, which crawl dangerously up between the sheer wall on the one hand and the sheer Fall on the other, entering it at opposite sides.

It stands out clear-cut from the gradual incline, that peculiar eminence; yet as the Master and Owd Bob debouched onto the Brae it was already invisible in the darkening night. Through the heather the two swung, the Master pondering on the identity of the Killer—for he was half of David's opinion as to Red Wull's innocence; and thanking his stars that so far Kenmuir had escaped, a piece of luck he attributed entirely to the vigilance of Th' Owd Un, who, sleeping in the porch, slipped out at all hours and went his rounds, warding off danger. And at the thought he looked down for the faithful dog who should be traveling at his side; yet could not see him, so thick hung the pall of night.

So he brushed his way along until, from the swell of the ground beneath his feet, he knew himself skirting the Giant's Chair. Now as he sped along the foot of the rise, of a sudden there burst on his ear the myriad patter of galloping feet. He turned, and at the second a swirl of sheep almost bore him down. It was velvet black, and they fled furiously by, yet he dimly discovered, driving at their trails, a vague houndlike form.

"The Killer, by thunder!" he ejaculated. "Bob, lad! Follow on!" And he swung round; but in the darkness could not see if the gray dog had obeyed.

The chase swept on into the night, and, far above him on the hillside, he could now hear the rattle of the flying feet. Recognizing the futility of following where he could not see his hand, he stood motionless, listening, and hoping Th' Owd Un was on the villain's heels.

He prayed for the moon; and, as though in answer, the lantern of the night lit the dour face of the Chair above him. The sheep had broken, and were scattered over the steep hillside, still galloping madly. In the rout one pair of darting figures caught and held his gaze: the foremost dodging, twisting, speeding upward; the hinder hard on the leader's heels, swift, remorseless. He looked for a third pursuing form; but none could he discern.

"He mun ha' missed him in the dark," he muttered.

Higher and higher sped those two dark specks, far out-topping the scattered remnant of the flock. Up and up, until of a sudden the sheer Fall dropped its relentless barrier in their path. On up the familiar track leading to the Scoop scudded the fugitive, bleating pitifully, nigh spent, the Killer hard on her now.

"He'll doon her in the Scoop!" cried the Master hoarsely. "Owd Un! Owd Un! Wheer iver are yo' gotten to?" But no Owd Un made reply.

As they reached the summit, just as he had prophesied, the two black dots were one; and down they rolled together into the hollow of the Scoop, out of the Master's ken. At the same instant the moon, as though loath to watch the last act of the bloody play, veiled her face.

It was his chance. "Noo!"—and up the hillside he sped, until the face of the Fall blocked his way. There he paused a moment and whistled a low call. He waited, all expectant, but no cold muzzle was shoved into his hand. Again he whistled. A pebble from above almost dropped on him, as if the criminal up there had moved to the brink of the Fall to listen.

He waited till all was still again, then crept, catlike, along the rock foot, and hit, at length, the ragged track. Up he crawled on hands and knees. The perspiration rolled off his face; one elbow brushed the rock perpetually; one hand plunged ever and anon into that naked emptiness on the other side.

He cursed his luck that Th' Owd Un had missed him in the dark; for now he must trust to chance, his own great strength, and his good oak stick. As he climbed, he laid his plan: to rush in on the Killer as he gorged and grapple with him. If in the darkness he missed—and in that narrow arena the contingency was improbable—the murderer might, in the panic of the moment, forget the one path to safety and leap over the Fall to his destruction.

At length the Master reached the summit and paused to draw breath. He crouched against the wet rock face and listened. No sound, and yet the murderer must be there. Ay, there was the tinkle of a dislodged stone; and again, the tread of stealthy feet. The Killer was moving; alarmed; was off.

Quick! The Master rose, gathered himself, and leapt. Something collided with him as he sprang; something wrestled madly with him; something wrenched from beneath him, and he heard the thud of a body striking ground far below, and the slithering and splattering of some creature speeding furiously down the hillside and away.

"Who the blazes?" roared he.

"What the devil?" screamed a little voice.

The moon shone out.

"Moore!"

"M'Adam!"

And there they were, struggling over the body of a dead sheep.

In a second they had disengaged and looked over the edge of the Fall. Nothing was to be seen, however, save an array of startled sheep on the hillside, mute witnesses of the murderer's escape. A pause, a careful scrutiny.

"There's blood on your coat."

"And on yours."

Together they turned back. There lay the murdered sheep in a pool of blood. Plain it was whence the marks on their coats came. The two men eyed one another suspiciously.

"What are yo' doin' here?"

"After the Killer. What are you?"

"After the Killer."

"Hoo did you come?"

"Up this path," pointing to the one behind him. "Hoo did you?"

"Up the other."

Silence; then, "I'd ha' had him but for yo'."

"I did have him, but ye tore me aff."

A pause again.

"Wheer's yer gray dog?" The challenge was unmistakable.

"I sent him after the Killer. Wheer's your Red Wull?"

"At hame, as I tell't ye before. When did yer dog leave ye?"

"When the Killer came past."

"Ye say he went after the Killer. Noo the Killer was here," pointing to the dead sheep. "Was your dog here, too?"

"If he had been he'd been here still."

"Onless he went over the Fall!"

"That was the Killer, yo' fule."

"Or your dog."

"There was only *one* beneath me. I felt him."

"Just so," said M'Adam, and laughed.

The two stared at one another, silent and stern, each trying to fathom the other's soul; then they turned to the brink of the Fall. Beneath them was the furrow in the shingle marking the Killer's line of retreat. They looked at one another again. Then each departed the way he had come to give his version of the story.

In the days that followed, both men were examined as to the minutest details of the matter. The whole countryside was placarded with huge bills now offering £100 for the capture of the criminal, dead or alive.

CHAPTER XI

MEANWHILE M'ADAM'S TAUNTS and gibes became more and more bitter, driving David almost to distraction. He longed to make it up with Maggie; he longed for that tender sympathy which the girl had always extended to him when his troubles with his father were heavy on him. The quarrel had lasted for months now, and he was weary of it, and ashamed. For, at least, he had the grace to acknowledge that no one was to blame but himself; and that it had been fostered solely by his ugly pride.

At length he could endure it no longer, and determined to ask the girl's forgiveness. As he walked on up the slope from the Wastrel, very slowly, heartening himself for his penance, he was aware of a strange disturbance in the yard above him: the noisy cackling of hens, the snorting of pigs disturbed, and above the rest the cry of a little child ringing out in shrill distress.

He sped up the slope as fast as his long legs would carry him. As he took the gate in his stride, he saw Maggie's little sister, Wee Anne, her fair hair streaming out behind, and one bare arm striking back at a great pursuing sow.

David shouted as he cleared the gate, but the brute paid no heed, and was almost touching the fugitive when Owd Bob came galloping round the corner, and in a second had flashed between pursuer and pursued. So close were the two that as he swung round on the startled sow, his tail brushed the child to the ground. David, leaving the old dog to secure the warrior pig, ran round to her; but he was anticipated. Maggie, rushing from the kitchen, already had Anne in her arms and was hurrying back with her to the house.

"Eh, ma pet, are yo' hurted?" David could hear her asking tearfully, as he crossed the yard and established himself in the door.

"Well," said he, in bantering tones, "yo'm a nice wench to ha' charge o' oor Anne!"

But the girl paid no heed to her tormentor in her joy at finding the child unhurt. "Theer! yo' bain't so much as scratted, ma precious. Rin oot agin, then," and the child scampered joyfully away. Maggie rose to her feet and stood with face averted. David's eyes dwelt lovingly upon her, admiring the pose of the neat head with its thatch of pretty brown hair.

"Ma word! If yo' dad should hear tell o' hoo his Anne—" he broke off into a long-drawn whistle.

Maggie's lips quivered, and the flush deepened on her cheek.

"I'm fear'd I'll ha' to tell him," the boy continued. "'Tis but ma duty. If it had not bin for me—"

"Yo', indeed!" she broke in contemptuously. "'Twas Owd Bob reskied her. Yo'd nowt to do wi' it."

"I tell yo'," David pursued stubbornly, "an' it had not bin for me yo' wouldn't have no sister by noo. She'd be lyin', she would, cold as ice, pore mite, wi' no breath in her. An' when yo' dad coom home there'd be no Wee Anne to rin to him, and climb on his knee. An' he'd say, 'What's gotten to oor Annie, as I left wi' yo'?' And then yo'd have to tell him, 'I never took no manner o' fash after her, Dad; d'reckly yo' back was turned, I—'"

The girl sat down, buried her face in her apron, and indulged in the rare luxury of tears. "Yo're the cruelest mon as iver was, David M'Adam," she sobbed, rocking to and fro.

He was at her side in a moment, tenderly bending over her. "Eh, Maggie, but I am sorry, lass—"

She wrenched away from him. "I hate yo'," she cried.

He gently removed her hands from before her tearstained face. "I was nob' but laffin', Maggie," he pleaded; "say yo' forgie me."

"I don't. I think yo're the hatefulest lad as iver lived."

The moment was critical; it was a time for heroic measures.

"No, yo' don't, lass," he remonstrated; and, releasing her wrists, lifted the little drooping face and, holding it between his two big hands, kissed it twice.

"Yo' coward!" she cried, a flood of warm red crimsoning her cheeks; and she struggled vainly to be free.

"Yo' used to let me when we was little uns," he reminded her. "And noo I mayn't so much as keek at yo' over a stone wall."

However that might be, he was keeking at her from closer range now. He looked so handsome—humble for once, penitent yet reproachful, his own eyes a little moist, and, withal, his old audacious self—that despite herself, her anger grew less hot.

"Say yo' forgie me and I'll let yo' go."

"I don't, nor niver shall," she answered firmly; but there was less conviction in her heart than voice.

"Iss yo' do, lass," he coaxed, and kissed her again.

She struggled faintly. "Hoo daur yo'?" she cried through her tears. But he was not to be moved.

"Will yo' noo?" he asked. And he kissed her again.

"Impidence!" she cried.

"Ay," said he, closing her mouth.

"I wonder at ye, Davie!" she said, surrendering.

AFTER THAT IT WAS UNDERSTOOD, though nothing definite had been said, that the boy and girl were courting. And in the Dale the unanimous opinion was that they would make "a gradely pair."

M'Adam was the last to hear the news. It was in the Sylvester Arms he heard it, and straightway fell into a frenzy.

"The daughter o' Moore o' Kenmuir, d'ye say? The daughter o' th' one man in the warld that's harmed me aboon the rest! Oh, David, David! I'd no ha' thocht it even o' you, ill son as ye've aye bin to me." Then the little man sat down and burst into tears.

Gradually, however, he resigned himself, and the more readily when he realized that David by his act had exposed a fresh wound into which he might plunge his barbed shafts.

"Is't true what they're sayin' that Maggie Moore's nae better than she should be?" the little man asked David one evening.

"They're not sayin' so, and if they were 'twad be a lie," the boy answered angrily.

M'Adam leaned back in his chair and nodded. "Ay, they tell't me that if ony man knew 'twad be David M'Adam."

David strode across the room. "Feyther," he said, "one day yo'll drive me too far."

THE SPRING WAS PASSING, marked throughout with the bloody trail of the Killer. The adventure in the Scoop scared him for a while into innocuousness; but then he resumed his game with re-doubled zest. There came at last a Saturday long to be remembered in the Dale.

For David the day started sensationally. Rising before cockcrow and going to the window, the first thing he saw in the misty dawn was Red Wull, hounding up the hill from the Stony Bottom; and in an instant his faith was shaken to its foundation.

The dog was traveling up at a long, slouching trot; and as he approached the house, David saw that his flanks were all splashed with red mud, his tongue out, and the foam dripping from his jaws, as though he had come far and fast. He leapt onto the sill of the unused back kitchen, pushed with his paw at the cranky old hatch-ment, and dropped within the house.

For the moment, excited as he was, David held his peace. Even the Black Killer took only second place in his thoughts. For that afternoon James Moore and Andrew would be over at Grammoch-town, and he was resolved to tackle Maggie and decide his fate. If she would have him—well, he would go next morning and thank God for it, kneeling beside her in the tiny village church; if not, he would leave the Grange and all its unhappiness behind, and straightway plunge out into the world.

Therefore, when, as he was breaking off work at noon, his father turned to him and said abruptly, "David, ye're to tak' the Cheviot lot o'er to Grammoch-town at once," he answered shortly, "Yo' mun tak' 'em yo'sel', if yo' wish 'em to go today." And with that he walked out.

Now it happened that on the previous day Maggie had given him a photograph of herself. As he left the room it dropped from his pocket. He failed to notice his loss, but directly he was gone M'Adam pounced on it.

"He! he! Wullie, what's this?" he giggled. "He! he! It's the jade hersel', I war'nt!" He held the picture down for the great dog to see, then walked out of the room, still sniggering.

Outside the house he collided against David. The boy had missed his treasure and was hurrying back for it.

"What yo' got theer?" he asked suspiciously.

"Only the pictur' o' some randy quean," his father answered.

"Gie it me!" David ordered fiercely. "It's mine."

"Na, na," the little man replied. "It's no for sic douce lads as dear David to ha' ony touch wi' leddies sic as this." He turned, still smiling, to Red Wull. "There ye are, Wullie!" He threw the photograph to the dog. "Tear her, Wullie, the Jezebel!"

The Tailless Tyke sprang on the picture, placed one big paw in the very center of the face, forcing it into the muck, and tore a corner off; then he chewed the scrap with slobbering gluttony.

David dashed forward. "Touch it, if ye daur, ye brute!" he yelled; but his father seized him and held him back.

"Whist, David, whist!" soothed the little man. "Rin aff wi' ye noo to Kenmuir. She'll mak' it up to ye, I war'nt."

"An' yo' gie me much more o' your sauce," David roared, "I'll gang reet awa', I warn yo', and leave you and yer Wullie to yer lone."

The little man began to whimper. "It'll brak' yer auld dad's heart, lad," he said.

"Nay; yo've got none. But 'twill ruin yo', please God. For yo' and yer Wullie'll get ne'er a soul to work for yo'!"

The little man burst into affected tears, rocking to and fro, his face in his hands. "Alas, Wullie! d'ye hear him? He's gaein' to leave us—the son o' my bosom! My little Davie!"

David started down the hill, then, "I'll gie yo' a word o' warnin'," he shouted back. "I'd advise yo' to keep a closer eye to yer Wullie's goings on, 'specially o' nights, or happen yo'll wake to a surprise one mornin'."

"And why that?" asked the little man, following down the hill.

"I'll tell yo'. When I wak' this mornin' I walked to the window, and what d'yo' think I see? Why, your Wullie gollopin' up from the Bottom, all foamin', too, and red-splashed, as if he'd coom from the Screes. What had he bin up to, I'd like to know?"

"What should he be doin'," the little man replied, "but havin' an eye to the stock? And that when the Killer might be oot."

David laughed harshly. "Ay, the Killer was oot, I'll go bail, and yo' may hear o't soon, ma man"; and he turned away again.

As HE HAD FORESEEN, David found Maggie alone. But in the heat of his indignation against his father he seemed to have forgotten his original intent, and instead poured his latest troubles into the girl's sympathetic ear.

"There's but one mon in the world he wishes worse nor me," he was saying. Maggie sat in her father's chair by the fire, knitting, while he lounged on the kitchen table, swinging his long legs.

"And who may that be?" the girl asked.

"Why, Mr. Moore, to be sure, and Th' Owd Un, too."

"But why, David?" she asked anxiously.

David nodded toward the Dale Cup which rested on the mantelpiece in silvery majesty. "It's yon done it," he said. "And if Th'

Owd Un wins agin, as win he will, bless him, why, look out for 'me and ma Wullie,' that's all."

Maggie shuddered, and thought of the face at the window.

"'Me and ma Wullie,'" David continued; "It's aye the same—as if I never put ma hand to a stroke! Why, 'twas nob' but yester' morn' he says in his nasty way, 'David, ma gran' fellow, hoo ye work! Ye 'stonish me!' And on ma word, Maggie, ma back was nigh broke wi' toilin'."

Maggie's knitting dropped into her lap and she looked up, her soft eyes for once flashing. "It's cruel, David, so 'tis! I wonder yo' bide wi' him. If he treated me so, I'd no stay anither minute."

David jumped off the table. "Han' yo' niver guessed why I stop, lass?" he asked eagerly.

"Hoo should I know?" Maggie asked innocently.

"Nor care, neither, I s'pose," he said in reproachful accents. "Yo' want me to go and leave yo', and go reet awa'; I see hoo 'tis. Yo' wouldna mind if yo' was niver to see pore David agin."

"Yo' silly lad," the girl murmured, knitting steadfastly.

"Then yo' do," he cried, triumphant. "I knew yo' did." He approached close to her chair, his face clouded with eager anxiety. "But d'yo' like me more'n just *likin*', Maggie? D'yo'?"

The girl cuddled over her work so that he could not see her face.

"If yo' won't tell me yo' can show me," he coaxed. "There's other things besides words."

He stood before her, one hand on the chairback on either side. She sat thus, caged between his arms, with drooping eyes and heightened color.

"Do'ee move away a wee," she implored.

"Not till yo've showed me," he said, relentless.

"Tak' your hands away, then," she cried, laughing.

"Nay, not till yo've showed me."

"Do'ee, Davie," she supplicated.

"Do'ee," he pleaded.

She tilted her face provokingly, but her eyes were still down.

"It's no manner o' use, Davie."

"Please," he coaxed.

"Well, then—" She looked up, at last, shy, trustful, happy; and the sweet lips were tilted to meet his. And thus they were situated, loverlike, when a low, rapt voice broke in on them—

> "*A dear-lov'd lad, convenience snug,*
> *A treacherous inclination.*"

It was little M'Adam. He was leaning in at the open window, leering at the young couple. "The creetical moment! And I interfere! David, ye'll never forgie me."

The boy jumped round with an oath; and Maggie, her face flaming, started to her feet.

"By thunder! I'll teach yo' to come spyin' on me!" roared David. And grabbing a pail of soapy water that stood close by, he splashed its contents at the face in the window.

The little man started back, but the dirty torrent soused him through. The bucket followed, struck him full on the chest, and rolled him over in the mud. After it with a rush came David.

"I'll let yo' know, spyin' on me!" he yelled. "I'll—" Maggie, white-faced, clung to him, hampering him.

"Dinna, David, dinna!" she implored. "He's yer ain dad."

At the moment Sam'l Todd came round the corner, closely followed by 'Enry. They picked up the draggled little man and hustled him out of the yard like a thief. As they forced him through the gate, he struggled round. "By Him that made ye! Ye shall pay for this, David M'Adam, you and yer—"

But Sam'l's big hand descended on his mouth, and he was borne away before that last ill word had flitted into being.

CHAPTER XII

ALL THAT EVENING AT THE Sylvester Arms M'Adam's imprecations against David had made even the hardest shudder. When, at length, he staggered home, there was no light in the kitchen of the Grange, and the fire burnt low. So dark was the room that a piece of white paper pinned onto the table escaped his remark.

The little man sat down heavily, his clothes still sodden, and prepared to wait. His hand sought the pocket of his coat and fingered tenderly a small stone bottle, the fond companion of his widowhood. He pulled it out, uncorked it, and took a long pull; then placed it on the table by his side. Gradually he dozed off into a heavy sleep, while Red Wull watched at his feet.

An hour later David returned to the house. He struck a match and stood in the kitchen doorway peering in. "Not home, bain't he?" he muttered. "By gum! 'Twas lucky for him I didna get ma hand on him this evenin'." He held the tiny light above his head.

Two yellow eyes, glowing in the darkness, and a small dim figure bunched in a chair, told him his surmise was wrong. Many a time had he seen his father in such case before, and he muttered contemptuously, "Drunk, the leetle swab! Sleepin' it off, I reck'n."

Then he saw his mistake. There was no sound, no movement; only those two unwinking eyes were fixed on him. At length a small voice broke the quiet. "Drunk—the—leetle—swab!"

"I thowt yo' was sleepin'," said David lamely.

"Ay, so ye said. 'Sleepin' it aff'; I heard ye." Then, in the same small voice, "Wad ye obleege me, sir, by leetin' the lamp? Or d'ye think 'twad be soilin' yer dainty fingers? They're mair used, I'm told, to danderin' wi' the bonnie brown hair o' yer—"

"I'll not ha' ye talk o' ma Maggie so," interposed the boy passionately, and began to trim the lamp with trembling fingers.

As the lamp was lit, the strip of paper, pinned onto the table, caught M'Adam's eye. "What's this?" he muttered, and unloosed the nail that clamped it down. This is what he read:

Adam Mackadam yer warned to mak' an end to yer Red Wull will be best for him and the Sheep. This is the first yoll have two more the third will be the last— ◁━┣▥▥

It was written in pencil, and the only signature was a dagger, rudely limned in red.

M'Adam stared at it with whitening face and pursed lips. Then he stole a glance at David's broad back.

"What d'ye ken o' this, David?" he asked, holding up the slip.

David took up the paper and read it.

"It's coom to this, has it?" he said harshly, with blanching face.

"Ye ken what it means. I daresay ye pit it there, perhaps writ it. Ye'll explain it." M'Adam's eyes never moved off his son's face.

"It's plain as day. Ha' ye no heard?"

"I've heard naethin'."

"It's this thin. Tupper lost a sheep to the Killer last night."

"And what if he did?" The little man rose smoothly to his feet, his face dead-white.

"Why, he—lost it—on the Red—Screes." David drawled the words out, dwelling almost lovingly on each.

"What of it?" The little man's voice was calm as a summer sea.

"Why, your Wullie—as I told yo'—was on the Screes last night. And this," holding up the paper, "tells you that they ken, as I ken noo, as maist o' them ha' kent this mony a day, that your Wullie, Red Wull—the Terror—"

"Go on, David."

"Is the Black Killer."

It was spoken.

The frayed string was snapped at last. The little man's hand flashed to the bottle that stood before him.

"Ye—liar!" he shrieked, and threw it with all his strength at the boy's head. David dodged and ducked, and the bottle hurtled over his shoulder. Crash! It whizzed into the lamp behind, and broke on the wall beyond, its contents trickling down the wall to the floor. For a moment, darkness. Then the spirits met the lamp's smoldering wick and blazed into flame.

By the sudden light David saw his father on the far side of the table, pointing with crooked forefinger. By his side Red Wull was standing alert, hackles up, yellow fangs bared.

"Oot o' ma hoose! Back to Kenmuir! Back to yer—" The unpardonable word, unmistakable, hovered for a second on his lips.

"No mither this time!" panted David, racing round the table. "Wullie!"

The Terror leapt to the attack; but David overturned the table as he ran, opposing a momentary barrier in the dog's path.

"Stan' off, ye—!" screeched the little man, seizing a chair in both hands; "stan' off, or I'll brain ye!" But David was on him.

"Wullie, Wullie, to me!"

Again the Terror came with a roar like the sea. But David, with a mighty kick catching him full on the jaw, repelled the attack. Then he gripped his father round the waist and lifted him up. The little man, cursing, struggling in those iron arms, battered at the face above him, kicking and biting in his frenzy.

"The Killer! Wad ye ken wha's the Killer? Go and ask 'em at Kenmuir! Ask yer—"

David swayed slightly, crushing the body in his arms till it seemed every rib must break; then hurled it from him. The little man fell with a crash and a groan.

The blaze of the lamp flared, flickered, and died. There was hell-black darkness, and silence of the dead. David stood against the wall, panting. In the corner lay the body of his father, limp and still; and in the room one other living thing was moving.

He clung close to the wall, pressing it with wet hands. The horror of it all, the darkness, the man in the corner, that moving something, petrified him. "Feyther!" he whispered in hoarse agony, "are yo' hurt?"

The words were stifled in his throat. A chair overturned with a crash; a great body struck him on the chest; a hot breath volleyed in his face, and wolfish teeth were reaching for his throat.

"Come on, Killer!" he screamed. The horror of suspense was past. It had come, and with it he was himself again. Back, back, back, along the wall he was borne. His hands entwined themselves around a hairy throat; he forced the great head back; he braced himself for the effort, lifted the huge body at his breast, and heaved it from him. It struck the wall and fell with a soft thud.

As he recoiled a hand clutched his ankle and sought to trip him. David kicked back and down with all his strength. There was one awful groan, and he staggered against the door and out. He closed the door and paused, leaning against the wall to breathe. He struck a match and lifted his foot to see where the hand had clutched him.

God! There was blood on his heel.

Then a great fear laid hold on him. He crept back to the kitchen door and listened. Not a sound.

Fearfully he opened it a crack.

Silence of the tomb.

He banged it to. It opened behind him, and the fact lent wings to his feet. He turned and plunged out into the night, and ran through the blackness for his life.

In the village even the Black Killer and the murder on the Screes were forgotten in this new sensation. The mystery in which the affair was wrapped whetted the general interest. There had been a fight; M'Adam and the Terror had been mauled; and David had disappeared—those were the facts. But what was the origin of the affray no one knew, though one or two of the Dalesmen had, indeed, a shrewd suspicion.

Injured as he had been, M'Adam was yet sufficiently recovered to appear in the Sylvester Arms on the Saturday following the battle. He entered the taproom silently; one arm was in a sling and his head bandaged. He eyed every man present critically.

"Onythin' the matter?" asked Jem, at length, rather lamely, in view of the plain evidences of battle.

"Na, na; naethin' oot o' the ordinar'. Only David set on me, and me sleepin'. And," with a shrug, "here I am noo." The little man sat down, wagging his bandaged head. And nothing further could they get from him, except that if David reappeared it was M'Adam's firm resolve to hand him over to the police for attempted parricide.

The general verdict was that M'Adam had brought his punishment entirely on his own head. Tammas told him straight: "It served yo' well reet. An' I nob' but wish he'd made an end to yo'."

"He did his best, puir lad," M'Adam reminded him gently.

"We've had enough o' yo'," continued the uncompromising old man. "I'm fair grieved he didna slice yer throat, too."

At that M'Adam raised his eyebrows, stared, and then broke into a low whistle. "That's it, is it?" he muttered, as though a new light was dawning on him. "Ah, noo I see."

THE DAYS PASSED ON. THERE WAS STILL no news of the missing one, and Maggie's face became pitifully white and haggard. Of course she did not believe that David had attempted to murder his father, desperately tried as she knew he had been. Still, it was a terrible thought to her that he might at any moment be arrested; and her girlish imagination was perpetually conjuring up pictures of a trial, conviction, and the things that followed.

Then Sam'l started a wild theory that M'Adam had murdered his son, and thrown the body down the dry well at the Grange. The story was, of course, preposterous, yet it set the cap on the girl's fears; and she resolved, at whatever cost, to visit the Grange. Her intent she concealed from her father, knowing he would gently but firmly forbid it; and on an afternoon some fortnight after David's disappearance, choosing her opportunity, she threw a shawl over her head and fled down the slope to the Wastrel.

The little plank bridge rattled as she tripped across it and she started guiltily round. It proved, however, to be only Owd Bob, sweeping after. "Comin' wi' me, lad?" she asked as the old dog cantered up, thankful to have that gray protector with her.

Round Langholm fled the two; over the summer-clad lower slopes of the Pike, until they reached the Stony Bottom. Down the bramble-covered bank the girl slid, picked her way from stone to stone across the streamlet, and scrambled up the far bank.

At the top she halted, and her heart failed her. In her whole life she had never spoken to M'Adam. Yet she knew him well enough from all David's accounts—ay, and hated him for David's sake. She feared him, too, and, with a shudder, she recalled the dim face at the window. But even M'Adam could hardly harm a girl coming, broken-hearted, to seek her lover. Besides, was not Owd Bob with her? She clenched her teeth, drew the shawl about her, and set off running up the hill.

Soon the run dwindled to a crawl, and her heart pattered against her side. "Keep close, lad," she whispered to her gray guardian. And the old dog ranged up beside her, shoving into her skirt, as though to let her feel his presence.

So they reached the top of the hill; and the house stood before them, grim, unfriendly. The girl paused and lifted a warning finger, bidding her companion halt without. She tapped on the door. There was no answer. Her heart stood still, but she turned the handle and entered, leaving a crack open behind.

On the far side of the room a little man was sitting. His head was swathed in dirty bandages, and a bottle was on the table beside him. He was leaning forward, and there was a stare of naked horror in his eyes. One hand grasped the great dog who stood at his side, yellow teeth glinting; with the other he pointed a palsied finger at her.

"Ma God! Wha are ye?" he cried hoarsely.

The girl stood hard against the door, her fingers still on the handle; trembling like an aspen at the sight of that uncanny pair. The look in the little man's eyes petrified her. Rumors of his insanity tided back on her memory.

"I'm—I—" the words came in trembling gasps.

At the first utterance, however, the little man's hand dropped; he leaned back in his chair and gave a sigh of relief. No woman had crossed that threshold since his wife died; and, for a moment, he had thought this shawl-clad figure was the spirit of one he had loved long since and lost, come to reproach him with a broken troth.

"Speak up, I canna hear," he said, in tones mild compared with those last wild words.

"I—I'm Maggie Moore," the girl quavered.

"Moore! Maggie Moore, d'ye say?" he cried, half rising from his chair, a flush of color sweeping across his face, "the daughter o' James Moore?" He paused for an answer, glowering at her, and she shrank, trembling, against the door.

The little man leaned back in his chair. Gradually a grim smile crept across his countenance. "Weel, Maggie Moore," he said, half amused, "ony gate ye're a good plucked un."

At that the girl's courage returned with a rush. After all, this little man was not so very terrible. Perhaps he would be kind.

There was not to be peace yet, however. For a dark muzzle flecked with gray pushed in at the crack of the door and two anxious gray eyes followed.

With a roar Red Wull tore himself from his master's restraining hand, and dashed across the room.

"Back, Bob!" screamed Maggie, and the dark head withdrew. The door slammed with a crash as Red Wull flung himself against it, and Maggie was hurled into a corner.

M'Adam was on his feet, pointing, his face diabolical.

"Did you bring him? Did you bring *that* to ma door?"

Maggie huddled in the corner, her eyes gleaming big and black in the white face peering from the shawl.

"I brought him to protect me. I—I was afraid."

M'Adam sat down and laughed abruptly. "Afraid! I wonder ye were na afraid to bring him here. It's the first time iver he's set foot on ma land, and 't had best be the last." He turned to the great dog, who was snarling horribly, his nose to the bottom of the door. "Wullie, Wullie, come here. Lay ye doon—so—under ma chair—good lad. Noo's no the time to settle wi' him." Then, turning to Maggie, "If ye want him to mak' a show at the Trials two months hence, he'd best not come here agin. If he does, he'll no leave ma land alive; Wullie'll see to that."

The girl in the corner was scared almost out of her senses, but she saw before her now only the father of the man she loved; and a wave of emotion surged up in her breast. She advanced timidly toward him, holding out her hands.

"Eh, Mr. M'Adam," she pleaded, "I come to ask ye after David. Will ye no tell me wheer he is? I'd not trouble yo', but I've bin waitin' a waefu' while, it seems, and I'm wearyin' for news o' him."

The little man looked at her curiously. "Ah, noo I mind me—you're the lass as is thinkin' o' marryin' him?"

"We're promised," the girl answered simply.

"Weel," the other remarked, "as I said afore, ye're a good plucked un." Then, in a tone in which cynicism and indefinable sadness were blended, "If he mak's you as good a husband as he mad' son to me, ye'll ha' made a remairkable match, my dear."

Maggie fired in a moment. "A good feyther makes a good son," she answered almost pertly; and then, with infinite tenderness, "and I'm prayin' a good wife'll make a good husband."

"I'm feared that'll no help ye much," he said, scoffingly.

But the girl never heeded this last sneer, so set was she on her purpose. She had heard of the one tender place in the heart of this little man, and she resolved to appeal to it.

"Yo' loved a lass yo'sel' aince, Mr. M'Adam," she said. "Hoo would yo' ha' felt had she gone away and left yo'? Yo'd ha' bin mad; yo' know yo' would. And, Mr. M'Adam, I love the lad yer wife loved." She was kneeling at his feet now with both hands on his knees, looking up at him.

The little man was visibly touched. "Ay, ay, lass, that's enough," he said, trying to avoid those beseeching eyes. "I canna tell ye, for I dinna ken."

The girl's last hopes were dashed. And she remembered that this was the man whose persistent cruelty had driven her love into exile. She rose to her feet. "Nor ken, nor care!" she cried bitterly.

At the words all the softness fled from the little man's face. "Ye do me a wrang, lass," he said, looking up at her with an assumed ingenuousness. "If I kent where the lad was I'd be the vairy first to tell you, and the p'lice, too; eh, Wullie! he! he!" He chuckled at his wit and rubbed his knee. "I canna tell ye where he is now, but ye'd perhaps care to hear o' when I saw him last." He turned his chair the better to address her. "'Twas like so: I was sittin' in this vairy chair it was, asleep, when he crep' up behind an' lep' on ma back. I knew naethin' o't till I found masel' on the floor an' him kneelin' on me——"

The girl waved her hand at him disdainfully. "If David did strike you, you drove him to it," she said. "Yo' know, none so well, whether yo've bin a good feyther to him, and him no mither, poor laddie! Whether yo've bin to him what she'd ha' had yo' be. Ask yer conscience, Mr. M'Adam. An' if he was a wee aggravatin' at times, had he no reason?"

The little man pointed to the door, but the girl paid no heed.

"D'yo' think when yo' were cruel to him, jeerin' and fleerin', he never felt it, because he was too proud to show ye? He'd a big saft heart, had David, beneath the varnish. Mony's the time when mither was alive, I've seen him throw himsel' into her arms, sob-bin', and cry, 'Eh, if I had but mither! 'Twas different when mither was alive; he was kinder to me then. An' noo I've no one.' "

The clear, girlish voice shook. M'Adam, sitting with face averted, waved to her, mutely ordering her to be gone. But she held on, gentle, sorrowful, relentless.

"An' what'll yo' say to his mither when yo' meet her, as yo' must soon noo, and she asks yo', 'An' what o' th' lad I left wi' yo', Adam, to guard and keep for me?' And then yo'll ha' to speak the truth, God's truth, and yo'll ha' to answer, 'Sin' the day yo' left me I niver said a kind word to the lad. I niver bore wi' him, and niver tried to. And in the end I drove him by persecution to try and murder me.' Then maybe she'll look at yo'—yo' best ken hoo—and she'll say, 'Adam, Adam! is this what I deserved fra yo' ?' "

The gentle, implacable voice ceased. The girl turned and slipped softly out of the room, and M'Adam was left alone to his thoughts and his dead wife's memory.

"Mither and father, baith! Mither and father, baith!" rang remorselessly in his ears.

CHAPTER XIII

THE BLACK KILLER STILL CURSED the land. The £100 reward offered had brought no issue, and the Dalesmen were in despair. There was no proof; no hope that the end was near. As for the Tailless Tyke, the only evidence against him had flown with David, who had divulged what he had seen to no man.

Then, as a last resource, Jim Mason took a holiday from his duties and disappeared into the wilderness. Three days and three nights no man saw him. On the morning of the fourth he reappeared, a furtive look in his eyes, irritable, who had never been irritable before—to confess his failure. Cross-examined, he said with unaccustomed fierceness, "I seed nowt. Who's the liar as said I did?"

But that night his missus heard him in his sleep conning over something in a fearful whisper, "Two on 'em; one ahint t'other.

The first big—bull-like; t'ither—" At which point Mrs. Mason smote him in the ribs, and he woke in a sweat, crying, "Who said I seed—"

THE DAYS WERE SLIPPING AWAY; the summer was hot upon the land, and everything sank into oblivion before the all-absorbing interest of the coming Dale Trials. Soon the justice of Th' Owd Un's claim to the Shepherds' Trophy would be settled. If he won, he won outright—a thing unprecedented in the annals of the Cup. Win or lose, it was to be the last public appearance of the Gray Dog, the last event in the long struggle 'twixt Red and Gray.

Many a man would lose more than he cared to contemplate were Th' Owd Un beat. But he'd not be! Nay; he was older than his great rival; still, "What's the odds agin Owd Bob o' Kenmuir? I'm takin' 'em. Who'll lay agin Th' Owd Un?"

And with the air saturated with this perpetual talk of the gray dog and his certain victory, M'Adam became again the silent man of six months since—morose, brooding, suspicious. At the Sylvester Arms he usually sat isolated in a far corner, with Red Wull at his feet. Now and then he burst into a paroxysm of insane giggling, slapping his thigh, and muttering, "Ay, it's likely they'll beat us, Wullie. Yet there's a wee somethin' we ken and they dinna."

Meantime, there was no news of David. Some said he'd enlisted, some that he'd gone to sea. With no gleam of consolation, Maggie's misery was such as to rouse compassion in all hearts.

M'Adam also felt acutely the boy's loss. It may have been he missed the ever-present butt; it may have been a nobler feeling. Alone with Red Wull, too late he felt his loneliness. Sometimes, sitting in the kitchen, thinking of the past, he experienced sharp pangs of remorse; and this was all the more the case after Maggie's visit. After that day the little man, to do him justice, was never known to hint by word or look an ill thing of his enemy's daughter.

Yet his hatred for the father had never been so uncompromising. He grew reckless in his assertions. Now he openly stated his conviction that, on the eventful night of the fight, James Moore had egged David on to murder him.

"Then why don't yo' go and tell him so, yo' muckle liar?" roared Tammas at last.

"I will!" said M'Adam. And he did.

It was on the day preceding the great summer sheep fair at Grammoch-town that he fulfilled his vow.

That is always a big field day at Kenmuir; and on this occasion James Moore and Owd Bob had been up from the rising of the sun, rounding up, cutting out, drafting. It was already noon when the flock started from the yard.

On the gate by the stile, as the party came up, sat M'Adam. "I've a word to say to you, James Moore," he announced.

"Say it then, and quick. I've no time to stand gossipin' here."

"Queer thing, James Moore, you should be the only one to escape this Killer."

"Yo' forget yoursel', M'Adam."

"Ay, there's me. But you—hoo d'yo' 'count for *your* luck?"

James Moore swung round and pointed proudly at the gray dog. "There's my luck!" he said.

M'Adam laughed unpleasantly. "And I s'pose ye're thinkin' that yer luck will win you the Cup for certain a month hence."

"I hope so!" said the Master.

"Strange if he should not after all," mused the little man.

"What d'yo' mean?" James Moore asked suspiciously.

M'Adam shrugged. "There's mony a slip 'twixt Cup and lip, that's a'. I was only thinkin' some mischance might come to him."

The Master recalled the many rumors he had heard, and the attempt on the old dog early in the year. "I canna think ony one would be coward enough to murder him," he said.

M'Adam leaned forward. "Ye'd no think ony one'd be cooard enough to set the son to murder the father. Yet someone did. He failed at me, and next, I suppose, he'll try at Wullie!" There was a vindictive ring in the thin voice. "One way or t'ither, fair or foul, Wullie or me has got to go afore Cup Day, eh, James Moore?"

The Master put his hand on the latch of the gate. "That'll do, M'Adam," he said. "Noo git off this gate, yo're trespassin' as 'tis."

He shook the gate. M'Adam tumbled off, and went sprawling into the sheep clustered below. Picking himself up, he dashed on through the flock, scattering confusion everywhere.

"Just wait till I'm thro' wi' 'em, will yo'?" shouted the Master.

It was a request which, according to the etiquette of shepherding, one man was bound to grant another. But M'Adam burst his way through regardless, dancing and gesticulating. Save for the lightning vigilance of Owd Bob, the flock must have broken.

"I think yo' might ha' waited!" remonstrated the Master.

"Noo, I've forgot somethin'!" the other cried, and back he started as he had gone.

It was more than human nature could tolerate.

"Bob, keep him off!" A flash of teeth; a blaze of gray eyes; and the old dog had leapt forward to oppose the little man's advance, while his master opened the gate and put the flock through.

"Oot o' ma path, or I'll strike!" shouted the little man in a fury, as the last sheep passed through the gate.

"I'd not," warned the Master.

"But I will!" yelled M'Adam; and, darting forward as the gate swung to, struck furiously at his opponent. He missed, and the gray dog charged at him like a mail train. Over he went like a toppled wheelbarrow, while the old dog raced at the gate, took it in his stride, and galloped up the lane after his master.

"Served yo' properly!" James Moore called back. "He'll larn ye yet it's not wise to tamper wi' a gray dog or his sheep. Not the first time he's downed ye, I'm thinkin'!"

The little man raised himself painfully to his elbow and crawled toward the gate. Another moment, and a head was poked through the bars of the gate, and a devilish little face looked through.

"Downed me, he did!" the little man cried passionately. "I owed ye baith somethin' before this, and noo, James Moore, I owe ye somethin' more. An' mind ye, Adam M'Adam pays his debts!"

IT WAS ONLY THREE SHORT WEEKS before Cup Day that one afternoon Jim Mason brought a letter to Kenmuir. It was from Long Kirby—still in retirement—begging James Moore to keep Owd

Bob safe within doors at nights till after the great event. This was how the smith concluded his ill-spelt note: *Look out for M'Adam i tell you i know hel tri at thowd un afore cup day—failin im you. so for the luv o God keep yer eyes wide.*

The Master handed the letter to the postman, who read it carefully. "I tell yo' what," said Jim at length, speaking with an earnestness that made the other stare, "I wish yo'd do what he asks yo': keep Th' Owd Un in o' nights, I mean, just for the present."

The Master laughed, tearing the letter to pieces. "Nay," said he; "M'Adam or no M'Adam, Cup or no Cup, Th' Owd Un has the run o' ma land same as he's had since a puppy. Why, Jim, the first night I shut him up, that night the Killer comes, I'll lay."

Jim turned wearily away, and the Master stood looking after him, wondering what had come of late to his former cheery friend.

Those two were not the only warnings James Moore received in the weeks immediately preceding the Trials. One of the dairy-maids gave notice, avowing that, on several occasions in the early morning, she had seen a bogie flitting down the slope to the Wastrel—a sure portent, Sam'l declared, of an approaching death in the house. And once a shearer, coming up from the village, reported having seen, in the twilight of dawn, a little ghostly figure stealing silently from tree to tree in the larch copse by the lane.

The Master, however, irritated by these alarms, dismissed the story summarily. "One thing I'm sartin o'," said he. "There's not a critter moves on Kenmuir at nights but Th' Owd Un knows it."

Yet, even as he said it, a little man, draggled, weary-eyed, smeared with dew and dust, was limping into a house barely a mile away. "Nae luck, Wullie!" he cried, throwing himself into a chair. "An' yet I'm sure o't as I am that there's a God in heaven."

WHATEVER M'ADAM'S FAULTS, there formerly had been no harder-working man in the countryside. Of late, however, he never put his hand to the plough, and with none to help him the land was left wholly untended. He sat all day in his kitchen, brooding over his wrongs and brewing vengeance.

Even the Sylvester Arms knew him no more; for he stayed where he was with his dog and his bottle. Only, when the shroud of night had come down to cover him, he slipped out on some errand and not even Red Wull accompanied him.

So the time glided on, till the Sunday before the Trials came round.

All that day M'Adam sat in his kitchen, drinking, muttering, hatching revenge. "Curse it, Wullie! The time's slippin'! Thursday next—but three days mair! and I haena the proof!"—and he rocked to and fro, biting his nails in the agony of his impotence.

At midnight he arose, a desperate plan looming through his fuddled brain.

"I swore I'd pay him, Wullie, and I will. I haena the proof, but I *know*—I *know*!" He groped his way to the mantelpiece, and took down the old blunderbuss that hung there.

"Wullie," he whispered, chuckling hideously, "you and I—" But the Tailless Tyke was not there. At nightfall he had slouched silently out of the house on business he best wot of. So his master crept out of the room alone—on tiptoe, still chuckling.

The cool night air refreshed him, and he stepped stealthily along, his quaint weapon over his shoulder, till he reached the plank bridge over the Wastrel. He crossed it safely, then he stole up the slope like a hunter stalking his prey. Arrived at the gate, he raised himself cautiously, and peered over into the moonlit yard. The little gray house slept peacefully, all unaware of the man with murder in his heart laboriously climbing the gate.

The door of the porch was wide, the chain hanging limply down, unused; and M'Adam could see within, the moon shining on the iron studs of the inner door, and the blanket of him who should have slept there, *and did not*.

"He's no there, Wullie! He's no there!"

He jumped down from the gate, and reeled recklessly across the yard. The drunken fever of anticipated victory flushed his veins.

Another moment, and he was in front of the good oak door, battering at it madly, screaming vengeance. "Where is he? What's he at? Come and tell me that, James Moore!"

The quiet farmyard, startled from its sleep, awoke in an uproar.

Cattle shifted in their stalls; horses whinnied; fowls chattered, and above the rest, loud and piercing, the shrill cry of a terrified child. Maggie, wakened from a vivid dream of David chasing the police, hurried a shawl around her, and in a minute had Wee Anne in her arms and was comforting her.

James Moore flung open a window and leaned out.

M'Adam heard the noise and glanced up. "There ye are, are ye? Curse ye for a coward! Come doon, James Moore! I daur ye to it!"

The Master thought that the little man's brain had gone. "What is't yo' want?" he asked, as calmly as he could.

"*What is't I want?* Hark to him!" screamed the madman. "He robs me o' ma Cup; he pits ma son on to murder me! Gie me back the Cup ye stole. Gie me back ma son! And there's anither thing. What's yer gray dog doin'?"

"I'll coom doon and talk things over wi' yo'," the Master said soothingly. But before he could withdraw from the window, M'Adam aimed his weapon full at his enemy's head.

The threatened man looked down the gun's great quivering mouth, wholly unmoved. "Yo' mun hold it steadier, little mon, if yo'd hit!" he said grimly. "There, I'll coom help yo'!" He withdrew slowly, wondering where the gray dog was.

In another moment he was downstairs, undoing the bolts and bars of the door. On the other side stood M'Adam, his blunderbuss at his shoulder, his finger trembling on the trigger, waiting.

"Feyther! Feyther! Git yo' back!" screamed Maggie, who saw it all from the window above the door.

Her cry was too late! The blunderbuss went off with a roar, belching out sparks and smoke. The shot peppered the door like hail.

"Aw! Oh! Ma gummy! A'm a goner! A'm shot! 'Elp! Murder!" bellowed a lusty voice from the loft on the other side of the yard.

The little man lay quite still upon the ground, with another figure standing over him. As he had stood, finger on trigger, waiting for that last bolt to be drawn, a gray form had suddenly and silently attacked him from behind, and jerked him backward to the ground. With the shock of the fall the blunderbuss had gone off.

The last bolt was thrown back with a clatter, and the Master emerged. "Yo', was't, Bob, lad?" he said. "I was wonderin' wheer yo' were. Yo' came just at the reet moment, as yo' aye do!" Then, in a loud voice, "Yo're not hurt, Sam'l Todd—I can tell that by yer noise. Coom away doon from that loft and gie me a hand."

He walked up to M'Adam, who still lay gasping on the ground. The shock of the fall and recoil of the weapon had knocked the breath out of him; beyond that he was barely hurt.

The Master stood over his fallen enemy and looked sternly down at him.

"I've put up wi' more from you, M'Adam, than I would from ony ither mon," he said. "But this is too much. If yo' were half a man I'd gie yo' the finest thrashin' iver yo' had in yer life. Why yo've got this down on me yo' ken best. I niver did yo' or ony ither mon a harm. As to the Cup, I've got it and I'm goin' to do ma best to keep it—it's for yo' to win it from me if yo' can o' Thursday. As for what yo' say o' David, yo' know it's a lie. Noo I'm goin' to lock yo' up, yo're not safe abroad. I'm thinkin' I'll ha' to hand ye o'er to the p'lice."

With Sam'l's help he half dragged, half supported the stunned little man across the yard and shoved him into a tiny room, used for the storage of coal, at the end of the farm buildings.

"Yo' think it over that side, ma lad," called the Master grimly, as he turned the key, "and I will this." And with that he retired to bed.

EARLY IN THE MORNING James Moore went to release his prisoner. But he was a minute too late. For scuttling down the slope was a little black-begrimed, tottering figure with white hair blowing in the wind. M'Adam had broken away a wooden hatchment which covered a manhole in the wall of his prison, squeezed through, and so escaped.

"Happen it's as well," thought the Master, watching the flying figure. Then, "Hi, Bob, lad!" he called; for the gray dog, ears back, tail streaming, was racing after the fugitive.

On the bridge Owd Bob halted, then turned and trotted back to his master.

"Yo' nob' but served him right, I'm thinkin'," said the Master. "Like as not he came here wi' the intent to mak' an end to yo'. Well, after Thursday, I pray God we'll ha' peace. It's gettin' above a joke." The two turned back into the yard.

CHAPTER XIV

CUP DAY BROKE CALM AND BEAUTIFUL, no cloud on the horizon, no threat of storm in the air; a fitting day on which the Shepherds' Trophy must be won outright.

And well it was so. For never since the founding of the Dale Trials had such a concourse been gathered together on the north bank of the Silver Lea. By noon the paddock at the back of the Dalesman's Daughter was packed with animated groups of farmers, sharp-faced townsmen, loud-voiced bookmakers, giggling girls, amorous boys; whilst here and there, on the outskirts of the crowd, a lonely man and wise-faced dog, come from afar to wrest his proud title from the best sheep dog in the North.

On the other side of the stream was a little group of judges, inspecting the course. The line laid out ran thus: the sheep must first be found in the big enclosure to the right of the starting flag; then up the slope and away from the spectators; round a flag and obliquely down the hill again; through a gap in the wall; along the hillside, parallel to the Silver Lea; abruptly to the left through a pair of flags—the trickiest turn of them all; then down the slope to the pen, which was set up close to the bridge over the stream.

The proceedings began with the Local Stakes. These were followed by the Open Juveniles, and it was late in the afternoon when, at length, the great event of the meeting was reached. In the paddock the clamor of the crowd increased tenfold, and the yells of the bookmakers were redoubled.

"Walk up, gen'lemen, walk up! Rasper? Yesser—twenty to one bar two! Bob? What price Bob? Even money, sir—no, not a penny longer, couldn't do it! Red Wull? 'oo says Red Wull?"

On the far side of the stream is clustered about the starting flag the finest array of sheep dogs ever seen together. There, beside the tall form of his master, stands Owd Bob o' Kenmuir. His silvery brush fans the air, and he holds his dark head high as he scans his challengers. Below him, the small, mean-looking, smooth-coated black dog is the unbeaten Pip, winner of the renowned Cambrian Stakes at Llangollen—as many think, the best of all the good dogs that have come from sheep-dotted Wales. Beside him, that handsome sable collie, with the tremendous coat and slash of white on throat and face, is the famous MacCallum More, fresh from his victory at the Highland meeting. Tupper's big blue Rasper is there; Londesley's Lassie; and many more—and not a bad dog there.

And alone, his back to the others, stands a little bowed, conspicuous figure—Adam M'Adam; while the great dog beside him, a hideous incarnation of scowling defiance, is Red Wull, the Terror o' the Border.

The babel had subsided now. The battle for the Cup had begun—little Pip leading the dance. Hucksters left their wares and bookmakers their stools to watch the struggle. Every eye was intent on the moving figures of man and dog and three sheep across the stream. One after one the competitors ran their course and penned their sheep. And all received their just meed of applause, save only Adam M'Adam's Red Wull.

Last of all, when Owd Bob trotted out to uphold his title, there went up such a shout as made Maggie's wan cheeks to blush with pleasure, and Wee Anne to scream right lustily.

His was an incomparable exhibition. Sheep should be humored rather than hurried; coaxed, rather than coerced. And that sheep dog has attained the summit of his art who subdues his own personality and leads his sheep in pretending to be led. Well might the bosoms of the Dalesmen swell with pride as they watched their favorite at his work; well might Tammas pull out that hackneyed phrase, "The brains of a mon and the way of a woman."

But of this part it is enough to say that Pip, Owd Bob, and Red Wull were selected to fight out the struggle afresh.

The course was altered and stiffened. On the far side of the stream it remained as before; but the pen was removed from its former position, carried over the bridge, up the near slope, and the hurdles put together at the very foot of the spectators.

The sheep had to be driven over the plank bridge, and the penning done beneath the very nose of the crowd. A stiff course, if ever there was one; and the time allowed, ten short minutes.

Evan Jones and little Pip led off. Those two, who had won on many a hard-fought field, worked together as they had never worked before. Round the flag, through the gap, they brought their sheep. Down between the two flags—accomplishing right well that awkward turn; and back to the bridge.

There they stopped: the sheep would not face that narrow way. Once, twice, and again, they broke; and each time the gallant little Pip, his tongue out and tail quivering, brought them back to the bridgehead. At length one faced it; then another, and—it was too late. Time was up. The judges signaled; and the Welshman called off his dog and withdrew.

Out of sight of mortal eye, Evan Jones sat down and took the small dark head between his knees—and you may be sure the dog's heart was heavy as the man's. "We did our pest, Pip," he cried brokenly, "but we're peat—the first time ever we've been!"

No TIME TO DALLY. James Moore and Owd Bob were off on their last run.

No applause this time; not a voice was raised; anxious faces; twitching fingers; the whole crowd tense as a stretched wire. A false turn, a willful sheep, a cantankerous judge, and the gray dog would be beat. And not a man there but knew it.

Yet over the stream master and dog went about their business, for all the world as though they were rounding up a flock on the Muir Pike. The old dog found his sheep in a twinkling, and a wild, scared trio they proved. Rounding the first flag, one bright-eyed wether made a dash for the open. He was quick, but the gray dog was quicker; a splendid recover.

Down the slope they came for the gap in the wall. A little below the opening, James Moore took his stand to stop and turn them; while a distance behind his sheep loitered Owd Bob, seeming to follow rather than drive, yet bringing them rapidly along, through the gap, along the hill parallel to the spectators. A wide sweep for the turn at the flags, and the sheep wheeled, dropped through them, and traveled rapidly for the bridge.

"Steady!" whispered the crowd.

"Hold 'em, for God's sake!" croaked Long Kirby, who had come back for the Trials.

The pace down the hill had grown quicker—too quick. Close on the bridge the three sheep made an effort to break. A dash—and two were checked; but the third went away like the wind, and after him Owd Bob, a gray streak against the green.

Tammas was cursing silently; Kirby was white to the lips; and in the stillness you could plainly hear the Dalesmen's sobbing breath.

"Gallop! They say he's old and slow!" muttered the Parson. "Dash! Look at that!" For the gray dog, racing like the Nor'easter over the sea, had already retrieved the fugitive.

Man and dog were coaxing the three a step at a time toward the bridge. One ventured—the others followed.

In the middle the leader stopped and tried to turn—and time was flying, flying, and the penning alone must take minutes.

"We're beat, Tammas!" groaned Sam'l. "I told yo' th' owd tyke—" Then breaking into a bellow, his honest face crimson with enthusiasm: "Coom on, Master! Good for yo', Owd Un! Yon's the style!"

For the gray dog had leapt on the back of the hindmost sheep; it had surged forward against the next, and they were over, and making up the slope amidst a thunder of applause.

At the pen it was a sight to see shepherd and dog working together. The Master, his face stern and a little whiter than its wont, casting forward with both hands, herding the sheep in; the gray dog dropping to hand; crawling and creeping, closer and closer. And the last sheep reluctantly passed through—on the stroke of time.

The mob surged forward, roaring.

"Back, please!" the stewards ordered. "M'Adam's to come!"

From the far bank the little man watched the scene. His coat and cap were off, his sleeves rolled up; and his face was twitching but set as he stood—ready.

The hubbub over the stream at length subsided. One of the judges nodded to him.

"Noo, Wullie, noo or niver! 'Scots wha hae'!" And they were off.

"Back, gentlemen! Back! He's off—he's coming! M'Adam's coming!"

The great dog was onto his sheep before the crowd knew it. Up the slope swept the three sheep, with him right on their backs, and round the first flag, already galloping. Down the hill for the gap, and M'Adam was flying ahead to turn them. But they passed him like a hurricane, and Red Wull was in front with a rush and turned them alone. Through the gap they rattled, ears back, feet twinkling like the wings of driven grouse.

"He's lost 'em! They'll break! They're away!" was the cry.

The sheep were tearing along the hillside. After them raced Red Wull. And last of all, leaping over the ground like a demoniac, making for the plank bridge, the white-haired figure of M'Adam. Red Wull was now racing parallel to the fugitives and above them. All four were traveling at a terrific rate, while the two flags were barely twenty yards in front, below the line of flight and almost parallel to it. To effect the turn a change of direction must be made almost through a right angle.

"He's beat! M'Adam's beat! Can't make it nohow!" was the roar.

From over the stream a yell—"Turn 'em, Wullie!"

At the word the great dog swerved down on the flying three. They turned, still at the gallop, like a troop of cavalry, and dropped, clean and neat, between the flags; and down to the stream they rattled, passing M'Adam on the way.

"Weel done, Wullie!" came his scream; and from the crowd went up an involuntary burst of applause.

"Ma word!"

"Did yo' see that?"

A shade later, and they must have overshot the mark; a shade sooner, and a miss. Right onto the center of the bridge the leading sheep galloped and—stopped abruptly.

In the crowd there was utter silence. The sweat was dripping off Long Kirby's face; and, at the back, a green-coated bookmaker slipped his notebook in his pocket, and glanced behind him. James Moore, standing in front of them all, was the calmest there.

Like his forerunner Red Wull leapt on the back of the hindmost sheep. But the red dog was heavy where the gray was light. The sheep staggered, slipped, and fell. Almost before it had touched the water, M'Adam, his face afire, was in the stream. In a second he had hold of the struggling creature, and, with an almost super-human effort, had half thrown, half shoved it onto the bank.

Again a tribute of admiration, led by James Moore.

The little man scrambled, panting, onto the bank and raced after sheep and dog. They were up to the pen, and the last wrestle began. The crowd craned forward to watch the uncanny little man and the huge dog, working so close below them. M'Adam tapped with his stick on the ground like a blind man, coaxing the sheep in. And the Tailless Tyke, his tongue out and flanks heaving, crept and worked up to the opening, patient as never before. They were in at last.

There was a lukewarm, halfhearted cheer: then silence. Exhausted and trembling, M'Adam leaned against the pen, one hand on it; while Red Wull, his flanks still heaving, gently licked the other. Quite close stood James Moore and the gray dog; above was the wall of people, utterly still; below, the judges comparing notes.

Then one of the judges went up to James Moore and shook his hand. Owd Bob o' Kenmuir had won the Shepherds' Trophy outright.

A second's palpitating silence; then shouts, screams, hat-tossings, back-clappings blended in a mighty din. Maggie's face flushed scarlet. Squire and parson were boisterously shaking hands. Long Kirby, who had not prayed for thirty years, ejaculated earnestly, "Thank God!" Some Dalesmen laughed and some cried; all joined in that roar of victory.

To little M'Adam, standing with his back to the crowd, that storm of cheering came as the first announcement of defeat. A wintry smile crept across his face. "We might a kent it, Wullie," he muttered, soft and low. The tension loosed, the battle lost, the little man almost broke down. There were red dabs of color in his face; his eyes were big; his lips pitifully quivering.

An old man—utterly alone—he had staked his all on a throw—and lost.

Lady Eleanour marked the forlorn little figure, standing solitary on the fringe of the uproarious mob. She noticed the expression on his face; and her tender heart went out to the lone man in his defeat. She went up to him and laid a hand upon his arm.

"Mr. M'Adam," she said timidly, "won't you come and sit down in the tent? You look *so* tired! I can find you a corner where no one shall disturb you."

The little man wrenched roughly away. The unexpected kindness was almost too much for him. A few paces off he turned again.

"It's reel kind o' yer ladyship," he said huskily; and tottered away to be alone with Red Wull.

About the victors surged a continually changing throng, shaking the man's hand, patting the dog; and now, elbowing through the press, came squire and parson.

"The first time ever the Dale Cup's been won outright!" said the parson. "And I think Kenmuir's the very fittest place for its final home, and a Gray Dog of Kenmuir for its winner."

"Oh, by the by!" burst in the squire. "I've fixed the Manor dinner for today fortnight, James. Tell Saunderson and Tupper, will you? Want all the tenants there. And tell your Maggie perhaps you'll have news for her after it—eh! eh!"—and he was gone.

Last of all, M'Adam approached James Moore. "I maun congratulate ye, Mr. Moore. Ye've beat us—you and the gentlemen—judges."

" 'Twas a close thing, M'Adam," the other answered. "An' yo' made a gran' fight. In ma life I niver saw a finer turn than yours by the two flags yonder. I hope yo' bear no malice."

"Malice! Me? Is it likely? Na, na. 'Do onto ivery man as he does onto you—and somethin' over,' that's my motter. I owe ye mony a good turn, which I'll pay ye yet. Na, na; there's nae good fechtin' again fate—and the judges. Weel, I wush you well o' yer victory. Perhaps 'twill be oor turn next."

In giving the Cup away, Lady Eleanour made a pretty speech. Yet all the while she was haunted by a white, miserable face, and was conscious of two black moving dots in the Murk Muir Pass opposite her—solitary, desolate, a contrast to the huzzahing crowd.

That is how the champion challenge Dale Cup came to wander no more; won outright by the last of the Gray Dogs of Kenmuir—Owd Bob.

Why he was the last of the Gray Dogs is now to be told.

CHAPTER XV

The sun was hiding behind the Pike. Over the lowlands the feathery breath of night hovered still, and the hillside shivered in the chillness of dawn. Down on the dewy sward beside the Stony Bottom there lay the ruffled body of a dead sheep. All about the victim the bracken was trampled down; stones displaced as though by striving feet; the whole spotted with the all-pervading red.

A score of yards up the hill, in a writhing confusion of red and gray, two dogs at death grips. While yet higher, a pack of wild-eyed hill sheep watched, fascinated, the bloody drama.

The first cold flicker of dawn stole across the green. The rising sun peered over the shoulder of the Pike. And from the sleeping dale there arose the yodeling of a man driving his cattle home.

Day was upon them.

James Moore was waked by a little whimpering cry beneath his window. He leapt out of bed and rushed to look. In a moment he was downstairs and out, examining the old dog.

"Poor old lad, yo've caught it this time!" he cried. There was a ragged tear on the dog's cheek; a gash in his throat from which the blood still welled, while head and neck were clotted with red.

Hastily the Master summoned Maggie. After her, Andrew came hurrying down. They doctored the old warrior on the table in the kitchen. Maggie tenderly washed and dressed his wounds; and he stood all the while grateful yet fidgeting, looking up into his master's face as if imploring to be gone.

"He mun a had a rare tussle wi' someone—eh, Dad?" said the girl as she worked.

"Ay; and wi' whom? 'Twasn't for nowt he got fightin', I war'nt. Nay; he's a tale to tell, has The Owd Un, and— Ah-h-h! I thowt as much. Look 'ee!" For bathing the bloody jaws, he had come upon a cluster of tawny red hairs. To but one creature could they belong—the Tailless Tyke.

"He mun a bin trespassin'!" cried Andrew.

"Ay," the Master answered. "But Th' Owd Un shall show us."

Owd Bob's hurts proved less severe than had seemed possible. And at length, the wounds washed and sewn up, he jumped down from the table and made for the door.

"Noo, owd lad, yo' may show us," said the Master, and, with Andrew, hurried after him down the hill, along the stream, and over Langholm How. And as they neared the Stony Bottom, the sheep, herding in groups, raised frightened heads to stare.

Of a sudden a cloud of poisonous flies rose up, buzzing, before them; and there in a dimple of the ground lay a murdered sheep.

At last the Black Killer had visited Kenmuir.

"I guessed as much," said the Master, standing over the mangled body. "Well, it's the worst night's work ever the Killer done. I reck'n Th' Owd Un come on him while he was at it; and then they fought. And, ma word! It mun ha' bin a fight too." For all around were traces of that terrible struggle.

James Moore walked slowly over the battlefield, stooping down as though he were gleaning. And gleaning he was.

A long time he bent so, and at length raised himself.

"The Killer has killed his last," he muttered. "Run yo' home,

Andrew, and fetch the men to carry yon away," pointing to the carcass. "And Bob, lad, yo've done your work well; go yo' home wi' him."

Then he turned and crossed the Stony Bottom, his face set like a rock. At length the proof was in his hand. As he stalked up the hill, a dark head appeared at his knee.

"Eh, Owd Un, but yo' should ha' gone wi' Andrew," the Master said. "Hooiver, as yo' are here, come along." And he strode away up the hill, with the gray dog at his heels.

As they approached the house, M'Adam was standing in the door, sucking his eternal twig. His sour face betrayed nothing but sarcasm, surprise, challenge. As man and dog passed through the gap in the hedge, he started forward. "James Moore, as I live!" he cried, as though welcoming a long-lost brother. " 'Deed and it's a weary while sin' ye've honored ma puir hoose." And, in fact, it was nigh twenty years. "Come in and let's ha' a crack. James Moore kens weel hoo welcome he aye is in ma bit biggin'."

The Master ignored the greeting, and announced shortly, "One o' ma sheep been killed back o' t' Dyke."

"The Killer?"

"The Killer."

The cordiality beaming in every wrinkle of the little man's face gave place to sorrowful sympathy. "Dear, dear! it's come to that, has it—at last?" he said gently, and his eyes wandered to the gray dog and dwelt mournfully upon him. "Man, I'm sorry—I canna tell ye I'm surprised. Masel', I kent it all alang. Weel, weel, he's lived his life, if ony dog iver did; and noo he maun gang where he's sent a many before him. Puir mon! Puir tyke!"

James Moore listened to this harangue at first puzzled. Then he caught the other's meaning, and his eyes flashed. "Ye fool, M'Adam! Did ye hear iver tell o' a sheep dog worryin' his master's sheep?"

The little man rubbed his hands softly together. "Ye're right, I never did. But your dog is not as ither dogs—'There's none like him—none,' I've heard ye say so yersel, many a time. An' I'm wi' ye. There's none like him—for devilment." His voice began to quiver and his face to blaze. "It's his cursed cunning that's deceived ivery one but me—whelp o' Satan that he is!" He shouldered up to his tall adversary. "If not him, wha else had done it?" he asked, looking up into the other's face as if daring him to speak.

The Master's shaggy eyebrows lowered. "Wha, ye ask?" he replied coldly, "and I answer you. Your Red Wull, M'Adam!"

At that all the little man's affected good humor fled. "Ye lee, mon! Ye lee!" he screamed. "I see what ye're at. Ye've found at last—blind that ye've been!—that it's yer ain hell's tyke that's the Killer; and noo ye think by yer leein' impitations to throw the blame on ma Wullie. Ye rob me o' ma Cup, ye rob me o' ma son, ye wrang me in everything; there's but ae thing left me—Wullie. And noo ye're set on takin' him awa'." He was all a-shake, and almost sobbing. "Ha' ye no wranged me enough wi'oot that?" he cried. "Ye say it's Wullie. Where's yer proof?"

The Master was now as calm as his foe was passionate. "Where?" he replied sternly. "Why, there!" holding out his right hand. "Yon's proof enough to hang a hunner'd." For lying in his broad palm was a little bundle of that damning red hair.

"Let's see it!" The little man bent to look closer. "There's for yer proof!" he cried, and spat deliberately down into the other's naked palm. Then he stood back, facing his enemy.

James Moore strode forward. It looked as if he was about to make an end of his miserable adversary, so strongly was he moved. But just at that moment, who should come stalking round the corner of the house but the Tailless Tyke? He limped sorely, his head and neck were swathed in bandages, and the little eyes gleamed out fiery and bloodshot.

At sight of the visitors, he halted abruptly. His hackles ran up, and a snarl, like a rusty brake shoved hard down, escaped from between his teeth. Then he trotted heavily forward, his head sinking low and lower as he came.

And Owd Bob, eager to take up the gage of battle, advanced, glad and gallant, to meet him. But the war-worn warriors were not to be allowed their will.

"Wullie, Wullie, wad ye!" cried the little man.

"Bob, lad, coom in!" called the other. Then he turned and looked down at the man beside him, contempt flaunting in every feature.

"Well?" he said shortly.

M'Adam's face was quite white beneath the tan, but he spoke calmly. "I'll tell ye the truth," he said slowly. "I was up there the morn"—pointing to the window above—"and I see Wullie crouchin' down alongside the Stony Bottom. In a minnit I see anither dog squatterin' alang on your side the Bottom. He creeps up to the sheep on th' hillside, chases 'em, and doons one. The sun was risen by then, and I see the dog clear as I see you noo. It was that dog there—I swear it!" And he pointed an accusing finger at Owd Bob.

"Noo, Wullie! thinks I. And afore ye could clap yer hands, Wullie was over the Bottom and onto him as he gorged—the bloody-minded murderer! They fought and fought. I watched till I could watch nae langer, and, all in a sweat, I rin doon the stairs and oot. When I got there, there was yer tyke makin' fu' split for Kenmuir, and Wullie comin' up the hill to me. It's God's truth, James Moore. Tak' him hame, and let his dinner be an ounce o' lead. 'Twill be the best day's work iver ye done."

The little man spoke with an earnestness that might have convinced one who knew him less well. But the Master only looked down on him with a great scorn. "It's Monday today," he said coldly. "I gie yo' till Saturday. If yo've not done your duty by then—and well you know what 'tis—I shall come do it for ye. I'll remind ye agin o' Thursday—yo'll be at the Manor dinner, I suppose. I'm sorry for ye, but I've ma duty to do—so've you. Till Saturday I shall breathe no word to ony soul o' this business, so that if you put him oot o' the way wi'oot bother, no one need iver know as hoo Adam M'Adam's Red Wull was the Black Killer."

He turned away. But the little man sprang after him.

"Look ye here, James Moore!" he cried. "Ye're big, I'm sma'; ye've ivery one to your back, I've niver a one; you tell your story, and they'll believe ye—for you gae to church; I'll tell mine, and they'll think I lie—for I dinna. But if iver agin I catch ye on ma land I'll no spare ye. You ken best if I'm in earnest or no."

ON THURSDAY MORNING, James Moore and Andrew came down arrayed in all their best. It was the day of the squire's annual dinner to his tenants. The sun had reached its highest when the two wayfarers passed through the gray portals of the Manor.

In the stately entrance hall were gathered now the many tenants of the wide March Mere Estate. Weatherbeaten, rent-paying sons of the soil; most of them native born, many of them like James Moore, whose fathers had for generations owned and farmed the land they now leased at the hands of the Sylvesters—there in the old hall they were assembled, a mighty host. And apart from the others, a little lost figure, stood M'Adam.

The door at the far end of the hall opened and the squire entered, beaming on everyone. "Here you are—eh, eh! How are you all? Glad to see ye! Bringin' a friend with me—eh, eh!" and he stood aside to let by his agent, Parson Leggy, and last of all, shy and blushing, a fair-haired young giant.

"If it bain't David!" was the cry. "Eh, lad, we's fain to see yo'! And yo'm lookin' hearty, surely!" And they thronged about the boy, shaking him by the hand and asking him his story.

'Twas but a simple tale. After his flight on the eventful night he had gone south, drovering. He had written to Maggie, and been hurt to receive no reply. Too proud to write again, he had remained ignorant of his father's recovery, neither caring nor daring to return. Then, by mere chance, he had met the squire at the York cattle show; and that kind man, who knew his story, had eased his fears and obtained from him a promise to return as soon as the term of his engagement had expired. And there he was.

Of all the Dalesmen present, only one seemed unmoved, and that was M'Adam. When first David had entered he had started forward, a flush of color warming his thin cheeks; but no one had noticed his emotion; and now, back again in his place, he watched the scene, a sour smile playing about his lips.

Then the gong rang out, and the squire led the way into the

great dining hall. At the one end of the long table, heavy with all the solid delicacies of such a feast, he took his seat with the Master of Kenmuir upon his right. At the other end was Parson Leggy. At first the stalwart Dalesmen talked but little, awed like children. But the squire's ringing laugh and the parson's cheery tones soon put them at their ease, and a babel of voices rose. Only M'Adam sat silent, and his hand crept oftener to his glass than his plate.

Toward the end of the meal there was loud tapping on the table, calls for silence, and men pushed back their chairs. The squire rose to make his annual speech. He started by telling them how glad he was to see them there. He made an allusion to Owd Bob and the Shepherds' Trophy which was heartily applauded. He touched on the Black Killer, and said he had a remedy to propose: that Th' Owd Un should be set upon the criminal's track—a suggestion which was received with enthusiasm, while M'Adam's cackling laugh could be heard high above the rest.

From that he dwelt at length upon the existing conditions of agriculture, and thanked God that there had never been any friction between him and his people (cheers); and he wished to give them a toast, "The Queen! God bless her!" and—wait a minute!—to couple with her Majesty's name—he was sure that gracious lady would wish it—that of "Owd Bob o' Kenmuir!" Then he sat down abruptly amid thundering applause.

The toasts duly honored, James Moore, as Master of Kenmuir, rose to answer. He began by saying that he spoke "as representing all the tenants"—but he was interrupted.

"Na," came a shrill voice from halfway down the table. "Ye'll except me, James Moore. I'd as soon be represented by Judas!"

There were cries of "Hold ye gab, little mon!" and the squire's voice, "That'll do, Mr. M'Adam!"

The little man restrained his tongue, but his eyes gleamed like a ferret's; and the Master continued his speech. All the while M'Adam kept up a low-voiced, running commentary. At length, half rising from his chair, he cried, "Sit doon, James Moore! Hoo daur ye stan' there like an honest man. Sit doon, I say, or"—threateningly—"wad ye hae me come to ye?"

At that the squire's voice rang out sharp and stern. "Keep silence and sit down, sir! D'you hear me? If I have to speak to you again it will be to order you to leave the room."

M'Adam obeyed, sullen and vengeful, like a beaten cat.

The Master concluded his speech by calling on all present to give three cheers for the squire and her ladyship. The call was responded to enthusiastically, every man standing. Just as the noise was at its zenith, Lady Eleanour herself glided into the gallery at the end of the hall; whereat the cheering became deafening.

Slowly the clamor subsided. One by one the tenants sat down. At length there was left standing one solitary figure—M'Adam. His face was set, and he gripped the chair in front of him with thin, nervous hands. "Mr. Sylvester," he began in a low yet clear voice, "I'll tak' the liberty, wi' yer permission, to say a word. It's maybe the last time I'll be wi' ye, so I hope ye'll listen to me."

The Dalesmen looked surprised, and the squire uneasy. Nevertheless he nodded assent.

The little man straightened. All the passion had fled from his face, and left behind was a strange, ennobling earnestness.

"Gentlemen," he began, "I've bin amang ye noo a score years, and I can truly say there's not a man in this room I can ca' 'Friend.' Not one as'd back me like a comrade if a trouble came upon me." There was no rebuke in the grave voice—it merely stated a hard fact. "There's I doot no one amang ye but has someone—friend or blood—wham he can turn to when things are sair wi' him. I've no one.

"I bear alane my lade o' care—

alane wi' Wullie, who stands to me, blaw or snaw, rain or shine. And whiles I'm feared he'll be took from me." He spoke this last half to himself, a grieved, puzzled expression on his face, as though lately he had dreamed some ill dream.

"Besides Wullie, I've no friend on God's earth. And, mind ye, a bad man aften mak's a good friend—but ye've never given me the chance. I dinna blame ye. There's somethin' bred in me, it seems, as sets ivery one agin me. It's the same wi' Wullie and the

tykes—they're doon on him same as men are on me. I suppose
we was made so. Sin' I was a lad it's aye bin the same.

"In ma life I've had three friends. Ma mither—and she went;
then ma wife"—he gave a great swallow—"and she's awa'; and
I may say they're the only two human bein's as ha' lived on God's
earth in ma time that iver tried to bear wi' me—and Wullie. A
man's mither—a man's wife—a man's dog! It's aften a' he has
in this world; and the more he prizes them the more like they are
to be took from him." The earnest voice shook, and the dim eyes
puckered and filled. "Sin' I've bin amang ye—twenty-odd years—
can any man here mind speakin' any word that wasna ill to me?"
He paused; there was no reply.

"Still, her ladyship spoke kindly to me, God bless her!" He
glanced up into the gallery.

"Weel, we'll be gaein' in a wee while noo, Wullie and me, alane
and togither, as we've aye done. And when I'm gone what'll ye say
o' me? 'He was a drunkard.' I am. 'He was a sinner.' I am. 'He was
everything he shouldna be.' I am. 'We're glad he's gone.' That's
what ye'll say o' me. And it's but ma deserts."

The gentle, condemning voice ceased, and began again. "That's
what I am. If things had been differ', perhaps I'd ha' bin differ'.
D'ye ken Robbie Burns? That's a man I've read, and read, and read.
D'ye ken why I love him as some o' you do yer Bibles? Because
there's a humanity about him. A weak man hissel', aye slippin',
slippin', slippin', and tryin' to hold up; sorrowin' ae minute, sin-
nin' the next; doin' ill deeds and wishin' 'em undone—just a plain
human man, a sinner. And that's why I'm thinkin' he's tender for
us as is like him.. *He understood.* It's what he wrote—after ain o' his
tumbles, I'm thinkin'—that I was goin' to tell ye:

> *"Then gently scan yer brother man,*
> *Still gentler sister woman,*
> *Though they may gang a kennin' wrang,*
> *To step aside is human—*

the doctrine o' Charity. Gie him his chance, says Robbie, though he
be a sinner; and I'm wi' him. Ye see me here—a bad man wi' still a

streak o' good in him. If I'd had ma chance, perhaps 'twad be—a good man wi' just a spice o' the devil in him. A' the differ' betune what is and what might ha' bin."

HE SAT DOWN. In the great hall there was silence, save for a tiny sound from the gallery like a sob suppressed.

The squire rose hurriedly and left the room. After him, one by one, trailed the tenants. At length, two only remained—M'Adam and Parson Leggy, stern, upright, motionless. The parson rose, and strode across the silent hall.

"M'Adam," he said, "I've listened to what you've said, as I think we all have, with a sore heart. You hit hard—but I think you were right. I've not done my duty by you as I ought—it's now my duty as God's minister to be the first to say I'm sorry." And it was evident from his face what an effort the words cost him.

It was the old M'Adam who looked up. The thin lips were curled; a grin was crawling across the mocking face. "Mr. Hornbut, I believe ye thocht me in earnest, 'deed and I do!" He leaned back in his chair and laughed softly. "Ye swallered it all down like best butter." Then, stretching forward, "Mr. Hornbut, I was playin' wi' ye."

The parson's face, as he listened, was ugly to watch. He shot out a hand to grab the scoffer by his coat; then dropped it again and turned abruptly away. As he passed through the door a little sneering voice called after him:

"Mr. Hornbut, I ask ye hoo you, a minister, can reconcile it to yer conscience to think—though it be but for a minute—that there can be ony good in a man and him no churchgoer?" He sniggered to himself, and his hand crept to a half-emptied wine decanter.

AN HOUR LATER, JAMES MOORE, his business with the squire completed, passed through the hall on his way out. Its only occupant was now M'Adam, and the Master walked straight up to his enemy.

"M'Adam," he said gruffly, holding out a sinewy hand, "I'd like to say —"

The little man knocked aside the token of friendship.

"Na, na. No cant, if ye please, James Moore. I ken you and you ken me, and all the whitewash i' th' warld'll no deceive us."

The Master turned away. But M'Adam pursued him. "I was nigh forgettin'," he said. "I've a surprise for ye. But I hear it's yer birthday on Sunday, and I'll keep it till then—he! he!"

"Ye'll see me before Sunday, M'Adam," the other answered. "On Saturday I'm comin' to see if yo've done yer duty."

At the door of the hall the Master met David. "Noo, lad, yo're comin' along wi' Andrew and me," he said; "Maggie'll niver forgie us if we dinna bring yo' home wi' us."

"Thank you kindly, Mr. Moore," the boy replied. "I've to see squire first; and then yo' may be sure I'll be after you."

The Master faltered a moment. "David, ha'n' yo' spoke to yer father yet?" he asked in low voice. "Yo' should, lad."

The boy made a gesture of dissent. "I canna," he said.

"I would, lad," the other advised. "An' yo' don't yo' may be sorry after."

As he turned away he heard the boy's steps crossing the hall; then a thin, mock-cordial voice in the emptiness.

IT HAD BEEN LONG DARK when the Master and Andrew emerged from the Dalesman's Daughter and plunged out into the night. As they crossed the Silver Lea and trudged over that familiar ground, where a fortnight since had been fought out the battle of the Cup, the wind fluttered past them in spasmodic gasps.

"There's trouble in the wind," said the Master.

"Ay," answered his laconic son.

All day there had been no breath of air, and the sky dangerously blue. But now a leaden blackness was surging up from the horizon, smothering the starlit night; and small dark clouds were driving tempestuously forward—the vanguard of the storm. In the distance was a low rumbling like heavy tumbrils on the floor of heaven. All about, the wind sounded hollow like a mighty scythe on corn. There was now no glimmer of light; and as they ascended the Pass they felt blindly along the rock face.

The wind rose and roared past them up the rocky track. And the

water gates of heaven were flung wide. Wet and weary, they battled on. Once they halted for a moment, finding a miserable shelter
in a crevice of the rock. "It's a Black Killer's night," panted the
Master. "I reck'n he's oot."

"Ay," the boy gasped, "reck'n he is."

Up and up they climbed, blind and buffeted. The eternal thunder
of the rain was all about them, the clamor of the gale above. Once,
in a lull in the storm, the Master turned and peered back into the
blackness along the path they had come.

"I thowt I heard a step!" he cried. But nothing could he see.

Then the wind leaped to life again, drowning all sound with its
hurricane voice; and they bent to their task. Nearing the summit,
the Master turned once more. "There it was again!" he called; but
his words were swept away on the storm.

At length, nigh spent, they topped the last pitch of the Pass, and
emerged into the Devil's Bowl. There they flung themselves onto
the soaking ground to draw breath. Behind them the wind rushed
with a sullen roar up the funnel of the Pass.

As they lay there, still panting, the moon gleamed down in
momentary graciousness. In front, through the lashing rain, they
could discern the hillocks that squat, haglike, round the Devil's
Bowl; and lying in its bosom, its white waters, usually so still,
ploughed now into a thousand furrows, the Lone Tarn.

Of a sudden the Master reared himself onto his arms, and stayed
motionless a while. Then he dropped as though dead, forcing down
Andrew with an iron hand.

"Lad, did'st see?" he whispered.

"Nay; what was't?" the boy replied, roused by his father's tone.
"There!"

And as the Master pointed forward, Andrew saw indeed.

There, in front, by the fretting waters of the Tarn, packed in a
solid phalanx, with every head turned in the same direction, was a
flock of sheep, staring with horror-bulging eyes. Beyond them, not
fifty yards away, crouched a humpbacked boulder, casting a long,
misshapen shadow in the moonlight. And beneath it were two
black objects, one still struggling feebly.

"The Killer!" gasped the boy, all ablaze with excitement.

Above them a huddle of clouds flung in furious rout across the night, and the moon was veiled.

"Follow, lad!" ordered the Master, and, one behind the other, they began to crawl silently over the sodden ground, lying prone during the blinks of moon, stealing forward in the dark; till, at length, the swish of the rain on the waters of the Tarn, and the sobbing of the flock in front, warned them they were near. And still the gracious moon hid their approach, and the drunken wind drowned with its revelry the sound of their coming.

So they stole on, on hands and knees, with hearts aghast and fluttering breath; until, in a lull of wind, they could hear, right before them, the smack of lips, chewing a bloody meal.

"Say thy prayers, Red Wull. Thy last minute's come!" muttered the Master, rising to his knees. Then, in Andrew's ear, "When I rush, lad, follow!" For he thought, when the moon came out, to jump in on the great dog, and, surprising him as he lay gorged and unsuspicious, to deal him one terrible swashing blow.

The moon flung off its veil of cloud. White and cold, it stared down into the Devil's Bowl; on murderer and murdered.

Within a hand's cast of the avengers humped the black boulder. On the border of its shadow lay a dead sheep; and standing beside the body, his coat all ruffled by the hand of the storm—Owd Bob—Owd Bob o' Kenmuir.

Then the light went in, and darkness covered the land.

CHAPTER XVII

It was Owd Bob. There could be no mistaking. In the wide world there was but one Owd Bob o' Kenmuir. The silver moon gleamed down on the dark head and rough gray coat, and lit the white escutcheon on his chest.

And in the darkness James Moore was lying with his face pressed downward that he might not see.

Then the darkness lifted a moment, and he stole a furtive glance at the scene in front. It was no dream; clear and cruel in the moonlight the humpbacked boulder; the dead sheep; and that gray figure, beautiful, motionless, damned for all eternity.

The Master turned his face and looked at Andrew, a dumb, pitiful entreaty in his eyes; but in the boy's white, horror-stricken countenance was no comfort. Then his head lolled down again, and the strong man was whimpering.

"He! he! he! 'Scuse ma laffin', Mr. Moore—he! he! he!"

A little man, all wet and shrunk, sat hunching on a mound above them, rocking to and fro in the agony of his merriment.

"Ye raskil—he! he! Ye rogue—he! he!" and he shook his fist waggishly at the motionless gray dog.

The man below him rose heavily to his feet, and tumbled toward the mocker as though in blind delirium, moaning still as he went. And there was that on his face which no man can mistake. Boy that he was, Andrew knew it.

"Feyther! Feyther! Do'ee not!" he pleaded, running after his father and laying impotent hands on him.

But the strong man shook him off like a fly, and rolled on with that awful expression plain to see in the moonlight.

In front the little man squatted in the rain and took no thought to flee. "Come on, James Moore! Come on!" he laughed, malignant joy in his voice; and something gleamed bright in his right hand, and was hid again. "I've bin waitin' this a weary while noo."

Of a sudden, there sounded the splash of a man's foot, falling heavily behind; a hand like a falling tree smote the Master on the shoulder; and a voice roared above the noise of the storm:

"Mr. Moore! Look, man! Look!"

The Master tried to shake off that detaining grasp; but it pinned him where he was, immovable.

"Look, I tell yo'!" cried that great voice again.

With dull, uncomprehending gaze James Moore stared as bidden. There was the gray dog in the moonlight, heedless still of any witnesses; there the murdered sheep, lying within and without that distorted shade; and there the humpbacked boulder.

He stared into the shadow, and still stared. Then he started as

though struck. The shadow of the boulder had moved! Ay, ay, ay;
he was sure of it—a huge dim outline as of a lion *couchant*, in the
very thickest of the blackness. Clearer every moment grew that
crouching figure; till at length they plainly could discern the line of
arching loins, the massive, wagging head. No mistake this time.
There he lay in the deepest black, reveling in his horrid debauch—
the Black Killer.

They watched him at his feast, and the moon caught his wicked,
rolling eye and the red shreds of flesh dripping from his jaw. While
all the time the gray dog stood before him as though carved in
stone.

At last, as the murderer turned his head from side to side, he
saw that still figure. He leaped back, dismayed. Then with a roar
he was up and across his victim with fangs bared, his coat standing
erect in wet, rigid furrows from topknot to tail.

So the two stood, face to face, with perhaps a yard of rain-
pierced air between them. An age, it seemed, they waited so. Then
a voice, clear yet low and far away, broke the silence.

"Eh, Wullie!" it said.

There was no anger in the tones, only an incomparable reproach; the sound of the cracking of a man's heart.

At the call the great dog leapt round. He saw the small, familiar
figure, clear-cut against the tumbling sky; and for the only time
in his life Red Wull was afraid. His blood foe was forgotten; the
dead sheep was forgotten; everything was sunk in the agony of that
moment. He cowered upon the ground, and a cry like that of a
lost soul was wrung from him.

On the mound above stood his master. The little man's white
hair was bared to the night wind; the rain trickled down his face;
his hands were folded behind his back. And there was such an
expression on his face as I cannot describe.

"Wullie, Wullie, to me!" he cried at length; and his voice
sounded weak and far, like a distant memory.

At that, the huge brute came crawling toward him on his belly,
whimpering as he came, very pitiful in his distress. For his pain,
insufferable, was that this, his friend and father, who had trusted

him, should have found him in his sin. So he crept up to his master's feet; and the little man never moved. "Wullie!" he said very gently. "They've aye bin agin me and you! A man's mither—a man's wife—a man's dog! They're all I've iver had, and noo ain o' they has turned agin me! Indeed I am alone!"

At that the great dog raised himself, and placing his forepaws on his master's chest tenderly, lest he should hurt him who was already hurt past healing, stood towering above him; while the little man laid his two cold hands on the dog's shoulders.

So they stood, looking at one another, like a man and his love.

At M'Adam's words, Owd Bob looked up, and for the first time saw his master.

He seemed in nowise startled, but trotted over to him. There was nothing fearful in his carriage, no haunting blood guiltiness in the true gray eyes. Yet his tail was low, and, as he stopped at his master's feet, he was quivering. For weeks he had tracked the Killer; yet always had lost him on the Marches. Now, at last, he had run him to ground.

"I thowt it had bin yo', lad," the Master whispered, his hand on the dark head at his knee—"I thowt it had bin yo'!"

Rooted to the ground, the three watched the scene between M'Adam and his Wull. The Master was trembling; Andrew crying; and David turned his back. At length, silent, they moved away.

"Had I—should I go to him?" asked David hoarsely, nodding toward his father.

"Nay, nay, lad," the Master replied. "Yon's not a matter for a mon's friends."

So they marched out of the Devil's Bowl, and left those two alone together.

A little later, as they tramped along, James Moore heard staggering footsteps behind. He stopped, and the other two went on.

"Man," a voice whispered, and a face, white and pitiful, looked into his—"Man, ye'll no tell them a'? I'd no like 'em to ken 'twas ma Wullie."

"You may trust me!" the other answered thickly.

The little man stretched out a palsied hand. "Gie us yer hand on't. And G-God bless ye, James Moore!"

So these two shook hands in the moonlight, with none to witness it but the God who made them.

And that is why the mystery of the Black Killer is yet unsolved in the Daleland. Only one other knows—knows now which of those two he saw upon a summer night was guilty. And Postie Jim tells no man.

ON THE FOLLOWING MORNING there was a sheep auction at the Dalesman's Daughter.

Early as many of the farmers arrived, there was one earlier. Tupper, the first man to enter the sand-floored parlor, found M'Adam before him. He was sitting a little forward in his chair; his thin hands rested on his knees; and on his face was a gentle, dreamy expression.

"When I coom doon this mornin'," whispered Teddy Bolstock, "I found 'im sittin' just so. And he's nor moved nor spoke since."

"Where's th' Terror, then?" asked Tupper, awed somehow into like hushed tones.

"In t' paddock at back," Teddy answered, "marchin' hoop and doon for a' the world like a sentry-soger."

Then Londesley entered, and after him Rob Saunderson, Jim Mason, and others, each with his dog. Each man remarked the little lone figure for once without its huge attendant genius. And all the time M'Adam sat as though he neither heard nor saw, lost in some sweet, sad dream.

After the first glance, however, the farmers paid him little heed, clustering round the publican at the farther end of the room to hear the latest story of Owd Bob. It appeared that, a week previously, James Moore with a pack of sheep had met the new Grammoch-town butcher at the Dalesman's Daughter. A bargain concluded, the butcher started with the flock for home. As he had no dog, the Master offered him Th' Owd Un. "And he'll pick me up i' th' town tomorrow," said he.

Now the butcher was a stranger in the land. Of course he had heard of Owd Bob o' Kenmuir, yet it never struck him that this handsome creature, who handled sheep as he had never seen them handled, was that hero—"the best sheep dog in the North."

Certain it is that by the time the flock was penned behind the shop, he coveted the dog—ay, would even offer ten pounds for him! Forthwith the butcher locked him up in an outhouse—summit of indignity; resolving to make his offer on the morrow.

When the morrow came he found no dog in the outhouse, and, worse, no sheep in the pen. A sprung board showed the way of escape of the one, and a displaced hurdle that of the other. And as he was making the discovery, a gray dog and a flock of sheep, traveling along the road toward the Dalesman's Daughter, met the Master.

From the first, Owd Bob had mistrusted the man. His master's sheep were not for such a rogue; and he worked his own way out and took the sheep with him. The story was told to a running chorus of—"Ma word! Good, Owd Un!—Ho! ho! Did he thot?"

Of them all, only M'Adam sat silent.

Rob Saunderson remarked it. "And what d'yo' think o' that, Mr. M'Adam, for a wunnerfu' story of a wunnerfu' tyke?" he asked.

"It's a gude tale, a vera gude tale," the little man answered dreamily. "And James Moore didna invent it; he had it from the Christmas number o' the *Flock-keeper*." (On the following Sunday, old Rob, from sheer curiosity, reached down from his shelf the specified number of the paper. To his amazement he found the little man was right. There was the story almost identically. None the less it is also true of Owd Bob o' Kenmuir.)

"Ay, ay," the little man continued, "and in a day or twa James Moore'll ha' a better tale to tell ye—a mair laffable. And yet—ay—no—I'll no believe it! I niver loved James Moore, but I think, as Mr. Hornbut aince said, he'd rather die than lie. Owd Bob o' Kenmuir!" he continued in a whisper. "Up till the end I canna shake him aff. I half think that where I'm gaein' to there'll be gray dogs sneakin' around me in the twilight."

Now Teddy Bolstock lifted his hand for silence.

"D'yo hear thot?— Thunder!"

They listened; and from without came a gurgling, jarring roar, horrible to hear.

"No thunder thot! More like the Lea in flood. And yet—"

M'Adam had moved at last. He was on his feet, staring about him, wild-eyed. "Where's yer dogs?" he almost screamed.

"Here's ma— Nay, by thunder! He's not!" was the astonished cry.

No man had noticed that his dog had risen from his side; no one had noticed a file of shaggy figures creeping out of the room.

"I tell ye it's the tykes! They're on ma Wullie—fifty to one they're on him! My God! My God! And me not there!"

At that moment Bessie Bolstock rushed in, white-faced. "Hi! Feyther! Mr. Saunderson! All o' you! T' tykes fightin' mad! Hark!"

Each man seized his stick and rushed for the door; and M'Adam led them all.

A RARE THING IT WAS for M'Adam and Red Wull to be apart. So rare, that others besides the men in that little taproom noticed it. Saunderson's old Shep, for one, walked quietly to the back door and looked out. There on the slope below him he saw what he sought, stalking up and down. And as the old dog watched, his tail was gently swaying as though he were well pleased.

He walked back into the taproom. From dog to dog he went, stopping at each; then he made for the door again. One by one the others rose and trailed out after him: big blue Rasper, Londesley's Lassie, Grip and Grapple, the publican's bull terriers; Jim Mason's Gyp, foolish and flirting even now; and others there were.

Out of the house they pattered, silent and unseen, with murder in their hearts. At last they had found their enemy alone. And slowly, in a black cloud, they dropped down the slope upon him.

And he saw them coming, knew their errand—as who should better than the Terror of the Border?—and was glad. Death it might be, and such an one as he would wish to die—at least distraction from that long-drawn, haunting pain. He looked grimly at the approaching crowd, and saw there was not one there but he had humbled in his time. He awaited them, his great head high, daring them to come on.

And on they came, slow, certain, murderous, opening out to cut him off on every side. There was no need. He never thought to move.

They were up to him now; walking round him on their toes, their backs a little humped, heads averted; yet eyeing him askance. And he remained stock-still, nor looked at them. His chin was cocked, and his muzzle wrinkled in a dreadful grin. As he stood there, shivering a little, his eyes rolling back, every bristle on end, he looked a devil indeed.

Alongside him crop-eared Grip and Grapple looked up at the line above them where hairy neck and shoulder joined. Behind was big Rasper, and close to him Lassie. Of the others, each had marked his place, each taken up his post. Last of all, old Shep took his stand full in front of his enemy, their shoulders almost rubbing, head past head.

So the two stood a moment, as though they were whispering; then like lightning each struck. Rearing high, they wrestled with striving paws and the expression of fiends incarnate. Down they went, Shep underneath, and the great dog with a dozen of these wolves of hell upon him.

And there, where a fortnight before he had fought and lost the battle of the Cup, Red Wull now battled for his life. The hate of years came bubbling forth, and he went in to fight, reveling in the red lust of killing. His one chance lay in quickness, to prevent the swarming crew getting their hold till he had diminished their numbers.

Then it was a sight to see the great brute, fighting with feet and body and teeth—every inch of him at war. More than once he broke right through the mob, only to turn again and face it. No flight for him, nor thought of it. Up and down the slope the dark mass tossed, worrying at that great centerpiece. Up and down, roaming wide, leaving everywhere a trail of red.

Gyp he had pinned and hurled over his shoulder. Grip followed; he shook her till she rattled, then flung her afar; and she fell with a horrid thud, not to rise. While Grapple, the death to avenge, hung tighter.

So they fought on. And ever and anon a great figure rose up from the heaving inferno all around; rearing to his full height, his head ragged and bleeding. Then down he would go again, smothered beneath the weight of numbers, yet struggled up again, his little tail like the gallant stump of a flagstaff shot away.

Long odds! It could not last. And down he went at length, silent still—never a cry should they wring from him in his agony: Rasper beneath him now; three at his throat; two at his ears; a crowd on flanks and body. The Terror of the Border was down at last!

"Wullie, ma Wullie!" screamed M'Adam, bounding down the slope a crook's length in front of the rest. "Wullie! Wullie! To me!"

At the shrill cry the huddle below heaved and swayed and dragged to and fro, and a great tossing head, bloody past recognition, flung out from the ruck. One quick glance he shot at the little flying form in front; then with a roar like a waterfall plunged toward it, shaking off the bloody leeches as he went.

"Wullie! I'm wi' ye!" cried that little voice, now so near.

Through—through—through! An incomparable effort and his last. They hung to his throat, they clung to his muzzle, they were round and about him. And down he went again, shooting up at his master one quick, beseeching glance as the sea of blood closed over him—tearing, like foxhounds at the kill.

THEY LEFT THE DEAD and pulled away the living. And it was no light task, for the pack were mad for blood.

At the bottom of the heap was old Shep, stone-dead. And as Saunderson pulled the body out, his face was working; for no man can lose the friend of a dozen years and remain unmoved.

Big Rasper was gasping out his life. Two more came crawling out to find a quiet spot where they might lay them down to die. Before the night had fallen another had gone to his account. While not a dog who fought upon that day but carried the scars of it with him to his grave.

The Terror o' th' Border, terrible in his life, like Samson, was yet more terrible in his dying.

At the sight of that which once had been his Red Wull the little man neither raved nor swore; it was past that for him. He sat down, heedless of the soaking ground, and took the mangled head in his lap very tenderly.

"They've done ye at last, Wullie," he said quietly, unalterably convinced that the attack had been organized while he was detained in the taproom.

On hearing the loved voice, the dog gave one weary wag of his stump tail. And with that the Tailless Tyke, Adam M'Adam's Red Wull, the Black Killer, went to his long home.

ONE BY ONE THE DALESMEN took away their dead, and the little man was left alone with the body of his last friend.

Dry-eyed he sat there, nursing the dead dog's head; hour after hour—alone—crooning to himself:

> "Monie a sair daurk we twa hae wrought,
> An' wi' the weary warl' fought!
> An' monie an anxious day I thought
> We wad be beat.

An' noo we are, Wullie—noo we are!"

He sat there, muttering, and stroking the poor head upon his lap, bending over it, like a mother over a sick child. And no man approached him.

It was long past noon when at length he rose, laying the dog's head reverently down, and tottered away toward that bridge which once the dead thing on the slope had held against a thousand.

He crossed it and turned; there was a look upon his face, half hopeful, half fearful, very piteous to see.

"Wullie, Wullie, to me!" he cried.

A while he waited in vain. Then he recrossed the bridge, walking blindly like a sobbing child, and yet dry-eyed. Over the dead body he bent, slung it on his back, and staggered away. Limp and hideous, the carcass hung down from the little man's shoulders. The huge head, with wide eyes and lolling tongue, jolted and swagged with the motion, seeming to grin defiance at the world it had left, as the two passed out of its ken.

IN THE DEVIL'S BOWL, NEXT DAY, they found the pair: Adam M'Adam and his Red Wull, face-to-face; dead, not divided; each, save for the other, alone. M'Adam, lying on his back, his dim dead eyes staring up at the heaven, still clasped a crumpled photograph; the weary body at rest at last, the mocking face—mocking no longer—alight with a transfiguring happiness.

POSTSCRIPT

ADAM M'ADAM AND HIS RED WULL lie buried together, one just within, the other just without, the consecrated pale.

The only mourners at the funeral were David, James Moore, Maggie, and a gray dog peering through the lych-gate.

During the service Lady Eleanour joined the little group about the grave to pay a last tribute to the dead. And there was more than usual solemnity in the parson's voice as he intoned the anthem.

WHEN YOU WANDER in the gray hill country of the North, in the loneliest corner of that lonely land you may chance upon a low farmhouse, lying in the shadow of the Muir Pike.

Entering, a tall old man comes out to greet you—the Master of Kenmuir. His shoulders are bent now; the hair is frosted; but the blue-gray eyes look you as proudly in the face as of yore.

And while food is being prepared for you, you will notice on the mantelpiece, standing solitary, a massive silver cup, dented. That is the world-known Shepherds' Trophy, won outright, as the old man will tell you, by Owd Bob, last and best of the Gray Dogs of Kenmuir.

When at length you take your leave, the old man accompanies you to the top of the slope to point you your way. "Yo' cross the stream; over Langholm How, yonder; past the Bottom; and oop th' hill on far side. Yo'll come on th' house o' top. And happen yo'll meet Th' Owd Un on the road. Good-day to you, sir, good-day."

So you go as he has bidden you. On the way you come upon

an old gray dog, trotting soberly along. Th' Owd Un, indeed, seems to spend the evening of his life going thus between Kenmuir and the Grange. The black muzzle is almost white now; the gait is stiff and slow; venerable, indeed, is he of whom men still talk as the best sheep dog in the North.

As he passes, he pauses to scan you. The noble head is high, and one foot raised; and you look into two big gray eyes such as you have never seen before—soft, a little dim, and infinitely sad.

That is Owd Bob o' Kenmuir, of whom the tales are many as the flowers on the May. With him dies the last of the immortal line of the Gray Dogs of Kenmuir.

You travel on up the hill, something pensive, and knock at the door of the house on the top.

A woman opens to you. And nestling in her arms is a little boy with golden hair and happy face.

You ask the child his name. He kicks and crows, and looks up at his mother; and in the end lisps roguishly, "Adum Mataddum."

OLIVER TWIST

Oliver Twist

A condensation of the book by
CHARLES DICKENS

George Cruikshank

With the celebrated illustrations of
George Cruikshank

In *Oliver Twist* Charles Dickens produced one of the most color-ful and fantastic galleries of rogues in all of literature. Here are the villainous Fagin and his gang of adolescent thieves, the murderous Bill Sykes, the shadowy and evil Monks, all painted against a backdrop of nineteenth-century London—its slums, its murky back alleys, its dens of crime, its teeming underworld where innumerable orphans wandered, homeless and hungry, to become the exploited victims of unscrupulous men.

Dickens wrote of *Oliver Twist* that his aim was to show these people as they really were, "forever skulking uneasily through the dirtiest paths of life, with the great black ghastly gallows closing up their prospect, turn them where they might." To do this, he felt, would be a service to society.

No one could have been better qualified to write the story of the waif Oliver. At the tender age of twelve, with his father in Marshalsea debtor's prison, the young Charles went to work in a factory, labeling blacking bottles for a few shillings a week. By the age of fifteen, however, he had succeeded in breaking out of this miserable way of life to become a solicitor's clerk. His work brought him into the courts and soon he turned to court reporting. From this he passed eventually to reporting the proceedings in the House of Commons for a number of news-papers.

His first published original writing was a series of sketches that appeared under the name "Boz." They were illustrated by Cruikshank, whose famous illustrations for *Oliver Twist* appear in these pages. But it was the publication of the *Pickwick Papers* that catapulted Dickens into an uninterrupted period of wealth and fame.

In the thirty-odd years that remained to him, Dickens became one of the world's most beloved authors, writing innumerable books that have charmed, thrilled, and frightened generations of readers.

···◉· CHAPTER I ·◉···

AMONG OTHER PUBLIC BUILDINGS in a certain town, which for many reasons it will be prudent to refrain from mentioning, there is a workhouse; and in this workhouse was born, on a day and date which I need not trouble myself to repeat, the item of mortality whose name is prefixed to this book, Oliver Twist.

For a long time after it was ushered into this world by the parish surgeon, it remained a matter of doubt whether the child would survive to bear any name at all. The fact is that there was considerable difficulty in inducing Oliver to take upon himself the office of respiration—a practice which custom has rendered necessary to our existence; and for some time he lay gasping on a little flock mattress, rather unequally poised between this world and the next—the balance being decidedly in favor of the latter. Now if during this brief period Oliver had been surrounded by careful grandmothers, anxious aunts, experienced nurses, and doctors of profound wisdom, he would most inevitably have been killed in no time. There being nobody by, however, but an old pauper woman, who was rendered rather misty by an unwonted allowance of beer, and a parish surgeon who did such matters by contract, Oliver and nature fought out the point between them. The result was that after a few struggles Oliver breathed, sneezed, and with a loud cry proceeded to advertise to the inmates of the workhouse the fact of a new burden having been imposed upon the parish.

As Oliver gave this first proof of the free and proper action of his lungs, the patchwork coverlet upon the iron bedstead rustled; the pale face of a young woman was raised feebly from the pillow, and a faint voice said, "Let me see the child, and die."

The surgeon had been warming his hands by the fire. As the young woman spoke he turned and said, with more kindness than might have been expected of him, "Oh, you must not talk about dying yet."

"Lor bless her dear heart, no!" interposed the pauper nurse. "When she has lived as long as I have, sir, and had thirteen children of her own, and all on 'em dead except two, and them in the wurkus with me, she'll know better than to take on in that way, bless her dear heart! Think what it is to be a mother, there's a dear lamb, do."

Apparently this consolatory perspective of a mother's prospects failed in producing its due effect. The patient shook her head and stretched out her hand towards the child. The surgeon deposited it in her arms. She imprinted her cold white lips passionately on its forehead, passed her hands over her face, gazed wildly round, shuddered, fell back—and died. They chafed her breast, hands, and temples; but the blood had stopped forever.

"It's all over, Mrs. Thingummy!" said the surgeon at last. He put on his gloves and hat; then, pausing by the bedside, he added, "She was a good-looking girl, too. Where did she come from?"

"She was found last night lying in the street, and was brought here," replied the old woman. "She had walked some distance, for her shoes were worn to pieces; but where she came from, nobody knows."

The surgeon leaned over the body and raised the left hand. "The old story," he said, shaking his head. "No wedding ring, I see. Good night!"

The medical gentleman walked away to dinner; and the nurse sat down on a low chair before the fire and proceeded to dress the infant.

Oliver cried lustily. If he could have known that he was an

orphan, left to the tender mercies of churchwardens and overseers, to be cuffed and buffeted through the world—despised by all, and pitied by none, perhaps he would have cried the louder.

FROM THIS DAY ON, for quite a few years, Oliver was the victim of a systematic course of treachery and deception. Since there was no female domiciled in the workhouse who was in a situation to impart to him the nourishment of which he stood in need, the parish authorities magnanimously resolved that he should be "farmed," or, in other words, he should be dispatched to a branch workhouse some three miles off, where some twenty or thirty other juvenile offenders against the poor laws rolled about the floor without the inconvenience of too much food or too much clothing. This they did under the parental superintendence of an elderly female, who received the culprits for the consideration of sevenpence-halfpenny per small head per week. Now a great deal of food may be got for sevenpence-halfpenny, quite enough to overload a child's stomach and make it uncomfortable. The elderly female knew what was good for children, and she had a very accurate perception of what was good for herself. So she appropriated the greater part of the weekly stipend to her own use and consigned the rising parochial generation to an even shorter allowance than was originally provided for them.

It cannot be expected that this system of farming would produce any very extraordinary or luxuriant crop. Oliver Twist's ninth birthday found him a pale thin child, somewhat diminutive in stature and decidedly small in circumference. But nature or inheritance had implanted a good sturdy spirit in his breast; and perhaps to this circumstance may be attributed his having any ninth birthday at all. Be this as it may, it *was* his ninth birthday; and he was keeping it in the coal cellar with a select party of two other young gentlemen, who, often participating with him in a sound thrashing, had been locked up for atrociously presuming to be hungry, when Mrs. Mann, the good lady of the house, was unexpectedly startled by the apparition of Mr. Bumble, the workhouse beadle, striving to undo the wicket of the garden gate.

"Goodness gracious, is that you, Mr. Bumble, sir?" said Mrs. Mann, thrusting her head out of the window in well-affected ecstasies of joy. "(Susan, take Oliver and them two brats upstairs and wash 'em directly.) My heart alive! Mr. Bumble, how glad I am to see you, sure-ly! Lor, only think," she said, running out, "that I should have forgotten the gate was bolted on account of them dear children! Walk in, pray, Mr. Bumble, do, sir."

Although this invitation was accompanied with a curtsy that might have softened the heart of a churchwarden, it by no means mollified the beadle, who was a fat man and a choleric one. He gave the little wicket a tremendous shake. "Do you think this respectful conduct, Mrs. Mann," he inquired, "to keep parish officers a-waiting at your garden gate, when they come here on porochial business connected with the porochial orphans?"

"I'm sure, Mr. Bumble, that I was only a-telling one or two of the dear children as is so fond of you that it was you a-coming," replied Mrs. Mann with humility.

"Well, well, Mrs. Mann," he replied in a calmer tone, "it may be as you say. Lead the way in, for I come on business, and have something to say."

Mrs. Mann ushered the beadle into a small parlor, placed a seat for him, and officiously deposited his cocked hat and cane on the table before him. Mr. Bumble wiped from his forehead the perspiration which his walk had engendered, glanced complacently at the cocked hat, and smiled.

"You've had a long walk, or I wouldn't mention it," observed Mrs. Mann, with captivating sweetness. "Now, will you take a drop of somethink, Mr. Bumble?"

"Not a drop. Not a drop," said Mr. Bumble, waving his right hand in a dignified manner.

"Just a leetle drop, with a little cold water and a lump of sugar," said Mrs. Mann persuasively.

"What is it?" inquired the beadle.

"Why, it's what I keep a little of in the house to put into the blessed infants' Daffy when they ain't well, Mr. Bumble," replied Mrs. Mann, as she opened a corner cupboard and took down a bottle and glass. "It's gin. I'll not deceive you, Mr. B. It's gin."

"Do you give the children Daffy, Mrs. Mann?" inquired Bumble, following with his eyes the interesting process of mixing.

"Ah, bless 'em, that I do, dear as it is," replied the nurse. "I couldn't see 'em suffer before my eyes, you know, sir."

"No," said Mr. Bumble approvingly, "no, you could not. You are a humane woman, Mrs. Mann." (Here she set down the glass.) "I shall take a early opportunity of mentioning it to the board, Mrs. Mann." (He stirred the gin and water.) "I drink your health with cheerfulness, Mrs. Mann," and he swallowed half of it.

"And now about business," he said, taking out a pocketbook. "The child that we named Oliver Twist is nine years old today."

"Bless him!" interposed Mrs. Mann, inflaming her left eye with the corner of her apron.

"And notwithstanding a offered reward of ten pound, and not-withstanding the most superlative exertions on the part of this parish," said Bumble, "we have never been able to discover who is his father or what was his mother's name or con-dition."

Mrs. Mann raised her hands in astonishment. "How comes he to have any name at all, then?"

The beadle drew himself up with pride and said, "I inwented it."

"You, Mr. Bumble!"

"I, Mrs. Mann. We name our foundlings in alphabetical order. The last was a S—Swubble, I named him. This was a T—Twist, I named *him*. The next one as comes will be Unwin, and the next Vilkins."

"Why, you're quite a literary character, sir!" said Mrs. Mann.

"Well, well," said the beadle, evidently gratified with the com-pliment, "perhaps I may be, Mrs. Mann." He finished the gin and water and added, "Oliver being now too old to remain here, the board have determined to have him back into the house. I have come out myself to take him there. So let me see him at once."

"I'll fetch him directly," said Mrs. Mann.

Oliver, having had by this time as much of the outer coat of dirt which encrusted his face and hands removed as could be scrubbed off in one washing, was led into the room by his protectress.

"Make a bow to the gentleman, Oliver," said Mrs. Mann.

Oliver made a bow which was divided between the beadle on the chair and the cocked hat on the table.

"Will you go along with me, Oliver?" said Mr. Bumble, in a majestic voice.

Oliver was about to say that he would go along with anybody with great readiness when, glancing upward, he caught sight of Mrs. Mann, who had got behind the beadle's chair and was shaking her fist at him with a furious countenance. He took the hint at once, for the fist had been too often impressed upon his body not to be deeply impressed upon his recollection.

"Will *she* go with me?" inquired poor Oliver.

"No, she can't," replied Mr. Bumble. "But she'll come and see you sometimes."

This was no very great consolation to the child. Young as he was, however, he had sense enough to make a feint of feeling great regret at going away. It was no very difficult matter for the boy to call tears into his eyes. Hunger and recent ill-usage are great assistants if you want to cry, and Oliver cried very naturally indeed. Mrs. Mann gave him a thousand embraces, and what Oliver wanted a great deal more, a piece of bread and butter, lest he should seem too hungry when he got to the workhouse. With the slice of bread in his hand and the little brown cloth parish cap on his head, Oliver was then led away by Mr. Bumble from the wretched home where one kind word or look had never lighted the gloom of his infant years. And yet he burst into an agony of grief as the cottage gate closed after him. Wretched as were the little companions in misery he was leaving behind, they were the only friends he had ever known; and a sense of his loneliness in the great wide world sank into the child's heart for the first time.

At the workhouse Oliver was handed over to the care of an old woman, but within a quarter of an hour Mr. Bumble returned and informed him that the board had said he was to appear before it forthwith. Not having a very clearly defined notion of what a live board was, Oliver was rather astounded by this intelligence and was not quite certain whether he ought to laugh or cry. He had no time to think about the matter, however, for Mr. Bumble gave him a tap on the back with his cane to make him lively, and conducted him into a large whitewashed room where eight or ten fat gentlemen were sitting round a table. At the top of the table, seated in an armchair rather higher than the rest, was a particularly fat gentleman with a very red face.

"Bow to the board," said Bumble. Oliver brushed away two or three tears that were lingering in his eyes, and seeing no board but the table, fortunately bowed to that.

"What's your name, boy?" asked the gentleman in the high chair.

Oliver was frightened at the sight of so many gentlemen, which made him tremble; and the beadle gave him another tap behind, which made him cry; whereupon a gentleman in a white waistcoat said he was a fool.

"Hush," said the gentleman in the high chair. "Boy, listen to me. You know you're an orphan, I suppose?"

"What's that, sir?" inquired poor Oliver.

"You know you've got no father or mother, and that you were brought up by the parish, don't you?"

"Yes, sir," replied Oliver, weeping bitterly.

"What are you crying for?" inquired the gentleman in the white waistcoat. "The boy *is* a fool—I thought he was."

"I hope you say your prayers every night," said another gentleman gruffly, "and pray for the people who take care of you."

"Yes, sir," stammered the boy. But he hadn't, because nobody had taught him.

"Well! You have come here to be educated and taught a useful trade," said the red-faced gentleman in the high chair.

"So you'll begin to pick oakum tomorrow morning at six o'clock," added the surly one in the white waistcoat.

For the combination of these blessings Oliver bowed low at the direction of the beadle, and was then hurried away to a large ward where, on a rough, hard bed, he sobbed himself to sleep.

Poor Oliver! He little thought, as he lay sleeping in happy unconsciousness of all around him, that the board had that very day arrived at a decision which would exercise the most material influence over all his future fortunes. But they had. And this was it: they had found out that the poor people liked the workhouse! It was a tavern for them where there was nothing to pay; a public breakfast, dinner, tea, and supper the year round; a brick and mortar elysium, where it was all play and no work. So the board established the rule that poor people should have the alternative (for they would compel nobody, not they) of being starved by a gradual process in the house, or by a quick one out of it. With this view they contracted with the waterworks to lay on an unlimited supply of water, and with a corn-factor to supply periodically small quantities of oatmeal; and they issued three meals of thin gruel a day, with an onion twice a week, and half a roll on Sundays.

For the first six months after Oliver Twist came to the workhouse the system was in full operation. It was rather expensive at first, in consequence of the increase in the undertaker's bill, and the necessity of taking in the clothes of the paupers, which fluttered loosely on their shrunken forms. But the number of workhouse inmates got thin as well; and the board were in ecstasies.

The room in which the boys were fed was a large stone hall, with a copper pot at one end, out of which the master, dressed in an apron for the purpose and assisted by two women, ladled the gruel at mealtimes. Of this festive composition each boy had one portion and no more—except on occasions of great public rejoicing, when he had two ounces and a quarter of bread besides. Their bowls never wanted washing. The boys polished them with their spoons till they shone again; and when they had performed this operation, they would sit staring at the pot with eager eyes as if they could have devoured it, meanwhile sucking their fingers assiduously, with the view of catching up any stray splashes of gruel.

Boys have generally excellent appetites. Oliver Twist and his companions suffered the tortures of slow starvation for three more months; but at last they got so voracious that one boy, who was tall for his age, hinted darkly to his companions that unless he had another basin of gruel *per diem*, he was afraid he might some night happen to eat the boy who slept next him, who happened to be a weakly youth of tender age. He had a wild, hungry eye and they implicitly believed him. A council was held; lots were cast to determine who should walk up to the master after supper that evening and ask for more; and it fell to Oliver Twist.

The evening arrived; the boys took their places. The master, in his cook's uniform, stationed himself at the copper; the gruel was served out, and a long grace was said over the short portions. The gruel disappeared; the boys whispered to each other, and Oliver's neighbors nudged him. Child as he was, he was desperate with hunger and reckless with misery. He rose from the table, and advancing to the master, bowl and spoon in hand, said, somewhat alarmed at his own temerity:

"Please, sir, I want some more."

The master, a fat, healthy man, turned pale. He gazed stupefied on the small rebel for some seconds and then clung for support to the copper. His pauper assistants were paralyzed with wonder, the boys with fear.

"*What?*" said the master at length, in a faint voice.

"Please, sir," replied Oliver, "I want some more."

The master aimed a blow at Oliver's head with the ladle, pinioned him in his arms, and shrieked aloud for the beadle.

The board were sitting in solemn conclave when Mr. Bumble rushed into the room, and addressing the gentleman in the high chair, said, "Mr. Limbkins, I beg your pardon, sir! Oliver Twist has asked for more!"

There was a general start. Horror was depicted on every countenance. "For *more!*" said Mr. Limbkins. "Compose yourself, Bumble, and answer me distinctly. Do I understand that he asked for more, after he had eaten the supper allotted by the dietary?"

"He did, sir," replied Bumble.

"That boy will be hung," said the gentleman in the white waistcoat. "I know that boy will be hung."

Nobody controverted the prophetic gentleman's opinion. An animated discussion took place. Oliver was ordered into instant confinement, and a notice was next morning pasted on the outside of the gate, offering a reward of five pounds to anybody who would take Oliver Twist off the hands of the parish.

Oliver asking for More

FOR A WEEK after the commission of the impious offense of asking for more, Oliver remained a close prisoner in the dark and solitary room to which he was consigned by the wisdom and mercy of the board. He cried bitterly all day; and, when the long, dismal night came on, he spread his little hands before his eyes to shut out the darkness, and crouching in the corner, tried to sleep, waking with a start and tremble, and drawing himself close to the wall, as if to feel even its cold hard surface were a protection in the gloom and loneliness which surrounded him. But let it not be supposed that during the period of his incarceration Oliver was denied the pleasure of society or the advantages of religious consolation. As for society, he was carried every other day into the hall where the boys dined and there sociably flogged as a public example. And far from being denied the advantages of religious consolation, he was kicked into the same apartment every evening at prayer time and there permitted to listen to a general supplication of the boys, containing a special clause inserted by the board, in which they asked to be made virtuous, and to be guarded from the sins and vices of Oliver Twist.

It chanced one morning, while Oliver's affairs were in this auspicious state, that Mr. Bumble encountered at the gate no less a person than Mr. Sowerberry, the parochial undertaker. Mr. Sowerberry was a tall, gaunt, large-jointed man, attired in a suit of threadbare black, with darned cotton stockings of the same color. His step was elastic and his face betokened inward pleasantry as he shook Mr. Bumble cordially by the hand.

"I have taken the measure of the two women that died last night, Mr. Bumble," he said.

"You'll make your fortune, Mr. Sowerberry," said the beadle, as he thrust his thumb and forefinger into the undertaker's proffered snuffbox, which was an ingenious little model of a coffin.

"Think so?" said the undertaker. "The prices allowed by the board are very small, Mr. Bumble."

"So are the coffins," replied the beadle, with precisely as near an approach to a laugh as a great official ought to indulge in.

Mr. Sowerberry was much tickled at this, and laughed a long time without cessation. "Well, well, Mr. Bumble," he said at length, "there's no denying that, since the new system of feeding has come in, the coffins are something narrower and more shallow than they used to be; but we must have some profit, Mr. Bumble. Well-seasoned timber is an expensive article, sir."

Mr. Bumble thought it advisable to change the subject. Oliver Twist being uppermost in his mind, he made him his theme. "Bye the bye," said Mr. Bumble, "you don't know anybody who wants a boy, do you? A porochial 'prentis, who is at present a deadweight—a millstone round the porochial throat? Liberal terms, Mr. Sowerberry, liberal terms!" As Mr. Bumble spoke, he raised his cane to the notice above him and gave three distinct raps on the words FIVE POUNDS.

"That's just the very thing I wanted to speak to you about," said the undertaker, taking Mr. Bumble by the gilt-edged lapel of his official coat. "You know—dear me, what a very elegant button this is, Mr. Bumble! I never noticed it before."

"Yes, I think it is rather pretty," said the beadle, glancing proudly downward at the large brass buttons which embellished his coat. "The die is the same as the porochial seal—the Good Samaritan healing the sick and bruised man. The board presented it to me, Mr. Sowerberry. Well, what about the boy?"

"Well," replied the undertaker, "I was thinking that as I pay a good deal towards the poor's rates, I've a right to get as much out of 'em as I can—and so—I think I'll take the boy."

Mr. Bumble grasped the undertaker by the arm and led him into the building. Mr. Sowerberry was closeted with the board for five minutes; and it was arranged that Oliver should go to him that afternoon "upon liking"—which means, in the case of a parish apprentice, that if the master find upon a short trial that he can get enough work out of a boy without putting too much food into him, he shall have him for a term of years, to do what he likes with.

When little Oliver was taken before "the gentlemen" that evening and informed that he was to go as general house lad to a coffin-maker's, he evinced so little emotion that they by common consent pronounced him a hardened young rascal, and ordered Mr. Bumble to remove him forthwith. The simple fact was that Oliver, instead of possessing too little feeling, possessed rather too much; and was in a fair way of being reduced, for life, to a state of brutal stupidity by the ill-usage he had received. He heard the news in perfect silence; and, having had his luggage put into his hand—which was not difficult to carry, inasmuch as it was all comprised within the limits of a small brown paper parcel—he was led away by the beadle to a new scene of suffering.

For some time Mr. Bumble drew Oliver along without notice or remark, and, it being a windy day, little Oliver was completely enshrouded by the skirts of Mr. Bumble's coat as they blew open, disclosing to great advantage his flapped waistcoat and drab plush knee breeches. As they drew near their destination, however, Mr. Bumble thought it expedient to look down and see that the boy was in good order for inspection by his new master.

"Oliver!" said Mr. Bumble.

"Yes, sir," replied Oliver in a low, tremulous voice.

"Pull that cap off your eyes and hold up your head, sir."

Although Oliver did as he was desired at once, and passed the back of his unoccupied hand briskly across his eyes, a tear rolled down his cheek. It was followed by another, and another. He made a strong effort, but it was unsuccessful. Withdrawing his other hand from Mr. Bumble's, he covered his face with both, and wept until the tears sprang out between his bony fingers.

"Well!" exclaimed Mr. Bumble, stopping short and darting at his little charge a look of intense malignity. "Well! Of *all* the ungratefulest boys as ever I see, Oliver, you are the—"

"No, no, sir," sobbed Oliver, clinging to the hand which held the well-known cane, "no, no, sir, I will be good, indeed I will, sir! I am a very little boy, sir, and it is so lonely, sir! So very lonely! Everybody hates me. Oh, sir, don't pray be cross to me!"

The child beat his hand upon his heart and looked in his companion's face with tears of real agony. Mr. Bumble regarded Oliver's piteous look with astonishment, hemmed three or four times in a husky manner, and bade Oliver dry his eyes and be a good boy. Then once more taking his hand, he walked on with him in silence.

The undertaker, who had just put up the shutters of his shop, was making some entries in his daybook by the light of a most appropriate dismal candle when Mr. Bumble entered.

"I've brought the boy, Mr. Sowerberry," announced the beadle. Oliver made a bow.

"Oh, that's the boy, is it?" said the undertaker, raising the candle above his head to get a better view of Oliver. "Mrs. Sowerberry, will you come here a moment, my dear?"

Mrs. Sowerberry, a short, thin, squeezed-up woman with a vixenish countenance, emerged from a little room behind the shop.

"My dear," said Mr. Sowerberry deferentially, "this is the boy from the workhouse." Oliver bowed again.

"Dear me!" she said. "He's very small."

"Why, he *is* rather small," replied Mr. Bumble, looking at Oliver as if it were his fault that he was no bigger. "There's no denying it. But he'll grow, Mrs. Sowerberry—he'll grow."

"I daresay he will," replied the lady pettishly, "on *our* victuals. Parish children always cost more to keep than they're worth. However, men always think they know best. There! Get downstairs, little bag o' bones."

With this the undertaker's wife opened a side door and pushed Oliver down a steep flight of stairs into a stone cell, damp and dark, and denominated "kitchen," wherein sat a slatternly girl, in shoes down-at-heel and blue worsted stockings very much out of repair. "Here, Charlotte," said Mrs. Sowerberry, following Oliver down, "give this boy some of the cold bits of meat that were put by for Trip. I daresay the boy isn't too dainty to eat 'em—are you, boy?"

Oliver, whose eyes had glistened at the mention of meat and who was trembling with eagerness to devour it, replied in the negative, and a plateful of coarse broken victuals that the dog had neglected was set before him. Oliver tore the bits asunder with all the ferocity of famine.

"Well," said the undertaker's wife when Oliver had finished his supper, which she had regarded in silent horror and with fearful auguries of his future appetite, "have you done?"

There being nothing else eatable within his reach, Oliver replied in the affirmative.

"Then come with me," said Mrs. Sowerberry, taking up a lamp and leading the way upstairs. "Your bed's under the counter. You don't mind sleeping among the coffins, I suppose? It doesn't much matter whether you do or don't, for you can't sleep anywhere else. Come, don't keep me here all night!"

Meekly, Oliver followed his new mistress upstairs.

OLIVER, BEING LEFT TO HIMSELF in the undertaker's shop, set the lamp down on a workman's bench and gazed timidly about with a feeling of awe and dread, which many people a good deal older than he will be at no loss to understand. An unfinished coffin on black trestles, which stood in the middle of the shop, looked so gloomy and deathlike that a cold tremble came over him every time his eyes wandered in its direction, and from it he almost expected to see some frightful form slowly rear its head to drive him mad with terror. Against the wall were ranged a long row of elm boards cut into the same shape, looking in the dim light like high-shouldered ghosts with their hands in their pockets. The shop was close and hot. The atmosphere seemed tainted with the smell of coffins. The recess beneath the counter in which his mattress was thrust looked like a grave.

Nor were these the only dismal feelings which depressed Oliver. He was alone in a strange place, and we all know how chilled and desolate the best of us will sometimes feel in such a situation. The boy had no friends to care for, or to care for him. And as he crept into his narrow bed, he wished it were his coffin, and that he could be lain in a calm and lasting sleep in the churchyard ground, with the sound of the old deep bell to soothe him in his sleep.

Oliver was awakened in the morning by a loud kicking at the outside of the shop door, which, before he could huddle on his clothes, was repeated in an angry and impetuous manner about twenty-five times. When he began to undo the chain, the legs desisted and a voice cried, "Open the door, will yer?"

"I will, directly, sir," replied Oliver, turning the key.

"I suppose yer the new boy, ain't yer?" said the voice.

"Yes, sir," replied Oliver.

"How old are yer?" inquired the voice.

"Ten, sir," replied Oliver.

"Then I'll whop yer when I get in," said the voice; "you just see if I don't!" And, having made this obliging promise, the voice began to whistle.

Oliver drew back the bolts with a trembling hand and opened the door. A big charity boy was sitting on a post in front of the house, eating a slice of bread and butter, which he cut into wedges with a clasp knife and then consumed with great dexterity.

"I beg your pardon, sir," said Oliver innocently. "Did you want a coffin?"

At this the boy looked monstrous fierce and said that Oliver would want one before long if he made jokes with his superiors in that way. "Yer don't know who I am, I suppose, Work'us?" said the charity boy in continuation.

"No, sir," rejoined Oliver.

"I'm Mister Noah Claypole, and you're under me. Take down the shutters, yer idle young ruffian!" With this, Mr. Claypole administered a kick to Oliver and entered the shop with a dignified air which did him great credit. It is difficult for a large-headed, small-eyed, lumbering youth to look dignified under any circumstances, but it is more especially so when added to these personal attractions are a red nose and yellow smalls.

Oliver, having taken down the shutters, and broken a pane of glass in his efforts to stagger away beneath the weight of the first one, was graciously assisted by Noah, who assured him that "he'd catch it." Mr. and Mrs. Sowerberry came down soon after. Oliver, having "caught it" in fulfillment of Noah's prediction, followed that young gentleman down the stairs to breakfast.

"Come near the fire, Noah," said Charlotte. "I saved a nice bit of bacon for you from Master's breakfast. Oliver, take them bits that

I've put out on the cover of the bread pan, and take your tea away to that box in the corner and drink it there. Make haste, for they'll want you to mind the shop."

"D'ye hear, Work'us?" said Noah Claypole.

"Lor, Noah!" said Charlotte. "What a rum creature you are! Why don't you let the boy alone?"

"Let him alone!" said Noah. "Why, everybody lets him alone, for that matter. Neither his father nor his mother nor his relations will ever interfere with him. Eh, Charlotte? He! He!"

"Oh, you queer soul!" said Charlotte, bursting into a hearty laugh in which she was joined by Noah; after which they both looked scornfully at poor Oliver Twist, as he sat on his box and ate the stale pieces which had been specially reserved for him.

Noah was a charity boy, but not a workhouse orphan. No chance child was he, for he could trace his genealogy; his parents lived hard by; his mother being a washerwoman and his father a drunken soldier, discharged with a wooden leg and a diurnal pension of twopence-halfpenny. The shop boys in the neighborhood had branded Noah with the ignominious epithet of "charity," and now that fortune had cast in his way a nameless orphan, he retorted on him with interest. This shows us how beautiful human nature may be made to be, and how impartially the same amiable qualities are developed in the finest lord and the dirtiest charity boy.

Oliver had been sojourning at the undertaker's some three weeks or a month. Mr. and Mrs. Sowerberry—the shop being shut up—were taking their supper in the little back parlor when Mr. Sowerberry, after several deferential glances at his wife, said, "About young Twist, my dear. A very good-looking boy."

"He need be, for he eats enough," observed the lady.

"There's an expression of melancholy in his face, my dear," resumed Mr. Sowerberry, "which is very interesting. He would make a delightful mute, my love."

Mrs. Sowerberry looked up with an expression of wonderment.

"I don't mean a regular mute to attend grown-up people, my dear, but only for children's funerals. It would be very new to have a mute in proportion. It would have a superb effect."

Mrs. Sowerberry, who had a good deal of taste in the undertaking way, was much struck by the novelty of this idea; but, as it would have been compromising her dignity to have said so, she merely inquired with sharpness why such an obvious suggestion had not presented itself to her husband's mind before. It was speedily determined, therefore, that Oliver should be at once initiated into the mysteries of the trade, and accompany his master on the very next occasion when his services were required.

It was a nice sickly season just at this time. Coffins were looking up, and in the course of a few weeks Oliver acquired a great deal of experience. The success of Mr. Sowerberry's ingenious speculation exceeded even his most sanguine hopes. The oldest inhabitants recollected no period at which measles had been so prevalent or so fatal to infant existence, and many were the mournful processions which little Oliver headed, in a hatband reaching down to his knees, to the indescribable admiration and emotion of all the mothers in the town.

Oliver accompanied his master in most of his adult expeditions, too, in order that he might acquire that equanimity of demeanor and command of nerve which are essential to a finished undertaker. At the same time he continued meekly to submit to the ill-treatment of Noah Claypole. Noah used him far worse than before, now that his jealousy was roused by seeing the new boy promoted to the black stick and hatband while he, the old one, remained stationary in muffin cap and leathers. Charlotte treated him ill because Noah did, and Mrs. Sowerberry was his decided enemy because Mr. Sowerberry was disposed to be his friend; so, between these three on one side and a glut of funerals on the other, Oliver was not altogether comfortable.

And now comes a very important passage in Oliver's history, slight and unimportant perhaps in appearance, but which indirectly produced a material change in all his prospects and proceedings.

One day Oliver and Noah had descended into the kitchen at the usual dinner hour to banquet on a small joint of mutton—a pound and a half of the worst end of the neck—when, Charlotte being called out of the way, there ensued a brief interval of time which

Noah Claypole, being hungry and vicious, considered he could not possibly devote to a worthier purpose than aggravating and tantalizing young Oliver.

Intent upon this innocent amusement, Noah put his feet on the tablecloth; pulled Oliver's hair; twitched his ears; and furthermore announced his intention of coming to see him hanged, whenever that desirable event should take place. When none of these taunts produced the desired effect of making Oliver cry, Noah attempted to be more facetious still, and did what many small wits with far greater reputations sometimes do to this day when they want to be funny. He got rather personal.

"Work'us," said Noah, "how's your mother?"

"She's dead," replied Oliver. "Don't you say anything about her to me!" Oliver's color rose as he said this; he breathed quickly, and there was a curious working of the mouth and nostrils.

"What did she die of, Work'us?" persisted Noah.

"Of a broken heart, some of our old nurses told me," replied Oliver, more as if he were talking to himself than answering Noah. "I think I know what it must be to die of that."

"Tol-de-rol, Work'us," said Noah, as a tear rolled down Oliver's cheek. "What's set you a-sniveling now?"

"Not *you*," replied Oliver, hastily brushing the tear away. "And that's enough. Don't say anything more to me about my mother; you'd better not!"

"Better not!" jeered Noah. "Work'us, don't be impudent. Yer must know, Work'us, yer mother was a regular right-down bad un."

"What did you say?" inquired Oliver, looking up very quickly.

"A regular right-down bad un, Work'us," replied Noah coolly. "And it's a great deal better, Work'us, that she died when she did, or else she'd have been in prison by now; or else transported, or hung, which is more likely than either, isn't it?"

Crimson with fury, Oliver started up; seized Noah by the throat; shook him, in the violence of his rage, till his teeth chattered in his head; and, collecting his whole force into one heavy blow, felled him to the ground. His spirit had been roused at last; the cruel insult to his dead mother had set his blood on fire. His breast heaved,

his eyes grew bright, and he stood glaring over the cowardly tormentor who now lay crouching at his feet.

"He'll murder me!" blubbered Noah. "Charlotte! Missis! Help!
Oliver's gone mad! Char—lotte!"

Noah's shouts were responded to by screams from Charlotte and
Mrs. Sowerberry, the former of whom rushed into the kitchen, while
the latter paused on the staircase till she was quite certain that it was
consistent with the preservation of human life to come down.

"Oh, you little wretch!" screamed Charlotte, seizing Oliver with
her utmost force, which was about equal to that of a moderately
strong man in good training. "Oh, you little un-grate-ful, mur-de-
rous villain!" And between every syllable Charlotte gave Oliver a
blow with all her might. Her fist was by no means a light one, but,
lest it should not be effectual in calming Oliver's wrath, Mrs.
Sowerberry plunged into the kitchen and assisted to hold him with
one hand while she scratched his face with the other. In this favorable position of affairs Noah rose and pommeled him behind.

When they were all wearied out and could tear and beat no longer,
they dragged Oliver, struggling but nothing daunted, into the
cellar and there locked him up. This being done, Mrs. Sowerberry
sank into a chair and burst into tears.

"Oh, Charlotte," she said, speaking as well as she could through
a deficiency of breath, "what a mercy we have not all been murdered in our beds!"

"Ah, mercy indeed, ma'am," was the reply. "Poor Noah! He was
all but killed, ma'am, when I come in."

"Poor fellow!" said Mrs. Sowerberry, looking piteously on the
charity boy. Noah, whose top waistcoat button might have been
somewhere on a level with the crown of Oliver's head, rubbed his
eyes and performed some affecting tears and sniffs.

"What's to be done?" exclaimed Mrs. Sowerberry. "Your master's not at home; there's not a man in the house, and he'll kick that
door down in ten minutes." Oliver's vigorous plunges against the
bit of timber in question rendered this occurrence highly probable.
"Run to Mr. Bumble, Noah, and tell him to come here directly.
Never mind your cap! Make haste!"

Oliver plucks up a Spirit

Noah started off at his fullest speed, and paused not once for breath until he reached the workhouse gate. Having rested here to collect a good burst of sobs and an imposing show of tears and terror, he knocked loudly at the wicket, which was opened by an aged pauper.

"Mr. Bumble! Mr. Bumble!" cried Noah, in tones so loud and agitated that they alarmed Mr. Bumble, who happened to be hard by. He rushed into the yard without his cocked hat—which is a remarkable circumstance, as showing that even a beadle may be afflicted momentarily with a loss of self-possession.

"Oh, Mr. Bumble, sir!" said Noah. "Oliver, sir, has—"

"What? What?" interposed Mr. Bumble, with a gleam of pleasure in his metallic eyes. "He hasn't run away, has he, Noah?"

"No, sir, but he's turned wicious," replied Noah. "He tried to murder me, sir, and Charlotte, and Missis. Oh, what dreadful pain it is, such agony, sir!" And here Noah twisted his body into an extensive variety of eellike positions, thereby giving Mr. Bumble to understand that from the violent onset of Oliver Twist he had sustained severe internal injury and damage, from which he was suffering the acutest torture.

Noah saw that the intelligence he communicated perfectly paralyzed Mr. Bumble, and when he observed a gentleman in a white waistcoat crossing the yard, he was more tragic in his lamentations than ever, rightly conceiving it highly expedient to attract the notice of the gentleman aforesaid. The gentleman's notice was very soon attracted, for he had not walked three paces when he turned angrily round and inquired what that young cur was howling for.

"It's a poor boy from the free school, sir," replied Mr. Bumble, "who has been all but murdered, sir, by young Twist."

"By Jove!" exclaimed the gentleman in the white waistcoat, stopping short. "I knew it! I felt a strange presentiment from the very first that that audacious young savage would come to be hung!"

"He has likewise attempted, sir, to murder the female servant," said Mr. Bumble, with a face of ashy paleness.

"And his missis," interposed Mr. Claypole.

"And his master, too, I think you said, Noah?" added Mr. Bumble.

"No! He's out, but he said he wanted to," replied Noah.

"Ah! Said he wanted to, did he, my boy?" inquired the gentleman in the white waistcoat.

"Yes, sir," replied Noah. "And, please, sir, Missis wants to know whether Mr. Bumble can spare time to step up there, directly, and flog him—'cause Master's out."

"Certainly, my boy, certainly," said the gentleman in the white waistcoat, smiling benignly and patting Noah's head, which was about three inches higher than his own. "You're a good boy. Here's a penny for you. Bumble, just step up to Sowerberry's with your cane. And don't spare him, Bumble."

"No, I will not, sir," replied the beadle, adjusting the wax end which was twisted round the bottom of his cane for the purpose of parochial flagellation.

"Tell Sowerberry not to spare him either. They'll never do anything with him without stripes and bruises."

"I'll take care, sir," replied the beadle; and he and Noah betook themselves with all speed to the undertaker's shop.

Here the position of affairs had not at all improved. Sowerberry had not yet returned, and Oliver continued to kick with vigor at the cellar door. Mr. Bumble judged it prudent to parley before opening the door. With this view, applying his mouth to the keyhole, he said in a deep and impressive tone, "Oliver!"

"Come; you let me out!" replied Oliver.

"Do you know this here voice?" said Mr. Bumble.

"Yes!" replied Oliver.

"Ain't you afraid of it, sir? Ain't you a-trembling?"

"No!" replied Oliver boldly.

An answer so different from the kind he was in the habit of receiving staggered Mr. Bumble not a little. He stepped back from the keyhole, drew himself up to his full height and looked from one to another of the three bystanders in mute astonishment.

"Oh, Mr. Bumble, he must be mad," said Mrs. Sowerberry. "No boy in half his senses could venture to speak so to you."

"It's not Madness, ma'am," replied Mr. Bumble after a few moments of deep meditation. "It's Meat. You've overfed him, ma'am. You've raised a artificial soul and spirit in him, ma'am, unbecoming a person of his condition, as the board, Mrs. Sowerberry, who are practical philosophers, will tell you. If you had kept the boy on gruel, ma'am, this would never have happened."

"Dear, dear!" ejaculated Mrs. Sowerberry, piously raising her eyes to the ceiling. "This comes of being so liberal!"

"Ah," said Mr. Bumble, when the lady brought her eyes down to earth again, "the only thing that can be done now is to leave him in the cellar for a day, till he's a little starved down, and then keep him on gruel all through his apprenticeship. He comes of a bad family. Excitable natures, Mrs. Sowerberry! Both the nurse and doctor said that his mother made her way here against difficulties and pain that would have killed any well-disposed woman weeks before."

At this point, Oliver, just hearing enough to know that some new allusion was being made to his mother, recommenced kicking with a violence that rendered every other sound inaudible. Sowerberry returned at this juncture. Oliver's offense having been explained to him with such exaggerations as the ladies thought best calculated to rouse his ire, he unlocked the cellar door and dragged his rebellious apprentice out by the collar.

Oliver's clothes had been torn in the beating he had received, his face was bruised and scratched, and his hair scattered over his forehead. The angry flush had not disappeared, however, and he scowled boldly at Noah.

"Now, you are a nice young fellow, ain't you?" said Sowerberry, giving Oliver a shake and a box on the ear.

"He called my mother names," replied Oliver.

"Well, and what if he did, you little ungrateful wretch?" said Mrs. Sowerberry. "She deserved what he said, and worse."

"She didn't," said Oliver.

"She did," said Mrs. Sowerberry.

"It's a lie!" said Oliver.

Mrs. Sowerberry burst into a flood of tears.

This flood of tears left Mr. Sowerberry no alternative. If he had hesitated for one instant to punish Oliver most severely, it must be quite clear to every experienced reader that he would have been, according to all precedents established in matrimony, an unnatural husband. To do him justice, he was, as far as his power went, kindly disposed towards the boy. The flood of tears, however, left him no resource, so he at once gave Oliver a drubbing which satisfied even Mrs. Sowerberry herself and rendered Mr. Bumble's subsequent application of the parochial cane rather unnecessary.

For the rest of the day Oliver was shut up in the back kitchen; and that night Mrs. Sowerberry, after making various remarks by no means complimentary to the memory of his mother, ordered him upstairs to his dismal bed.

It was not until he was left alone in the gloomy workshop of the undertaker that Oliver gave way to the feelings which the day's treatment may be supposed likely to have awakened in a mere child. He had listened to their taunts with a look of contempt; he had borne the lash without a cry: for he felt a pride swelling in his heart which would have kept down a shriek to the last. But now, when there was none to see or hear him, he fell upon his knees and, hiding his face in his hands, wept.

For a long time Oliver remained motionless in this attitude. His single candle was burning low in the socket when he rose to his feet. Having gazed cautiously round him and listened intently, he gently undid the fastenings of the door, and looked abroad.

It was a cold, dark night. The stars seemed, to the boy's eyes, farther from the earth than he had ever seen them before; there was no wind, and the somber shadows of the trees looked sepulchral and deathlike. He softly reclosed the door. Having availed himself of the expiring light of the candle to tie up in a handkerchief his few articles of wearing apparel, he sat himself down on a bench to wait for morning.

With the first ray of light that struggled through the crevices in the shutters, Oliver arose and again unbarred the door. One timid look around—one moment's hesitation—and he had closed it behind him and was in the open street.

He looked to the right and to the left, uncertain whither to fly.

He remembered to have seen wagons as they went out of town toiling up the hill. He took the same route, and arriving at a footpath across the fields, struck into it and walked quickly on.

Along this same footpath Oliver well remembered he had trotted beside Mr. Bumble, when Mr. Bumble first led him to the workhouse from the farm. His way lay directly in front of the cottage. His heart beat quickly when he bethought himself of this, but it was so early that there was very little fear of his being seen, so he walked on.

He reached the cottage. There was no appearance of its inmates stirring at that hour. Oliver stopped and peeped into the garden. A child was weeding one of the beds; he raised his pale face and disclosed the features of one of his former companions. Oliver felt glad to see him, for, though younger than himself, the boy had been his little friend and playmate. They had been beaten and starved and shut up together many and many a time.

"Hush, Dick!" said Oliver, as the boy ran to the gate and thrust his thin arm between the rails to greet him. "Is anyone up?"

"Nobody but me," replied the child.

"You mustn't say you saw me, Dick," said Oliver. "I am running away. They beat and ill-use me, and I am going to seek my fortune some long way off. I don't know where. How pale you are!"

"I heard the doctor tell them I was dying," said the child with a faint smile. "I am very glad to see you, dear, but don't stop, don't stop!"

"Yes, I will, to say good-by to you. I shall see you again, Dick, and you will be well and happy!"

"After I am dead, but not before," replied the child. "I know the doctor must be right, Oliver, because I dream so much of heaven, and angels and kind faces. Kiss me," said the child, climbing up the low gate and flinging his little arms around Oliver's neck. "Good-by, dear! God bless you!"

The blessing was from a young child's lips, but it was the first that Oliver had ever heard invoked upon his head; and through all the struggles and sufferings and troubles of his life after that, he never once forgot it.

Wʜᴇɴ Oʟɪᴠᴇʀ ʀᴇᴀᴄʜᴇᴅ the end of the path and gained the high-road it was eight o'clock. Now, though he was nearly five miles away from the town, he feared that he might be pursued and over-taken; and so he ran, and hid behind the hedges by turns, till noon. Then he sat down to rest by the side of a milestone and began to think, for the first time, about where he had better go and try to live.

The milestone bore in large characters an intimation that it was seventy miles to London. The name awakened a new train of ideas in the boy's mind. London—that great large place—nobody, not even Mr. Bumble, could ever find him there! And he had heard the old men in the workhouse say that no lad of spirit need want in London, that there were ways of living in that vast city which those from country parts had no idea of. As these things passed through his thoughts, he jumped to his feet and again walked forward.

Oliver walked twenty miles that day, and all that time tasted nothing but a single crust of dry bread which he had in his pocket and a few draughts of water which he begged at cottage doors. When night came, he turned into a meadow and crept close under a hayrick. He felt frightened at first, for the wind moaned dismally and he was cold and hungry, and more alone than he had ever been before. Being very tired with his walk, however, he soon fell asleep and forgot his troubles.

He felt cold and stiff next morning, and so hungry that he was obliged to exchange his only money—one penny—for a small loaf of bread in the very first village through which he passed. He had walked no more than twelve miles when night closed in again. His feet were sore, and his legs so weak that they trembled. Another night passed in the bleak damp air made him worse; when he set forward the next morning he could hardly crawl along.

He was hungrier than ever, but when he showed his nose in a shop, they talked about the beadle, which brought Oliver's heart into his mouth—very often the only thing he had there for many hours together. In fact, if it had not been for a good-hearted turnpikeman and a benevolent old lady, he would most assuredly have fallen dead on the king's highway. But the turnpikeman gave him a meal of bread and cheese; and the old lady took pity on the poor orphan and gave him what little she could afford—and more—with gentle words and tears of sympathy.

Early on the seventh morning Oliver limped slowly into the little town of Barnet. The window shutters were closed; the street was empty; not a soul had awakened to the business of the day. The sun was rising in all its splendid beauty; but the light only served to show the boy his own lonesomeness and desolation as he sat, with bleeding feet and covered with dust, upon a doorstep.

By degrees, the shutters were opened; and people began passing to and fro. Some turned round to stare at him as they hurried by; but none relieved him, or troubled themselves to inquire how he came there. He had no heart to beg. And there he sat.

He had been crouching there for some time, gazing listlessly at the passing coaches and thinking how strange it seemed that they could do in a few hours what it had taken him a whole week to accomplish, when he was roused by observing that a boy was surveying him earnestly from the opposite side of the way. Oliver raised his head and returned the steady look. Upon this, the boy crossed over; and, walking close up to Oliver he said, "Hullo, my covey! What's the row?"

The boy was about his own age, but one of the queerest-looking boys Oliver had ever seen. He was a snub-nosed, flat-browed, common-faced boy enough, and as dirty a juvenile as one would wish to see; but he had about him all the airs and manners of a man. He was short for his age, with bowlegs and little, sharp, ugly eyes. His hat was stuck on the top of his head so lightly that it threatened to fall off every moment. He wore a man's coat reaching nearly to his heels. He had turned the cuffs back, halfway up his arm, apparently with the ultimate view of thrusting his hands into the pockets of his corduroy trousers, for there he kept them.

"What's the row?" said this strange young gentleman to Oliver.

"I am very hungry and tired," replied Oliver, the tears standing in his eyes. "I have been walking seven days."

"Walking sivin days!" said the young gentleman. "Beak's order, eh? But," he added, noticing Oliver's surprise, "I suppose you don't know what a beak is, my flash com-pan-i-on?"

Oliver mildly replied that he had always heard a bird's mouth described by the term in question.

"My eyes, how green!" exclaimed the young gentleman. "Why, a beak's a madgst'rate. But come, you want grub, and you shall have it. I'm at low-water mark myself—only one bob and a magpie; but *as* far *as* it goes, I'll fork out and stump. Up on your pins."

Assisting Oliver to rise, the young gentleman took him to an adjacent shop, where he purchased a sufficiency of ham and a half loaf of bread. Then he led the way to the taproom of a nearby public house. Here a pot of beer was brought in; and Oliver, falling to at his new friend's bidding, made a long and hearty meal, during which the strange boy eyed him with great attention. "Going to London?" he asked when Oliver had at length concluded.

"Yes."

"Got any lodgings?"

"No."

"Money?"

"No."

The strange boy whistled and put his arms into his pockets as far as the big coat sleeves would let them go.

"Do you live in London?" inquired Oliver.

"Yes—when I'm at home," replied the boy. "I suppose you want some place to sleep tonight, don't you?"

"I do, indeed," answered Oliver. "I have not slept under a roof since I left the country."

"Don't fret your eyelids on that score," said the young gentleman. "I know a 'spectable old genelman as lives in London wot'll give you lodgings for nothink—that is, if any genelman he knows interduces you. And don't he know me? Oh, no! Certainly not!"

This unexpected offer of shelter was too tempting to be resisted, especially as it was followed up by the assurance that the old gentleman referred to would doubtless provide Oliver with comfortable employment. This led to a more friendly and confidential dialogue, from which Oliver discovered that his friend's name was Jack Dawkins and that he was a pet and protégé of the elderly gentleman. Mr. Dawkins's appearance did not say a vast deal in favor of the comforts which his patron's interest obtained for those whom he took under his protection; but, as he had a rather flighty and dissolute mode of conversing, and furthermore avowed that among his intimate friends he was better known by the sobriquet of "The Artful Dodger," Oliver concluded that the moral precepts of his benefactor had hitherto been thrown away on him. Under this impression, he secretly resolved to cultivate the good opinion of the old gentleman as quickly as possible, and if he found the Dodger incorrigible, to decline the honor of his further acquaintance.

As John Dawkins objected to their entering London before nightfall, it was nearly eleven o'clock when they reached the turnpike at Islington. They crossed into St. John's Road, struck down several dark alleys, thence into Saffron Hill, along which the Dodger scudded at a rapid pace, directing Oliver to follow close at his heels. A dirtier or more wretched place Oliver had never seen. The streets were narrow and muddy, and the air was impregnated with filthy odors. Heaps of children, even at that time of night, were crawling in and out of the doors of the small shops, or screaming from the inside. The sole places that seemed to prosper were the public houses, where the lowest orders were wrangling with might and main. Covered ways and yards disclosed little knots of houses where drunken men and women were positively wallowing in filth; and from several doorways great ill-looking fellows cautiously emerged, bound, to all appearance, on no very well disposed or harmless errands.

Oliver was just considering whether he hadn't better run away when they reached the bottom of a hill in Clerkenwell. His conductor, catching him by the arm, pushed open the door of a house near Field Lane; and, drawing him into the passage, closed it behind them.

"Now, then!" cried a voice from below, in reply to a whistle from the Dodger.

"Plummy and slam!" was the reply.

This seemed to be some watchword or signal that all was right, for the light of a feeble candle gleamed at the remote end of the passage, and a man's face peeped out from where a balustrade of the old kitchen staircase had been broken away.

"There's two on you," said the man. "Who's the t'other one?"

"A new pal," replied Jack Dawkins. "Is Fagin upstairs?"

"Yes, he's a-sortin' the wipes. Up with you!" The candle was drawn back, and the face disappeared.

Oliver, groping his way with one hand and having the other firmly grasped by his companion, ascended with difficulty the dark and broken stairs. His conductor threw open the door of a back room and drew Oliver in after him.

The walls and ceiling of the room were black with age and dirt. There was a table before the fire; on it were a candle, stuck in a ginger-beer bottle, two or three pewter pots, and a loaf and butter. In a frying pan on the fire some sausages were cooking; and standing over them, with a toasting fork in his hand, was a very old shriveled Jew, whose villainous-looking and repulsive face was obscured by a quantity of matted red hair. He was dressed in a greasy flannel gown, and was dividing his attention between the frying pan and a clotheshorse, over which hung a number of silk handkerchiefs. Several beds made of old sacks were huddled on the floor. Seated round the table were four or five boys, none older than the Dodger, smoking long clay pipes and drinking spirits with the air of middle-aged men. These all crowded about their associate as he whispered a few words to the Jew and then turned and grinned at Oliver. So did the Jew himself, toasting fork in hand.

"This is him, Fagin," said Dawkins, "my friend Oliver Twist."

Fagin grinned, and, making a low obeisance to Oliver, took him by the hand and hoped he should have the honor of his intimate acquaintance. Upon this, the young gentlemen with the pipes came round him and shook both his hands very hard—especially the hand in which he held his little bundle. One young gentleman was very anxious to hang up his cap for him; and another was so obliging as to put his hands in his pockets, in order that he might not have the trouble of emptying them himself when he went to bed. These civilities would probably have been extended much further but for a liberal exercise of the old man's toasting fork on the heads and shoulders of the affectionate youths.

"We are very glad to see you, Oliver, very," said Fagin. "Dodger, take off the sausages and draw a chair near the fire for Oliver. Ah, you're a-staring at the pocket handkerchiefs, eh, my dear? We've just looked 'em out, ready for the wash; that's all, Oliver, that's all. Ha! Ha! Ha!"

The latter part of this speech was hailed by a boisterous shout, in the midst of which they all sat down to supper. Oliver ate his share, and the old man then mixed him a glass of hot gin and water, telling him he must drink it off directly. Oliver did as he was desired. Immediately afterwards he felt himself gently lifted onto one of the sacks, and then he sank into a deep sleep.

IT WAS LATE NEXT MORNING when Oliver awoke. There was no other person in the room but the old Jew, who was boiling some coffee in a saucepan and whistling softly to himself as he stirred it with an iron spoon. He would stop every now and then to listen when there was the least noise below; and then he would go on whistling and stirring again as before.

Although Oliver had roused himself from sleep, he was not thoroughly awake, and he watched Fagin with half-closed eyes. When the coffee was done, Fagin drew the saucepan to the hob. Standing then in an irresolute attitude, he looked at Oliver and called him by his name. Oliver did not answer, and was to all appearance asleep. After satisfying himself on this head, Fagin gently fastened the door. He drew forth from a trap in the floor a small box which he placed carefully on the table. His eyes glistened as he raised the lid and looked in. Sitting down, he then took from the box a magnificent gold watch sparkling with jewels.

"Aha," said the old man, shrugging up his shoulders and distorting every feature with a hideous grin.

At least half a dozen more watches were drawn forth from the same box and surveyed with equal pleasure, besides rings, bracelets, and other articles of jewelry, of such magnificent materials and costly workmanship that Oliver had no idea even of their names.

Having replaced these trinkets, Fagin took out another—so small that it lay in the palm of his hand—and pored over it long and earnestly. At length he put it down, and, leaning back in his chair, muttered, "What a fine thing capital punishment is! Dead men never bring awkward stories to light. Five of 'em strung up in a row, and none left to play booty or turn white-livered!"

As Fagin uttered these words, his bright dark eyes fell on Oliver's face. The boy's eyes were fixed on his in mute curiosity, and it was enough to show the old man that he had been observed. He closed the lid of the box with a loud crash, and, laying his hand on a bread knife which was on the table, started furiously up.

"What's that?" he cried. "What do you watch me for? Why are you awake? What have you seen? Speak out, boy! Quick!"

"I wasn't able to sleep any longer, sir," replied Oliver meekly. "I am very sorry if I have disturbed you, sir."

"You were not awake an hour ago?" said Fagin, scowling.

"No, indeed!"

"Are you sure?" cried Fagin, with a still fiercer look than before, and a threatening attitude.

"Upon my word I was not, sir," replied Oliver earnestly. "I was not, indeed, sir."

"Tush, tush, my dear!" said the old man, abruptly resuming his former manner and playing with the knife a little before he laid it down, as if he had caught it up in mere sport. "Of course I know that, my dear. I only tried to frighten you. Ha! Ha! You're a brave boy, Oliver!" Fagin chuckled and rubbed his hands, but glanced uneasily at the box, notwithstanding. "Did you see any of these pretty things, my dear?" he asked.

"Yes, sir," replied Oliver.

"Ah," said Fagin, turning rather pale. "They—they're mine, Oliver, my little property. All I have to live on in my old age. The folks call me a miser, my dear."

Oliver thought the old gentleman must be a decided miser to live in such a dirty place, with so many watches; but he only cast a deferential look at the old man and asked if he might get up.

"Certainly, my dear, certainly," replied the old gentleman. "There's a pitcher of water in the corner by the door. Bring it here, and I'll give you a basin to wash in, my dear."

Oliver got up, walked across the room, and stooped to raise the pitcher. When he turned his head, the box was gone.

He had scarcely washed himself, and made everything tidy at Fagin's directions by emptying the basin out of the window, when the Dodger returned, accompanied by a very sprightly young friend whom Oliver had seen smoking on the previous night, and who was now formally introduced to him as Charley Bates. The four sat down to breakfast on the coffee and some hot rolls and ham which the Dodger had brought home in the crown of his hat.

"Well," said Fagin, glancing slyly at Oliver and addressing the Dodger, "I hope you've been at work this morning, my dears?"

"Hard," replied the Dodger.

"As nails," added Charley Bates.

"Good boys!" said Fagin. "What have *you* got, Dodger?"

"A couple of pocketbooks," replied that young gentleman.

"Lined?" inquired Fagin with eagerness.

"Pretty well," said the Dodger, producing them.

"Not so heavy as they might be," said Fagin, after looking at the insides carefully, "but very neat and nicely made. Ingenious workman, ain't he, Oliver?"

"Very, indeed, sir," said Oliver. At which Mr. Charles Bates laughed uproariously, very much to the amazement of Oliver.

"And what have you got, my dear?" said Fagin to Charley Bates.

"Wipes," replied Master Bates, at the same time producing four pocket-handkerchiefs.

"Well," said Fagin, inspecting them closely, "they're very good ones. You haven't marked them well, though, Charley, so the marks shall be picked out with a needle, and we'll teach Oliver how to do it. Shall us, Oliver, eh? Ha! Ha! You'd like to be able to make pocket-handkerchiefs as easy as Charley Bates, wouldn't you, my dear?"

"Very much, indeed, if you'll teach me, sir," replied Oliver.

Master Bates saw something so exquisitely ludicrous in this

reply that he burst into another laugh; which laugh, meeting the coffee he was drinking, and carrying it down some wrong channel, very nearly terminated in his premature suffocation.

"He is so jolly green!" said Charley when he recovered.

The Dodger said nothing, but he smoothed Oliver's hair over his eyes and said he'd know better by and by.

When the breakfast was cleared away, the merry old gentleman and the two boys played at a very curious and uncommon game, which was performed in this way. The merry old gentleman, placing a snuffbox in one pocket of his trousers, a notecase in the other and a watch in his waistcoat pocket with a guard chain round his neck, and sticking a mock-diamond pin in his shirt, buttoned his coat tight round him, and putting his spectacle case and handkerchief in his pockets, trotted up and down the room with a stick in imitation of the manner in which old gentlemen walk about the streets. Sometimes he stopped at the fireplace and sometimes at the door, making believe that he was staring into shopwindows. At such times he would look constantly round him, for fear of thieves, and would keep slapping all his pockets in turn to see that he hadn't lost anything, in such a very funny and natural manner that Oliver laughed till the tears ran down his face.

All this time the two boys followed him closely about, getting out of his sight so nimbly every time he turned round that it was impossible to follow their motions. At last the Dodger trod on his toes, or ran on his boot accidentally, while Charley stumbled up against him from behind; and in that one moment they took from him, with extraordinary rapidity, snuffbox, notecase, watch, guard chain, shirt pin, pocket-handkerchief, and even the spectacle case. If the old gentleman felt a hand in any one of his pockets, he cried out where it was, and the game began all over again.

When this game had been played a great many times, a couple of young ladies called, one of whom was named Bet and the other Nancy. They wore a good deal of hair, not very neatly turned up behind, and were rather untidy about the shoes and stockings. They were not exactly pretty, perhaps, but they had a great deal of color in their faces and looked quite hearty. Since they were remarkably agreeable in their manners, Oliver thought them very nice girls indeed.

These visitors stopped a long time. Spirits were produced, and the conversation took a very convivial and improving turn. At length Charley Bates expressed his opinion that it was time to pad the hoof. This, it occurred to Oliver, must be French for going out, for directly afterwards the Dodger, Charley, and the two young ladies went away together, having been kindly furnished by the amiable old gentleman with money to spend.

"There, my dear," said Fagin. "That's a pleasant life, isn't it? They have gone out for the day."

"Have they finished work, sir?" inquired Oliver.

"Yes," said Fagin. "That is, unless they should unexpectedly come across any when they are out, and they won't neglect it if they do, my dear, depend on it. Make 'em your models, my dear. Take their advice in all matters—especially the Dodger's, my dear. He'll be a great man himself and will make you one, too. Is my handkerchief hanging out of my pocket, my dear?" said Fagin, stopping short.

"Yes, sir," said Oliver.

"See if you can take it out without my feeling it, as you saw them do when we were at play this morning."

Oliver held up the bottom of the pocket with one hand, as he had seen the Dodger hold it, and drew the handkerchief lightly out of it with the other.

"Is it gone?" cried Fagin.

"Here it is, sir," said Oliver, showing it in his hand.

"You're a clever boy, my dear," said the playful old gentleman, patting Oliver on the head approvingly. "I never saw a sharper lad. Here's a shilling for you. If you go on in this way, you'll be the greatest man of the time. And now come here, and I'll show you how to take the marks out of the handkerchiefs."

Oliver wondered what picking the old gentleman's pocket in play had to do with his chances of being a great man. But thinking that Fagin, being so much his senior, must know best, he followed him to the table and was soon deeply involved in his new study.

FOR MANY DAYS Oliver remained in Fagin's room, picking the marks out of the numerous pocket-handkerchiefs and sometimes taking part in the game already described. At length he began to languish for fresh air, and earnestly entreated the old gentleman to allow him to go out to work with his two companions.

Oliver was rendered the more anxious to be actively employed by what he had seen of the stern morality of the old gentleman's character. Whenever the Dodger or Charley Bates came home empty-handed, he would expatiate vehemently on the misery of idle habits and would enforce upon them the necessity of an active life by sending them supperless to bed. On one occasion, indeed, he even went so far as to knock them both down a flight of stairs.

At length, one morning, Oliver obtained the permission he had so eagerly sought, and the old gentleman placed him under the guardianship of Charley Bates and the Dodger. The three boys sallied out, the Dodger with his coat sleeves tucked up and his hat cocked as usual, Master Bates sauntering along with his hands in his pockets, and Oliver between them wondering where they were going and what branch of manufacture he would be instructed in first.

The pace at which they went was such a very lazy saunter that Oliver began to think his companions were going to deceive the old gentleman by not going to work at all. The Dodger had a vicious propensity, too, of pulling the caps from the heads of small boys and tossing them away, while Charley Bates exhibited some very loose notions concerning the rights of property by pilfering apples and onions from market stalls and thrusting them into pockets which were surprisingly capacious. These things looked so bad that Oliver was on the point of declaring his intention of seeking his way back as best he could, when his thoughts were suddenly directed into another channel by a very mysterious change of behavior on the part of the Dodger.

They were just emerging from a narrow court in Clerkenwell

when the Dodger made a sudden stop, and, laying his finger on his lip, drew his companions back again with the greatest caution.

"Do you see that old cove at the bookstall?" said the Dodger.

"The old gentleman over the way?" said Oliver. "I see him."

"He'll do," said the Dodger.

"A prime plant," observed Master Charley Bates.

Oliver looked from one to the other with the greatest surprise; but he was not permitted to make any inquiries, for the two boys walked stealthily across the road and slunk close behind the old gentleman. Oliver walked a few paces after them, and, not knowing whether to advance or retire, stood looking on in silent amazement.

The old gentleman was a very respectable-looking personage, with a powdered head and gold spectacles. He was dressed in a bottle-green coat with a black velvet collar, wore white trousers, and carried a small bamboo cane under his arm. He had taken up a book from the stall, and there he stood, reading away, as hard as if he were in his chair in his own study. It was plain from his abstraction that he saw not the bookstall, nor the street, nor the boys, nor anything but the book itself.

What was Oliver's horror and alarm as he stood a few paces off, looking on with his eyelids as wide open as they would possibly go, to see the Dodger plunge his hand into the old gentleman's pocket and draw from thence a handkerchief! To see him hand the same to Charley Bates, and finally to behold them both running away round the corner at full speed!

In an instant the whole mystery of the handkerchiefs, the watches, and the jewels rushed upon the boy's mind. He stood for a moment with the blood so tingling through all his veins from terror that he felt as if he were in a burning fire. Then, confused and frightened, he took to his heels, and, not knowing what he did, made off as fast as he could lay his feet to the ground.

In the very instant when Oliver began to run, the old gentleman, putting his hand to his pocket and missing his handkerchief, turned sharp round. Seeing the boy scudding away, he very naturally concluded him to be the depredator, and shouting "Stop thief!" with all his might, made off after him, book in hand.

Oliver amazed at the Dodger's Mode of "going to work"

But the old gentleman was not the only person who raised the hue and cry. The Dodger and Master Bates, unwilling to attract public attention by running down the open street, had merely retired into the very first doorway round the corner. They no sooner heard the cry and saw Oliver running than they issued forth with great promptitude, and shouting "Stop thief!" too, joined in the pursuit like good citizens.

"Stop thief! Stop thief!" There is a magic in the sound. The tradesman leaves his counter and the trucker his wagon; the butcher throws down his cleaver, the baker his basket, the milkman his pail, the errand boy his parcels, the schoolboy his marbles. Away they run, pell-mell, helter-skelter, slap-dash: tearing, yelling, screaming, knocking down the passersby as they turn the corners, rousing up the dogs, and astonishing the fowls; and streets, squares, and alleys re-echo with the sound.

"Stop thief! Stop thief!" The cry is taken up by a hundred voices, and the crowd accumulate at every turning. Away they fly, splashing through the mud and rattling along the pavements; up go the windows, out run the people, onward bear the mob.

"Stop thief!" There is a passion *for hunting something* deeply implanted in the human breast. One wretched breathless child— panting with exhaustion, terror in his eyes, perspiration streaming down his face—strains every nerve to make head upon his pursuers. And as they gain upon him, they hail his decreasing strength with still louder shouts, and whoop with joy. "Stop thief!" Aye, stop him for God's sake, were it only in mercy!

Stopped at last! A clever blow. He is down upon the pavement, and the crowd eagerly gather round him, jostling to catch a glimpse. "Stand aside!" "Give him a little air!" "Nonsense, he don't deserve it!" "Where's the gentleman?" "Here he is." "Make room there for the gentleman!" "Is this the boy, sir?" "Yes."

Oliver lay, covered with mud and dust and bleeding from the mouth, looking wildly round upon the heap of faces that surrounded him, when the old gentleman was officiously dragged into the circle by the foremost of the pursuers.

"Yes," said the gentleman, "I am afraid it is the boy."

"Afraid!" murmured the crowd. "That's a good un!"

"Poor fellow!" said the gentleman. "He has hurt himself."

"*I* did that, sir," said a great lubberly fellow, stepping forward. "*I* stopped him, sir."

The fellow touched his hat with a grin, expecting something for his pains; but the old gentleman, eyeing him with an expression of dislike, looked as if he contemplated running away himself— which he might possibly have attempted to do, had not a police officer (who is generally the last person to arrive in such cases) at that moment made his way through the crowd and seized Oliver by the collar.

"Come, get up," he said roughly.

"It wasn't me indeed, sir. It was two other boys," said Oliver, clasping his hands passionately. "They are here somewhere."

"Oh no, they ain't," said the officer. He meant this to be ironical, but it was true besides, for the Dodger and Charley Bates had filed off down the first convenient alley they had come to. "Now, will you stand upon your legs, you young devil?"

Oliver made a shift to raise himself to his feet. He was at once lugged along at a rapid pace by the police officer, who held him by his jacket collar. The gentleman walked by the officer's side, and as many of the crowd as could achieve the feat got a little ahead and stared back at Oliver.

The offense had been committed in the immediate neighborhood of a very notorious metropolitan police office. Hence the crowd had only the satisfaction of accompanying Oliver through two or three streets when he was led beneath a low archway and up a dirty alley into this dispensary of summary justice. Here stood a stout man with a bunch of whiskers on his face and a bunch of keys in his hand.

"What's the matter now?" he asked carelessly.

"A young pickpocket," replied the officer who had Oliver in charge.

"Are you the party that's been robbed, sir?" inquired the man with the keys.

"Yes, I am," replied the old gentleman, "but I am not sure that this boy actually took the handkerchief. I—I would rather not press the case."

"Must go before the magistrate now, sir," replied the man. "His worship will be disengaged in half a minute. Now, young gallows!"

This was an invitation for Oliver to enter through a door which led into a stone cell. This cell was the size and shape of a coal cellar and intolerably dirty. Here Oliver was searched, and nothing being found upon him, locked up.

The old gentleman looked almost as rueful as Oliver when the key grated in the lock. "There is something in that boy's face," he said to himself as he walked slowly away, tapping his chin with the cover of his book in a thoughtful manner, "something that touches and interests me. *Can* he be innocent? He looked like— Bless my soul! Where have I seen that look before?"

After musing for some minutes the old gentleman walked into a waiting room of the police office and there, retiring into a corner, called up before his mind's eye a vast amphitheater of faces over which a dusky curtain had hung for many years. "No," he said, shaking his head, "it must be my imagination." For he could recall no one countenance of which Oliver's features bore a trace. So he heaved a sigh over the recollections he had awakened, and being, happily for himself, an absent old gentleman, buried them again in the pages of the musty book.

He was roused by a touch on the shoulder from the man with the keys. He closed his book hastily, and was at once ushered into the imposing presence of the renowned Mr. Fang. Mr. Fang sat behind a bar at the end of the room, and on one side was a sort of wooden pen in which poor little Oliver had been deposited, trembling very much at the awfulness of the scene.

Mr. Fang was a lean, long-backed, stiff-necked, middle-sized man with no great quantity of hair. His face was stern and much flushed.

The old gentleman bowed respectfully, and advancing to the magistrate's desk, said, putting down his card, "That is my name and address, sir." He then withdrew a pace or two and waited to be questioned.

Now, it happened that Mr. Fang was perusing an article in a newspaper adverting to some recent decision of his and commending him, for the three hundred and fiftieth time, to the special and particular notice of the Secretary of State for the Home Department. He was out of temper, and he looked up with an angry scowl.

"Who are you?" said Mr. Fang.

The old gentleman pointed, with some surprise, to his card.

"Officer!" said Mr. Fang, tossing the card contemptuously away with the newspaper. "Who is this fellow?"

"My name, sir," said the old gentleman, speaking *like* a gentleman, "my name, sir, is Brownlow. Permit me to inquire the name of the magistrate who offers a gratuitous and unprovoked insult to a respectable person, under the protection of the bench." Mr. Brownlow looked round the office in search of some person who would afford him the required information.

"Officer," said Mr. Fang, "what's this fellow charged with?"

"He's not charged at all, your worship," replied the officer. "He appears against the boy, your worship."

"Appears against the boy, does he?" said Fang, surveying Mr. Brownlow contemptuously from head to foot. "Swear him!"

"Before I am sworn, I must beg to say one word," said Mr. Brownlow, "and that is that I really never, without actual experience, could have believed—"

"Hold your tongue, sir!" said Mr. Fang peremptorily.

"I will not, sir!" replied the old gentleman.

"Hold your tongue this instant, or I'll have you turned out of the office!" said Mr. Fang. "Swear this person! I'll not hear another word. Swear him."

Mr. Brownlow's indignation was greatly roused, but reflecting perhaps that he might only injure the boy by giving vent to it, he suppressed his feelings and submitted to be sworn.

"Now," said Fang, "what's the charge against the boy? What have you got to say, sir?"

"I was standing at a bookstall—" Mr. Brownlow began.

"Hold your tongue, sir," said Mr. Fang. "Policeman! Here, swear this policeman. Now, what is this?"

The policeman, with becoming humility, related how he had taken the charge, how he had searched Oliver and found nothing on his person, and how that was all he knew about it.

"Are there any witnesses?" inquired Mr. Fang.

"None, your worship," replied the policeman.

Mr. Fang, turning to Mr. Brownlow, said in a towering passion, "Do you mean to state what your complaint against this boy is, or do you not? You have been sworn. Now, if you stand there, refusing to give evidence, I'll punish you for disrespect to the bench!"

With many interruptions and repeated insults, Mr. Brownlow contrived to state his case, observing that in the surprise of the moment he had run after the boy because he saw him running away, and expressing his hope that the magistrate would deal leniently with him.

"He has been hurt already," said the old gentleman in conclusion, looking toward the bar. "And I really fear that he is ill."

"Oh, yes, I daresay!" said Mr. Fang with a sneer. "Come, none of your tricks here, you young vagabond. What's your name?"

Oliver tried to reply, but his tongue failed him. He was deadly pale, and the whole place seemed turning round and round.

"What's your name, you hardened scoundrel?" demanded Mr. Fang. "Officer, what's his name?"

This was addressed to a bluff old fellow in a striped waistcoat who was standing by the bar. He bent over Oliver and repeated the inquiry, but finding him really incapable of understanding the question, and knowing that his not replying would only infuriate the magistrate the more and add to the severity of his sentence, he hazarded a guess. "He says his name's Tom White, your worship," said this kindhearted thieftaker.

"Oh, he won't speak out, won't he?" said Fang. "Very well, very well. Where does he live?"

"Where he can, your worship," replied the officer, again pretending to receive Oliver's answer.

"Has he any parents?" inquired Mr. Fang.

"He says they died in his infancy, your worship," said the officer, hazarding the usual reply.

At this point of the inquiry Oliver raised his head and murmured a feeble prayer for a draught of water.

"Stuff and nonsense!" said Mr. Fang.

"I think he really is ill, your worship," remonstrated the officer.

"Take care of him, officer," said the old gentleman, raising his hands instinctively. "He'll fall down."

"Stand away, officer," cried Fang. "Let him fall, if he likes."

Oliver availed himself of the kind permission and fell to the floor in a fainting fit.

"I knew he was shamming," said Fang, as if this were incontestable proof of the fact. "Let him lie there; he'll soon be tired of that."

"How do you propose to deal with the case, sir?" inquired the clerk in a low voice.

"Summarily," replied Mr. Fang. "He stands committed for three months—hard labor of course. Clear the office."

A couple of men were preparing to carry the insensible boy to his cell when an elderly man, of decent but poor appearance, rushed hastily into the office.

"Stop, stop! Don't take him away! For heaven's sake, stop a moment!" cried the newcomer, breathless with haste.

Mr. Fang was not a little indignant to see an unbidden guest enter in such irreverent disorder. "What is this? Who is this? Turn this man out. Clear the office!" he cried.

"I *will* speak!" cried the man. "I will not be turned out. I saw it all. I keep the bookstall. I demand to be sworn, Mr. Fang."

The man was right. His manner was determined, and the matter was growing rather too serious to be hushed up.

"Swear the man," growled Mr. Fang with ill grace. "Now, man, what have you got to say?"

"This," he said. "I saw three boys, two others and the prisoner, loitering on the opposite side of the way when this gentleman was reading. The robbery was committed by another boy. I saw it done, and I saw that this boy was amazed and stupefied by it."

"Why didn't you come here before?" said Fang.

"I hadn't a soul to mind the shop till five minutes ago. Everybody had joined in the pursuit. I've run here all the way."

"The plaintiff was reading, was he?" inquired Fang.

"Yes," replied the man. "The very book he has in his hand."

"Oh, that book, eh?" said Fang. "Is it paid for?"

"No, it is not," replied the man, with a smile.

"Dear me, I forgot all about it!" exclaimed the absent old gentleman innocently.

"A nice person to prefer a charge against a poor boy!" said Fang, with a comical effort to look humane. "I consider, sir, that you have obtained possession of that book under very suspicious circumstances, and you may think yourself very fortunate that the owner apparently declines to prosecute. Let this be a lesson to you, my man, or the law will overtake you yet. The boy is discharged. Clear the office."

"Damme!" cried the old gentleman, bursting out with the rage he had kept down so long. "Damme! I'll—"

"Clear the office!" said the magistrate.

The mandate was obeyed, and the indignant Mr. Brownlow was conveyed out, with the book in one hand and the bamboo cane in the other, in a perfect frenzy of rage and defiance. He reached the yard, and his passion vanished in a moment. Little Oliver Twist lay on his back on the pavement, whence he had been carried, with his shirt unbuttoned, his temples bathed with water, his face a deadly white, and a cold tremble convulsing his whole frame.

"Poor boy!" said Mr. Brownlow, bending over him. "Call a coach, somebody, pray. Directly!"

A coach was obtained, and Oliver having been carefully laid on the seat, the old gentleman got in, and away they drove.

THE COACH STOPPED at length before a neat house in a quiet shady street near Pentonville. Here a bed was prepared without loss of time, in which Mr. Brownlow saw his young charge carefully deposited, and here he was tended with a kindness and solicitude that knew no bounds.

But for many days Oliver remained insensible to all the goodness of his new friends. The sun rose and sank many times, and still the boy lay stretched on his uneasy bed, dwindling away beneath the dry and wasting heat of fever. Weak and pallid, he awoke at last from what seemed to have been a long and troubled dream. Feebly raising himself in the bed, he looked anxiously around.

"What room is this? Where have I been brought to?" said Oliver in a faint voice. "This is not the place I went to sleep in."

The curtain at the bed's head was hastily drawn back, and a neatly dressed, motherly old lady rose, as she undrew it, from an armchair close by.

"Hush, my dear," said the old lady softly. "You have been very ill. Lie down again, there's a dear!" With those words, she gently placed Oliver's head on the pillow; and, smoothing back his hair from his forehead, looked so kindly and lovingly into his face that he could not help placing his little withered hand in hers.

"Save us!" said the old lady, with tears in her eyes. "What a grateful little dear it is. Pretty creetur! What would his mother feel if she had sat by him as I have and could see him now!"

"Perhaps she does see me," whispered Oliver. "Perhaps she has sat by me. I almost feel as if she had."

"That was the fever, my dear," said the old lady mildly.

"I suppose it was," replied Oliver, "because heaven is a long way off. But if she knew I was ill, she must have pitied me, even there, for she was very ill herself before she died. She can't know anything about me though," added Oliver after a moment's silence. "If she had seen me hurt, it would have made her sorrowful, and her face has always looked happy when I have dreamed of her."

The old lady made no reply, but wiping her eyes, she brought some cool stuff for Oliver to drink. Then, patting him on the cheek, she told him he must lie very quiet or he would be ill again. So Oliver kept very still, partly because he was anxious to obey the kind old lady and partly because he was exhausted with what he had already said. He soon fell into a doze from which he was awakened by the light of a candle, which showed him a gentleman with a large and loud-ticking gold watch in his hand, who felt his pulse and said he was a great deal better.

"You *are* a great deal better, are you not, my dear?" said the gentleman.

"Yes, thank you, sir," replied Oliver.

"Yes, I know you are," said the gentleman. "You're hungry, too, a'n't you?"

"No, sir," answered Oliver.

"Hem!" said the gentleman. "No, I know you're not. He is not hungry, Mrs. Bedwin," said the gentleman, looking very wise.

The old lady made a respectful inclination of the head, which seemed to say that she thought the doctor was a very clever man. The doctor appeared much of the same opinion himself.

"You're not thirsty. Are you?" said the doctor.

"Yes, sir, rather thirsty," answered Oliver.

"Just as I expected, Mrs. Bedwin," said the doctor. "It's very natural that he should be thirsty. You may give him a little tea, ma'am, and some dry toast without any butter. Don't keep him too warm, ma'am; but be careful that you don't let him be too cold."

The old lady dropped a curtsy. The doctor hurried away, his boots creaking in a very important and wealthy manner as he went downstairs. Gradually Oliver fell into that deep tranquil sleep which ease from recent suffering alone imparts. The night passed, and it had been bright day for hours when he again opened his eyes; he felt cheerful and happy. The crisis of the disease was safely past. He belonged to the world again.

In three days' time he was able to sit in an easy chair, well propped up with pillows, and Mrs. Bedwin had him carried downstairs into the little housekeeper's room, which belonged to her. Having him set here, by the fireside, the good old lady sat herself down too; and, being in a state of considerable delight at seeing him so much better, forthwith began to cry most violently.

"Never mind me, my dear," said the old lady. "I'm only having a regular good cry. There, it's all over now."

"You're very, very kind to me, ma'am," said Oliver.

"Well, never you mind that, my dear," said the old lady. "It's time you had your broth, for the doctor says Mr. Brownlow may come in to see you this morning, and we must get up our best looks." And with this, the old lady applied herself to warming up in a little saucepan a bowlful of broth.

"Are you fond of pictures, dear?" inquired the old lady, seeing that Oliver had fixed his eyes most intently on a portrait which hung against the wall opposite his chair.

"I don't quite know, ma'am," said Oliver, without taking his eyes from the canvas. "I have seen so few that I hardly know. What a beautiful, mild face that lady's is! Is—is it a likeness, ma'am?"

"Yes," said the old lady, "that's a portrait."

"Whose, ma'am?" asked Oliver.

"Why, really, my dear, I don't know," answered the old lady. "It's not a likeness of anybody that you or I know, I expect. Why, sure you're not afraid of it?" she added, observing the look of awe with which the child regarded the painting.

"Oh no, no," returned Oliver quickly. "But the eyes look so sorrowful, and where I sit, they seem fixed on me. It makes my heart beat, as if it were alive and wanted to speak to me."

"Lord save us!" exclaimed the old lady, starting. "Don't talk in that way, child. You're weak and nervous after your illness. Let me wheel your chair to the other side, and then you won't see it. There!" said the old lady, suiting the action to the word.

Oliver *did* see it in his mind's eye as distinctly as if he had not altered his position, but he thought it better not to worry the kind old lady, so he smiled gently when she looked at him; and Mrs. Bedwin, satisfied, salted and broke bits of toasted bread into his broth. Oliver got through the preparation with extraordinary expedition. He had scarcely swallowed the last spoonful when there came a soft rap at the door. "Come in," said the old lady, and in walked Mr. Brownlow.

Now the old gentleman came in as brisk as need be, but he had no sooner raised his spectacles on his forehead to take a good long look at Oliver than his countenance underwent a very great variety of odd contortions. Oliver, looking very worn and shadowy from sickness, made an ineffectual attempt to stand up out of respect to his benefactor, which terminated in his sinking back into the chair again; and the fact is that Mr. Brownlow's heart, being large enough for any six ordinary old gentlemen of humane disposition, pumped a supply of tears into his eyes.

"Poor boy!" said Mr. Brownlow, clearing his throat. "I'm rather hoarse this morning, Mrs. Bedwin. I'm afraid I have caught cold."

"I hope not, sir," said Mrs. Bedwin.

"I don't know, Bedwin, I don't know," said Mr. Brownlow. "I rather think I had a damp napkin at dinnertime yesterday. But never mind that. How do you feel, my dear?"

"Very happy, sir," replied Oliver. "And very grateful indeed, sir, for your goodness to me."

"Good boy," said Mr. Brownlow stoutly. "Have you given him any nourishment, Bedwin?"

"He has just had a bowl of beautiful strong broth, sir," replied Mrs. Bedwin.

"Ugh!" said Mr. Brownlow with a shudder. "A couple of glasses of port wine would have done him a great deal more good. Wouldn't they, Tom White, eh?"

"My name is Oliver, sir," replied the little invalid, with a look of astonishment.

"Oliver," said Mr. Brownlow. "Oliver what? Oliver White, eh?"

"No, sir, Twist. Oliver Twist."

"Queer name!" said the old gentleman. "What made you tell the magistrate your name was White?"

"I never told him so, sir," returned Oliver in amazement.

This sounded so like a falsehood that the old gentleman looked sternly in Oliver's face. But it was impossible to doubt him: there was truth in every one of its sharpened lineaments.

"Some mistake," said Mr. Brownlow. Although his motive for looking steadily at Oliver no longer existed, the old idea of the resemblance between his features and some familiar face came upon him so strongly that he could not withdraw his gaze.

"I hope you are not angry with me, sir?" said Oliver, raising his eyes beseechingly.

"No, no," replied the old gentleman. "Why, what's this? Bedwin, look there!"

As he spoke, he pointed hastily to the picture above Oliver's head and then to the boy's face. There was its living copy. The eyes, the head, the mouth; every feature was the same. The expression was, for the instant, so precisely alike that the minutest line seemed copied with startling accuracy!

Oliver knew not the cause of this sudden exclamation; for, not being strong enough to bear the start it gave him, he fainted away.

··꘎· CHAPTER V ·꘎··

WHEN THE DODGER and his accomplished friend Master Bates joined in the hue and cry which was raised at Oliver's heels, as has been already described, they were actuated by a laudable regard for themselves; forasmuch as the liberty of the individual is one of the proudest boasts of a truehearted Englishman, and if any further proof were wanted of the strictly philosophical nature of the conduct of these young gentlemen, it would be found in the fact of their quitting the pursuit when the general attention was fixed on Oliver, and making for their home by the shortest possible cut.

The noise of their footsteps on the creaking stairs roused the merry old gentleman as he sat over the fire. There was a rascally smile on his white face as he bent his ear towards the door. "Why, how's this?" muttered Fagin, changing countenance. "Only two of 'em? Where's the third? They can't have got into trouble!"

The door was slowly opened and the Dodger and Charley Bates entered, closing it behind them.

"Where's Oliver?" asked Fagin, rising with a menacing look.

The young thieves eyed their preceptor in alarm, but they made no reply.

"What's become of the boy?" asked Fagin again, seizing the Dodger tightly by the collar. "Speak out or I'll throttle you!"

Mr. Fagin looked so much in earnest that Charley Bates, who conceived it by no means improbable that it might be his turn to be throttled second, dropped on his knees and raised a loud, well-sustained roar.

"Will you speak?" thundered Fagin, shaking the Dodger so that his keeping in the big coat at all seemed miraculous.

"Why, the traps have got him," said the Dodger sullenly. "Let go o' me, will you!" And swinging himself at one jerk clean out of the big coat, which he left in Fagin's hands, the Dodger snatched up the toasting fork and made a pass at the merry old gentleman's waistcoat. Fagin stepped back, and seizing a pot of beer, prepared to hurl it at his assailant's head. But Charley Bates at this moment calling his attention by a perfectly terrific howl, he suddenly altered its destination and flung it full at that young gentleman.

"Why, wot the blazes is in the wind now!" growled a deep voice. "Who pitched that 'ere at me? It's well it's the beer and not the pot as hit me, or I'd have settled somebody. Wot's it all about, Fagin?"

The man who growled out these words was a stoutly built fellow of about five and thirty, in a black velveteen coat, very soiled drab breeches, lace-up half boots, and gray cotton stockings which enclosed a bulky pair of legs with large, swelling calves. He had a brown hat on his head and a dirty handkerchief round his neck, with the long frayed ends of which he smeared the beer from his face as he spoke. He disclosed, when he had done so, a broad heavy countenance with a beard of three days' growth, and two scowling eyes, one of which displayed various parti-colored symptoms of having been recently damaged by a blow.

"Come in, d'ye hear, you sneaking warmint?" growled this engaging ruffian.

A white shaggy dog, with his face scratched and torn in twenty different places, skulked into the room.

"Why didn't you come in afore?" said the man. "You're getting too proud to own me afore company, are you? Lie down!"

This command was accompanied with a kick which sent the animal to the other end of the room. He appeared well used to it, however, for he coiled himself up in a corner without uttering a sound.

"Wot are you up to? Ill-treating the boys, you covetous, avaricious, in-sa-ti-a-ble old fence?" asked the man, seating himself deliberately. "I wonder they don't murder you! *I* would if I was them. If I'd been your 'prentis, I'd have done it long ago."

"Hush! Hush! Mr. Sikes," said the Jew, trembling; "don't speak so loud."

"None of your mistering," replied the ruffian. "You always

mean mischief when you come that. You know my name. Out with it!"

"Well, well, then—Bill Sikes," said Fagin, with abject humility. "You seem out of humor, Bill."

"Perhaps I am," replied Sikes. "I should think *you* was rather out of sorts too, unless you mean as little harm when you throw pewter pots about as you do when you blab, and—"

"Are you mad?" said Fagin, catching the man by the sleeve and pointing towards the boys.

Mr. Sikes contented himself with tying an imaginary knot under his left ear and jerking his head over on the right shoulder; a piece of dumb show which Fagin appeared to understand perfectly. He then demanded a glass of liquor. "And mind you don't poison it," he said, laying his hat on the table.

After swallowing two or three glasses of spirits, Mr. Sikes condescended to take some notice of the young gentlemen; which gracious act led to a conversation, in which the cause and manner of Oliver's capture were detailed, with such alterations and improvements on the truth as appeared advisable to the Dodger.

"I'm afraid," said Fagin, "that he may say something which will get us into trouble. And I'm afraid," added the old man, regarding Sikes closely as he did so, "that if the game was up with us, it might be up with a good many more, and that it would come out rather worse for you than it would for me, my dear."

The man started, and turned round on Fagin. But the old gentleman's eyes were vacantly staring on the opposite wall.

"Somebody must find out wot's been done at the police office," said Mr. Sikes, in a lower tone.

Fagin nodded assent.

"If he hasn't peached and is committed, there's no fear till he comes out again," said Mr. Sikes, "and then he must be taken care on. You must get hold of him somehow."

Again Fagin nodded. The prudence of this line of action, indeed, was obvious; but, unfortunately, there was one very strong objection to its being adopted. This was that the Dodger and Charley Bates and Fagin and Mr. William Sikes happened, one and all, to entertain a violent and deeply rooted antipathy to going near a police office on any ground or pretext whatever. How long they might have sat and looked at each other, in a state of uncertainty not the most pleasant of its kind, it is difficult to guess. But the sudden entrance of the two young ladies whom Oliver had seen on a former occasion caused the conversation to flow afresh.

"The very thing!" said Fagin. "Bet will go, won't you, my dear?"

"Where?" inquired the young lady.

"Only just up to the police office, my dear," said Fagin coaxingly.

It is due to the young lady to say that she did not positively affirm that she would not, but that she merely expressed an emphatic and earnest desire to be "blessed" if she would. Fagin's countenance fell. He turned from this young lady, who was gaily, not to say gorgeously, attired in a red gown, green boots and yellow curl papers, to the other female.

"Nancy, my dear," he said in a soothing manner, "what do *you* say?"

"That it won't do; so it's no use a-trying it on, Fagin."

"Why, you're just the very person for it," reasoned Mr. Sikes. "Nobody about here knows anything of you."

"And as I don't want 'em to, neither," replied Nancy in the same composed manner, "it's rather more no than yes with me, Bill."

"She'll go, Fagin," said Sikes.

"No, she won't, Fagin," said Nancy.

"Yes, she will, Fagin," said Sikes.

And Mr. Sikes was right. By dint of alternate threats and bribes, the lady in question was ultimately prevailed upon to undertake the commission.

Accordingly, with a clean white apron tied over her gown and her curl papers tucked up under a straw bonnet—both articles of dress being provided from an inexhaustible stock of garments kept by Fagin—Miss Nancy prepared to issue forth on her errand.

"Stop a minute, my dear," said Fagin, producing a little covered basket and a large street-door key. "Carry these. It looks more respectable, my dear. There, very good indeed!"

"Oh, my brother! My poor, sweet, innocent little brother!" exclaimed Nancy, bursting into tears. "What has become of him? Where have they taken him to? Oh, do have pity and tell me, if you please, gentlemen!"

Having uttered these words in a most lamentable and heart-broken tone, to the immeasurable delight of her hearers, Miss Nancy paused, winked to the company, nodded, and disappeared.

"Ah, she's a clever girl, my dears," said Fagin, turning round to his young friends and shaking his head, as if in mute admonition to them to follow her bright example.

"She's a honor to her sex," said Mr. Sikes, filling his glass, and smiting the table with his enormous fist. "Here's her health, and wishing they was all like her!"

While these and many other encomiums were being passed on the accomplished Nancy, that young lady made her way to the police office, whither she made straight up to the bluff officer in the striped waistcoat, and with the most piteous wailings and lamentations, demanded her own dear brother.

"*I* haven't got him, my dear," said the officer. "The gentleman's got him."

"What gentleman? Oh, gracious heavens! What gentleman?"

In reply to this incoherent question, the officer informed the deeply affected sister that Oliver had been taken ill in the office, and discharged in consequence of a witness having proved the robbery to have been committed by another boy; and that the plaintiff had carried him away, in an insensible condition, to his own residence, which was somewhere at Pentonville, as he had heard that word mentioned in the directions to the coachman.

In a dreadful state of doubt and uncertainty, the agonized young woman staggered to the gate and then, exchanging her faltering walk for a swift run, returned to Fagin's domicile by the most devious route she could think of.

Mr. Bill Sikes no sooner heard the account of the expedition than he hastily called the white dog and, putting on his hat, expeditiously departed.

"We must know where he is, my dears; he must be found," said Fagin, greatly excited. "Charley, do nothing but skulk about till you bring home some news of him! Nancy, my dear, I must have him found. I trust to you and the Artful for everything! Stay, stay," he added, unlocking a drawer with a shaking hand, "there's money, my dears. I shall shut up this shop tonight. You'll know where to find me! Don't stop here a minute, my dears!"

With these words he pushed the three of them from the room, and, carefully barring the door behind them, drew from its place of concealment the box which he had unintentionally disclosed to Oliver. Then he hastily proceeded to dispose the watches and jewelry beneath his clothing.

A rap at the door startled him in this occupation. "Who's there?" he cried in a shrill tone.

"Me!" replied the voice of the Dodger through the keyhole.

"What now?" cried Fagin impatiently.

"Is he to be kidnaped to your other place? Nancy says."

"Yes," replied Fagin, "wherever she lays hands on him. Find him, that's all! I shall know what to do next; never fear."

The Dodger murmured a reply and hurried downstairs after his companions.

"He has not peached so far," said Fagin, as he pursued his occupation. "If he means to blab us among his new friends, we may stop his mouth yet."

··~⊙· CHAPTER VI ·⊙~··

OLIVER SOON RECOVERED from the fainting fit into which Mr. Brownlow's abrupt exclamation had thrown him; and the subject of the picture was carefully avoided, both by the old gentleman and Mrs. Bedwin, in the conversation that ensued—which was confined to such topics as might amuse without exciting him. He was still too weak to get up to breakfast, but when he came down into the housekeeper's room next day, his first act was to cast an eager glance at the wall in the hope of again looking on the face of the beautiful lady. But his expectations were disappointed, for the picture had been removed.

"Ah!" said the housekeeper, watching the direction of Oliver's eyes. "It is gone, you see."

"I see it is, ma'am. Why have they taken it away?"

"Mr. Brownlow said that as it seemed to worry you, perhaps it might prevent your getting well," rejoined the old lady.

"Oh, no, indeed. It didn't worry me, ma'am," said Oliver. "I liked to see it. I quite loved it."

"Well, well," said the old lady good-humoredly, "you get well as fast as you can, dear, and it shall be hung up again."

This was all the information Oliver could obtain about the picture at that time. So, as the old lady had been so kind to him in his illness, he listened attentively to a great many stories she told him. When the old lady had expatiated a long while on the excellences of her children, and the merits of her husband, who had been dead and gone just six and twenty years, it was time to have tea. After tea she began to teach Oliver cribbage, and they played, with great interest and gravity, until it was time for the invalid to have some warm wine and water, with a slice of dry toast, and then to go cozily to bed.

They were happy days, those of Oliver's recovery. Everything was so quiet and orderly, everybody was so gentle, that after the noise and turbulence in the midst of which he had always lived it seemed like heaven itself. He was no sooner strong enough to put his clothes on properly than Mr. Brownlow caused a complete new suit, and a new cap, and a new pair of shoes, to be provided for him. As Oliver was told that he might do what he liked with the old clothes, he gave them to a servant who had been very kind to him and asked her to sell them and keep the money for herself. This she very readily did, and Oliver felt quite delighted to think that there was now no possible danger of his ever being able to wear them again. He had never had a new suit before.

One evening, about a week after the affair of the picture, as he was sitting talking to Mrs. Bedwin, there came a message down from Mr. Brownlow that if Oliver felt pretty well, he should like to see him in his study and talk to him a while.

"Bless us and save us! Wash your hands, and let me part your hair nicely for you, child," said Mrs. Bedwin. "Dear heart alive! If we had known he would have asked for you, we would have put a clean collar on you."

Oliver did as the old lady bade him, and he looked so delicate and handsome that she went so far as to say, looking at him with great complacency from head to foot, that she really didn't think it would have been possible, on the longest notice, to have made much difference in him for the better.

Thus encouraged, Oliver tapped at the study door. On Mr. Brownlow calling to him to come in, he found himself in a little back room quite full of books, with a window looking into some pleasant gardens. Mr. Brownlow was seated reading before the window. When he saw Oliver, he told him to come and sit down. Oliver complied, marveling where the people could be found to read such a great number of books as seemed to be written to make the world wiser.

"There are a good many books, are there not, my boy?" asked Mr. Brownlow, observing the curiosity with which Oliver surveyed the shelves that reached from the floor to the ceiling.

"A great number, sir," replied Oliver. "I never saw so many."

"You shall read them if you behave well. How should you like to grow up a clever man and write books, eh?"

"I think I would rather read them, sir," replied Oliver.

"What, wouldn't you like to be a book writer?"

Oliver considered a little while and at last said he should think it would be a much better thing to be a bookseller, upon which the old gentleman laughed heartily and declared he had said a very good thing. "Don't be afraid," he continued, "we won't make an author of you while there's an honest trade to be learnt."

"Thank you, sir," said Oliver, and at the earnest manner of his reply the old gentleman laughed again.

"Now," said Mr. Brownlow, speaking if possible in a kinder but at the same time in a much more serious manner, "I want you to pay great attention, my boy, to what I am going to say. I shall talk to you without any reserve, because I am sure you are as well able to understand me as many older persons would be."

"Oh, don't tell me you are going to send me away, sir, pray!" exclaimed Oliver, alarmed at the old gentleman's serious tone. "Don't send me back to the wretched place I came from. Let me stay here and be a servant. Have mercy on a poor boy, sir!"

"My dear child," said the old gentleman, moved by the warmth of Oliver's sudden appeal, "you need not be afraid of my deserting you, unless you give me cause."

"I never, never will, sir," interposed Oliver.

"I hope not," rejoined the old gentleman. "I have been deceived before in the objects whom I have endeavored to benefit, but I feel strongly disposed to trust you; and I am more interested in you than I can account for even to myself. You say you are a friendless orphan. Let me hear your story: where you come from, who brought you up, and how you got into the company in which I found you. Speak the truth, and you shall not be friendless while I live."

Just as Oliver was on the point of beginning to relate how he had been brought up at the farm, and carried to the workhouse by Mr. Bumble, a peculiarly impatient little double knock was heard at the street door, and the servant, running upstairs, announced Mr. Grimwig.

"Is he coming up?" inquired Mr. Brownlow.

"Yes, sir," replied the servant. "He asked if there were any muffins in the house, and when I told him yes, he said he had come to tea."

Mr. Brownlow smiled, and said to Oliver that Mr. Grimwig was an old friend of his; and he must not mind his being a little rough in his manners, for he was a worthy creature at bottom.

At this moment there walked into the room, supporting himself by a thick stick, a stout old gentleman rather lame in one leg. He was dressed in a blue coat, striped waistcoat, nankeen breeches and a broad-brimmed white hat with the sides turned up with green. A plaited shirt frill stuck out from his waistcoat, and a very long steel watch chain, with nothing but a key at the end, dangled below it. He had a manner of screwing his head on one side when he spoke, and of looking out of the corners of his eyes at the same time, which irresistibly reminded the beholder of a parrot. In this attitude he fixed himself the moment he made his appearance, and holding out a small piece of orange peel at arm's length, exclaimed in a growling, discontented voice, "Look here, do you see this! Isn't it a most wonderful and extraordinary thing that I can't call at a man's house but I find a piece of this on the staircase? I've been lamed with orange peel once, and I know orange peel will be my death at last. It will, sir; or I'll be content to eat my own head, sir!"

This was the handsome offer with which Mr. Grimwig backed and confirmed nearly every assertion he made, and it was the more singular in his case, because even admitting for the sake of argument the possibility of scientific improvements being ever brought to pass which will enable a gentleman to eat his own head in the event of his being so disposed, Mr. Grimwig's head was such a particularly large one that the most sanguine man alive could hardly entertain a hope of being able to get through it at a sitting.

"I'll eat my head, sir," repeated Mr. Grimwig, striking his stick on the floor. "Hallo, what's that!" looking at Oliver, and retreating a pace or two.

"This is young Oliver Twist, whom we were speaking about," said Mr. Brownlow. Oliver bowed.

"You don't mean to say that's the boy who had the fever?" said Mr. Grimwig, recoiling a little more. "Wait a minute! Don't speak! Stop—" continued Mr. Grimwig abruptly. "If that's not the boy, sir, who had the orange and threw this bit of peel on the staircase, I'll eat my head and his, too!"

"No, no, he has not had one," said Mr. Brownlow, laughing. "Come! Put down your hat and speak to my young friend."

"I feel strongly on this subject, sir," said the irritable old gentleman, drawing off his gloves. "There's always more or less orange peel on the pavement in our street, and I *know* it's put there by the surgeon's boy at the corner. He's an assassin! So he is. If he is not—" Here the irascible old gentleman gave a great knock on the floor with his stick, which was always understood by his friends to imply the customary offer whenever it was not expressed in words. Then he sat down, and opening a double eyeglass, which he wore attached to a broad black riband, took a view of Oliver, who, seeing that he was the object of inspection, colored and bowed again.

"That's the boy, is it?" said Mr. Grimwig at length.

"That is the boy," replied Mr. Brownlow.

"How are you, boy?" asked Mr. Grimwig.

"A great deal better, thank you, sir," replied Oliver.

Mr. Brownlow, seeming to apprehend that his singular friend was about to say something disagreeable, asked Oliver to tell Mrs. Bedwin they were ready for tea—which, as Oliver did not half like the visitor's manner, he was very happy to do.

"He is a nice-looking boy, is he not?" inquired Mr. Brownlow.

"I don't know," replied Mr. Grimwig pettishly. "Where does he come from? Who is he? What is he? He has had a fever. What of that? Fevers are not peculiar to good people, are they? Bad people have fevers sometimes, haven't they, eh? Pooh! Nonsense!"

When Mr. Brownlow admitted that he had postponed any investigation into Oliver's previous history until he thought the boy was strong enough to bear it, Mr. Grimwig chuckled maliciously. And he demanded with a sneer whether the housekeeper was in the habit of counting the plate at night, because if she didn't find a tablespoon or two missing some sunshiny morning, why, he would be content to—and so forth.

All this Mr. Brownlow, knowing his friend's peculiarities, bore with great good humor. Mr. Grimwig, at tea, was graciously pleased to express his entire approval of the muffins, and Oliver, who made one of the party, began to feel more at his ease than he had yet done in the fierce old gentleman's presence.

"And when are you going to hear a full, true and particular account of the life of Oliver Twist?" asked Grimwig of Mr. Brownlow at the conclusion of the meal, looking sideways at Oliver.

"Tomorrow morning," replied Mr. Brownlow. "I would rather he was alone with me at the time. Come up to me tomorrow morning at ten o'clock, my dear."

"Yes, sir," Oliver answered with some hesitation, because he was confused by Mr. Grimwig's looking so hard at him.

"I'll tell you what," whispered that gentleman to Mr. Brownlow; "he won't come up to you tomorrow morning. I saw him hesitate. He is deceiving you, my good friend."

"I'll swear he is not," replied Mr. Brownlow warmly.

"If he is not," said Mr. Grimwig, "I'll—" and down went the stick.

"I'll answer for that boy's truth with my life!" said Mr. Brownlow, knocking the table.

"And I for his falsehood with my head!" rejoined Mr. Grimwig, with a provoking smile, knocking the table also.

As fate would have it, Mrs. Bedwin chanced to bring in at this moment a small parcel of books, which Mr. Brownlow had that morning purchased of the identical bookstall-keeper who has already figured in this history. Having laid them on the table, she prepared to leave the room.

"Call after the delivery boy, Mrs. Bedwin!" said Mr. Brownlow. "It's particular. They are not paid for, and the bookseller is a poor man. There are some books to be taken back, too."

The street door was opened. Oliver ran one way; the girl ran another; and Mrs. Bedwin stood on the step. Oliver and the girl returned, breathless, to report that there were no tidings of the boy.

"Dear me, I am sorry for that," exclaimed Mr. Brownlow. "I particularly wished those books to be returned tonight."

"Send Oliver with them," said Mr. Grimwig, with an ironical smile. "He will be sure to deliver them safely, you know."

"Yes, do let me take them, please, sir," said Oliver.

The old gentleman was just going to say that Oliver should not go out on any account when a most malicious cough from Mr. Grimwig determined him that he should, and that he should prove to Mr. Grimwig the injustice of his suspicions at once.

"You *shall* go, my dear," said the old gentleman. "The books are on a chair by my table. Fetch them down."

Oliver, delighted to be of use, brought down the books and waited, cap in hand, to hear what message he was to take.

"You are to say," said Mr. Brownlow, glancing steadily at Grimwig, "that you have brought those books back and that you have come to pay the four pound ten I owe him. This is a five-pound note, so you will have to bring me back ten shillings change."

"I won't be twenty minutes, sir," replied Oliver eagerly. Having buttoned up the bank note in his jacket pocket and placed the books carefully under his arm, he made a respectful bow and left the room. Mrs. Bedwin followed him to the door, giving him many directions about the nearest way and the names of the bookseller and the street, all of which Oliver said he clearly understood. Having super-added many injunctions to be sure and not take cold, the old lady at length permitted him to depart.

"Bless his sweet face!" said the old lady, looking after him. "I can't bear, somehow, to let him go out of my sight."

At this moment Oliver looked gaily round and waved. The old lady smilingly returned his salutation.

"Let me see, he'll be back in thirty minutes at the longest," said Mr. Brownlow, pulling out his watch and placing it on the table. "It will be dark by that time."

"You really expect him to come back, do you?" inquired Mr. Grimwig.

"Don't you?" asked Mr. Brownlow, smiling.

"No," he said, smiting the table with his fist, "I do not. The boy has a new suit of clothes on his back, a set of valuable books under his arm, and a five-pound note in his pocket. He'll join his old friends the thieves, and laugh at you. If ever that boy returns to this house, sir, I'll eat my head."

With these words he drew his chair closer to the table, and there the two friends sat, in silent expectation, with the watch between them.

·· CHAPTER VII ··

IN THE OBSCURE PARLOR of a low public house, a dark and gloomy den, there sat, brooding over a small glass, a man in a velveteen coat, drab shorts and half boots. Even by that dim light no experienced agent of police would have hesitated to recognize him as

Mr. William Sikes. At his feet sat a white-coated, red-eyed dog who occupied himself alternately in winking and in licking himself.

"Keep quiet, you warmint! Keep quiet!" said Mr. Sikes, bestowing a kick and a curse simultaneously upon the dog. The dog at once fixed his teeth in one of the half boots. Having given it a hearty shake, he retired, growling, under a bench.

"You would, would you?" said Sikes, seizing a poker in one hand and deliberately opening with the other a large clasp knife. "Come here, you devil! Come here! D'ye hear?" Then, dropping on his knees, he began to assail the animal most furiously, when, the door suddenly opening, the dog darted out, leaving Bill Sikes with the poker and the clasp knife in his hands. Mr. Sikes at once transferred his anger to the newcomer.

"Wot the devil do you come in between me and my dog for?" he said with a fierce gesture.

"I didn't know, my dear, I didn't know," replied Fagin humbly; for he was the newcomer. He was followed by Nancy, who was decorated with the bonnet, apron, basket, and door key, complete.

"You are on the scent, are you, Nancy?" inquired Sikes, proffering a glass of liquor.

"Yes, I am, Bill," replied the young lady, disposing of the contents of the glass, "and tired enough of it I am, too. The young brat's been ill and confined; and—"

"Ah, Nancy, dear," said Fagin, looking up.

Now, whether a peculiar contraction of Fagin's red eyebrows, and a half closing of his deeply set eyes, warned Miss Nancy that she was too communicative, is not a matter of much importance. The fact is that she suddenly checked herself, pulled her shawl over her shoulders, and declared it was time to go. Mr. Sikes accompanied her; and they went away together, followed at a little distance by the dog, who slunk out of a neighboring yard.

Fagin thrust his head out of the room door when Sikes had left it; shook his clenched fist; muttered a deep curse; and then, with a horrible grin, seated himself at the table.

Meanwhile Oliver Twist, little dreaming that he was within so very short a distance of the merry old gentleman, was on his way to the bookstall. When he got into Clerkenwell, he accidentally turned down a bystreet which was not exactly in his way; but he was walking along, thinking how happy and contented he felt, when he was startled by a young woman screaming out very loud: "Oh, my dear brother!" And he had hardly looked up to see what the matter was when a pair of arms were thrown tight around his neck.

"Don't," cried Oliver, struggling. "Let go of me. Who is it?"

The only reply to this was a great number of loud lamentations from the young woman who had embraced him and who had a little basket and door key in her hand. "I've found him!" she cried. "Oh, Oliver, Oliver, you naughty boy, to make me suffer sich distress! Come home, dear, come!" The young woman then got so dreadfully hysterical that a couple of women looking on asked what was the matter.

"Oh, ma'am," replied the young woman, "he ran away near a month ago from his parents, who are hardworking and respectable people, and went and joined a set of thieves and bad characters, and almost broke his mother's heart."

"Young wretch!" said one woman.

"Go home, little brute," said the other.

"I am not," replied Oliver, greatly alarmed. "I don't know her. I haven't any sister, or father and mother either. I'm an orphan; I live at Pentonville."

"Only hear him, how he braves it out!" cried the young woman.

"Why, it's Nancy!" exclaimed Oliver, who now saw her face for the first time. He started back in astonishment.

"You see, he knows me!" cried Nancy, appealing to the bystanders. "He can't help himself."

"Wot the devil's this?" said a man, bursting out of a beer shop with a white dog at his heels. "Young Oliver! Come home to your poor mother. Come home directly!"

"I don't belong to them. I don't know them. Help! Help!" cried Oliver, struggling in the man's powerful grasp.

"Help?" repeated the man. "Yes, I'll help you, you young rascal! Wot books are these? You've been a-stealing 'em, have you? Give 'em here." With these words the man tore the volumes from

Oliver and struck him on the head. "Come on, you young villain! Here, Bull's-eye, mind him, boy! Mind him!"

In another moment Oliver was dragged into a labyrinth of dark narrow alleys and was forced along them at a pace which rendered his cries unintelligible.

The gas lamps were lighted, meanwhile; Mrs. Bedwin waited anxiously at the open door; the servant had run up the street twenty times to see if there were any traces of Oliver; and still the two old gentlemen sat, perseveringly, in the dark parlor, with the watch between them.

SIKES AND NANCY WALKED ON, with Oliver, by little-frequented and dirty ways, for a full half hour, meeting very few people. At length they turned into a narrow street of old-clothes shops and stopped before the door of a shop that was closed and apparently untenanted. The house was in ruinous condition.

"All right," cried Sikes, glancing cautiously about.

Nancy stooped below the shutters, and Oliver heard the sound of a bell. They crossed the street and stood for a few moments under a lamp. A noise, as if a sash window were raised, was heard, and soon afterwards the door softly opened. Mr. Sikes then seized the terrified boy by the collar, and all three were quickly inside the house. The passage was perfectly dark. They waited while the person who had let them in chained and barred the door.

"Is the old un here?" asked Sikes.

"Yes," replied a voice, "and precious down in the mouth he has been. Won't he be glad to see you? Oh, no!"

The style of this reply, as well as the voice which delivered it, seemed familiar to Oliver's ears, but it was impossible to distinguish even the form of the speaker in the darkness.

"Let's have a glim," said Sikes, "or we shall go breaking our necks."

"Stand still a moment and I'll get one," replied the voice. The receding footsteps of the speaker were heard, and in another minute the form of Mr. John Dawkins, otherwise the Artful Dodger, appeared bearing a tallow candle.

The young gentleman did not stop to bestow any other mark of recognition on Oliver than a humorous grin, but, turning away, he beckoned the visitors to follow him down a flight of stairs. They crossed an empty kitchen, and opening the door of a low earthy-smelling room which seemed to have been built in a small back-yard, were received with a shout of laughter.

"Oh, my wig, my wig!" cried Master Charles Bates, from whose lungs the laughter had proceeded. "Here he is! Oh, Fagin, do look at him! I can't bear it. Hold me, somebody, while I laugh it out."

With this irrepressible ebullition of mirth, Master Bates laid himself flat on the floor and kicked convulsively in an ecstasy of facetious joy. Then, jumping to his feet, he snatched the candle from the Dodger and viewed Oliver round and round, while Fagin, taking off his nightcap, made a great number of low bows to the bewildered boy. The Artful, meantime, who seldom gave way to merriment when it interfered with business, rifled Oliver's pockets with steady assiduity.

"Look at his togs, Fagin!" said Charley, putting the light so close to his new jacket as nearly to set him on fire. "Superfine cloth, and the heavy swell cut! Oh, my eye, what a game! Nothing but a gentleman, Fagin!"

"Delighted to see you looking so well, my dear," said the old man, bowing with mock humility. "The Artful shall give you an-other suit, my dear, for fear you should spoil that Sunday one. Why didn't you write, my dear, and say you were coming? We'd have got something warm for supper."

At this Master Bates roared again, so loud that Fagin himself relaxed and even the Dodger smiled. But as the Artful drew forth the five-pound note at that instant, it is doubtful whether the sally or the discovery awakened his merriment.

"Hallo, wot's that?" inquired Sikes, stepping forward as Fagin seized the note. "That's mine, Fagin."

"No, no, my dear," said the old man. "Mine, Bill, mine. You shall have the books."

"If that ain't mine and Nancy's," said Bill Sikes, putting on his hat with a determined air, "I'll take the boy back again."

Oliver's Reception by Fagin and the Boys

Fagin started. Oliver started, too, for he hoped that the dispute might really end in his being taken back.

"Come! Hand over, I tell you!" said Sikes. "Do you think Nancy and me has got nothing else to do with our time but to spend it in scouting arter every boy as gets grabbed through you? Give it here, you avaricious old skeleton!"

With this gentle remonstrance, Mr. Sikes plucked the note from between the old man's finger and thumb, folded it up small and tied it in his neckerchief. "That's for our share of the trouble," said Sikes, "and not half enough, neither. You may keep the books if you're that fond of reading. If you a'n't, sell 'em."

"They belong to the old gentleman," said Oliver, wringing his hands, "to the good, kind old gentleman who had me nursed when I was near dying. Oh, pray send him back the books and money! He'll think I stole them. Keep me here all my life, but pray, pray send them back!" With those words, which were uttered with all the energy of passionate grief, Oliver fell on his knees at Fagin's feet and beat his hands together in desperation.

"The boy's right," remarked Fagin, looking covertly round and knitting his shaggy eyebrows into a hard knot. "You're right, Oliver; they *will* think you have stolen 'em. Ha! Ha!" he chuckled. "It couldn't have happened better if we had chosen our time!"

"Of course it couldn't," replied Sikes. "I know'd that, directly I see him coming through Clerkenwell with the books under his arm. They're softhearted psalm-singers, or they wouldn't have taken him in. They'll ask no questions, fear they should be obliged to prosecute and so get him lagged. He's safe enough."

Oliver had looked from one to the other while these words were being spoken, as if he could scarcely understand what passed; but when Bill Sikes concluded, he jumped suddenly to his feet and tore wildly from the room, uttering shrieks for help which made the bare old house echo to the roof.

"Keep back the dog, Bill!" cried Nancy, springing before the door and closing it as Fagin and his two pupils darted out in pursuit. "Keep back the dog; he'll tear the boy to pieces."

"Serve him right!" cried Sikes, struggling to disengage himself from the girl's grasp. "Stand off from me, or I'll split your head against the wall."

"I don't care for that, Bill, I don't care for that!" screamed the girl, struggling violently with the man. "The child shan't be torn down by the dog, unless you kill me first!"

"Shan't he!" said Sikes, setting his teeth. "I'll soon do that if you don't keep off."

The housebreaker flung the girl from him to the farther end of the room just as Fagin and the two boys returned, dragging Oliver.

"What's the matter here!" said Fagin, looking round.

"The girl's gone mad, I think," replied Sikes savagely.

"No, she hasn't," said Nancy, pale and breathless.

"Then keep quiet," said Fagin, with a threatening look. He turned to Oliver. "So you wanted to get away, my dear?" he said, taking up a jagged club which lay in a corner of the fireplace.

Oliver made no reply. But he watched the old man's motions and breathed quickly.

"Wanted to get assistance, call for the police, did you?" sneered Fagin. "We'll cure you of that, my young master!"

He inflicted a smart blow on Oliver's shoulders with the club and was raising it for a second, when the girl, rushing forward, wrested it from his hand and flung it into the fire.

"I won't stand by and see it done, Fagin!" cried the girl. "You've got the boy, and what more would you have? Let him be—or I shall put that mark on some of you that will bring me to the gallows before my time!" She stamped her foot violently on the floor, and with her lips compressed and her hands clenched, looked alternately at Fagin and the other robber.

"Why, Nancy," said Fagin in a soothing tone, "you—you're more clever than ever tonight. Ha! Ha! My dear, you are acting beautifully!"

"Am I?" said the girl. "Take care I don't overdo it! You will be the worse for it if I do."

There is something about a roused woman, especially if she add to all her other passions the fierce impulses of recklessness and despair, which few men like to provoke. Fagin, shrinking back a few paces, cast a glance, half imploring and half cowardly, at Sikes. Mr. Sikes, thus mutely appealed to, and possibly feeling his personal pride and influence interested in the reduction of Miss Nancy to reason, gave utterance to a couple of score of curses and threats. As they produced no visible effect on the object against whom they were discharged he resorted to more tangible arguments.

"Wot do you mean by this?" said Sikes. "Do you know who you are and wot you are?"

"Oh, yes, I know," replied the girl, laughing hysterically.

"Well, then, keep quiet," rejoined Sikes, with a growl like that he was accustomed to use when addressing his dog. "You're a nice one to take up the gen-teel side! A pretty subject for the child to make a friend of!"

"God Almighty help me, I am!" cried the girl. "And I wish I had been struck dead in the street before I had lent a hand in bringing him here. He's a thief, a liar, a devil, all that's bad, from this night forth. Isn't that enough for the old wretch, without blows?"

"Come, come, Sikes," said Fagin, motioning toward the boys, who were eagerly attentive to all that passed, "we must have civil words; civil words, Bill."

"Civil words!" cried the girl, whose passion had become frightful to see. "Civil words, you villain! I thieved for you when I was a child not half as old as this!" pointing to Oliver. "I have been in the same trade and in the same service for twelve years since. Don't you know it? Speak out! Don't you know it?"

"Well, well," replied Fagin, with an attempt at pacification, "and if you have, it's your living!"

"Aye, it is my living!" returned the girl, pouring out the words in one continuous and vehement scream. "And the cold, wet, dirty streets are my home, and you're the wretch that drove me to them long ago, and that'll keep me there, day and night, day and night, till I die!"

"I shall do you a mischief worse than that," interposed Fagin, goaded by these reproaches, "if you say much more!"

The girl said nothing more, but, tearing her hair and dress in a transport of passion, made a rush at Fagin. She would probably have left signal marks of her revenge on him had not her wrists been seized by Sikes at the right moment; whereupon she made a few ineffectual struggles, and fainted.

"She's all right now," said Sikes, laying her down in a corner. "She's uncommon strong in the arms when she's up in this way."

"It's the worst of having to do with women," said the old man, replacing his club. "But they're clever, and we can't get on in our line without 'em. Charley, show Oliver to bed."

"I suppose he'd better not wear his best clothes tomorrow, Fagin, had he?" inquired Charley Bates.

"Certainly not," replied Fagin, reciprocating the grin with which Charley put the question.

Master Bates, apparently much delighted with his commission, took the candle and led Oliver into an adjacent kitchen, where there were two or three beds. Here, with many bursts of laughter, Charley produced the identical old suit of clothes which Oliver had so much congratulated himself on leaving off at Mr. Brownlow's. It was the accidental display of them to Fagin, by the secondhand man who purchased them from Mr. Brownlow's maid, that had been the first clue received of his whereabouts.

"Pull off the smart ones," said Charley, "and I'll give 'em to Fagin to take care of. What fun!"

Poor Oliver unwillingly complied. Master Bates, rolling up the new clothes under his arm, left Oliver in the dark, locking the door behind him.

··ᴇᴠᴏ· CHAPTER VIII ·ᴏᴠᴇ··

A FEW DAYS after these events, Mr. Bumble made an official trip to London to represent the board at a legal action at the Quarter Sessions at Clerkenwell. At six o'clock in the morning, having exchanged his cocked hat for a round one, he took his place in the coach; and in due course of time he arrived in London. There he sat himself down in the house at which the coach stopped, and took a temperate dinner of steaks, oyster sauce, and porter. After that, putting a glass of hot gin and water on the chimneypiece, he drew his chair to the fire and composed himself to read the paper.

The very first paragraph on which Mr. Bumble's eye rested was the following advertisement:

FIVE GUINEAS REWARD

Whereas a young boy, named Oliver Twist, absconded, or was enticed, on Thursday evening last, from his home at Pentonville, and has not since been heard of, the above reward will be paid to any person who will give such information as will lead to the discovery of the said Oliver Twist, or tend to throw any light upon his previous history, in which the advertiser is, for many reasons, warmly interested.

And then followed a full description of Oliver's dress and person, with the name and address of Mr. Brownlow.

Mr. Bumble opened his eyes; read the advertisement carefully three times; and in something more than five minutes was on his way to Pentonville, having actually, in his excitement, left the glass of hot gin and water untasted.

"Is Mr. Brownlow at home?" inquired Mr. Bumble of the girl who opened the door.

In reply the girl asked the nature of his errand, and he had no sooner uttered Oliver's name than Mrs. Bedwin, who had been listening at the parlor door, hastened into the passage.

"Come in, come in," said the old lady. "I knew we should hear of him—bless his heart! I said so, all along."

Having said this, the worthy old lady burst into tears. The girl had run upstairs meanwhile and now returned with a request that Mr. Bumble would follow her immediately. He was shown into the little back study, where sat Mr. Brownlow and his friend Mr. Grimwig with decanters and glasses before them. The latter gentleman at once burst into the exclamation:

"A beadle! A parish beadle, or I'll eat my head."

"Pray don't interrupt just now," said Mr. Brownlow. "Take a seat, will you?"

Mr. Bumble sat himself down, quite confounded by the oddity of Mr. Grimwig's manner. Mr. Brownlow moved the lamp so as to obtain a view of the beadle's countenance and said, "Now, sir, you come in consequence of having seen the advertisement. You know where this poor boy is?"

"No more than nobody," replied Mr. Bumble.

"Well, what *do* you know of him?" inquired the old gentleman.

"You don't happen to know any good of him, do you?" said Mr. Grimwig caustically.

Mr. Bumble, catching at the inquiry quickly, shook his head with portentous solemnity.

"You see?" said Mr. Grimwig, looking triumphantly at Mr. Brownlow.

Mr. Brownlow looked apprehensively at Mr. Bumble's pursed-up countenance and requested him to communicate what he knew regarding Oliver in as few words as possible.

Mr. Bumble put down his hat, unbuttoned his coat, folded his arms, and after a few moments' reflection commenced his story. It occupied some twenty minutes in the telling, but the sum and substance of it was: that Oliver was a foundling born of low and vicious parents; that he had from birth displayed no better qualities than treachery, ingratitude and malice; and that he had terminated his brief career in the place of his birth by making a sanguinary and cowardly attack on an unoffending lad and running away in the nighttime from his master's house. In proof of his really being the person he represented himself, Mr. Bumble laid upon the table the papers he had brought to town.

"I fear it is all too true," said Mr. Brownlow sorrowfully, after looking over the papers. "This is not much to give you for your intelligence; but I would have given you treble the money if it had been favorable to the boy."

It is not improbable that if Mr. Bumble had been possessed of this information at an earlier period of the interview he might have imparted a different coloring to his little history. It was too late to do it now, however, so he shook his head gravely, and, pocketing the five guineas, he withdrew.

Mr. Brownlow paced the room to and fro for some minutes, evidently so much disturbed that even Mr. Grimwig forbore to vex him further. At length he stopped and rang the bell violently. "Mrs. Bedwin," said Mr. Brownlow when the housekeeper appeared, "that boy, Oliver, is an impostor."

"It can't be, sir. It cannot be," said the old lady energetically.

"I tell you he is!" retorted the old gentleman. "We have just heard a full account of him from his birth, and he has been a thorough-paced little villain all his life."

"I never will believe it, sir," replied the old lady firmly. "Never! He was a dear, grateful, gentle child. I know what children are, sir, and have these forty years. People who can't say the same shouldn't say anything about them. That's my opinion!"

This was a hard hit at Mr. Grimwig, who was a bachelor.

"Silence!" said Mr. Brownlow, feigning an anger he was far from feeling. "Never let me hear that boy's name again! I rang to tell you that. Never, on any pretense. Remember!"

There were sad hearts at Mr. Brownlow's that night.

ABOUT NOON NEXT DAY, when the Dodger and Master Bates had gone out to pursue their customary avocations, Mr. Fagin took the opportunity of reading Oliver a long lecture on the crying sin of ingratitude, of which he clearly demonstrated he had been guilty to no ordinary extent in willfully absenting himself from the society of his anxious friends. Mr. Fagin laid great stress on the fact of his having taken Oliver in and cherished him when, without his timely aid, he might have perished with hunger, and he related the dismal and affecting history of a young lad whom he had succored under parallel circumstances but who, proving unworthy of his confidence and evincing a desire to communicate with the police, had unfortunately come to be hanged at the Old Bailey. Mr. Fagin concluded by drawing a rather disagreeable picture of the discomforts of hanging, and with great politeness of manner, expressed his anxious hopes that he might never be obliged to submit Oliver Twist to that unpleasant operation.

Little Oliver's blood ran cold as he listened to the old man's dark threats. Glancing timidly up and meeting Fagin's searching look, he felt that his pale face and trembling limbs were neither unnoticed nor unrelished by that wary old gentleman.

Fagin, smiling hideously, patted Oliver on the head and said, that if he kept quiet and applied himself to business, he saw they would be very good friends yet. Then, taking his hat and an old patched greatcoat, he went out, and locked the door behind him.

And so Oliver remained all that day and many subsequent days, seeing nobody between early morning and midnight, and left during the long hours to commune with his own thoughts— which, never failing to revert to his kind friends and the opinion they must long ago have formed of him, were sad indeed.

After the lapse of a week or so Fagin left the room door un- locked, and Oliver was at liberty to wander about the house. The moldering shutters were fast closed, and the only light which was admitted stole its way through round holes at the top, making the rooms more gloomy and filling them with strange shadows. The house was a very dirty place. Spiders had built webs in the angles of the walls and ceilings, and sometimes mice would scam- per across the floors. With these exceptions, there was neither sight nor sound of any living thing; and often, when it grew dark, Oliver would crouch in the corner of the passage by the street door to be as near living people as he could, and would remain there until Fagin or the boys returned.

One afternoon, the Dodger and Master Bates being engaged that evening, the first-named young gentleman took it into his head to evince some anxiety regarding the decoration of his person, and with this aim, condescendingly commanded Oliver to assist him in his toilet. Oliver was only too glad to make himself useful, and only too happy to have some faces, however bad, to look on. So, kneeling on the floor while the Dodger sat on the table, he applied himself to a process which Mr. Dawkins designated as "japanning his trotter cases"—in plain English, cleaning his boots.

The Dodger looked down on Oliver with a thoughtful coun- tenance for a brief space and then, heaving a sigh, he said to Master Bates:

"What a pity it is he isn't a prig"—by which he meant "thief."

"Ah," said Master Bates, "he don't know what's good for him."

The Dodger sighed again and said, "Now *I* am a prig. So are you, Charley. So's Fagin. So's Sikes. So's Nancy. So's Bet. So we all are, down to the dog."

"And he's the downiest one of the lot."

"And the least given to peaching," added the Dodger.

"Why don't you put yourself under Fagin, Oliver?" asked Charley.

"And make your fortun'?" said the Dodger.

"And so be able to retire on your property and do the genteel, as I mean to in the very next leap year but four," said Charley.

"I don't like it," rejoined Oliver timidly. "I wish they would let me go. I—I—would rather go."

"Go?" exclaimed the Dodger. "Why, where's your spirit? Would you go and be dependent on your friends? *I* couldn't do it."

"*You* can leave your friends, though," said Oliver as he went on with his boot-cleaning, "and let them be punished for what you did."

"That," rejoined the Dodger, with a wave of his pipe, "was all out of consideration for Fagin, 'cause the traps know that we work together, and he might have got into trouble if we hadn't made our lucky. That was the move, wasn't it, Charley?"

Master Bates nodded assent.

"You've been brought up bad, Oliver," continued the Dodger, surveying his polished boots with satisfaction. "Fagin will make something of you, though, or you'll be the first he ever had that turned out unprofitable. You'd better begin at once."

Master Bates backed this advice with sundry moral admonitions of his own; and then he and his friend Mr. Dawkins launched into a glowing description of the numerous pleasures incidental to the life they led.

"And put this in your pipe, Nolly," said the Dodger as Fagin was heard unlocking the door above, "if you don't take fogles and tickers . . ."

"He don't know what you mean," interposed Master Bates.

"If you don't take pocket-handkechers and watches," said the Dodger, reducing his conversation to Oliver's level, "some other cove will, and you've just as good a right to them as they have."

"To be sure!" said Fagin, who had entered unseen by Oliver. "It all lies in a nutshell, my dear, take the Dodger's word for it. He understands the catechism of his trade." The old man rubbed his hands gleefully together as he corroborated the Dodger's reasoning, and chuckled with delight at his pupil's proficiency.

The conversation proceeded no further at this time, for the old man had returned home accompanied by a gentleman whom Oliver had never seen before. This gentleman was accosted by the Dodger as Tom Chitling. Mr. Chitling was older than the Dodger in years, having perhaps numbered eighteen winters. But there was a degree of deference in his deportment toward that young gentleman which seemed to indicate that he felt himself conscious of a slight inferiority in point of professional acquirements. He had small twinkling eyes and a pockmarked face, wore a fur cap, a dark corduroy jacket, greasy fustian trousers, and an apron. His wardrobe was, in truth, rather out of repair, but he excused himself by stating that his "time" was only out an hour before; and that, in consequence of having worn the regimentals for six weeks past, he had not been able to bestow any attention on his private clothes. Mr. Chitling added that he had not touched a drop of anything for forty-two mortal long hardworking days, and that he wished he might be busted if he "warn't as dry as a lime basket."

"Where do you think the gentleman has come from, Oliver?" inquired Fagin, as Charley put a bottle of spirits on the table.

"I—I—don't know, sir," replied Oliver.

"Who's that?" inquired Tom Chitling, casting a contemptuous look at Oliver.

"A young friend of mine, my dear," replied Fagin.

"He's in luck then," said the young man, with a meaning look at Fagin. "Never mind where I came from, young un; you'll find your way there soon enough, I'll bet a crown!"

At this sally the boys laughed. They exchanged a few short whispers with Fagin and then withdrew. Chitling and Fagin drew their chairs towards the fire, and the old man, telling Oliver to come and sit by him, led the conversation to the great advantages of the trade, the proficiency of the Dodger, the amiability of Charley Bates, and the liberality of Fagin himself.

From this day Oliver was seldom left alone, but was placed in almost constant communication with the two boys. They played the old game with the Jew every day—whether for their own improvement or Oliver's, Mr. Fagin best knew. At other times the old man would tell them stories of robberies he had committed in his younger days, mixed up with so much that was droll and curious that Oliver could not help laughing heartily and showing that he was amused in spite of all his better feelings. In short, the wily old man had the boy in his toils. Having prepared his mind by solitude and gloom to prefer any society to the companionship of his own sad thoughts, Fagin was now slowly instilling into his soul the poison which he hoped would blacken it forever.

··⚬· CHAPTER IX ·⚬··

ONE CHILL, DAMP, WINDY NIGHT Fagin, buttoning his greatcoat tight round his shriveled body and pulling the collar up so as to obscure the lower part of his face, emerged from his den. He paused on the step as the door was locked and chained behind him, and having listened until the boys' retreating footsteps were no longer audible, slunk quickly down the street.

The house to which Oliver had been conveyed was in the neighborhood of Whitechapel. Fagin struck off in the direction of Spitalfields. The mud lay thick upon the stones; a black mist hung over the streets, and the rain fell sluggishly down. It seemed just the night when it befitted such a being as Fagin to be abroad. As he glided stealthily along, creeping beneath the shelter of the walls and doorways, he seemed like some loathsome reptile, engendered in the slime and darkness, crawling forth by night in search of some rich offal for a meal. He kept on his course through many winding and narrow ways until he reached Bethnal Green; then he turned off into a maze of the mean and dirty streets which abound in that densely populated quarter. He was evidently too familiar with the ground he traversed to be at all bewildered either by the darkness of the night or the intricacies of the way. At length he turned into a street lighted only by a single lamp at the farther end. At the door of a house in this street he knocked. Having exchanged a few muttered words with the person who opened the door, he walked upstairs. A dog growled as he touched the handle of a room door, and a man's voice demanded who was there.

"Only me, Bill. Only me, my dear," said Fagin, looking into the meanly furnished apartment. Nothing there indicated that its occupier was anything but a working man, and no more suspicious articles were displayed to view than two or three heavy bludgeons which stood in a corner.

"Bring in your body then," said Sikes. "Lie down, you stupid brute! Don't you know the devil when he's got a greatcoat on?"

Apparently the dog had been somewhat deceived by Mr. Fagin's outer garment; but as the old man unbuttoned it and threw it over the back of a chair, he retired to the corner from which he had risen, wagging his tail to show that he was as well satisfied as it was in his nature to be.

"Well!" said Sikes.

"Well, my dear," replied Fagin. "Ah, Nancy!"

The latter recognition was uttered with just enough of embarrassment to imply a doubt of its reception; for Mr. Fagin and his young friend had not met since she had interfered in behalf of Oliver. But all doubts on the subject, if he had any, were speedily removed by the young lady's behavior. She took her feet off the fender, pushed back her chair, and bade Fagin draw up his, for it was a cold night and no mistake.

"It *is* cold, Nancy, dear," said Fagin as he warmed his skinny hands over the fire. "It seems to go right through one."

"It must be a piercer if it finds its way through *your* heart," said Mr. Sikes. "Give him something to drink, Nancy. Make haste. It's enough to turn a man ill to see his ugly old carcass shivering like a ghost just rose from the grave."

Nancy quickly brought a bottle from a cupboard. Sikes, pouring out a glass of brandy, bade Fagin drink it.

"Thankye, Bill," replied the old man, putting down the glass after setting his lips to it. "And now about the crib at Chertsey," he went on, drawing his chair forward and speaking in a low voice.

"Yes, wot about it?" inquired Sikes.

"When is it to be done? Such plate, my dear, such plate!" said Fagin, rubbing his hands in a rapture of anticipation.

"Not at all," replied Sikes coldly.

"Not to be done at all!" echoed Fagin, leaning back in his chair.

"No, not at all," rejoined Sikes. "At least, it can't be a put-up job, as we expected."

"Then it hasn't been properly gone about," said Fagin, turning pale with anger. "Don't tell me!"

"But I will tell you," retorted Sikes. "Toby Crackit has been hanging about the place for a fortnight, and he can't get one of the servants into line."

"Do you mean to tell me, Bill," said Fagin, softening as the other grew heated, "that neither of the two men in the house can be got over?"

"Yes, I do mean to tell you so," replied Sikes. "The old lady has had 'em twenty year, and if you were to give 'em five hundred pound, they wouldn't be in it."

"But do you mean to say, my dear," remonstrated Fagin, "that even the women servants can't be got over?"

"Not a bit of it," replied Sikes.

"Not even by flash Toby Crackit?" said Fagin incredulously.

"No, not even by flash Toby Crackit," replied Sikes. "He says he's worn sham whiskers and a canary waistcoat the whole blessed time he's been loitering there, and it's all of no use."

After ruminating for some minutes with his chin sunk on his breast, Fagin raised his head and said with a deep sigh, "It's a sad thing, my dear, to lose so much when we had set our hearts on it."

"So it is," said Mr. Sikes. "Worse luck!"

A long silence ensued, during which Fagin was plunged in deep thought. Sikes eyed him furtively from time to time. Nancy sat with her eyes fixed on the fire, as if she had been deaf to all that passed.

"Fagin," said Sikes, abruptly breaking the stillness, "is it worth fifty shiners extra if it's safely done from the outside?"

"Yes," said Fagin, as suddenly rousing himself.

"Then," said Sikes, "let it come off as soon as you like. Toby and me were over the garden wall the night afore last, sounding the panels of the door and shutters. The crib's barred up at night like a jail; but there's one part we can crack, safe and softly."

"Which is that, Bill?" asked Fagin eagerly.

"Why, as you cross the lawn —"

"Yes?" said Fagin, bending forward.

"Umph!" cried Sikes, stopping short. "Never mind which part it is. You can't do it without me, I know. But it's best to be on the safe side when one deals with you."

"As you like, my dear, as you like," replied Fagin. "Is there no help wanted but yours and Toby's?"

"None," said Sikes, " 'cept a boy; and he mustn't be a big un."

"A boy!" exclaimed Fagin. He nodded his head towards Nancy, who was still gazing at the fire, and intimated by a sign that he would have her told to leave the room. Sikes shrugged impatiently.

"Why, you don't mind the old girl, do you, Fagin?" he asked. "She ain't one to blab. Are you, Nancy?"

"*I* should think not!" replied the young lady, drawing her chair up to the table and putting her elbows on it.

"No, no, my dear, I know you're not," said Fagin. "But I didn't know whether you mightn't p'r'aps be out of sorts, you know, my dear, as you were the other night."

At this confession Miss Nancy burst into a loud laugh, and, swallowing a glass of brandy, shook her head with an air of defiance, which seemed to have the effect of reassuring both gentlemen.

"Now, Fagin," said Nancy. "Tell Bill at once about Oliver!"

"Ha! You're a clever one, my dear, the sharpest girl I ever saw!" said Fagin, patting her on the neck. "It *was* about Oliver I was going to speak, sure enough. Ha! Ha! Ha!"

"What about him?" demanded Sikes.

"He's the boy for you, my dear," replied the old man, laying his finger on the side of his nose and grinning frightfully. "He's been in good training these last few weeks, and it's time he began to work for his bread. Besides, the others are all too big."

"Well, he is just the size I want," said Mr. Sikes, ruminating.

"And will do everything you want, Bill, my dear," interposed Fagin. "That is, if you frighten him enough."

"Frighten him!" echoed Sikes. "It'll be no sham frightening, mind you. If there's anything queer about him when we once get into the work, you won't see him alive again, Fagin. Think of that before you send him."

"I've thought of it all," said the Jew with energy. "I've—I've had my eye on him, my dears. Once let him feel that he is one of us, once fill his mind with the idea that he has been a thief, and he's ours for life. Oho! It couldn't have come about better!" The old man crossed his arms, and drawing his head and shoulders into a heap, literally hugged himself for joy.

"Ours?" said Sikes. "Yours, you mean."

"Perhaps I do, my dear," said Fagin, with a shrill chuckle.

"And wot," said Sikes, scowling fiercely on his agreeable friend, "wot makes you take so much pains about one chalk-faced kid, when you know there are fifty boys snoozing about Common Garden every night as you might pick and choose from?"

"Because they're of no use to me, my dear," replied Fagin, with some confusion. "Their looks convict 'em when they get into trouble, and I lose 'em. With this boy, properly managed, my dears, I could do what I couldn't with twenty of them. Besides," said the old man, recovering his self-possession, "he has us now if he gets away again. He *must* be in the same boat with us. Never mind how he came there, it's quite enough for my power over him that he was in a robbery; that's all I want. Now, when is it to be done, Bill?"

"I planned with Toby, the night arter tomorrow, if he heerd nothing to the contrary," rejoined Sikes in a surly voice. "You'd better bring the boy here tomorrow night. Then you hold your tongue and keep the melting pot ready for the loot."

After some discussion, it was decided that Nancy should repair to Fagin's next evening and bring Oliver away with her; Fagin craftily observing that Oliver would be more willing to accompany the girl who had so recently interfered in his behalf, than anybody else. It was also solemnly arranged that poor Oliver should, for the purposes of the contemplated expedition, be unreservedly consigned to the care and custody of Mr. William Sikes, and further, that the said Sikes should deal with him as he thought fit, and should not be held responsible by Fagin for any mischance or evil that might befall him, or any punishment which it might be necessary to visit on him.

These preliminaries adjusted, Mr. Sikes proceeded to drink brandy at a furious rate, yelling forth at the same time most unmusical snatches of song mingled with wild execrations, until he fell on the floor and went to sleep where he fell.

"Good night, Nancy," said Fagin, muffling himself up as before.

"Good night."

Their eyes met, and Fagin scrutinized her narrowly. There was no flinching about the girl. She was as true and earnest in the matter as Toby Crackit himself could be. He again bade her good night, and bestowing a sly kick on the prostrate form of Mr. Sikes while her back was turned, groped downstairs.

"Always the way!" muttered the old man to himself. "The worst of these women is that a very little thing serves to call up some long-forgotten feeling, and the best of them is that it never lasts. Ha! Ha! The man against the child, for a bag of gold!"

Beguiling the time with these pleasant reflections, Mr. Fagin wended his way through mud and mire to his gloomy abode, where the Dodger was sitting up, impatiently awaiting his return. "Is Oliver abed? I want to speak to him," was Fagin's first remark.

"Hours ago," replied the Dodger, throwing open a door. "Here he is!"

The boy was lying fast asleep on a rude bed on the floor, so pale with anxiety and sadness that he looked like death—not death as it shows in shroud and coffin but in the guise it wears when life has just departed; when a young and gentle spirit has, but an instant, fled to heaven, and the gross air of the world has not had time to breathe on the changing dust it hallowed.

"Not now," said Fagin, turning softly away. "Tomorrow. Tomorrow."

··❧· CHAPTER X ·☙··

WHEN OLIVER AWOKE in the morning he was a good deal surprised to find that a new pair of shoes, with strong thick soles, had been placed at his bedside. At first he was pleased with the discovery, hoping that it might be the forerunner of his release; but such thoughts were quickly dispelled on his sitting down to breakfast with Fagin, who told him that he was to be taken to the residence of Bill Sikes that night.

"To—to—stop there, sir?" asked Oliver, alarmed.

"No, no, my dear. Not to stop there," replied Fagin. "We shouldn't like to lose you. Don't be afraid, Oliver, you shall come back to us again. Ha! Ha! Ha! We won't send you away, my dear. Oh, no, no!" The old man, who was stooping over the fire toasting a piece of bread, looked round as he bantered Oliver thus. "I suppose," he said, chuckling, "you want to know what you're going to Bill's for—eh, my dear?"

Oliver colored, but boldly said yes, he did want to know.

"Why, do you think?" inquired Fagin, parrying the question.

"Indeed, I don't know, sir," replied Oliver.

"Bah!" said Fagin, turning away, seemingly vexed at Oliver for not expressing any greater curiosity. "Wait till Bill tells you, then."

After that Fagin remained surly and silent till night, when he prepared to go abroad. "You may burn a candle," he said then, putting one on the table. "And here's a book for you to read till they come to fetch you. Good night!"

"Good night!" replied Oliver softly.

Fagin, pointing to the candle, motioned him to light it. He did so, and as he placed the candlestick on the table saw that Fagin was gazing fixedly at him with lowering and contracted brows.

"Take heed, Oliver!" said the old man, shaking his right hand before him in a warning manner. "He's a rough man and thinks nothing of blood when his own is up. Whatever falls out, do what he bids you. Mind!" Placing a strong emphasis on the last word, he suffered his features gradually to resolve themselves into a ghastly grin, and, nodding his head, left the room.

Oliver leaned his head on his hand when the old man disappeared, and pondered with a trembling heart on the words he had just heard. He could think of no bad object to be attained by sending him to Sikes which would not be equally well answered by his remaining with Fagin; and after meditating for a long time, he concluded that he had been selected to perform some ordinary menial offices for the housebreaker until another boy better suited for his purpose could be engaged. He was too well accustomed to suffering, and had suffered too much where he was, to bewail the prospect of change very severely.

He remained lost in thought for some minutes and then, taking up the book which Fagin had left, began to read. It was a history of the lives and trials of great criminals, and the pages were soiled and thumbed with use. Here he read of dreadful crimes that made the blood run cold, of secret murders committed by the lonely wayside, of men who had been tempted and led on by their own bad thoughts to such dreadful bloodshed as it made the flesh creep to think of. The terrible descriptions were so real and vivid that the sallow pages seemed to turn red with gore, and the words on them to be whispered in his ears as if they were murmured by the spirits of the dead.

In a paroxysm of fear, the boy closed the book and thrust it from him. Then, falling on his knees, he prayed Heaven that he should die at once rather than be reserved for crimes so fearful and appalling. By degrees he grew more calm, and besought in a low and broken voice that he might be rescued from his present dangers, and that if any aid were to be raised up for a poor outcast boy it might come to him now, when, desolate and deserted, he stood alone in the midst of wickedness and guilt.

He remained on his knees, with his head buried in his hands, when a rustling noise aroused him. "What's that!" he cried, starting up, and catching sight of a figure by the door. "Who's there?"

"Only me," replied a tremulous voice.

Oliver raised the candle above his head and looked. It was Nancy.

"Put down the light," said the girl, turning away her head. "It hurts my eyes."

Oliver saw that she was very pale, and gently inquired if she were ill. The girl threw herself into a chair and wrung her hands, but made no reply. "God forgive me!" she cried after a while. "I never thought of this."

"Has anything happened?" asked Oliver. "Can I help you?"

She rocked herself to and fro, caught her throat, and gasped for breath.

"Nancy!" cried Oliver. "What is it?"

The girl drew her shawl close round her and shivered with cold. Oliver stirred the fire. Drawing her chair close to it, she sat there for a time without speaking, but at length she raised her head.

"I don't know what comes over me sometimes," said she, affecting to busy herself in arranging her dress. "It's this damp, dirty room, I think. Now, Nolly, dear, are you ready?"

"Am I to go with you?" asked Oliver.

"Yes. I have come from Bill," replied the girl.

"What for?" asked Oliver, recoiling.

"What for?" echoed the girl, averting her eyes. "Oh! For no harm."

"I don't believe it," said Oliver, who had watched her closely.

"Have it your own way," rejoined the girl, affecting to laugh. "For no good then."

Oliver could see that he had some power over the girl's better feelings, and for an instant thought of appealing to her compassion. But then the thought darted across his mind that it was barely eleven o'clock, and that many people were still in the streets, of whom surely some might be found to give credence to his tale. He stepped forward and said, somewhat hastily, that he was ready. Neither his brief consideration nor its purport was lost on his companion. She eyed him narrowly while he spoke, and cast on him a look of intelligence which sufficiently showed that she guessed what had been passing in his thoughts.

"Hush!" said the girl, pointing to the door as she looked cautiously round. "You can't help yourself. I have tried hard for you, but all to no purpose. If ever you are to get loose from here, this is not the time."

Struck by the energy of her manner, Oliver looked up in her face with great surprise. She seemed to speak the truth; her countenance was white and agitated, and she trembled with very earnestness.

"I have saved you from being ill-used once, and I will again, and I do now," continued the girl; "for those who would have fetched you, if I had not, would have been far more rough than me. I have promised for your being silent; if you are not, you will not only do harm to yourself, but to me, too, and perhaps be my death. See here! I have borne all this for you already!" She pointed hastily to some livid bruises on her neck and arms, and continued, "If I could help you now, I would; but I have not the power. They don't mean to harm you; whatever they make you do is no fault of yours. Hush! Give me your hand. Make haste!"

She caught the hand which Oliver instinctively placed in hers, and, blowing out the light, drew him after her up the stairs. The door was opened quickly by someone shrouded in the darkness, and was as quickly closed when they had passed out. A hackney cabriolet was waiting. The girl pulled him in with her and drew the curtains close. The driver wanted no directions, but lashed his horse into full speed, without the delay of an instant. All was so quick and hurried that Oliver had scarcely time to recollect where he was before the carriage stopped at the house to which Fagin's steps had been directed on the previous evening. For one brief moment Oliver cast a hurried glance along the empty street, and a cry for help hung on his lips. But the girl's voice was in his ear, beseeching him in such tones of agony to remember her that he had not the heart to utter it. Then the opportunity was gone; he was already in the house and the door was shut.

"This way," said the girl, releasing her hold. "Bill!"

"Hallo!" replied Sikes, appearing at the head of the stairs with a candle. "Oh! That's the time of day. Come on!"

This was a very strong expression of approbation, an uncommonly hearty welcome, from a person of Mr. Sikes's temperament. Nancy, appearing much gratified thereby, saluted him cordially.

"Bull's-eye's gone home with Tom," observed Sikes. "He'd have been in the way. So you've got the kid," he added, when they had all reached his room. "Did he come quiet?"

"Like a lamb," rejoined Nancy.

"I'm glad to hear it," said Sikes, looking grimly at Oliver, "for the sake of his young carcass, as would otherways have suffered for it. Come here, young un, and let me read you a lectur', which is as well got over at once."

Thus addressing his new pupil, Mr. Sikes pulled off Oliver's cap and threw it into a corner; and then, taking him by the shoulder, sat himself down by the table and stood the boy in front of him.

"Now, first, do you know wot this is?" inquired Sikes, taking up a pistol which lay on the table.

Oliver replied in the affirmative.

"Well, then, look here," continued Sikes. "This is powder, that 'ere's a bullet, and this is a little bit of a old hat for waddin'."

Oliver murmured his comprehension of the different bodies referred to, and Mr. Sikes proceeded to load the pistol with great nicety. "Now it's loaded," he said when he had finished, and grasping Oliver's wrist, he put the barrel so close to his temple that they touched. The boy could not repress a start. "If you speak a word when you're out o' doors with me except when I speak to you, that loading will be in your head without notice. So if you *do* make up your mind to speak without leave, say your prayers first. As near as I know, there isn't anybody as would be asking very partickler arter you, if you *was* disposed of; so I needn't take this devil and all of trouble to explain matters to you if it warn't for your own good. D'ye hear me?"

"The short and the long of what you mean," said Nancy to Bill, speaking emphatically, and slightly frowning at Oliver, as if to bespeak his serious attention to her words, "is, that if you're crossed by him in this job you have on hand, you'll prevent his ever telling tales afterwards by shooting him through the head, and you will take your chance of swinging for it, as you do for a great many other things in the way of business, every month of your life."

"That's it!" observed Mr. Sikes approvingly. "Women can always put things in fewest words—except when it's blowing up, and then they lengthens it out. And now that he's thoroughly up to it, let's have some supper and get a snooze before starting."

In pursuance of this request Nancy quickly laid the cloth; and, disappearing for a few minutes, she presently returned with a pot of porter and a dish of sheepsheads. The worthy Mr. Sikes drank all the beer at a draught and did not utter, on a rough calculation, more than fourscore oaths during the whole meal. Supper being ended, he then disposed of a couple of glasses of spirits and water and threw himself on the bed, ordering Nancy, with many imprecations in case of failure, to call him at five precisely. Oliver, by command, stretched himself in his clothes on a mattress on the floor; and the girl, mending the fire, sat before it, in readiness to rouse them at the appointed time.

For a long time Oliver lay awake; but, weary with watching and anxiety, he at length fell asleep. When he awoke Sikes was thrusting various articles into the pockets of his greatcoat, which hung over the back of a chair. Nancy was busily engaged in preparing breakfast. It was not yet daylight; the candle was still burning. A sharp rain was beating against the windowpanes, and the sky outside looked black and cloudy.

"Now, then!" growled Sikes, as Oliver started up. "Half past five! Look sharp or you'll get no breakfast, for it's late."

Oliver was not long in making his toilet; having taken some breakfast, he replied to a surly inquiry from Sikes by saying that he was quite ready. Nancy threw him a handkerchief to tie round his throat; Sikes gave him a large rough cape to button over his shoulders. Thus attired, he gave his hand to the robber, who, merely pausing to show him with a menacing gesture that he had that same pistol in a side pocket of his greatcoat, clasped it firmly in his, and, exchanging a farewell with Nancy, led him away. Oliver turned when they reached the door, in the hope of meeting a look from the girl. But she had resumed her old seat in front of the fire and sat perfectly motionless before it.

It was a cheerless morning when they got into the street, blowing and raining hard, and the clouds looking dull and stormy. There was a faint glimmering of the coming day in the sky, but the somber light only served to pale that which the streetlamps afforded, without shedding any warmer or brighter tints on the wet housetops and dreary streets. There appeared to be nobody stirring; and the streets through which they passed were noiseless and empty.

By the time they had turned into the Bethnal Green Road, the day had fairly begun to break. Many of the lamps were already extinguished; a few wagons were slowly toiling on toward London; and now and then a stagecoach covered with mud rattled by. The public houses, with gaslights burning inside, were already open. By degrees other shops began to be unclosed, and a few scattered people were met with. Then came straggling groups of laborers going to their work; then men and women with fish baskets on their heads; donkey carts laden with vegetables; milk-women with pails; an unbroken concourse of people trudging out with various supplies to the eastern suburbs. As they threaded the streets of the City, the traffic swelled into a roar of sound. The busy morning of half the London population had begun.

Crossing Finsbury Square, Mr. Sikes struck presently into Smithfield, from which place arose a tumult of discordant sounds that filled Oliver Twist with amazement. It was market morning. The ground was covered with filth and mire; a thick steam, rising from the reeking bodies of the cattle, and mingling with the fog which seemed to rest upon the chimney tops, hung heavily above. All the pens in the center of the large area were filled with sheep; and tied up to posts by the gutterside were long lines of beasts and oxen, three or four deep. Countrymen, butchers, drovers, thieves, idlers, and vagabonds of every grade were massed together; the whistling of drovers, the barking of dogs, the bellowing and plunging of oxen, the bleating of sheep, the grunting and squeaking of pigs, the cries of hawkers, the shouts, oaths, and quarreling on all sides, the hideous and discordant din that resounded from every corner of the market, and the squalid figures constantly running to and fro, rendered it a stunning and bewildering scene.

Mr. Sikes, dragging Oliver after him, elbowed his way through the thickest of the crowd, nodding twice or thrice to a passing friend, and pressed steadily onward until they were clear of the turmoil and had made their way into Holborn.

"Now, young un!" said Sikes, looking up at the clock of St. Andrew's Church. "Hard on seven! Come, you must step out."

Mr. Sikes accompanied this speech with a jerk at his little companion's wrist. Oliver, quickening his pace into a kind of trot between a fast walk and a run, kept up with the rapid strides of the housebreaker as well as he could.

They held their course at this rate until they had passed Hyde Park Corner. Sikes then relaxed his pace until an empty cart which was at a distance behind them came up. Seeing HOUNSLOW written on it, he asked the driver with as much civility as he could assume if he would give them a lift as far as Isleworth.

"Jump up," said the man. "Is that your boy?"

"Yes, he's my boy," replied Sikes, looking hard at Oliver and putting his hand abstractedly into the pocket where the pistol was.

"Your father walks rather too quick for you, don't he, my man?" inquired the driver, seeing that Oliver was out of breath.

"Not a bit of it," replied Sikes, interposing. "He's used to it. Here, take hold of my hand, Ned. In with you!"

Thus addressing Oliver, he helped him into the cart, and the driver, pointing to a heap of sacks, told him to lie down there and rest himself.

As they passed the different milestones Oliver wondered more and more where his companion meant to take him. Kensington, Hammersmith, Chiswick were all passed, and yet they went on as steadily as if they had only just begun their journey. At length they came to a crossroads, and here the cart stopped. Sikes dismounted and lifted Oliver down.

"Good-by, boy," said the man.

"He's sulky," replied Sikes, giving Oliver a shake. "Don't mind him."

"Not I!" rejoined the other, and he drove away.

Sikes waited until he had fairly gone, and then once again led Oliver onward on his journey. Taking the right-hand road, they walked on for a long time, passing many large gardens and gentlemen's houses, and stopping for nothing until they reached a town. Here against the wall of a house Oliver saw written up in large letters, HAMPTON. They lingered about in the fields for some hours. At length they came back into the town and, turning into an old public house, ordered dinner by the kitchen fire.

The kitchen was an old low-roofed room, with a great beam across the middle of the ceiling, and benches with high backs by the fire. Sikes and his young comrade sat in a corner by themselves without being troubled by other customers. They had some cold meat for dinner, and sat so long after it, while Mr. Sikes indulged himself with three or four pipes, that Oliver began to feel certain they were not going any farther. Being quite overpowered by fatigue, he fell asleep.

It was dark when he was awakened by a push from Sikes. Rousing himself, he found that worthy in close fellowship and communication with a laboring man over a pint of ale.

"So you're going to Lower Halliford, are you?" inquired Sikes. "Could you give me and my boy a lift as far as there?"

"If you're going directly, I can," said the man, who seemed a little the worse—or better, as the case might be—for drinking. "And not slow about it neither. My horse is a good un. Here's luck to him!"

They bade the company good night and went out. The horse whose health had just been drunk was standing outside, ready harnessed to the cart. Oliver and Sikes got in, and the man, defying the hostler and the world to produce the horse's equal, mounted also. The horse being given his head made very unpleasant use of it, tossing it into the air, and after supporting himself for a short time on his hind legs, he started off at a great speed and rattled out of the town right gallantly.

The night was very dark. A damp mist rose from the marshy ground and spread itself over the dreary fields. It was piercing cold, too; all was gloomy and black. Oliver sat huddled in a corner of the cart, bewildered with alarm and apprehension.

Finally the cart stopped. Sikes alighted and took Oliver by the hand, and they once again walked on. Passing through Shepperton and continuing in mud and darkness through gloomy lanes, they came within sight of the lights of another town at no great distance. On looking intently forward, Oliver saw that there was water just beyond them and that they were coming to a bridge. Sikes then turned suddenly down a bank on the left.

The water! thought Oliver, turning sick with fear. He has brought me to this lonely place to murder me!

He was about to make a last struggle for his young life when he saw that they stood before a solitary house. There was a window on each side of the dilapidated entrance and one story above. The house was dark, dismantled, and, to all appearance, uninhabited.

Sikes, with Oliver's hand still in his, softly approached the low porch and raised the latch. The door yielded to the pressure, and they passed in together.

·· ❧ · CHAPTER XI · ❧ ··

"HALLO!" cried a loud, hoarse voice as soon as they set foot in the passage.

"Don't make such a row," said Sikes, bolting the door. "Show a glim, Toby."

"Aha, my pal!" cried the same voice. "A glim, Barney, a glim! Show the gentleman in. Wake up first, if convenient."

The speaker appeared to throw a bootjack or some such article at the person he addressed, for the noise of a wooden object falling violently was heard.

"Do you hear?" cried the same voice. "There's Bill Sikes in the passage with nobody to do the civil to him, and you sleeping there as if you took laudanum with your meals. Are you any fresher now?"

A pair of slipshod feet shuffled hastily across the bare floor of the room as this interrogatory was put, and there issued from a door on the right hand, first, a feeble candle, and next, the form of an individual who soon demonstrated that he was laboring under the infirmity of speaking through his nose.

"Bister Sikes!" exclaimed this individual, whose name was Barney. "Cub id, sir, cub id."

"You get on first," said Sikes, putting Oliver in front of him, and they entered a low dark room with a smoky fire, two or three broken chairs, a table, and a very old couch on which, with his legs much higher than his head, a man was reposing at full length, smoking a long clay pipe. He was dressed in a smartly cut snuff-colored coat with large brass buttons, an orange neckerchief, a coarse, staring, shawl-pattern waistcoat, and drab breeches. Mr. Crackit (for he it was) had no very great quantity of hair, but what he had was of a reddish dye and tortured into long corkscrew curls. He was a trifle above the middle size and apparently rather weak in the legs, but this circumstance by no means detracted from his own admiration of his top boots, which he contemplated, in their elevated situation, with lively satisfaction.

"Bill, my boy," said this figure, turning his head towards the door, "I'm glad to see you. I was almost afraid you'd given it up, in which case I should have made a personal wentur. Hallo!"

Uttering this exclamation in a tone of great surprise as his eye rested on Oliver, Mr. Toby Crackit brought himself into a sitting posture and demanded who that was.

"The boy. Only the boy," replied Sikes, drawing a chair towards the fire.

"Wud of Bister Fagid's lads!" exclaimed Barney with a grin.

"Fagin's, eh!" exclaimed Toby, looking at Oliver. "Wot an inwalable boy that'll make for the old ladies' pockets in chapels! His mug is a fortun' to him."

"There—there's enough of that," interposed Sikes impatiently, and stooping towards his friend, he whispered a few words in his ear, at which Mr. Crackit laughed immensely and honored Oliver with a long stare of astonishment.

"Now," said Sikes, as he resumed his seat, "if you'll give us something to eat and drink, you'll put some heart in us. Sit down by the fire, younker, and rest yourself, for you'll have to go out with us again tonight."

Oliver looked at Sikes in mute and timid wonder, and drawing a stool to the fire, sat with his aching head on his hands, scarcely knowing where he was or what was passing around him.

"Here," said Toby, as Barney placed some fragments of food and a bottle on the table. "Success to the crack!" He rose to honor the toast, filled a glass with spirits, and drank off its contents. Mr. Sikes did the same.

"A dram for the boy," said Toby, half-filling a wineglass. "Down with it, innocence."

"Indeed," said Oliver, looking piteously up into the man's face, "indeed, I—"

"Down with it!" echoed Toby. "Do you think I don't know what's good for you? Tell him to drink it, Bill."

"Burn my body, he had better!" said Sikes, clapping his hand on his pocket. "Drink it, you perwerse imp, drink it!"

Frightened by the menacing gestures of the two men, Oliver hastily swallowed the contents of the glass and immediately fell into a violent fit of coughing, which delighted all three of them.

This done, and Sikes having satisfied his appetite (Oliver could eat nothing but a crust of bread which they made him swallow), the two men laid themselves down on chairs for a short nap. Oliver retained his stool by the fire; Barney, wrapped in a blanket, stretched himself on the floor. Nobody stirred for some time but Barney, who rose once or twice to throw coals on the fire.

Oliver had fallen into a heavy doze when he was roused by Toby Crackit jumping up and declaring it was half past one. In an instant the other two were on their feet, and all were engaged in busy preparation. Sikes and his companion enveloped their necks and chins in large dark shawls and drew on their greatcoats. Barney, opening a cupboard, brought forth several articles which he hastily crammed into the coat pockets.

"Barkers for me, Barney," said Toby Crackit.

"Here they are," replied Barney, producing a pair of pistols. "You loaded them yourself."

"All right!" replied Toby, stowing them away. "Persuaders, crape, keys, center bits, darkies—nothing forgotten?" he inquired, fastening a small crowbar to a loop inside his coat.

"All right," rejoined his companion. "Bring them bits of timber, Barney. That's the time of day." With these words he took a thick stick from Barney's hands. Barney, having delivered another stick to Toby, fastened Oliver's cape.

"Now then!" said Sikes, holding out his hand.

Oliver, who was completely stupefied by the unwonted exercise, and the air, and the drink which had been forced upon him, put his hand mechanically into that which Sikes extended.

"Take his other hand, Toby," said Sikes. "Look out, Barney."

The man went to the door and returned to announce that all was quiet. The two robbers issued forth with Oliver between them. Barney, having made all fast, rolled himself up and was soon asleep again.

It was now intensely dark. The mist was much heavier than it had been earlier, and within a few minutes Oliver's hair and eyebrows became stiff with half-frozen moisture. They crossed the bridge and kept on briskly towards the lights which he had seen before. They were at no great distance off, and they soon arrived at Chertsey.

"We'll go slap through the town," whispered Sikes. "There'll be nobody in the way tonight to see us."

Toby acquiesced; and they hurried through the main street of the little town, which at that late hour was wholly deserted. They cleared the town as the church bell struck two. Quickening their pace, they turned up a road on the left. After walking about a quarter of a mile, they stopped before a detached house surrounded by a wall, to the top of which Toby Crackit, scarcely pausing to take breath, climbed in a twinkling.

"Hoist the boy up next," said Toby. "I'll catch hold of him."

Before Oliver had time to look round, Sikes had caught him under the arms, and in three or four seconds he and Toby were lying on the grass on the other side. Sikes followed directly. They then stole cautiously towards the house.

And now for the first time Oliver, well-nigh mad with grief and terror, saw that housebreaking and robbery, if not murder, were the objects of the expedition. He clasped his hands together and involuntarily uttered a subdued exclamation of horror. A mist came before his eyes; his limbs failed him, and he sank upon his knees.

"Get up!" murmured Sikes, trembling with rage and drawing the pistol from his pocket. "Get up, or I'll strew your brains on the grass!"

"Oh, for God's sake, let me go!" cried Oliver. "Let me run away and die in the fields. I will never come near London—never, never! Have mercy on me and do not make me steal, for the love of all the bright angels that rest in heaven!"

The man to whom this appeal was made swore a dreadful oath and had cocked the pistol when Toby, striking it from his grasp, placed his hand on the boy's mouth and dragged him to the house.

"Hush!" cried the man. "It won't answer here. Say another word and I'll do your business myself with a crack on the head. Here, Bill, wrench the shutter open. He's game enough now, I'll engage. I've seen older hands took the same way for a minute or two on a cold night."

Sikes, invoking terrific imprecations on Fagin's head for sending Oliver on such an errand, plied the crowbar vigorously, but with little noise. After some assistance from Toby, the shutter swung open on its hinges. It was a little lattice window, about five feet and a half above the ground, which belonged to a scullery. The aperture was so small that the inmates had probably not thought it worth while to defend it more securely; but it was large enough to admit a boy of Oliver's size nevertheless. A very brief exercise of Mr. Sikes's art sufficed to overcome the fastening of the lattice, and it soon stood wide open also.

"Now listen, you young limb," whispered Sikes, drawing a dark lantern from his pocket and throwing the glare full on Oliver's face, "I'm a-going to put you through there. Take this light, go softly up the steps straight afore you and along the little hall to the street door, unfasten it and let us in."

Toby now planted himself firmly with his head against the wall beneath the window, and with his hands upon his knees, so as to make a step of his back. This was no sooner done than Sikes, mounting on him, put Oliver gently through the window with his feet first, and, without leaving hold of his collar, planted him safely on the floor inside.

"Take this lantern," said Sikes, looking into the room. "You see the stairs afore you?"

Oliver, more dead than alive, gasped out, "Yes." Sikes, pointing to the street door with the pistol barrel, briefly advised him to take notice that he was within shot all the way and that if he faltered he would fall dead that instant.

"It's done in a minute," said Sikes in the same low whisper. "Directly I leave go of you, do your work. Hark!"

"What's that?" whispered the other man.

They listened intently.

"Nothing," said Sikes, releasing his hold of Oliver. "Now!"

In the short time he had had to collect his senses, the boy had firmly resolved that, whether he died in the attempt or not, he would make one effort to dart upstairs from the hall and alarm the family. Filled with this idea, he advanced at once, but stealthily.

"Come back!" suddenly cried Sikes aloud. "Back! Back!"

Scared by the sudden breaking of the dead stillness of the place and by a loud cry which followed it, Oliver let his lantern fall and knew not whether to advance or fly.

The cry was repeated, a light appeared, a vision of two terrified half-dressed men at the top of the steps swam before his eyes—a flash, a loud noise, smoke, a crash somewhere—and he staggered back.

Sikes had disappeared for an instant, but he was up again and had Oliver by the collar before the smoke had cleared away. He fired his own pistol after the two men, who were already retreating, and dragged the boy up.

"Clasp your arm tighter," said Sikes as he drew him through the

The Burglary

window. "Give me a shawl here. They've hit him. Quick! How the boy bleeds!"

Then came the loud ringing of a bell, mingled with the noise of firearms and the shouts of men, and the sensation of being carried over uneven ground at a rapid pace. And then the noises grew confused in the distance; and a cold deadly feeling crept over the boy's heart; and he saw or heard no more.

···&·· CHAPTER XII ·&···

THE NIGHT WAS BITTER COLD. Snow lay on the ground, and a sharp wind howled abroad. Such was the aspect of out-of-doors affairs when Mrs. Corney, the widow matron of the workhouse to which our readers have been already introduced as the birthplace of Oliver Twist, sat herself down before a cheerful fire in her own little room. In fact, Mrs. Corney was about to solace herself with a cup of tea. She had just thrust a silver spoon (private property) into her two-ounce tea caddy when she was disturbed by a soft tap at the door.

"Oh, come in with you!" she said sharply. "Some of the old women dying, I suppose. They always die when I'm at meals. Don't stand there letting the cold air in. What's amiss now, eh?"

"If you please, Mistress," said a withered old female pauper, putting her head in at the door, "old Sally is a-going fast."

"Well, what's that to me?" angrily demanded the matron. "I can't keep her alive, can I?"

"No, no, Mistress," replied the old woman, "nobody can; she's far beyond the reach of help. But she's troubled in her mind; she says she has got something to tell which you must hear. She'll never die quiet till you come, Mistress."

At this intelligence Mrs. Corney muttered a variety of invectives against old women who couldn't even die without annoying their betters, and, muffling herself in a thick shawl, she followed the messenger from the room, scolding all the way. The old crone tottered along the passages and up the stairs to the room where the

OLIVER TWIST

sick woman lay. It was a bare garret, with a dim light burning at the
farther end. Another old woman was watching by the bed.

"Did she say any more, Anny, dear, while I was gone?" inquired
the messenger.

"Not a word," replied the other old woman.

At this the patient raised herself upright and stretched out her
arms. "I *will* tell her!" she cried, struggling. "Come here! Nearer!
Let me whisper in your ear." She clutched the matron by the arm,
and was about to speak, when looking round, she caught sight of
the two old women bending forward in the attitude of eager listeners. "Turn them away," she said. "Make haste!"

The matron pushed the old women from the room and closed
the door. On being excluded, they crouched at the keyhole.

"Now listen to me," said the dying woman, as if making a great
effort to revive one latent spark of energy. "In this very room—in
this very bed—I once nursed a pretty young creetur that was
brought into the house with her feet cut and bruised with walking
and soiled with dust and blood. She gave birth to a boy, and died.
Now what was the year!"

"Never mind that," said the impatient matron. "What about
her?"

"Aye," murmured the sick woman, relapsing into drowsiness,
"what about her? I know!" she cried, sitting up fiercely, her face
flushed and her eyes starting from her head. "I robbed her, so
I did! I tell you she wasn't cold when I stole it!"

"Stole what, for God's sake?" cried the matron.

"*It!*" replied the woman. "The only thing she had. She lacked
clothes to keep her warm and food to eat, but she had kept *it*
safe in her bosom. It was gold, I tell you! Rich gold that might
have saved her life!"

"Gold?" echoed the matron, bending eagerly over the woman
as she fell back. "Go on, what of it? Who was the mother?"

"She charged me to keep it safe," replied the woman with a
groan, "and trusted me as the only woman about her, and now the
child's death, perhaps, is on me besides! They would have treated
him better if they had known it all!"

"Known what?" asked the other. "Speak!"

"The boy grew so like his mother," said the woman, rambling on and not heeding the question, "that I could never forget it when I saw his face. Poor girl! She was so young, too! Such a gentle lamb! Wait, there's more to tell."

"Be quick," replied the matron, inclining her head to catch the words as they came more faintly from the dying woman. "Or it may be too late!"

"The mother," said the woman, making a more violent effort than before, "the mother, when the pains of death first came on her, whispered in my ear that if her baby was born alive, and thrived, the day might come when it would not feel so much disgraced to hear its poor young mother named. 'And, oh, kind Heaven!' she said, folding her thin hands together, 'whether it be boy or girl, raise up some friends for it in this troubled world and take pity on a lonely desolate child abandoned to its mercy!'"

"The boy's name?" demanded the matron.

"They *called* him Oliver," replied the woman feebly. "The gold I stole was . . ."

"Yes, yes—what?" cried the other. She was bending eagerly over the woman to hear her reply; but drew back, instinctively, as the woman once again rose slowly and stiffly into a sitting posture; then, clutching the coverlet with both hands, the woman muttered some indistinct sounds in her throat and fell lifeless on the bed.

"Stone dead!" said one of the other old women, hurrying in as soon as the door was opened.

"And nothing to tell, after all," said the matron, walking carelessly away.

The two crones, to all appearance too busily occupied in the preparations for their dreadful duties to make any reply, were left alone, hovering about the body.

WHILE THESE THINGS were passing in the country workhouse, Mr. Fagin sat in the old den—the same from which Oliver had been removed by the girl—brooding abstractedly over a dull, smoky fire, his chin resting on his thumbs.

At a table behind him sat the Artful Dodger, Master Charles Bates, and Mr. Chitling, all intent on a game of whist. It being a cold night, the Dodger wore his hat, as indeed was often his custom within doors. His countenance, peculiarly intelligent at all times, acquired additional interest from his close observance of the game and his attentive perusal of Mr. Chitling's hand, on which from time to time he bestowed earnest glances, wisely regulating his own play by the result of his observations of his neighbor's cards.

"That's two doubles and the rub," said Mr. Chitling with a very long face, as he drew half a crown from his pocket. "I never see such a feller as you, Dodger; you win everything. Even when we've good cards, Charley and I can't make nothing of 'em."

Either the matter or the manner of this remark, which was made very ruefully, delighted Charley Bates so much that his consequent shout of laughter roused Fagin from his reverie, and induced him to inquire what was the matter.

"Matter, Fagin!" cried Charley. "I wish you had watched the play. Tommy Chitling hasn't won a point!"

"Ha! Ha! My dear," said Fagin, with a grin. "You must get up very early in the morning to win against the Dodger."

The Artful Dodger received this compliment with philosophy, and offered to cut any gentleman in company for the first picture card at a shilling a time. At this moment the bell rang. "Hark!" he cried. "I heard the tinkler." Catching up the light, he crept softly upstairs.

The bell was rung again with some impatience while the party were in darkness. After a short pause the Dodger reappeared and whispered to Fagin mysteriously.

"What!" cried the old man. "Alone?"

The Dodger nodded, fixed his eyes on Fagin's face and awaited directions. The old man bit his yellow fingers and meditated for some seconds, his face working with agitation. At length he raised his head. "Where is he?" he asked.

The Dodger pointed to the floor above.

"Bring him down," said Fagin. "And you, Charley, Tom—scarce!"

This brief direction was softly and immediately obeyed. There was no sound of the other two's whereabouts when the Dodger descended the stairs, bearing the light in his hand, and followed by a man in a coarse smock frock. This man, after casting a hurried glance round the room, pulled off a large wrapper which had concealed the lower portion of his face and disclosed, all haggard, unwashed and unshorn, the features of flash Toby Crackit.

"How are you, Faguey?" said this worthy. "Pop that shawl away, Dodger, so that I may know where to find it when I cut; that's the time of day!" With these words he pulled up the smock frock, and, winding it round his middle, drew a chair to the fire. "I can't talk about business till I've eat and drank," he went on; "so produce the sustainance, Faguey, and let's have a quiet fill-out for the first time these three days!"

Fagin motioned to the Dodger to place what eatables there were on the table, and seating himself opposite the housebreaker, waited his leisure. To judge from appearances, Toby was by no means in a hurry to open the conversation. At first Fagin contented himself with patiently watching his countenance, as if to gain from its expression some clue to the intelligence he brought; but in vain. He looked tired and worn, but through dirt and beard and whisker there still shone, unimpaired, the self-satisfied smirk of flash Toby Crackit. Then Fagin started pacing up and down the room in an agony of impatience. It was all of no use. Toby continued to eat until he could eat no more; then, ordering the Dodger out, he closed the door, mixed a glass of spirits and water; and composed himself for talking.

"First and foremost, Faguey," he said, "how's Bill?"

"What!" screamed Fagin. He had drawn up his chair, but now started from his seat.

"Why, you don't mean to say—" began Toby, turning pale.

"Mean?" cried Fagin, stamping furiously. "Where are they? Sikes and the boy! Why have they not been here?"

"The crack failed," said Toby faintly.

"I know it," replied the Jew, tearing a newspaper from his pocket and pointing to it. "What more?"

"They fired and hit the boy. We cut over the fields—straight as the crow flies—through hedge and ditch. They gave chase. Damme! The whole country was awake, and the dogs upon us."

"The boy!"

"Bill had him on his back and scudded like the wind. We stopped to take him between us; his head hung down and he was cold. They were close on our heels; every man for himself, and each from the gallows! We parted company, and left the youngster lying in a ditch. Alive or dead, that's all I know about him."

Fagin stopped to hear no more, but uttering a loud yell and twining his hands in his hair, rushed from the room and from the house. Gaining the street, he pressed onward for a time in the same wild and disordered manner. When he began to recover from the effect of Toby Crackit's intelligence, however, he began to skulk through byways and alleys. At length he turned into a narrow and dismal alley leading to Saffron Hill.

In the filthy shops of this lane are exposed for sale huge bunches of secondhand silk handkerchiefs, of all sizes and patterns; for here reside the traders who purchase them from pickpockets. Fagin was well known to the lane's sallow denizens; many nodded as he passed; he replied to their salutations in the same way, but bestowed no closer recognition until he reached the farther end of the alley. There he stopped to address a man of small stature who was smoking a pipe at a warehouse door; and pointing in the direction of Saffron Hill, he inquired whether anyone was up yonder tonight.

"At the Cripples?" inquired the man. "Yes, there's some half dozen of 'em gone in. But I don't think your friend's there."

"Sikes is not, I suppose?" inquired Fagin, with a disappointed countenance.

"*Non istwentus*, as the lawyers say," replied the little man, shaking his head, and Fagin turned away.

The Three Cripples, or rather the Cripples, which was the sign by which the establishment was familiarly known to its patrons, was the public house in which Mr. Sikes and his dog have already figured. Entering it, Fagin made a sign to a man at the bar and walked straight upstairs. There, opening the door of a room and insinuating himself into it, he looked anxiously about as if in search of some particular person.

The room was illuminated by two gaslights, but the place was so full of dense tobacco smoke that at first it was scarcely possible to discern anything more. By degrees, however, an assemblage of heads, as confused as the noises that greeted the ear, might be made out. Fagin looked from face to face until he succeeded, at length, in catching the eye of the landlord. He beckoned to him slightly, and left the room as quietly as he had entered it.

"What can I do for you, Mr. Fagin?" inquired the man, as he followed him out to the landing.

Fagin said in a whisper, "Is *he* here?"

"No," replied the man.

"And no news of Barney?" inquired Fagin.

"None," replied the landlord. "He won't stir till it's all safe. Depend on it, they're on the scent down there; but he's all right, Barney is, else I should have heard of him."

"Will *he* be here tonight?" asked Fagin, laying the same emphasis on the pronoun as before.

"Monks, do you mean?" inquired the landlord, hesitating.

"Hush!" said Fagin. "Yes."

"Certain," replied the man, drawing a gold watch from his fob. "I expected him here before now. If you'll wait ten minutes, he'll be—"

"No, no," said Fagin hastily; as though, however desirous he might be to see the person in question, he was nevertheless relieved by his absence. "Tell him I came here to see him; and that he must come to me tonight. No, say tomorrow. As he is not here, tomorrow will be time enough."

"Good!" said the man. "Nothing more?"

"Not a word," said Fagin, descending the stairs.

The landlord returned to his guests, and Fagin, after a brief reflection, called a hack. Bidding the man drive toward Bethnal Green, he dismissed him a quarter of a mile from Mr. Sikes's residence, and performed the remainder of the distance on foot.

"Now," he muttered, as he crept up the stairs, "if there is any deep play here, I shall have it out of you, my girl, cunning as you are!"

He entered the room without ceremony. Nancy was alone, lying with her head on the table and her hair straggling over it. "She has been drinking," he thought coolly, and turned to close the door. The noise thus occasioned roused the girl. She eyed his crafty face narrowly as she inquired whether there was any news. After she had listened to his recital of Toby Crackit's story she sank into her former attitude, but spoke not a word.

During the silence, Fagin looked restlessly about the room, as if to assure himself that there were no appearances of Sikes having covertly returned. He was apparently satisfied with his inspection, and at length he said, in a most conciliatory tone, "And where should you think Bill was now, my dear?"

The girl moaned out that she could not tell.

"And the boy?" said Fagin, straining his eyes to catch a glimpse of her face. "Poor leetle child! Left in a ditch, Nance; only think!"

"The child," said the girl, suddenly looking up, "is better off where he is than among us; and if no harm comes to Bill from it, I hope Oliver lies dead in the ditch."

"What?" cried Fagin in amazement.

"Aye, I do," returned the girl, meeting his gaze. "I shall be glad to have him away from my eyes, and to know that the worst is over. The sight of him turns me against myself and all of you."

"You're drunk!" exclaimed Fagin, exasperated. "I must have the boy back. So listen to me, you drab! If Sikes comes back, and leaves the boy behind him; or if he gets off free and fails to restore Oliver to me, murder him yourself if you would have him escape the hangman!"

"What is all this?" cried the girl involuntarily.

"What is it?" pursued Fagin, mad with rage. "The boy's worth hundreds of pounds to me. Am I to lose him then through the whims of a drunken gang? And me bound, too, to a born devil that has the power to, to—"

Panting for breath, the old man stammered for a word, and in that instant checked his wrath. A moment before, with eyes dilated and face grown livid with passion, his hands had grasped the air, but now he shrunk cowering into a chair and trembled with the apprehension of having disclosed some hidden villainy. "Nancy, dear," he croaked in his usual voice. "Did you mind me?"

"Don't worry me now, Fagin," replied the girl, raising her head languidly. "If Bill has not done it this time, he will another. He has done many a good job for you and will do many more."

"Regarding this boy, my dear?" said the old man, rubbing the palms of his hands nervously together.

"The boy must take his chance with the rest," said Nancy hastily. "And I say again, I hope he is dead and out of harm's way—that is, if Bill comes to no harm. And if Toby got clear off, Bill's pretty sure to be safe, for Bill's worth two of Toby any time."

"And about what I was saying, my dear?" observed Fagin, keeping his glistening eye on her.

"You must say it all over again if it's anything you want me to do," rejoined Nancy. "And if it is, you had better wait till tomorrow. You put me up for a minute, but now I'm stupid again."

Fagin put several other questions, all with the same drift of ascertaining whether the girl had profited by his unguarded hints; but she was so utterly unmoved that his impression of her being more than a trifle in liquor was confirmed. Having eased his mind by this discovery, he again turned his face homeward, leaving his young friend asleep with her head on the table.

It was within an hour of midnight. A sharp wind scoured the streets, and he went straight before it, trembling and shivering as every fresh gust drove him rudely on his way. He had reached the corner of his own street when a dark figure emerged from deep shadow, and, crossing the road, glided up to him unperceived.

"Fagin!" whispered a voice close to his ear.

"Ah," said the old man, turning quickly, "is that—"

"Yes!" interrupted the stranger. "I have been here these two hours. Where the devil have you been?"

"On your business, my dear," replied Fagin, glancing uneasily at his companion. "On your business all night."

"Oh, of course!" sneered the stranger. "Well, and what's come of it?"

"Nothing good."

"Nothing bad, I hope?" said the stranger, stopping short and turning a startled look on his companion.

The old man was about to reply when the stranger motioned to the house, remarking that he had better say what he had got to say under cover. Fagin unlocked the door and requested his companion to close it softly while he got a light. As he spoke, it closed with a loud noise.

"That wasn't my doing," said the other man. "The wind blew it to. Look sharp with the light, or I shall knock my brains out in this confounded hole."

Fagin stealthily descended the kitchen stairs. After a short absence he returned with a lighted candle and the news that Toby Crackit was asleep in the back room below and the boys in the front one. Beckoning the man to follow him, he led the way upstairs.

"We can say the few words we've got to say in here, my dear," he said, throwing open a door on the second floor, "and as there are holes in the shutters, and we never show lights to our neighbors, we'll set the candle on the stairs. There!"

With those words, Fagin placed the candle on an upper flight of stairs, opposite to the room door. This done, he led the way into the apartment, which was destitute of all movables save a broken armchair, and an old sofa without covering. Upon this piece of furniture the stranger sat himself with the air of a weary man; and Fagin drawing up the armchair opposite, they sat face-to-face and conversed for some time in whispers. Fagin appeared to be defending himself against some remarks of the stranger; and the latter appeared to be in a state of considerable irritation. They might have been talking thus for a quarter of an hour or more when Monks—by which name Fagin had designated the strange man several times in the course of their colloquy—said, raising his voice a little:

"I tell you again, it was badly planned. Why not have kept him here, and made a sneaking, sniveling pickpocket of him at once?

Haven't you done it with other boys scores of times? If you had had patience for a twelvemonth at most, couldn't you have got him convicted and sent safely out of the kingdom, perhaps for life?"

"Whose turn would that have served, my dear?" inquired Fagin humbly.

"Mine," replied Monks.

"But not mine. When there are two parties to a bargain, it is only reasonable that the interests of both should be consulted. I saw it was not easy to train him to the business; he was not like other boys in the same circumstances. I had nothing to frighten him with; and we always must have that in the beginning. What could I do? Send him out with the Dodger and Charley? We had enough of that at first, my dear; I trembled for us all."

"*That* was not my doing," observed Monks.

"No, no, my dear!" renewed Fagin. "And I don't quarrel with it now—because if it had never happened, you might never have clapped eyes on the boy and so discovered that it was him you were looking for. Well! I got him back for you by means of the girl; and then *she* begins to favor him."

"Throttle the girl!" said Monks impatiently.

"Why, we can't afford to do that just now, my dear," replied Fagin, smiling. "And, besides, I know what these girls are, Monks. As soon as the boy begins to harden, she'll care no more for him. You want him made a thief. If he is alive, I can make him one from this time; and if—if—it's not likely, mind—but if the worst comes to the worst, and he is dead—"

"It's no fault of mine if he is!" interposed the other man, clasping Fagin's arm with trembling hands. "Mind that, Fagin! I had no hand in it. Anything but his death, I told you from the first. I won't shed blood; it's always found out, and haunts a man besides. If they shot him dead, I was not the cause; do you hear me? Oh, this infernal den! What's that?"

"What?" cried Fagin, springing to his feet. "Where?"

"Yonder!" replied the man, glaring at the opposite wall. "I saw the shadow of a woman, in a cloak and bonnet, pass along the wainscot!"

The two men rushed from the room. The candle, wasted by the draft, was standing where it had been placed. It showed them only the empty staircase and their own white faces. They listened intently; a profound silence reigned throughout the house.

"It's your fancy," said Fagin, taking up the light, and, telling his associate he could follow if he pleased, he ascended the stairs. They looked into all the rooms: they were cold, bare and empty. They descended into the passage and thence into the cellars. The green damp hung on the low walls; the tracks of the snail and slug glistened in the light of the candle; but all was still as death.

"What do you think now?" asked Fagin when they had regained the passage. "Besides ourselves, there's not a creature in the house except Toby and the boys; and I locked them in their rooms when I first went downstairs."

Mr. Monks gave vent to several grim laughs and confessed it could only have been his excited imagination. He declined any renewal of the conversation, however, for that night, for he suddenly remembered that it was past one o'clock. So the amiable couple parted.

And now that they have done so, let us set on foot a few inquiries after young Oliver Twist, and ascertain whether he be still lying in the ditch where Toby Crackit left him.

··◉· CHAPTER XIII ·◉··

"WOLVES TEAR YOUR THROATS!" muttered Sikes, grinding his teeth. "I wish I was among some of you; you'd howl the hoarser for it."

As Sikes growled forth this imprecation, he rested the body of the wounded boy across his bended knee and turned to look back at his pursuers. There was little to be made out in the mist and darkness, but the loud shouting of men vibrated through the air and the barking of dogs resounded in every direction.

"Stop, you white-livered hound!" cried Sikes to Toby Crackit, who, making the best use of his long legs, was already ahead. "Stop!"

The repetition of the word brought Toby to a standstill. He was not quite satisfied that he was beyond the range of pistol shot, and Sikes was in no mood to be played with.

"Bear a hand with the boy," cried Sikes furiously. "Come back!"

Toby made a show of returning, but intimated considerable reluctance. "Quicker!" cried Sikes, laying the boy in a dry ditch at his feet, and drawing a pistol from his pocket.

At this moment the noise grew louder. Sikes, again looking round, could discern that the men who had given chase were climbing the gate of the field in which he stood, and that a couple of dogs were some paces in advance of them.

"It's all up, Bill!" cried Toby. "Drop the kid and show 'em your heels!"

With this parting advice, Mr. Crackit, preferring the chance of being shot by his friend to the certainty of being taken by his enemies, turned tail and darted off. Sikes clenched his teeth, took another look round, and threw over the prostrate form of Oliver the cape in which he had been hurriedly muffled. He then ran along a nearby hedge, as if to distract the attention of those behind from the spot where the boy lay, until he reached another hedge which met it at right angles. Whirling his pistol high in the air, he cleared it at a bound and was gone.

"Pincher! Neptune!" cried a tremulous voice in the rear. "Come here, come here!"

The dogs, who in common with their masters seemed to have no particular relish for the sport in which they were engaged, readily answered to the command. Three men, who had by this time advanced some distance into the field, stopped to take counsel together.

"My advice, or leastways I should say my *orders*, is," said the fattest man of the party, "that we 'mediately go home again."

"I am agreeable to anything which is agreeable to Mr. Giles," said a shorter man, who was very pale in the face and very polite, as frightened men frequently are.

"Mr. Giles ought to know," said the third, who had called the dogs back.

"Certainly," replied the shorter man, "and it isn't our place to contradict Mr. Giles. No, no, I know my sitiwation!"

"You are afraid, Brittles," said Mr. Giles.

"I a'n't," said Brittles.

"You are," said Giles.

"You're a falsehood, Mr. Giles," said Brittles.

The third man brought the dispute to a close most philosophically. "I'll tell you what it is, gentlemen," said he. "We're all afraid. It's natural and proper to be afraid under such circumstances. *I* am."

This dialogue was held between the two men who had surprised the burglars and a traveling tinker, who had been sleeping in an outhouse and who had been roused, together with his two mongrel curs, to join in the pursuit of the burglars. Mr. Giles acted in the double capacity of butler and steward to the old lady of the mansion; Brittles was a lad-of-all-work who, having entered her service a mere child, was treated as a promising young boy still, though he was something past thirty.

Encouraging each other with such converse as this, keeping very close together and looking apprehensively round whenever a fresh gust of wind rattled through the boughs, the three men made their way home at a good round trot.

The air grew colder as day came slowly on, and the mist rolled along the ground like a dense cloud of smoke. Still Oliver lay motionless and insensible on the spot where Sikes had left him. Morning drew on apace; its first dull hue glimmered faintly in the sky. The rain came down thick and fast and pattered noisily among the leafless bushes. But Oliver felt it not as it beat against him.

At length, uttering a low cry of pain, the boy awoke. His left arm, rudely bandaged in a shawl, hung heavy and useless at his side; the bandage was saturated with blood. He was so weak that he could scarcely raise himself into a sitting posture; when he had done so he looked feebly round for help and groaned with pain. Trembling in every joint from cold and exhaustion, he made an effort to stand upright; but he fell prostrate on the ground. After a short return of the same stupor, however, urged by a sickness at his heart which seemed to warn him that if he lay there he must surely die, he got to his feet again and essayed to walk. His head was dizzy, and he staggered like a drunken man. But he kept up nevertheless and, languidly, went stumbling onward, creeping through hedge gaps as they came in his way, until he reached a road.

Here the rain began to fall so heavily that it roused him. He looked about and saw that at no great distance there was a house which perhaps he could reach. Though wearied and tormented with pain, he summoned up all his strength and bent his faltering steps towards it.

As he drew nearer to the house, a feeling came over him that he had seen it before. He remembered nothing of its details, but the shape and aspect of the building seemed familiar to him.

That garden wall! On the grass inside he had fallen on his knees last night and prayed the two men's mercy. It was the very house they had attempted to rob!

Oliver felt such fear come over him that, for the instant, he forgot the agony of his wound and thought only of flight. But even if he were stronger, whither could he fly? He pushed against the garden gate, tottered across the lawn, climbed the steps, knocked faintly at the door, and sank down against one of the pillars of the little portico.

It happened that about this time Mr. Giles, Brittles, and the tinker were recruiting themselves, after the fatigues and terrors of the night, with tea and sundries in the kitchen. Not that it was Mr. Giles's habit to admit to too great familiarity the humbler servants; but death, fires, and burglary make all men equals; so Mr. Giles sat with his legs stretched out before the kitchen fender, leaning his left arm on the table while with his right he illustrated a circumstantial and minute account of the robbery to which his hearers (but especially the cook and housemaid, who were of the party) listened with breathless interest.

"It was about half past two," said Mr. Giles, "when I woke up and fancied I heerd a noise, and I sat up in bed and listened."

The cook and housemaid simultaneously ejaculated, "Lor!" and drew their chairs closer together.

"I tossed off the bedclothes," continued Giles, "got softly out of bed, drew on a pair of—"

"Ladies present, Mr. Giles," murmured the tinker.

"—of *shoes*, sir," said Giles, turning on him, "seized the loaded pistol that always goes upstairs with the plate basket, and went to wake Brittles. 'Brittles,' I says when I had woke him, 'we're dead men, I think, but don't be frightened.'"

"*Was* he frightened?" asked the cook.

"Not a bit of it," replied Mr. Giles. "He was as firm—ah!—pretty near as firm as I was."

"I should have died at once, I'm sure, if it had been me," observed the housemaid.

"You're a woman," retorted Brittles, plucking up a little.

"Brittles is right," said Mr. Giles, nodding his head approvingly. "From a woman, nothing else was to be expected. We, being men, took a dark lantern and groped our way downstairs in the pitch dark, as it might be so."

Mr. Giles had risen and taken two steps with his eyes shut to accompany his description with appropriate action, when he started violently, in common with the rest of the company, and hurried back to his chair. The cook and housemaid screamed.

"It was a knock," said Mr. Giles, assuming perfect serenity. "Open the door, somebody."

Nobody moved.

"It seems a strange sort of thing, at such a time," said Mr. Giles, surveying the pale faces which surrounded him, "but the door must be opened. Do you hear, somebody?"

He looked at Brittles; but that young man, being naturally modest, probably considered himself nobody, and so held the inquiry could not have any application to him; at all events, he tendered no reply. Mr. Giles directed an appealing glance at the tinker, but he had suddenly fallen asleep. The women were out of the question.

"If Brittles would rather open the door in the presence of witnesses," said Mr. Giles, "I am ready to make one."

"So am I," said the tinker, waking up as suddenly as he had fallen asleep.

Oliver at Mrs. Maylie's Door

Brittles capitulated on these terms; and the party took their way upstairs with the dogs in front. The two women brought up the rear. By the advice of Mr. Giles, they all talked very loud to warn any evil-disposed person outside that they were strong in numbers; and by a master stroke of policy of the same ingenious gentleman, the dogs' tails were well pinched in the hall to make them bark savagely.

These precautions having been taken, Mr. Giles held on fast by the tinker's arm and gave the word of command to open the door. Brittles obeyed. The group, peeping timorously over each other's shoulders, beheld no more formidable object than poor little Oliver Twist, huddled against a pillar, speechless and exhausted, who raised his heavy eyes and mutely solicited their compassion.

"A boy!" exclaimed Mr. Giles, valiantly pushing the tinker into the background. "What's the matter with the—eh? Why—Brittles, look here—don't you know?"

Brittles no sooner saw Oliver than he uttered a loud cry. Mr. Giles, seizing the boy by one leg and one arm (fortunately not the broken limb), lugged him into the hall and deposited him at full length on the floor.

"Here he is!" bawled Giles, calling in great excitement up the staircase. "Here's one of the thieves, ma'am. Wounded. I shot him, miss, and Brittles held the light."

The two women servants ran upstairs to carry the intelligence that Mr. Giles had captured a robber, and the tinker busied himself in endeavoring to restore Oliver, lest he should die before he could be hanged. In the midst of all this noise and commotion there was heard a sweet female voice which quelled it in an instant.

"Giles," whispered the voice from the stairhead.

"I'm here, miss," replied Mr. Giles. "Don't be frightened, miss. He didn't make a very desperate resistance!"

"Hush!" replied the young lady. "You frighten my aunt as much as the thieves did. Is the poor creature much hurt?"

"Wounded desperate, miss!" replied Giles with complacency.

"Wait one instant while I speak to Aunt," said the lady.

With a footstep as soft and gentle as the voice, the speaker tripped away. She soon returned with the direction that the wounded person was to be carried carefully upstairs to Mr. Giles's room, and that Brittles was to saddle the pony and betake himself to Chertsey to fetch a constable and a doctor.

"But won't you take one look at him first, miss?" asked Mr. Giles, with as much pride as if Oliver were some bird of rare plumage that he had skillfully brought down.

"Not now, for the world," replied the young lady. "Poor fellow! Oh, treat him kindly, Giles, for my sake!"

The old servant looked up at the speaker, as she turned away, with a glance as proud and admiring as if she had been his own child. Then, bending over Oliver, he helped to carry him upstairs with the care and solicitude of a woman.

IN A HANDSOME ROOM—though its furniture had rather the air of old-fashioned comfort than of modern elegance—there sat two ladies at a well-spread breakfast table. Mr. Giles, in a full suit of black, was in attendance on them.

Of the two ladies, one was well advanced in years, but the high-backed oaken chair in which she sat was not more upright than she. Dressed with the utmost nicety and precision, in a quaint mixture of bygone costume, with some slight concessions to the prevailing taste, she sat in a stately manner, with her hands folded on the table before her.

The younger lady was in the bloom and springtime of woman-hood. Not past seventeen, she was cast in so slight and exquisite a mold, and was so pure and beautiful, that earth seemed not her element. The very intelligence that shone in her deep blue eyes seemed scarcely of the world; and yet the changing expression of sweetness and good humor that played about her face, above all, the cheerful smile, were made for home, and fireside peace and happiness. She was busily engaged in the little offices of the table.

"And Brittles has been gone upwards of an hour, has he?" asked the old lady, after a pause.

"An hour and twelve minutes, ma'am," replied Mr. Giles, referring to a silver watch, which he drew forth by a black ribbon.

As he spoke, a gig drove up to the garden gate; out of it jumped a fat gentleman who ran straight up to the door, and, getting into the house by some mysterious process, burst into the room and nearly overturned Mr. Giles and the breakfast table together.

"I never heard of such a thing!" exclaimed the fat gentleman. "My dear Mrs. Maylie—bless my soul!—in the silence of the night, too—I *never* heard of such a thing!"

With these expressions of condolence the fat gentleman shook hands with both ladies, and drawing up a chair, inquired how they found themselves. "You ought to be positively dead with the fright," he said. "Why didn't you send? Bless me, I should have come in a minute. Dear, dear! So unexpected! In the silence of the night, too! And you, Miss Rose," said the doctor, turning to the young lady, "I—"

"Oh, very much so, indeed," said Rose, interrupting him. "But there is a poor creature upstairs whom Aunt wishes you to see."

"Ah, to be sure!" replied the doctor. "So there is. Where is he? Show me the way. I'll look in again as I come down, Mrs. Maylie."

Talking all the way, Dr. Losberne, the neighborhood surgeon, followed Mr. Giles upstairs. Known for ten miles round as "the doctor," he had grown fat more from good humor than from good living, and was as kind and hearty and withal as eccentric an old bachelor as will be found in five times that space.

The doctor was absent much longer than either he or the ladies had anticipated. A large flat box was fetched out of the gig; a bedroom bell was rung often, and the servants ran up and down stairs perpetually. At length the doctor returned, and in reply to an anxious inquiry after his patient, looked very mysterious and closed the door.

"This is a very extraordinary thing, Mrs. Maylie," he said.

"He is not in danger, I hope?" said the old lady.

"I don't think he is," replied the doctor. "Have you seen this thief?"

"No," said the old lady. "Rose wished to see the man, but I wouldn't hear of it."

"Humph!" rejoined the doctor. "There is nothing very alarming in his appearance. Have you any objection to seeing him in my presence?"

"If it be necessary," replied the old lady, "certainly not."

"Then I think it is necessary," said the doctor. "At all events, I am quite sure that you would deeply regret not having done so if you postponed it. He is perfectly quiet and comfortable now. Allow me—Miss Rose, will you permit me? Not the slightest fear, I pledge you my honor!"

With many loquacious assurances that they would be agreeably surprised in the aspect of the criminal, the doctor drew the young lady's arm through one of his, and offering his disengaged hand to Mrs. Maylie, led them upstairs. "Now," said the doctor in a whisper, as he softly turned the handle of a bedroom door, "let us hear what you think of him. He has not been shaved very recently, but he don't look at all ferocious notwithstanding."

Motioning them to advance, he gently drew back the curtains of the bed. Upon it, in lieu of the dogged black-visaged ruffian they had expected to behold, there lay a mere child, worn with pain and exhaustion and sunk into a deep sleep. His wounded arm, bound and splintered up, was crossed upon his breast; his head reclined upon the other arm, which was half hidden by his long hair as it streamed over the pillow.

While the doctor looked on his patient for a minute or so, in silence, the younger lady glided softly past, and seating herself by the bedside, gathered Oliver's hair from his face. As she stooped over him, her tears fell on his forehead.

"What can this mean?" exclaimed the elder lady. "This poor child can never have been the pupil of robbers!"

The surgeon mournfully shook his head. "Crime, like death, is not confined to the old and withered," he rejoined. "The youngest and fairest are too often its chosen victims."

"But can you really believe that this delicate boy has been the voluntary associate of the worst outcasts of society?" asked Rose.

The surgeon shook his head in a manner which intimated that he feared it was very possible, and observing that they might disturb the patient, led the way into an adjoining apartment.

"But even if he has been wicked," pursued Rose, "think how young he is; think that he may never have known a mother's love or the comfort of a home, and that ill-usage and blows, or the want of bread, may have driven him to herd with men who have forced him to guilt! Aunt, dear Aunt, think of this before you let them drag this sick child to a prison. As you love me and know that I have never felt the want of parents in your goodness and affection, but that I might have been equally helpless and unprotected with this poor child, have pity on him before it is too late!"

"My dear love," said the elder lady, as she folded the weeping girl to her bosom, "do you think I would harm a hair of his head? What can I do to save him, sir?"

"Let me think, ma'am," said the doctor.

Dr. Losberne thrust his hands into his pockets and took several turns up and down the room, often stopping, and balancing himself on his toes, and frowning frightfully. At length he made a dead halt and spoke. "I think if you give me a full commission to bully Giles and Brittles, I can manage it. Giles is a faithful old servant, I know, but you can make it up to him in a thousand ways, and reward him for being such a good shot besides. You don't object to that?"

"Unless there is some other way of preserving the child," replied Mrs. Maylie.

"There is no other," said the doctor. "But the great point of our agreement is yet to come. When the boy awakes, although I have told that thickheaded constable fellow downstairs that he mustn't be moved or spoken to on peril of his life, I think we may converse with him without danger. Now, I make this stipulation—that I shall examine him in your presence and that if from what he says we judge that he is a real and thorough bad one (which is more than possible), he shall be left to his fate without any further interference."

"Oh, no, Aunt!" entreated Rose. "He cannot be hardened in vice! It is impossible."

"Very good," retorted the doctor. "Then so much the more reason for acceding to my proposition."

Finally the treaty was entered into, and the parties thereunto sat down to wait until Oliver should awake.

Hour after hour passed, and still Oliver slumbered heavily. It was evening, indeed, before the kindhearted doctor brought the two ladies the intelligence that he was at length sufficiently restored to be spoken to. The boy was very ill, he said, and weak from loss of blood, but his mind was so troubled with anxiety to disclose something, that the doctor deemed it better to give him the opportunity now than to insist on his remaining quiet until next morning.

The conference was a long one. Oliver told them all his simple history, though he was often compelled to stop by pain and want of strength. It was a solemn thing to hear, in the darkened room, the feeble voice of the sick child recounting the catalogue of evils and calamities which hard men had brought on him.

Oliver's pillow was smoothed by gentle hands that night, and loveliness and virtue watched him as he slept at last, calm and happy. He was no sooner at rest than the doctor, after wiping his eyes, betook himself downstairs to open up on Mr. Giles.

Assembled in the kitchen were the women servants, Mr. Brittles, Mr. Giles, the tinker (who had received a special invitation to regale himself for the remainder of the day in consideration of his services), and the local constable. The latter gentleman had a large staff, a large head, large features, and large half boots, and he looked as if he had been taking a proportionate allowance of ale— as indeed he had.

The adventures of the previous night were still under discussion when the doctor entered. "Sit still!" he said, waving his hand.

"Thank you, sir," said Mr. Giles. "How is the patient, sir?"

"So-so," returned the doctor. "I am afraid you have got yourself into a scrape there, Mr. Giles."

"I hope you don't mean to say, sir," said Mr. Giles, trembling, "that he's going to die? I wouldn't cut a boy off, no, not for all the plate in the county, sir."

"That's not the point," said the doctor mysteriously. "Tell me this, both of you! Are you going to take upon yourselves to swear that the boy upstairs is the boy that was put through the little window last night? Out with it! Come! We are prepared for you!"

The doctor, who was universally considered one of the best-tempered creatures on earth, made this demand in such a tone of anger that Giles and Brittles, who were considerably muddled by ale and excitement, stared at each other in stupefaction.

"Pay attention to the reply, Constable, will you?" said the doctor, shaking his forefinger with great solemnity. "Something may come of this before long."

The constable looked as wise as he could and took up his staff of office.

"It's a simple question of identity, you will observe," said the doctor.

"That's what it is, sir," replied the constable, coughing with great violence, for he had finished his ale in a hurry and some of it had gone the wrong way.

"Here's a house broken into," said the doctor, "and a couple of men catch one moment's glimpse of a boy, in the midst of gunpowder smoke, and in all the distraction of alarm and darkness. Here's a boy comes to that very same house next morning; and because he happens to have his arm tied up, these men lay violent hands on him—by doing which they place his life in great danger—and swear he is the thief. Now, the question is whether these men are justified by the fact; if not, in what situation do they place themselves?"

The constable nodded profoundly. He said if that wasn't law, he would be glad to know what was.

"I ask you again!" thundered the doctor. "Are you, on your solemn oaths, able to identify that boy?"

Brittles looked doubtfully at Mr. Giles; Mr. Giles looked doubtfully at Brittles; the constable put his hand behind his ear to catch the reply.

"It was all done for the—for the best, sir!" answered Giles. "I am sure I thought it was the boy. They—they certainly had a boy."

"Well? Do you think it's the *same* boy?" inquired the doctor.

"I don't know, I really don't, sir," said Giles, with a rueful countenance. "I couldn't swear to him."

Brittles, on being questioned, then involved himself and his respected superior in such a wonderful maze of fresh contradictions and impossibilities as tended to throw no particular light on anything, except his declarations that he shouldn't know the real boy if he were put before him that instant, and that he had only taken Oliver to be he because Mr. Giles had said he was.

The question was then raised as to whether Mr. Giles had really shot anybody. And upon the constable's examining the fellow pistol to that which he had fired, it turned out to have no more destructive loading than gunpowder and brown paper—a discovery which made a considerable impression on everybody but the doctor, who had drawn the ball out about ten minutes before. On no one, however, did it make a greater impression than on Mr. Giles, who, after laboring under the fear of having mortally wounded a fellow creature, eagerly favored this new idea.

After some more examination and a great deal more conversation, the constable was persuaded to ignore Oliver's existence; and, being rewarded with a couple of guineas, he returned to town.

··✦◎· CHAPTER XIV ·◎✦··

OLIVER GRADUALLY throve and prospered under the united care of Mrs. Maylie, Rose, and Dr. Losberne. Still his ailings were neither slight nor few. In addition to the pain attendant on a broken limb, his exposure to the wet and cold had brought on a fever which hung about him for many weeks and reduced him sadly. But at length he began by slow degrees to get better and to be able to say sometimes, in a few tearful words, how deeply he felt the goodness of the two sweet ladies, and how ardently he hoped that when he grew strong and well again, he could do something to show his gratitude—something, however slight, which would prove to them that he was eager to serve them with his whole heart and soul.

"Poor fellow!" said Rose, when Oliver had been one day feebly endeavoring to utter words of thankfulness. "You shall have many opportunities of serving us. We are going into the country, and my aunt intends that you shall accompany us. The quiet place, the pure air, and all the beauties of spring will restore you. We will employ you in a hundred ways, when you can bear the trouble."

"The trouble!" cried Oliver. "Oh, dear lady, if I could but work for you—what would I give to do it!"

"You shall give nothing at all," replied Miss Maylie, smiling. "And if you only take half the trouble to please us that you promise now, you will make me happy. To think that my aunt should have been the means of rescuing anyone from such sad misery as you have described to us would be an unspeakable pleasure to me, but to know that the object of her compassion was sincerely grateful would delight me more than you can well imagine. Do you understand me?" she inquired, watching Oliver's thoughtful face.

"Oh yes, ma'am, yes!" replied Oliver eagerly. "But I was thinking that I am ungrateful now."

"To whom?" inquired the young lady.

"To the kind gentleman, Mr. Brownlow, and the dear old nurse, who took so much care of me before. If they knew how happy I am, they would be pleased, I am sure."

"I am sure they would," rejoined Oliver's benefactress, "and Dr. Losberne has already promised that when you are well enough to bear the journey, he will carry you to see them."

"Has he, ma'am?" cried Oliver, his face brightening. "I don't know what I shall do for joy when I see their kind faces again!"

In a short time Oliver was sufficiently recovered to undergo the fatigue of this expedition. One morning he and Dr. Losberne set out accordingly in Mrs. Maylie's little carriage.

When at length the coach turned into the street in which Mr. Brownlow resided, Oliver's heart beat so violently that he could scarcely draw his breath.

"Now, my boy, which house is it?" inquired Dr. Losberne.

"That white house!" replied Oliver, pointing eagerly out of the window. "Oh! Pray make haste! I feel as if I should die, it makes me tremble so."

The coach rolled on. It stopped. No, that was the wrong house;

the next door. The coach went on a few paces and stopped again. Oliver looked up at the windows with tears of happy expectation coursing down his face.

Alas! The white house was empty and there was a sign in the window: To LET.

"Knock next door," cried Dr. Losberne to the coachman. When a servant appeared, he asked, "What has become of Mr. Brownlow, who used to live in the adjoining house?"

The servant said that Mr. Brownlow had gone to the West Indies six weeks before. "The old gentleman, the housekeeper, and a gentleman who was a friend of Mr. Brownlow's all went together."

Oliver clasped his hands and sank feebly backwards.

"Turn towards home again," said Dr. Losberne to the driver, "and don't stop till you get out of this confounded London!"

This bitter disappointment caused Oliver much grief even in the midst of his happiness, for he had pleased himself many times during his illness thinking of Mr. Brownlow and Mrs. Bedwin, and what delight it would be to tell them how many long days and nights he had passed bewailing his cruel separation from them. The hope of explaining how he had been forced away had sustained him in many of his recent trials; and now, the idea that they should have gone so far and carried with them the belief that he was an impostor and a robber—a belief which might remain uncontradicted to his dying day—was almost more than he could bear.

The circumstance occasioned no alteration, however, in the behavior of his benefactors. After another fortnight, when the fine warm weather had fairly begun and every tree and flower was putting forth its young leaves and rich blossoms, they made preparations for quitting the house near Chertsey for some months. Sending the plate, which had so excited Fagin's cupidity, to the banker's, they departed to a cottage at some distance in the country and took Oliver with them.

It was a lovely spot to which they repaired, and Oliver seemed to enter on a new existence there. The rose and honeysuckle clung to the cottage walls, the ivy crept round the trunks of the trees, and the garden flowers perfumed the air. Hard by was a little churchyard full of humble green mounds, beneath which the old people of the village lay at rest. Oliver often wandered here, and, thinking of the wretched grave in which his mother lay, would sometimes sit down and weep for her.

But it was a happy time. The days were serene; the nights brought with them nothing but pleasant thoughts. In the morning Oliver would be afoot by six o'clock, roaming the fields for nosegays of wild flowers which he would bring home for the embellishment of the breakfast table. Later every morning he went to a white-headed old gentleman who lived nearby, who taught him to read better and to write, and who spoke so kindly and took such pains that Oliver could never try enough to please him. He would walk with Mrs. Maylie and Rose, or sit near them in some shady place and listen while the young lady read. Then he had his own lesson for the next day to prepare, and at this he would work hard in a little room which looked into the garden, till evening came slowly on. Then the ladies would walk out again and he with them, listening with great pleasure to all they said, and very happy if they had forgotten anything which he could run to fetch. When it became quite dark and they returned home, Rose would sit down to the piano and play some pleasant air, or sing in a gentle voice some old song which it pleased her aunt to hear, and Oliver would sit by one of the windows, listening in a perfect rapture.

And when Sunday came, how differently the day was spent from any way in which he had ever spent it yet, and how happily too! There was the little church in the morning, with the birds singing without, and the sweet-smelling air filling the homely building with its fragrance while the poor people knelt reverently in prayer. There were the walks as usual, and at night Oliver read a chapter or two from the Bible, which he had been studying all the week; and in the performance of this duty he felt more proud and pleased than if he had been the clergyman himself.

SPRING FLEW SWIFTLY BY and summer came. The same quiet life went on at the little cottage, and the same cheerful serenity prevailed among its inmates. Oliver, long since grown stout and healthy, had become completely domesticated with the old lady and her niece, and the fervent attachment of his young and sensitive heart was repaid by their pride in and attachment to himself.

One beautiful night, they had taken a longer walk than was customary with them, for the day had been unusually warm, there was a brilliant moon, and a refreshing wind had sprung up. Rose had been in high spirits, and they had walked on in merry conversation until they had far exceeded their ordinary bounds. Mrs. Maylie being fatigued, they returned more slowly home. Rose sat down to the piano as usual and fell into a low and solemn air. Then as she played they heard a sound as if she were weeping.

"Rose, my love!" cried Mrs. Maylie, rising hastily and bending over her. "What is this? My dear child, what distresses you?"

"Nothing, Aunt, nothing," replied the young lady. "I don't know what it is. I can't describe it; but I feel—"

"Not ill, my love?" interposed Mrs. Maylie.

Rose shuddered, as though some deadly chillness were passing over her, and, covering her face with her hands, she sank upon a sofa and gave vent to the tears which she was now unable to repress. "I can't help it," she said. "I fear I *am* ill, Aunt."

She was indeed; for, when candles were brought, they saw that the hue of her countenance had changed to a marble whiteness, and there was a haggard look about the gentle face which it had never worn before. Another minute and it was suffused with a crimson flush. Again this disappeared, like the shadow thrown by a passing cloud, and she was once more deadly pale.

Oliver anxiously observed that the old lady was alarmed by these appearances, and so in truth was he; but seeing that she affected to make light of them, he endeavored to do the same, and when Rose was persuaded by her aunt to retire for the night, she assured them that she felt certain she should rise in the morning quite well.

"I hope," said Oliver, when Mrs. Maylie returned, "that nothing is the matter?"

"I hope not, Oliver," the old lady said in a trembling voice. "I have been very happy with her. Too happy, perhaps. My dear, dear Rose. Oh, what should I do without her!"

An anxious night ensued. When morning came, Rose was in the first stage of a high and dangerous fever.

"We must be active, Oliver, and not give way to useless grief," said Mrs. Maylie. "This letter must be sent with all possible expedition to Dr. Losberne. It must be carried to the market town by the footpath across the fields. There the people at the inn will dispatch it by an express on horseback to Chertsey. I can trust you to see it done, I know."

Oliver could make no reply, but looked his anxiety to be gone at once.

"Here is another letter," said Mrs. Maylie, pausing to reflect. "But whether to send it now or wait until I see how Rose goes on, I scarcely know. I would not forward it unless I feared the worst."

Oliver saw that it was directed to Harry Maylie, Esquire, at some lord's house in the country.

"Shall it go, ma'am?" asked Oliver, impatient to execute his commission.

"I think not," replied Mrs. Maylie. "I will wait until tomorrow."

With these words she gave Oliver her purse, and he started off without more delay. Swiftly he ran across the fields, nor did he stop, save now and then to recover breath, until he came to the little marketplace of the town. He hastened to the inn, where a postboy, who had been dozing under the gateway, referred him to the hostler; who, after hearing what he wanted, referred him to the landlord. This gentleman walked with much deliberation into the bar to make out the bill, and after it was ready and paid, a horse had to be saddled and a man to be dressed, which took up ten good minutes more. But at length all was ready, and the letter having been handed up with many entreaties for its speedy delivery, the man set spurs to his horse and was out of the town and galloping along the turnpike road in a couple of minutes.

Oliver was hurrying out of the inn with a somewhat lighter heart when he accidentally stumbled against a tall man wrapped in a cloak who was at that moment coming out of the inn door.

"Hah!" cried the man, fixing his eyes on Oliver, and suddenly recoiling. "What the devil's this?"

"I beg your pardon, sir," said Oliver. "I was in a hurry and didn't see you."

"Death!" muttered the man, glaring at the boy. "Who would have thought it! Grind him to ashes, and he'd start up from a stone coffin to come in my way!"

"I am sorry," stammered Oliver, confused by the strange man's wild look. "I hope I have not hurt you!"

"Rot you!" murmured the man between his clenched teeth. "If I had only had the courage to say the word, I might have been free of you. Curses on your head, you imp! What are you doing here?"

The man shook his fist and advanced towards Oliver, as if intending to aim a blow at him, but instead fell violently on the ground, writhing and foaming in a fit. Oliver gazed for a moment at the struggles of the madman (for such he supposed him to be), and then darted into the house for help. Having seen the stranger safely carried into the hotel, he turned his face homewards, running as fast as he could and recalling the man's extraordinary behavior with a great deal of astonishment and some fear.

The circumstance did not dwell in his recollection long, however, for when he reached the cottage he found that Rose Maylie had rapidly grown worse. Before midnight she was delirious. A medical practitioner who resided on the spot was in constant attendance on her, and he had pronounced her disorder to be one of a most alarming nature. "In fact," he said to Mrs. Maylie, "it will be little short of a miracle if she recovers."

How often did Oliver start from his bed that night, listening for the slightest sound! How often did cold drops of terror start on his brow, when a sudden trampling of feet caused him to fear that something too dreadful to think of had occurred!

Morning came; and the little cottage was still. People spoke in whispers. All the livelong day and for hours after it had grown dark, Oliver paced softly up and down the garden, raising his eyes often to the sick chamber and shuddering to see the darkened window looking as if death lay stretched inside. Late at night Dr. Losberne arrived. "It is hard," said the good doctor, turning away as he spoke. "So young, so much beloved. But there is little hope."

And hearing Dr. Losberne's opinion, Mrs. Maylie dispatched Giles to deliver her second letter.

Another morning. The sun shone as brightly as if it looked on no misery. And with every leaf and flower in full bloom about her, with life and health surrounding her, the fair young creature lay, wasting fast. Oliver crept away to the old churchyard, and sitting down on one of the green mounds, wept and prayed.

When he reached home, Mrs. Maylie was sitting in the little parlor. Oliver's heart sank at the sight, for she had never left the bedside of her niece. He learned that Rose had fallen into a deep sleep from which she would waken either to recovery and life or to bid them farewell and die.

They sat, listening, and afraid to speak, for hours. Outside, the sun sank lower and lower and at length cast over sky and earth those brilliant hues which herald its departure. Their quick ears caught the sound of an approaching footstep. They both involuntarily darted to the door as Dr. Losberne entered.

"What of Rose?" cried the old lady. "My dear child! She is dead!"

"No!" cried the doctor passionately. "As God is good and merciful, she will live to bless us all for years to come."

It was almost too much happiness to bear. Oliver felt stunned by the unexpected intelligence. He could not weep or speak or rest until, after a long ramble in the quiet evening air, a burst of tears came to his relief, and he seemed to awaken, all at once, to a full sense of the joyful change that had occurred.

The night was fast closing in when he returned homewards, laden with flowers which he had culled for the sick chamber. As he walked along the road he heard behind him the noise of a vehicle approaching at a furious pace. Looking round, he saw that it was a post chaise, and as the horses were galloping, and the road was narrow, he stood leaning against a gate until it should pass him.

As it dashed on, Oliver caught a glimpse of a man in a white nightcap. In a second or two, the nightcap was thrust out of the chaise window while a stentorian voice bellowed to the driver to stop. "Master Oliver," cried the voice, when the horses were pulled up. "What's the news? Miss Rose!"

"Is it you, Giles?" cried Oliver, running up to the chaise.

Giles was suddenly pulled back by a young gentleman who also occupied the chaise and who eagerly demanded what was the news.

"Better—much better!" replied Oliver. "The change took place only a few hours ago, and Dr. Losberne says that all danger is at an end."

The gentleman opened the chaise door, leaped out, and taking Oliver hurriedly by the arm, led him aside.

"You are quite certain, my boy?" demanded the gentleman in a tremulous voice. "Do not deceive me by awakening vain hopes."

"I would not for the world, sir," replied Oliver. "Dr. Losberne's words were that she would live to bless us all for many years to come. I heard him say so." The tears stood in Oliver's eyes as he recalled the scene. The gentleman turned his face away and remained silent for some minutes. Oliver thought he heard him sob, but he feared to interrupt him, and so stood apart. All this time Mr. Giles, with the white nightcap on, sat on the steps of the chaise, wiping his eyes with a blue handkerchief dotted with white spots.

At last the gentleman turned to Giles and addressed him. "I think you had better go on to my mother's in the chaise," he said. "I would rather walk. You can say I am coming. Only first exchange that nightcap for some more appropriate covering or we shall be taken for madmen!"

Reminded of his unbecoming costume, Mr. Giles substituted a hat of sober shape, which he took out of the chaise. This done, the postboy drove off.

As they walked along, Oliver glanced from time to time with much curiosity at the newcomer. He seemed about five and twenty years of age and was of middle height; his countenance was frank and handsome and his demeanor easy and prepossessing. Notwithstanding the difference between youth and age, he bore so strong a likeness to the old lady that Oliver would have had no great difficulty in imagining their relationship if he had not already spoken of her as his mother.

Mrs. Maylie was anxiously waiting to receive her son when he reached the cottage. The meeting did not take place without great emotion on both sides. "Mother!" whispered the young man. "Why did you not write before?"

"I did," replied Mrs. Maylie. "But I kept back the letter until I had heard Dr. Losberne's opinion."

"But why?" said the young man. "If Rose had—if this illness had terminated differently, how could I ever have known happiness again?"

"If that *had* been the case, Harry," said Mrs. Maylie, "I fear that your arrival here a day sooner or a day later would have been of very little import."

"But you must know, Mother, that on Rose, sweet gentle girl, my heart is set," rejoined the young man.

"I know that she deserves the best and purest love the heart of man can offer," said Mrs. Maylie. "I know that the devotion and affection of her nature require no ordinary return, but one that shall be deep and lasting."

"That is unkind, Mother," said Harry. "Do you still suppose that I am a boy ignorant of my own mind and mistaking the impulses of my own soul?"

"I think, my dear son," returned Mrs. Maylie, laying her hand on his shoulder, "that youth has many generous impulses which do not last. Above all, I think that if an ardent and ambitious man marry a wife on whose name there is a stain which, though it originated in no fault of hers, may be visited by sordid people on her and on his children and be made the subject of sneers against him, he may, no matter how generous and good his nature, one day repent of the connection he formed in early life. And she may have the pain of knowing that he does so."

"Mother," said the young man impatiently, "he would be a selfish brute, unworthy alike of the name of man and of the woman you describe, who acted thus."

"You think so now, Harry," replied his mother.

"And ever will!" said the young man. "The mental agony I have just suffered wrings from me the avowal to you of a passion which is not one of yesterday, nor one I have lightly formed. I have no thought, no hope in life, beyond her; and if you oppose me in this, you cast my peace and happiness to the wind."

"Harry," said Mrs. Maylie, "it is because I think so much of warm and sensitive hearts that I would spare them from being wounded."

"Let it rest with Rose, then," interposed Harry. "My feelings remain unchanged, as they ever will; and before I leave this place, Rose shall hear me."

"She shall," said Mrs. Maylie.

"There is something in your manner which would almost imply that she will hear me coldly, Mother," said the young man.

"Not coldly," rejoined the old lady. "Far from it! You have too strong a hold on her affections already. But before you suffer yourself to be carried to the highest point of hope, reflect for a few moments, my dear child, on Rose's history, and consider what effect the knowledge of her doubtful birth may have on her decision, devoted as she is to us with that perfect sacrifice of self which has always been her characteristic."

"What do you mean?"

"That I leave you to discover," replied Mrs. Maylie. "I must go back to her now. God bless you!"

"You will tell her I am here?" asked Harry. "And say how anxious I have been, and how I long to see her? You will not refuse to do this, Mother?"

"No," said the old lady. "I will tell her." And pressing her son's hand affectionately, she hastened from the room.

Dr. Losberne and Oliver had remained at another end of the apartment while this conversation was proceeding. The former now held out his hand to Harry Maylie, and hearty salutations were exchanged. The remainder of the evening then passed cheerfully away, and it was late before they retired, with light and thankful hearts, to take that rest of which, after the doubt and suspense they had recently undergone, they stood much in need.

Oliver rose next morning and went about his usual early occupations with more hope and pleasure than he had known for many days. The sweetest wild flowers that could be found were once more gathered to gladden Rose with their beauty. It is worthy of remark, and Oliver did not fail to note it at the time, that after that first morning his expeditions were no longer made alone.

Harry Maylie, meeting Oliver coming laden home, was seized with such a passion for flowers and displayed such a taste in their arrangement as left his young companion far behind. Oliver, however, knew where the best flowers were to be found, and morning after morning they scoured the country together. The window of the young lady's chamber was opened now, for she loved to feel the rich summer air revive her with its freshness; but there always stood, just inside the lattice, one particular little bunch of flowers which was made up with great care every morning; and Oliver could not help noticing that the withered ones were never thrown away.

And so the days were flying by, and Rose was rapidly recovering. Nor did Oliver's time hang heavy on his hands. He applied himself with redoubled assiduity to the instructions of the white-headed old gentleman, and labored so hard that his quick progress surprised even himself. It was while he was engaged in this pursuit that he was greatly startled by a most unexpected occurrence.

The little room in which he was accustomed to sit when busy at his books was on the ground floor at the back of the house. Its lattice window looked into a garden, whence a wicket gate opened into a small paddock; beyond was fine meadowland and wood. There was no other dwelling near.

One sultry evening, when the first shades of twilight were settling on the earth, Oliver, who had been poring over his books for some time, fell asleep. It was that kind of sleep which, while it holds the body prisoner, does not free the mind from a sense of things about it. Oliver knew perfectly well that he was in his own little room, that his books were lying on the table before him, and that the sweet air was stirring among the plants outside. And yet he was asleep. Suddenly the scene changed; the air became close and confined; and he thought, with a glow of terror, that he was in Fagin's house again. There sat the hideous old man in his accustomed corner, pointing at him and whispering to another man, with his face averted, who sat beside him.

"Hush, my dear!" he thought he heard Fagin say. "It is he, sure enough. Come away."

"He!" the other man seemed to answer. "Could I mistake him, think you? If you buried him fifty feet deep and took me across his grave, I fancy I should know, if there wasn't a mark above it, that he lay buried there!"

The man seemed to say this with such dreadful hatred that Oliver awoke with fear and started up.

Good heaven! What was that which sent the blood tingling to his heart? There—at the window—so close that he could have almost touched him—with his eyes peering and meeting his—there stood Fagin! And beside him, white with rage or fear or both, was the very man who had accosted him in the inn yard!

It was but an instant, a flash before his eyes; and they were gone. But they had recognized him, and he them. And their look was as firmly impressed on his memory as if it had been deeply carved in stone and set before him from his birth. He stood transfixed for a moment. Then, leaping from the window into the garden, Oliver called loudly for help.

···⚙· CHAPTER XV ·⚙··

WHEN THE INMATES of the house, attracted by Oliver's cries, hurried to the spot, they found him, pale and agitated, pointing in the direction of the meadows, and scarcely able to articulate the words: "Fagin! Fagin!"

Harry Maylie, who had heard Oliver's history from his mother, understood him at once. "What direction did he take?" he asked, catching up a heavy stick.

"That," replied Oliver, pointing out their course. "It was Fagin and another man."

"Then they are in the ditch!" said Harry. "Follow! And keep as near me as you can."

So saying, he sprang over the hedge and darted off with a speed which rendered it exceedingly difficult for Giles and Oliver to keep

Monks and the Jew

near him. In a minute or two Dr. Losberne, who had been out walking and just then returned, tumbled over the hedge after them, shouting to know what was the matter. On they all went until the leader, striking off into an angle of the field indicated by Oliver, began to search narrowly the ditch and hedge adjoining, which afforded time for the remainder of the party to come up, and for Oliver to communicate to Dr. Losberne the circumstances that had led to so vigorous a pursuit.

The search was in vain. There were not even the traces of recent footsteps to be seen. They stood now on the summit of a little hill commanding the open fields in every direction for three or four miles. There was the village in the hollow on the left, but in order to gain that after pursuing the track Oliver had pointed out, the men must have made a circuit of open ground, which was impossible in so short a time. Nor could they have gained the thick wood in another direction for the same reason.

"It must have been a dream, Oliver," said Harry Maylie.

"Oh no, indeed, sir," replied Oliver, shuddering at the very recollection of the old wretch's countenance. "I saw them both as plainly as I see you now."

"Who was the other?" inquired Harry and Dr. Losberne together.

"The very same man I told you of, who came so suddenly upon me at the inn," said Oliver. "We had our eyes fixed full on each other, and I could swear to him."

The two gentlemen watched Oliver's earnest face as he spoke and, looking from him to each other, seemed to feel satisfied of the accuracy of what he said. Still in no direction were there any appearances of the trampling of men in hurried flight.

"This is strange!" said Harry.

Notwithstanding the evidently useless nature of their search, they did not desist until the coming on of night rendered its further prosecution hopeless. Giles was then dispatched to the alehouses in the village, furnished with the best description Oliver could give of the appearance and dress of the strangers, but he returned without any intelligence calculated to lessen the mystery.

On the next day the inquiries were renewed, but with no better success, and after a few days the affair began to be forgotten.

Meanwhile, Rose was rapidly recovering. She had left her room, was able to go out, and mixing once more with the family, carried joy into the hearts of all.

But although this happy change had a visible effect on the little circle, and although cheerful voices and merry laughter were once more heard in the cottage, there was at times an unwonted restraint on some which Oliver could not fail to remark. Mrs. Maylie and her son were often closeted together, and more than once Rose appeared with traces of tears on her face. After Dr. Losberne had fixed a day for his departure to Chertsey, and Harry had announced that he might depart with the doctor, these symptoms increased.

At length one morning, when Rose was alone in the parlor, Harry Maylie entered, and, with some hesitation, begged permission to speak with her for a few moments.

"What I shall have to say, Rose," said the young man, drawing his chair towards her, "has already presented itself to your mind; the most cherished hopes of my heart are not unknown to you, though from my lips you have not yet heard them stated."

Rose had been very pale from the moment of his entrance, but that might have been the effect of her recent illness. She merely bowed, and bending over some plants that stood near, waited in silence for him to proceed.

"I—I ought to have left here before," said Harry.

"You should indeed," replied Rose, and a tear fell upon one of the flowers over which she bent. "I mean you should have left so that you might have turned to high and noble pursuits again—to pursuits well worthy of you."

"There is no pursuit more worthy than the struggle to win such a heart as yours," said the young man, taking her hand. "Rose, my own dear Rose! For years I have loved you, hoping to win my way to fame and then come proudly home and tell you it had been pursued only for you to share. That time has not arrived, but here, with no fame won, I offer you the heart so long your own, and stake my all on the words with which you greet the offer!"

"Your behavior has ever been kind and noble," said Rose, mastering the emotions by which she was agitated. "As you believe that I am not insensible or ungrateful, so hear my answer."

"It is that I may endeavor to deserve you?"

"It is that you must endeavor to forget me," replied Rose. "Not as your old and dearly attached companion, for that would wound me deeply, but as the object of your love."

There was a pause, during which Rose gave free vent to her tears, covering her face with one hand. Harry retained the other.

"And your reasons for this decision?" he asked at length.

"You have a right to know them," rejoined Rose. "But you can say nothing to alter my resolution. It is a duty that I must perform. I owe it to myself that I, a girl with such a blight on my name, should not give your friends reason to suspect that I had sordidly yielded to your first passion and fastened myself, a clog, on all your hopes and projects. I owe it to you and yours not to become an obstacle to your progress in the world."

"If your inclinations chime with your sense of duty—"

"They do not," replied Rose, coloring deeply.

"Then you return my love?" asked Harry. "Say but that, dear Rose, and soften the bitterness of this disappointment!"

"If I could have done so without doing heavy wrong to him I loved," rejoined Rose, "I could have—"

"Have received this declaration very differently?" asked Harry.

"I could," said Rose, disengaging her hand. "But why should we prolong this painful interview? As we have met today, we must meet no more. Farewell, Harry! The prospect before you is a brilliant one. All the honors to which great talents and powerful connections can help men in public life are in store for you. But those connections are proud, and I will neither mingle with such as may hold in scorn the mother who gave me life, nor bring disgrace on the son of her who has so well supplied that mother's place."

"One word more, dearest Rose!" cried Harry, throwing himself before her. "If I had been less—less fortunate, the world would call it—if some obscure and peaceful life had been my destiny, would you have turned from me then? Or has my probable advancement to riches and honor given this scruple birth?"

"Do not press me to reply," answered Rose. "The question does not arise and never will. It is unkind to urge it."

"If your answer be what I almost dare to hope it is," retorted Harry, "it will shed a gleam of happiness upon my lonely way. Rose, in the name of my attachment, in the name of all I have suffered for you and all you doom me to undergo, answer me this one question!"

"Then, if your lot had been differently cast," rejoined Rose, "if I could have been a help and comfort to you in any humble scene, and not a blot and drawback in ambitious and distinguished crowds, I should have been spared this trial."

"I ask one promise," said Harry. "Once, and only once more— say within a year, but it may be sooner—may I speak to you again on this subject, for the last time? I will lay at your feet whatever of station or fortune I may possess, and if you still adhere to your present resolution, I will not seek by word or act to change it."

"It will be useless," rejoined Rose. "But let it be so."

She extended her hand. But the young man caught her to his bosom, and imprinting one kiss on her beautiful forehead, hurried from the room.

"AND SO YOU ARE RESOLVED to be my traveling companion, eh?" said the doctor, as Harry Maylie joined him and Oliver at the breakfast table the following morning. "Why, you are not in the same mind two half hours together!"

"You will tell me a different tale one of these days," said Harry, coloring without any perceptible reason.

"I hope I may have good cause to do so," replied Dr. Losberne, "though I confess I don't think I shall. For yesterday morning you had made up your mind, in a great hurry, to stay here. Before noon you announce that you are going to accompany me as far as I go on your road to London. And at night you urge me with great mystery to start before the ladies are stirring, the consequence of which is that young Oliver here is pinned down to his breakfast when he ought to be ranging the meadows after botanical phenomena. Too bad, isn't it, Oliver?"

"I should have been very sorry not to have been at home when you and Mr. Maylie went away, sir," rejoined Oliver.

"That's a fine fellow," said the doctor. "But, to speak seriously, Harry—has any communication from the great nobs produced this sudden anxiety on your part to be gone?"

"The great nobs," replied Harry, "under which designation I presume you include my most stately uncle, have not communicated with me at all since I have been here."

"Well," said the doctor, "you are a queer fellow. But of course they will get you into Parliament at the election before Christmas, and these sudden shiftings and changes are no bad preparation for political life."

Harry Maylie looked as if he could have made one or two remarks, but he contented himself with saying, "We shall see." The post chaise drove up to the door shortly afterwards, and the good doctor bustled out to see the luggage packed.

"Oliver, let me speak a word with you," said Harry in a low voice, beckoning Oliver into the window recess. "You can write well now?"

"I hope so, sir," replied Oliver.

"I shall not be at home again for some time, and I wish you would write to me—say once a fortnight. Will you?"

"Certainly, sir; I shall be proud to do it!" exclaimed Oliver.

"I should like to know how—how my mother and Miss Maylie are," said the young man. "You can tell me what walks you take and whether she—they, I mean—seem happy and well. You understand me? I would rather you did not mention it to them. Let it be a secret between you and me. I depend on you."

Oliver, elated and honored by a sense of his importance, promised to be secret and explicit in his communications; and Mr. Maylie took leave of him. The doctor was already in the chaise; Harry cast one slight glance at the latticed window and jumped in.

"Drive on!" he cried. "Fast, full gallop! Nothing short of flying will keep pace with me today."

Jingling and clattering till distance rendered its noise inaudible, the vehicle wound its way along the road until even its dusty cloud was no longer to be seen. But there was one looker-on who remained with eyes fixed on the spot where the carriage disappeared long after it was many miles away. Behind the white curtain which had shrouded her from view when Harry raised his eyes towards the window, sat Rose.

···&·· CHAPTER XVI ·&···

MR. BUMBLE SAT moodily in the workhouse parlor, meditating, and from time to time he heaved a deep sigh.

There were other appearances besides Mr. Bumble's gloom which announced that a great change had taken place in the position of his affairs. The laced coat and the cocked hat, where were they? He still wore knee breeches, but they were not *the* breeches. The coat was wide-skirted, but, oh, how different from *the* coat! The mighty cocked hat was replaced by a modest round one. Mr. Bumble was no longer a beadle.

Mr. Bumble had been promoted, or so he thought. He had married the matron of the workhouse, Mrs. Corney, and he was now master of the workhouse. Another beadle had come into power. On him the cocked hat, gold-laced coat, and staff had descended.

"And tomorrow two months it was done!" said Mr. Bumble with a sigh. "It seems a age."

Mr. Bumble might have meant that he had concentrated a whole existence of happiness into the short space of eight weeks, but the sigh—there was a vast deal of meaning in the sigh.

"I sold myself," said Mr. Bumble, "for what I thought she had. I sold myself for a small quantity of secondhand furniture and twenty pound in money. I went very reasonable. Cheap, dirt cheap!"

"Cheap?" cried a shrill voice in Mr. Bumble's ear. "You would have been dear at any price; and dear I paid for you, the Lord knows that!"

Mr. Bumble turned and encountered the face of his consort.

"Mrs. Bumble, ma'am!" said Mr. Bumble with sentimental sternness.

282

"Well!" cried the lady.

"Have the goodness to look at me," said Mr. Bumble, fixing his eyes on her. ("If she stands such a eye as that," he said to himself, "she can stand anything.")

Whether the former Mrs. Corney was particularly proof against eagle glances is a matter of opinion. The fact is that she treated the glance with great disdain and even raised a genuine laugh thereat. On hearing this most unexpected sound Mr. Bumble looked incredulous. He then relapsed into his former state; nor did he rouse himself until his attention was again awakened by the voice of his partner.

"Are you going to sit snoring there all day?" inquired Mrs. Bumble.

"I am going to sit here as long as I think proper, ma'am," rejoined Mr. Bumble. "And although I was *not* snoring, I shall snore, gape, sneeze, laugh, or cry, as the humor strikes me; such being my prerogative."

"*Your* prerogative!" sneered Mrs. Bumble, with ineffable contempt.

"I said the word, ma'am," said Mr. Bumble. "The prerogative of a man is to command."

"And what's the prerogative of a woman, in the name of goodness?" cried the relict of Mr. Corney deceased.

"To obey, ma'am!" thundered Mr. Bumble. "Your late unfortunate husband should have taught it you, and then perhaps he might have been alive now. I wish he was, poor man!"

Mrs. Bumble, seeing at a glance that the decisive moment had now arrived and that a blow struck for the mastership on one side or other must necessarily be conclusive, dropped into a chair and fell into a paroxysm of tears. But tears were not the things to find their way to Mr. Bumble's soul; his heart was waterproof. He eyed his lady with a look of satisfaction and begged, in an encouraging manner, that she should cry her hardest.

"It opens the lungs, washes the countenance, exercises the eyes, and softens down the temper," said Mr. Bumble. "So cry away!"

As he discharged himself of this pleasantry, Mr. Bumble took his hat from a peg, and putting it on, rather rakishly, on one side, thrust his hands into his pockets and sauntered towards the door.

Now Mrs. Bumble had tried the tears because they were less troublesome than a manual assault, but she was quite prepared to make trial of the latter mode of proceeding. The first proof Mr. Bumble experienced of the fact was conveyed in a hollow sound, immediately succeeded by the sudden flying off of his hat. His lady, clasping him tightly round the throat with one hand, then inflicted a shower of blows on his head with the other. This done, she created a little variety by scratching his face and tearing his hair, and, having inflicted as much punishment as she deemed necessary, she pushed him over a chair and defied him to talk about his prerogative again, if he dared.

"Get up!" she ended. "And take yourself away from here, unless you want me to do something desperate."

Mr. Bumble rose with a very rueful countenance, wondering what "something desperate" might be. Picking up his hat, he darted out of the room, leaving the former Mrs. Corney in full possession of the field. He had been fairly taken by surprise, and fairly beaten. He had a decided propensity for bullying and derived considerable pleasure from the exercise of petty cruelty, and he was, consequently (it is needless to say), a coward. And now Mr. Bumble had fallen from all the height and pomp of beadleship to the lowest depth of the most snubbed henpeckery.

"All in two months!" said Mr. Bumble, filled with dismal thoughts. It was too much. He boxed the ears of the boy who opened the gate for him, and walked distractedly into the street.

He walked until exercise had abated the first passion of his grief; and then the revulsion of feeling made him thirsty. He came to a public house in a byway whose parlor, as he gathered from a hasty peep over the blinds, was deserted save by one solitary customer. Mr. Bumble stepped in, and ordering something to drink as he passed the bar, entered the apartment into which he had looked from the street.

The man seated there was tall and dark and wore a large cloak. He had the air of a stranger, and seemed, by the dusty soils on his dress, to have traveled some distance. He scarcely deigned to nod his head in acknowledgment of Mr. Bumble's salutation. Mr. Bumble had quite dignity enough for two, so he drank his gin and water in silence.

It so happened, however, that Mr. Bumble felt every now and then a powerful inducement to steal a look at the stranger, and that whenever he did so he withdrew his eyes in some confusion, finding that the stranger was at that moment stealing a look at him. The stranger's eye was keen and bright, but shadowed by a scowl of distrust and suspicion repulsive to behold. When they had encountered each other's glance several times in this way, the stranger, in a harsh, deep voice, broke silence.

"Were you looking for me," he said, "when you peered in at the window?"

"Not that I am aware of, unless you're Mr.—" Mr. Bumble stopped short, for he was curious to know the man's name.

"I see you were not," said the stranger, an expression of quiet sarcasm playing about his mouth, "or you would have known my name. I would recommend you not to ask for it."

"I meant no harm, young man," observed Mr. Bumble majestically.

"I have seen you before, I think," said the stranger, after another silence. "I only passed you in the street, but I should know you again. You were beadle here once, were you not?"

"I was," said Mr. Bumble in some surprise, "porochial beadle."

"Just so," said the other, nodding his head. "What are you now?"

"Master of the workhouse, young man!" rejoined Mr. Bumble impressively, to check any undue familiarity the stranger might assume.

"You have the same eye to your own interest that you always had, I doubt not?" resumed the stranger, looking keenly at Mr. Bumble. "Answer freely, man. I know you pretty well, you see."

"I suppose a married man," replied Mr. Bumble in evident perplexity, "is not more averse to turning an honest penny when he can than a single one. Porochial officers are not so well paid that they can afford to refuse any little extra fee when it comes to them in a civil and proper manner."

The stranger smiled and nodded again, as much as to say he had not mistaken his man. Then he rang the bell. "Fill this glass again," he said, handing Mr. Bumble's empty tumbler to the landlord. "Let it be strong and hot. You like it so, I suppose?"

"Not too strong," replied Mr. Bumble with a delicate cough.

"You understand what that means, landlord!" said the stranger.

The host smiled, disappeared, and returned with a steaming jug, of which the first gulp brought the water to Mr. Bumble's eyes.

"Now listen to me," said the stranger. "I came down to this place to find you, and by chance you walked into the very room I was sitting in. I want some information from you. I don't ask you to give it for nothing. There's that, to begin with."

As he spoke, he pushed a couple of sovereigns across the table to his companion. When Mr. Bumble had put them in his waistcoat pocket, he went on: "Carry your memory back—let me see—ten or eleven years. The season, winter. The scene, the workhouse. The time, night. And the place, the crazy hole in which miserable drabs gave birth to puling children for the parish to rear—and hid their shame, rot 'em, in the grave!"

"The lying-in room, I suppose?" asked Mr. Bumble.

"Yes," said the stranger. "A boy was born there."

"Many boys," observed Mr. Bumble, despondingly.

"I speak of one," cried the stranger, "a meek-looking, pale-faced boy, who was apprenticed here to a coffin-maker—and who ran away to London."

"Why, you mean Oliver! Young Twist!" said Mr. Bumble. "I remember him. There wasn't a obstinater young rascal—"

"It's not of him I want to hear; I've heard enough of him," said the stranger. "It's of a woman, the hag that nursed his mother. Where is she?"

"Where is she?" said Mr. Bumble, whom the gin and water had rendered facetious. "It would be hard to tell. There's no midwifery there, whichever place she's gone to, so I suppose she's out of employment."

"What do you mean?" demanded the stranger.

"That she died last winter," rejoined Mr. Bumble.

The man looked fixedly at him. For some time he appeared doubtful whether he ought to be relieved or disappointed by the intelligence; and at length he observed that it was no great matter.

But Mr. Bumble was cunning enough to see that an opportunity was opened for the lucrative disposal of the secret in the possession of his better half. His wife had told him a little about old Sally's death, and although she had never fully confided Sally's disclosure to him, he had heard enough from her to know that it related to the last moments of the young mother of Oliver Twist. Calling this to mind, he informed the stranger, with an air of mystery, that one woman had been closeted with the old harridan shortly before she died, and that she could throw some light on the subject.

"How can I find her?" asked the stranger, plainly showing that all his fears (whatever they were) were aroused afresh by this news.

"Only through me," rejoined Mr. Bumble.

"When?" cried the stranger.

"Tomorrow," said Bumble.

"At nine in the evening," said the stranger, producing a scrap of paper and writing on it an address, "bring her to me there. I needn't tell you to be secret. It's to your interest."

With these words he led the way to the door. Bumble observed that the address contained no name.

"What name am I to ask for?" he asked.

"Monks!" rejoined the stranger, and strode hastily away.

It was a dull, close, overcast summer evening. The dense clouds which seemed to presage a violent thunderstorm were already yielding large drops of rain when Mr. and Mrs. Bumble, turning out of the main street of the town, directed their course towards a scattered little colony of ruinous houses erected on a swamp bordering the river. The husband carried an unlighted lantern, and trudged on, a few paces ahead of his wife, towards their destination.

This colony had long been known as the residence of low ruffians who subsisted chiefly on plunder and crime. In the heart of it stood a large building formerly used as a factory, but long since gone to ruin. The rat, the worm, and the damp had weakened and rotted the piles on which it stood, and a considerable portion of the building had already sunk down into the water, while the remainder, bending over the dark stream, seemed to wait a favorable opportunity of following and involving itself in the same fate.

It was before this tottering ruin that the worthy couple paused, as the first peal of thunder reverberated in the air and the rain commenced pouring violently down.

"The place should be somewhere here," said Bumble, consulting a scrap of paper in his hand.

"Halloa!" cried a voice from above. "I'll be with you directly."

"Is that the man?" asked Mr. Bumble's lady.

Mr. Bumble nodded.

"Then mind what I told you," said the matron, "and say as little as you can, or you'll betray us at once."

Mr. Bumble, who eyed the building with rueful looks, was about to express some doubts relative to the advisability of proceeding any further with the enterprise, when he was prevented by the appearance of Monks, who opened a small door near them.

"Come in!" he cried impatiently. "Don't keep me here!"

They walked in. Beckoning them to follow him, the man led the way up a ladder to the floor above. There a lantern, which hung on a rope from a heavy beam, cast a dim light on an old table and three chairs that were placed beneath it.

"Now," said Monks, when they had seated themselves, "the sooner we come to our business, the better for all. The woman knows what it is, does she?"

The question was addressed to Bumble, but his wife intimated that she was perfectly acquainted with it.

"He is right in saying that you were with this hag the night she died and that she told you something—"

"About the mother of the boy you named," replied the matron, interrupting him. "Yes."

"The first question is, of what nature was her communication?" asked Monks.

"That's the second question," observed the woman with deliberation. "The first is, what may the communication be worth?"

"Who the devil can tell that, without knowing of what kind it is?" asked Monks.

"Nobody better than you, I am persuaded," answered Mrs. Bumble, who did not want for spirit, as her yokefellow could abundantly testify.

"Humph!" said Monks significantly. "There may be money's worth to get, eh? Something that was taken from her? Something that she wore? Something that—"

"You had better bid," interrupted Mrs. Bumble. "I have heard enough to assure me that you are the man I ought to talk to."

Mr. Bumble, who had not yet been admitted by his better half into the full secret, listened to this dialogue in undisguised astonishment which increased, if possible, when Monks demanded what sum was required for the disclosure.

"What's it worth to you?" asked the woman collectedly.

"It may be nothing—or it may be twenty pounds," replied Monks. "Speak out, and let me know which."

"Give me five and twenty pounds in gold," said the woman, "and I'll tell you all I know. Not before. It's not a large sum."

"Not a large sum for a paltry secret that may be nothing when it's told," cried Monks impatiently, "and which has been lying dead for ten years past and more?"

"Such matters keep well, and, like good wine, often double their value in the course of time," answered the matron, still preserving a resolute indifference.

"What if I pay it for nothing?" asked Monks, hesitating.

"You can easily take the money away again from me," replied the matron. "I am but a woman, alone and unprotected."

"Not alone, my dear, nor unprotected neither," submitted Mr. Bumble in a voice tremulous with fear. "And besides, Mr. Monks is too much of a gentleman to attempt any violence on porochial persons. Mr. Monks is aware that I am not a young man, my dear, and that I am a little run to seed. But I have no doubt Mr. Monks has heerd, my dear, that I am a very determined officer with very uncommon strength if I'm once roused. I only want a little rousing, that's all."

As Mr. Bumble spoke, he made a melancholy feint of grasping his lantern with fierce determination and plainly showed, by the alarmed expression of every feature, that he *did* want a little rousing, prior to making any very warlike demonstration.

"You are a fool," said Mrs. Bumble in reply, "and had better hold your tongue."

"So! He's your husband, eh?" said Monks grimly. "So much the better; I have less hesitation in dealing with two people when I find that there's only one will between them. I'm in earnest. See here!"

He thrust his hand into a pocket, and producing a canvas bag, counted out twenty-five sovereigns on the table and pushed them over to the woman.

"Now," he said, "gather them up; and let's hear your story."

The faces of the three nearly touched as the two men leaned over the small table in their eagerness to hear the woman's whisper. The sickly rays of the suspended lantern aggravated the paleness of their countenances which, encircled by gloom and darkness, looked ghastly in the extreme.

"When this woman that we called old Sally died," the matron began, "she spoke of a young creature who had brought a child into the world some years before, not merely in the same room but in the same bed in which she then lay dying. The child was the one you named to him last night." The matron nodded carelessly towards her husband. "This nurse had robbed the mother. She stole from the corpse, when it had hardly turned to one, that which the dead mother had prayed her, with her last breath, to keep for her infant's sake."

"Did she sell it?" cried Monks with desperate eagerness. "Where? When?"

"As she told me with great difficulty that she had done this," said the matron, "the nurse fell back and died."

"Without saying more?" cried Monks in a voice which, from its very suppression, seemed only the more furious. "It's a lie! I'll not be played with. She said more!"

"She didn't utter another word," said the woman, unmoved, "but she clutched my gown with one hand which was partly closed, and when I saw that she was dead and removed the hand, I found that it clasped a scrap of dirty paper."

"Which contained?" interposed Monks, stretching forward.

"It was a pawnbroker's ticket," replied the woman. "The time was out in two days, and I thought something might one day come of it, so I redeemed the pledge."

"Where is it now?" asked Monks quickly.

"*There!*" replied the woman. And as if glad to be relieved of it, she threw on the table a small kid bag. Monks, pouncing upon it, tore it open with trembling hands. It contained a gold locket, in which were two locks of hair and a plain gold wedding ring.

"It has the word 'Agnes' engraved on the inside," said the woman. "There is a blank left for the surname, and then follows the date, which is within a year before the child was born."

"And this is all?" said Monks, after a close and eager scrutiny of the contents of the little packet.

"All," replied the woman.

Mr. Bumble drew a long breath, as if he were glad to find that the story was over and no mention made of taking the twenty-five pounds back again, and he took courage to wipe off the perspiration which had been trickling over his nose unchecked.

"I know nothing of the story beyond what I can guess at," said his wife, addressing Monks after a short silence. "And I want to know nothing, for it's safer. But may I ask two questions?"

"You may ask," said Monks with some show of surprise, "but whether I answer or not is another question."

"First, is that what you expected to get from me?"

"It is," replied Monks. "The other question?"

"What do you propose to do with it? Can it be used against me?"

"Never," rejoined Monks, "nor against me either. See!"

With these words, he suddenly wheeled the table aside and released a large trapdoor which opened close to Mr. Bumble's feet, and caused that gentleman to retire several paces backward with great precipitation.

"Look down," said Monks, lowering the lantern into the gulf. "Don't fear me. I could have let you down quietly enough, when you were seated over it, if that had been my game."

Thus encouraged, the matron drew near to the brink, and even Mr. Bumble himself, impelled by curiosity, ventured to do the same. The turbid water, swollen by the heavy rain, was rushing rapidly on below, plashing and foaming against the green and slimy piles.

"If you flung a man's body down there, where would it be tomorrow morning?" asked Monks, swinging the lantern to and fro in the dark well.

"Twelve miles down the river," replied Bumble, recoiling at the thought.

Monks drew the little packet from his breast, where he had hurriedly thrust it, and tying it to a leaden weight which was lying on the floor, he dropped it into the stream. It fell straight and true, clove the water with a scarcely audible splash, and was gone. The three, looking into each other's faces, seemed to breathe more freely.

"There!" said Monks, closing the trapdoor. "If the sea ever gives up its dead, as books say, it will keep its gold to itself, and that trash among it. And now we may break up our pleasant party."

"By all means," observed Mr. Bumble with great alacrity.

"You'll keep a quiet tongue in your head, will you?" said Monks, with a threatening look. "I am not afraid of your wife."

"You may depend on me, young man," answered Mr. Bumble, bowing himself gradually toward the ladder.

"I am glad, for your sake, to hear it," remarked Monks. "Now get away from here as fast as you can."

It was fortunate that the conversation terminated at this point or Mr. Bumble, who had bowed himself to within six inches of the ladder, would infallibly have pitched headlong into the room below. He lighted his lantern, and making no effort to prolong the discourse, descended in silence, followed by his wife. Monks brought up the rear. They traversed the lower room slowly—Mr. Bumble, holding his lantern a foot above the ground, walked with remarkable care, looking nervously about him for hidden trapdoors.

The door at which they had entered was softly unfastened by Monks, and, exchanging a nod with their mysterious acquaintance, the couple emerged into the wet and darkness outside.

·•ᴇᴠ⊙· CHAPTER XVII ·⊙ᴠᴇ·

ON THE EVENING following that on which these three worthies disposed of their little matter of business, Mr. William Sikes, awakening from a nap, drowsily growled forth an inquiry as to what time it was.

The room in which Mr. Sikes propounded this question was not one of those he had tenanted previous to the Chertsey expedition, although it was situated at no great distance from his former lodgings. It was an apartment of very limited size, lighted only by one small window in the shelving roof. Nor were there wanting other indications of the good gentleman's having gone down in the world of late, for a great scarcity of furniture and of all such small movables as spare clothes and linen bespoke a state of extreme poverty. The condition of Mr. Sikes himself confirmed these symptoms. Lying on the bed, wrapped in his white greatcoat, he displayed a set of features in no degree improved by the cadaverous hue of illness, a soiled nightcap, and a stiff black beard of a week's growth. The dog sat at the bedside, now eyeing his master and now pricking his ears and uttering a low growl as some noise in the street attracted his attention. Seated by the window, engaged in patching an old waistcoat, was a female so pale and reduced with privation that there would have been considerable difficulty in recognizing her as the same Nancy who has already figured in this tale, but for the voice in which she replied to Mr. Sikes.

"Not long gone seven," said the girl. "How do you feel, Bill?"

"As weak as water," replied Mr. Sikes with an imprecation. "Here, lend us a hand and let me get off this thundering bed."

Illness had not improved Mr. Sikes's temper; as the girl raised him to a chair he cursed her awkwardness and struck her.

"Whining, are you?" said Sikes. "Come! Don't stand sniveling there. D'ye hear me?"

"Why, don't be hard on me tonight, Bill," said the girl, with a touch of tenderness. "Such a number of nights as I've been nursing and caring for you—and this the first that I've seen you like yourself. You wouldn't have served me as you did just now if you'd thought of that, would you? Say you wouldn't."

"Well, then, I wouldn't. But get up and bustle about, and don't come over me with your woman's nonsense!"

At any other time this remonstrance would have had the desired effect; but the girl, being really weak and exhausted, sank into a chair, dropped her head and fainted before Mr. Sikes could get out a few appropriate oaths. Not knowing what to do in this uncommon emergency, Mr. Sikes tried a little blasphemy, and finding that mode of treatment ineffectual, called for assistance.

"What's the matter here, my dear?" said Fagin, looking in.

"Lend a hand to the girl, can't you?" replied Sikes impatiently.

With an exclamation of surprise, Fagin hastened to the girl's assistance, while Mr. John Dawkins (otherwise the Artful Dodger), who had followed his venerable friend into the room, hastily deposited on the floor a bundle with which he was laden, and snatching a bottle from the grasp of Master Charles Bates, who came close at his heels, uncorked it with his teeth and poured a portion of its contents down the patient's throat, previously taking a taste himself to prevent mistakes.

"Give her a whiff of fresh air with the bellows, Charley," said Mr. Dawkins, "and you slap her hands, Fagin, while Bill undoes the petticuts."

These united restoratives, administered with great energy, were not long in producing the desired effect. The girl gradually recovered her senses, and staggering to a chair by the bedside, hid her face on the pillow, leaving Mr. Sikes to confront the newcomers.

"What evil wind has blowed you here?" he asked Fagin, in some astonishment at their unlooked-for appearance.

"No evil wind at all, my dear, for I've brought something good that you'll be glad to see. Dodger, my dear, open the bundle and

Mr. Fagin and his Pupils recovering Nancy

give Bill the trifles that we spent our money on this morning."

The Artful untied his huge bundle and handed the articles it contained to Charley Bates, who placed them on the table.

"Sich a rabbit pie, Bill!" exclaimed that young gentleman, disclosing to view a huge pasty. "And here's half a pound of seven-and-sixpenny tea; a pound and a half of sugar; two half-quartern bran loaves; a pound of best fresh butter; a piece of double Glo'ster cheese; and, to wind up all, some of the richest sort you ever lushed!" Uttering this last panegyric, Master Bates produced a bottle of wine, while Mr. Dawkins poured out a glass of raw spirits from the bottle he carried, which the invalid tossed down his throat without a moment's hesitation.

"Ah!" said Fagin, rubbing his hands with satisfaction. "You'll do, Bill; you'll do now."

"Do!" exclaimed Mr. Sikes. "I might have been done for, afore you'd have done anything to help me. What do you mean by leaving a man in this state, three weeks and more, you false-hearted wagabond? If it hadn't been for the girl, I might have died."

"Only hear him, boys!" said Fagin, shrugging. "And us come to bring him all these beau-ti-ful things!"

"The things is well enough in their way," observed Mr. Sikes, a little soothed as he glanced over the table. Cutting himself a piece of the pie, he began to wash it down with applications from the spirit bottle. "But I must have some blunt from you tonight."

"I haven't a piece of coin about me," replied Fagin.

"Then you've got lots at home," retorted Sikes, "and I must have some from there tonight, and that's flat."

"Well, well," said Fagin with a sigh, "I'll send the Artful round."

"You won't do nothing of the kind," rejoined Mr. Sikes. "The Artful's a deal too artful. Nancy shall go to the ken and fetch it, to make all sure."

After a great deal of haggling, Fagin beat down the required amount from five pounds to three pounds four and sixpence. Then he returned homeward, attended by Nancy and the boys, while Mr. Sikes flung himself on the bed to sleep away the time until the young lady returned.

In due course they arrived at Fagin's abode, where they found Toby Crackit and Mr. Chitling intent upon their fifteenth game at cribbage.

"Has nobody been, Toby?" asked Fagin.

"Not a living leg," answered Mr. Crackit. "It's been dull as swipes." And with this Mr. Crackit swept up his winnings and swaggered elegantly out of the room.

"Ah!" cried Tom Chitling. "He's cleaned me out. But I can go and earn some more when I like, can't I, Fagin?"

"To be sure you can; and the sooner you go the better, Tom; so don't lose any more time! Dodger! Charley! It's time you were on the lay. It's near ten, and nothing done yet."

In obedience to this hint, the boys, nodding to Nancy, took up their hats and left the room.

"Now," said Fagin, "I'll go and get you that cash, Nancy. This is only the key of a little cupboard where I keep a few odd things the boys get, my dear. I never lock up my money, for I've got none to lock up, my dear— Ha! Ha! Ha! It's a poor trade, Nancy, but I'm fond of seeing the young people about me; and I bear it all, I bear it all. Hush," he said, hastily concealing the key in his breast; "who's that? Listen!"

The girl appeared in no way interested in whether anyone came or went until the murmur of a man's voice reached her ears. Then she tore off her bonnet and shawl with the rapidity of lightning and thrust them under the table, muttering a complaint of the heat. Her action, however, had been unobserved by Fagin, who had his back towards her.

"Bah," he whispered, as though nettled by the interruption; "it's the man I expected before; he's coming down. Not a word about the money while he's here, Nance."

Laying his skinny forefinger on his lip, Fagin carried a candle to the door. The visitor, coming hastily into the room, was close upon the girl before he observed her.

It was Monks.

"Only one of my young people," said Fagin, observing that Monks drew back on beholding a stranger. "Don't move, Nancy."

The girl drew closer to the table and glanced carelessly at Monks; but as he turned towards Fagin she stole another look, keen and searching and full of purpose.

"Any news?" inquired Fagin.

"Great," replied Monks with a smile. "I have been prompt enough this time. Let me have a word with you."

Fagin pointed upwards and took Monks out of the room. Nancy could hear by the creaking of the boards that Fagin seemed to be leading his companion to the second story.

Before the sound of their footsteps had ceased to echo through the house, the girl slipped off her shoes, glided silently from the room, ascended the stairs and was lost in the gloom above.

The room remained deserted for a quarter of an hour; then the girl glided back with the same soft tread; and immediately afterwards the two men were heard descending. Monks went at once into the street, and Fagin crawled upstairs again for the money. When he returned, the girl was adjusting her shawl and bonnet.

"Why, Nance," exclaimed the old man, starting back as he put down the candle, "how pale you are! What have you been doing to yourself?"

"Nothing that I know of, except sitting in this close place for I don't know how long," replied the girl carelessly. "Come, let me get back; that's a dear."

With a sigh for every piece of money, Fagin counted the amount into her hand. They parted without more conversation.

When the girl got into the open street she sat down on a doorstep, and seemed, for a few moments, wholly bewildered. Suddenly she arose, and hurrying in a direction quite opposite to that in which Sikes was awaiting her return, quickened her pace until it resolved into a violent run. After completely exhausting herself, she stopped to take breath; wrung her hands, and burst into tears.

It might be that she felt then the full hopelessness of her condition; but she turned back; and hurrying now in the contrary direction, soon reached the dwelling where she had left the housebreaker.

If she betrayed any agitation when she presented herself to

Mr. Sikes, he did not observe it. Merely inquiring if she had brought the money, and receiving an affirmative reply, he uttered a growl of satisfaction and resumed the slumbers which her arrival had interrupted.

It was fortunate for her that the possession of money had so beneficial an effect in smoothing down his temper next day that he had no inclination to be very critical about her behavior. That she had all the abstracted and nervous manner of one who is on the eve of some bold and hazardous step would have been obvious to the lynx-eyed Fagin; but Mr. Sikes, lacking the niceties of discrimination and being in an unusually amiable condition, saw nothing unusual in her demeanor. As night came on, however, while she sat watching until the housebreaker should drink himself asleep, there was a paleness in her cheek and a fire in her eye that even Sikes observed.

"Why, burn my body!" he said, staring at the girl. "You look like a corpse come to life. Wot's the matter?"

"Nothing," replied the girl. "Why do you look at me so hard?"

"I tell you wot it is," said Sikes. "If you haven't caught the fever. there's something more than usual in the wind—no, damme! It must be the fever coming on."

Fortifying himself with this assurance, Sikes drained his glass and then, with many oaths, called for his physic. The girl jumped up, poured it out with her back towards him, and held the vessel to his lips while he drank off the contents. Sikes fell back on the pillow. His eyes closed and opened again; he shifted his position restlessly, and, after dozing again, and again springing up, he was suddenly stricken, as it were, while in the very attitude of rising, into a deep and heavy sleep.

The girl hastily dressed herself in her bonnet and shawl, looking fearfully round from time to time as if, despite the sleeping draught she had put in the physic, she expected every moment to feel the pressure of Sikes's heavy hand on her shoulder. Stooping softly over the bed, she kissed the robber's lips, and then opening and closing the door with noiseless touch, hurried from the house.

Gliding rapidly down the street, she tracked her way towards the West End of London. Over an hour later she reached her destination. It was a family hotel in a quiet, handsome street near Hyde Park. As the brilliant light of the lamp which burned before its door guided her to the spot, the clock struck eleven. She stepped into the hall and looked round with an air of incertitude.

"Now, young woman," said a smartly dressed female, looking out from the office, "who do you want here?"

"A lady who is stopping here—Miss Maylie," said Nancy.

The woman, noting her appearance, replied only by a look of virtuous disdain, and summoned a waiter to answer her. To him Nancy repeated her request.

"What name and business am I to say?" asked the waiter.

"It's of no use saying any," replied Nancy. "I must see the lady."

"Come!" said the man, pushing her toward the door. "None of this. Take yourself off."

"I shall be carried out if I go!" said the girl violently. "Isn't there anybody here that will see a simple message carried for a poor wretch like me?"

This appeal produced an effect on a softhearted man cook, who added his intercession, and the result was that the waiter at last undertook to deliver the message. "What's it to be?" he asked, with one foot on the stairs.

"That a young woman earnestly asks to speak to Miss Maylie alone," said Nancy, "and that if the lady will only hear the first word she has to say, she will know whether to hear her business or to have her turned out of doors."

"I say," said the man, "you're coming it strong!"

He ran upstairs. Soon he returned and said she was to walk up. Nancy followed him with trembling limbs to a small antechamber, and here he left her.

NANCY'S LIFE HAD BEEN SQUANDERED among the most noisome of the stews and dens of London, but there was something of the woman's original nature in her still. When she heard a light step approaching the door, and thought of the wide contrast which the small room would in another moment contain, she felt burdened with the sense of her own deep shame, and she shrank as though she could scarcely bear the presence of her with whom she had sought this interview.

But struggling with these better feelings was pride. Even this degraded companion of thieves and ruffians felt too proud to betray a feeble gleam of the womanly feeling which she thought a weakness.

She raised her eyes sufficiently to observe that the figure which presented itself was that of a slight and beautiful girl; then tossing her head with affected carelessness, she said, "It's a hard matter to get to see you, lady. If I had taken offense and gone away, as many would have done, you'd have been sorry for it one day."

"I am very sorry if anyone has behaved harshly to you," replied Rose. "Tell me why you wished to see me."

The kind tone of this answer, the gentle manner, and the absence of any haughtiness took the girl completely by surprise. She burst into tears. "Oh, lady, lady," she said, clasping her hands, "if there was more like you, there would be fewer like me!"

"Sit down," said Rose earnestly. "If you are in poverty or affliction I shall be truly glad to relieve you if I can—I shall indeed."

"Let me stand, lady," said the girl, still weeping, "and do not speak to me so kindly till you know me better. I am the girl that dragged little Oliver back to old Fagin's on the night he went out from the house in Pentonville."

"You!" said Rose Maylie.

"I, lady! I am the infamous creature you have heard of that lives among thieves, and that never has known any better life or kinder words than they have given me, so help me God! Do not mind shrinking openly from me, lady. I am well used to it. But thank Heaven that you were never in the midst of cold and hunger, and riot and drunkenness—and worse—as I have been from my birth."

"I pity you!" said Rose in a broken voice. "It wrings my heart to hear you!"

"Heaven bless you for your goodness!" rejoined the girl. "Now I must tell you that I am about to put my life and the lives of others in your hands. I have stolen away from those who would surely murder me, if they knew I had been here, to tell you what I have overheard. Do you know a man named Monks?"

"No," said Rose.

"He knows you," replied the girl, "and knew you were here, for it was by hearing him tell your address that I found you. Some time ago, soon after Oliver was put into your house on the night of the robbery, I—suspecting this man—listened to a conversation held between him and Fagin in the dark. I heard that Monks had seen Oliver accidentally with two of our boys on the day we first lost him, and had known him directly to be a particular child that he was watching for, though I couldn't make out why. A bargain was struck with Fagin that if Oliver was got back, Fagin should have a certain sum; and he was to have more for making Oliver a thief, which this Monks wanted for some purpose of his own."

"For what purpose?" asked Rose.

"I do not know," said the girl. "But last night he came again. Again they went upstairs, and again I listened at the door. The first words I heard Monks say were these: 'So the only proofs of the boy's identity lie at the bottom of the river.' They laughed, and Monks, talking on about the boy, and getting very wild, said that though he had got the young devil's money safely now, he'd rather have had it the other way; for what a game it would have been to have brought down the boast of the father's will by driving him through every jail in town, and then hauling him up for some capital felony, which Fagin could manage after having made a good profit of him besides."

"What is all this!" said Rose.

"The truth, lady, though it comes from my lips," replied the girl. "Then Monks said that if he could gratify his hatred by taking the boy's life without bringing his own neck in danger, he would; but as he couldn't, if he took advantage of the boy's birth and history, he might harm him yet. 'In short, Fagin,' he says, 'even you never laid such snares as I'll contrive for my young brother, Oliver!'"

"His brother!" exclaimed Rose.

"Those were his words," said Nancy, glancing uneasily round, as she had scarcely ceased to do since she began to speak, for a vision of Sikes haunted her perpetually. "And more. He said it seemed contrived by Heaven or the devil against him that Oliver should come into your hands; but there was comfort in that too, for how many hundreds of thousands of pounds would you not give, if you had them, to know who your two-legged spaniel was. But it is growing late, and I have to reach home without suspicion of having been on such an errand as this. I must get back quickly."

"Back?" said Rose. "But what can I do? To what use can I turn this communication without you? Why do you wish to return to such companions? If you repeat this information to a gentleman who is in the next room, you can be consigned to some place of safety within half an hour."

"I must go back," said the girl, "because—how can I tell such things to you?—because there is one man, the most desperate among them all, that I can't leave; no, not even to be saved from the life I am leading. It is too late!"

"It is never too late," said Rose, "for penitence and atonement."

"It is!" cried the girl, writhing in the agony of her mind. "I cannot leave him now! I could not be his death, and if I told others what I have told you and led to their being taken, he would be sure to die. He is the boldest, and he has been so cruel!"

"Is it possible," cried Rose, "that for such a man as this you can resign every future hope? It is madness!"

"I don't know what it is," answered the girl. "I only know that it is so. I am drawn back to him through every suffering; and I should be, I believe, if I knew that I was to die by his hand at last."

"What am I to do?" said Rose. "This mystery must be investigated, or how will its disclosure benefit Oliver, whom you are anxious to serve?"

"You must have some kind gentleman about you that will advise you what to do," rejoined the girl.

"But where can I find you again when it is necessary?"

"Will you promise me that you will have my secret strictly kept, and come alone, or with the only other person that knows it, and that I shall not be watched or followed?" asked the girl.

"I promise you solemnly," answered Rose.

"Every Sunday night, from eleven until twelve," said the girl without hesitation, "I will walk on London Bridge if I am alive."

"Stay another moment," said Rose, as Nancy moved towards the door. "You will at least take some money which may enable you to live without dishonesty—at all events until we meet again?"

"Not a penny," replied the girl. "But may God bless you, sweet lady, and send as much happiness on your head as I have brought shame on mine!" Sobbing aloud, the unhappy creature turned away; while Rose, overpowered by this extraordinary interview, sank into a chair and endeavored to collect her thoughts.

Rose's situation was, indeed, one of no common difficulty. While she felt the most eager desire to penetrate the mystery in which Oliver's history was enveloped, she could not but hold sacred the confidence which the miserable woman had reposed in her. Her words and manner had touched Rose's heart.

She and her aunt and Oliver had proposed remaining in London only three days, prior to departing for some weeks to a distant part of the coast. It was now midnight of the first day. What course of action could she determine upon, which could be adopted in eight and forty hours? Or how could she postpone the journey without exciting suspicion?

Dr. Losberne was with them, but Rose was too well acquainted with this excellent gentleman's impetuosity, and the wrath with which he would receive the news, to trust him with the secret. The thought occurred to her of seeking assistance from Harry, but this awakened the recollection of their last parting, and it seemed unworthy of her to call him back.

She passed a sleepless night. But after more communing with herself next day, she arrived at the desperate conclusion of consulting Harry. She had taken up her pen and laid it down again fifty times, without writing the first word, when Oliver, who had been walking in the streets with Giles for a bodyguard, entered the room in such agitation as seemed to betoken some new cause of alarm.

"What makes you look so flurried?" asked Rose.

"I feel as if I should choke," replied the boy, scarcely able to articulate. "Oh dear! I have seen the gentleman who was so good to me—Mr. Brownlow! He was getting out of a coach and going into a house. I didn't speak to him—I couldn't, I trembled so. But Giles asked for me whether he lived there, and they said he did. Look, here it is," said Oliver, opening a scrap of paper.

At once Rose determined to turn this discovery to account.

"Quick!" she said. "Tell them to fetch a hackney coach. I will take you there without a minute's loss of time."

Oliver needed no prompting, and in a few minutes they were on their way to Craven Street in the Strand. When they arrived, Rose left Oliver in the coach, under pretense of preparing the old gentleman to receive him, and sending up her card, requested to see Mr. Brownlow on pressing business. The servant soon returned, and following him into an upper room, Miss Maylie was presented to an elderly gentleman of benevolent appearance in a bottle-green coat. Another old gentleman, who did not look particularly benevolent, was also seated there, with his hands clasped on the top of a thick stick.

"Mr. Brownlow, I believe, sir?" asked Rose.

"That is my name," said the first gentleman, rising with great politeness. "Be seated, pray. This is my friend Mr. Grimwig." Grimwig rose, made a stiff bow and dropped into his chair again.

"I shall surprise you, I have no doubt," said Rose, "but you once showed great goodness to a very dear young friend of mine, and I am sure you will take an interest in hearing of him again."

"Indeed!" said Mr. Brownlow. "And who is he?"

"Oliver Twist," replied Rose.

The words no sooner escaped her lips than Mr. Grimwig discharged from his features every expression but one of unmitigated wonder, and emitted a long whistle.

Mr. Brownlow was no less surprised, although his astonishment was not expressed in the same eccentric manner. He drew his chair nearer to Miss Maylie's and said, "My dear young lady, if you can produce any evidence which will alter the unfavorable opinion I was once induced to entertain of that poor child, in Heaven's name put me in possession of it."

"A bad one! I'll eat my head if he is not a bad one," growled Mr. Grimwig.

"He is a child of a noble nature and a warm heart," said Rose, coloring.

"Do not heed my friend, Miss Maylie," said Mr. Brownlow. "He does not mean what he says."

"Yes, he does," growled Mr. Grimwig.

"No, he does not," said Mr. Brownlow.

"He'll eat his head if he doesn't," growled Mr. Grimwig.

"He would deserve to have it knocked off if he does," said Mr. Brownlow. "Now, Miss Maylie, will you let me know what intelligence you have of this poor child?"

Rose at once related, in a few words, all that had befallen Oliver since he left Mr. Brownlow's house, reserving Nancy's information for that gentleman's private ear, and concluding with the assurance that Oliver's only sorrow, for some months past, had been the not being able to meet with his former benefactor.

"Thank God!" said the old gentleman. "This is great happiness to me. But where is he now, Miss Maylie?"

"He is waiting in a coach at the door," replied Rose.

"At this door!" cried the old gentleman. And with this he hurried out of the room, down the stairs and into the coach without another word. He soon returned, accompanied by Oliver, whom Mr. Grimwig received graciously.

"There is somebody else who should not be forgotten," said Mr. Brownlow, ringing the bell. "Send Mrs. Bedwin here, if you please."

The old housekeeper answered the summons with all dispatch, and dropping a curtsy at the door, waited for orders.

"Why, you get blinder every day, Bedwin," said Mr. Brownlow testily. "Put on your glasses and see if you can't find out what you were wanted for, will you?"

The old lady began to rummage in her pocket for her spectacles. But Oliver's patience was not proof against this, and, yielding to his first impulse, he sprang into her arms.

"God be good to me!" cried the old lady, embracing him. "It is my innocent boy!"

"My dear old nurse!" cried Oliver.

"I knew he would come back," said the old lady, holding him in her arms. "How well he looks, and how like a gentleman's son he is dressed again! Where have you been this long, long while? Ah, the same sweet face, but not so pale; the same soft eye, but not so sad." Running on thus, the good soul laughed and wept by turns.

Leaving her and Oliver to compare notes at leisure, Mr. Brownlow led Rose into another room and there heard a full narration of her interview with Nancy, which occasioned him no little surprise and perplexity. Rose also explained her reasons for not confiding in Dr. Losberne. The old gentleman considered that she had acted prudently and undertook to hold conference with the worthy doctor himself. It was arranged that he should call at the hotel at eight o'clock that evening, and that in the meantime Mrs. Maylie should be cautiously informed of all that had occurred. These preliminaries adjusted, Rose and Oliver returned home.

Rose had by no means overrated the measure of the good doctor's wrath. Nancy's history was no sooner unfolded to him that evening than he poured forth a shower of mingled threats and execrations, said he would make her the first victim of the police, and actually put on his hat preparatory to sallying forth to obtain their assistance. But he was restrained by Mr. Brownlow.

"Then what the devil is to be done?" said the impetuous doctor. "Are we to pass a vote of thanks to all these vagabonds, and beg them to accept a hundred pounds or so apiece as some slight acknowledgment of their kindness to Oliver?"

"Not exactly that," rejoined Mr. Brownlow, laughing. "But we must proceed gently and with great care."

"Gentleness and care?" exclaimed the doctor. "I'd send them one and all to—"

"Never mind where," interposed Mr. Brownlow. "But reflect whether sending them anywhere is likely to attain the object we have in view. Our object, after all, is simply to discover Oliver's parentage and regain for him the inheritance of which, if this story be true, he has been fraudulently deprived. It is quite clear that we shall have extreme difficulty in getting to the bottom of this mystery unless we can bring this man Monks to his knees. That can only be done by stratagem and by catching him when he is not surrounded by these people. For, suppose he were apprehended, we have no proof against him. He is not even (so far as we know) concerned with the gang in any of their robberies. We must then catch him ourselves. Before we can resolve on any precise course of action, therefore, it will be necessary to see the girl; to ascertain from her whether she will point out this Monks to us, on the understanding that Monks is to be dealt with by us and not by the law; or, if she cannot do that, to procure from her such an account of his haunts and description of his person as will enable us to identify him. She cannot be seen until next Sunday night; this is Tuesday. I would suggest that in the meantime we remain perfectly quiet and keep these matters secret even from Oliver himself."

Although Dr. Losberne made many wry faces on receiving a proposal which involved a delay of five whole days, he was fain to admit that no better course occurred to him just then; and as both Rose and Mrs. Maylie sided very strongly with Mr. Brownlow, that gentleman's proposition was carried unanimously.

"I should like," he said, "to call in the aid of my friend Grimwig. He is a strange creature, but a shrewd one, and a lawyer, and might prove of material assistance to us."

"I have no objection to your calling in your friend if I may call in mine," said the doctor. "He is Mrs. Maylie's son, and this young lady's—very old friend," said the doctor.

Rose blushed deeply, but she did not make any audible objection to this motion. Harry Maylie and Mr. Grimwig were accordingly added to the committee.

"We stay in town, of course," said Mrs. Maylie, "while there remains the slightest prospect of prosecuting this inquiry with a chance of success."

"Good," rejoined Mr. Brownlow. "And as I see on the faces about me a disposition to inquire how it happened that I was not here to corroborate Oliver's tale, having so suddenly left the kingdom, let me stipulate that I shall be asked no questions until such time as I may deem it expedient to tell my own story. But come! Supper has been announced, and young Oliver is waiting."

CHAPTER XVIII

ADEPT AS SHE WAS in the arts of cunning and dissimulation, Nancy could not wholly conceal the effect which the knowledge of the step she had taken wrought on her mind. She remembered that Fagin and Sikes had confided to her schemes which had been hidden from all others, in the full confidence that she was trustworthy. Vile as those schemes were, desperate as were their originators, and bitter as were her feelings towards Fagin, who had led her, step by step, into an abyss of crime and misery, still there were times when even towards him she felt some relenting, lest he should fall at last by her hand. But she was resolved not to be turned aside by any consideration. Her fears for Sikes would have been more powerful inducements to recoil while there was yet time; but she had stipulated that her secret should be rigidly kept, she had dropped no clue which could lead to his discovery, she had refused, for his sake, a refuge from all the guilt and wretchedness that encompassed her—what more could she do! She was resolved.

Though all her mental struggles terminated in this conclusion, they left their traces too. She grew much paler and thinner, even within a few days. At times she laughed without merriment; at others, she sat silent and dejected.

It was Sunday night, and the bell of the nearest church struck the hour. Sikes and Fagin were talking in the housebreaker's room, but they paused to listen. The girl looked up from her low seat and listened too. Eleven.

"An hour this side of midnight," said Sikes, raising the blind to look out and then returning to his seat. "Dark and heavy it is too. A good night for business, this."

"What a pity, Bill, my dear, that there's none quite ready to be done." Fagin sighed and shook his head despondingly. Then, pulling Sikes by the sleeve, he pointed towards Nancy, who had put on her bonnet and was leaving the room.

"Hallo!" cried Sikes. "Nance. Where's the gal going at this hour?"

"Not far."

"Wot answer's that? I say where are you going?"

"I don't know where," replied the girl.

"Then I do," said Sikes, more in the spirit of obstinacy than because he had any real objection to the girl going out. "Nowhere. Sit down."

"I'm not well. I told you that before. I want a breath of air."

"Put your head out of the winder," returned Sikes.

"There's not enough there. I want it in the street."

"Then you won't have it," replied Sikes. With which assurance he rose, locked the door, took the key out, and pulling her bonnet from her head, flung it on the table. "There—now stop quietly where you are, will you?"

"What do you mean, Bill?" said the girl. "Do you know what you're doing?"

"Know wot I'm—" cried Sikes, turning to Fagin. "She's out of her senses, you know, or she daren't talk to me in that way."

"You'll drive me to something desperate," muttered the girl, placing both hands on her breast, as though to keep down by force some violent outbreak. "Let me go, will you, this instant!"

"No!" cried Sikes, seizing her roughly by the arm. "Cut my limbs off one by one, if I don't think the gal's stark raving mad!"

He suddenly pinioned her hands and dragged her into a small adjoining room, where he thrust her into a chair and held her down by force. She struggled and implored by turns until twelve o'clock had struck, and then, exhausted, ceased to contest the point. With many oaths Sikes left her to recover and rejoined Fagin.

"Whew!" said the housebreaker, wiping the perspiration from his face. "Wot a precious strange gal that is! Wot did she take it into her head to go out tonight for, do you think?"

"Obstinacy, woman's obstinacy, I suppose," replied Fagin.

"Well, I suppose it is," growled Sikes. "I thought I had tamed her, but she's as bad as ever."

"Worse," said Fagin thoughtfully. "I never knew her like this for such a little cause."

"Nor I. I think she's got a touch of fever. I'll let her a little blood without troubling the doctor, if she's took that way again."

Fagin nodded an expressive approval of this mode of treatment.

Just then the girl herself appeared and resumed her former seat. Her eyes were swollen and red. She rocked herself to and fro, tossed her head, and after a little time burst out laughing.

"Why, now she's on the other tack!" exclaimed Sikes, turning a look of excessive surprise on his companion.

Fagin nodded to him to take no further notice just then, and the girl soon subsided. Then he bade Sikes good night, and asked if somebody would light him down the dark stairs.

"Light him down," said Sikes to the girl. "It's a pity he should break his neck himself and disappoint the sightseers."

Nancy followed the old man downstairs with a candle. When they reached the passage, he laid his finger on his lip, and drawing close to her, said in a whisper, "What is it, Nancy, dear? If *he*"—he pointed with his skinny forefinger up the stairs—"is so hard with you, why don't you—"

"Well?" she said, as Fagin paused, with his eyes looking into hers.

"No matter just now. We'll talk of this again. You have a friend in me, Nance, a staunch friend. If you want revenge on those that treat you like a dog—worse than his dog, for he humors him sometimes—come to me. You know me of old, Nance."

"I know you well," she replied, without manifesting the least emotion. She said good night in a steady voice, answered his parting look with a nod of intelligence, and closed the door between them.

Fagin walked towards home, intent on the thoughts that were working within his brain. The idea had come to him that Nancy, wearied of the housebreaker's brutality, had conceived an attachment for some new friend. Her altered manner, and her desperate impatience to leave home that night at a particular hour, favored the supposition. The object of this new liking was not among Fagin's myrmidons. He would be a valuable acquisition with such an assistant as Nancy, and must be secured without delay.

There was another, and a darker, object to be gained. Sikes knew too much, and his ruffian taunts often galled Fagin. The girl must know that if she shook him off she could never be safe from his fury. "With a little persuasion," thought Fagin, "what more likely than that she would consent to poison him? Women have done such things, and worse, to secure the same object before now. There would be the dangerous villain gone—another secured in his place—and my influence over the girl, with a knowledge of this crime to back it, unlimited."

But perhaps she would recoil from a plot to take the life of Sikes. "How," thought Fagin as he crept homeward, "can I increase my influence with her? What new power can I acquire?"

Such brains are fertile in expedients. If, Fagin thought, he laid a watch, discovered the object of her altered regard, and threatened to reveal the whole history to Sikes, could he not secure her compliance?

"I can," he said, almost aloud. "She durst not refuse me then. Not for her life, not for her life. I shall have her yet!"

FAGIN WAS UP, betimes, next morning, and waited impatiently for the appearance of a new associate. This young man's name was Morris Bolter. He was a long-legged, knock-kneed, shambling young man with a red nose, recently come to London from the country, and he was not yet acquainted with Nancy. At length he presented himself and commenced a voracious assault on the breakfast provided by Fagin.

"I want you, Bolter," said Fagin, seating himself opposite him, "to do a piece of work for me, my dear, that needs great care and caution. You are to dodge a woman. I need you to tell me where she goes, who she sees, and, if possible, what she says."

"Who is she?" inquired Bolter, cutting a monstrous slice of bread.

"One of us. But she has found out some new friends, my dear, and I must know who they are."

"Of course," replied Bolter, after taking a series of large bites. "Where is she? Where am I to wait for her? Where am I to go?"

"All that, my dear, you shall hear from me at the proper time," said Fagin. "Keep ready and leave the rest to me."

That night, and the next, and the next again, the spy sat booted and dressed in countryman's clothes, ready to turn out at a word from Fagin. Six long nights passed, and on each, Fagin came home with a disappointed face, and briefly intimated that it was not yet time. On the seventh, he returned earlier, and with an exultation he could not conceal.

"She goes abroad tonight," said Fagin, "and on the right errand, I'm sure; for the man she is afraid of will not be back much before daybreak. Come with me. Quick!"

They left the house stealthily and hurried to Sikes's house. It was past eleven o'clock when they arrived. A few minutes later the door opened, and Nancy came out.

"Is that the woman?" asked Bolter, scarcely above his breath.

Fagin nodded. "Now, follow her, and keep to the other side of the street!"

By the light of the lamps Bolter followed the girl. She looked nervously round twice or thrice, but seemed to gather courage as she went on. The spy preserved a prudent distance.

The clocks were chiming three quarters past eleven as the two figures emerged on London Bridge. The young woman advanced with a rapid step, now looking eagerly about her as though expecting someone; the young man slunk along in deepest shadow, accommodating his pace to hers. At nearly the center of the bridge, she stopped. The man stopped too.

It was a very dark night; a mist hung over the river. There were few people stirring, and such as there were hurried quickly past.

The girl had taken a few restless turns to and fro—closely watched by her hidden observer—when the heavy bell of St. Paul's tolled midnight. A moment later a young lady, accompanied by a gray-haired gentleman, alighted from a hackney carriage and dismissed it. They had scarcely set foot on the pavement when the girl started and made towards them. As the girl joined them they halted with an exclamation of surprise. At that moment the man in countryman's garments brushed against them, roughly asked what they took up the whole pavement for, and passed on.

"I'm afraid to speak to you here," said the girl hurriedly to the lady and the gentleman. "Come down the steps yonder!"

The Meeting

The girl pointed towards some steps that formed a landing stairs from the river. These stairs consisted of three flights, and the steps of the lowest flight widened so that a person turning that second angle of the stone wall would be unseen by any others on the stairs above him. To this spot the spy, ahead of the others, now hastened unobserved. Here he concealed himself, pretty certain that they would come no lower. Soon he heard the sound of footsteps and of voices almost close at his ear.

"This is far enough," said the voice of the gentleman. "I will not suffer the young lady to go any farther. Many people would have distrusted you too much to have come even so far. Why not have let me speak to you above, where it is light?"

"I told you I was afraid to speak to you there," said the voice of the girl. "I have such a fear and dread on me I can hardly stand."

"A fear of what?" asked the gentleman.

"I scarcely know of what," replied the girl. "I wish I did. Horrible thoughts of death, and shrouds with blood upon them, and a fear that has made me burn as if I was on fire."

"Imagination," said the gentleman.

"Speak to her kindly," said the young lady. "Poor creature!"

"You were not here last Sunday night," said the gentleman.

"I couldn't come," replied Nancy. "I was kept by force. By him that I told the young lady of before."

"You were not suspected of holding any communication with anybody on the subject which has brought us here tonight, I hope?" asked the gentleman.

"No," replied the girl. "But it's not easy for me to leave him unless he knows why—I couldn't have gone to see the lady when I did, but that I gave him a drink of laudanum. But neither he nor any of them suspect me."

"Good," said the gentleman. "Now listen to me. This young lady has communicated to me and to some other friends, who can be safely trusted, what you told her. We now propose to extort the secret, whatever it may be, from this man Monks. But if he cannot be secured or, if secured, cannot be acted upon as we wish, you must deliver up Fagin."

"Fagin!" cried the girl, recoiling. "I will never do it! Devil that he is, I will never do that!"

"Tell me why," said the gentleman.

"Because," rejoined the girl firmly, "bad life as he has led, I have led a bad life too—there are many of us who have kept the same courses together, and I'll not turn on them who might have turned on me, but didn't, bad as they are."

"Then," said the gentleman quickly, as if he had been aiming to attain this point, "put Monks into my hands, and leave him to me to deal with."

"What if he turns against the others?"

"I promise you that if the truth is forced from him, there the matter will rest. There must be circumstances in Oliver's little history which it would be painful to drag before the public eye, and if the truth is once elicited, they shall go scot-free."

"And if it is not?" suggested the girl.

"Then," pursued the gentleman, "Fagin shall not be brought to justice without your consent."

"Have I the lady's promise for that?" asked the girl.

"You have," replied Rose. "My true and faithful pledge."

"Monks would never learn how you knew what you do?" asked the girl.

"Never," replied the gentleman. "We will so act that he will never even be able to guess."

"I have been a liar and among liars from a little child," said the girl after an interval of silence, "but I will take your word."

She then proceeded, in a voice so low it was difficult for the listener to hear, to describe, by name and situation, the public house of The Three Cripples, and the night and hour on which Monks was most in the habit of frequenting it.

"He is tall," said the girl, "and a strongly made man; he has a lurking walk, and he constantly looks over his shoulder. His eyes are sunk in his head much deeper than any other man's. His face is dark, like his hair and eyes, and, although he can't be more than six and twenty, withered and haggard. His lips are often disfigured with the marks of teeth, for he has desperate fits and sometimes even bites his hands and covers them with wounds—why did you start?" said the girl, stopping suddenly.

The gentleman replied, in a hurried manner, that he was not conscious of having done so, and he begged her to proceed.

"And on his throat," she added, "so high that you can see it beneath his neckerchief when he turns his face, there is—"

"A broad red mark, like a burn?" cried the old gentleman.

"How's this?" asked the girl. "You know him!"

The young lady uttered a cry of surprise.

"I think I do," said the gentleman. "But many people are singularly like each other. We shall see." He took a step or two nearer the concealed spy. "Now," he continued after a pause, "you have given us most valuable assistance, young woman, and I wish you to be the better for it. What can I do to serve you?"

"Nothing," replied Nancy, weeping now. "I am past all hope!"

"You put yourself beyond its pale," said the gentleman. "It is in our power now—and it is our most anxious wish—to offer you a quiet asylum either in England or, if you fear to remain here, in some foreign country. Before the dawn you could be placed entirely beyond the reach of your former associates. Come! Quit them all while there is time and opportunity!"

"She will be persuaded now!" cried the young lady. "She hesitates, I am sure."

"No, I do not," replied the girl after a short struggle. "I am chained to my old life. I loathe and hate it now, but I cannot leave it. I have gone too far to turn back. I must go home."

"Home!" repeated the young lady.

"Home, lady," rejoined the girl. "To such a home as I have raised for myself with the work of my life. Let us part. I shall be watched or seen. Go! If I have done you any service, all I ask is that you leave me and let me go my way alone."

"It is useless," said the gentleman with a sigh, turning away. "We compromise her safety, perhaps, by staying here."

"Yes, yes," urged the girl.

"This purse," cried the young lady. "Take it for my sake, that you may have some resource in an hour of need and trouble."

"No!" replied the girl. "I have not done this for money. Let me have that to think of. And yet I should like to have something that belonged to you, sweet lady—no, no, not a ring—your handkerchief. There. God bless you. Good night, good night!"

The voices ceased; the sound of retreating footsteps was audible. The astonished listener remained motionless at his post for some minutes afterwards. Then, peeping out to make sure that he was unobserved, he darted away and made for Fagin's house as fast as his legs would carry him.

IT WAS NEARLY TWO HOURS before daybreak; that time which in the autumn of the year may be truly called the dead of night; when the streets are silent and deserted. It was at this still hour that Fagin sat watching in his old lair, with face so distorted and pale, and eyes so bloodshot, that he looked like some hideous phantom, moist from the grave. He crouched over a cold hearth, wrapped in a torn coverlet, with his face turned towards a candle that stood on a table by his side. Stretched on the floor lay Morris Bolter, fast asleep. Towards him the old man sometimes directed his eyes for an instant and then brought them back again to the candle, which, with a long-burned wick and grease dripping upon the table, plainly showed that his thoughts were busy elsewhere.

Indeed they were. Mortification at the overthrow of his scheme; hatred of the girl who had dared to palter with strangers; utter distrust of the sincerity of her refusal to yield him up; bitter disappointment at the loss of his revenge on Sikes; fear of detection and ruin and death; and deadly rage; these were the passionate considerations which shot through the brain of Fagin as every evil thought and blackest purpose lay working at his heart.

He sat without appearing to take the smallest heed of time until his ear was attracted by a footstep in the street. "At last," he muttered. The bell rang as he spoke. He crept upstairs to the door and presently returned, accompanied by a man muffled to the chin. It was Sikes, and he carried a bundle under one arm.

"There!" Sikes said, laying the bundle on the table. "Take care of that. It's been trouble enough to get."

Fagin locked the bundle in the cupboard and sat down again without speaking. But he did not take his eyes off the robber for an instant. His lips were quivering so violently and his face was so altered by emotion that the housebreaker drew back in fright.

"Wot now?" cried Sikes. "Wot do you look at a man so for?"

Fagin shook his trembling forefinger in the air, but his passion was so great that the power of speech was for the moment gone.

"Damme!" said Sikes, with a look of alarm, feeling in his pocket. "He's gone mad. I must look to myself!"

"No, no," rejoined Fagin, finding his voice. "It's not—you're not the person, Bill. I've no fault to find with you."

"Oh, you haven't, haven't you?" said Sikes, ostentatiously passing a pistol into a more convenient pocket. "That's lucky."

"I've got that to tell you, Bill, will make you worse than me."

"Aye?" returned the robber with an incredulous air. "Tell away! Look sharp, or Nance will think I'm lost."

"Lost!" cried Fagin. "She has pretty well settled that in her own mind already."

Sikes looked with great perplexity into Fagin's face, and reading no satisfactory explanation of the riddle there, clenched his coat collar and shook him soundly. "Speak, will you!" he said. "Say wot you've got to say in plain words. Out with it, you old cur!"

"Suppose that lad that's lying there—" Fagin began.

Sikes turned to where Bolter was sleeping. "Well?" he asked.

"Suppose that lad," pursued Fagin, "was to peach—to blow upon us all—first seeking out the right folks for the purpose and then having a meeting with 'em in the street to paint our likenesses, describe every mark that they might know us by, and the crib where we might be most easily taken. Suppose he was to do all this, and besides to blow on a plant we've all been in—suppose he did all this!" cried Fagin, his eyes flashing with rage. "What then?"

"Wot then!" replied Sikes with a tremendous oath. "I'd grind his skull under the iron heel of my boot!"

"What if *I* did it?" cried Fagin, almost in a yell. "*I*, that know so much and could hang so many besides myself?"

Sikes turned white at the mere suggestion. "I should have such strength," he muttered, poising his brawny arm, "that I would smash your head as if a loaded wagon had gone over it."

"You would?"

"Would I!"

"If it was Charley, or the Dodger, or Bet, or—"

"I don't care who," replied Sikes impatiently. "Whoever it was, I'd serve them the same!"

Fagin looked hard at the robber, and motioning him to be silent, stooped and shook the sleeper. "Bolter, Bolter! Poor lad!" said Fagin, looking up with an expression of devilish anticipation. "He's tired—tired with watching *her* so long—watching *her*, Bill!"

"Wot d'ye mean?" asked Sikes, drawing back.

Fagin made no answer but hauled the sleeper into a sitting posture. Bolter, yawning, looked sleepily about. "Tell me that again— just for him to hear," said Fagin, pointing to Sikes as he spoke.

"Tell yer what?" asked the sleepy Bolter.

"That about—NANCY," said Fagin, clutching Sikes by the wrist as if to prevent his leaving before he had heard. "You followed her?"

"Yes."

"To London Bridge, where she met two people?"

"So she did."

"A gentleman and a lady, that she had gone to of her own accord before, who asked her to give up all her pals, and Monks first, which she did—and to describe him, and to tell what house it was that we meet at, which she did—and what time he went there, which she did. She told it all, every word, without a threat, without a murmur—she did—did she not?" cried Fagin.

"All right," replied Bolter. "That's just what it was!"

"What did they say about last Sunday?"

"Why, I told yer that before," replied Bolter.

"Again. Tell it again!" Fagin tightened his grasp on Sikes and brandished his other hand aloft as the foam flew from his lips.

"They asked her," said Bolter, who seemed to have a dawning perception who Sikes was, "why she didn't come last Sunday as she promised. She said she was forcibly kept at home by the man she had told them of before."

"What more of him? Tell him that!"

"Why, that she couldn't easily get out of doors unless he knew where she was going," said Bolter, "and so the first time she went to see the lady, she gave him a drink of laudanum."

"Hell's fire!" cried Sikes. "Let me go!" Flinging the old man from him, he rushed out and darted wildly up the stairs.

"Bill, Bill!" cried Fagin, following him hastily and catching him at the door. "You won't be—too—violent, Bill?" The day was breaking and there was light enough for them to see each other's faces. There was fire in the eyes of both, which could not be mistaken. "I mean," said Fagin, "not too violent for safety. Be crafty, Bill, and not too bold."

Sikes made no reply, but pulled open the door and dashed into the silent streets. Without one pause, or moment's consideration, but looking straight before him with savage resolution, he held on his headlong course until he reached his own door. Striding lightly up the stairs and entering his room, he double-locked the door. Then he drew back the curtain of the bed.

The girl was lying, half dressed, on the bed. He had roused her from sleep, for she raised herself with a startled look.

"Get up!" said the man.

"It *is* you, Bill!" said the girl with an expression of pleasure.

"It is," was the reply. "Get up!"

Seeing the faint light of day without, the girl rose to undraw the curtain.

"Let it be," said Sikes, thrusting his hand before her. "There's light enough for wot I've got to do."

"Bill," said the girl in a low voice of alarm, "why do you look like that at me!"

The robber regarded her for a few seconds with dilated nostrils and heaving breast; then, grasping her by the head and throat, he dragged her into the middle of the room.

"Bill, Bill!" gasped the girl, wrestling with the strength of mortal fear. "I—speak to me—tell me what I have done!"

"You know, you she-devil!" he said, suppressing his breath. "You were watched tonight—every word you said was heard."

"Then spare my life for the love of Heaven, as I spared yours!" rejoined the girl, clinging to him. "Bill, dear Bill, you cannot have the heart to kill me! Oh, think of all I have given up, only this night, for you! Bill, Bill, for dear God's sake, for your own, for mine, stop! I have been true to you, on my guilty soul I have!"

The man struggled violently to release his arms, but those of the girl were clasped round his, and he could not tear them away.

"Bill," cried the girl, striving to lay her head on his breast, "the gentleman and that dear lady told me tonight that I could end my days in peace in some foreign country. Let me see them again, and beg them to show the same mercy and goodness to you; and let us both leave this dreadful place, and lead better lives. It is never too late to repent—but we must have time—a little, little time!"

The housebreaker freed one arm and grasped his pistol. But the certainty of immediate detection if he fired flashed across his mind even in the midst of his fury; and he beat it twice with all the force he could summon upon the girl's upturned face.

She staggered and fell, nearly blinded with the blood that rained down from a deep gash in her forehead. But raising herself with difficulty on her knees, she drew from her bosom a white handkerchief—Rose Maylie's—and holding it up in her folded hands as high towards heaven as her feeble strength would allow, breathed one prayer for mercy to her Maker.

It was a ghastly figure to look upon. The murderer, staggering backwards to the wall, and shutting out the sight with his hand, seized a heavy club and struck her down.

···· CHAPTER XIX ·····

THE SUN—the bright sun that brings back not light alone, but new hope and freshness to man—burst upon the crowded city in clear and radiant glory. Through costly glass and paper-mended window, it shed its equal ray. It lighted up the room where the murdered woman lay. It did. He tried to shut it out, but it would stream in.

He had not moved; he had been afraid to stir. Once he had thrown a rug over the body, but it was worse to imagine the eyes moving towards him than to see them glaring upwards. He had plucked the rug off again. And there was the body—mere flesh and blood no more—but such flesh, and so much blood!

He kindled a fire, and thrust the club into it; he held the weapon till it broke, and then piled it on the coals to smolder into ashes. He washed himself and rubbed his clothes; there were spots that would not be removed. He cut the pieces out, and burned them. How those stains were dispersed about the room! The very feet of the dog were bloody.

All this time he had never once turned his back on the corpse; no, not for a moment. Such preparations completed, he moved backwards towards the door, dragging the dog with him lest he should soil his feet anew and carry evidences of the crime into the streets. He shut the door softly, locked it, took the key and left the house. He glanced up at the window, to be sure that nothing was visible from the outside. There was the curtain still drawn. He whistled to the dog and walked rapidly away.

Unsteady of purpose and uncertain where to go, he struck off through Islington towards Hampstead Heath. Traversing the hollow by the Vale of Health, he made along the heath to the fields at North End, in one of which he lay down under a hedge and slept. Soon he was up again and away—into the country—then back again—then over another part of the same ground—then wandering up and down in fields and lying in ditches to rest, and starting on again. In this way he wandered over miles and miles of ground. Morning and noon had passed and the day was on the wane, and still he rambled. At last, at nine o'clock that night, quite tired out, and followed by the dog, limping and lame from the unaccustomed exercise, he crept into a public house in a quiet village. There was a fire in the taproom, and some country laborers were drinking before it. They made room for the stranger, but he sat down in the farthest corner, and ate and drank alone, or rather with his dog, to whom he cast a morsel of food from time to time.

When he had finished, he plunged into the solitude and darkness of the road again. He felt a dread and awe creeping on him, and every object before him took the semblance of some fearful thing; but these fears were nothing compared to the sense that haunted him of that morning's ghastly figure following at his heels. He could trace its shadow in the gloom, hear its garments rustling in the leaves, and every breath of wind came laden with that last low cry. If he stopped, it did the same. If he ran, it followed, as if borne on one slow melancholy wind that never rose or fell. At times he turned, with desperate determination, resolved to beat this phantom off, but the hair rose on his head and his blood stood still, for it had turned with him and was behind him then. He had kept it before him that morning, but it was behind now—always.

There was a shed in a field that offered shelter for the night. Before the door were three tall poplar trees, which made it very dark within, and the wind moaned through them with a dismal wail. Here he stretched himself close to the wall—to undergo new torture. For now a terrible vision came before him of those widely staring eyes, so lusterless and so glassy, in the midst of the darkness. There were but two, but they were everywhere.

He got up and rushed into the field. The phantom was again behind him. He re-entered the shed and shrank down once more. The eyes were there. And here he remained in terror, trembling in every limb, and the cold sweat starting from every pore, when suddenly there arose upon the night wind the noise of distant shouting, and the roar of voices mingled in alarm.

Springing to his feet, he rushed again into the open air. The broad sky seemed on fire. Rising into the air with showers of sparks were sheets of flame and clouds of smoke. The shouts grew louder, and the man could hear the cry of "Fire!" mingled with the ringing of an alarm bell and the crackling of flames. It was like new life to him. He darted onward—leaping gate and fence as madly as his dog. He came upon the spot. There were half-dressed figures tearing to and fro, some endeavoring to drag frightened horses from the stables, others coming laden from the burning house, amidst falling sparks and the tumbling down of red-hot beams. Women and children shrieked; the clanking of pumps, the hissing of water, as it fell upon the blazing wood, added to the tremendous roar. He shouted too, and flying from memory and himself, plunged into the throng.

Hither and thither he dived that night, now working at the pumps, now hurrying through the smoke and flame, over floors that trembled with his weight, under the lee of falling bricks. But he bore a charmed life, and had neither scratch nor bruise, till morning dawned again and only blackened ruins remained.

This mad excitement over, there returned with tenfold force the dreadful consciousness of his crime. He looked suspiciously about him, for he feared to be the subject of some talk. The dog obeyed the beck of his finger, and they drew off together. As he passed near an engine the firemen called to him to share their refreshment. He took some bread and meat and heard the men, who were from London, talking about the murder. "He's gone to Birmingham, they say, but they'll have him yet. The scouts are out, and by tomorrow night there'll be a cry all through the country."

He hurried off, and walked till he almost dropped upon the ground; then he lay down in a lane, and had a long but uneasy sleep. Wandering on again, irresolute and undecided, he became oppressed with the fear of another solitary night. Suddenly he took the desperate resolution of going back to London.

"There's somebody to speak to there, at all events," he thought. "A good hiding place, too. They'll never expect to nab me there, after this country scent. Why can't I lie by for a week or so, and, forcing blunt from Fagin, get abroad to France? Damme, I'll risk it."

He chose the least frequented roads and began his journey back, resolved to enter the metropolis at dusk by a circuitous route. The dog, though. If any descriptions of him were out, it would not be forgotten that the dog was missing and had probably gone with him. He resolved to drown him, and looked about for a pond, picking up a heavy stone and tying it to his handkerchief as he went. But perhaps the animal's instinct apprehended something of the purpose of these preparations; for he skulked a little farther in the rear than usual, and when his master halted at the brink of a pool, he stopped outright.

"Come here!" cried Sikes.

The animal came up from force of habit, but as Sikes stooped to attach the handkerchief to his throat, he uttered a low growl and started back.

"Come here!" said the robber.

The dog wagged his tail, but moved not. Sikes made a running noose and called him again.

The dog advanced, retreated, paused an instant, turned, and scoured away at his hardest speed.

The man whistled again and again, and sat down and waited in the expectation that he would return. But no dog appeared, and at length he resumed his journey.

THE TWILIGHT WAS BEGINNING to close in when Mr. Brownlow alighted from a hackney coach at his own door and knocked. The door being opened, a sturdy man got out of the coach and another dismounted from the box. At a sign from Mr. Brownlow, they helped out a third man, and taking him between them, hurried him into the house. This man was Monks. They walked in the same manner up the stairs, and Mr. Brownlow, preceding them, led the way into a back room. At the door of this apartment, Monks, who had come with evident reluctance, stopped. The two men looked to the old gentleman for instructions.

"He knows the alternative," said Mr. Brownlow. "If he moves a finger but as you bid him, drag him into the street, call for the police, and impeach him as a felon in my name."

"How dare you say this of me?" asked Monks.

"How dare you urge me to it, young man?" replied Mr. Brownlow, confronting him with a steady look. "Are you mad enough to leave this house? Unhand him. There, sir. You are free to go, but I warn you, by all I hold most sacred, that the instant you set foot in the street, I will have you apprehended on a charge of fraud and robbery."

"By what authority am I kidnaped on the street and brought here by these dogs?" asked Monks, looking at the men beside him.

"By mine," replied Mr. Brownlow. "Those persons are indem-

nified by me. If you complain of being deprived of your liberty—
and you deemed it advisable to remain quiet as you came along
—throw yourself for protection on the law."

Monks was plainly disconcerted, and he hesitated.

"You will decide quickly," said Mr. Brownlow with composure.
"If you wish me to prefer my charges publicly, you know the way.
If not, and you appeal to my forbearance, and the mercy of those
you have deeply injured, seat yourself in that chair."

"Is there—" demanded Monks with a faltering tongue, "is
there—no middle course?"

"None."

Monks looked at the old gentleman, but, reading in his countenance nothing but severity and determination, he walked into
the room, and, shrugging his shoulders, sat down.

"Lock the door on the outside," said Mr. Brownlow to the
attendants, "and come when I ring."

The men obeyed, and the two were left alone together.

"This is pretty treatment, sir," said Monks, "from my father's
oldest friend."

"It is because I was your father's oldest friend, young man,"
returned Mr. Brownlow; "it is because the hopes of young and
happy years were bound up with him and that fair creature, his
only sister, who rejoined her God in youth, and left me here a
lonely man; it is because he knelt with me beside her deathbed on
the morning that would—but Heaven willed otherwise—have
made her my wife; it is because my seared heart clung to him from
that time forth, through all his trials and errors, till he died; it is
because old recollections have filled my heart, and even the sight
of you brings with it old thoughts of him; it is because of all these
things that I am moved to treat you gently now—yes, Edward
Leeford, even now—and blush for your unworthiness who bear
the name."

"What has the name to do with it?" asked the other. "What is
the name to me?"

"Nothing," replied Mr. Brownlow, "nothing to you. But it was
hers, and even at this distance of time brings back to me, an old

man, the glow and thrill which I once felt only to hear it repeated by a stranger. I am very glad you have changed it—very."

"This is all mighty fine," said Monks (to retain his assumed designation), "but what do you want with me?"

"You have a brother," said Mr. Brownlow, "the whisper of whose name in your ear in the street was, in itself, almost enough to make you accompany me hither in alarm."

"I have no brother," replied Monks. "You know I was an only child."

"Attend to what I do know and you may not," said Mr. Brownlow. "I shall interest you by and by. I know that, of the wretched marriage into which family pride forced your unhappy father when a mere boy, you were the sole and most unnatural issue. But I also know the misery, the slow torture, the protracted anguish of that ill-assorted union. I know how indifference gave place to dislike, dislike to hate, and hate to loathing, until at last your father and mother wrenched asunder the chain that bound them, and, retiring a wide space apart, carried each a galling fragment, to hide it in new society beneath the gayest looks they could assume. Your mother succeeded; she forgot it soon. But it rusted and cankered at your father's heart for years."

"Well, they were separated," said Monks, "and what of that?"

"When they had been separated for some time," returned Mr. Brownlow, "and your mother, wholly given up to continental frivolities, had forgotten the young husband ten years her junior who, with prospects blighted, lingered on at home, he fell among new friends. *This* circumstance, at least, you know already."

"Not I," said Monks, turning away his eyes and beating his foot on the floor, as if determined to deny everything.

"Your manner, no less than your actions, assures me that you have never forgotten it, or ceased to think of it with bitterness," returned Mr. Brownlow. "I speak of thirteen years ago, when you were but twelve or thirteen years old, and your father but one and thirty. Must I go back to events which cast a shade on the memory of your parent, or will you disclose to me the truth?"

"I have nothing to disclose," rejoined Monks.

"These new friends, then," said Mr. Brownlow, "were a naval officer retired from active service, whose wife had died and left him with two daughters; one a beautiful creature of nineteen, and the other a mere child of three or four. They resided in the same part of the country in which your father had taken up his abode. Acquaintance, intimacy, friendship, followed on each other. Your father was gifted as few men are. As the old officer knew him more, he grew to love him. I would that it had ended there. But his daughter did the same."

The old gentleman paused. Monks was biting his lips, with his eyes fixed on the floor. Seeing this, Mr. Brownlow resumed: "The end of a year found your father solemnly contracted to that daughter; the object of the first, true, ardent passion of a guileless girl. At length a rich relation died and left your father a considerable amount of money. It was necessary that he should immediately repair to Rome, where this relation had died, leaving his affairs in great confusion. Your father was seized with a mortal illness there. He was followed, the moment the news reached Paris, by your mother, who took you with her. He died the day after her arrival, leaving no will—*no will*—so that the whole property fell to her and you."

Monks held his breath and listened with intense eagerness, though his eyes were not directed towards the speaker. As Mr. Brownlow paused, he changed his position with an air of sudden relief and wiped his hot face and hands.

"Before he went abroad, and as he passed through London on his way," said Mr. Brownlow slowly, and fixing his eyes on the other's face, "your father came to me."

"I never heard of that," interrupted Monks in a tone intended to appear incredulous, but savoring more of disagreeable surprise.

"He left with me, among some other things, a portrait painted by himself of this poor girl, which he could not carry on his hasty journey. He was worn by anxiety almost to a shadow; talked in a wild, distracted way of ruin and dishonor worked by himself; confided to me his intention to convert his whole property into money, and, having settled on his wife and you a portion of his recent acquisition, to fly the country—I guessed too well he would not fly alone. Even from me, his old and early friend, he withheld any more particular confession, promising to write and tell me all, and after that to see me once again, for the last time. Alas! *That* was the last time. I had no letter, and I never saw him again.

"I went, when all was over, to the scene of his—I will use the term the world would freely use—of his guilty love, resolved, if my fears were realized, that the erring child should find one heart and home to shelter her. But the family had left that part a week before. Why, or whither, none could tell."

Monks drew his breath more freely, and looked round with a smile of triumph.

"When your brother," said Mr. Brownlow, drawing nearer the other, "a feeble, ragged, neglected child, was cast in my way by a stronger hand than chance, and rescued by me from a life of vice and infamy—"

"What?" cried Monks.

"By me," said Mr. Brownlow. "I told you I should interest you before long. I see that your cunning associate suppressed my name, although for aught he knew it would be strange to your ears. When your brother was rescued by me, then, and lay recovering from sickness in my house, his strong resemblance to this picture I have spoken of struck me with astonishment. Even when I first saw him in all his dirt and misery, there was a lingering expression in his face that came on me like a glimpse of some old friend flashing in a vivid dream. I need not tell you he was snared away before I knew his history—"

"Why not?" asked Monks hastily.

"Because you know it well," replied Mr. Brownlow.

"You—you—can't prove anything against me," stammered Monks. "I defy you to do it!"

"We shall see," returned the old gentleman, with a searching glance. "I lost the boy, and no efforts of mine could recover him. Your mother being dead, I knew that you alone could solve the mystery if anybody could, and as when I had last heard of you, you were on your estate in the West Indies—whither you retired upon your mother's death to escape the consequences of vicious courses here—I made the voyage. You had left it months before and were supposed to be in London. I returned. Your agents said you came and went as strangely as you had ever done, keeping the same low haunts and mingling with the same infamous herd who had been your associates when an ungovernable boy. I paced the streets by night and day, but until two hours ago all my efforts to find you were fruitless, and I never saw you for an instant."

"And now you do see me," said Monks, rising boldly, "what then? Fraud and robbery are high-sounding words—justified, you think, by a fancied resemblance in some young imp to a dead man's daub. Brother! You don't even know that a child was born of this maudlin pair; you don't even know that!"

"I *did not*," replied Mr. Brownlow, rising too. "But within the last fortnight I have learned it all. You have a brother; and you know him. There was a will, which your mother destroyed, leaving the secret and the gain to you at her own death. It contained a reference to some child likely to be the result of this sad connection, which child was born, and accidentally encountered by you, when your suspicions were first awakened by his resemblance to his father. You repaired to the place of his birth. There existed proofs of his birth and parentage. Those proofs were destroyed by you, and now, in your own words to your accomplice Fagin, '*the only proofs of the boy's identity lie at the bottom of the river.*' Unworthy son, coward, liar—you, who hold your councils with thieves and murderers in dark rooms at night—you, whose evil plots and wiles have brought a violent death on the head of one worth millions such as you—you, who from your cradle were gall and bitterness to your own father's heart—you, Edward Leeford, do you still brave me?"

"No, no, no!" returned the coward, overwhelmed by these accumulated charges.

"Every word," cried the old gentleman, "that has passed between you and this villain Fagin is known to me! Shadows have caught your whispers and brought them to my ear. The sight of the persecuted child has turned vice itself, and given it the courage and almost the attributes of virtue. Murder has been done, to which you were morally if not really a party!"

"No, no!" interposed Monks. "I know nothing of that. I thought the cause was a common quarrel."

"It was the partial disclosure of *your* secrets," replied Mr. Brownlow. "Will you now disclose the whole?"

"Yes, I will."

"Set your hand to a statement of truth and facts, and repeat it before witnesses?"

"That I promise too."

"You must do more than that," said Mr. Brownlow. "Make restitution to an innocent and unoffending child, for such he is, although the offspring of a guilty love. You have not forgotten the provisions of the will. Carry them into execution so far as your brother is concerned, and then go where you please."

Monks rose and started to pace up and down, meditating with dark and evil looks on this proposal, torn by his fears on the one hand and his hatred on the other, when the door was hurriedly unlocked, and Dr. Losberne entered the room in violent agitation. "The man will be taken," he cried. "He will be taken tonight!"

"The murderer?" asked Mr. Brownlow.

"Yes, yes," replied the other. "His dog has been seen lurking about some old haunt, and there seems little doubt that his master either is or will be there, under cover of darkness. Spies are hovering about in every direction. He cannot escape. A reward of a hundred pounds is proclaimed by Government tonight."

"I will give fifty more," said Mr. Brownlow, "and proclaim it with my own lips upon the spot, if I can reach it. Where is Mr. Maylie?"

"Harry? As soon as he had seen this man safe in a coach with you," replied the doctor, "he hurried off to where he heard this. Mounting his horse, he then sallied forth to join the first party at some place in the outskirts."

"Fagin," said Mr. Brownlow. "What of him?"

"When I last heard, he had not been taken, but he will be, or is, by this time. They're sure of him."

"Have you made up your mind?" asked Mr. Brownlow, in a low voice, of Monks.

"Yes," replied Monks. "You—you—will be secret with me?"

"I will. Remain here till I return. It is your only hope of safety." He and Dr. Losberne left the room, and the door was locked.

"What have you done?" asked the doctor in a whisper.

"All that I could hope to do. I left him no loophole of escape. Write and appoint the evening after tomorrow, at seven, for the meeting. But my blood boils to avenge that poor murdered girl. Which way have they taken?"

"Drive straight to the police office and you will be in time. I will remain here," said Dr. Losberne.

The two gentlemen hastily separated in a fever of excitement.

CHAPTER XX

NEAR A CERTAIN PART of the Thames in the borough of Southwark, where the buildings on the banks and the vessels on the river are dirtiest, there exists the filthiest, strangest locality in London. Offensive sights and smells come forth from the narrow alleys, and deafening clashes from the ponderous wagons that bear merchandise from the warehouses. In the remoter and less frequented streets there is every sign of desolation and neglect; tottering housefronts project over the pavement, and dismantled walls seem hesitating to fall.

In this neighborhood stands Jacob's Island, surrounded by a ditch eight feet deep and twenty wide when the tide is in, called Folly Ditch. The ditch is an inlet from the Thames and can be crossed by several wooden bridges. At high tide the inhabitants of the houses on either side lower, from their back doors and windows, buckets and pails in which they haul up water. The houses themselves have crazy wooden galleries, with holes which look down upon the slime beneath; and every repulsive indication of filth, rot, and poverty ornaments the banks of Folly Ditch.

In Jacob's Island itself the warehouses are roofless and empty;

the houses have no owners; they are broken open and entered upon by those who have the courage. They must have powerful motives for a secret residence, or be reduced to a destitute condition indeed, who seek a refuge in desolate Jacob's Island.

In an upper room of one of these houses whose back commanded the ditch—a detached house of fair size, ruinous in other respects but strongly defended at door and window—were two men who, regarding each other every now and then with perplexity, sat for some time in gloomy silence. One of these was Toby Crackit; the other was Mr. Tom Chitling.

"I wish," said Toby to Mr. Chitling, "that you had picked out some other crib when the two old ones got too warm, and had not come here to join me. Well, when was Fagin took?"

"Two o'clock this afternoon. Charley and I made our lucky up the wash'us chimney, and Bolter got into the empty water butt, head downward, but his legs were so precious long that they stuck out at the top, and so they took him, too."

"And the Dodger?"

"Also taken."

"And Bet?"

"Poor Bet! She went to see the body," replied Chitling, his countenance falling more and more, "and went off mad, screaming and raving; so that they put a strait-weskut on her and took her to the hospital—and there she is."

"And wot's come of young Charley Bates?"

"He hung about, not to come over here afore dark, but he'll be here soon. There's nowhere else to go to now, for the people at the Cripples are all in custody, and the bar is filled with traps."

"This is a smash," observed Toby, biting his lips. "They can prove Fagin an accessory before the fact, and he'll swing in six days, by God!"

"You should have heard the people roar," said Chitling. "They'd have torn Fagin away. You should have seen how he clung to the officers as if they were his dearest friends. I can see 'em now, dragging him along; the people jumping up, and snarling with their teeth and making at him; I can see the blood upon his hair and beard, and hear the women crying that they'd tear his heart out!"

The horror-stricken witness of this scene pressed his hands on his ears, got up and paced violently to and fro. While he was thus engaged, a pattering noise was heard on the stairs, and Sikes's dog bounded into the room through an open window.

"What's the meaning of this?" said Toby. "Sikes can't be coming here. I—I—hope not!"

"If he was coming here, he'd have come with the dog. He—he can't have made away with himself. What do you think?" said Chitling.

Toby shook his head.

The dog, creeping under a chair, coiled himself up to sleep. It being now dark, the shutter was closed, and a candle lighted and placed on the table. The terrible events of the last two days had made a deep impression on the two men. They drew their chairs close together, starting at every sound, as silent and awe-stricken as if the remains of the murdered woman lay in the next room.

They had sat thus some time when suddenly they heard a hurried knocking at the door below. The dog was on the alert in an instant and ran whining to the door. The knocking came again. Crackit went to the window over the narrow street; then, shaking all over, he drew in his head. There was no need to say who it was; his pale face was enough.

"We must let him in," he said, taking up the candle.

"Isn't there any help for it?" asked the other man in a hoarse voice.

"None. He *must* come in."

Crackit went down to the door, and returned followed by a man with the lower part of his face buried in a handkerchief. He drew the handkerchief slowly off. Blanched face, sunken eyes, hollow cheeks, three days' beard, wasted flesh; it was the very ghost of Sikes.

He laid his hand upon a chair which stood in the middle of the room; but as he was about to drop into it he shuddered, and glancing over his shoulder, he dragged it back close to the wall—as close as it would go—ground it against it—and sat down.

Not a word had been exchanged. He looked from one to the other in silence. If an eye were furtively raised and met his, it was instantly averted. When his hollow voice broke silence, both the others started.

"How came that dog here?" he asked.

"Alone. Three hours ago."

"Tonight's paper says that Fagin's took. Is it true?"

"True."

They were silent again.

"Damn you both!" said Sikes, passing his hand across his forehead. "Have you nothing to say to me?"

There was an uneasy movement, but neither spoke.

"You keep this house," said Sikes to Crackit. "Will you let me lie here till this hunt is over?"

"You may stop here, if you think it safe," returned the person addressed, after some hesitation.

Sikes looked behind him at the wall and said, "Is—is—the body—is it buried?"

They shook their heads.

"Why isn't it?" he retorted, with the same glance behind him. "Wot do they keep such ugly things above the ground for? Who's that knocking?"

Crackit intimated, by a motion of his hand as he left the room, that there was nothing to fear, and directly came back with Charley Bates behind him. The moment the boy saw Sikes he fell back.

"Toby," said the boy, "why didn't you tell me this downstairs?"

There had been something so tremendous in the shrinking off of the other two that the wretched man was willing to propitiate even this lad. He made as though he would shake hands with him.

"Let me go into some other room," said the boy, retreating.

"Charley!" said Sikes. "Don't you—don't you know me?"

"Don't come near me!" answered the boy, retreating, and looking with horror on the murderer's face. "You monster!"

Sikes stopped. They looked at each other, but Sikes's eyes sank gradually to the floor.

"Witness, you two!" cried the boy, shaking his clenched fist and becoming more excited as he spoke. "I'm not afraid of him—if they come here after him, I'll give him up, I will! He may kill me for it, but if I am here I'll give him up! Murder! Help! Murder!"

Pouring out these cries, and accompanying them with violent gesticulation, the boy actually threw himself, single-handed, upon the strong man, and in the intensity of his energy and the suddenness of his surprise, brought him heavily to the floor.

The two spectators seemed quite stupefied. They offered no interference, and the boy and man rolled on the floor together, the former never ceasing to call for help with all his might. The contest, however, was too unequal to last long. Sikes had Charley down, and his knee was on his throat, when Crackit pulled him back with a look of alarm and pointed to the window. There were lights gleaming below, loud voices, and the tramp of hurried footsteps crossing the nearest wooden bridge. The gleam of lights increased; the footsteps came more thickly. Then came a loud knocking at the door, and a hoarse murmur from a multitude of angry voices.

"Help!" shrieked the boy in a voice that rent the air. "He's here! Break down the door!"

Strokes, thick and heavy, rattled on the door and lower window shutters, and a loud huzzah burst from the crowd.

"Open the door of some place where I can lock this screeching hell-babe," cried Sikes, now dragging the boy as easily as if he were an empty sack. "That door. Quick!" He flung the boy through the door and turned the key. "Is the downstairs door fast?"

"Double-locked and chained," replied Crackit, still seeming bewildered.

"And the windows, too?"

"Yes."

"Damn you!" cried the desperate ruffian, throwing up the sash and menacing the crowd below. "Do your worst! I'll cheat you yet!"

Of all the terrific yells that ever fell on mortal ears, none could exceed the answering cry of the infuriated throng. Some shouted to those who were nearest to set the house on fire; others roared to the officers to shoot him dead. One man on horseback cried, beneath the window, in a voice that rose above all others, "Twenty guineas to the man who brings a ladder!" The nearest voices took up the cry, and hundreds echoed it. Some called for ladders, some for sledgehammers; some ran with torches to and fro as if to seek them; some pressed forward with the ecstasy of madmen; and all joined in one loud furious roar.

"The tide," cried the murderer, as he staggered back into the room and shut the faces out. "The tide was in as I came up. Give me a long rope. They're all in front. I may drop into the Folly Ditch and clear off that way. Give me a rope!"

Crackit pointed to where such articles were kept. The murderer, hastily selecting the longest and strongest cord, hurried to the housetop. There he planted a board, which he had carried up with him, so firmly against the door in the roof that it must be matter of great difficulty to open it from the inside; and creeping over the tiles, he looked over the low parapet.

The water was out, and the ditch a bed of mud.

The crowd had seen him come out on the roof, and some had begun to stream round the house. They had been hushed for a few moments, watching his motions and doubtful of his purpose. But the instant they perceived it and knew it was defeated, they raised a cry of triumphant execration to which all their previous shouting had been whispers. It seemed as though the whole city had poured its population out to curse him. The houses on the opposite side of the ditch had now been entered by the mob; there were tiers of faces in every window; and cluster upon cluster of people clung to every housetop. Each little bridge bent beneath the weight upon it.

"They have him now," cried a man on the nearest bridge. "Hurrah!"

"I will give fifty pounds," cried an old gentleman from the same quarter, "to the man who takes him alive!"

Sikes had shrunk down, quelled by the ferocity of the crowd, and the impossibility of escape; but now he sprang to his feet, determined to make one last effort for his life by dropping into the ditch, and, at the risk of being stifled in the mud, endeavoring to get away in the darkness and confusion. Roused into new strength

The Last Chance

and energy, and stimulated by noise within the house which announced that an entrance had been effected, he fastened one end of the rope firmly round a chimney stack, and with the other made a strong running noose. He could let himself down by the rope to within a short distance of the ground, and he had his knife ready in his hand to cut it then and drop.

At the very instant when he brought the loop over his head previous to slipping it beneath his armpits—at that very instant, however—the murderer, looking behind him on the roof, threw his arms above his head and uttered a yell of terror.

"The eyes again!" he cried in an unearthly screech.

Staggering as if struck by lightning, he lost his balance and tumbled over the parapet. The noose was on his neck. It ran up with his weight, tight as a bowstring, as he fell for five and thirty feet. There was a sudden jerk, a terrific convulsion of the limbs; and the murderer swung lifeless against the wall with the open knife clutched in his stiffening hand.

A dog, which had lain concealed till now, ran backwards and forwards on the parapet with a dismal howl, and collecting himself for a spring, jumped for the dead man's shoulders. Missing his aim, he fell into the ditch, turning completely over as he went, and striking his head against a stone, dashed out his brains.

··❧· CHAPTER XXI ·❦··

TWO DAYS after these events Oliver found himself, at three o'clock in the afternoon, in a carriage rolling fast towards his native town. Mrs. Maylie, Rose, Mrs. Bedwin, and the good doctor were with him; and Mr. Brownlow followed in a post chaise, accompanied by one other person whose name had not been mentioned.

Oliver was in a flutter of agitation and uncertainty which almost deprived him of speech. He and the two ladies had been very carefully made acquainted by Mr. Brownlow with the nature of the admissions which had been forced from Monks, and although they knew that the object of their present journey was to complete the work which had been begun, still the whole matter was enveloped in enough mystery to leave them in the most intense suspense.

Mr. Brownlow had also, with Dr. Losberne's assistance, cautiously stopped all channels of communication through which they could receive intelligence of the dreadful occurrences that had so recently taken place. So they traveled on in silence, each busied with reflections and no one disposed to give utterance to his thoughts.

But if Oliver had remained silent while they journeyed, what a crowd of emotions and recollections were wakened in his breast when they turned into that road which he had traversed on foot, a poor, homeless, wandering boy, without a friend to help him! "See there, there!" he cried, eagerly clasping Rose's hand and pointing out of the carriage window. "That's the stile I came over, there are the hedges I crept behind for fear anyone should overtake me and force me back! Yonder is the path across the fields, leading to the cottage where I was a little child! Oh Dick, Dick, my dear old friend, if I could only see you now!"

"You will see him soon," replied Rose, gently taking his folded hands between her own. "You shall tell him how happy you are, and how rich you have grown, and that in all your happiness you have none so great as the coming back to make him happy too."

"Yes, yes," said Oliver, "and we'll—we'll take him away from here, and have him clothed and taught, and send him to some quiet country place where he may grow strong and well—shall we?"

Rose nodded "Yes," for the boy was smiling through such happy tears that she could not speak.

"He said 'God bless you' to me when I ran away," cried the boy, with a burst of affectionate emotion; "and I will say 'God bless *you*' now, and show him how I love him for it!"

As they approached the town and at length drove through its narrow streets, it became matter of no small difficulty to restrain the boy within reasonable bounds. There was Sowerberry's, the undertaker's, smaller and less imposing than he remembered it; there was the workhouse, with its dismal windows frowning on the street; there was the same porter standing at the gate, at sight of whom Oliver involuntarily shrank back, and then laughed at himself for being so foolish; there was nearly everything as if he had left it but yesterday, and all his recent life had been but a dream.

But it was pure, earnest, joyful reality. They drove straight to the door of the chief hotel (which Oliver used to think a mighty palace, but which had somehow fallen off in grandeur); and here was Mr. Grimwig all ready to receive them when they got out of the coach, all smiles and kindness, and not once offering to eat his head. There was dinner prepared, and there were bedrooms ready, and everything was arranged as if by magic.

Notwithstanding all this, when the hurry of the first half hour was over, the same silence and constraint prevailed that had marked their journey down. Mr. Brownlow did not join them at dinner, but remained in a separate room. The two other gentlemen hurried in and out and conversed apart. Once Mrs. Maylie was called away, and after being absent for nearly an hour, returned with eyes swollen with weeping. These things made Rose and Oliver nervous and uncomfortable, and they sat wondering in silence, or spoke in whispers.

At length, when nine o'clock had come and they began to think they were to hear no more that night, Dr. Losberne and Mr. Grimwig entered the room, followed by Mr. Brownlow and a man whom Oliver almost shrieked with surprise to see; for they told him it was his brother, and it was the same man he had met at the market town, and seen looking in with Fagin at the window of his little room. Monks cast a look of hate at the astonished boy and sat down near the door. Mr. Brownlow, who had papers in his hand, walked towards him.

"This is a painful task," he said, "but these declarations, which have been signed in London before many gentlemen, must be in substance repeated here. We must hear them from your own lips before we part, and you know why."

"Go on," said the person addressed, turning away his face. "I have done enough, I think. Don't keep me here."

"This child," said Mr. Brownlow, drawing Oliver to him and laying his hand on his head, "is your half brother, the illegitimate son of your father, my dear friend Edwin Leeford, by poor young Agnes Fleming, who died in giving him birth."

"Yes," said Monks, scowling at the trembling boy, the beating of whose heart he might have heard. "That is their bastard child."

"The term you use," said Mr. Brownlow sternly, "is a reproach to those who long since passed beyond the feeble censure of the world. It reflects disgrace on no one living except you who use it. Let that pass. He was born in this town."

"In the workhouse of this town," was the sullen reply. "His father, being taken ill at Rome, was joined by his wife, my mother, from whom he had been long separated, who took me with her from Paris. He knew nothing of us, for his senses were gone, and the next day he died. Among the papers in his desk were two dated on the night his illness first came on, directed to yourself"—he here addressed himself to Mr. Brownlow—"and enclosed in a few short lines to you, with an intimation on the cover of the package that it was not to be forwarded till after he was dead. One of these papers was a letter to this girl Agnes; the other a will."

"What of the letter?" asked Mr. Brownlow.

"The letter? A penitent confession. He had palmed a tale on the girl that some secret mystery prevented his marrying her just then; and so she had gone on, trusting patiently to him, until she trusted too far, and lost what none could ever give her back. She was, at that time, within a few months of her confinement. He told her all he had meant to do, to hide her shame, if he had lived, and prayed her, if he died, not to curse his memory. He reminded her of the day he had given her the little locket and the ring with her Christian name engraved upon it, and a blank left for his name which he hoped one day to have bestowed on her—prayed her yet to wear it next her heart—and then ran on, wildly, as if he had gone distracted. I believe he had."

"The will?" said Mr. Brownlow as Oliver's tears fell fast.

Monks was silent.

"The will," said Mr. Brownlow, speaking for him, "was in the same spirit as the letter. He talked of miseries which his wife had brought on him; of the rebellious disposition, vice, and malice of you his only son, who had been trained to hate him; and left you and your mother each an annuity of eight hundred pounds. The bulk of his property he divided into two equal portions—one for Agnes Fleming, and the other for their child, if it should be born alive, and ever come of age. If it were a girl, it was to inherit the money unconditionally; but if a boy, only on the stipulation that in his minority he should never have stained his name with any public act of dishonor, meanness, cowardice, or wrong. He did this, he said, to mark his confidence in the mother, and his conviction that the child would share her gentle heart and noble nature. If he were disappointed in this expectation, then the money was to come to you: for then, and not till then, when both children were equal, would he recognize your prior claim upon his purse, who had none upon his heart, but had, from infancy, repulsed him."

"My mother," said Monks in a louder tone, "did what a woman should have done. She burned this will. The letter never reached its destination, but that and other proofs she kept, in case they ever tried to lie away the blot. The girl's father had the truth from my mother, with every aggravation that her violent hate could add. Goaded by shame and dishonor, he fled with his children into a remote corner of Wales, changing his very name so that his friends might never know of his retreat. But the girl left her home in secret. He searched for her in every town and village near; but he returned home convinced that she had destroyed herself to hide her shame and his; and on that night his old heart broke, and he was found dead in his bed."

There was a short silence here, until Mr. Brownlow took up the thread of the narrative.

"Years after this," he said, "this man's—Edward Leeford's—mother came to me. He had left her, when he was only eighteen; had robbed her of jewels and money; gambled, squandered, forged, and fled to London, where for two years he had associated with the lowest outcasts. She was sinking under an incurable disease, and wished to recover him before she died. Inquiries and searches were made, which were ultimately successful, and he went back with her to France."

"There she died," said Monks, "and on her deathbed she bequeathed these secrets to me, together with her deadly hatred of all whom they involved—though I had inherited the hatred long be-fore. She would not believe that the girl had destroyed herself and the child too, but was filled with the impression that a male child had been born and was alive. I swore to her, if ever it crossed my path, to hunt it down; to pursue it with the bitterest hatred; and to spit on that insulting will by dragging the child, if I could, to the very gallows foot. She was right. He came in my way at last. I began well; and but for babbling drabs, I would have finished as I began!"

As the villain folded his arms together, impotently muttering curses, Mr. Brownlow turned to the terrified group and explained that Fagin, who had been Monks's accomplice, had received a large reward for keeping Oliver ensnared. Some part of this reward was to be given up in the event of Oliver's being rescued; and a dispute on this head had led to their visit to the country house for the pur-pose of identifying him.

"The locket and ring?" said Mr. Brownlow, turning to Monks.

"I bought them from the man and woman I told you of, who stole them from the nurse, who stole them from the corpse," an-swered Monks. "You know what became of them."

Mr. Brownlow merely nodded to Mr. Grimwig, who, disap-pearing with alacrity, shortly returned, pushing in Mrs. Bumble and dragging her unwilling consort after him.

"Do my eyes deceive me," cried Mr. Bumble with ill-feigned enthusiasm, "or is that little Oliver? Oh, O-li-ver, if you know'd how I've been a-grieving for you—"

"Hold your tongue, fool," murmured Mrs. Bumble.

"Can't I be supposed to feel?" remonstrated the workhouse mas-ter. "*I* as brought him up porochially—when I see him a-setting here among ladies and gentlemen of the very affablest description!"

"Do you know that person?" asked Mr. Brownlow, pointing to Monks.

"No," replied Mrs. Bumble flatly.

"Perhaps *you* don't?" said Mr. Brownlow, addressing her spouse.

"I never saw him in all my life," said Mr. Bumble.

"Nor sold him anything, perhaps?"

"No," replied Mrs. Bumble.

"You never had, perhaps, a certain gold locket and ring?" said Mr. Brownlow.

"Certainly not," replied the matron. "Why are we brought here to answer to such nonsense as this?"

Again Mr. Brownlow nodded to Mr. Grimwig, and again that gentleman limped away. This time he led in two palsied old women, who shook and tottered as they walked.

"You shut the door the night old Sally died," said the foremost one, raising her shriveled hand, "but you couldn't shut out the sound, or stop the chinks."

"No, no," said the other, wagging her toothless jaws. "No, no, no."

"We heard old Sally try to tell you what she'd done, and saw you take a paper from her hand, and watched you, too, next day, when you went to the pawnbroker's shop," said the first.

"Yes," added the second, "it was a locket and gold ring. We found out that, and saw it given you. We were by. Oh, we were by!"

"And we know more than that," resumed the first, "for Sally told us long ago that the young mother had told her that, after being taken ill, she was on her way to die near the grave of the father of the child, feeling she should never get over it."

"Would you like to see the pawnbroker himself?" asked Mr. Grimwig, with a motion toward the door.

"No," replied Mrs. Bumble. "If he"—she pointed to Monks—"has been coward enough to confess, as I see he has, and you have found these hags, I have nothing more to say. I *did* sell the locket and ring, and they're where you'll never get them. What then?"

"Nothing," replied Mr. Brownlow, "except that it remains for us to take care that neither of you is employed in a situation of trust again. You may leave the room."

"I hope," said Mr. Bumble, looking about him with great ruefulness as Mr. Grimwig disappeared with the two old women, "that this unfortunate little circumstance will not deprive me of my porochial office?"

"Indeed it will," replied Mr. Brownlow. "You may make up your mind to that."

"It was all Mrs. Bumble. She *would* do it," urged Mr. Bumble, first ascertaining that his partner had left the room.

"That is no excuse," replied Mr. Brownlow. "You were present on the occasion of the destruction of these trinkets, and are the more guilty of the two, in the eye of the law, for the law supposes that your wife acts under your direction."

"If the law supposes that," said Mr. Bumble, squeezing his hat emphatically in both hands, "the law is a idiot! If that's the eye of the law, the law is a bachelor. And the worst I wish the law is, that his eye may be opened by experience—by experience."

Mr. Bumble fixed his hat on and followed his helpmate.

"Young lady," said Mr. Brownlow, turning to Rose, "give me your hand. Do not tremble. You need not fear to hear the few remaining words we have to say."

"If they have any reference to me," said Rose, "pray let me hear them at some other time. I have not strength or spirits now."

"Nay," returned the old gentleman, drawing her arm through his, "you have more fortitude than this, I am sure. Do you know this young lady, sir?"

"Yes," replied Monks.

"I never saw you before," said Rose faintly.

"I have seen you often," returned Monks.

"The father of the unhappy Agnes had *two* daughters," said Mr. Brownlow. "What was the fate of the other—the child?"

"The child," replied Monks, "when her father died in Wales, in a strange place, under a strange name, without a letter, book, or scrap of paper that yielded the faintest clue by which his friends or relatives could be traced—the child was taken by some wretched cottagers, who reared her as their own."

"Go on," said Mr. Brownlow, signing to Mrs. Maylie to approach. "Go on."

"You couldn't find the spot to which these people had repaired," said Monks, "but my mother found it, and found the child."

"She took it, did she?"

"No. The people were poor and began to sicken of their fine humanity; but she left the child with them, giving them a small present of money, and promised more, which she never meant to send. She didn't quite rely, however, on their discontent and poverty for the child's unhappiness, but told the history of the sister's shame with such alterations as suited her; bade them take good heed of the child, for she came of bad blood; and told them she was illegitimate, and sure to go wrong at some time or other. The circumstances countenanced all this; the people believed it; and there the child dragged on an existence miserable enough to satisfy us until a widow lady, residing then at Chester, saw the girl by chance, pitied her, and took her home. In spite of all our efforts she remained there and was happy. I lost sight of her two or three years ago, and saw her no more until a few months back."

"Do you see her now?"

"Yes. Leaning on your arm."

"But not the less my niece," cried Mrs. Maylie, folding the girl in her arms, "not the less my dearest child! I would not lose her now, for all the treasures of the world!"

"The only friend I ever had," cried Rose, clinging to her. "The kindest, best of friends. My heart will burst. I cannot bear all this."

"You have borne more, and have been the best and gentlest creature that ever shed happiness on everyone she knew," said Mrs. Maylie tenderly. "Come, my love, remember who this is who waits to clasp you in his arms! Look, my dear!"

"Not Aunt," cried Oliver, throwing his arms about her neck. "I'll never call her Aunt—but sister, my own dear sister, that something taught my heart to love so dearly from the first! Rose, dear, darling Rose!"

Let the tears which fell, and the broken words which were exchanged in the long close embrace between the orphans, be sacred. A father, sister, and mother were gained, and lost, in that one moment. Joy and grief were mingled in the cup. All the others left the room, and they were a long, long time alone.

At length a soft tap at the door announced that someone else was without. Oliver opened it, glided away, and gave place to Harry Maylie.

"Dear Rose, I know it all," he said, taking a seat beside the girl.

"Do you guess that I have come to remind you of a promise? You gave me leave, at any time within a year, to renew the subject of our last discourse."

"I did," said Rose.

"I was to lay whatever of station or fortune I might possess at your feet, and if you still adhered to your former determination, I pledged myself by no word or act to seek to change it."

"The same reasons which influenced me then will influence me now," said Rose firmly. "The disclosure of tonight leaves me in the same position, with reference to you, as that in which I stood before."

"You harden your heart against me, Rose," urged her lover.

"Oh, Harry," said the young lady, bursting into tears, "I wish I could, and spare myself this pain."

"Then why inflict it on yourself?" said Harry, taking her hand. "Think, dear Rose, think what you have heard tonight."

"And what have I heard?" cried Rose. "That a sense of his deep disgrace so worked on my own father that he shunned all—there, we have said enough, Harry."

"Not yet," said the young man, detaining her as she rose. "My hopes, my wishes, my prospects—every thought in life except my love for you—have undergone a change. I offer you, now, no distinction among a bustling crowd, no mingling with a world of malice and detraction, but a home—a heart and home—yes, dearest Rose, and those, and those alone, are *all* I have to offer."

"What do you mean?" she asked.

"I mean this—that when I left you last, I left you with a firm determination to level all fancied barriers between yourself and me, resolved that if my world could not be yours, I would make yours mine. This I have done. Such power and patronage, such relatives of influence and rank as smiled upon me, look coldly now. But in England's richest county, and by one village church—mine, Rose, my church now—there stands a rustic dwelling which you can make me prouder of than all the hopes I have renounced, measured a thousandfold. This church—this dwelling—is *my* rank and station now, and here I lay it down!"

"IT'S A TRYING THING waiting supper for lovers," said Mr. Grimwig, waking up, and pulling his pocket-handkerchief from over his head.

Truth to tell, the supper had been waiting a most unreasonable time. Neither Mrs. Maylie, nor Harry, nor Rose (who now came in together) could offer a word in extenuation.

"I had serious thoughts of eating my head tonight," said Mr. Grimwig, "for I began to think I should get nothing else. I'll take the liberty, if you'll allow me, of saluting the bride that is to be."

Mr. Grimwig lost no time in carrying this notice into effect on the blushing girl, and the example, being contagious, was followed both by the doctor and Mr. Brownlow. Some people affirm that Harry Maylie had been observed to set the example originally, in a dark room adjoining; but the best authorities consider this downright scandal—he being young and a clergyman.

"Oliver, my child," said Mrs. Maylie, "where have you been, and why do you look so sad? There are tears stealing down your face at this moment. What is the matter?"

It is a world of disappointment; often to the hopes we most cherish, and hopes that do our nature the greatest honor.

Poor Dick was dead!

·•❧· CHAPTER XXII ·☙•·

THE COURTROOM WAS PAVED, from floor to roof, with human faces. From the rail before the dock, away into the smallest corner in the galleries, all looks were fixed upon one man—Fagin. He seemed to stand surrounded by a firmament bright with gleaming eyes.

He stood there, in all this glare of living light, with one hand resting on the wooden slab before him, the other held to his ear and his head thrust forward, to enable him to catch with greater distinctness every word of the presiding judge, who was delivering his charge to the jury. At times he turned his eyes sharply upon the jurymen to observe the effect of the slightest featherweight in his favor. Beyond this he stirred not hand or foot. He had scarcely moved since the trial began, and now that the judge ceased to speak, he still remained in the same strained attitude of close attention.

A slight bustle in the court recalled him to himself, and he saw that the jurymen had turned together to consider their verdict. As his eyes wandered to the gallery, he could see the people rising above each other to see his face. A few there were who seemed unmindful of him and looked only to the jury, but in no one face could he read the faintest sympathy with himself, or any feeling but one of all-absorbing interest that he should be condemned.

He looked wistfully into the faces of the jurors, one by one, when they passed out, as though to see which way the greater number leaned; but that was fruitless. The jailer touched his shoulder and motioned him to a chair. Mechanically he sat down. He looked up into the gallery again. Some of the people were eating, and one young man was sketching his face in a little notebook. He wondered if it was a good likeness, and looked on when the artist broke his pencil point and made another with his knife, as any idle spectator might have done. In the same way he turned his eyes towards the judge, and his mind began to busy itself with the fashion of his dress. Not that, all this time, his mind was for an instant free from an overwhelming sense of the grave that opened at his feet; and yet he could not fix his thoughts on it. Thus, even while he trembled, and turned burning hot at the idea of speedy death, he fell to counting the iron spikes before him, and wondering how the head of one had been broken off. Then he thought of all the horrors of the gallows and the scaffold—and stopped to watch a man sprinkling the floor to cool it—and then went on to think again.

At length there was a cry of silence, and a breathless look from all towards the door. The jury returned. He could glean nothing from their faces; they might as well have been of stone. Perfect stillness ensued—not a rustle—not a breath. Guilty.

The building rang with a tremendous shout, and another, and another; the echoes gathered strength, swelling out like angry thunder. It was a peal of joy from the populace outside, greeting the news that he would die on Monday.

The noise subsided, and he was asked if he had anything to say why sentence of death should not be passed on him. Standing once more, he had resumed his listening attitude, but the demand was twice repeated before he seemed to hear it, and then he only muttered that he was an old man—an old man—and so, dropping into a whisper, he was silent again.

The judge assumed the black cap. The address was solemn and impressive; the sentence fearful to hear. The prisoner now stood like a marble figure; and his haggard face was still thrust forward, his eyes staring out before him, when the jailer put his hand on his arm and beckoned him away. He gazed stupidly about him for an instant, and obeyed.

They led him through a paved room under the court, where some prisoners were waiting till their turns came, and as he passed they fell back, to render him more visible to the people who were clinging to the bars; and they assailed him with opprobrious names, and screeched and hissed. He shook his fist, and his conductors hurried him on through a gloomy passage into the interior of the prison. Here he was searched, that he might not have about him the means of anticipating the law. Then they led him to one of the condemned cells, and left him there—alone.

He sat down on a stone bench, which served for seat and bedstead, and casting his bloodshot eyes upon the floor, tried to collect his thoughts. After a while he began to remember what the judge had said, though it had seemed to him, at the time, that he could not hear a word. To be hanged by the neck till he was dead—that was the end.

As it came on very dark he began to think of all the men he had known who had died on the scaffold, some of them through his means. He had seen some of them die—and had joked, too, because they had died with prayers on their lips. With what a rattling noise the drop went down; and how suddenly they changed from vigorous men to dangling heaps of clothes! Some of them might have inhabited that very cell—sat upon that very spot. It was very dark; why didn't they bring a light? Scores of men must have passed their last hours here. Light, light!

At length, when his hands were raw with beating against the

Fagin in the Condemned Cell

heavy door, two men appeared, one bearing a candle, which he thrust into an iron candlestick fixed against the wall, the other dragging in a mattress on which to pass the night; for the prisoner was to be left alone no more. Then came dark, dismal night; and the sound of the church clocks striking brought despair. The boom of every iron bell came laden with the one hollow sound—Death.

The day was gone as soon as come—and night came on again, night so long and yet so short. Venerable men of his own persuasion came to pray beside him, but he drove them away with curses.

Saturday night. He had only one night more to live. And as he thought of this, the day broke—Sunday. It was not until the night of this last awful day that a withering sense of his helpless, desperate state came in its full intensity upon his blighted soul. With gasping mouth and burning skin he hurried to and fro in a paroxysm of fear and wrath. His red hair hung down on his bloodless face; his beard was twisted into knots; his eyes shone with a feverish light. He grew so terrible in all the tortures of his evil conscience that one man could not bear to sit there eyeing him alone, so two kept watch together.

As night fell, the space before the prison was cleared, and a few strong barriers had been already thrown across the road to break the pressure of the expected crowd, when Mr. Brownlow and Oliver appeared at the wicket and presented an order of admission to the prisoner.

"Is the young gentleman to come too, sir?" said the man who was to conduct them. "It's not a sight for children, sir."

"It is not indeed, my friend," rejoined Mr. Brownlow, "but my business with this man is intimately connected with him, and as this child has seen him in the full career of his success and villainy, I think it as well—even at the cost of some pain and fear—that he should see him now."

These few words had been said apart, so as to be inaudible to Oliver. The man glanced at Oliver with some curiosity, and led them through dark and winding ways towards the cells. Finally he motioned them to follow him into a cell. They did so.

The condemned criminal was seated on his bed, rocking himself from side to side, with a countenance more like that of a snared beast than the face of a man. His mind was evidently wandering to his old life, for he continued to mutter without appearing conscious of their presence other than as a part of his vision.

"Good boy, Charley—well done—" he mumbled. "Oliver too—quite the gentleman now—quite the—take that boy away to bed! Do you hear me? He has been the—the—somehow the cause of all this. It's worth the money to bring him up to it."

"Fagin," said the jailer.

"That's me!" he cried, falling, instantly, into the attitude of listening he had assumed upon his trial. "An old man, my lord; a very old, old man!"

"Here's somebody wants to see you," said the jailer. "Fagin, Fagin! Are you a man?"

"I shan't be one long," he replied, looking up with no human expression but rage and terror. "Strike them all dead! What right have they to butcher me?"

As he spoke he caught sight of Oliver and Mr. Brownlow and shrank to the farthest corner of the seat.

"Steady," said the jailer. "Now sir, tell him what you want."

"You have some papers," said Mr. Brownlow, "which were placed in your hands for better security by a man called Monks."

"It's all a lie," replied Fagin. "I haven't one—not one!"

"For the love of God," said Mr. Brownlow solemnly, "do not say that now, on the very verge of death, but tell me where they are. Sikes is dead; Monks has confessed. Where are those papers?"

"Oliver," cried Fagin, beckoning to him. "Here, here! Let me whisper to you."

"I am not afraid," said Oliver in a low voice as he relinquished Mr. Brownlow's hand.

"The papers," said Fagin, drawing Oliver towards him, "are in a canvas bag, in a hole a little way up the chimney in the top front room. I want to talk to you, my dear. I want to talk to you."

"Yes, yes," returned Oliver. "Let me say a prayer. Do! And we will talk till morning."

OLIVER TWIST

"Outside, outside!" replied Fagin, pushing the boy before him towards the door. "You can get me out, if you take me so. Now!"

"Oh, God, forgive this wretched man!" cried the boy with a burst of tears.

"That's right, that'll help us," said Fagin. "This door first. Hurry!"

"You had better leave, sir," said the jailer to Mr. Brownlow. The door of the cell opened, and the two attendants entered.

"Press on, press on," cried Fagin. "Faster!"

The men laid hands on him, and disengaging Oliver from his grasp, held him back. He struggled with the power of desperation for an instant, and then sent up cry upon cry that rang in their ears until they reached the open yard.

It was some time before they left the prison. Oliver was so weak that for an hour he had not the strength to walk.

Day was dawning when they emerged. A great multitude had already assembled; the windows were filled with people; the crowd were pushing, quarreling, joking. Everything told of life and animation, except one dark cluster of objects in the center of all—the black stage, the crossbeam, the rope, and all the hideous apparatus of death.

THE FORTUNES OF THOSE who have figured in this tale are nearly closed. The little that remains to relate of them is told in few and simple words.

Before three months had passed, Rose Fleming and Harry Maylie were married in the village church which was henceforth to be the scene of the young clergyman's labors. On the same day they entered into possession of their new and happy home.

Mrs. Maylie took up her abode with her son and daughter-in-law, to enjoy, during the tranquil remainder of her days, the contemplation of the happiness of those on whom the warmest affections of her well-spent life had been unceasingly bestowed.

It appeared on full and careful investigation, that if the wreck of property remaining in the custody of Monks were equally divided between himself and Oliver, it would yield, to each, little more than three thousand pounds. By the provisions of his father's will, Oliver would have been entitled to the whole; but Mr. Brownlow, unwilling to deprive the elder son of the opportunity of retrieving himself and of pursuing an honest career, proposed this mode of distribution, to which his young charge joyfully acceded.

Monks, still bearing that assumed name, retired with his portion to a distant part of the New World; where, having quickly squandered it, he once more fell into his old courses, and, after undergoing a long confinement for some fresh act of knavery, at length died in prison. As, indeed, died the chief remaining members of his friend Fagin's gang.

Mr. Brownlow adopted Oliver as his son. Removing with him and the old housekeeper to within a mile of the parsonage house where his dear friends resided, he gratified the only remaining wish of Oliver's warm and earnest heart, and thus linked together a little society, whose condition approached as nearly to one of perfect happiness as can ever be known in this changing world.

Soon after the marriage of the young people, the worthy doctor returned to Chertsey, where for two or three months he contented himself with hinting that he feared the air began to disagree with him. Then, finding that the place really no longer was to him what it had been, he settled his business on his assistant, took a bachelor's cottage outside the village of which his young friend was pastor, and instantaneously recovered. He had managed to contract a strong friendship for Mr. Grimwig, which that eccentric gentleman cordially reciprocated, and he is accordingly visited by Mr. Grimwig a great many times in the course of the year.

Mr. and Mrs. Bumble, deprived of their situations, were gradually reduced to great indigence and misery, and finally became paupers in that very same workhouse in which they had once lorded it over others. Mr. Bumble has been heard to say that in this degradation he has not even spirits to be thankful for being separated from his wife.

As to Mr. Giles and Brittles, they still remain in their old posts, at the parsonage, but divide their attentions so equally among its inmates, and Oliver, and Mr. Brownlow, and Dr. Losberne, that to this day the villagers have never been able to discover to which establishment they properly belong.

Master Charles Bates, appalled by Sikes's crime, fell into a train of reflection whether an honest life was not, after all, the best. Arriving at the conclusion that it was, he turned his back upon the past. He struggled hard and suffered much for some time; but succeeded in the end, and, from being a farmer's drudge and a carrier's lad, is now the merriest young grazier in all Northamptonshire.

How Mr. Brownlow went on from day to day, becoming more and more attached to his adopted child as his nature showed the thriving seeds of all he wished him to become—how he traced in him new traits of his early friend that awakened old remembrances, melancholy and yet sweet—how the two orphans remembered the lessons of adversity in mercy to others, and mutual love, and fervent thanks to Him who had protected them—these are all matters which need not to be told; I have said that they were truly happy, and they were.

Within the altar of the old village church there stands a white marble tablet which bears as yet but one word: AGNES. There is no coffin in that tomb; and may it be many, many years before another name is placed above it! But if the spirits of the dead ever come back to earth to visit spots hallowed by the love—the love beyond the grave—of those whom they knew in life, then surely the shade of Agnes sometimes hovers round that solemn nook. I believe it none the less because that nook is in a church, and she was weak and erring.

A Selection of

MODERN
AMERICAN
POETRY

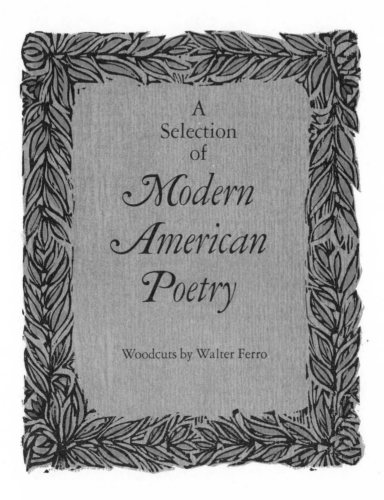

A
Selection
of

Modern

American

Poetry

Woodcuts by Walter Ferro

A poet is a rather special kind of philosopher—a person who looks behind the face of everyday things for the realities of life, the truths of existence. A poet expresses the truths he finds in verbal images—some drawn from nature, including human nature, some from his imagination. There is nothing in human experience that the poet may not touch on—humor, despair, beauty, the craftsman's skill, love, loneliness, death.

In this country during the eighteenth and nineteenth centuries a great many poets were writing, but most of their work was imitative of the British verse of the time. It was not until the advent of Walt Whitman and Emily Dickinson that the voice of a truly original and distinctive American poetry began to be heard. They were the first "modern" American poets, and their work has had a profound influence on later writers here and abroad.

In this brief selection of poetry, then, we have included only poems written by Americans during the last hundred years or so. The thoughts and feelings they express, however, are timeless and have no geographical boundaries. They speak to all men in all places, and so they can be called universal.

It is the hope of the editors that every reader will find here some poem that seems addressed particularly to him, and that this small selection will tempt him to explore on his own the world's rich heritage of poetry.

John Updike
1932–

Youth's Progress

Dick Schneider of Wisconsin . . . was elected "Greek
God" for an interfraternity ball.   —*Life*

When I was born, my mother taped my ears
So they lay flat. When I had aged ten years,
My teeth were firmly braced and much improved.
Two years went by; my tonsils were removed.

At fourteen, I began to comb my hair
A fancy way. Though nothing much was there,
I shaved my upper lip—next year, my chin.
At seventeen, the freckles left my skin.

Just turned nineteen, a nicely molded lad,
I said goodbye to Sis and Mother; Dad
Drove me to Wisconsin and set me loose.
At twenty-one, I was elected Zeus.

E. E. Cummings
1894–1962

in Just-

in Just-
spring   when the world is mud-
luscious the little
lame balloonman

whistles   far   and wee

and eddieandbill come
running from marbles and
piracies and it's
spring

when the world is puddle-wonderful

the queer
old balloonman whistles
far   and   wee
and bettyandisbel come dancing

from hop-scotch and jump-rope and

it's
spring
and
    the

          goat-footed

balloonMan   whistles
far
and
wee

---

i am a little church

i am a little church(no great cathedral)
far from the splendor and squalor of hurrying cities
—i do not worry if briefer days grow briefest,
i am not sorry when sun and rain make april

my life is the life of the reaper and the sower;
my prayers are prayers of earth's own clumsily striving
(finding and losing and laughing and crying)children
whose any sadness or joy is my grief or my gladness

around me surges a miracle of unceasing
birth and glory and death and resurrection:
over my sleeping self float flaming symbols
of hope,and i wake to a perfect patience of mountains

i am a little church(far from the frantic
world with its rapture and anguish)at peace with nature
—i do not worry if longer nights grow longest;
i am not sorry when silence becomes singing

winter by spring,i lift my diminutive spire to
merciful Him Whose only now is forever:
standing erect in the deathless truth of His presence
(welcoming humbly His light and proudly His darkness)

maggie and milly and molly and may

maggie and milly and molly and may
went down to the beach(to play one day)

and maggie discovered a shell that sang
so sweetly she couldn't remember her troubles,and

milly befriended a stranded star
whose rays five languid fingers were;

and molly was chased by a horrible thing
which raced sideways while blowing bubbles:and

may came home with a smooth round stone
as small as a world and as large as alone.

For whatever we lose(like a you or a me)
it's always ourselves we find in the sea

Rosemary and Stephen Vincent Benét
1900–1962   1898–1943

Nancy Hanks

If Nancy Hanks
Came back as a ghost,
Seeking news
Of what she loved most,
She'd ask first
"Where's my son?
What's happened to Abe?
What's he done?

"Poor little Abe,
Left all alone
Except for Tom,
Who's a rolling stone;
He was only nine
The year I died.
I remember still
How hard he cried.

"Scraping along
In a little shack,
With hardly a shirt
To cover his back,
And a prairie wind
To blow him down,
Or pinching times
If he went to town.

"You wouldn't know
About my son?
Did he grow tall?
Did he have fun?
Did he learn to read?
Did he get to town?
Do you know his name?
Did he get on?"

Stephen Vincent Benét

The Ballad of William Sycamore

My father, he was a mountaineer,
His fist was a knotty hammer;
He was quick on his feet as a running deer,
And he spoke with a Yankee stammer.

My mother, she was merry and brave,
And so she came to her labor,
With a tall green fir for her doctor grave
And a stream for her comforting neighbor.

And some are wrapped in the linen fine,
And some like a godling's scion;
But I was cradled on twigs of pine
In the skin of a mountain lion.

And some remember a white, starched lap
And a ewer with silver handles;
But I remember a coonskin cap
And the smell of bayberry candles.

The cabin logs, with the bark still rough,
And my mother who laughed at trifles,
And the tall, lank visitors, brown as snuff,
With their long, straight squirrel-rifles.

I can hear them dance, like a foggy song,
Through the deepest one of my slumbers,
The fiddle squeaking the boots along
And my father calling the numbers.

The quick feet shaking the puncheon-floor,
And the fiddle squealing and squealing,
Till the dried herbs rattled above the door
And the dust went up to the ceiling.

There are children lucky from dawn till dusk,
But never a child so lucky!
For I cut my teeth on "Money Musk"
In the Bloody Ground of Kentucky!

When I grew tall as the Indian corn,
My father had little to lend me,
But he gave me his great, old powder-horn
And his woodsman's skill to befriend me.

With a leather shirt to cover my back,
And a redskin nose to unravel
Each forest sign, I carried my pack
As far as a scout could travel.

Till I lost my boyhood and found my wife,
A girl like a Salem clipper!
A woman straight as a hunting-knife
With eyes as bright as the Dipper!

We cleared our camp where the buffalo feed,
Unheard-of streams were our flagons;
And I sowed my sons like the apple-seed
On the trail of the Western wagons.

They were right, tight boys, never sulky or slow,
A fruitful, a goodly muster.
The eldest died at the Alamo.
The youngest fell with Custer.

The letter that told it burned my hand.
Yet we smiled and said, "So be it!"
But I could not live when they fenced the land,
For it broke my heart to see it.

I saddled a red, unbroken colt
And rode him into the day there;
And he threw me down like a thunderbolt
And rolled on me as I lay there.

The hunter's whistle hummed in my ear
As the city-men tried to move me,
And I died in my boots like a pioneer
With the whole wide sky above me.

Now I lie in the heart of the fat, black soil,
Like the seed of a prairie-thistle;
It has washed my bones with honey and oil
And picked them clean as a whistle.

And my youth returns, like the rains of Spring,
And my sons, like the wild-geese flying;
And I lie and hear the meadow-lark sing
And have much content in my dying.

Go play with the towns you have built of blocks,
The towns where you would have bound me!
I sleep in my earth like a tired fox,
And my buffalo have found me.

Emily Dickinson
1830–1886

Much Madness Is Divinest Sense

Much madness is divinest sense
To a discerning eye;
Much sense the starkest madness.
'Tis the majority
In this, as all, prevails.
Assent, and you are sane;
Demur,—you're straightway dangerous,
And handled with a chain.

Hope Is the Thing with Feathers

Hope is the thing with feathers
That perches in the soul,
And sings the tune without the words
And never stops at all,

And sweetest in the gale is heard;
And sore must be the storm
That could abash the little bird
That kept so many warm.

I've heard it in the chillest land,
And on the strangest sea;
Yet, never, in extremity,
It asked a crumb of me.

There Is No Frigate Like a Book

There is no frigate like a book
  To take us lands away,
Nor any coursers like a page
  Of prancing poetry.

This traverse may the poorest take
  Without oppress of toll;
How frugal is the chariot
  That bears a human soul!

I Never Saw a Moor

I never saw a moor,
I never saw the sea;
Yet know I how the heather looks,
And what a wave must be.

I never spoke with God,
Nor visited in heaven;
Yet certain am I of the spot
As if the chart were given.

Edwin Arlington Robinson
1869–1935

Cliff Klingenhagen

Cliff Klingenhagen had me in to dine
With him one day; and after soup and meat,
And all the other things there were to eat,

Cliff took two glasses and filled one with wine
And one with wormwood. Then, without a sign
For me to choose at all, he took the draught
Of bitterness himself, and lightly quaffed
It off, and said the other one was mine.

And when I asked him what the deuce he meant
By doing that, he only looked at me
And smiled, and said it was a way of his.
And though I know the fellow, I have spent
Long time a-wondering when I shall be
As happy as Cliff Klingenhagen is.

Miniver Cheevy

Miniver Cheevy, child of scorn,
    Grew lean while he assailed the seasons;
He wept that he was ever born,
    And he had reasons.

Miniver loved the days of old
    When swords were bright and steeds were prancing;
The vision of a warrior bold
    Would set him dancing.

Miniver sighed for what was not,
    And dreamed, and rested from his labors;
He dreamed of Thebes and Camelot,
    And Priam's neighbors.

Miniver mourned the ripe renown
    That made so many a name so fragrant;

He mourned Romance, now on the town,
  And Art, a vagrant.

Miniver loved the Medici,
  Albeit he had never seen one;
He would have sinned incessantly
  Could he have been one.

Miniver cursed the commonplace
  And eyed a khaki suit with loathing;
He missed the mediaeval grace
  Of iron clothing.

Miniver scorned the gold he sought,
  But sore annoyed was he without it;
Miniver thought, and thought, and thought,
  And thought about it.

Miniver Cheevy, born too late,
  Scratched his head and kept on thinking;
Miniver coughed, and called it fate,
  And kept on drinking.

Phyllis McGinley
1905–

Launcelot with Bicycle

Her window looks upon the lane.
From it, anonymous and shy,
Twice daily she can see him plain,
Wheeling heroic by.

She droops her cheek against the pane
And gives a little sigh.

Above him maples at their bloom
Shake April pollen down like stars
While he goes whistling past her room
Toward unimagined wars,
A tennis visor for his plume,
Scornful of handlebars.

And, counting over in her mind
His favors, gleaned like windfall fruit
(A morning when he spoke her kind,
An afterschool salute,
A number that she helped him find,
Once, for his paper route),

Sadly she twists a stubby braid
And closer to the casement leans—
A wistful and a lily maid
In moccasins and jeans,
Despairing from the seventh grade
To match his lordly teens.

And so she grieves in Astolat
(Where other girls have grieved the same)
For being young and therefore not
Sufficient to his fame—
Who will by summer have forgot
Grief, April, and his name.

Countee Cullen
1903–1946

Incident

(*For Eric Walrond*)

Once riding in old Baltimore,
　Heart-filled, head-filled with glee,
I saw a Baltimorean
　Keep looking straight at me.

Now I was eight and very small,
  And he was no whit bigger,
And so I smiled, but he poked out
  His tongue, and called me, "Nigger."

I saw the whole of Baltimore
  From May until December;
Of all the things that happened there
  That's all that I remember.

A Negro Mother's Lullaby

(*After visiting John Brown's grave*)

Hushaby, hushaby, dark one at my knee;
Slumber you softly, nor pucker, nor frown;
Though some may be bonded, you shall be free,
Thanks to a man . . . Osawatamie Brown.
  His sons are high fellows,
  An Archangel is he,
  And they doff their bright haloes
  To none but the Three.

Hushaby, hushaby, sweet darkness at rest,
Two there have been who their lives laid down
That you might be beautiful here at my breast:
Our Jesus and . . . Osawatamie Brown.
  His sons are high fellows,
  An Archangel is he,
  And they doff their bright haloes
  To none but the Three.

Hushaby, hushaby, when a man, not a slave,
    With freedom for wings you go through the town,
    Let your love be dew on his evergreen grave;
    Sleep, in the name of Osawatamie Brown.

        Rich counsel he's giving
        Close by the throne,
        Tall he was living
        But now taller grown.
        His sons are high fellows,
        An Archangel is he,
        And they doff their bright haloes
        To none but the Three.

T. S. Eliot
1888–1965

Preludes: I

The winter evening settles down
With smell of steaks in passageways.
Six o'clock.
The burnt-out ends of smoky days.
And now a gusty shower wraps
The grimy scraps
Of withered leaves about your feet
And newspapers from vacant lots;
The showers beat
On broken blinds and chimney-pots,
And at the corner of the street
A lonely cab-horse steams and stamps.

And then the lighting of the lamps.

Landscapes: New Hampshire

Children's voices in the orchard
Between the blossom- and the fruit-time:
Golden head, crimson head,
Between the green tip and the root.
Black wing, brown wing, hover over;
Twenty years and the spring is over;
To-day grieves, to-morrow grieves,
Cover me over, light-in-leaves;
Golden head, black wing,
Cling, swing,
Spring, sing,
Swing up into the apple-tree.

The Rum Tum Tugger

The Rum Tum Tugger is a Curious Cat:
If you offer him pheasant he would rather have grouse.
If you put him in a house he would much prefer a flat,
If you put him in a flat then he'd rather have a house.
If you set him on a mouse then he only wants a rat,
If you set him on a rat then he'd rather chase a mouse.
Yes the Rum Tum Tugger is a Curious Cat—
   And there isn't any call for me to shout it:
    For he will do
    As he do do
      And there's no doing anything about it!

The Rum Tum Tugger is a terrible bore:
When you let him in, then he wants to be out;
He's always on the wrong side of every door,
And as soon as he's at home, then he'd like to get about.
He likes to lie in the bureau drawer,
But he makes such a fuss if he can't get out.
Yes the Rum Tum Tugger is a Curious Cat—
    And it isn't any use for you to doubt it:
        For he will do
        As he do do
            And there's no doing anything about it!

The Rum Tum Tugger is a curious beast:
His disobliging ways are a matter of habit.
If you offer him fish then he always wants a feast;
When there isn't any fish then he won't eat rabbit.
If you offer him cream then he sniffs and sneers,
For he only likes what he finds for himself;
So you'll catch him in it right up to the ears,
If you put it away on the larder shelf.
The Rum Tum Tugger is artful and knowing,
The Rum Tum Tugger doesn't care for a cuddle;
But he'll leap on your lap in the middle of your sewing,
For there's nothing he enjoys like a horrible muddle.
Yes the Rum Tum Tugger is a Curious Cat—
    And there isn't any need for me to spout it:
        For he will do
        As he do do
            And there's no doing anything about it!

Hart Crane
1899–1932

March

Awake to the cold light
of wet wind running
twigs in tremors. Walls
are naked. Twilights raw—
and when the sun taps steeples
their glistenings dwindle
upward . . .

      March
slips along the ground
like a mouse under pussy
willows, a little hungry.

The vagrant ghost of winter,
is it this that keeps the chimney
busy still? For something still
nudges shingles and windows:

but waveringly,—this ghost,
this slate-eyed saintly wraith
of winter wanes
and knows its waning.

October-November

Indian-summer-sun
With crimson feathers whips away the mists,—
Dives through the filter of trellises
And gilds the silver on the blotched arbor-seats.

Now gold and purple scintillate
On trees that seem dancing
In delirium;
Then the moon
In a mad orange flare
Floods the grape-hung night.

Fear

The host, he says that all is well
And the fire-wood glow is bright;
The food has a warm and tempting smell,—
But on the window licks the night.

Pile on the logs. . . . Give me your hands,
Friends! No,—it is not fright. . . .
But hold me . . . somewhere I heard demands. . . .
And on the window licks the night.

Amy Lowell
1874-1925

The Pike

In the brown water,
Thick and silver-sheened in the sunshine,
Liquid and cool in the shade of the reeds,
A pike dozed.
Lost among the shadows of stems
He lay unnoticed.
Suddenly he flicked his tail,
And a green-and-copper brightness
Ran under the water.

Out from under the reeds
Came the olive-green light,
And orange flashed up
Through the sun-thickened water.
So the fish passed across the pool,
Green and copper,
A darkness and a gleam,
And the blurred reflections of the willows
    on the opposite bank
Received it.

A Lady

You are beautiful and faded
Like an old opera tune
Played upon a harpsichord;
Or like the sun-flooded silks
Of an eighteenth-century boudoir.
In your eyes
Smoulder the fallen roses of out-lived minutes,
And the perfume of your soul
Is vague and suffusing,
With the pungence of sealed spice-jars.
Your half-tones delight me,
And I grow mad with gazing
At your blent colours.

My vigour is a new-minted penny,
Which I cast at your feet.
Gather it up from the dust,
That its sparkle may amuse you.

Misericordia

He earned his bread by making wooden soldiers,
With beautiful golden instruments,
Riding dapple-grey horses.
But when he heard the fanfare of trumpets
And the long rattle of drums
As the army marched out of the city,
He took all his soldiers
And burned them in the grate;
And that night he fashioned a ballet-dancer
Out of tinted tissue paper,
And the next day he started to carve a Pietà
On the steel hilt
Of a cavalry sword.

Delmore Schwartz
1913–1966

The Would-Be Hungarian

Come, let us meditate upon the fate of a little boy who wished to
be
Hungarian! Having been moved with his family to a new suburb,
having been sent to a new school, the only Catholic school in
the new suburb,
Where all the other children were Hungarian,

He felt very sad and separate on the first day, he felt more and
more separated and isolated
Because all the other boys and girls pitied and were sorry for him
since he was not

Hungarian! Hence they pitied and were sorry for him so much
    they gave him handsome gifts,
Presents of comic books, marbles and foreign coins, peppermints
    and candy, a pistol, and also their devoted sympathy, pity
    and friendship

Making him sadder still since now he saw how all Hungarians
    were very kind and generous, and he was not

Hungarian! Hence he was an immigrant, an alien: he was and
    he would be,
Forever, no matter what, he could never become Hungarian!
Hungarian! Hence he went home on the first day, bearing his gifts
    and telling his parents how much he wished to be
Hungarian: in anguish, in anger,
Accusing them of depriving him, and misusing him: amusing
    them,
So that he rose to higher fury, shouting and accusing them

—Because of you I am a stranger, monster, orang-outang!
Because of you (his hot tears say) I am an orang-outang! and not
Hungarian! Worse than to have no bicycle, no shoes . . .
        Behold how this poor boy, who wished so passionately to
          be Hungarian
        Suffered and knew the fate of being American.
        Whether on Ellis Island, Plymouth Rock,
        Or in the secret places of the mind and heart
        This is America—as poetry and hope
        This is the fame, the game and the names of our fate:
        This we must suffer or must celebrate.

Vachel Lindsay
1879-1931

The Flower-Fed Buffaloes

The flower-fed buffaloes of the spring
In the days of long ago,
Ranged where the locomotives sing
And the prairie flowers lie low:—
The tossing, blooming, perfumed grass
Is swept away by the wheat,
Wheels and wheels and wheels spin by
In the spring that still is sweet.
But the flower-fed buffaloes of the spring
Left us, long ago.
They gore no more, they bellow no more,
They trundle around the hills no more:—
With the Blackfeet, lying low,
With the Pawnees, lying low,
Lying low.

The Leaden-Eyed

Let not young souls be smothered out before
They do quaint deeds and fully flaunt their pride.
It is the world's one crime its babes grow dull,
Its poor are ox-like, limp and leaden-eyed.

Not that they starve, but starve so dreamlessly,
Not that they sow, but that they seldom reap,
Not that they serve, but have no gods to serve,
Not that they die but that they die like sheep.

The Broncho That Would Not Be Broken

A little colt—broncho, loaned to the farm
To be broken in time without fury or harm,
Yet black crows flew past you, shouting alarm,
Calling "Beware," with lugubrious singing . . .
The butterflies there in the bush were romancing,
The smell of the grass caught your soul in a trance,
So why be a-fearing the spurs and the traces,
O broncho that would not be broken of dancing?

You were born with the pride of the lords great and olden
Who danced, through the ages, in corridors golden.
In all the wide farm-place the person most human.
You spoke out so plainly with squealing and capering,
With whinnying, snorting contorting and prancing,
As you dodged your pursuers, looking askance,
With Greek-footed figures, and Parthenon paces,
O broncho that would not be broken of dancing.

The grasshoppers cheered. "Keep whirling," they said.
The insolent sparrows called from the shed
"If men will not laugh, make them wish they were dead."
But arch were your thoughts, all malice displacing,
Though the horse-killers came, with snake-whips advancing
You bantered and cantered away your last chance.
And they scourged you, with Hell in their speech and their faces,
O broncho that would not be broken of dancing.

"Nobody cares for you," rattled the crows,
As you dragged the whole reaper, next day, down the rows.
The three mules held back, yet you danced on your toes.
You pulled like a racer, and kept the mules chasing,
You tangled the harness with bright eyes side-glancing,

While the drunk driver bled you—a pole for a lance—
And the giant mules bit at you—keeping their places.
O broncho that would not be broken of dancing.

In that last afternoon your boyish heart broke.
The hot wind came down like a sledge-hammer stroke.
The blood-sucking flies to a rare feast awoke.
And they searched out your wounds, your death-warrant tracing.
And the merciful men, their religion enhancing,
Stopped the red reaper, to give you a chance.
Then you died on the prairie, and scorned all disgraces,
O broncho that would not be broken of dancing.

Sara Teasdale
1884–1933

I Have Loved Hours at Sea

I have loved hours at sea, gray cities,
   The fragile secret of a flower,
Music, the making of a poem
   That gave me heaven for an hour;

First stars above a snowy hill,
   Voices of people kindly and wise,
And the great look of love, long hidden,
   Found at last in meeting eyes.

I have loved much and been loved deeply—
   Oh when my spirit's fire burns low,
Leave me the darkness and the stillness,
   I shall be tired and glad to go.

The Falling Star

I saw a star slide down the sky,
Blinding the north as it went by,
Too burning and too quick to hold,
Too lovely to be bought or sold,
Good only to make wishes on
And then forever to be gone.

May Sarton
1912–

A Celebration

I never saw my father old;
I never saw my father cold.
His stride, staccato, vital,
His talk struck from pure metal
Simple as gold, and all his learning
Only to light a passion's burning.
So, beaming like a lesser god,
He bounced upon the earth he trod,
And people marvelled on the street
At this stout man's impetuous feet.

Loved donkeys, children, awkward ducks,
Loved to retell old simple jokes;
Lived in a world of innocence
Where loneliness could be intense;
Wrote letters until very late,
Found comfort in an orange cat—
Rufus and George exchanged no word,
But while George worked his Rufus purred—
And neighbors looked up at his light
Warmed by the scholar working late.

I never saw my father passive;
He was electrically massive.
He never hurried, so he said,
And yet a fire burned in his head;
He worked as poets work, for love,
And gathered in a world alive,
While black and white above his door
Spoke Mystery, the avatar—
An Arabic inscription flowed
Like singing: "In the name of God."

And when he died, he died so swift
His death was like a final gift.
He went out when the tide was full,
Still undiminished, bountiful;
The scholar and the gentle soul,
The passion and the life were whole.
And now death's wake is only praise,
As when a neighbor writes and says:
"I did not know your father, but
His light was there. I miss the light."

Langston Hughes
1902–1967

Daybreak in Alabama

When I get to be a composer
I'm gonna write me some music about
Daybreak in Alabama
And I'm gonna put the purtiest songs in it
Rising out of the ground like a swamp mist
And falling out of heaven like soft dew.
I'm gonna put some tall tall trees in it
And the scent of pine needles
And the smell of red clay after rain

And long red necks
And poppy colored faces
And big brown arms
And the field daisy eyes
Of black and white black white black people
And I'm gonna put white hands
And black hands and brown and yellow hands
And red clay earth hands in it
Touching everybody with kind fingers
And touching each other natural as dew
In that dawn of music when I
Get to be a composer
And write about daybreak
In Alabama.

Walt Whitman
1819–1892

Miracles

Why, who makes much of a miracle?
As to me I know of nothing else but miracles,
Whether I walk the streets of Manhattan,
Or dart my sight over the roofs of houses toward the sky,
Or wade with naked feet along the beach just in the edge of the
    water,
Or stand under trees in the woods,
Or talk by day with any one I love, or sleep in the bed at night
    with any one I love,
Or sit at table at dinner with the rest,
Or look at strangers opposite me riding in the car,

Or watch honey-bees busy around the hive of a summer
    forenoon,
Or animals feeding in the fields,
Or birds, or the wonderfulness of insects in the air,
Or the wonderfulness of the sundown, or of stars shining so quiet
    and bright,
Or the exquisite delicate thin curve of the new moon in spring;
These with the rest, one and all, are to me miracles,
The whole referring, yet each distinct and in its place.

To me every hour of the light and dark is a miracle,
Every cubic inch of space is a miracle,
Every square yard of the surface of the earth is spread with
    the same,
Every foot of the interior swarms with the same;
Every spear of grass—the frames, limbs, organs, of men and
    women, and all that concerns them,
All these to me are unspeakably perfect miracles.

To me the sea is a continual miracle,
The fishes that swim—the rocks—the motion of the waves—the
    ships with men in them,
What stranger miracles are there?

When I Heard the Learn'd Astronomer

When I heard the learn'd astronomer,
When the proofs, the figures, were ranged in columns before me,
When I was shown the charts and diagrams, to add, divide, and
    measure them,
When I sitting heard the astronomer where he lectured with much
    applause in the lecture-room,

How soon unaccountable I became tired and sick,
Till rising and gliding out I wander'd off by myself,
In the mystical moist night-air, and from time to time,
Look'd up in perfect silence at the stars.

A Red Squaw Came One Breakfast-time

A red squaw came one breakfast-time to the old homestead,
On her back she carried a bundle of rushes for rush-bottoming
chairs,
Her hair, straight, shiny, coarse, black, profuse, half-envelop'd
her face,
Her step was free and elastic, and her voice sounded exquisitely as
she spoke.

My mother look'd in delight and amazement at the stranger,
She look'd at the freshness of her tall-borne face and full and
pliant limbs,
The more she look'd upon her she loved her,
Never before had she seen such wonderful beauty and purity,
She made her sit on a bench by the jamb of the fireplace, she
cook'd food for her,
She had no work to give her, but she gave her remembrance and
fondness.

The red squaw staid all the forenoon, and toward the middle of
the afternoon she went away,
O my mother was loth to have her go away,
All the week she thought of her, she watch'd for her many a
month,
She remember'd her many a winter and many a summer,
But the red squaw never came nor was heard of there again.

Ogden Nash
1902—

The Octopus

Tell me, O Octopus, I begs,
Is those things arms, or is they legs?
I marvel at thee, Octopus;
If I were thou, I'd call me Us.

The Termite

Some primal termite knocked on wood
And tasted it, and found it good,
And that is why your Cousin May
Fell through the parlor floor today.

Celery

Celery, raw,
Develops the jaw,
But celery, stewed,
Is more quietly chewed.

The Parsnip

The parsnip, children, I repeat,
Is simply an anemic beet.
Some people call the parsnip edible;
Myself, I find this claim incredible.

The Purist

I give you now Professor Twist,
A conscientious scientist.
Trustees exclaimed, "He never bungles!"
And sent him off to distant jungles.
Camped on a tropic riverside,
One day he missed his loving bride.
She had, the guide informed him later,
Been eaten by an alligator.
Professor Twist could not but smile.
"You mean," he said, "a crocodile."

Boy at the Window

Seeing the snowman standing all alone
In dusk and cold is more than he can bear.
The small boy weeps to hear the wind prepare
A night of gnashings and enormous moan.
His tearful sight can hardly reach to where
The pale-faced figure with bitumen eyes
Returns him such a god-forsaken stare
As outcast Adam gave to Paradise.

The man of snow is, nonetheless, content,
Having no wish to go inside and die.
Still, he is moved to see the youngster cry.
Though frozen water is his element,
He melts enough to drop from one soft eye

A trickle of the purest rain, a tear
For the child at the bright pane surrounded by
Such warmth, such light, such love, and so much fear.

Edgar Lee Masters
1869–1950

George Gray

I have studied many times
The marble which was chiseled for me—
A boat with a furled sail at rest in a harbor.
In truth it pictures not my destination
But my life.
For love was offered me and I shrank from its disillusionment;
Sorrow knocked at my door, but I was afraid;
Ambition called to me, but I dreaded the chances.
Yet all the while I hungered for meaning in my life.
And now I know that we must lift the sail
And catch the winds of destiny
Wherever they drive the boat.
To put meaning in one's life may end in madness,
But life without meaning is the torture
Of restlessness and vague desire—
It is a boat longing for the sea and yet afraid.

Lucinda Matlock

I went to the dances at Chandlerville,
And played snap-out at Winchester.
One time we changed partners,
Driving home in the moonlight of middle June,

And then I found Davis.
We were married and lived together for seventy years,
Enjoying, working, raising the twelve children,
Eight of whom we lost
Ere I had reached the age of sixty.
I spun, I wove, I kept the house, I nursed the sick,
I made the garden, and for holiday
Rambled over the fields where sang the larks,
And by Spoon River gathering many a shell,
And many a flower and medicinal weed—
Shouting to the wooded hills, singing to the green valleys.
At ninety-six I had lived enough, that is all,
And passed to a sweet repose.
What is this I hear of sorrow and weariness,
Anger, discontent and drooping hopes?
Degenerate sons and daughters,
Life is too strong for you—
It takes life to love Life.

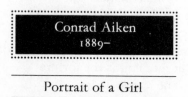

Conrad Aiken
1889–

Portrait of a Girl

This is the shape of the leaf, and this of the flower,
And this the pale bole of the tree
Which watches its bough in a pool of unwavering water
In a land we never shall see.

The thrush on the bough is silent, the dew falls softly,
In the evening is hardly a sound.

And the three beautiful pilgrims who come here together
Touch lightly the dust of the ground,

Touch it with feet that trouble the dust but as wings do,
Come shyly together, are still,
Like dancers who wait, in a pause of the music, for music
The exquisite silence to fill.

This is the thought of the first, and this of the second,
And this the grave thought of the third:
'Linger we thus for a moment, palely expectant,
And silence will end, and the bird

'Sing the pure phrase, sweet phrase, clear phrase in the twilight
To fill the blue bell of the world;
And we, who on music so leaflike have drifted together,
Leaflike apart shall be whirled

'Into what but the beauty of silence, silence forever?' . . .
. . . This is the shape of the tree,
And the flower, and the leaf, and the three pale beautiful pilgrims;
This is what you are to me.

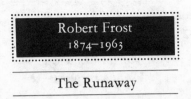

Robert Frost
1874–1963

The Runaway

Once when the snow of the year was beginning to fall,
We stopped by a mountain pasture to say, 'Whose colt?'
A little Morgan had one forefoot on the wall,
The other curled at his breast. He dipped his head

And snorted at us. And then he had to bolt.
We heard the miniature thunder where he fled,
And we saw him, or thought we saw him, dim and gray,
Like a shadow against the curtain of falling flakes.
'I think the little fellow's afraid of the snow.
He isn't winter-broken. It isn't play
With the little fellow at all. He's running away.
I doubt if even his mother could tell him, "Sakes,
It's only weather." He'd think she didn't know!
Where is his mother? He can't be out alone.'
And now he comes again with clatter of stone,
And mounts the wall again with whited eyes
And all his tail that isn't hair up straight.
He shudders his coat as if to throw off flies.
'Whoever it is that leaves him out so late,
When other creatures have gone to stall and bin,
Ought to be told to come and take him in.'

Dust of Snow

The way a crow
Shook down on me
The dust of snow
From a hemlock tree

Has given my heart
A change of mood
And saved some part
Of a day I had rued.

Birches

When I see birches bend to left and right
Across the lines of straighter darker trees,
I like to think some boy's been swinging them.
But swinging doesn't bend them down to stay
As ice-storms do. Often you must have seen them
Loaded with ice a sunny winter morning
After a rain. They click upon themselves
As the breeze rises, and turn many-colored
As the stir cracks and crazes their enamel.
Soon the sun's warmth makes them shed crystal shells
Shattering and avalanching on the snow-crust—

Such heaps of broken glass to sweep away
You'd think the inner dome of heaven had fallen.
They are dragged to the withered bracken by the load,
And they seem not to break; though once they are bowed
So low for long, they never right themselves:
You may see their trunks arching in the woods
Years afterwards, trailing their leaves on the ground
Like girls on hands and knees that throw their hair
Before them over their heads to dry in the sun.
But I was going to say when Truth broke in
With all her matter-of-fact about the ice-storm
I should prefer to have some boy bend them
As he went out and in to fetch the cows—
Some boy too far from town to learn baseball,
Whose only play was what he found himself,
Summer or winter, and could play alone.
One by one he subdued his father's trees
By riding them down over and over again
Until he took the stiffness out of them,
And not one but hung limp, not one was left
For him to conquer. He learned all there was
To learn about not launching out too soon
And so not carrying the tree away
Clear to the ground. He always kept his poise
To the top branches, climbing carefully
With the same pains you use to fill a cup
Up to the brim, and even above the brim.
Then he flung outward, feet first, with a swish,
Kicking his way down through the air to the ground.
So was I once myself a swinger of birches.
And so I dream of going back to be.
It's when I'm weary of considerations,
And life is too much like a pathless wood

Where your face burns and tickles with the cobwebs
Broken across it, and one eye is weeping
From a twig's having lashed across it open.
I'd like to get away from earth awhile
And then come back to it and begin over.
May no fate willfully misunderstand me
And half grant what I wish and snatch me away
Not to return. Earth's the right place for love:
I don't know where it's likely to go better.
I'd like to go by climbing a birch tree,
And climb black branches up a snow-white trunk
Toward heaven, till the tree could bear no more,
But dipped its top and set me down again.
That would be good both going and coming back.
One could do worse than be a swinger of birches.

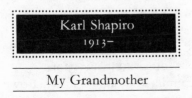

Karl Shapiro
1913–

My Grandmother

My grandmother moves to my mind in context of sorrow
And, as if apprehensive of near death, in black;
Whether erect in chair, her dry and corded throat harangued
  by grief,
Or at ragged book bent in Hebrew prayer,
Or gentle, submissive, and in tears to strangers;
Whether in sunny parlor or back of drawn blinds.

Though time and tongue made any love disparate,
On daguerreotype with classic perspective

Beauty I sigh and soften at is hers.
I pity her life of deaths, the agony of her own,
But most that history moved her through
Stranger lands and many houses,
Taking her exile for granted, confusing
The tongues and tasks of her children's children.

Elinor Wylie
1885–1928

Wild Peaches

When the world turns completely upside down
You say we'll emigrate to the Eastern Shore
Aboard a river-boat from Baltimore;
We'll live among wild peach trees, miles from town,
You'll wear a coonskin cap, and I a gown
Homespun, dyed butternut's dark gold colour.
Lost, like your lotus-eating ancestor,
We'll swim in milk and honey till we drown.

The winter will be short, the summer long,
The autumn amber-hued, sunny and hot,
Tasting of cider and of scuppernong;
All seasons sweet, but autumn best of all.
The squirrels in their silver fur will fall
Like falling leaves, like fruit, before your shot.

The autumn frosts will lie upon the grass
Like bloom on grapes of purple-brown and gold.
The misted early mornings will be cold;
The little puddles will be roofed with glass.
The sun, which burns from copper into brass,
Melts these at noon, and makes the boys unfold
Their knitted mufflers; full as they can hold,
Fat pockets dribble chestnuts as they pass.

Peaches grow wild, and pigs can live in clover;
A barrel of salted herrings lasts a year;
The spring begins before the winter's over.
By February you may find the skins
Of garter snakes and water moccasins
Dwindled and harsh, dead-white and cloudy-clear.

When April pours the colours of a shell
Upon the hills, when every little creek
Is shot with silver from the Chesapeake
In shoals new-minted by the ocean swell,
When strawberries go begging, and the sleek
Blue plums lie open to the blackbird's beak,
We shall live well—we shall live very well.

The months between the cherries and the peaches
Are brimming cornucopias which spill
Fruits red and purple, sombre-bloomed and black;

Then, down rich fields and frosty river beaches
We'll trample bright persimmons, while you kill
Bronze partridge, speckled quail, and canvasback.

Down to the Puritan marrow of my bones
There's something in this richness that I hate.
I love the look, austere, immaculate,
Of landscapes drawn in pearly monotones.
There's something in my very blood that owns
Bare hills, cold silver on a sky of slate,
A thread of water, churned to milky spate
Streaming through slanted pastures fenced with stones.

I love those skies, thin blue or snowy gray,
Those fields sparse-planted, rendering meagre sheaves;
That spring, briefer than apple-blossom's breath,
Summer, so much too beautiful to stay,
Swift autumn, like a bonfire of leaves,
And sleepy winter, like the sleep of death.

Ezra Pound
1885–

Meditatio

When I carefully consider the curious habits of dogs
I am compelled to conclude
That man is the superior animal.

When I consider the curious habits of man
I confess, my friend, I am puzzled.

Above the Dock

Above the quiet dock in mid night,
Tangled in the tall mast's corded height,
Hangs the moon. What seemed so far away
Is but a child's balloon, forgotten after play.

Autumn

A touch of cold in the Autumn night—
I walked abroad,
And saw the ruddy moon lean over a hedge
Like a red-faced farmer.
I did not stop to speak, but nodded,
And round about were the wistful stars
With white faces like town children.

May Swenson
1919–

The Centaur

The summer that I was ten—
Can it be there was only one
summer that I was ten? It must

have been a long one then—
each day I'd go out to choose
a fresh horse from my stable

which was a willow grove
down by the old canal.
I'd go on my two bare feet.

But when, with my brother's jack-knife,
I had cut me a long limber horse
with a good thick knob for a head,

and peeled him slick and clean
except a few leaves for the tail,
and cinched my brother's belt

around his head for a rein,
I'd straddle and canter him fast
up the grass bank to the path,

trot along in the lovely dust
that talcumed over his hoofs,
hiding my toes, and turning

his feet to swift half-moons.
The willow knob with the strap
jouncing between my thighs

was the pommel and yet the poll
of my nickering pony's head.
My head and my neck were mine,

yet they were shaped like a horse.
My hair flopped to the side
like the mane of a horse in the wind.

My forelock swung in my eyes,
my neck arched and I snorted.
I shied and skittered and reared,

stopped and raised my knees,
pawed at the ground and quivered.
My teeth bared as we wheeled

and swished through the dust again.
I was the horse and the rider,
and the leather I slapped to his rump

spanked my own behind.
Doubled, my two hoofs beat
a gallop along the bank,

the wind twanged in my mane,
my mouth squared to the bit.
And yet I sat on my steed

quiet, negligent riding,
my toes standing the stirrups,
my thighs hugging his ribs.

At a walk we drew up to the porch.
I tethered him to a paling.
Dismounting, I smoothed my skirt

and entered the dusky hall.
My feet on the clean linoleum
left ghostly toes in the hall.

Where have you been? said my mother.
Been riding, I said from the sink,
and filled me a glass of water.

What's that in your pocket? she said.
Just my knife. It weighted my pocket
and stretched my dress awry.

Go tie back your hair, said my mother,
and *Why is your mouth all green?*
*Rob Roy, he pulled some clover
as we crossed the field,* I told her.

Stephen Crane
1871–1900

There Was a Man with Tongue of Wood

There was a man with tongue of wood
Who essayed to sing,
And in truth it was lamentable.
But there was one who heard
The clip-clapper of this tongue of wood
And knew what the man
Wished to sing,
And with that the singer was content.

Once I Saw Mountains Angry

Once I saw mountains angry,
And ranged in battle-front.
Against them stood a little man;

Ay, he was no bigger than my finger.
I laughed, and spoke to one near me,
"Will he prevail?"
"Surely," replied this other;
"His grandfathers beat them many times."
Then did I see much virtue in grandfathers—
At least, for the little man
Who stood against the mountains.

Blades of Grass

In heaven,
Some little blades of grass
Stood before God.
"What did you do?"
Then all save one of the little blades
Began eagerly to relate
The merits of their lives.
This one stayed a small way behind,
Ashamed.

Presently, God said,
"And what did you do?"
The little blade answered, "O my lord,
Memory is bitter to me,
For, if I did good deeds,
I know not of them."
Then God, in all His splendour,
Arose from His throne.
"O best little blade of grass!" He said.

Robinson Jeffers
1887–1962

Carmel Point

The extraordinary patience of things!
This beautiful place defaced with a crop of suburban houses—
How beautiful when we first beheld it,
Unbroken field of poppy and lupin walled with clean cliffs;
No intrusion but two or three horses pasturing,
Or a few milch cows rubbing their flanks on the outcrop
   rockheads—

Now the spoiler has come: does it care?
Not faintly. It has all time. It knows the people are a tide
That swells and in time will ebb, and all
Their works dissolve. Meanwhile the image of the pristine
    beauty
Lives in the very grain of the granite,
Safe as the endless ocean that climbs our cliff. —As for us:
We must uncenter our minds from ourselves;
We must unhumanize our views a little, and become confident
As the rock and ocean that we were made from.

Hurt Hawks

I

The broken pillar of the wing jags from the clotted shoulder,
The wing trails like a banner in defeat,
No more to use the sky forever but live with famine
And pain a few days: cat nor coyote
Will shorten the week of waiting for death, there is game
    without talons.
He stands under the oak-bush and waits
The lame feet of salvation; at night he remembers freedom
And flies in a dream, the dawns ruin it.
He is strong and pain is worse to the strong, incapacity
    is worse.
The curs of the day come and torment him
At distance, no one but death the redeemer will humble
    that head,
The intrepid readiness, the terrible eyes.
The wild God of the world is sometimes merciful to those
That ask mercy, not often to the arrogant.

You do not know him, you communal people, or you have forgotten him;
Intemperate and savage, the hawk remembers him;
Beautiful and wild, the hawks, and men that are dying, remember
   him.

II

I'd sooner, except the penalties, kill a man than a hawk; but the
   great redtail
Had nothing left but unable misery
From the bone too shattered for mending, the wing that trailed
   under his talons when he moved.
We had fed him six weeks, I gave him freedom,
He wandered over the foreland hill and returned in the evening,
   asking for death,
Not like a beggar, still eyed with the old
Implacable arrogance. I gave him the lead gift in the twilight. What
   fell was relaxed,
Owl-downy, soft feminine feathers; but what
Soared: the fierce rush: the night-herons by the flooded river cried
   fear at its rising
Before it was quite unsheathed from reality.

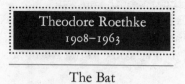

Theodore Roethke
1908–1963

The Bat

By day the bat is cousin to the mouse.
He likes the attic of an aging house.

His fingers make a hat about his head.
His pulse beat is so slow we think him dead.

He loops in crazy figures half the night
Among the trees that face the corner light.

But when he brushes up against a screen,
We are afraid of what our eyes have seen:

For something is amiss or out of place
When mice with wings can wear a human face.

Child on Top of a Greenhouse

The wind billowing out the seat of my britches,
My feet crackling splinters of glass and dried putty,
The half-grown chrysanthemums staring up like accusers,
Up through the streaked glass, flashing with sunlight,
A few white clouds all rushing eastward,
A line of elms plunging and tossing like horses,
And everyone, everyone pointing up and shouting!

Adelaide Crapsey
1878–1914

Youth

But me
They cannot touch,
Old Age and death . . . the strange
And ignominious end of old
Dead folk!

November Night

Listen.
With faint dry sound,
Like steps of passing ghosts,
The leaves, frost-crisp'd, break from the trees
And fall.

The Warning

Just now,
Out of the strange
Still dusk . . . as strange, as still . . .
A white moth flew. Why am I grown
So cold?

Archibald MacLeish
1892–

Eleven

And summer mornings the mute child, rebellious,
Stupid, hating the words, the meanings, hating
The Think now, Think, the Oh but Think! would leave
On tiptoe the three chairs on the verandah
And crossing tree by tree the empty lawn
Push back the shed door and upon the sill
Stand pressing out the sunlight from his eyes
And enter and with outstretched fingers feel
The grindstone and behind it the bare wall
And turn and in the corner on the cool

Hard earth sit listening. And one by one,
Out of the dazzled shadow in the room,
The shapes would gather, the brown plowshare, spades,
Mattocks, the polished helves of picks, a scythe
Hung from the rafters, shovels, slender tines
Glinting across the curve of sickles—shapes
Older than men were, the wise tools, the iron
Friendly with earth. And sit there, quiet, breathing
The harsh dry smell of withered bulbs, the faint
Odor of dung, the silence. And outside
Beyond the half-shut door the blind leaves
And the corn moving. And at noon would come,
Up from the garden, his hard crooked hands
Gentle with earth, his knees still earth-stained, smelling
Of sun, of summer, the old gardener, like
A priest, like an interpreter, and bend
Over his baskets.

                 And they would not speak:
They would say nothing. And the child would sit there
Happy as though he had no name, as though
He had been no one: like a leaf, a stem,
Like a root growing—

Crossing

At five precisely in the afternoon
The dining car cook on the Boston and Albany
Through train to somewhere leaned and waved
At the little girl on the crossing at Ghent, New York—
The one with the doll carriage.

                              Who understood it best?
She, going home to her supper, telling her Pa?
The Negro cook, shutting the vestibule window,
Thinking: She waved right back she did? Or I,
Writing it down and wondering as I write it
Why a forgotten touch of human grace
Is more alive forgotten than its memory
Pressed between two pages in this place?

Where the Hayfields Were

Coming down the mountain in the twilight—
April it was and quiet in the air—
I saw an old man and his little daughter
Burning the meadows where the hayfields were.

Forksful of flame he scattered in the meadows.
Sparkles of fire in the quiet air
Burned in their circles and the silver flowers
Danced like candles where the hayfields were,—

Danced as she did in enchanted circles,
Curtseyed and danced along the quiet air:
Slightly she danced in the stillness, in the twilight,
Dancing in the meadows where the hayfields were.

John Ciardi
1916–

I Wouldn't

There's a mouse house
In the hall wall
With a small door
By the hall floor
Where the fat cat
Sits all day,
Sits that way
All day
Every day
Just to say,
"Come out and play"
To the nice mice
In the mouse house
In the hall wall
With the small door
By the hall floor.

And do they
Come out and play
When the fat cat
Asks them to?

Well, would you?

Edna St. Vincent Millay
1892–1950

Recuerdo

We were very tired, we were very merry—
We had gone back and forth all night on the ferry.
It was bare and bright, and smelled like a stable—
But we looked into a fire, we leaned across a table,
We lay on a hill-top underneath the moon;
And the whistles kept blowing, and the dawn came soon.

We were very tired, we were very merry—
We had gone back and forth all night on the ferry;
And you ate an apple, and I ate a pear,
From a dozen of each we had bought somewhere;
And the sky went wan, and the wind came cold,
And the sun rose dripping, a bucketful of gold.

We were very tired, we were very merry,
We had gone back and forth all night on the ferry.
We hailed, "Good morrow, mother!" to a shawl-covered head,

And bought a morning paper, which neither of us read;
And she wept, "God bless you!" for the apples and pears,
And we gave her all our money but our subway fares.

God's World

O World, I cannot hold thee close enough!
    Thy winds, thy wide grey skies!
    Thy mists, that roll and rise!
Thy woods, this autumn day, that ache and sag
And all but cry with colour! That gaunt crag
To crush! To lift the lean of that black bluff!
World, World, I cannot get thee close enough!

Long have I known a glory in it all,
        But never knew I this:
        Here such a passion is
As stretcheth me apart,—Lord, I do fear
Thou'st made the world too beautiful this year;
My soul is all but out of me,—let fall
No burning leaf; prithee, let no bird call.

The Buck in the Snow

White sky, over the hemlocks bowed with snow,
Saw you not at the beginning of evening the antlered
    buck and his doe
Standing in the apple-orchard? I saw them. I saw them
    suddenly go,
Tails up, with long leaps lovely and slow,
Over the stone-wall into the wood of hemlocks bowed
    with snow.

Now lies he here, his wild blood scalding the snow.

How strange a thing is death, bringing to his knees,
  bringing to his antlers
The buck in the snow.
How strange a thing,—a mile away by now, it may be,
Under the heavy hemlocks that as the moments pass
Shift their loads a little, letting fall a feather of snow—
Life, looking out attentive from the eyes of the doe.

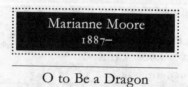

Marianne Moore
1887–

O to Be a Dragon

If I, like Solomon, . . .
could have my wish—

my wish . . . O to be a dragon,
a symbol of the power of Heaven—of silkworm
size or immense; at times invisible.
Felicitous phenomenon!

A Jellyfish

Visible, invisible,
  a fluctuating charm
an amber-tinctured amethyst
  inhabits it, your arm

approaches and it opens
　　and it closes; you had meant
to catch it and it quivers;
　　you abandon your intent.

Carl Sandburg
1878–1967

Losers

If I should pass the tomb of Jonah
I would stop there and sit for a while;
Because I was swallowed one time deep in the dark
And came out alive after all.

If I pass the burial spot of Nero
I shall say to the wind, "Well, well!"—
I who have fiddled in a world on fire,
I who have done so many stunts not worth doing.

I am looking for the grave of Sinbad too.
I want to shake his ghost-hand and say,
"Neither of us died very early, did we?"

And the last sleeping-place of Nebuchadnezzar—
When I arrive there I shall tell the wind:
"You ate grass; I have eaten crow—
Who is better off now or next year?"

Jack Cade, John Brown, Jesse James,
There too I could sit down and stop for a while.

I think I could tell their headstones:
"God, let me remember all good losers."

I could ask people to throw ashes on their heads
In the name of that sergeant at Belleau Woods,
Walking into the drumfires, calling his men,
"Come on, you . . . Do you want to live forever?"

Primer Lesson

Look out how you use proud words.
When you let proud words go, it is
    not easy to call them back.
They wear long boots, hard boots; they
    walk off proud; they can't hear you
    calling—
Look out how you use proud words.

Arithmetic

Arithmetic is where numbers fly like pigeons in and out of your
    head.
Arithmetic tells you how many you lose or win if you know how
    many you had before you lost or won.
Arithmetic is seven eleven all good children go to heaven—or five
    six bundle of sticks.
Arithmetic is numbers you squeeze from your head to your hand
    to your pencil to your paper till you get the answer.
Arithmetic is where the answer is right and everything is nice and
    you can look out of the window and see the blue sky—or the

answer is wrong and you have to start all over and try again
and see how it comes out this time.

If you take a number and double it and double it again and then
double it a few more times, the number gets bigger and bigger
and goes higher and higher and only arithmetic can tell you
what the number is when you decide to quit doubling.

Arithmetic is where you have to multiply—and you carry the
multiplication table in your head and hope you won't lose it.

If you have two animal crackers, one good and one bad, and you
eat one and a striped zebra with streaks all over him eats the
other, how many animal crackers will you have if somebody
offers you five six seven and you say No no no and you say
Nay nay nay and you say Nix nix nix?

If you ask your mother for one fried egg for breakfast and she
gives you two fried eggs and you eat both of them, who is
better in arithmetic, you or your mother?

A Father Sees a Son Nearing Manhood

A father sees a son nearing manhood.
What shall he tell that son?
"Life is hard; be steel; be a rock."
And this might stand him for the storms
and serve him for humdrum and monotony
and guide him amid sudden betrayals
and tighten him for slack moments.
"Life is a soft loam; be gentle; go easy."
And this too might serve him.
Brutes have been gentled where lashes failed.
The growth of a frail flower in a path up
has sometimes shattered and split a rock.

A tough will counts. So does desire.
So does a rich soft wanting.
Without rich wanting nothing arrives.
Tell him too much money has killed men
and left them dead years before burial:
the quest of lucre beyond a few easy needs
has twisted good enough men
sometimes into dry thwarted worms.
Tell him time as a stuff can be wasted.
Tell him to be a fool every so often
and to have no shame over having been a fool
yet learning something out of every folly
hoping to repeat none of the cheap follies
thus arriving at intimate understanding
of a world numbering many fools.
Tell him to be alone often and get at himself
and above all tell himself no lies about himself
whatever the white lies and protective fronts
he may use amongst other people.
Tell him solitude is creative if he is strong
and the final decisions are made in silent rooms.
Tell him to be different from other people
if it comes natural and easy being different.
Let him have lazy days seeking his deeper motives.
Let him seek deep for where he is a born natural.
    Then he may understand Shakespeare
    and the Wright brothers, Pasteur, Pavlov,
    Michael Faraday and free imaginations
bringing changes into a world resenting change.
        He will be lonely enough
        to have time for the work
        he knows as his own.

CRY,
THE BELOVED
COUNTRY

CRY,
THE BELOVED
COUNTRY

A CONDENSATION
OF THE BOOK BY

Alan Paton

ILLUSTRATED BY

DENVER GILLEN

In this story of a simple African parson's search for his erring son thousands of readers have found an unforgettable quality of truth and inspiration. The powerful narrative moves with swift pace and almost Biblical eloquence from the primitive countryside around the town of Ixopo, deep in the Zulu country of South Africa, to the Shanty Town warrens of Johannesburg's slums. It is a measure of the greatness of the book, which has been called "one of the best novels of our time," that this unfamiliar background and the characters who people it become intimately known and compellingly real.

Ixopo, as it happens, played an important part in Alan Paton's own life, for it was there, his formal education completed, that he first went to teach. Yet it was to be another twenty-five years before he started to write *Cry, the Beloved Country*. Born in Natal in 1903, the son of parents who believed in practicing their religion, Paton grew up with a conviction of the worth of all men, regardless of their color, and his life and work are a testament to this conviction. In 1935, after ten years of teaching, he became principal of the Diepkloof Reformatory near Johannesburg, then the largest on the African continent; and here, over the opposition of a staff suspicious of his "dangerous" ideas, he revolutionized the old punitive treatment of prisoners, seeking instead to reclaim them for a useful life in society. His experience in these years provided the stuff of this novel.

Cry, the Beloved Country was published in 1948. It has since been translated into twenty-five languages, and in South Africa itself once outsold every other work except the Bible. At first rather bewildered by such international enthusiasm, Alan Paton has since accounted for it in the following words:

"I do believe there is a level at which one can state an overwhelming truth that a man just cannot deny. After he has confronted the truth in that fashion, he is not the same man again."

THERE IS A LOVELY ROAD that runs from Ixopo into the hills. These hills are grass-covered and rolling, and they are lovely beyond any singing of it. The road climbs seven miles into them, to Carisbrooke; and from there, if there is no mist, you look down on one of the fairest valleys of Africa. About you there is grass and bracken and you may hear the forlorn crying of the titihoya,* one of the birds of the veld. Below you is the valley of the Umzimkulu, on its journey from the Drakensberg to the sea; and beyond and behind the river, great hill after great hill; and beyond and behind them, the mountains of Ingeli and East Griqualand.

The grass is rich and matted, you cannot see the soil. It holds the rain and the mist, and they seep into the ground, feeding the streams in every kloof. It is well tended, and not too many cattle

---

*A glossary of special South African terms will be found on page 591.

feed upon it; not too many fires burn it, laying bare the soil. Stand unshod upon it, for the ground is holy, being even as it came from the Creator. Keep it, guard it, care for it, for it keeps men, guards men, cares for men. Destroy it and man is destroyed.

Where you stand the grass is rich and matted, you cannot see the soil. But the rich green hills break down. They fall to the valley below, and falling, change their nature. For they grow red and bare; they cannot hold the rain and mist, and the streams are dry in the kloofs. Too many cattle feed upon the grass, and too many fires have burned it. Stand shod upon it, for it is coarse and sharp, and the stones cut under the feet. It is not kept, or guarded, or cared for, it no longer keeps men, guards men, cares for men. The titihoya does not cry here any more.

The great red hills stand desolate, and the earth has torn away like flesh. The lightning flashes over them, the clouds pour down upon them, the dead streams come to life, full of the red blood of the earth. Down in the valleys women scratch the soil that is left, and the maize hardly reaches the height of a man. They are valleys of old men and old women, of mothers and children. The men are away, the young men and the girls are away. The soil cannot keep them any more.

THE SMALL CHILD ran importantly to the wood-and-iron church with the letter in her hand. Next to the church was a house and she knocked timidly on the door. The Reverend Stephen Kumalo looked up from the table where he was writing, and he called, Come in.

The small child opened the door, carefully, like one who is afraid to open carelessly the door of so important a house, and stepped timidly in.

—I bring a letter, umfundisi.

—A letter, eh? Where did you get it, my child?

—From the store, umfundisi. The white man asked me to bring it to you.

—That was good of you. Go well, small one.

But she did not go at once. She rubbed one bare foot against the other, she rubbed one finger along the edge of the table.

—Perhaps you might be hungry, small one.

—Not very hungry, umfundisi.

—Perhaps a little hungry.

—Yes, a little hungry, umfundisi.

—Go to the mother then. Perhaps she has some food.

—I thank you, umfundisi.

She walked delicately, as though her feet might do harm in so great a house with tables and chairs, and a clock, and a plant in a pot, and many books, more even than the books at the school.

Kumalo looked at his letter. It was dirty, especially about the stamp. It had been in many hands, no doubt. It came from Johannesburg; now there in Johannesburg were many of his own people. His brother John, who was a carpenter, had gone there, and had a business of his own in Sophiatown, Johannesburg. His sister Gertrude, twenty-five years younger than he, and the child of his parents' age, had gone there with her small son to look for the husband who had never come back from the mines. His only child Absalom had gone there, to look for his aunt Gertrude, and he had never returned. And indeed many other relatives were there, though none so near as these. It was hard to say from whom this letter came, for it was so long since any of these had written that one did not well remember their writing.

He turned the letter over, but there was nothing to show from whom it came. He was reluctant to open it, for once such a thing is opened, it cannot be shut again.

He called to his wife, Has the child gone?

—She is eating, Stephen.

—Let her eat then. She brought a letter. Do you know anything about a letter?

—How should I know, Stephen?

—No, that I do not know. Look at it.

She took the letter and she felt it. But there was nothing in the touch to tell from whom it might be. She read out the address slowly and carefully—

Rev. Stephen Kumalo,
St. Mark's Church.
Ndotsheni.
NATAL.

She mustered up her courage, and said, It is not from our son.
—No, he said. And he sighed. It is not from our son.
—Perhaps it concerns him, she said.
—Yes, he said. That may be so.
—It is not from Gertrude, she said.
—Perhaps it is my brother John.
—It is not from John, she said.
They were silent, and she said, How we desire such a letter, and when it comes, we fear to open it.
—Who is afraid? he said. Open it.
She opened it, slowly and carefully, for she did not open so many letters. She spread it out open, and read it slowly and carefully, so that he did not hear all that she said. Read it aloud, he said.
She read it aloud, reading as a Zulu who reads English.

The Mission House,
Sophiatown,
Johannesburg.

25/9/46.

MY DEAR BROTHER IN CHRIST,
I have had the experience of meeting a young woman here in Johannesburg. Her name is Gertrude Kumalo, and I understand she is the sister of the Rev. Stephen Kumalo, St. Mark's Church, Ndotsheni. This young woman is very sick, and therefore I ask you to come quickly to Johannesburg. Come to the Rev. Theophilus Msimangu, the Mission House, Sophiatown, and there I shall give you some advices. I shall also find accommodation for you, where the expenditure will not be very serious.
I am, dear brother in Christ,
Yours faithfully,
THEOPHILUS MSIMANGU.

438

They were both silent till at long last he said, Has the child eaten?

She went to the kitchen and came back with the child.

—Have you eaten, my child?

—Yes, umfundisi.

—Then go well. And thank you for bringing the letter.

When the child was gone, she said to him, What will you do, Stephen?

He sighed. Bring me the St. Chad's money, he said.

She went out, and came back with a tin, of the kind in which they sell coffee, or cocoa, and this she gave to him. He held it in his hand, studying it, as though there might be some answer in it, till at last she said, It must be done, Stephen.

—How can I use it? he said. This money was to send Absalom to St. Chad's.

—Absalom will never go now to St. Chad's.

—How can you say such a thing? he said sharply.

—He is in Johannesburg, she said wearily. When people go to Johannesburg, they do not come back.

—You have said it, he said. It is said now. This money which was saved for that purpose will never be used for it. You have opened a door, and because you have opened it, we must go through. And *Tixo* alone knows where we shall go.

—It was not I who opened it, she said, hurt by his accusation. It has a long time been open, but you would not see.

—We had a son, he said harshly. Zulus have many children, but we had only one son. He went to Johannesburg, and as you said—when people go to Johannesburg, they do not come back. They do not even write any more. They do not go to St. Chad's, to learn that knowledge without which no black man can live. They go to Johannesburg, and there they are lost, and no one hears of them at all. And this money . . .

He held out the tin to her. Open it, he said.

With trembling hands she took the tin and opened it. She emptied it out over the table, some old and dirty notes, and a flood of silver and copper.

—Count it, he said.

She counted it laboriously, turning over the notes and the coins to make sure what they were.

—Twelve pounds, five shillings and sevenpence.

—I shall take eight pounds, and the shillings and pence, he said.

—Take it all, Stephen. There may be doctors, hospitals, other troubles. Take it all. And take the Post Office Book—there is ten pounds in it—you must take that also.

—I have been saving that for your stove, he said.

—That cannot be helped, she said. And that other money, though we saved it for St. Chad's, I had meant it for your new black clothes, and a new black hat, and new white collars.

—That cannot be helped either. Let me see, I shall go . . .

—Tomorrow, she said. From Carisbrooke.

—I shall write to the Bishop now, and tell him I do not know how long I shall be gone.

He rose heavily to his feet, and went and stood before her. I am sorry I hurt you, he said. I shall go and pray in the church.

He went out of the door, and she watched him through the little window, walking slowly to the door of the church. Then she sat down at his table, and put her head on it, and was silent, with the patient suffering of black women, with the suffering of oxen, with the suffering of any that are mute.

I T IS INTERESTING to wait for the train at Carisbrooke, while it climbs up out of the great valley. Those who know can tell you with each whistle where it is, at what road, what farm, what river. But though Stephen Kumalo has been there a full hour before he need, he does not listen to these things. This is a long way to go, and a lot of money to pay. And who knows how sick his sister may be, and what money that may cost? And if he has to bring her back, what will that cost too? And Johannesburg is a great city, with so many streets they say that a man can spend his days going up one and down another, and never the same one twice. One must catch buses too, but not as here, where the only bus that comes is the right bus. For there there is a multitude of buses, and only one bus in ten, one bus in twenty maybe, is the right bus. If you take the wrong bus, you may travel to quite some other place. And they say it is danger to cross the street, yet one must needs cross it. For there the wife of Mpanza of Ndotsheni, who had gone there when Mpanza was dying, saw her son Michael killed in the street. Twelve years old and moved by excitement, he stepped out into danger, but she was hesitant and stayed at the curb. And under her eyes the great lorry crushed the life out of her son.

And the great fear too—the greatest fear since it was so seldom spoken. Where was their son? Why did he not write any more?

There is a last whistle and the train is near at last. The parson turns to his companion.

—Friend, I thank you for your help.

—Umfundisi, I was glad to help you. You could not have done it alone. This bag is heavy.

The train is nearer, it will soon be in.

—Umfundisi, I have a favor to ask.

—Ask it then.

—You know Sibeko?

—Yes.

—Well, Sibeko's daughter worked here for the white man uSmith in Ixopo. And when the daughter of uSmith married, she went to Johannesburg, and Sibeko's daughter went with them to work. The address is here, with the new name of this married woman. But Sibeko has heard no word of his daughter this ten, twelve months. And he asks you to inquire.

Kumalo took the paper and looked at it. Springs, he said. I have heard of the place. But it is not Johannesburg, though they say it is near. Friend, the train is here. I shall do what I can.

Kumalo climbed into the carriage for non-Europeans, already full of the humbler people of his race, some with assortments of European garments, some with blankets over their primitive dress, though these were all women. Men traveled no longer in primitive dress.

The journey had begun. And now the fear back again, the fear of the unknown, the fear of the great city where boys were killed crossing the street, the fear of Gertrude's sickness. Deep down the fear for his son. Deep down the fear of a man who lives in a world not made for him, whose own world is slipping away, dying, being destroyed, beyond any recall.

The humble man reached in his pocket for his sacred book, and began to read. It was this world alone that was certain.

A day and night have passed, and the train is running now through the outskirts of Johannesburg.

RAILWAY LINES, railway lines, it is a wonder. To the left, to the right, so many that he cannot count. A train rushes past, with a sudden roaring of sound that makes him jump in his seat. Another races alongside, but drops slowly behind. Stations, stations, more than he has ever imagined. People are waiting there in hundreds, but the train rushes past, leaving them disappointed. The buildings get higher, the streets more uncountable. How does one find one's way in such a confusion? It is dusk, and the lights are coming on in the streets. One of the passengers points for him.

—Johannesburg, umfundisi.

He sees great high buildings; there are red and green lights on them, almost as tall as the buildings. They go on and off. Water comes out of a bottle, till the glass is full. Then the lights go out. And when they come on again, lo the bottle is full and upright, and the glass empty. And there goes the bottle over again. Black and white, it says, black and white, though it is red and green.

It is too much to understand.

He is silent, his head aches, he is afraid. There is this railway station to come, this great place with all its tunnels under the ground. The train stops, under a great roof, and there are thousands of people. Steps go down into the earth, and here is the tunnel under the ground. Black people, white people, some going, some coming, so many that the tunnel is full. He goes carefully that he may not bump anybody, holding tightly onto his bag. He comes out into a great hall, and the stream goes up the steps, and here he is out in the street. The noise is immense. Cars and buses one behind the other, more than he has ever imagined. The stream goes over the street, but remembering Mpanza's son, he is afraid to follow. Lights change from green to red, and back again to green. He has heard that. When it is green, you may go. But when he starts across, a great bus swings across the path. There is some law of it that he does not understand, and he retreats again. He finds himself a place against the wall; he will look as though he is waiting for some purpose. His heart beats like that of a child, there is nothing to do or think to stop it. *Tixo*, watch over me, he says to himself. *Tixo*, watch over me.

A YOUNG MAN CAME to him and spoke to him in a language that he did not understand.

—I do not understand, he said.

—You are a Xosa, then, umfundisi?

—A Zulu, he said.

—Where do you want to go, umfundisi?

—To Sophiatown, young man.

—Come with me then and I shall show you.

He was grateful for this kindness, but half of him was afraid. He was glad the young man did not offer to carry his bag, but he spoke courteously, though in a strange Zulu.

The lights turned green, and his guide started across the street. Another car swung across the path, but the guide did not falter, and the car came to a stop. It made one feel confidence.

He could not follow the turnings that they made under the high buildings, but at last, his arm tired beyond endurance by the bag, they came to a place of many buses.

—You must stand in line, umfundisi. Have you your money for the ticket?

Quickly, eagerly, as though he must show this young man that he appreciated his kindness, he put down his bag, took out his purse, and took a pound from it.

—Shall I get your ticket for you, umfundisi? Then you need not lose your place in the line, while I go to the ticket office.

—Thank you, he said.

The young man took the pound and walked to the corner. As he turned it, Kumalo was afraid. The line moved forward and he with it, clutching his bag. And again forward, and soon he must enter a bus, but still he had no ticket. As though he had suddenly thought of something he left the line, and walked to the corner, but there was no sign of the young man. He sought courage to speak to someone, and went to an elderly man, decently and cleanly dressed.

—Where is the ticket office, my friend?

—What ticket office, umfundisi?

—For the ticket for the bus.

—You get your ticket on the bus. There is no ticket office.

—I gave a pound to a young man, the parson said, and he told me he would get my ticket at the ticket office.

—You have been cheated, umfundisi. Can you see the young man? No, you will not see him again. Look, come with me. Where are you going, Sophiatown?

—Yes, Sophiatown. To the Mission House.

—Oh, yes. I too am an Anglican. I was waiting for someone, but I shall wait no longer. I shall come with you myself. Do you know the Reverend Msimangu?

—Indeed, I have a letter from him.

In due time they took their places in the bus. And it in its turn swung out into the confusion of the streets. The driver smoked carelessly, and it was impossible not to admire such courage. Street after street, light after light, as though they would never end, at times at such speed that the bus swayed from side to side, and the engine roared in the ears.

They alighted at a small street, and there were still thousands of people about. They walked a great distance, through streets crowded with people. At last they stopped before a lighted house, and knocked. A young tall man in clerical dress opened the door.

—Mr. Msimangu, I bring a friend to you, the Reverend Kumalo from Ndotsheni.

—Come in, come in, my friends. Mr. Kumalo, I am glad to greet you. Is this your first visit to Johannesburg?

Kumalo spoke humbly. I am much confused, he said. I owe much to our friend.

—You fell into good hands. This is Mr. Mafolo, one of our big businessmen, and a good son of the Church. You are no doubt hungry, Mr. Kumalo. Mr. Mafolo, will you stay for some food?

But Mr. Mafolo would not wait. The door shut after him, and Kumalo settled himself in a big chair, and accepted a cigarette though it was not his custom to smoke. The room was light, and the great bewildering town shut out. He puffed like a child at his smoke, and was thankful. The long journey to Johannesburg was over, and he had taken a liking to this young, confident man. In good time no doubt they would come to discuss the reason for this pilgrimage safely at an end. For the moment it was enough to feel welcome and secure.

I HAVE A PLACE for you to sleep, my friend, in the house of an old woman, a Mrs. Lithebe, who is a good member of our church. She is an Msutu, but she speaks Zulu well. She will think it an honor to have a priest in the house. It is cheap, only three shillings a week, and you can have your meals with the people of the Mission. Now there is the bell. Would you like to wash your hands?

They washed their hands in a modern place, with a white basin, and water cold and hot, and towels worn but very white, and a modern lavatory too. When you were finished, you pressed a little rod, and the water rushed in as though something was broken. It would have frightened you if you had not heard of such things before.

They went into a room where a table was laid, and there he met many priests, both white and black, and they sat down after grace and ate together. He was a bit nervous of the many plates and knives and forks, but watched what others did, and used the things likewise.

He sat next to a young rosy-cheeked priest from England, who asked him where he came from, and what it was like there. And another black priest cried out, I am also from Ixopo. My father and mother are still alive there, in the valley of the Lufafa. How is it there?

And he told them about the great hills and valleys of that far country. And the love of them must have been in his voice, for they were all silent and listened to him. He told them too of the sickness of the land, and how the grass had disappeared, and of the dongas that ran from hill to valley, and valley to hill; how it was a land of old men and women, and mothers and children; how the maize grew barely to the height of a man; how the tribe was broken, and the house broken, and the man broken; how when they went away, many never came back, many never wrote.

So they all talked of the sickness of the land, of the broken tribe and the broken house, of young men and young girls that went away and forgot their customs, and lived loose and idle lives. They talked of young criminal children, and older and more dangerous criminals, of how white Johannesburg was afraid of black crime. One of them went and got him a newspaper, the *Johannesburg Mail*, and showed him in bold black letters: OLD COUPLE ROBBED AND BEATEN IN LONELY HOUSE. FOUR NATIVES ARRESTED.

—That happens nearly every day, he said. And it is not only the Europeans who are afraid. We are also afraid, right here in Sophiatown.

—You will learn much here in Johannesburg, said the rosy-cheeked priest. It is not only in your place that there is destruction. I want to hear again about your country, but I must go now.

So they broke up, and Msimangu said he would take his visitor to his own private room.

—We have much to talk about, he said.

They went to the room, and when Msimangu had shut the door they sat themselves down. Kumalo said to him, You will pardon me if I am hasty, but I am anxious to hear about my sister.

—Yes, yes, said Msimangu. I am sure you are anxious. You must think I am thoughtless. But you will pardon me if I ask you first, why did she come to Johannesburg?

Kumalo, though disturbed by this question, answered obediently. She came to look for her husband who was recruited for the mines. But when his time was up, he did not return, nor did he write at all. She did not know if he were dead perhaps. So she took her small child and went to look for him.

Then because Msimangu did not speak, he asked anxiously, Is she very sick?

Msimangu said gravely, Yes, she is very sick. But it is not that kind of sickness. It is another, a worse kind of sickness. I sent for you firstly because she is a woman that is alone, and secondly because her brother is a priest. I do not know if she ever found her husband, but she has no husband now. He looked at Kumalo. It would be truer to say, he said, that she has many husbands.

Kumalo said, *Tixo! Tixo!*

—She lives in Claremont, not far from here. It is one of the worst places in Johannesburg. After the police have been there, you can see the liquor running in the streets. You can smell it, you can smell nothing else, wherever you go in that place.

He leant over to Kumalo. I used to drink liquor, he said, but it was good liquor, such as our fathers made. But now I have vowed to touch no liquor any more. This is bad liquor here, made strong with all manner of things that our people have never used. And that is her work, she makes and sells it. I shall hide nothing from you, though it is painful for me. These women sleep with any man for their price. A man has been killed at her place. They gamble and drink and stab. She has been in prison, more than once.

He leant back in his chair and moved a book forward and backward on the table. This is terrible news for you, he said.

Kumalo nodded dumbly, and Msimangu brought out his cigarettes. Will you smoke? he said.

Kumalo shook his head. I do not really smoke, he said. And they were both silent, as though a word had been spoken that made it hard to speak another. At last Kumalo said, Where is the child?

—The child is there. But it is no place for a child. And that too is why I sent for you. Perhaps if you cannot save the mother, you can save the child.

—Where is this place?

447

—It is not far from here. I shall take you tomorrow.

—I have another great sorrow.

—You may tell me.

—I shall be glad to tell you.

But then he was silent, and tried to speak and could not, so Msimangu said to him, Take your time, my brother.

—It is not easy. It is our greatest sorrow.

—A son, maybe. Or a daughter?

—It is a son.

—I am listening.

—Absalom was his name. He too went away, to look for my sister, but he never returned, nor after a while did he write any more. Our letters, his mother's and mine, all came back to us. And now after what you tell me, I am still more afraid.

—We shall try to find him, my brother. Perhaps your sister will know. You are tired, and I should take you to the room I have got for you.

—Yes, that would be better.

They rose, and Kumalo said, It is my habit to pray in the church. Maybe you will show me.

—It is on the way.

Kumalo said humbly, Maybe you will pray for me.

—I shall do it gladly. My brother, I have of course my work to do, but so long as you are here, my hands are yours.

—You are kind.

Something in the humble voice must have touched Msimangu, for he said, I am not kind. I am a selfish and sinful man, but God put His hands on me, that is all.

He picked up Kumalo's bag, but before they reached the door Kumalo stopped him.

—I have one more thing to tell you.

—Yes.

—I have a brother also, here in Johannesburg. He too does not write any more. John Kumalo, a carpenter.

Msimangu smiled. I know him, he said. He is too busy to write. He is one of our great politicians.

—A politician? My brother?

—Yes, he is a great man in politics.

Msimangu paused. I hope I shall not hurt you further. Your brother has no use for the Church any more. He says that what God has not done for South Africa, man must do. That is what he says.

—This is a bitter journey.

—I can believe it.

—Sometimes I fear—what will the Bishop say when he hears? One of his priests?

—What can a Bishop say? Something is happening that no Bishop can stop. They must go on.

—How can you say they must go on?

—They must go on, said Msimangu gravely. You cannot stop the world from going on. My friend, I am a Christian. It is not in my heart to hate a white man. It was a white man who brought my father out of darkness. But you will pardon me if I talk frankly to you. The tragedy is not that things are broken. The tragedy is that they are not mended again. The white man has broken the tribe. And it is my belief—and again I ask your pardon—that it cannot be mended again. But the house that is broken, and the man that falls apart when the house is broken, these are the tragic things. That is why children break the law, and old white people are robbed and beaten. He passed his hand across his brow.

—It suited the white man to break the tribe, he continued gravely. But it has not suited him to build something in the place of what is broken. I have pondered this for many hours, and I must speak it, for it is the truth for me. They are not all so. There are some white men who give their lives to build up what is broken.

—But they are not enough, he said. They are afraid, that is the truth. It is fear that rules this land.

He laughed apologetically. These things are too many to talk about now. They are things to talk over quietly and patiently. You must get Father Vincent to talk about them. He is a white man and can say what must be said. He is the one with the boy's cheeks, the one who wants to hear more about your country. But come, let us go to the church.

449

MRS. LITHEBE, I BRING my friend to you. The Reverend Stephen Kumalo.

—Umfundisi, you are welcome. The room is small, but clean.

—I am sure of it.

—Good night, my brother, said Msimangu. Shall I see you in the church tomorrow at seven?

—Assuredly.

—And after that I shall take you to eat. Stay well, my friend. Stay well, Mrs. Lithebe.

—Go well, my friend.

—Go well, umfundisi.

She took him to the small clean room and lit a candle for him.

—If there is anything, you will ask, umfundisi.

—I thank you.

—Sleep well, umfundisi.

—Sleep well, mother.

He stood a moment in the room. Forty-eight hours ago he and his wife had been packing his bag in faraway Ndotsheni. Twenty-four hours ago the train had been thundering through an unseen country. And now outside, the stir and movement of people, but behind them, through them, one could hear the roar of a great city. Johannesburg. Johannesburg. Who could believe it?

IT IS NOT FAR to Claremont. They lie together; Sophiatown, where any may own property, Western Native Township which belongs to the Municipality of Johannesburg, and Claremont, the garbage heap of the proud city. These three are bounded on the west by the European district of Newlands, and on the east by the European district of Westdene.

—That is a pity, says Msimangu. I am not a man for segregation, but it is a pity that we are not apart. They run trams from the center of the city, and part is for Europeans and part for us. But we are often thrown off the trams by young hooligans. And our hooligans are ready for trouble too.

—But the authorities, do they allow that?

—They do not. But they cannot watch every tram. And if a trouble develops, who can find how it began, and who will tell the truth? It is a pity we are not apart.

So they walked till they came to Claremont and Kumalo was shocked by its shabbiness and dirtiness, and the closeness of the houses, and the filth in the streets.

—Do you see that woman, my friend?

—I see her.

—She is one of the queens, the liquor sellers. They say she is one of the richest of our people in Johannesburg.

—And these children? Why are they not at school?

—Some because they do not care, and some because their parents do not care, but many because the schools are full.

They walked down Lily Street, and turned off into Hyacinth Street, for the names there are very beautiful.

—It is here, brother. Number Eleven. Do you go in alone?

—It would be better.

—When you are ready, you will find me next door at Number Thirteen. There is a woman of our church there, and a good woman who tries with her husband to bring up good children. But it is hard. Their eldest daughter whom I prepared for confirmation has run away, and lives in Pimville, with a young loafer of the streets. Knock there, my friend. You know where to find me.

There is laughter in the house, the kind of laughter of which one is afraid. Perhaps because one is afraid already, perhaps because it is in truth bad laughter. A woman's voice, and men's voices. But he knocks, and she opens.

—It is I, my sister.

Have no doubt it is fear in her eyes. She draws back a step, and makes no move towards him. She turns and says something that he cannot hear. Chairs are moved, and other things are taken. She turns to him.

—I am making ready, my brother.

They stand and look at each other, he anxious, she afraid. She turns and looks back into the room. A door closes, and she says, Come in, my brother.

Only then does she reach her hand to him. It is cold and wet, there is no life in it. They sit down, she is silent upon her chair.

—I have come, he said.

—It is good.

—You did not write.

—No, I did not write.

—Where is your husband?

—I have not found him, my brother.

—But you did not write.

—I had no money to write.

—Not two pennies for a stamp?

She does not answer him. She does not look at him.

—But I hear you are rich.

—I am not rich.

—I hear you have been in prison.

—That is true indeed.

—Was it for liquor?

A spark of life comes into her. She must do something, she cannot keep so silent. She tells him she was not guilty. There was some other woman.

—You stayed with this woman?

—Yes.

—Why did you stay with such a woman?

—I had no other place.

—And you helped her with her trade?

—I had to have money for the child.

—Where is the child?

She looks round vaguely. She gets up and goes to the yard. She calls, but the voice that was once so sweet has a new quality in it, the quality of the laughter that he heard in the house. She is revealing herself to him.

—I have sent for the child, she says.

—Where is it?

—It shall be fetched, she says. There is discomfort in her eyes, and she stands fingering the wall. The anger wells up in him.

—Where shall I sleep? he asks.

The fear in her eyes is unmistakable. Now she will reveal herself, but his anger masters him, and he does not wait for it.

—You have shamed us, he says in a low voice, not wishing to make it known to the world. A liquor seller, a prostitute, with a child and you do not know where it is. Your brother a priest. How could you do this to us?

She looks at him sullenly, like an animal that is tormented.

—I have come to take you back. She falls on the floor and cries; her cries become louder and louder, she has no shame.

—They will hear us, he says urgently.

She tries to control her sobs.

—Do you wish to come back?

She nods her head. I do not like Johannesburg, she says. I am sick here. The child is sick also.

—Do you wish with your heart to come back?

She nods her head again. She sobs too. She looks at him with eyes of distress, and his heart quickens with hope. I am a bad woman, my brother. I am no woman to go back.

His eyes fill with tears, his deep gentleness returns to him. He goes to her and lifts her from the floor to the chair. Inarticulately he strokes her face, his heart filled with pity.

—God forgives us, he says. Who am I not to forgive? Let us pray.

They knelt down, and he prayed, quietly so that the neighbors might not hear, and she punctuated his petitions with Amens. And when he had finished, she burst into a torrent of prayer, of self-denunciation, and urgent petition. And thus reconciled, they sat hand in hand.

—And now I ask you for help, he said.

—What is it, my brother?

—Our child, have you not heard of him?

—I did hear of him, brother. He was working at some big place in Johannesburg, and he lived in Sophiatown, but where I am not sure. But I know who will know. The son of our brother John and your son were often together. John will know.

—I shall go there. And now, my sister, I must see if Mrs. Lithebe has a room for you. Have you many things?

—Not many. This table and those chairs, and a bed. And some few dishes and pots. That is all.

—I shall find someone to fetch them. You will be ready?

—My brother, here is the child.

Into the room, shepherded by an older girl, came his little nephew. His clothes were dirty and his nose running, and he put his finger in his mouth, and gazed at his uncle out of wide saucerlike eyes. Kumalo lifted him up, and wiped his nose clean, and kissed and fondled him.

—It will be better for the child, he said. He will go to a place where the wind blows, and where there is a school for him.

—It will be better, she agreed.

—I must go, he said. There is much to do.

He went out into the street, and curious neighbors stared at him. It was an umfundisi that was here. He found his friend, and poured out his news, and asked him where they could find a man to fetch his sister, her child and possessions.

—We shall go now, said Msimangu. I am glad for your sake, my friend.

—There is a great load off my mind, my friend. Please God the other will be as successful.

He fetched her with a lorry that afternoon, amidst a crowd of interested neighbors, who discussed the affair loudly and frankly, some with approval, and some with the strange laughter of the towns. He was glad when the lorry was loaded, and they left.

Mrs. Lithebe showed them their room, and gave the mother and child their food while Kumalo went down to the Mission. And that night they held prayers in the dining room, and Mrs. Lithebe and Gertrude punctuated his petitions with Amens. Kumalo himself was lighthearted and gay like a boy; one day in Johannesburg, and already the tribe was being rebuilt, the house and the soul restored.

GERTRUDE'S DRESS, for all that she might once have been rich, was dirty, and the black greasy knitted cap that she wore on her head made him ashamed. Although his money was little, he bought her a red dress and a white thing that they called a turban for her head. Also a shirt, a pair of short trousers, and a jersey for the boy; and a couple of stout handkerchiefs for his mother to use on his nose. In his pocket was his Post Office Book, and there was ten pounds there that he and his wife were saving to buy the stove, for that, like any woman, she had long been wanting to have. To save ten pounds from a stipend of eight pounds a month takes much patience and time, especially for a parson, who must dress in good black clothes. His clerical collars were brown and frayed, but they must wait now a while. It was a pity about the ten pounds, that it would sooner or later have to be broken into, but the trains did not carry for nothing, and they would no doubt get a pound or two for her things. Strange that she had saved nothing from her sad employment, which brought in much money, it was said.

But this day would begin the search for his son. There was Msimangu coming up the street.

—Are you ready, my friend?

—Yes, I am ready.

They walked up the street, and down another, and up yet another. It was true what they said, that you could go up one street and down another till the end of your days, and never walk the same one twice.

—Here is your brother's shop. You see his name.

—Yes, I see it.

—Shall I come with you?

—Yes, I think it would be right.

His brother John was sitting there on a chair, talking to two other men. He had grown fat, and sat with his hands on his knees like a chief. He did not recognize Kumalo, for the light from the street was on the backs of his visitors.

—Good morning, my brother.

—Good morning, sir.

—Good morning, my brother, son of our mother.

John Kumalo looked closely at him, and stood up with a great hearty smile. My own brother, he said. Well, well, who can believe? What are you doing in Johannesburg?

Kumalo looked at the visitors. I come on business, he said.

—I am sure my friends will excuse us. My own brother, the son of our mother, has come.

The two men rose, and they all said, Stay well and go well.

—Do you know the Reverend Msimangu, my brother?

—Well, well, he is known to everybody. Everybody knows the Reverend Msimangu. Sit down, gentlemen. I think we must have some tea. He went to the door and called into the place behind.

—Is your wife Esther well, my brother?

John Kumalo smiled his jolly and knowing smile. My wife Esther has left me these ten years, my brother.

—And have you married again?

—Well, well, not what the Church calls married, you know. But she is a good woman.

—You wrote nothing of this, brother.

—No, how could I write? You people in Ndotsheni do not understand the way life is in Johannesburg. I thought it better not to write.

—That is why you stopped writing.

—Well, well, that could be why I stopped. Trouble, brother, unnecessary trouble.

—But I do not understand. How is life different in Johannesburg?

—Well, that is difficult. Do you mind if I speak in English? I can explain these things better in English.

—Speak in English, then, brother.

—You see I have had an experience here in Johannesburg. It is not like Ndotsheni. One must live here to understand it. He looked at his brother. Something new is happening here, he said.

He did not sit down, but began to speak in a strange voice. He walked about, and looked through the window into the street, and up at the ceiling, and into the corners of the room as though something were there, and must be brought out.

—Down in Ndotsheni I am nobody, even as you are nobody, my brother. I am subject to the chief, who is an ignorant man. I must salute him and bow to him, but he is an uneducated man. Here in Johannesburg I am a man of some importance, of some influence. I have my own business, and when it is good, I can make ten, twelve pounds a week. He began to sway to and fro, he was not speaking to them, he was speaking to people who were not there.

—I do not say we are free here. I do not say we are free as men should be. But at least I am free of the chief. At least I am free of an old and ignorant man, who is nothing but a white man's dog. He is a trick, a trick to hold together something that the white man desires to hold together. He smiled his cunning and knowing smile, and for a moment addressed himself to his visitors.

—But it is not being held together, he said. It is breaking apart, your tribal society. It is here in Johannesburg that the new society is being built. Something is happening here, my brother.

He paused for a moment, then he said, I do not wish to offend you gentlemen, but the Church too is like the chief. You must do so and so and so. You are not free to have an experience. A man must be faithful and meek and obedient, and he must obey the laws, whatever the laws may be. It is true that the Church speaks with a fine voice, and that the Bishops speak against the laws. But this they have been doing for fifty years, and things get worse, not better.

His voice grew louder, and he was again addressing people who were not there. Here in Johannesburg it is the mines, he said, everything is the mines. These high buildings, this wonderful City Hall, this beautiful Parktown with its beautiful houses, all this is built with the gold from the mines. This wonderful hospital for Europeans, the biggest hospital south of the equator, it is built with the gold from the mines.

There was a change in his voice, it became louder like the voice of a bull or a lion. Go to our hospital, he said, and see our people lying on the floors. They lie so close you cannot step over them. But it is they who dig the gold. For three shillings a day. We live in the compounds, we must leave our wives and families behind. And when the new gold is found, it is not we who will get more for our labor. It is the white man's shares that will rise, you will read it in all the papers. They go mad when new gold is found. They bring more of us to live in the compounds, to dig under the ground for three shillings a day. They do not think, here is a chance to pay more for our labor. They think only, here is a chance to build a bigger house and buy a bigger car. It is important to find gold, they say, for all South Africa is built on the mines.

He growled, and his voice grew deep, it was like thunder that was rolling. But it is not built on the mines, he said, it is built on our backs, on our sweat, on our labor. Every factory, every theater, every beautiful house, they are all built by us. And what does a chief know about that? But here in Johannesburg they know.

He stopped, and was silent. And his visitors were silent also, for there was something in this voice that compelled one to be silent. Then Kumalo spoke to this new brother that he saw.

—I have listened attentively to you, my brother. Much of what you say saddens me, partly because of the way you say it, and partly because much of it is true. And now I have something to ask of you. But I must tell you first that Gertrude is with me here. She is coming back to Ndotsheni.

—Well, well, I shall not say it is a bad thing. Johannesburg is not a place for a woman alone. I myself tried to persuade her, but she did not agree, so we did not meet any more.

—And now I must ask you. Where is my son?

There is something like discomfort in John's eyes. He takes out a large red handkerchief to wipe his face.

—Well, you have heard no doubt he was friendly with my son.

—I have heard that.

—Well, you know how these young men are. I do not blame them altogether. You see, my son did not agree well with his second mother. What it was about I could never discover. Nor did he agree with his mother's children. Many times I tried to arrange matters, but I did not succeed. So he said he would leave. He had good work so I did not stop him. And your son went with him.

—Where, my brother?

—I do not rightly know. But I heard that they had a room in Alexandra. Now wait a minute. They were both working for a factory. I remember. Wait till I look in the telephone book.

He went to a table and there Kumalo saw the telephone. He felt a little pride to be the brother of a man who had such a thing.

—There it is. Doornfontein Textiles Company, 14 Krause Street. I shall write it down for you, my brother.

—Can we not telephone them? asked Kumalo hesitantly.

His brother laughed. What for? he asked. To ask if Absalom Kumalo is working there? Or to ask if they will call him to the telephone? They do not do such things for a black man, my brother.

—It does not matter, said Msimangu. My hands are yours, my friend.

They said their farewells and went out into the street.

—He is a big man, in this place, your brother, said Msimangu. His shop is always full of men, talking as you have heard. But they say you must hear him at a meeting. They say he speaks like a bull, and growls in his throat like a lion, and could make men mad if he would. But for that they say he has not enough courage, for he would surely be sent to prison.

—I shall tell you one thing, Msimangu continued. Many of the things that he said are true.

He stopped in the street and spoke quietly and earnestly to his companion. Because the white man has power, we too want power, he said. But when a black man gets power, when he gets money, he is a great man if he is not corrupted. I have seen it often. He seeks power and money to put right what is wrong, and when he gets them, why, he enjoys the power and the money. Now he can gratify his lusts, now he can arrange ways to get white man's liquor, and the power has no heart in it. There is only one thing that has power completely, and that is love.

—I see only one hope for our country, and that is when white men and black men, desiring neither power nor money, but desiring only the good of their country, come together to work for it.

He was grave and silent, and then he said somberly, I have one great fear in my heart, that one day when they are turned to loving, they will find we are turned to hating.

—This is not the way to get to Doornfontein, he said. Come, let us hurry.

And Kumalo followed him silently, oppressed by the grave and somber words.

BUT THEY WERE NOT SUCCESSFUL at Doornfontein, although the white men treated them with consideration. Msimangu knew how to arrange things with white men, and they went to a great deal of trouble, and found that Absalom Kumalo had left them some twelve months before.

One of them remembered that Absalom had been friendly with one of their workmen, Dhlamini, and this man was sent for. He told them that, when he had last heard, Absalom was staying with a Mrs. Ndlela, of End Street, Sophiatown, the street that separates Sophiatown from the European suburb of Westdene. He was not sure, but he thought that the number of the house was 105.

So they returned to Sophiatown, and indeed found Mrs. Ndlela at 105 End Street. She received them with a quiet kindness, and her children hid behind her skirts, and peeped out at the visitors. But Absalom was not there, she said. But wait, she had had a letter from him, asking about the things he had left behind. So while Kumalo played with her children, and Msimangu talked to her husband, she brought out a big box full of papers and other belongings, and looked for the letter. And while she was searching, and Msimangu was watching her kind and tired face, he saw her stop in her search for a moment, and look at Kumalo for a moment, half curiously, and half with pity. At last she found the letter, and she showed them the address, c/o Mrs. Mkize, 79 Twenty-third Avenue, Alexandra.

Then they must drink a cup of tea, and it was dark before they rose to leave, and the husband stepped out with Kumalo into the street.

—Why did you look at my friend with pity? asked Msimangu of the woman.

She dropped her eyes, then raised them again. He is an umfundisi, she said.

—Yes.

—I did not like his son's friends. Nor did my husband. That is why he left us.

—I understand you. Was there anything worse than that?

—No. I saw nothing. But I did not like his friends.

Out in the street they said farewell to the husband, and set off back to the Mission House.

—Tomorrow, said Msimangu, we go to Alexandra.

Kumalo put his hand on his friend's arm. The things are not happy that brought me to Johannesburg, he said, but I have found much pleasure in your company.

—Huh, said Msimangu, huh, we must hurry or we shall be late for our food.

T HE NEXT MORNING, after they had eaten at the Mission House, Msimangu and Kumalo set off for the great wide road that led to Alexandra.

They walked, through many streets full of cars and buses and people, till they reached the bus rank for Alexandra. But here they met an unexpected obstacle, for a man came up to them and said to Msimangu, Are you going to Alexandra, umfundisi?

—Yes, my friend.

—We are here to stop you, umfundisi. Not by force, you see— he pointed—the police are there to prevent that. But by persuasion. If you use this bus you are weakening the cause of the black people. We have determined not to use these buses until the fare is brought back again to fourpence.

—Yes, indeed, I have heard of it.

He turned to Kumalo.

—I was very foolish, my friend. I had forgotten the boycott of the buses.

—Our business is very urgent, said Kumalo humbly.

—This boycott is also urgent, said the man politely. They want us to pay sixpence, that is one shilling a day. Six shillings a week, and some of us only get thirty-five or forty shillings.

—Is it far to walk? asked Kumalo.

—It is a long way, umfundisi. Eleven miles.

—That is a long way, for an old man.

—Men as old as you are doing it every day, umfundisi. I cannot stop you taking a bus, umfundisi, but this is a cause to fight for.

If we lose it, then they will have to pay more in Sophiatown and Claremont and Kliptown and Pimville.

—I understand you well. We shall not use the bus.

The man thanked them and went to another would-be traveler.

—That man has a silver tongue, said Kumalo.

—That is the famous Dubula, said Msimangu quietly. A friend of your brother John. But they say—excuse me, my friend—that Tomlinson has the brains, and your brother the voice, but that this man has the heart. Well, my friend, what do we do now?

—I am willing to walk.

—Eleven miles, and eleven miles back. It is a long journey.

—I am willing. You understand I am anxious, my friend. This Johannesburg—it is no place for a boy to be alone.

—Good. Let us begin then.

So they walked many miles through the European city, up Twist Street to the Clarendon Circle, and down Louis Botha towards Orange Grove. And the cars and lorries never ceased, going one way or the other. After a long time a car stopped and a white man spoke to them. Where are you two going? he asked.

—To Alexandra, sir, said Msimangu, taking off his hat.

—I thought you might be. Climb in.

That was a great help to them, and at the turnoff to Alexandra they expressed their thanks.

—It is a long journey, said the white man. And I know that you have no buses.

They stood to watch him go on, but he did not go on. He swung round, and was soon on the road back to Johannesburg.

—Huh, said Msimangu, that is something to marvel at.

It was still a long way to Twenty-third Avenue, and as they walked, Msimangu explained that Alexandra was outside the boundaries of Johannesburg, and was a place where a black man could buy land and own a house. But the streets were not cared for, and there were no lights, and so great was the demand for accommodation that every man, if he could, built rooms in his yard and sublet them to others. Many of these rooms were hideouts for robbers, and there was much prostitution and brewing of illicit liquor.

—These things are very bad, said Msimangu. One of our young boys snatched a bag there from an old white woman, and she fell to the ground, and died there of shock and fear. And there was a terrible case of a white woman who lived by herself in a house not far from here, and because she resisted some of our young men who broke in, they killed her. Sometimes, too, white men and women sit in their cars in the dark under the trees on the Pretoria Road; and some of our young men sometimes rob and assault them, sometimes even the women. It is true that they are often bad women, but that is the one crime we dare not speak of.

—The white people of Orange Grove and Norwood and Highlands North got up a great petition to do away with Alexandra altogether. But our white friends fought against this petition, for they said that the good things of the place were more than the bad. That it was something to have a place of one's own, and a house to bring up children in, and a place to have a voice in, so that a man is something in the land where he was born. Professor Hoernle—he is dead, God rest his soul—he was the great fighter for us. Huh, I am sorry you cannot hear him. When he spoke, there was no white man that could speak against him.

He took out his handkerchief and wiped his face. I have talked a great deal, he said, right up to the very house we are seeking.

A woman opened the door to them. She gave them no greeting, and when they stated their business, it was with reluctance that she let them in.

—You say the boy has gone, Mrs. Mkize?

—Yes, I do not know where he is gone.

—When did he go?

—These many months. A year it must be.

—And had he a friend?

—Yes, another Kumalo. The son of his father's brother. But they left together.

—And you do not know where they went?

—They talked of many places. But you know how these young men talk.

—How did he behave himself, this young man Absalom?

Have no doubt it is fear in her eyes. Have no doubt it is fear now in his eyes also. It is fear, here in this house.

—I saw nothing wrong, she said.

—But you guessed there was something wrong.

—There was nothing wrong, she said.

—Then why are you afraid? Kumalo asked her.

—I am not afraid, she said. She looked at them sullenly, watchfully.

—We thank you, said Msimangu. Stay well.

—Go well, she said.

Out in the street Kumalo spoke. There is something wrong, he said.

—I do not deny it. My friend, two of us are too many together. Turn left at the big street and go up the hill, and you will find a place for refreshment. Wait for me there.

Heavyhearted the old man went, and Msimangu followed him slowly till he turned at the corner. Then he returned to the house.

She opened again to him, as sullen as before; now that she had recovered, there was more sullenness than fear.

—I am not from the police, he said. I have nothing to do with the police, I wish to have nothing to do with them. But there is an old man suffering because he cannot find his son.

—That is a bad thing, she said, but she spoke as one speaks who must speak so.

—It is a bad thing, he said, and I cannot leave you until you have told what you would not tell.

—I have nothing to tell, she said.

—You have nothing to tell because you are afraid. I shall not leave you till I discover it. And if it is necessary, I shall go to the police after all, because there will be no other place to go.

—It is hard for a woman who is alone, she said resentfully.

—It is hard for an old man seeking his son.

—I am afraid, she said.

—He is afraid also. Could you not see he is afraid?

—I could see it, umfundisi.

—Then tell me, what sort of life did they lead here, these two young men? But she kept silent, with the fear in her eyes, and tears near to them. He could see she would be hard to move.

—I am a priest. Would you not take my word? But she kept silent.

—Have you a Bible?

—I have a Bible.

—Then I will swear to you on the Bible.

But she kept silent till he said again, I will swear to you on the Bible. So getting no peace, she rose irresolute, and went to a room behind, and after some time she returned with the Bible.

—I am a priest, he said. My yea has always been yea, and my nay, nay. But because you desire it, and because an old man is afraid, I swear to you on this Book that no trouble will come to you of this, for we seek only a boy. So help me *Tixo*.

—What sort of life did they lead? he asked.

—They brought many things here, umfundisi, in the late hours of the night. They were clothes, and watches, and money, and food in bottles, and many other things.

—Was there ever blood on them?

—I never saw blood on them, umfundisi.

—That is something. Only a little, but something.

—And why did they leave? he asked.

—I do not know, umfundisi. But I think they were near to being discovered.

—And they left when?

—About a year since, umfundisi. Indeed as I told you.

—And here on this Book you will swear you do not know where they are gone?

She reached for the Book, but, It does not matter, he said. He said farewell to her, and hurried out after his friend. But she called after him, They were friendly with the taxi driver Hlabeni. Near the bus rank he lives. Everyone knows him.

—For that I give you thanks. Stay well, Mrs. Mkize.

At the refreshment stall he found his friend.

—Did you find anything further? asked the old man eagerly.

—I heard of a friend of theirs, the taxi driver Hlabeni. Let me first eat, and we shall find him out.

When Msimangu had eaten, he went to ask a man where he could find Hlabeni, the taxi driver. There he is on the corner sitting in his taxi, said the man. Msimangu walked over to the taxi, and said to the man sitting in it, Good afternoon, my friend.

—Good afternoon, umfundisi.

—I want a taxi, my friend. What do you charge to Johannesburg? For myself and a friend?

—For you, umfundisi, I should charge eleven shillings.

—It is a lot of money.

—Another taxi would charge fifteen or twenty shillings.

—My companion is old and tired. I shall pay you eleven shillings.

The man made to start his engine, but Msimangu stopped him. I am told, he said, that you can help me to find a young man Absalom Kumalo.

Have no doubt too that this man is afraid. But Msimangu was quick to reassure him. I am not here for trouble, he said. I give you my word that I am seeking trouble neither for you nor for myself. But my companion, the old man who is tired, is the father of this young man, and he has come from Natal to find him. Everywhere we go, we are told to go somewhere else, and the old man is anxious.

—Yes, I knew this young man.

—And where is he now, my friend?

—I heard he was gone to Orlando, and lives there amongst the squatters in Shanty Town. But further than that I do not know.

—Orlando is a big place, said Msimangu.

—Where the squatters live is not so big, umfundisi. It should not be hard to find him. There are people from the Municipality working among the squatters, and they know them all. Could you not ask one of those people?

—There you have helped me, my friend. I know some of those people. Come, we shall take your taxi. Another day we shall find him.

AND THIS IS SHANTY TOWN, my friend.

Even here the children laugh in the narrow lanes that run between these tragic habitations. A sheet of iron, a few planks, hessian and grass, an old door from some forgotten house. Smoke curls from vents cunningly contrived, there is a smell of food, there is a sound of voices, not raised in anger or pain, but talking of ordinary things, of this one that is born and that one that has died, of this one that does so well at school and that one who is now in prison. There is drought over the land, and the sun shines warmly down from the cloudless sky. But what will they do when it rains, what will they do when it is winter?

—It is sad for me to see.

—Yet see them building over there. And that they have not done for many a year. Some good may come of this. And this too is Dubula's work.

—He is everywhere, it seems.

—See, there is one of our nurses. Does she not look well in her red and white, and her cap upon her head?

—She looks well indeed.

—The white people are training more and more of them. It is strange how we move forward in some things, and stand still in others, and go backward in yet others. Yet in this matter of nurses we have many friends amongst the white people. There was a great outcry when it was decided to allow some of our young people to train as doctors at the European University of the Witwatersrand. But our friends stood firm, and they will train there until we have a place of our own. Good morning, nurse.

—Good morning, umfundisi.

—Nurse, have you been working here long?

—Yes, as long as the place is here.

—And did you ever know a young man, Absalom Kumalo?

—Yes, that I did. But he is not here now. And I can tell where he stayed. He stayed with the Hlatshwayos, and they are still here. Do you see the place where there are many stones so that they cannot build? See, there is a small boy standing there.

—Yes, I see it.

—And beyond it the house with the pipe, where the smoke is coming out?

—Yes, I see it.

—Go down that lane, and you will find the Hlatshwayos in the third or fourth house, on the side of the hand that you eat with.

—Thank you, nurse, we shall go.

Her directions were so clear that they had no difficulty in finding the house.

—Good morning, mother.

The woman was clean and nice-looking, and she smiled at them in a friendly way. Good morning, umfundisi, she said.

—Mother, we are looking for a lad, Absalom Kumalo.

—He stayed with me, umfundisi. We took pity on him because he had no place to go. But I am sorry to tell you that they took him away, and I heard that the magistrate had sent him to the reformatory.

—The reformatory?

—Yes, the big school over there, beyond the soldiers' hospital. It is not too far to walk.

—I must thank you, mother. Stay well. Come, my friend. They walked on in silence, for neither of them had any words. Kumalo would have stumbled, though the road was straight and even, and Msimangu took his arm.

—Have courage, my brother.

He glanced at his friend, but Kumalo's eyes were on the ground. Although Msimangu could not see his face, he could see the drop that fell on the ground, and he tightened his grip on the arm.

—Have courage, my brother.

—Sometimes it seems that I have no more courage.

—I have heard of this reformatory. Your friend the priest from England speaks well of it. I have heard him say that if any boy wishes to amend, there is help for him there. So take courage.

—I was afraid of this.

—Yes, I too was afraid of it.

—Yes, you became afraid in Alexandra, when you sent me on, and you returned to speak again to the woman.

—I see that I cannot hide from you.

—That is not because I am so wise. Only because it is my son. What did the woman say to you, my friend?

469

—She said that these two young men were in some mischief. Many goods, white people's goods, came to the house.

—This reformatory, can they reform there?

—I do not know it well. Some people say one thing, some the other. But your friend speaks well of it.

And after a long while, during which Msimangu's thoughts had wandered elsewhere, Kumalo said again, It is my hope that they can reform there.

—It is my hope also, my brother.

After a walk of about one hour, they came to the road that led up to the reformatory. It was midday when they arrived, and from all directions there came boys marching, into the gates of the reformatory. From every place they came, until it seemed that the marching would never end.

—There are very many here, my friend.

—Yes, I did not know there would be so many.

One of their own people, a pleasant fellow with a smiling face, came up to them and asked them what they wanted, and they told him they were searching for one Absalom Kumalo. So this man took them to an office, where a young white man inquired of them in Afrikaans what was their business.

—We are looking, sir, for the son of my friend, one Absalom Kumalo, said Msimangu in the same language.

—Absalom Kumalo. Yes, I know him well. Strange, he told me he had no people.

—Your son told him, my friend, that he had no people, said Msimangu in Zulu.

—He was no doubt ashamed, said Kumalo. I am sorry, he said to Msimangu in Zulu, that I speak no Afrikaans. For he had heard that sometimes they do not like black people who speak no Afrikaans.

—You may speak what you will, said the young man. Your son did well here, he said. He became one of our senior boys, and I have great hope for his future.

—You mean, sir, that he is gone?

—Gone, yes, only one month ago. We made an exception in his

case, partly because of his good behavior, partly because of his age, but mainly because there was a girl who was pregnant by him. She came here to see him, and he seemed fond of her, and anxious about the child that would be born. And the girl too seemed fond of him, so with all these things in mind, and with his solemn undertaking that he would work for his child and its mother, we asked the Minister to let him go. Of course we do not succeed in all these cases, but where there seems to be real affection between the parties, we take the chance, hoping that good will come of it. One thing is certain, that if it fails, nothing could have succeeded.

—And is he now married, sir?

—No, umfundisi, he is not. But everything is arranged for the marriage. This girl has no people, and your son told us he had no people, so I myself and my native assistant have arranged it.

—That is good of you, sir. I thank you for them.

—It is our work. You must not worry too much about this matter, and the fact that they were not married, the young man said kindly. The real question is whether he will care for them, and lead a decent life.

—That I can see, although it is a shock to me.

—I understand that. Now I can help you in this matter. If you will sit outside while I finish my work, I will take you to Pimville, where Absalom and this girl are living. He will not be there, because I have found work for him in the town, and they have given me good reports of him. I persuaded him to open a Post Office Book, and he already has three or four pounds in it.

—Indeed I cannot thank you, sir.

—It is our work, said the young man. Now if you will leave me, I shall finish what I have to do, and then take you to Pimville.

Outside the pleasant-faced man came and spoke to them and, hearing their plans, invited them to his house, where he and his wife had a number of boys in their charge, boys who had left the big reformatory building and were living outside in these free houses. He gave them some tea and food, and he too told them that Absalom had become a head boy, and had behaved well during his stay at the reformatory. So they talked about the reformatory,

471

and the children that were growing up in Johannesburg without home or school or custom, and about the broken tribe and the sickness of the land, until a messenger came from the young man to say that he was ready.

It was not long before the motorcar had reached Pimville, which is a village of half-tanks used as houses, set up many years before in emergency, and used ever since. For there have never been houses enough for all the people who came to Johannesburg. At the gate they asked permission to enter, for a white man may not go into these places without permission.

They stopped at one of these half-tank houses, and the young white man took them in, where they were greeted by a young girl, who herself seemed no more than a child.

—We have come to inquire after Absalom, said the young white man. This umfundisi is his father.

—He went on Saturday to Springs, and he has not yet returned.

The young man was silent awhile, and he frowned in perplexity. But this is Tuesday, he said. Have you heard nothing from him?

—Nothing, she said.

—When will he return? he asked.

—I do not know, she said.

—Will he ever return? he asked, indifferently, carelessly.

—I do not know, she said. She said it tonelessly, hopelessly, as one who is used to waiting, to desertion. She said it as one who expects nothing from her years upon the earth. No rebellion will come out of her, no demands, no fierceness. Nothing will come out of her at all, save the children of men who will use her, leave her, forget her. And so slight was her body, and so few her years, that Kumalo for all his suffering was moved to compassion.

—What will you do? he asked.

—I do not know, she said.

—Perhaps you will find another man, said Msimangu bitterly. And before Kumalo could speak, to steal away the bitterness and hide it from her—I do not know, she said.

And again before Kumalo could speak, Msimangu turned his back on the girl, and spoke to him privately.

—You can do nothing here, he said. Let us go.

—My friend . . .

—I tell you, you can do nothing. Have you not troubles enough of your own? I tell you there are thousands such in Johannesburg. And were your back as broad as heaven, and your purse full of gold, and did your compassion reach from here to hell itself, there is nothing you can do.

Silently they withdrew. All of them were silent, the young white man heavy with failure, the old man with grief, Msimangu still bitter with his words. Kumalo stood at the car though the others were already seated.

—You do not understand. The child will be my grandchild.

—Even that you do not know, said Msimangu angrily. His bitterness mastered him again. And if he were, he said, how many more such have you? Shall we search them out, day after day, hour after hour? Will it ever end?

Kumalo stood in the dust like one who has been struck. Then without speaking any more he took his seat in the car.

Again they stopped at the gate of the village, and the young white man got out and went into the office of the European super-intendent. He came back, his face set and unhappy.

—I have telephoned the factory, he said. It is true. He has not been at work this week.

At the gates of Orlando they stopped yet again.

—Would you like to get out here? the young man asked. They climbed out, and the young man spoke to Kumalo.

—I am sorry for this, he said.

—Yes, it is very heavy. As if his English had left him, he spoke in Zulu to Msimangu. I am sorry too for this end to his work, he said.

—He too is sorry for this end to your work, said Msimangu in Afrikaans.

—Yes, it is my work, but it is his son. He turned to Kumalo and spoke in English. It has happened sometimes that a boy is ar-rested, he said, or is injured and taken to hospital, and we do not know. Do not give up hope, umfundisi. I will not give up the search.

473

They watched him drive away. He is a good man, said Kumalo. Come, let us walk.

But Msimangu did not move.

—I am ashamed to walk with you, he said. His face was twisted, like that of a man much distressed.

Kumalo looked at him astonished.

—I ask your forgiveness for my ugly words, said Msimangu.

—You mean about the search?

—You understood, then?

—I am old, and have learnt something. You are forgiven.

IT WAS A PLEASANT EVENING at the Mission House. Father Vincent, the rosy-cheeked priest, was there, and they talked about the place where Kumalo lived and worked. And the white man in his turn spoke about his own country, about the hedges and the fields, and Westminster Abbey, and the great cathedrals up and down the land. Yet even this pleasure was not to be entire, for one of the white priests came in from the city with the *Evening Star*, and showed them the bold black lines: MURDER IN PARKWOLD. WELL-KNOWN CITY ENGINEER SHOT DEAD. ASSAILANTS THOUGHT TO BE NATIVES.

—This is a terrible loss for South Africa, said the white priest. For this Arthur Jarvis was a courageous young man, and a great fighter for justice. And it is a terrible loss for the Church too. He was one of the finest of all our young laymen.

—Jarvis? It is indeed a terrible thing, said Msimangu. He was the president of the African Boys' Club, here in Claremont, in Gladiolus Street.

—Perhaps you might have known him, said Father Vincent to Kumalo. It says that he was the only child of Mr. James Jarvis, of High Place, Carisbrooke.

—I know the father, said Kumalo sorrowfully. I mean I know him well by sight and name, but we have never spoken. His farm is in the hills above Ndotsheni, and he sometimes rode past our church. But I did not know the son.

He was silent, then he said, Yet I remember, there was a small bright boy, and he too sometimes rode on his horse past the church. A small bright boy, I remember, though I do not remember it well.

And he was silent again, for who is not silent when someone is dead, who was a small bright boy?

—Shall I read this? said Father Vincent.

At 1:30 p.m. today Mr. Arthur Jarvis, of Plantation Road, Parkwold, was shot dead in his house by an intruder, thought to be a native. It appears that Mrs. Jarvis and her two children were away for a holiday, and that Mr. Jarvis had telephoned his partners to say he would be staying at home with a slight cold. It would seem that a native, probably with two accomplices, entered by the kitchen, thinking no doubt there would be no one in the house. The native servant in the kitchen was knocked unconscious, and it would appear that Mr. Jarvis heard the disturbance and came down to investigate. He was shot dead at short range in the passageway leading from the stairs into the kitchen. There were no signs of any struggle.

Three native youths were seen lounging in Plantation Road shortly before the tragedy, and a strong force of detectives was immediately sent to the scene. Exhaustive inquiries are being made, and the plantations on Parkwold Ridge are being combed. The native servant, Richard Mpiring, is in the Non-European Hospital, and it is hoped that when he regains consciousness he will be able to furnish the police with important information.

The sound of the shot was heard by a neighbor, Mr. Michael Clarke, who investigated promptly and made the tragic discovery. The police were on the scene within a few minutes. On the table by the bed of the murdered man was found an unfinished manuscript on "The Truth about Native Crime," and it would appear that he was engaged in writing it when he got up to go to his death. The bowl of a pipe on the table was found still to be warm.

Mr. Jarvis leaves a widow, a nine-year-old son, and a five-year-old daughter. He was the only son of Mr. James Jarvis, of High Place Farm, Carisbrooke, Natal, and a partner in the city engineering firm of Davis, van der Walt and Jarvis. The dead man was well known for his interest in social problems, and for his efforts for the welfare of the non-European sections of the community.

A silence falls upon them all. This is no time to talk of hedges and fields, or the beauties of any country. Sadness and fear and hate, how they well up in the heart and mind, whenever one opens the pages of these messengers of doom. Cry for the broken tribe, for the law and the custom that is gone. Aye, and cry aloud for the man who is dead, for the woman and children bereaved. Cry, the beloved country, these things are not yet at an end. The sun pours down on the earth, on the lovely land that man cannot enjoy.

Kumalo rose. I shall go to my room, he said. Good night to you all.

—I shall walk with you, my friend.

They walked to the gate of the little house of Mrs. Lithebe. Kumalo lifted to his friend a face that was full of suffering.

—This thing, he said. This thing. Here in my heart there is nothing but fear. Fear, fear, fear.

—I understand. Yet it is nevertheless foolish to fear that one thing in this great city, with its thousands and thousands of people.

—It is not a question of wisdom and foolishness. It is just fear.

HAVE NO DOUBT it is fear in the land. For what can men do when so many have grown lawless? Who can enjoy the lovely land, who can enjoy the seventy years, and the sun that pours down on the earth, when there is fear in the heart? Who can walk quietly in the shadow of the jacarandas, when their beauty is grown to danger? Who can lie peacefully abed, when the darkness holds some secret? What lovers can lie sweetly under the stars, when menace grows with the measure of their seclusion?

There are voices crying what must be done, a hundred, a thousand voices. But what do they help if one seeks for counsel, for one cries this, and one cries that, and another cries something that is neither this nor that.

IT'S A CRYING SCANDAL, ladies and gentlemen, that we get so few police. This suburb pays more in taxes than most of the suburbs of Johannesburg, and what do we get for it? A third-class police station, with one man on the beat, and one at the telephone. This is the second outrage of its kind in six months, and we must demand more protection. (*Applause.*)

—Mr. McLaren, will you read us your resolution?

I SAY WE SHALL ALWAYS have native crime to fear until the native people of this country have worthy purposes to inspire them and worthy goals to work for. For it is only because they see neither purpose nor goal that they turn to drink and crime and prostitution. Which do we prefer, a law-abiding, industrious and purposeful native people, or a lawless, idle and purposeless people? The truth is that we do not know, for we fear them both. And so long as we vacillate, so long will we pay dearly for the dubious pleasure of not having to make up our minds. And the answer does not lie, except temporarily, in more police and more protection. (*Applause.*)

AND YOU THINK, Mr. de Villiers, that increased schooling facilities would cause a decrease in juvenile delinquency amongst native children?

—I am sure of it, Mr. Chairman.

—Have you the figures for the percentage of children at school, Mr. de Villiers?

—In Johannesburg, Mr. Chairman, not more than four out of ten are at school. But of those four not even one will reach his sixth standard. Six are being educated in the streets.

—May I ask Mr. de Villiers a question, Mr. Chairman?

—By all means, Mr. Scott.

—Who do you think should pay for this schooling, Mr. de Villiers?

—We should pay for it. If we wait till native parents can pay for it, we will pay more heavily in other ways.

—Don't you think, Mr. de Villiers, that more schooling simply means cleverer criminals?

—I am sure that is not true.

—Let me give you a case. I had a boy working for me who had

passed Standard Six. Perfect gentleman, bow tie, hat to the side, and the latest socks. I treated him well and paid him well. Now do you know, Mr. de Villiers, that this selfsame scoundrel . . .

WE WENT TO THE ZOO LAKE, my dear. But it's quite impossible. I really don't see why they can't have separate days for natives.

—I just don't go there any more on a Sunday, my dear. We take John and Penelope on some other day. But I like to be fair. Where can these poor creatures go?

—Why can't they make recreation places for them?

—When they wanted to make a recreation center on part of the Hillside Golf Course, there was such a fuss that they had to drop it.

—But, my dear, it would have been impossible. The noise would have been incredible.

—So they stay on the pavements and hang about the corners. And believe me, the noise is just as incredible there too. But that needn't worry you where you live.

—Don't be catty, my dear. Why can't they put up big recreation centers somewhere, and let them all go free on the buses?

—Where, for example?

—You do persist, my dear. Why not in the City?

—And how long will it take them to get there? And how long to get back? How many hours do you give your servants off on Sunday?

—Oh, it's too hot to argue. Get your racquet, my dear, they're calling us. Look, it's Mrs. Harvey and Thelma. You've got to play like a demon, do you hear?

AND SOME CRY for the cutting up of South Africa without delay into separate areas, where white can live without black, and black without white, where black can farm their own land and mine their own minerals and administer their own laws. And others cry away with the compound system, that brings men to the towns without their wives and children, and breaks up the tribe and the house and the man, and they ask for the establishment of villages for the laborers in mines and industry.

And the churches cry too. The English-speaking churches cry for more education, and more opportunity, and for a removal of the restrictions on native labor and enterprise. And the Afrikaans-speaking churches want to see the native people given opportunity to develop along their own lines, and remind their own people that the decay of family religion, where the servants took part in family devotions, has contributed in part to the moral decay of the native people. But there is to be no equality in church or state.

Yes, there are a hundred, and a thousand voices crying. But what does one do, when one cries this thing, and one cries another? Who knows how we shall fashion a land of peace where black outnumbers white so greatly? Some say that the earth has bounty enough for all, and that more for one does not mean less for another, that the advance of one does not mean the decline of another. They say that poor-paid labor means a poor nation, and that better-paid labor means greater markets and greater scope for industry and manufacture. And others say that this is a danger, for better-paid labor will not only buy more but will also read more, think more, ask more, and will not be content to be forever voiceless and inferior.

WE DO NOT KNOW, we do not know. We shall live from day to day, and put more locks on the doors, and get a fine fierce dog, and hold on to our handbags more tenaciously; and the beauty of the trees by night, and the raptures of lovers under the stars, these things we shall forego. We shall forego the evening walk over the starlit veld. We shall be careful, and knock this off our lives, and knock that off our lives, and hedge ourselves about with safety and precaution.

And our lives will shrink, but they shall be the lives of superior beings; and we shall live with fear, but at least it will not be a fear of the unknown. And the conscience shall be thrust down; the light of life shall not be extinguished, but be put under a bushel, to be preserved for a generation that will live by it again, in some day not yet come; and how it will come, and when it will come, we shall not think about at all.

THEY ARE HOLDING a meeting in Parkwold tonight, as they held one last night in Turffontein, and will hold one tomorrow night in Mayfair. And the people will ask for more police, and for heavier sentences for native housebreakers, and for the death penalty for all who carry weapons when they break in. And some will ask for a new native policy, that will show the natives who is the master.

And the Left Club is holding a meeting too, on "A Long Term Policy for Native Crime," and has invited both European and non-European speakers to present a symposium. And the Cathedral Guild is holding a meeting too, on "The Real Causes of Native Crime." But there will be a gloom over it, for the speaker of the evening, Mr. Arthur Jarvis, has just been shot dead in his house at Parkwold.

CRY, THE BELOVED COUNTRY, for the unborn child that is the inheritor of our fear. Let him not love the earth too deeply. Let him not laugh too gladly when the water runs through his fingers, nor stand too silent when the setting sun makes red the veld with fire. Let him not be too moved when the birds of his land are singing, nor give too much of his heart to a mountain or a valley. For fear will rob him of all if he gives too much.

MR. MSIMANGU?

—Ah, it is Mrs. Ndlela, of End Street.

—Mr. Msimangu, the police have been to me.

—The police?

—Yes, they want to know about the son of the old umfundisi. They are looking for him.

—For what, mother?

—They did not say, Mr. Msimangu.

—Is it bad, mother?

—It looks as if it were bad.

—And then, mother?

—I was frightened, umfundisi. So I gave them the address. Mrs. Mkize, 79 Twenty-third Avenue, Alexandra. And one said yes, this woman was known to deal in heavy matters.

—You gave them the address?

He stood silent in the door.

—Did I do wrong, umfundisi?

—You did no wrong, mother.

—I was afraid.

—It is the law, mother. We must uphold the law.

—I am glad, umfundisi.

He thanks the simple woman, and tells her to go well. He stands for a moment, then turns swiftly and goes to his room. He takes out an envelope from a drawer, and takes paper money from it. He looks at it ruefully, and then with decision puts it into his pocket, with decision takes down his hat. Then dressed, with indecision looks out of the window to the house of Mrs. Lithebe, and shakes his head. But he is too late, for as he opens his door, Kumalo stands before him.

—You are going out, my friend?

Msimangu is silent. I was going out, he says at last.

—But you said you would work in your room today.

And Msimangu would have said, Can I not do as I wish, but something prevented him. Come in, he said.

—I would not disturb you, my friend.

—Come in, said Msimangu, and he shut the door. My friend, I have just had a visit from Mrs. Ndlela, at the house we visited in End Street, here in Sophiatown.

Kumalo hears the earnest tones. There is news? he asks, but there is fear, not eagerness, in his voice.

—Only this, said Msimangu, that the police came to her house, looking for the boy. She gave them the address, Mrs. Mkize, at 79 Twenty-third Avenue in Alexandra.

—Why do they want the boy? asked Kumalo in a low and trembling voice.

—That we do not know. I was ready to go there when you came.

Kumalo looked at him out of sad and grateful eyes, so that the resentment of the other died out of him. You were going alone? the old man asked.

—I was going alone, yes. But now you may come also.

Mrs. Mkize!

She drew back, hostile.

—Have the police been here?

—They have been, not long since.

—And what did they want?

—They wanted the boy.

—And what did you say?

—I said it was a year since he left here.

—And where have they gone?

—To Shanty Town. She draws back again, remembering.

—To the address you did not know, he said coldly.

She looks at him sullenly. What could I do? she said. It was the police.

—No matter. What was the address?

—I did not know the address. Shanty Town, I told them.

Some fire came into her. I told you I did not know the address, she said.

Mrs. Hlatshwayo!

The pleasant-faced woman smiled at them, and drew aside for them to enter the hessian house.

—We shall not come in. Have the police been here?

—They were here, umfundisi. They wanted the boy.

—For what, mother?

—I do not know, umfundisi.

—And where have they gone?

—To the school, umfundisi.

—Tell me, he said privately, did it seem heavy?

—I could not say, umfundisi.

—Stay well, Mrs. Hlatshwayo.

—Go well, umfundisi.

Good morning, my friend.

—Good morning, umfundisi, said the native assistant at the reformatory.

—Where is the young white man?

482

—He is in the town. It was now, now, that he went.

—Have the police been here?

—They have been here. It was now, now, that they left.

—What did they want?

—They wanted the boy, Absalom Kumalo, the son of the old man there in the taxi.

—Why did they want him?

—I do not know. I had other work, and went out while they came in with the white man.

—Was the young white man—well, disturbed?

—He was disturbed.

—And where did they go?

—To Pimville, umfundisi. To the home of the girl.

MY CHILD!

—Umfundisi.

—Have the police been here?

—They have been here, now, now, they were here.

—And what did they want?

—They wanted Absalom, umfundisi.

—And what did you tell them?

—I told them I had not seen him since Saturday, umfundisi.

—And why did they want him? cried Kumalo in torment.

She drew back frightened. I do not know, she said.

—And why did you not ask? he cried.

The tears filled her eyes. I was afraid, she said.

Msimangu went to the taxi, and Kumalo followed him. And the girl ran after them, as one runs who is with child.

—They told me I must let them know if he comes. Her eyes were full of trouble. What shall I do? she said.

—That is what you ought to do, said Msimangu. And you will let us know also. Wait, you must go to the superintendent's office and ask him to telephone to the Mission House in Sophiatown. I shall write the number here for you: 49-3041.

—I shall do it, umfundisi.

—Tell me, did the police say where they would go?

483

—They did not say, umfundisi. But I heard them say, *die spoor loop dood*, the trail runs dead.

—Stay well, my child.

—Go well, umfundisi. She turned to say go well to the other, but he was already in the taxi, bowed over his stick.

THE FOLLOWING DAY Kumalo ate his midday meal at the Mission, and returned to Mrs. Lithebe's to play with Gertrude's son. There was great bargaining going on, for Mrs. Lithebe had found a buyer for Gertrude's table and chairs, and for the pots and pans. Everything was sold for three pounds, which was not a bad sum for a table that was badly marked and discolored, with what he did not ask. And the chairs too were weak, so that one had to sit carefully upon them.

Indeed the price was paid for the pots and pans, which were of the stuff called aluminum. Now the black people do not buy such pots and pans, but his sister said that they were the gift of a friend, and into that too he did not inquire.

When the last thing had been loaded, and the money paid, and the lorry had gone, he would have played with the small boy, but he saw, with the fear catching at him suddenly with a physical pain, Msimangu and the young white man from the reformatory walking up the street towards the house. With the habit born of experience, he forced himself to go to the gate, and noted with dread their set faces and the low tones in which they spoke.

—Good afternoon, umfundisi. Is there a place where we can talk? asked the young man.

—Come to my room, he said, hardly trusting to his voice.

In the room he shut the door, and stood not looking at them.

—I have heard what you fear, said the young man. It is true.

And Kumalo stood bowed, and could not look at them. He sat down in his chair and fixed his eyes upon the floor.

The young man shrugged his shoulders. This will be bad for the reformatory, he said more loudly, even indifferently.

And Kumalo nodded his head, not once, nor twice, but three

or four times, as though he too would say, Yes, it will be bad for the reformatory.

—Yes, said the young man, it will be bad for us. They will say we let him out too soon. Of course there is one thing. The other two were not reformatory boys. But it was he who fired the shot.

—My friend, said Msimangu, in as ordinary a voice as he could find, one of the two others is the son of your brother.

And so Kumalo nodded his head again, one, two, three, four times. And when that was finished, he began again, as though he too was saying, One of the two others is the son of my brother.

Then he stood up, and looked round the room, and they watched him. He took his coat from a nail, and put it on, and he put his hat on, and took his stick in his hand. And so dressed he turned to them, and nodded again. But this time they did not know what he said.

—You are going out, my friend? said Msimangu.

—Do you wish to come to the prison, umfundisi? I have arranged it for you. And Kumalo nodded. He turned and looked round the room again, and found that his coat was already on him, and his hat; he touched both coat and hat, and looked down at the stick that was in his hand.

—My brother first, he said, if you will show me the way only.

—I shall show you the way, my friend.

—And I shall wait at the Mission, said the young man.

Msimangu took his arm, and it was like walking with a child or with one that was sick. So they came to the shop of Kumalo's brother. And at the shop Kumalo turned, and closed his eyes, and his lips were moving. Then he opened his eyes and turned to Msimangu. Do not come further, he said. It is I who must do this.

And then he went into the shop.

Yes, the bull voice was there, loud and confident. His brother John was sitting there on a chair, talking to two other men, sitting there like a chief.

—Good afternoon, my brother.

—Ah, my brother, it is you. Well, well, I am glad to see you. Will you not come and join us?

Kumalo looked at the visitors. I am sorry, he said, but I come again on business, urgent business.

—I am sure my friends will excuse us. Excuse us, my friends.

So they all said, Go well, and the two men left them.

—Well, well, I am glad to see you, my brother. And your business, how does it progress? Have you found the prodigal?

—He is found, my brother. He is in prison, arrested for the murder of a white man.

—Murder? The man does not jest now. One does not jest about murder. Still less about the murder of a white man.

—Yes, murder. He broke into a house in a place they call Parkwold, and killed the white man who would have prevented him.

—What? Only a day or two since? On Tuesday? I remember!

Yes, he remembers. He remembers too that his own son and his brother's son are companions. The veins stand out on the bull neck, and the sweat forms on the brow. Have no doubt it is fear in the eyes. He wipes his brow with a cloth. There are many questions he could ask. All he says is, Yes, indeed, I do remember. His brother is filled with compassion for him. He will try gently to bring it to him.

—I am sorry, my brother.

What does one say? Does one say, Of course you are sorry? Does one say, Of course, it is your son? How can one say it, when one knows what it means? Keep silent then, but the eyes are upon one. One knows what they mean.

—You mean . . . ? he asked.

—Yes. He was there also.

John Kumalo whispers *Tixo, Tixo*. And again, *Tixo, Tixo*. Kumalo comes to him and puts his hands on his shoulders.

—There are many things I could say, he said. But I do not say them. I say only that I know what you suffer.

—Indeed, who could know better?

—There is a young white man at the Mission, and he is waiting to take me now to the prison. Perhaps he would take you also.

—Let me get my coat and hat, my brother.

They set out along the street to the Mission House. Msimangu, watching anxiously for their return, sees them coming. The old man walks now more firmly, it is the other who seems bowed and broken.

Father Vincent, the rosy-cheeked priest from England, takes Kumalo's hand in both his own. Anything, he says, anything. You have only to ask. I shall do anything.

THEY PASS THROUGH the great gate in the grim high wall. The young man from the reformatory talks for them, and it is arranged. John Kumalo is taken to one room, and the young man goes with Stephen Kumalo to another. There the son is brought to them.

They shake hands, indeed the old man takes his son's hand in both of his own, and the hot tears fall fast upon them. The boy stands unhappy, there is no gladness in his eyes. He twists his head from side to side, as though the loose clothing is too tight for him.

—My child, my child.

—Yes, my father.

—At last I have found you.

—Yes, my father.

—And it is too late.

To this the boy makes no answer. As though he may find some hope in this silence, the father presses him. Is it not too late? he asks. But there is no answer. Persistently, almost eagerly, Is it not too late? he asks. The boy turns his head from side to side, he meets the eyes of the young white man, and his own retreat swiftly. My father, it is what my father says, he answers.

—I have searched in every place for you.

To that also no answer. The old man loosens his hands, and his son's hand slips from them lifelessly. There is a barrier here, a wall, something that cuts off one from the other.

—Why did you do this terrible thing, my child?

The young white man stirs watchfully, the white warder makes no sign, perhaps he does not know this tongue. There is a moisture in the boy's eyes, he turns his head from side to side, and makes no answer.

—Answer me, my child.

—I do not know, he says.

—Why did you carry a revolver?

The white warder stirs too, for the word in Zulu is like the word in English and in Afrikaans. The boy too shows a sign of life.

—For safety, he says. This Johannesburg is a dangerous place. A man never knows when he will be attacked.

—But why did you take it to this house?

And this again cannot be answered.

—Have they got it, my child?

—Yes, my father.

—They have no doubt it was you?

—I told them, my father.

—What did you tell them?

—I told them I was frightened when the white man came. So I shot him. I did not mean to kill him.

—And your cousin. And the other?

—Yes, I told them. They came with me, but it was I who shot the white man.

—Did you go there to steal?

And this again cannot be answered.

—You were at the reformatory, my child?

The boy looked at his boot, and pushed it forward along the ground. I was there, he said.

—Did they treat you well?

Again there is a moisture in the eyes, again he turns his head from side to side, drops his eyes again to the boot pushing forward and backward on the ground. They treated me well, he said.

—And this is your repayment, my child?

And this again cannot be answered. The young white man comes over, for he knows that this does nothing, goes nowhere. Perhaps he does not like to see these two torturing each other.

—Well, Absalom?

—Sir?

—Why did you leave the work that I got for you?

And you too, young man, can get no answer. There are no answers to these things.

—And your girl. The one we let you go to, the girl you worried over, so that we took pity on you.

And again the tears in the eyes. Who knows if he weeps for the girl he has deserted? Who knows if he weeps for a promise broken? Who knows if he weeps for another self, that would work for a woman, pay his taxes, save his money, keep the laws, love his children, another self that has always been defeated? Or does he weep for himself alone, to be let alone, to be free of the merciless rain of questions, why, why, why, when he knows not why. They do not speak with him, they do not jest with him, they do not sit and let him be, but they ask, ask, ask, why, why, why—his father, the white man, the prison officers, the police, the magistrates— why, why, why.

The young white man shrugs his shoulders, smiles indifferently. But he is not indifferent, there is a mark of pain between his eyes.

—So the world goes, he says.

—Answer me one thing, my child. Will you answer me?

—I can answer, father.

—You wrote nothing, sent no message. You went with bad companions. You stole and broke in and—yes, you did these things. But why?

The boy seizes upon the word that is given him. It was bad companions, he said.

—I need not tell you that is no answer, said Kumalo. But he knows he will get no other this way. Yes, I see, he said, bad companions. Yes, I understand. But for you, yourself, what made you yourself do it?

How they torture one another. And the boy, tortured, shows again a sign of life. It was the devil, he said.

Oh boy, can you not say you fought the devil, wrestled with the devil, struggled with him night and day, till the sweat poured from you and no strength was left? Can you not say that you wept for your sins, and vowed to make amends, and stood upright, and stumbled, and fell again? It would be some comfort for this tortured man, who asks you, desperately, why did you not struggle against him?

And the boy looks down at his feet again, and says, I do not know.

The old man is exhausted, the boy is exhausted, and the time is nearly over. The young white man comes to them again. Does he still wish to marry the girl? he asks Kumalo.

—Do you wish to marry this girl, my son?

—Yes, my father.

—I shall see what I can do, says the young man. I think it is time for us to go.

—May we come again?

—Yes, you may come again. We shall ask the hours at the gate.

—Stay well, my child.

—Go well, my father.

—My child, I think you may write letters here. But do not write to your mother till I see you again. I must first write to her.

—It is good, my father.

They go, and outside the gate they meet John Kumalo. He is feeling better, the big bull man. Well, well, he says, we must go at once and see a lawyer.

—A lawyer, my brother. For what should we spend such money? The story is plain, there cannot be doubt about it.

—What is the story? asks John Kumalo.

—The story? These three lads went to a house that they thought was empty. They struck down the servant. The white man heard a noise and he came to see. And then . . . and then . . . my son . . . mine, not yours . . . shot at him. He was afraid, he says.

—Well, well, says John Kumalo, that is a story. He seems reassured. Well, well, that is a story. And he told you this in front of the others?

—Why not, if it is the truth?

John Kumalo seems reassured. Perhaps you do not need a lawyer, he said. If he shot the white man, there is perhaps nothing more to be said.

—Will you have a lawyer then?

John Kumalo smiles at his brother. Perhaps I shall need a lawyer, he says. For one thing, a lawyer can talk to my son in private.

He seems to think, then he says, You see, my brother, there is no proof that my son or this other young man was there at all. Yes, John Kumalo smiles at that, he seems quite recovered.

—Not there at all? But my son . . .

—Yes, yes, John Kumalo interrupts him, and smiles at him. Who will believe your son? he asks. He says it with meaning, with cruel and pitiless meaning.

Kumalo looks at his brother, but his brother does not look at him. Indeed he walks away. Wearily, wearily, Kumalo goes from the great gate in the wall to the street. *Tixo*, he says, *Tixo*, forsake me not. Father Vincent's words come back to him, Anything, anything, he said, you have only to ask. Then to Father Vincent he will go.

KUMALO RETURNED to Mrs. Lithebe's tired and dispirited. The two women were silent, and he had no desire to speak to them, and none to play with his small nephew. He withdrew into his room, and sat silent there, waiting till he could summon strength enough to go to the Mission House. But while he sat, there was a knock at his door, and Mrs. Lithebe stood there with the young white man.

Kumalo stood up, an old bowed man. He sought for humble and pleading words, but none came to him. And because he could not look at the young man, he fixed his eyes on the floor.

—Umfundisi.

—Sir?

The young man said, I think you must have a lawyer. Not because the truth must not be told, but because I do not trust your brother. You can see what is in his mind. His plan is to deny that his son and the third man were with your son. Now you and I do not know whether that will make matters worse or not, but a lawyer would know. And another thing also, Absalom says that he fired the revolver because he was afraid, with no intention of killing the white man. It needs a lawyer to make the court believe that that is true.

—Yes, I see that.

—Do you know of any lawyer, of your church maybe?

—No, sir, I do not. But it was my plan to go to see Father Vincent at the Mission House, when I had rested for a while.

So they walked to the Mission House, and there they talked for a long time with the rosy-cheeked priest from England.

—I think I could get a good man to take the case, said Father Vincent. I think we are all agreed that it is to be the truth and nothing but the truth, and that the defense will be that the shot was fired in fear and not to kill. Our lawyer will tell us what to do about this other matter, the possibility, my friend, that your nephew and the other young man will deny that they were there. For it appears that it is only your son who states that they were there. For us it is to be the truth, and nothing but the truth, and indeed, the man I am thinking of would not otherwise take the case. I shall see him as soon as possible.

—And what about the marriage? asked the young man.

—I shall ask him about that also. I do not know if it can be arranged, but I should gladly marry them if it can be.

So they rose to separate, and Father Vincent put his hand on the old man's arm. Be of good courage, he said. Whatever happens, your son will be severely punished, but if his defense is accepted, it will not be the extreme punishment. And while there is life, there is hope for amendment of life.

—That is now always in my mind, said Kumalo. But my hope is little.

—Stay here and speak with me, said Father Vincent.

—And I must go, said the young white man. But, umfundisi, I am ready to help if my help is needed.

When the young man had gone, Kumalo and the English priest sat down, and Kumalo said to the other, You can understand that this has been a sorrowful journey.

—I understand that, my friend.

—At first it was a search. I was anxious at first, but as the search went on, step by step, so did the anxiety turn to fear, and this fear grew deeper step by step. It was at Alexandra that I first grew afraid, but it was here in your House, when we heard of the murder, that my fear grew into something too great to be borne.

—To think, said Kumalo, that my wife and I lived out our lives in innocence, there in Ndotsheni, not knowing that this thing was coming, step by step. Why, he said, if one could only have been told, this step is taken, and this step is about to be taken. If only one could have been told that. But we were not told.

Father Vincent put his hand over his eyes, to hide them from the light, to hide them from the sight of the man who was speaking.

—There is a man sleeping in the grass, said Kumalo. And over him is gathering the greatest storm of all his days. Such lightning and thunder will come as have never been seen before, bringing death and destruction. People hurry past him, to places safe from danger. And whether they do not see him there in the grass, or whether they fear to halt even a moment, but they do not wake him, they let him be.

After that Kumalo seemed to have done with speaking, and they were silent a long time till Father Vincent said again, My friend.

—Father?

—My friend, your anxiety turned to fear, and your fear turned to sorrow. But sorrow is better than fear. For fear impoverishes always, while sorrow may enrich.

Kumalo looked at him, with an intensity of gaze that was strange in so humble a man, and hard to encounter.

—I do not know that I am enriched, he said.

—Sorrow is better than fear, said Father Vincent doggedly. Fear is a journey, a terrible journey, but sorrow is at least an arriving.

—And where have I arrived? asked Kumalo.

—No one can comprehend the ways of God, said Father Vincent desperately.

Kumalo looked at him, not bitterly or accusingly or reproachfully. It seems that God has turned from me, he said.

—That may seem to happen, said Father Vincent. But it does not happen, never, never, does it happen. Go and pray, go and rest.

Kumalo stood up. I have no hope any more. What did you say I must do? Yes, pray and rest.

There was no mockery in his voice, and Father Vincent knew that it was not in this man's nature to speak mockingly. But so mocking were the words that the white priest caught him by the arm, and said to him urgently, Sit down, I must speak to you as a priest.

When Kumalo had sat down, Father Vincent said to him, Yes, I said pray and rest. Even if it is only words that you pray, and even if your resting is only a lying on a bed. And do not pray for yourself, and do not pray to understand the ways of God. For they are secret. Who knows what life is, for life is a secret. And why you go on, when it would seem better to die, that is a secret. Do not pray and think about these things now, there will be other times. Pray for Gertrude, and for her child, and for the girl that is to be your son's wife, and for the child that will be your grandchild. Pray for your wife and all at Ndotsheni. Pray for the woman and the children that are bereaved. Pray for the soul of him who was killed. Pray for all white people, those who do justice, and those who would do justice if they were not afraid. And do not fear to pray for your son, and for his amendment.

—I hear you, said Kumalo humbly.

—And give thanks where you can give thanks. For nothing is better. Is there not your wife, and Mrs. Lithebe, and Msimangu, and this young white man at the reformatory? Now, for your son and his amendment, you will leave this to me and Msimangu; for you are too distraught to see God's will. And now, my son, go and pray, go and rest.

He helped the old man to his feet, and gave him his hat. And when Kumalo would have thanked him, he said, We do what is in us, and why it is in us, that is also a secret. It is Christ in us, crying that men may be succored and forgiven, even when He Himself is forsaken. I shall pray for you night and day. That I shall do and anything more that you ask.

THE NEXT DAY Kumalo, who was learning to find his way about the great city, took train to Pimville to see the girl who was with child by his son. He chose this time so that Msimangu would not be able to accompany him, because he felt he would do it better alone. He thought slowly and acted slowly, no doubt because he lived in the slow tribal rhythm; and he had seen that this could irritate those who were with him, and he had felt also that he could reach his goal more surely without them.

He found the house not without difficulty, and knocked at the door, and the girl opened to him. And she smiled at him uncertainly, with something that was fear, and something that was child-like and welcoming.

—And how are you, my child?

—I am well, umfundisi.

He sat down on the only chair in the room, sat down carefully on it, and wiped his brow. Have you heard of your husband? he asked. Only the word does not quite mean husband.

The smile went from her face. I have not heard, she said.

—What I have to say is heavy, he said. He is in prison.

—In prison? she said.

—He is in prison, for the most terrible deed that a man can do. But the girl did not understand him. She waited patiently for him to continue. She was surely but a child.

—He has killed a white man.

—Au! The exclamation burst from her. She put her hands over her face. And Kumalo himself could not continue, for the words were like knives, cutting into a wound that was still new and open.

She sat down on a box, and looked at the floor, and the tears started to run slowly down her cheeks.

—I do not wish to speak of it, my child. Can you read? The white man's newspaper?

—A little.

—Then I shall leave it with you. But do not show it to others.

—I shall not show it to others, umfundisi.

—I do not wish to speak of it any more. I have come to speak with you of another matter. Do you wish to marry my son?

—It is as the umfundisi sees it.

—I am asking you, my child.

—I can be willing.

—And why would you be willing?

495

She looked at him, for she could not understand such a question.

—Why do you wish to marry him? he persisted.

She picked little strips of wood from the box, smiling in her perplexedness. He is my husband, she said, with the word that does not quite mean husband.

—But you did not wish to marry him before?

The questions embarrassed her; she stood up, but there was nothing to do, and she sat down again, and fell to picking at the box.

—Speak, my child.

—I do not know what to say, umfundisi.

—Is it truly your wish to marry him?

—It is truly my wish, umfundisi.

—I must be certain. I do not wish to take you into my family if you are unwilling.

At those words she looked up at him eagerly. I am willing, she said.

—We live in a far place, he said. There are no streets and lights and buses there. There is only me and my wife, and the place is very quiet.

—I understand, umfundisi.

—I must say a hard thing to you.

—I am listening, umfundisi.

—What will you do in this quiet place when the desire is upon you? I am a parson, and live at my church, and our life is quiet and ordered. I do not wish to ask you something that you cannot do.

—I understand, umfundisi. I understand completely. She looked at him through her tears. You shall not be ashamed of me. You need not be afraid for me. You need not be afraid because it is quiet. Quietness is what I desire. And the word, the word desire, quickened her to brilliance. That shall be my desire, she said, that is the desire that will be upon me, so that he was astonished.

—You are cleverer than I thought, he said.

—I was clever at school, she said eagerly.

He was moved to sudden laughter, and stood wondering at the strangeness of its sound.

—What church are you?

496

—Church of England, umfundisi . . . this too, eagerly.

He laughed again at her simplicity, and was as suddenly solemn. I want one promise from you, he said, a heavy promise.

And she too was solemn. Yes, umfundisi?

—If you should ever repent of this plan, either here or when we are going to my home, you must not shut it up inside you, or run away. You will promise to tell me that you have repented.

—I promise, she said gravely, and then eagerly, I shall never repent.

And so he laughed again, and let go her hands and took up his hat. I shall come for you when everything is ready for the marriage. Have you clothes?

—I have some clothes, umfundisi. I shall prepare them.

—And you must not live here. Shall I find you a place near me?

—I would wish that, umfundisi. She clapped her hands like a child. Let it be soon, she said, and I shall give up my room at this house.

—Stay well, then, my child.

—Go well, umfundisi.

He went out of the house, and she followed him to the little gate. When he turned back to look at her, she was smiling at him. He walked on like a man from whom a pain has lifted a little, not altogether, but a little. He remembered too that he had laughed, and that it had pained him physically, as it pains a man who is ill and should not laugh. And he remembered too, with sudden and devastating shock, that Father Vincent had said, I shall pray, night and day. At the corner he turned and, looking back, saw that the girl was still watching him.

M RS. LITHEBE.
—Umfundisi?

—Mrs. Lithebe, you have been so kind, and I have another kindness to ask you.

—Perhaps it can be done.

—You have heard of this girl who is with child by my son.

—I have heard of her.

—She lives in Pimville, in a room in the house of other people. She wishes to marry my son, and I believe it can be arranged. Then—whatever may happen—she will go with me to Ndotsheni, and bear her child there in a clean and decent home. But I am anxious to get her away from this place, and I wondered . . . I do not like to trouble you, mother.

—You would like to bring her here, umfundisi?

—Indeed, that would be a great kindness.

—I will take her, said Mrs. Lithebe. She can sleep in the room where we eat. But I have no bed for her.

—That would not matter. It is better for her to sleep on the floor of a decent house, than to . . .

—Indeed, indeed.

—Mother, I am grateful. Indeed you are a mother to me.

—Why else do we live? she said.

HE PASSED AGAIN through the great gate in the grim high wall, and they brought the boy to him. Again he took the lifeless hand in his own, and was again moved to tears, this time by the dejection of his son.

—Are you in health, my son?

The son stood and moved his head to one side, and looked for a while at the one window, and then moved and looked at the other, but not at his father.

—I am in health, my father.

—I have some business for you, my son. Are you certain that you wish to marry this girl?

—I can marry her?

—There is a friend of mine, a white priest, and he will see if it can be arranged, and he will see the Bishop to see if it can be done quickly. And he will get a lawyer for you.

There is a spark of life in the eyes, of some hope maybe.

—You would like a lawyer?

—They say one can be helped by a lawyer.

—You told the police that these other two were with you?

—I told them. And now I have told them again.

—And then?

—And then they were angry with me, and cursed me in front of the police, and said that I was trying to bring them into trouble.

—And then?

—And then they asked what proof I had. And the only proof I had was that it was true, it was these two and no other and they stood there with me in the house, I here and they yonder.

He showed his father with his hands, and the tears came into his eyes, and he said, Then they cursed me again, and stood looking angrily at me, and said one to the other, How can he lie so about us?

—They were your friends?

—Yes, they were my friends.

—And they will leave you to suffer alone?

—Now I see it.

—And until this, were they friends you could trust?

—I could trust them.

—You mean they were the kind of friends that a good man could choose, upright, hardworking, obeying the law?

Old man, leave him alone. You lead him so far and then you spring upon him. He looks at you sullenly, soon he will not answer at all.

—Tell me, were they such friends?

But the boy made no answer.

—And now they leave you alone?

Silence, then—I see it, said the boy.

—Did you not see it before?

Reluctantly the boy said, I saw it. The old man was tempted to ask, Then why, why did you continue with them? But the boy's eyes were filled with tears, and the father's compassion struggled with the temptation and overcame it. He took his son's hands, and this time they were not quite lifeless, but there was some feeling in them, and he held them strongly and comfortingly.

—Be of courage, my son. Do not forget there is a lawyer. But it is only the truth you must tell him.

—I shall tell him only the truth, my father. He opened his mouth as though there were something he would say, but he did not say it.

—Do not fear to speak, my son.

—He must come soon, my father. He looked at the window, and his eyes filled again with tears. He tried to speak carelessly. Or it may be too late, he said.

—Have no fear of that. He will come soon. Shall I go now to see when he will come?

—Go now, soon, soon, my father.

—And Father Vincent will come to see you, so that you can make confession and amend your life.

—It is good, my father.

—And the marriage, that will be arranged if we can arrange it. And the girl—she will live with me in Sophiatown. And she will come back with me to Ndotsheni, and the child will be born there.

—It is good, my father.

—And you may write now to your mother.

—I shall write, my father.

—And wipe away your tears.

The boy stood up and wiped his eyes with the cloth that his father gave him. And they shook hands, and there was some life now in the hand of the boy. The warder said to the boy, You may stay here, there is a lawyer to see you. You, old man, you must go.

So Kumalo left him, and at the door stood a white man, ready to come in. He was tall and grave, like a man used to heavy matters, and the warder knew him and showed him much respect. He looked like a man used to great matters, much greater than the case of a black boy who has killed a man, and he went gravely into the room, even as a chief would go.

KUMALO RETURNED to the Mission House, and there had tea with Father Vincent. After the tea was over there was a knock at the door, and the tall grave man was shown into the room. And Father Vincent treated him also with respect, and called him sir, and then Mr. Carmichael. He introduced Kumalo to him, and Mr. Carmichael shook hands with him, and called him Mr. Kumalo, which

500

is not the custom. They had more tea, and fell to discussing the case.

—I shall take it for you, Mr. Kumalo, said Mr. Carmichael. I shall take it *pro deo*, as we say. It is a simple case, for the boy says simply that he fired because he was afraid, not meaning to kill. And it will depend entirely on the judge and his assessors, for I think we will ask for that, and not for a jury. But with regard to the other two boys, I do not know what to say. I hear, Mr. Kumalo, that your brother has found another lawyer for them, and indeed I could not defend them, for I understand that their defense will be that they were not there at all and that your son is, for reasons of his own, trying to implicate them. Whether that is true or not will be for the Court to decide, but I incline to the opinion that your son is speaking the truth, and has no motive for trying to implicate them. It is for me to persuade the Court that he is speaking the whole truth, and that he speaks the whole truth when he says that he fired because he was afraid, and therefore I obviously could not defend these two who maintain that he is not speaking the truth. Is that clear, Mr. Kumalo?

—It is clear, sir.

—I must have all the facts about your son, Mr. Kumalo, when and where he was born, and what sort of child he was, and whether he was obedient and truthful, and when and why he left home, and what he has done since he came to Johannesburg. You understand?

—I understand, sir.

—And now, Father Vincent, could you and I go into this matter of the school?

—With pleasure, sir. Mr. Kumalo, will you excuse us?

He took Kumalo to the door, and standing outside it, shut it.

—You may thank God that we have got this man, he said. He is a great man, and one of the greatest lawyers in South Africa, and one of the greatest friends of your people.

—I do thank God, and you too, father. But tell me, I have one anxiety, what will it cost? My little money is nearly exhausted.

—Did you not hear him say he would take the case *pro deo?* It is Latin, and it means for God. So it will cost you nothing, or at least very little.

—He takes it for God?

—That is what it meant in the old days of faith, though it has lost much of that meaning. But it still means that the case is taken for nothing.

Kumalo stammered. I have never met such kindness, he said. He turned away his face, for he wept easily in those days. Father Vincent smiled at him. Go well, he said, and went back to the lawyer who was taking the case for God.

THERE IS A LOVELY ROAD that runs from Ixopo into the hills. These hills are grass-covered and rolling, and they are lovely beyond any singing of it. The road climbs seven miles into them; and from there, if there is no mist, you look down on one of the fairest valleys of Africa.

Up here on the tops is a small and lovely valley, between two hills that shelter it. There is a house there, and flat ploughed fields; they will tell you that it is one of the finest farms of this countryside. It is called High Place, the farm and dwelling place of James Jarvis, Esquire, and it stands high above Ndotsheni, and the great valley of the Umzimkulu.

Jarvis watched the ploughing with a gloomy eye. The hot afternoon sun of October poured down on the fields, and there was no cloud in the sky. Rain, rain, there was no rain. The clods turned up hard and unbroken, and here and there the plough would ride uselessly over the iron soil. At the end of the field it stopped, and the oxen stood sweating and blowing in the heat.

—It is no use, umnumzana.

—Keep at it, Thomas. I shall go up to the tops and see what there is to see.

—You will see nothing, umnumzana. I know because I have looked already.

Jarvis grunted, and calling his dog, set out along the kaffir path that led up to the tops. There was no sign of drought there, for the grass was fed by the mists, and the breeze blew coolingly on his sweating face. But below the tops the grass was dry, and the hills of

Ndotsheni were red and bare, and the farmers on the tops had begun to fear that the desolation of them would eat back, year by year, mile by mile, until they too were overtaken.

It was a problem almost beyond solution. Some people said there must be more education of the natives, but a boy with education did not want to work on the farms, and went off to the towns to look for more congenial occupation. The work was done by old men and women, and when the grown men came back from the mines and the towns, they sat in the sun and drank their liquor and made endless conversation. Some said there was too little land anyway, and that the natives could not support themselves on it, even with the most progressive methods of agriculture. But there were many sides to such a question. For if they got more land, and treated it as they treated what they had already, the country would turn into a desert. And where was the land to come from, and who would pay for it?

Jarvis turned these old thoughts over in his mind as he climbed to the tops, and when he reached them he sat down on a stone and took off his hat, letting the breeze cool him. This was a view that a man could look at without tiring of it, this great valley of the Umzimkulu. He could look around on the green rich hills that he had inherited from his father, and down on the rich valley where he lived and farmed. It had been his wish that his son, the only child that had been born to them, would have taken it after him. But the young man had entertained other ideas, and had gone in for engineering, and well—good luck to him. He had married a fine girl, and had presented his parents with a pair of fine grandchildren. It had been a heavy blow when he decided against High Place, but his life was his own, and no other man had a right to put his hands on it.

Down in the valley below there was a car going up to the house. He recognized it as the police car from Ixopo, and it would probably be Binnendyk on his patrol, and a decent fellow for an Afrikaner. Indeed Ixopo was full of Afrikaners now, whereas once there had been none of them. For all the police were Afrikaners, and the post-office clerks, and the men at the railway station, and the village people got on well with them one way and the other.

His wife was coming out of the house to meet the car, and there were two policemen climbing out of it. One looked like the captain himself, van Jaarsveld, one of the most popular men in the village, a great Rugby player in his day, and a soldier of the Great War. They seemed to have come to see him, for his wife was pointing up to the tops. He called his dog, and set out along the path that would soon drop down steeply amongst the stones. When he reached a little plateau about halfway down to the fields, he found that van Jaarsveld and Binnendyk were already climbing the slope, and saw that they had brought their car down the rough track to the ploughing. They caught sight of him, and he waved to them, and sat down upon a stone to wait for them. Binnendyk dropped behind, and the captain came on above to meet him.

—Well, captain, have you brought some rain for us?

The captain turned to look over the valley to the mountains beyond.

—I don't see any, Mr. Jarvis, he said.

—Neither do I. What brings you out today?

They shook hands, and the captain looked at him.

—Mr. Jarvis.

—Yes.

—I have bad news for you.

—Bad news?

Jarvis sat down, his heart beating loudly. Is it my son? he asked.

—Yes, Mr. Jarvis.

—Is he dead?

—Yes, Mr. Jarvis. The captain paused. He was shot dead at one thirty this afternoon in Johannesburg.

Jarvis stood up, his mouth quivering. Shot dead? he asked. By whom?

—It is suspected by a native housebreaker. You know his wife was away?

—Yes, I knew that.

—And he stayed at home for the day, a slight indisposition. I suppose this native thought no one was at home. It appears that your son heard a noise, and came down to investigate. The native shot him dead. There was no sign of any struggle.

—My God!

—I'm sorry, Mr. Jarvis. I'm sorry to bring this news to you.

He offered his hand, but Jarvis had sat down again on the stone, and did not see it. My God, he said.

Van Jaarsveld stood silent while the older man tried to control himself.

—You didn't tell my wife, captain?

—No, Mr. Jarvis.

Jarvis knitted his brows as he thought of that task that must be performed. She isn't strong, he said. I don't know how she will stand it.

—Mr. Jarvis, I am instructed to offer you every assistance. Binnendyk can drive your car to Pietermaritzburg if you wish. You could catch the fast mail at nine o'clock. You will be in Johannesburg at eleven tomorrow morning. There's a private compartment reserved for you and Mrs. Jarvis.

—That was kind of you.

—I'll do anything you wish, Mr. Jarvis.

—What time is it?

—Half past three, Mr. Jarvis.

—Two hours ago.

—Yes, Mr. Jarvis.

—Three hours ago he was alive.

—Yes, Mr. Jarvis.

—My God!

—If you are to catch this train, you should leave at six. Or if you wish, you could take an airplane. There's one waiting at Pietermaritzburg. But we must let them know by four o'clock. You could be in Johannesburg at midnight.

—Yes, yes. You know, I cannot think.

—Yes, I can understand that.

—Which would be better?

—I think the airplane, Mr. Jarvis.

—Well, we'll take it. We must let them know, you say.

—I'll do that as soon as we get to the house. Can I telephone where Mrs. Jarvis won't hear me? I must hurry, you see.

—Yes, yes, you can do that.

—I think we should go.

But Jarvis sat without moving.

—Can you stand up, Mr. Jarvis? I don't want to help you. Your wife's watching us.

—She's wondering, captain. Even at this distance, she knows something is wrong.

—It's quite likely. Something she saw in my face, perhaps, though I tried not to show it.

Jarvis stood up. My God, he said. There's still that to do.

As they walked down the steep path, Binnendyk went ahead of them. Jarvis walked like a dazed man. Out of a cloudless sky these things come.

—Shot dead? he said.

—Yes, Mr. Jarvis.

—Did they catch the native?

—Not yet, Mr. Jarvis.

The tears filled the eyes, the teeth bit the lips. What does that matter? he said. They walked down the hill, they were near the field. Through the misted eyes he saw the plough turn over the clods, then ride high over the iron ground.

—Leave it, Thomas, he said. He was our only child, captain.

—I know that, Mr. Jarvis. They climbed into the car, and in a few minutes were at the house.

—James, what's the matter?

—Some trouble, my dear. Come with me to the office. Captain, you want to use the telephone. You know where it is?

—Yes, Mr. Jarvis.

The captain went to the telephone. It was a party line, and two neighbors were talking.

—Please put down your receivers, said the captain. This is an urgent call from the police. Please put down your receivers.

He rang viciously, and got no answer. There should be a special police call to exchange on these country lines. He rang more viciously. Exchange, he said, Police Pietermaritzburg. It is very urgent.

—You will be connected immediately, said exchange.

He started to talk to Pietermaritzburg about the airplane. His hand felt for the second earpiece, so that he could use that also, to shut out the sounds of the woman, of her crying and sobbing.

A YOUNG MAN met them at the airport.
—Mr. and Mrs. Jarvis?

—Yes.

—I'm John Harrison, Mary's brother. I don't think you remember me. I was only a youngster when you saw me last. Let me carry your things. I've a car here for you.

As they walked to the control building, the young man said, I needn't tell you how grieved we are, Mr. Jarvis. Arthur was the finest man I ever knew.

In the car he spoke to them again. Mary and the children are at my mother's and we're expecting you both to stay with us.

—How is Mary?

—She's suffering from the shock, Mr. Jarvis, but she's very brave.

—And the children?

—They've taken it very badly, Mr. Jarvis. And that has given Mary something to occupy herself.

They did not speak again. Jarvis held his wife's hand, but they all were silent with their own thoughts, until they drove through the gates of a suburban house, and came to a stop before a lighted porch. A young woman came out at the sound of the car, and embraced Mrs. Jarvis, and they wept together. Then she turned to Jarvis, and they embraced each other. This first meeting over, Mr. and Mrs. Harrison came out also, and after they had welcomed one another, and after the proper words had been spoken, they all went into the house.

Harrison turned to Jarvis. Would you like a drink? he asked.

—It would be welcome.

—Come to my study, then.

—And now, said Harrison, you must do as you wish. If there's anything we can do, you've only to ask us. If you would wish to go to the mortuary at once, John will go with you. Or you can go to-morrow morning if you wish. The police would like to see you, but they won't worry you tonight.

—I'll ask my wife, Harrison. You know, we've hardly spoken of it yet. I'll go to her, don't you worry to come.

—I'll wait for you here.

He found his wife and his daughter-in-law hand in hand, tip-toeing out of the room where his grandchildren were sleeping. He spoke to her, and she wept again and sobbed against him. Now, she said. He went back to Harrison, and swallowed his drink, and then he and his wife and their daughter-in-law went out to the car, where John Harrison was waiting for them.

While they were driving to the police laboratories, John Harri-son told Jarvis all that he knew about the crime, how the police were waiting for the houseboy to recover consciousness, and how they had combed the plantations on Parkwold Ridge. And he told him too of the paper that Arthur Jarvis had been writing, just be-fore he was killed, on "The Truth about Native Crime."

—I'd like to see it, said Jarvis.

—We'll get it for you tomorrow, Mr. Jarvis.

—My son and I didn't see eye to eye on the native question, John. In fact, he and I got quite heated about it on more than one occasion. But I'd like to see what he wrote.

—My father and I don't see eye to eye on the native question either, Mr. Jarvis. You know, Mr. Jarvis, there was no one in South Africa who thought so deeply about it, and no one who thought so clearly, as Arthur did. And what else is there to think deeply and clearly about in South Africa, he used to say.

So they came to the laboratories, and John Harrison stayed in the car, while the others went to do the hard thing that had to be done. And they came out silent but for the weeping of the two women, and drove back as silently to the house, where Mary's father opened the door to them.

—Another drink, Jarvis? Or do you want to go to bed?

—Margaret, do you want me to come up with you?

—No, my dear, stay and have your drink.

—Good night then, my dear.

—Good night, James.

He kissed her, and she clung to him for a moment. And thank you for all your help, she said. The tears came again into her eyes, and into his too for that matter. He watched her climb the stairs with their daughter-in-law, and when the door closed on them, he and Harrison turned to go to the study.

—It's always worse for the mother, Jarvis.

—Yes.

He pondered over it, and said then, I was very fond of my son. I was never ashamed of having him.

They settled down to their drinks, and Harrison told him that the murder had shocked the people of Parkwold, and how the messages had poured into the house.

—Messages from every conceivable place, every kind of person, he said. By the way, Jarvis, we arranged the funeral provisionally for tomorrow afternoon, after a service in the Parkwold Church. Three o'clock the service will be.

Jarvis nodded. Thank you, he said.

—And we kept all the messages for you. From the Bishop, and the Acting Prime Minister, and the Mayor, and from dozens of others. And from native organizations too, something called the Daughters of Africa, and a whole lot of others that I can't remember. And from colored people, and Indians, and Jews.

Jarvis felt a sad pride rising in him. He was clever, he said. That came from his mother.

—He was that right enough—you must hear John on it. But people liked him too, all sorts of people. You know he spoke Afrikaans like an Afrikaner?

—I knew he had learnt it.

—It's a lingo I know nothing about, thank God. But he thought he ought to know it, so he took lessons in it, and went to an Afrikaner farm. He spoke Zulu as you know, but he was talking of learning Sesuto. There was talk of getting him to stand at the next election.

—I didn't know that.

—Yes, he was always speaking here and there. You know the kind of thing. Native Crime, and more Native Schools, and he kicked up a hell of a dust in the papers about the conditions at the Non-European Hospital. And he was hot about the native compound system in the mines, and wanted the Chamber to come out one hundred percent for settled labor—you know, wife and family to come with the man.

Jarvis filled his pipe slowly, and listened to this tale of his son, to this tale of a stranger.

—Hathaway of the Chamber of Mines spoke to me about it, said Harrison. Asked me if I wouldn't warn the lad to pipe down a bit, because his firm did a lot of business with the mines. So I spoke to him, told him I knew he felt deeply about these things, but asked him to go slow a bit. Told him there was Mary to consider, and the children. I didn't speak on behalf of Mary, you understand? I don't poke my nose into young people's business.

—I understand.

—I've spoken to Mary, he said to me. She and I agree that it's more important to speak the truth than to make money.

Harrison laughed at that, but cut himself short, remembering the sadness of the occasion. My son John was there, he said, looking at Arthur as though he were God Almighty. So what could I say?

They smoked in silence awhile. I asked him, said Harrison, about his partners. After all their job was to sell machinery to the mines. I've discussed it with my partners, he said to me, and if there's any trouble, I've told them I'll get out. And what would you do? I asked him. What won't I do? he said. His face was sort of excited. Well, what could I say more?

Jarvis did not answer. For this boy of his had gone journeying in strange waters, further than his parents had known. Or perhaps his mother knew. It would not surprise him if his mother knew. But he himself had never done such journeying, and there was nothing he could say.

—Am I tiring you, Jarvis? Or is there perhaps something else you'd like to talk about? Or go to bed, perhaps?

—Harrison, you're doing me more good by talking.

—Well, that's how he was. He and I didn't talk much about these things. It's not my line of country. I try to treat a native decently, but he's not my food and drink. And these crimes put me off. I tell you, Jarvis, we're scared stiff in Johannesburg.

—Of crime?

—Yes, of native crime. There are too many of these murders and robberies and brutal attacks. I tell you we don't go to bed at night without barricading the house. It was at the Phillipsons', three doors down, that a gang of these roughs broke in; they knocked old Phillipson unconscious, and beat up his wife. It was lucky the girls were out at a dance, or one doesn't know what might have happened. I asked Arthur about that, but he reckoned we were to blame somehow. Can't say I always followed him, but he had a kind of sincerity. You sort of felt that if you had the time you could get some sort of sense out of it.

—There's one thing I don't get the sense of, said Jarvis. Why this should have happened . . .

—You mean . . . to him, of all people?

—Yes.

—That's one of the first things that we said. Here he was, day in and day out, on a kind of mission. And it was he who was killed.

—Mind you, said Jarvis, coming to a point, mind you, it's happened before. I mean, that missionaries were killed.

Harrison made no answer, and they smoked their pipes silently. A missionary, thought Jarvis, and thought how strange it was that he had called his son a missionary. For he had never thought much of missionaries. True, the Church made a lot of it, and there were special appeals to which he had given, but one did that kind of thing without believing much in missionaries. There was a mission near him, at Ndotsheni. But it was a sad place as he remembered it. A dirty old wood-and-iron church, patched and forlorn, and a dirty old parson, in a barren valley where the grass hardly grew. A dirty old school where he had heard them reciting, parrot fashion, on the

one or two occasions that he had ridden past there, reciting things
that could mean little to them.

—Bed, Jarvis? Or another drink?

—Bed, I think. Did you say the police were coming?

—They're coming at nine.

—And I'd like to see the house.

—I thought that you would. They'll take you there.

—Good. Then I'll go to bed. Will you say good night to your
wife for me?

—I'll do that. You know your room? And breakfast? Eight
thirty?

—Eight thirty. Good night, Harrison. And many thanks for
your kindnesses.

—No thanks are needed. Nothing is too much trouble. Good
night, Jarvis, and I hope you and Margaret will get some sleep.

Jarvis walked up the stairs, and went into the room. He walked
in quietly, and closed the door, and did not put on the light. The
moon was shining through the windows, and he stood there looking out on the world. All that he had heard went quietly through
his mind. His wife turned in the bed, and said, James.

—My dear.

—What were you thinking, my dear?

He was silent, searching for an answer. Of it all, he said.

—I thought you would never come.

He went to her quickly, and she caught at his hands. We were
talking of the boy, he said. All that he did, and tried to do. All the
people that are grieved.

—Tell me, my dear.

And so he told her in low tones all he had heard. She marveled a
little, for her husband was a quiet silent man, not given to much
talking. But tonight he told her all that Harrison had told him.

—It makes me proud, she whispered.

—But you always knew he was like that.

—Yes, I knew.

—I knew too that he was a decent man, he said. But you were
always nearer to him than I was.

—It's easier for a mother, James.

—I suppose so. But I wish now that I'd known more of him. You see, the things that he did, I've never had much to do with that sort of thing.

—Nor I either, James. His life was quite different from ours.

—It was a good life by all accounts.

He sat, she lay, in silence, with their thoughts and their memories and their grief.

—Although his life was different, he said, you understood it.

—Yes, James.

—I'm sorry I didn't understand it.

Then he said in a whisper, I didn't know it would ever be so important to understand it.

—My dear, my dear. Her arms went about him, and she wept. And he continued to whisper, There's one thing I don't understand, why it should have happened to him.

She lay there thinking of it, the pain was deep, deep and ineluctable. She tightened her arms about him. James, let's try to sleep, she said.

J ARVIS SAT IN THE CHAIR of his son, and his wife and Mary left him to return to the Harrisons. Books, books, books, more books than he had ever seen in a house! On the table papers, letters, and more books. Mr. Jarvis, will you speak at the Parkwold Methodist Guild? Mr. Jarvis, will you speak at the Anglican Young People's Association in Sophiatown? Mr. Jarvis, will you speak in a symposium at the University? No, Mr. Jarvis would be unable to speak at any of these.

On the walls between the books there were four pictures, of Christ crucified, and Abraham Lincoln, and the white gabled house of Vergelegen,* and a painting of leafless willows by a river in a wintry veld.

He rose from the chair to look at the books. Here were hundreds of books, all about Abraham Lincoln. He had not known that so

_____
*An historic South African homestead.

many books had been written about any one man. One bookcase was full of them. And another was full of books about South Africa, Sarah Gertrude Millin's *Life of Rhodes*, and her book about Smuts, and Engelenburg's *Life of Louis Botha*, and books on South African race problems, and books on South African birds, and the Kruger Park, and innumerable others. Another bookcase was full of Afrikaans books, but the titles conveyed nothing to him. And here were books about religion and Soviet Russia, and crime and criminals, and books of poems. He looked about for Shakespeare, and here was Shakespeare too.

He went back to the chair, and sat there looking long at the pictures of Christ crucified, and Abraham Lincoln, and Vergelegen, and the willows by the river. Then he drew some pieces of paper towards him.

The first was a letter to his son from the secretary of the Claremont African Boys' Club, Gladiolus Street, Claremont, regretting that Mr. Jarvis had not been able to attend the Annual Meeting of the Club, and informing him he had again been elected as President.

And the letter concluded, with quaintness of phrase—

I am compelled by the Annual Meeting to congratulate you with this matter, and to express considerable thanks to you for all the time you have been spending with us, and for the presents you have been giving the Club. How this Club would be arranged without your participation, would be a mystery to many minds amongst us. It is on these accounts that we desire to elect you again to the Presidency.

I am asking an apology for this writing-paper, but our Club writing-paper is lost owing to unforeseen circumstances.

I am,

Your obedient servant,

WASHINGTON LEFIFI.

The other papers were in his son's handwriting. They were obviously part of some larger whole, for the first line was the latter end of a sentence, and the last line was a sentence unfinished.

He looked for the rest of it, but finding nothing, settled down to read what he had:

was permissible. What we did when we came to South Africa was permissible. It was permissible to develop our great resources with the aid of what labor we could find. It was permissible to use unskilled men for unskilled work. But it is not permissible to keep men unskilled for the sake of unskilled work.

It was permissible when we discovered gold to bring labor to the mines. It was permissible to build compounds and to keep women and children away from the towns. It was permissible as an experiment, in the light of what we knew. But in the light of what we know now, with certain exceptions, it is no longer permissible. It is not permissible for us to go on destroying family life when we know that we are destroying it.

It was permissible to leave native education to those who wanted to develop it. It was permissible to doubt its benefits. But it is no longer permissible in the light of what we know. Partly because it made possible industrial development, and partly because it happened in spite of us, there is now a large urbanized native population. Now society has always, for reasons of self-interest if for no other, educated its children so that they grow up law-abiding.

There is no other way that it can be done. Yet we continue to leave the education of our native urban society to those few Europeans who feel strongly about it, and to deny opportunities and money for its expansion. That is not permissible. For reasons of self-interest alone, it is dangerous.

It was permissible to allow the destruction of a tribal system that impeded the growth of the country. It was permissible to believe that its destruction was inevitable. But it is not permissible to replace it by nothing, or by so little, that a whole people deteriorates, physically and morally. Our natives today produce criminals and prostitutes and drunkards, not because it is their nature to do so, but because their simple tribal system of order and tradition and convention has been destroyed by the impact of our own civilization. Our civilization has therefore an inescapable duty to set up another system of order and tradition and convention.

No one wishes to make the problem seem smaller than it is. No one wishes to make its solution seem easy. No one wishes to make light of the fears that beset us. But whether we be fearful or no, we shall never, because we are a Christian people, be able to evade the moral issues. It is time—

And there the manuscript and the page ended. Jarvis, who had become absorbed in the reading, searched again among the papers on the table, but he could find nothing to show that anything more than this had been written. He lit his pipe, and pulling the papers towards him, began to read them again.

After he had finished them the second time, he sat smoking his pipe and was lost in thought. Then he got up and went and stood in front of the Lincoln bookcase, and looked up at the picture of the man who had exercised such an influence over his son. He looked at the books, and slid aside the glass panel and took one of them out. Then he returned to his chair, and began to turn over its pages. One of the chapters was headed "The Famous Speech at Gettysburg." He turned over the preliminary pages till he came to the speech, and read it through carefully. That done, he smoked again, lost in a deep abstraction. After some time he rose and slipped the book into his pocket. He looked at his watch, knocked out his pipe in the fireplace, put on his hat, took up his stick. He walked slowly down the stairs, and opened the door into the fatal passage. He took off his hat and looked down at the dark stain on the floor.

Unasked, unwanted, the picture of the small boy came into his mind, the small boy at High Place, the small boy with the wooden guns. Unseeing he walked along the passage and out of the door through which death had come so suddenly. The policeman saluted him, and he answered him with words that meant nothing, that made no sense at all. He put on his hat, and walked to the gate. Undecided he looked up and down the road. Then with an effort he began to walk. With a sigh the policeman relaxed.

THE SERVICE IN THE Parkwold Church was over, and the church had been too small for all who wanted to come. White people, black people, colored people, Indians—it was the first time that

Jarvis and his wife had sat in a church with people who were not white. The Bishop himself had spoken, words that pained and uplifted. And the Bishop too had said that men did not understand this riddle, why a young man so full of promise was cut off in his youth, why a woman was widowed and children were orphaned, why a country was bereft of one who might have served it greatly. And the Bishop's voice rose when he spoke of South Africa, and he spoke in a language of beauty, and Jarvis listened for a while without pain, under the spell of the words.

And the Bishop said that here had been a life devoted to South Africa, of intelligence and courage, of love that cast out fear, so that the pride welled up in the heart, pride in the stranger who had been his son.

THE FUNERAL WAS OVER. The brass doors opened soundlessly, and the coffin slid soundlessly into the furnace that would reduce it to ashes. And people that he did not know shook hands with him, some speaking their sympathy in brief conventional phrases, some speaking simply of his son. The black people—yes, the black people also—it was the first time he had ever shaken hands with black people.

They returned to the house of the Harrisons, for the night that is supposed to be worst of all the nights that must come. For Margaret it would no doubt be so; he would not leave her again to go to bed alone. But for him it was over; he could sit quietly in Harrison's study, and drink his whisky and smoke his pipe, and talk about any matter that Harrison wanted to talk about, even about his son.

—How long will you stay, Jarvis? You're welcome to stay as long as you wish.

—Thank you, Harrison. I think Margaret will go back with Mary and the children, and we'll arrange for the son of one of my neighbors to stay with them. A nice lad, just out of the army. But I'll stay to wind up Arthur's affairs, at least in the preliminary stages.

—And what did the police say, if I may ask?

—They're still waiting for Arthur's servant to recover. They have hopes that he recognized one of them. Otherwise they say it will be very difficult. The whole thing was over so quickly. They hope too that someone may have seen them getting away. They think they were frightened and excited, and wouldn't have walked away normally.

—I hope to God they get them. And string 'em all up. Pardon me, Jarvis.

—I know exactly what you mean.

—God knows what's coming to the country. I don't. I'm not a nigger-hater, Jarvis. I try to give 'em a square deal, decent wages, and a clean room, and reasonable time off. Our servants stay with us for years. But the natives as a whole are getting out of hand. They've even started trade unions, did you know that?

—I didn't know that.

—Well, they have. They're threatening to strike here in the mines for ten shillings a day. They get about three shillings a shift now, and some of the mines are on the verge of closing down. They live in decent compounds—some of the latest compounds I wouldn't mind living in myself. They get good balanced food, far better than they'd ever get at home, free medical attention, and God knows what. I tell you, Jarvis, if mining costs go up much more there won't be any mines. And where will South Africa be then? And where would the natives be themselves? They'd die by the thousands of starvation.

—Am I intruding? asked John Harrison, coming into the study.

—Sit down, John, said Harrison.

So the young man sat down, and his father, who was growing warm and excited, proceeded to develop his theme.

—And where would the farmers be, Jarvis? Where would you sell your products, and who could afford to buy them? There wouldn't be any subsidies. There wouldn't be any industry either; industry depends on the mines to provide the money that will buy its products. And this government of ours soaks the mines every year for a cool seventy percent of the profits. And where would they be if there were no mines? Half the Afrikaners in the country would be out of work. There wouldn't be any civil service, either. Half of them would be out of work, too.

He poured out some more whisky for them both, and then resumed his subject.

—I tell you there wouldn't be any South Africa at all if it weren't for the mines. You could shut the place up, and give it back to the natives. That's what makes me so angry when people criticize the mines. Especially the Afrikaners. They have some fool notion that the mining people are foreign to the country, and are sucking the blood out of it, ready to clear out when the goose stops laying the eggs. I'm telling you that most of the mining shares are held here in the country itself, they're *our* mines. I get sick and tired of all this talk. Republic! Where would we be if we ever get a republic?

—Harrison, I'm going to bed. I don't want Margaret to go to bed alone.

—Old man, I'm sorry. I'm afraid I forgot myself.

—There's nothing to be sorry about. It's done me good to listen to you. I could have wished that my son was here tonight, that I could have heard him argue with you.

—You would have enjoyed it, Mr. Jarvis, said John Harrison eagerly, responding to this natural invitation to talk about a man not long since dead. I never heard anyone argue about these things as he could.

—I didn't agree with him, said Harrison, his discomfort passing, but I had a great respect for anything that he said.

—He was a good man, Harrison. I'm not sorry that we had him. Good night to you.

—Good night, Jarvis. Did you sleep last night? Did Margaret sleep?

—We both got some sleep.

—I hope you get some more tonight. Don't forget, the house is at your service.

—Thank you, good night. John?

—Yes, Mr. Jarvis.

—Do you know the Boys' Club in Gladiolus Street, Claremont?

—I know it well. It was our Club. Arthur's and mine.

—I should like to see it. Any time that suits.

—I'd be glad to take you, Mr. Jarvis.

—Thank you. Good night, Harrison. Good night, John.

The next morning Harrison waited for his guest at the foot of the stairs. Come into the study, he said. They went in, and Harrison closed the door behind him.

—The police have just telephoned, Jarvis. The servant recovered consciousness this morning. He says there were three right enough. They had their mouths and noses covered, but he is sure that the one that knocked him out was an old garden boy of Mary's. Mary had to get rid of him for some trouble or other. He recognized him because of some twitching about the eyes. When he left Mary, he got a job at some textile factory in Doornfontein. Then he left the factory, and no one can say where he went. But they got information about some other native who had been very friendly with him. They're after him now, hoping that he can tell them where to find the garden boy. They certainly seem to be moving.

—They do seem to be.

—And here is a copy of Arthur's manuscript on native crime. Shall I leave it on the table and you can read it in peace after breakfast?

—Thank you, leave it there.

After breakfast, Jarvis returned to his host's study, and began to read his son's manuscript. He turned first to the last page of it, and read with pain the last unfinished paragraph. This was almost the last thing that his son had done. When this was done he had been alive. Then at this moment, at this very word that hung in the air, he had got up and gone down the stairs to his death. If one could have cried then, Don't go down! If one could have cried, Stop, there is danger! But there was no one to cry. No one knew then what so many knew now. But these thoughts were unprofitable; it was not his habit to dwell on what might have been but what could never be. He wanted to understand his son, not to desire what was no more accessible to desire. So he compelled himself to read the last paragraph slowly—with his head, not his heart, so that he could understand it.

The truth is that our Christian civilization is riddled through and through with dilemma. We believe in the brotherhood of man, but we do not want it in South Africa. We believe that God endows men with diverse gifts, and that human life depends for its fullness on their employment and enjoyment, but we do not want it in South Africa. We believe in help for the underdog, but we want him to stay under. We go so far as to credit Almighty God with the intention of having created black men to hew wood and draw water for white men. We go so far as to assume that He blesses any action that is designed to prevent black men from the full employment of the gifts He gave them. Alongside of these very arguments we use others totally inconsistent, so that the accusation of repression may be refuted. We say we withhold education because the black child has not the intelligence to profit by it; we withhold opportunity to develop gifts because black people have no gifts; we justify our action by saying that it took us thousands of years to achieve our own advancement, and it would be foolish to suppose that it will take the black man any lesser time, and that therefore there is no need for hurry. We shift our ground again when a black man does achieve something remarkable, and feel deep pity for a man who is condemned to the loneliness of being remarkable, and decide that it is a Christian kindness not to let black men become remarkable. The truth is that our civilization is not Christian; it is a tragic compound of great ideal and fearful practice, of high assurance and desperate anxiety, of loving charity and fearful clutching of possessions. Allow me a minute . . .

Jarvis sat, deeply moved. Whether because this was his son, whether because this was almost the last act of his son, he could not say. Whether because there was some quality in the words, that too he could not say, for he had given little time in his life to the savoring and judging of words. Whether because there was some quality in the ideas, that too he could not say. For he had given little time to the study of these particular matters.

He picked up the page again, but for his son, not for the words or the ideas. He looked at the words. Allow me a minute . . .

And nothing more. Those fingers would not write any more. Allow me a minute, I hear a sound in the kitchen. Allow me a minute, while I go to my death. Allow me a thousand minutes, I am not coming back any more.

Jarvis shook it off, and put another match to his pipe, and after he had read the paper through, sat in a reverie, smoking.

—James.

He started. Yes, my dear, he said.

—You shouldn't sit by yourself, she said.

He smiled at her. It's not my nature to brood, he said.

—Then what have you been doing?

—Thinking. Not brooding, thinking. And reading. This is what I have been reading.

She took it, looked at it, and held it against her breast.

—Read it, he said quietly, it's worth reading.

So she sat down to read it, and he, watching her, knew what she would do. She turned to the last page, to the last words, Allow me a minute, and sat looking at them. She looked at him, she was going to speak, he accepted that. Pain does not go away so quickly.

THEY CALL FOR SILENCE in the Court, and the people stand. The Judge enters with his two assessors, and they sit, and then the people sit also. The Court is begun.

From the place of detention under the ground come the three that are to be judged, and all the people look at them. Some people think they look like murderers, they even whisper it, though it is forbidden to whisper. Some people think they do not look like murderers, and some think this one looks like a murderer, but that one does not.

A white man stands up and says that these three are accused of the murder of Arthur Trevelyan Jarvis, in his house at Plantation Road, Parkwold, Johannesburg, on Tuesday the eighth day of October, 1946, in the early afternoon. The first is Absalom Kumalo, the second is Matthew Kumalo, the third is Johannes Pafuri. They are called upon to plead guilty or not guilty, and the first says, I plead guilty to killing, but I did not mean to kill. The second says, I am not guilty, and the third likewise. Everything is said in

English and in Zulu, so that these three may understand. For though Pafuri is not a Zulu, he understands it well, he says.

The lawyer, the white man who is taking the case for God, says that Absalom Kumalo will plead guilty to culpable homicide, but not to murder, for he had no intention to kill. But the prosecutor says there is no charge of culpable homicide; for it is murder, and nothing less than murder, with which he is charged. So Absalom Kumalo pleads, like the two others, not guilty.

Then the prosecutor tells the Court the whole story of the crime. And Absalom Kumalo is still and silent, but the other two look grieved and shocked to think such things are said.

THEN AFTER THIS PLAN was made you decided on this day, the eighth day of October?

—That is so.

—Why did you choose this day?

—Because Johannes said that no one would be in the house.

—This same Johannes Pafuri?

—This same Johannes Pafuri who is charged with me now.

—And you chose this time of half past one?

—That is so.

—Was it not a bad time to choose? White people come home to eat at this time.

But the accused makes no answer.

—Why did you choose this time?

—It was Johannes who chose this time. He said it was told to him by a voice.

—What voice?

—No, that I do not know.

—An evil voice?

And again there is no answer.

—Then you three went to the back door of the house?

—That is so.

—You and these two who are charged with you?

—I and these very two.

—And then?

—Then we tied the handkerchiefs over our mouths.

—And then?

—Then we went into the kitchen.

—Who was there?

—The servant of the house was there.

—Richard Mpiring?

—No, I do not know his name.

—Is this the man here?

—Yes, that is the man.

—And then? Tell the Court what happened.

—This man was afraid. He saw my revolver. He stood back against the sink where he was working. He said, What do you want? Johannes said, We want money and clothes. This man said, You cannot do such a thing. Johannes said, Do you want to die? This man was afraid and did not speak. Johannes said, When I speak, people must tremble. Then he said again, Do you want to die? The man said nothing, but he suddenly called out, Master, master. Then Johannes struck him over the head with the iron bar that he had behind his back.

—How many times did he strike him?

—Once.

—Did he call out again?

—He made no sound.

—What did you do?

—No, we were silent. Johannes said we must be silent.

—What did you do? Did you listen?

—We listened.

—Did you hear anything?

—We heard nothing.

—Where was your revolver?

—In my hand.

—And then?

—Then a white man came into the passage.

—And then?

—I was frightened. I fired the revolver.

—And then?

The accused looked down. The white man fell, he said.
—And then?
—Johannes said quickly, We must go. So we all went quickly.
—To the back gate?
—Yes.
—And then over the road into the plantation?
—Yes.
—Did you stay together?
—No, I went alone.
—And when did you see these two again?
—At the house of Baby Mkize.
But the Judge interrupts. You may proceed shortly, Mr. Prosecutor. But I have one or two questions to ask the first accused.
—As your lordship pleases.
—Why did you carry this revolver? the Judge asked.
—It was to frighten the servant of the house.
—But why do you carry any revolver?
The boy is silent.
—You must answer my question.
—They told me to carry it.
—Who told you?
—No, they told me Johannesburg was dangerous.
—Who told you?
The boy is silent.
—You mean you were told by the kind of man who is engaged in this business of breaking in and stealing?
—No, I do not mean that.
—Well, who told you?
—I do not remember. It was said in some place where I was.
—You mean you were all sitting there, and some man said, One needs a revolver in Johannesburg, it is dangerous?
—Yes, I mean that.
—And you knew this revolver was loaded?
—Yes, I knew it.
—If this revolver is to frighten people, why must it be loaded?
But the boy does not answer.

—You were therefore ready to shoot with it?

—No, I would not have shot a decent person. I would have shot only if someone had shot at me.

—Would you have shot at a policeman if he had shot at you in the execution of his duty?

—No, not at a policeman.

The Judge pauses and everything is silent. Then he says gravely, And this white man you shot, was he not a decent person?

The accused looks down again at the floor. Then he answers in a low voice, I was afraid, I was afraid. I never meant to shoot him.

—Where did you get this revolver?

—I bought it from a man.

—Where?

—In Alexandra.

—Who is this man? What is his name?

—I do not know his name.

—Where does he live?

—I do not know where he lives.

—Could you find him?

—I could try to find him.

—Was this revolver loaded when you bought it?

—It had two bullets in it.

—How many bullets were in it when you went to this house?

—There was one bullet in it.

—What happened to the other?

—I took the revolver into one of the plantations in the hills beyond Alexandra, and I fired it there.

—What did you fire at?

—I fired at a tree.

—Did you hit this tree?

—Yes, I hit it.

—Then you thought, Now I can fire this revolver?

—Yes, that is so.

—Who carried the iron bar?

—Johannes carried it.

—Did you know he carried it?

—I knew it.

—You knew it was a dangerous weapon? That it could kill a man?

The boy's voice rises. It was not meant for killing or striking, he said. It was meant only for frightening.

—But you had a revolver for frightening?

—Yes, but Johannes took the bar. It had been blessed, he said.

—What did Johannes mean when he said the bar had been blessed?

—I do not know.

—Did he mean by a priest?

—I do not know.

—You did not ask?

—No, I did not ask.

—Your father is a priest?

The boy looks down at the floor and in a low voice he answers, Yes.

—Would he bless such a bar?

—No.

—You did not say to Johannes, You must not take this bar?

—No.

—You did not say to him, How can such a thing be blessed?

—No.

—Proceed, Mr. Prosecutor.

AND IF THESE TWO say there was no murder discussed at the house of Baby Mkize, they are lying?

—They are lying.

—And if they say that you made up this story after meeting them at the house of Mkize, they are lying?

—They are lying.

—And if Baby Mkize says that no murder was discussed in her presence, she is lying?

—She is lying. She was afraid, and said we must leave her house and never return to it.

—Did you leave together?

—No, I left first.

—And where did you go?

—I went into a plantation.

—And what did you do there?

—I buried the revolver.

—Is this the revolver before the Court?

The revolver is handed up to the accused and he examines it. This is the revolver, he says.

—How was it found?

—No, I told the police where to find it.

—And what did you do next?

—I prayed there.

The Prosecutor seems taken aback for a moment, but the Judge says, And what did you pray there?

—I prayed for forgiveness.

—And what else did you pray?

—No, there was nothing else that I wished to pray.

—And on the second day you walked again to Johannesburg?

—Yes.

—And you again walked amongst the people who were boycotting the buses?

—Yes.

—Were they still talking about the murder?

—They were still talking. Some said they heard it would soon be discovered.

—And then?

—I was afraid.

—So what did you do?

—That night I went to Germiston.

—But what did you do that day? Did you hide again?

—No, I bought a shirt, and then I walked about with the parcel.

—Why did you do that?

—I thought they would think I was a messenger.

—Was there anything else that you did?

—There was nothing else.

—Then you went to Germiston? To what place?

—To the house of Joseph Bhengu, at 12 Maseru Street.

—And then?

—While I was there the police came.

—What happened?

—They asked me if I was Absalom Kumalo. And I agreed, and I was afraid, and I had meant to go that day to confess to the police, and now I could see I had delayed foolishly.

—Did they arrest you?

—No, they asked if I could tell them where to find Johannes. I said no, I did not know, but it was not Johannes who had killed the white man, it was I myself. But it was Johannes who had struck down the servant of the house. And I told them that Matthew was there also. And I told them I would show them where I had hidden the revolver. And I told them that I had meant that day to confess, but had delayed foolishly, because I was afraid.

—You then made a statement before Andries Coetzee, Esquire, Additional Magistrate at Johannesburg?

—I do not know his name.

—Is this the statement?

The statement is handed up to the boy. He looks at it and says, Yes, that is the statement.

—And every word is true?

—Every word is true.

—There is no lie in it?

—There is no lie in it, for I said to myself, I shall not lie any more, all the rest of my days, nor do anything more that is evil.

—In fact you repented?

—Yes, I repented.

—Because you were in trouble?

—Yes, because I was in trouble.

—Did you have any other reason for repenting?

—No, I had no other reason.

THE PEOPLE STAND when the Court is adjourned, and while the Judge and his assessors leave the Court. Then they pass out through the doors at the back of the tiers of seats, the Europeans through their door, and the non-Europeans through their door, according to the custom.

Kumalo and Msimangu, Gertrude and Mrs. Lithebe come out together, and they hear people saying, There is the father of the white man who was killed. And Kumalo looks and sees that it is true, there is the father of the man who was murdered, the man who has the farm on the tops above Ndotsheni, the man he has seen riding past the church. And Kumalo trembles, and does not look at him any more. For how does one look at such a man?

JARVIS THOUGHT HE would go to the house again. It was foolish to go through the kitchen, past the stain on the floor, up the stairs that led to the bedroom. But that was the way he went. He went not to the bedroom but to the study that was so full of books. He looked at the pictures of the Christ crucified, and Abraham Lincoln, and Vergelegen, and the willows in the winter. He sat down at the table, where lay the invitations to do this and that, and the paper on what was permissible and what was not permissible in South Africa.

He opened the drawers of his son's table, and here were accounts, and here were papers and envelopes, and here were pens and pencils, and here were old checks stamped and returned by the bank.

And here in a deep drawer were typewritten articles, each neatly pinned together, and placed one on top of the other. Here was an article on "The Need for Social Centers," and one on "Birds of a Parkwold Garden," and another on "India and South Africa." And here was one called "Private Essay on the Evolution of a South African," and this he took out to read:

It is hard to be born a South African. One can be born an Afrikaner, or an English-speaking South African, or a colored man, or a Zulu. One can ride, as I rode when I was a boy, over green hills and into great valleys. One can see, as I saw when I was a boy, the reserves of the Bantu people and see nothing of what was happening there at all. One can hear, as I heard when I was a boy, that there are more Afrikaners than English-speaking people in

South Africa, and yet know nothing, see nothing, of them at all.

I was born on a farm, brought up by honorable parents, given all that a child could need or desire. They were upright and kind and law-abiding; they taught me my prayers and took me regularly to church; they had no trouble with servants and my father was never short of labor. From them I learned all that a child should learn of honor and charity and generosity. But of South Africa I learned nothing at all.

Shocked and hurt, Jarvis put down the papers. For a moment he felt something almost like anger, but he wiped his eyes with his fingers and shook it from him. But he was trembling and could read no further. He stood up and put on his hat, and went down the stairs, and as far as the stain on the floor. The policeman was ready to salute him, but he turned again, and went up the stairs, and sat down again at the table. He took up the papers and read them through to the end. Perhaps he was some judge of words after all, for the closing paragraphs moved him. Perhaps he was some judge of ideas after all.

Therefore I shall devote myself, my time, my energy, my talents, to the service of South Africa. I shall no longer ask myself if this or that is expedient, but only if it is right. I shall do this, not because I am noble or unselfish, but because life slips away, and because I need for the rest of my journey a star that will not play false to me, a compass that will not lie. I shall do this, not because I am a Negrophile and a hater of my own, but because I cannot find it in me to do anything else. I am lost when I balance this against that, I am lost when I ask if this is safe, I am lost when I ask if men, white men or black men, Englishmen or Afrikaners, Gentiles or Jews, will approve. Therefore I shall try to do what is right, and to speak what is true.

It would not be honest to pretend that it is solely an inverted selfishness that moves me. I am moved by something that is not my own, that moves me to do what is right, at whatever cost it may be. In this I am fortunate that I have married a wife who thinks as I do, who has tried to conquer her own fears and hates. Aspiration is thus made easy. My children are too young to understand. It would be grievous if they grew up to hate me or fear me, or to think of me as a betrayer of those things that I call our possessions. It would be a source of unending joy if they grew up to think as we do. It would be exciting, exhilarating, a matter for thanksgiving. But it cannot be bargained for. It must be given or withheld, and whether the one or the other, it must not alter the course that is right.

Jarvis sat a long time smoking, he did not read any more. He put the papers back in the drawer and closed it. He sat there till his pipe was finished. Then he put on his hat and came down the stairs. At the foot of the stairs he turned and walked towards the front door. He was not afraid of the passage and the stain on the floor; he was not going that way any more, that was all.

The front door was self-locking and he let himself out. He looked up at the sky from the farmer's habit, but these skies of a strange country told him nothing. He walked down the path and out of the gate. The policeman at the back door heard the door lock, and shook his head with understanding. He cannot face it any more, he said to himself, the old chap cannot face it any more.

O NE OF THE FAVORITE nieces of Margaret Jarvis, Barbara Smith by name, had married a man from Springs, and both Jarvis and his wife, on a day when the Court was not holding the case, went to spend a day with them. He had thought it would be a good thing for his wife, who had taken the death of their son even more hardly than he had feared. The two women talked of the people of Ixopo and Lufafa and Highflats and Umzimkulu, and he left them and walked in the garden, for he was a man of the soil. After a while they called to him to say they were going into the town, and asked if he wished to go with them. But he said that he would stay at the house, and read the newspaper while they were away, and this he did.

While he was reading there was a knock at the kitchen door, and he went out to find a native parson standing on the paved stone at the foot of the three stone steps that led up to the kitchen. The parson was old, and his black clothes were green with age, and his collar was brown with age or dirt. He took off his hat, showing the whiteness of his head, and he looked startled and afraid and he was trembling.

—Good morning, umfundisi, said Jarvis in Zulu, of which he was a master.

The parson answered in a trembling voice, Umnumzana, which means Sir, and to Jarvis's surprise, he sat down on the lowest step, as though he were ill or starving. Jarvis knew this was not rudeness, for the old man was humble and well mannered, so he came down the steps, saying, Are you ill, umfundisi? But the old man did not answer. He continued to tremble, and he looked down on the ground, so that Jarvis could not see his face, and could not have seen it unless he had lifted the chin with his hand, which he did not do, for such a thing is not lightly done.

—Are you ill, umfundisi?

—I shall recover, umnumzana.

—Do you wish water? Or is it food? Are you hungry?

—No, umnumzana, I shall recover.

Jarvis stood on the paved stone below the lowest step, but the old man was not quick to recover. He continued to tremble, and to look at the ground. It is not easy for a white man to be kept waiting, but Jarvis waited, for the old man was obviously ill and weak. The old man made an effort to rise, using his stick, but the stick slipped on the paved stone, and fell clattering on the stone. Jarvis picked it up and restored it to him, but the old man put it down as a hindrance, and he put down his hat also, and tried to lift himself up by pressing his hands on the steps. But his first effort failed, and he sat down again, and continued to tremble. Jarvis would have helped him, but such a thing is not so lightly done as picking up a stick; then the old man pressed his hands again on the steps, and lifted himself up. Then he lifted his face also and looked at Jarvis, and Jarvis saw that his face was full of a suffering that was of neither illness nor hunger. And Jarvis stooped, and picked up the hat and stick, and he held the hat carefully for it was old and dirty, and he restored them to the parson.

—I thank you, umnumzana.

—Are you sure you are not ill, umfundisi?

—I am recovered, umnumzana.

—And what are you seeking, umfundisi?

The old parson put his hat and his stick down again on the step, and with trembling hands pulled out a wallet from the inside pocket of the old green coat, and the papers fell out on the ground, because his hands would not be still.

—I am sorry, umnumzana. He stooped to pick up the papers, and because he was old he had to kneel, and the papers were old and dirty, and some that he had picked up fell out of his hands while he was picking up others, and the wallet fell too, and the hands were trembling and shaking. Jarvis was torn between compassion and irritation, and he stood and watched uncomfortably.

—I am sorry to detain you, umnumzana.

—It is no matter, umfundisi.

At last the papers were collected, and all were restored to the wallet except one, and this one he held out to Jarvis, and on it were the name and address of this place where they were.

—This is the place, umfundisi.

—I was asked to come here, umnumzana. There is a man named Sibeko of Ndotsheni—

—Ndotsheni, I know it. I come from Ndotsheni.

—And this man had a daughter, umnumzana, who worked for a white man uSmith in Ixopo . . .

—Yes, yes.

—And when the daughter of uSmith married, she married the white man whose name is on the paper.

—That is so.

—And they came to live here in Springs, and the daughter of Sibeko came here also to work for them. Now Sibeko has not heard of her for these twelve months, and I am asked to inquire about her.

Jarvis turned and went into the house, and returned with the boy who was working there. You may inquire from him, he said, and he turned again and went into the house. But when he was there it came suddenly to him that this was the old parson of Ndotsheni himself. So he came out again.

—Did you find what you wanted, umfundisi?

—This boy does not know her, umnumzana. When he came she had gone already.

—The mistress of the house is out, the daughter of uSmith. But she will soon be returning, and you may wait for her if you wish.

Jarvis dismissed the boy, and waited till he was gone.

—I know you, umfundisi, he said.

The suffering in the old man's face smote him, so that he said, Sit down, umfundisi. Then the old man would be able to look at the ground, and he would not need to look at Jarvis, and Jarvis would not need to look at him, for it was uncomfortable to look at him. So the old man sat down and Jarvis said to him, not looking at him, There is something between you and me, but I do not know what it is.

—Umnumzana.

—You are in fear of me, but I do not know what it is. You need not be in fear of me.

—It is true, umnumzana. You do not know what it is.

—I do not know but I desire to know.

—I doubt if I could tell it, umnumzana.

—You must tell it, umfundisi. Is it heavy?

—It is very heavy, umnumzana. It is the heaviest thing of all my years.

He lifted his face, and there was in it suffering that Jarvis had not seen before. Tell me, he said, it will lighten you.

—I am afraid, umnumzana.

—I see you are afraid, umfundisi. It is that which I do not understand. But I tell you, you need not be afraid. I shall not be angry. There will be no anger in me against you.

—Then, said the old man, this thing that is the heaviest thing of all my years, is the heaviest thing of all your years also.

Jarvis looked at him, at first bewildered, but then something came to him. You can only mean one thing, he said, you can only mean one thing. But I still do not understand.

—It was my son that killed your son, said the old man.

So they were silent. Jarvis left him and walked out into the trees of the garden. He stood at the wall and looked out over the veld, out to the great white dumps of the mines, like hills under the sun. When he turned to come back, he saw that the old man had risen, his hat in one hand, his stick in the other, his head bowed, his eyes on the ground. He went back to him.

—I have heard you, he said. I understand what I did not understand. There is no anger in me.

—Umnumzana.

—The mistress of the house is back, the daughter of uSmith. Do you wish to see her? Are you recovered?

—It was that that I came to do, umnumzana.

—I understand. And you were shocked when you saw me. You had no thought that I would be here. How did you know me?

—I have seen you riding past Ndotsheni, past the church where I work.

Jarvis listened to the sounds in the house. Then he spoke very quietly. Perhaps you saw the boy also, he said. He too used to ride past Ndotsheni. On a red horse with a white face. And he carried wooden guns, here in his belt, as small boys do.

The old man's face was working. He continued to look on the ground, and Jarvis could see that tears fell on it. He himself was moved and unmanned, and he would have brought the thing to an end, but he could find no quick voice for it.

—I remember, umnumzana. There was a brightness in him.

—Yes, yes, said Jarvis, there was a brightness in him.

—Umnumzana, it is a hard word to say. But my heart holds a deep sorrow for you, and for the inkosikazi, and for the young inkosikazi, and for the children.

—Yes, yes, said Jarvis. Yes, yes, he said fiercely. I shall call the mistress of the house.

He went in and brought her out with him. This old man, he said in English, has come to inquire about the daughter of a native named Sibeko, who used to work for you in Ixopo. They have heard nothing of her for months.

—I had to send her away, said Smith's daughter. She was good when she started, and I promised her father to look after her. But she went to the bad and started to brew liquor in her room. She was arrested and sent to jail for a month, and after that of course I could not take her back again.

—You do not know where she is? asked Jarvis.

—I'm sure I do not know, said Smith's daughter in English. And I do not care.

—She does not know, said Jarvis in Zulu. But he did not add that Smith's daughter did not care.

—I thank you, said the old man in Zulu. Stay well, umnumzana. And he bowed to Smith's daughter and she nodded her acknowledgment. He put on his hat and started to walk down the path to the back gate, according to the custom. Smith's daughter went into the house, and Jarvis followed the old man slowly, as though he were not following him. The old man opened the gate and went out through it and closed it behind him. As he turned to close it he saw that Jarvis had followed him, and he bowed to him.

—Go well, umfundisi, said Jarvis.

—Stay well, umnumzana. The old man raised his hat and put it back again on his head. Then he started to walk slowly down the road to the station, Jarvis watching him until he was out of sight. As he turned to come back, he saw that his wife was coming to join him, and he saw with a pang that she too walked as if she were old.

He walked to join her, and she put her arm in his.

—Why are you so disturbed, James? she asked. Why were you so disturbed when you came into the house?

—Something that came out of the past, he said. You know how it comes suddenly.

She was satisfied, and said, I know. She held his arm more closely. Barbara wants us for lunch, she said.

THE PEOPLE STAND when the great Judge comes into the Court, they stand more solemnly today, for this is the day of the judgment. The Judge sits, and then his two assessors, and then the people; and the three accused are brought from the place under the Court.

—I have given long thought and consideration to this case, says the Judge, and so have my assessors. We have listened carefully to all the evidence that has been brought forward, and have discussed it and tested it piece by piece.

And the interpreter interprets into Zulu what the Judge has said:

—The accused Absalom Kumalo has not sought to deny his guilt. He has told straightforwardly and simply the story of how he shot the late Arthur Jarvis in his house at Parkwold. He has maintained further that it was not his intention to kill or even to shoot, that the weapon was brought to intimidate the servant Richard Mpiring, that he supposed the murdered man to have been elsewhere. With this evidence we must later deal, but part of it is of the gravest importance in determining the guilt of the second and third accused. The first accused, Absalom Kumalo, states that the plan was put forward by the third accused, Johannes Pafuri, and that Pafuri struck the blow that rendered unconscious the servant Mpiring. In this he is supported by Mpiring himself, who says that he recognized Pafuri by the twitching of the eyes above the mask. It is further true that he picked out Pafuri from among ten men similarly disguised, more than one of whom suffered from a tic similar to that suffered by Pafuri. But the defense has pointed out that these tics were similar and not identical, and that Pafuri was well known to Mpiring. The defense has argued that the identification would have been valid only if all ten men had been of a similar build and had suffered from identical tics. The partial validity of the argument is clear; a marked characteristic like a tic can lead as easily to wrong identification as to correct identification, especially when the lower half of the face is concealed. It must be accepted that identification depends on the recognition of a pattern, of a whole, and that it becomes uncertain when the pattern is partially concealed. It would appear therefore that Mpiring's identification of his assailant is not of itself sufficient proof that Pafuri was that man.

—The prosecution has made much of the previous association of the three accused, and indeed has made out so strong a case that further investigation is called for into the nature of that association. But previous association, even of a criminal nature, is not in itself a proof of association in the grave crime of which these three persons stand accused.

—After long and thoughtful consideration, my assessors and I have come to the conclusion that the guilt of the second and third accused is not established, and they will be accordingly discharged. But I have no doubt that their previous criminal association will be exhaustively investigated.

There is a sigh in the Court. One act of this drama is over. The accused Absalom Kumalo makes no sign. He does not even look at the two who are now free. But Pafuri looks about as though he would say, This is right, this is just, what has been done.

—There remains the case against the first accused, the Judge continues. His learned Counsel pleads that he should not suffer the extreme penalty, argues that he is shocked and overwhelmed and stricken by his act, commends him for his truthful and straightforward confession, draws attention to his youth and to the disastrous effect of a great and wicked city on the character of a simple tribal boy. He has dealt profoundly with the disaster that has overwhelmed our native tribal society, and has argued cogently the case of our own complicity in this disaster. But even if it be true that we have, out of fear and selfishness and thoughtlessness, wrought a destruction that we have done little to repair, even if it be true that we should be ashamed of it and do something more courageous and forthright than we are doing, there is nevertheless a law, and it is one of the most monumental achievements of this defective society that it has made a law, and has set judges to administer it, and has freed those judges from any obligation whatsoever but to administer the law. A judge cannot, must not, dare not allow the existing defects of society to influence him to do anything but administer the law.

—The most important point to consider here is the accused's repeated assertion that he had no intention to kill, that the coming of the white man was unexpected, and that he fired the revolver out of panic and fear. If the Court could accept this as truth, then the Court must find that the accused did not commit murder.

—What are the facts of the case? How can one suppose otherwise than that here were three murderous and dangerous young men? It is true that they did not go to the house with the express intention of killing a man. But it is true that they took with them weapons the use of which might well result in the death of any man who interfered with the carrying out of their unlawful purpose.

—Are we to suppose that in this small room, where in this short and tragic space of time an innocent black man is cruelly struck down and an innocent white man is shot dead, that there was no intention to inflict grievous bodily harm of this kind should the terrible need for it arise? I cannot bring myself to entertain such a supposition.

They are silent in the Court. And the Judge too is silent. There is no sound there. No one coughs or moves or sighs. The Judge speaks:

—This Court finds you guilty, Absalom Kumalo, of the murder of Arthur Trevelyan Jarvis at his residence in Parkwold, on the afternoon of the eighth day of October, 1946. And this Court finds you, Matthew Kumalo, and Johannes Pafuri, not guilty, and you are accordingly discharged.

So these two go down the stairs into the place that is under the ground, and leave the other alone. He looks at them going, perhaps he is thinking, Now it is I alone.

The Judge speaks again. On what grounds, he asks, can this Court make any recommendation to mercy? I have given this long and serious thought, and I cannot find any extenuating circumstances. Therefore I can make no recommendation to mercy.

They are silent in the Court, but for all that a white man calls out in a loud voice for silence. Kumalo puts his face in his hands, he has heard what it means. Jarvis sits stern and erect. The young white man looks before him and frowns fiercely. The girl sits like the child she is, her eyes are fixed on the Judge, not on her lover.

—I sentence you, Absalom, to be returned to custody, and to be hanged by the neck until you are dead. And may the Lord have mercy upon your soul.

The Judge rises, and the people rise. But the guilty one falls to the floor, crying and sobbing. And there is a woman wailing, and an old man crying, *Tixo, Tixo.* No one calls for silence, though the Judge is not quite gone. For who can stop the heart from breaking?

T HEY PASSED AGAIN through the great gate in the grim high wall, Father Vincent and Kumalo, Gertrude and the girl and Msimangu. The boy was brought to them, and for a moment some great hope showed in his eyes, and he stood there trembling and shaking. But Kumalo said to him gently, We are come for the marriage, and the hope died out.

—My son, here is your wife that is to be.

The boy and the girl greeted each other like strangers, each giving hands without life, not to be shaken, but to be held loosely, so that the hands fell apart easily. They did not kiss after the European fashion, but stood looking at each other without words, bound in a great constraint. But at last she asked, Are you in health? and he answered, I am greatly. And he asked, Are you in health? and she answered, I am greatly also. But beyond that there was nothing spoken between them.

Father Vincent left them, and they all stood in the same constraint. Msimangu saw that Gertrude would soon break out into wailing and moaning, and he turned his back on the others and said to her gravely and privately, Heavy things have happened, but this is a marriage, and it were better to go at once than to wail or moan in this place. When she did not answer he said sternly and coldly, Do you understand me? And she said resentfully, I understand you. He left her and went to a window in the great grim wall, and she stood sullenly silent.

And Kumalo said desperately to his son, Are you in health? And the boy answered, I am greatly. Are you in health, my father? So Kumalo said, I am greatly. He longed for other things to say, but he could not find them. And indeed it was a mercy for them all, when a white man came to take them to the prison chapel.

Father Vincent was waiting there in his vestments, and he read to them from his book. Then he asked the boy if he took this woman, and he asked the girl if she took this man. And when they had answered as it is laid down in that book, for better for worse, for richer for poorer, in sickness and in health, till death did them part, he married them. Then he preached a few words to them, that they were to remain faithful, and to bring up what children there might be in the fear of God. So were they married and signed their names in the book.

After it was done, the two priests and the wife left father and son, and Kumalo said to him, I am glad you are married.

—I also am glad, my father.

—I shall care for your child, my son, even as if it were my own.

But when he realized what it was he had said, his mouth quivered and he would indeed have done that which he was determined not to do, had not the boy said out of his suffering, When does my father return to Ndotsheni?

—Tomorrow, my son.

—And you will tell my mother that I remember her.

Yes, indeed I shall tell her. Yes, indeed, I shall take her that message. Why yes indeed. But he did not speak those words, he only nodded his head.

—And my father.

—Yes, my son.

—I have money in a Post Office Book. Nearly four pounds is there. It is for the child. They will give it to my father at the office. I have arranged for it.

Yes, indeed I shall get it. Yes, indeed, even as you have arranged. Why yes indeed.

—And my father.

—Yes, my son.

—If the child is a son, I should like his name to be Peter.

And Kumalo said in a strangled voice, Peter.

—Yes, I should like it to be Peter.

—And if it is a daughter?

—No, if it is a daughter, I have not thought of any name. And my father.

—Yes, my son.

—I have a parcel at Germiston, at the home of Joseph Bhengu. I should be glad if it could be sold for my son.

—Yes, I hear you.

—There are other things that Pafuri had. But I think he will deny that they are mine.

—Pafuri? This same Pafuri?

—Yes, my father.

—It is better to forget them.

—It is as my father sees.

—And these things at Germiston, my son. I do not know how I could get them, for we leave tomorrow.

—Then it does not matter.

And because Kumalo could see that it did matter, he said, I shall speak to the Reverend Msimangu.

—That would be better.

—And this Pafuri, said Kumalo bitterly. And your cousin. I find it hard to forgive them.

The boy shrugged his shoulders hopelessly.

—They lied, my father. They were there, even as I said.

—Indeed they were there. But they are not here now.

—They are here, my father. There is another case against them.

—I did not mean that, my son. I mean they are not . . . they are not . . .

But he could not bring himself to say what he meant.

—They are here, said the boy not understanding. Here in this very place. Indeed, my father, it is I who go.

—Go?

—Yes. I must go . . . to . . .

Kumalo whispered, To Pretoria?

At those dread words the boy fell on the floor; he was crouched in the way that some of the Indians pray, and he began to sob, with great tearing sounds that convulsed him. For a boy is afraid of death. The old man, moved to it by that deep compassion which

544

was there within him, knelt by his son, and ran his hand over his head.

—Be of courage, my son.

—I am afraid, he cried. I am afraid.

—Be of courage, my son.

The boy reared up on his haunches. He hid nothing, his face was distorted by his cries. Au! au! I am afraid of the hanging, he sobbed, I am afraid of the hanging.

Still kneeling, the father took his son's hands, and they were not lifeless any more, but clung to his, seeking some comfort, some assurance. And the old man held them more strongly, and said again, Be of good courage, my son.

The white warder, hearing these cries, came in and said, but not with unkindness, Old man, you must go now.

—I am going, sir. I am going, sir. But give us a little time longer.

So the warder said, Well, only a little time longer, and he withdrew.

—My son, dry your tears.

So the boy took the cloth that was offered him and dried his tears. He kneeled on his knees, and though the sobbing was ended, the eyes were farseeing and troubled.

—My son, I must go now. Stay well, my son. I shall care for your wife and your child.

—It is good, he says. Yes, he says it is good, but his thoughts are not on any wife or child. Where his thoughts are there is no wife or child, where his eyes are there is no marriage.

—My son, I must go now.

He stood up, but the boy caught his father by the knees, and cried out to him, You must not leave me, you must not leave me. He broke out again into the terrible sobbing, and cried, No, no, you must not leave me.

The white warder came in again and said sternly, Old man, you must go now. And Kumalo would have gone, but the boy held him by the knees, crying out and sobbing. The warder tried to pull his arms away, but he could not, and he called another man to help him. Together they pulled the boy away, and Kumalo said desperately to him, Stay well, my son, but the boy did not hear him.

And so they parted.

Heavy with grief Kumalo left him, and went out to the gate in the wall where the others were waiting. And the girl came to him, and said shyly, but with a smile, Umfundisi.

—Yes, my child.

—I am now your daughter.

He forced himself to smile at her. It is true, he said. And she was eager to talk of it, but when she looked at him she could see that his thoughts were not of such matters. So she did not speak of it further.

I CANNOT THANK YOU enough, said Jarvis.

—We would have done more if we could, Jarvis.

John Harrison drove up, and Jarvis and Harrison stood for a moment outside the car.

—Our love to Margaret, and to Mary and the children, Jarvis. We'll come down and see you one of these days.

—You'll be welcome, Harrison, very welcome.

—One thing I wanted to say, Jarvis, said Harrison, dropping his voice. About the sentence. It can't bring the dead back, but it was right, absolutely right. It couldn't have been any other way so far as I'm concerned. If it had been any other way, I'd have felt there was no justice in the world. I'm only sorry the other two got off. The Crown made a mess of the case.

—Yes, I felt that way too. Well, good-by, and thank you again.

—I'm glad to do it.

At the station Jarvis gave John Harrison an envelope.

—Open it when I'm gone, he said.

So when the train had gone; young Harrison opened it. For your Club, it said. Do all the things you and Arthur wanted to do. If you like to call it the "Arthur Jarvis Club," I'll be pleased. But that is not a condition.

Young Harrison turned it over to look at the check underneath. He looked at the train as though he might have run after it. One thousand pounds, he said. Helen of Troy, one thousand pounds!

546

THEY HAD A PARTY at Mrs. Lithebe's at which Msimangu was the host. It was not a gay party, that was hardly to be thought of. But the food was plentiful, and there was some sad pleasure in it. Msimangu presided after the European fashion, and made a speech commending the virtues of his brother priest, and the motherly care that Mrs. Lithebe had given to all under her roof. Kumalo made a speech too, but it was stumbling and uncertain. But he thanked Msimangu and Mrs. Lithebe for all their kindnesses. Mrs. Lithebe would not speak, but giggled like a girl, and said that people were born to do such kindness. Then Msimangu told them that he had news for them, news that had been private until now, and that this was the first place where it would be told. He was retiring into a community, and would forswear the world and all possessions, and this was the first time that a black man had done such a thing in South Africa. There was clapping of hands, and all gave thanks for it. And Gertrude sat listening with enjoyment to the speeches, her small son asleep against her breast. And the girl listened also, with eager and smiling face, for in all her years she had never seen anything the like of this.

Then Msimangu said, We must all rise early to catch the train, my friends, and it is time we went to our beds.

Kumalo went with his friend to the gate, and Msimangu said, I am forsaking the world and all possessions, but I have saved a little money. I have no father or mother to depend on me, and I have the permission of the church to give this to you, my friend, to help you with all the money you have spent in Johannesburg, and all the new duties you have taken up. This book is in your name.

He put the book into Kumalo's hand, and Kumalo knew by the feeling of it that it was a Post Office Book. And Kumalo put his hands with the book on the top of the gate, and he put his head on his hands, and he wept bitterly. And Msimangu said to him, Do not spoil my pleasure, for I have never had a pleasure like this one. Which words of his made the old man break from weeping into sobbing, so that Msimangu said, There is a man coming, be silent, my brother.

They were silent till the man passed, and then Kumalo said, In all my days I have known no one as you are. And Msimangu said sharply, I am a weak and sinful man, but God put His hands on me, that is all. And as for the boy, he said, it is the Governor-General-in-Council who must decide if there will be mercy. As soon as Father Vincent hears, he will let you know.

—And if they decide against him?

—If they decide against him, said Msimangu soberly, one of us will go to Pretoria on that day, and let you know—when it is finished. And now I must go, my friend. But of you I ask a kindness.

—Ask all that I have, my friend.

—I ask that you will pray for me in this new thing I am about to do.

—I shall pray for you, morning and evening, all the days that are left.

—Good night, brother.

—Good night, Msimangu, friend of friends. And may God watch over you always.

—And you also.

Kumalo watched him go down the street and turn into the Mission House. Then he went into the room and lit his candle and opened the book. There was thirty-three pounds four shillings and fivepence in the book. He thanked God for all the kindnesses of men, and was comforted and uplifted. And these things done, he prayed for his son. Tomorrow they would all go home, all except his son. And he would stay in the place where they would put him, in the great prison in Pretoria, in the barred and solitary cell; and mercy failing, would stay there till he was hanged. Aye, but the hand that had murdered had once pressed the mother's breast into the thirsting mouth, had stolen into the father's hand when they went out into the dark. Aye, but the murderer afraid of death had once been a child afraid of the night.

In the morning he rose early, it was yet dark. He lit his candle, and suddenly remembering, went on his knees and prayed his prayer for Msimangu. He opened the door quietly, and shook the girl gently. It is time for us to rise, he said. She started up from the blankets. I shall not be long, she said. He smiled at the eagerness.

548

Ndotsheni, he said, tomorrow it is Ndotsheni. He opened Gertrude's door, and held up his candle. The little boy was there, the red dress and the white turban were there. But Gertrude was gone.

T HE ENGINE STEAMS and whistles over the veld of the Transvaal. The white flat hills of the mines drop behind, and the country rolls away as far as the eye can see. They sit all together, Kumalo, and the little boy on his knees, and the girl with her worldly possessions in one of those paper carriers that you find in the shops. The little boy has asked for his mother, but Kumalo tells him she has gone away, and he does not ask any more.

Darkness falls, and they thunder through the night, over battle-fields of long ago. They pass without seeing them the hills of Mooi River, Rosetta, Balgowan, lovely beyond any singing of it. As the sun rises they wind down the greatest hills of all, to Pietermaritz-burg. Here they enter another train, and the train runs along the valley of the Umsindusi, past the black slums, past Edendale, past Elandskop, and down into the great valley of the Umkomaas, where the tribes live, and the soil is sick almost beyond healing. And the people tell Kumalo that the rains will not fall; they cannot plough or plant, and there will be hunger in this valley.

At Donnybrook they enter still another train, the small toy train that runs to Ixopo through the green rolling hills of Eastwolds and Lufafa. And at Ixopo they alight, and people greet him and say, Au! but you have been a long time away.

There they enter the last train, that runs beside the lovely road that goes into the hills. Many people know him, and he is afraid of their questions. They talk like children, these people, and it is nothing to ask, who is this person, who is this girl, who is this child, where do they come from, where do they go? They will ask how is your sister, how is your son, so he takes his sacred book and reads in it, and they turn to another who has taste for conversation.

The sun is setting over the great valley of the Umzimkulu, behind the mountains of East Griqualand. His wife is there, and the friend to help the umfundisi with his bags. He goes to his wife quickly, and embraces her in the European fashion. He is glad to be home.

She looks her question, and he says to her, Our son is to die, perhaps there may be mercy, but let us not talk of it now.

—I understand you, she says.

—And Gertrude. All was ready for her to come. There we were all in the same house. But when I went to wake her, she was gone. Let us not talk of it now.

She bows her head.

—And this is the small boy, and this is our new daughter.

Kumalo's wife lifts the small boy and kisses him after the European fashion. You are my child, she says. She puts him down and goes to the girl who stands there humbly with her paper bag. She takes her in her arms after the European fashion, and says to her, You are my daughter. And the girl bursts suddenly into weeping, so that the woman must say to her, Hush, hush, do not cry. She says to her further, Our home is simple and quiet, there are no great things there. The girl looks up through her tears and says, Mother, that is all that I desire.

Something deep is touched here, something that is good and deep. Although it comes with tears, it is like a comfort in such desolation.

Kumalo shakes hands with his friend, and they all set out on the narrow path that leads into the setting sun, into the valley of Ndotsheni. But here a man calls, Umfundisi, you are back, it is a good thing that you have returned. And here a woman says to another, Look, it is the umfundisi that has returned. One woman dressed in European fashion throws her apron over her head, and runs to the hut, calling and crying more like a child than a woman, It is the umfundisi that has returned. She brings her children to the door and they peep out behind her dress to see the umfundisi that has returned.

A child comes into the path and stands before Kumalo so that he must stop. We are glad that the umfundisi is here again, she says.

The path is dropping now, from the green hills where the mist feeds the grass and the bracken. It runs between the stones, and one must walk carefully for it is steep. A woman with child must walk carefully, so Kumalo's wife goes before the girl, and tells her, Here is a stone, be careful that you do not slip. Night is falling, and the hills of East Griqualand are blue and dark against the sky.

The path is dropping into the red land of Ndotsheni. It is a wasted land, a land of old men and women and children, but it is home. The maize hardly grows to the height of a man, but it is home.

—It is dry here, umfundisi. We cry for rain.

—I have heard it, my friend.

—Our mealies are nearly finished, umfundisi. It is known to *Tixo* alone what we shall eat.

The path grows more level, it goes by the little stream that runs by the church. Kumalo stops to listen to it, but there is nothing to hear.

—The stream does not run, my friend.

—It has been dry for a month, umfundisi.

—Where do you get water, then?

—The women must go to the river, umfundisi, that comes from the place of uJarvis.

At the sound of the name of Jarvis, Kumalo feels fear and pain, but he makes himself say, How is uJarvis?

—He returned yesterday, umfundisi. I do not know how he is. But the inkosikazi returned some weeks ago, and they say she is sick and thin. I work there now, umfundisi.

Kumalo is silent, and cannot speak. But his friend says to him, It is known here, he says.

—Ah, it is known.

—It is known, umfundisi.

They do not speak again, and the path levels out, running past the huts, and the red empty fields. There is calling here, and in the dusk one voice calls to another in some far distant place. If you are a Zulu you can hear what they say, but if you are not, even if you know the language, you would find it hard to know what is being called. Some white men call it magic, but it is no magic, only an art perfected. It is Africa, the beloved country.

—They call that you are returned, umfundisi.

—I hear it, my friend.

—They are satisfied, umfundisi.

Indeed they are satisfied. They come from the huts along the road, they come running down from the hills in the dark. The boys are calling and crying, with the queer tremulous call that is known in this country.

—Umfundisi, you have returned.

—Umfundisi, we give thanks for your return.

—Umfundisi, you have been too long away.

A child calls to him, There is a new teacher at the school. A second child says to her, Foolish one, it is a long time since she came. A boy salutes as he has learned in the school, and cries, Umfundisi. He waits for no response, but turns away and gives the queer tremulous call, to no person at all, but to the air. He turns away and makes the first slow steps of a dance, for no person at all, but for himself.

There is a lamp outside the church, the lamp they light for the services. There are women of the church sitting on the red earth under the lamp; they are dressed in white dresses, each with a green cloth about her neck. They rise when the party approaches, and one breaks into a hymn, with a high note that cannot be sustained; but others come in underneath it, and support and sustain it, and some men come in too, with the deep notes and the true. Kumalo takes off his hat and he and his wife and his friend join in also, while the girl stands and watches in wonder. It is a hymn of thanksgiving, and the man remembers God in it, and prostrates himself and gives thanks for the Everlasting Mercy. And it echoes in the bare red hills and over the bare red fields of the broken tribe. And it is sung in love and humility and gratitude, and the humble simple people pour their lives into the song.

And Kumalo must pray. He prays, *Tixo*, we give thanks to Thee for Thy unending mercy. We give thanks to Thee for this safe return. We give thanks to Thee for the love of our friends and our families. We give thanks to Thee for all Thy mercies.

—*Tixo*, give us rain, we beseech Thee—

And here they say Amen, so many of them that he must wait till they are finished.

—*Tixo*, give us rain, we beseech Thee, that we may plough and sow our seed. And if there is no rain, protect us against hunger and starvation, we pray Thee.

And here they say Amen, so that he must wait again till they are finished. His heart is warmed that they have so welcomed him, so warmed that he casts out his fear, and prays that which is deep within him.

—*Tixo*, let this small boy be welcome in Ndotsheni, let him grow tall in this place. And his mother—

His voice stops as though he cannot say it, but he humbles himself, and lowers his voice.

—And his mother—forgive her her trespasses.

A woman moans, and Kumalo knows her, she is one of the great gossips of this place. So he adds quickly—

—Forgive us all, for we all have trespasses. And *Tixo*, let this girl be welcome in Ndotsheni, and deliver her child safely in this place.

He pauses, then says gently—

—Let her find what she seeks, and have what she desires.

And this is the hardest that must be prayed, but he humbles himself.

—And *Tixo*, my son—

They do not moan, they are silent. Even the woman who gossips does not moan. His voice drops to a whisper.

—Forgive him his trespasses.

It is done, it is out, the hard thing that was so feared. He knows it is not he, it is these people who have done it. Kneel, he says. So they kneel on the bare red earth, and he raises his hand, and his voice also, and strength comes into the old and broken man, for is he not a priest?

—The Lord bless you and keep you, and make His face to shine upon you, and give you peace, now and forever. And the grace of our Lord Jesus Christ, and the love of God, and the fellowship of the Holy Spirit, be with you and abide with you, and with all those that are dear to you, now and forevermore. Amen.

THE PEOPLE HAVE all gone now, and Kumalo turns to his friend.

—There are things I must tell you. Some day I shall tell you others, but some I must tell you now. My sister Gertrude was to come with us. We were all together, all ready in the house. But when I went to wake her, she was gone.

—Au! umfundisi.

—And my son, he is condemned to be hanged. He may be given mercy. They will let me know as soon as they hear.

—Au! umfundisi.

—You may tell your friends. And they will tell their friends. It is not a thing that can be hidden. Therefore you may tell them.

—I shall tell them, umfundisi.

—I do not know if I should stay here, my friend.

—Why, umfundisi?

—What, said Kumalo bitterly. With a sister who has left her child, and a son who has killed a man? Who am I to stay here?

—Umfundisi, it must be what you desire. But I tell you that there is not one man or woman that would desire it. There is not one man or woman here that has not grieved for you, that is not satisfied that you are returned. Why, could you not see? Could it not touch you?

—I have seen and it has touched me. It is something, after all that has been suffered. My friend, I do not desire to go. This is my home here. I have lived so long here, I could not desire to leave it.

—That is good, umfundisi. And I for my part have no desire to live without you. For I was in darkness—

—You touch me, my friend.

—Umfundisi, did you find out about Sibeko's daughter? You remember?

—Yes, I remember. And she too is gone. Where, there is not one that knows. They do not know, they said. Some bitterness came suddenly into him and he added, They said also, they do not care.

—Au! umfundisi.

—I am sorry, my friend.

The man sighed. I will go past Sibeko's, he said. I promised him as soon as I knew.

Kumalo walked soberly to the little house. Then he turned suddenly and called after his friend.

—I must explain to you, he said. It was the daughter of uSmith who said, she did not know, she did not care. She said it in English. And when uJarvis said it to me in Zulu, he said, She does not know. But uJarvis did not tell me that she said she did not care.

—I understand you, umfundisi.

—Go well, my friend.

—Stay well, umfundisi.

Kumalo turned again and entered the house, and his wife and the girl were eating.

—Where is the boy? he asked.

—Sleeping, Stephen. You have been a long time talking.

—Yes, there were many things to say.

—Did you put out the lamp?

—Let it burn a little longer.

—Has the church so much money, then?

He smiled at her. This is a special night, he said.

Her brow contracted with pain, he knew what she was thinking.

—I shall put it out, he said.

—Let it burn a little longer. Put it out when you have had your food.

—That will be right, he said soberly. Let it burn for what has happened here, let it be put out for what has happened otherwise.

He put his hand on the girl's head. Have you eaten, my child?

She looked up at him, smiling. I am satisfied, she said.

—To bed then, my child.

—Yes, father.

She got up from her chair. Sleep well, father, she said. Sleep well, mother.

—I shall take you to your room, my child.

When she came back, Kumalo was looking at the Post Office Book. He gave it to her and said, There is money there, more than you and I have ever had.

She opened it and cried out when she saw how much there was. Is it ours? she asked.

—It is ours, he said. It is a gift, from the best man of all my days.

—You will buy new clothes, she said. New black clothes, and new collars, and a new hat.

—And you will buy new clothes, also, he said. And a stove. Sit down, and I shall tell you about Msimangu, he said, and about other matters.

She sat down trembling.

—I am listening, she said.

KUMALO WAS IN HIS HOUSE, and there in the great heat he struggled with the church accounts, until he heard the sounds of a horse, and he heard it stop outside the church. He went out to see who might be riding in this merciless sun. And for a moment he caught his breath in astonishment; it was a small white boy on a red horse, a small white boy as like to another who had ridden here as any could be.

The small boy smiled at Kumalo and raised his cap and said, Good morning. And Kumalo felt a strange pride that it should be so, and a strange humility that it should be so, and an astonishment that the small boy should not know the custom.

—Good morning, inkosana, he said. It is a hot day for riding.

—I don't find it hot. Is this your church?

—Yes, this is my church.

—I go to a church school, St. Mark's. It's the best school in Johannesburg. We've a chapel there.

—St. Mark's, said Kumalo excited. This church is St. Mark's. But your chapel—it is no doubt better than this?

—Well—yes—it *is* better, said the small boy smiling. But it's in the town, you know. Is that your house?

—Yes, this is my house.

—Could I see inside it? I've never been inside a parson's house, I mean a native parson's house.

—You are welcome to see inside it, inkosana.

The small boy slipped off his horse and made it fast to the poles that were there for the horses of those that came to the church. He dusted his feet on the frayed mat outside Kumalo's door, and taking off his cap, entered the house.

—This is a nice house, he said. I didn't expect it would be so nice.

—Not all our houses are such, said Kumalo gently. But a priest must keep his house nice. You have seen some of our other houses, perhaps?

—Oh yes, I have. On my grandfather's farm. They're not so nice as this. Is that your work there?

—Yes, inkosana.

—It looks like arithmetic.

—It *is* arithmetic. They are the accounts of the church.

—I didn't know that churches had accounts. I thought only shops had those.

And Kumalo laughed at him. And having laughed once, he laughed again, so that the small boy said to him, Why are you laughing? But the small boy was laughing also, he took no offense.

—I am just laughing, inkosana.

—Inkosana? That's little inkosi, isn't it?

—It is little inkosi. Little master, it means.

—Yes, I know. And what are you called? What do I call you?

—Umfundisi.

—I see. Imfundisi.

—No. Umfundisi.

—Umfundisi. What does it mean?

—It means parson.

—May I sit down, umfundisi? The small boy pronounced the word slowly. Is that right? he said.

Kumalo swallowed the laughter. That is right, he said. Would you like a drink of water? You are hot.

—I would like a drink of milk, said the boy. Ice-cold, from the fridge, he said.

—Inkosana, there is no fridge in Ndotsheni.

—Just ordinary milk then, umfundisi.

—Inkosana, there is no milk in Ndotsheni.

The small boy flushed. I would like water, umfundisi, he said.

Kumalo brought him the water, and while he was drinking, asked him, How long are you staying here, inkosana?

—Not very long now, umfundisi.

He went on drinking his water, then he said, These are not our real holidays now. We are here for special reasons.

And Kumalo stood watching him, and said in his heart, O child bereaved, I know your reasons.

—Water is amanzi, umfundisi.

And because Kumalo did not answer him, he said, Umfundisi. And again, Umfundisi.

—My child.

—Water is amanzi, umfundisi.

Kumalo shook himself out of his reverie. He smiled at the small eager face, and he said, That is right, inkosana.

—And horse is ihashi.

—That is right also.

—And house is ikaya.

—Right also.

—And money is imali.

—Right also.

—And boy is umfana.

—Right also.

—And cow is inkomo.

Kumalo laughed outright. Wait, wait, he said, I am out of breath. And he pretended to puff and gasp, and sat down on the chair, and wiped his brow. You will soon talk Zulu, he said.

—Zulu is easy. What's the time, umfundisi?

—Twelve o'clock, inkosana.

—Jeepers creepers, it's time I was off. Thank you for the water, umfundisi.

The small boy went to his horse. Help me up, he cried. Kumalo helped him up, and the small boy said, I'll come and see you again, umfundisi. I'll talk more Zulu to you.

Kumalo laughed. You will be welcome, he said.

—Umfundisi?

—Inkosana?

—Why is there no milk in Ndotsheni? Is it because the people are poor?

—Yes, inkosana.

—And what do the children do?

Kumalo looked at him. They die, my child, he said. Some of them are dying now.

—Who is dying now?

—The small child of Kuluse.

—Didn't the doctor come?

—Yes, he came.

—And what did he say?

—He said the child must have milk, inkosana.

—And what did the parents say?

—They said, Doctor, we have heard what you say.

And the small boy said in a small voice, I see. He raised his cap and said solemnly, Good-by, umfundisi. He set off solemnly too, but it was not long before he was galloping wildly along the hot dusty road.

THE NIGHT BROUGHT coolness and respite. While they were having their meal, Kumalo and his wife, the girl and the small boy, there was a sound of wheels, and a knock at the door, and there was the friend who had carried the bags.

—Umfundisi. Mother.

—My friend. Will you eat?

—No indeed. I am on my way home. I have a message for you.

—For me?

—Yes, from uJarvis. Was the small white boy here today?

Kumalo had a dull sense of fear, realizing for the first time what had been done. He was here, he said.

—We were working in the trees, said the man, when this small boy came riding up. I do not understand English, umfundisi, but they were talking about Kuluse's child. And come and look what I have brought you.

There outside the door was the milk, in the shining cans in the cart.

—This milk is for small children only, for those who are not yet at school, said the man importantly. And it is to be given by you only. And these sacks must be put over the cans, and small boys must bring water to pour over the sacks. And each morning I shall take back the cans. This will be done till the grass comes and we have milk again.

The man lifted the cans from the cart and said, Where shall I put them, umfundisi? But Kumalo was dumb and stupid, and his wife said, We shall put them in the room that the umfundisi has in the church. So they put them there, and when they came back the man said, You would surely have a message for uJarvis, umfundisi? And Kumalo stuttered and stammered, and at last pointed his hand up at the sky. And the man said, *Tixo* will bless him, and Kumalo nodded.

A CHILD BROUGHT the four letters from the store to the school, and the headmaster sent them over to the house of the umfundisi. They were all letters from Johannesburg, one was from the boy Absalom to his wife, and another to his parents; they were both on His Majesty's Service, from the great prison in Pretoria. The third was from Msimangu himself, and the fourth from Mr. Carmichael. This one Kumalo opened fearfully, because it was from the lawyer who took the case for God, and would be about the mercy. And there the lawyer told him, in gentle and compassionate words, that there would be no mercy, and that his son would be hanged on the fifteenth day of that month. So he read no more but sat there an hour, two hours maybe. Indeed he neither saw sight nor heard sound till his wife said to him, It has come, then, Stephen.

And when he nodded, she said, Give it to me, Stephen. With shaking hands he gave it to her, and she read it also, and sat looking before her, with lost and terrible eyes, for this was the child of her womb, of her breasts. Yet she did not sit as long as he had done, for she stood up and said, It is not good to sit idle. Finish your letters, and go to see Kuluse's child, and the girl Elizabeth that is ill. And I shall do my work about the house.

—There is another letter, he said.

—From him? she said.

—From him.

He gave it to her, and she sat down again and opened it carefully and read it. The pain was in her eyes and her face and her hands, but he did not see it, for he stared before him on the floor, only his eyes were not looking at the floor but at no place at all, and his face was sunken, in the same mold of suffering from which it had escaped since his return to this valley.

—Stephen, she said sharply.

He looked at her.

—Read it, finish it, she said. Then let us go to our work.

He took the letter and read it, it was short and simple, and except for the first line, it was in Zulu, as is often the custom:

My dear Father and Mother,

I am hoping you are all in health even as I am. They told me this morning there will be no mercy for the thing that I have done. So I shall not see you or Ndotsheni again.

This is a good place. I am locked in, and no one may come and talk to me. But I may smoke and read and write letters, and the white men do not speak badly to me. There is a priest who comes to see me, a black priest from Pretoria. He is preparing me, and speaks well to me.

There is no more news here, so I close my letter. I think of you all at Ndotsheni, and if I were back there I should not leave it again.

Your son,

Absalom.

Is the child born? If it is a boy, I should like his name to be Peter. Have you heard of the case of Matthew and Johannes? I have been to the court to give evidence in this case, but they did not let me see it finish. My father, did you get the money in my Post Office Book?

When he had finished he went out to look at the clouds, for it was exciting to see them after weeks of pitiless sun. Indeed one or two of them were already sailing overhead, casting great shadows over the valley. It was close and sultry, and soon there would be thunder from across the Umzimkulu, for on this day the drought would break, with no doubt at all.

While Kumalo stood there he saw a motorcar coming down the road from Carisbrooke into the valley. It was a sight seldom seen, and the car went slowly because the road was not meant for cars, but only for carts and wagons and oxen. Then he saw that not far from the church there was a white man sitting still upon a horse. He seemed to be waiting for the car, and with something of a shock he realized that it was Jarvis. A white man climbed out of the car, and he saw with further surprise that it was the magistrate. Jarvis got down from his horse, and he shook hands with the magistrate, and with other white men that were climbing out of the car, bringing out with them sticks and flags. Then lo! from the other direction came riding the stout chief, in his fur cap and his riding breeches, surrounded by his counselors. The chief saluted the magistrate, and the magistrate the chief, and there were other salutes also. Then they all stayed and talked together, so that it was clear that they had met together for some purpose. There was pointing of hands, to places distant and to places at hand. Then one of the counselors began to cut down a small tree with straight clean branches. These branches he cut into lengths, and sharpened the ends, so that Kumalo stood more and more mystified. The white men brought out more sticks and flags from the car, and one of them set up a box on three legs, as though he would take photographs. Jarvis took some of the sticks and flags, and so did the magistrate, after he had taken off his coat because of the heat. They pointed to the clouds also, and Kumalo heard Jarvis say, It looks like rain at last.

Now the chief was not to be outdone by the white man, so he too got down from his horse and took some of the sticks, but Kumalo could see that he did not fully understand what was being done. Jarvis, who seemed to be in charge of these matters, planted one of the sticks in the ground, and the chief gave a stick to one of his counselors, and said something to him. So the counselor also planted the stick in the ground, but the white man with the box on the three legs called out, Not there, not there, take that stick away. The counselor was of two minds, and he looked hesitantly at the chief, who said angrily, Not there, not there, take it away. Then the chief, embarrassed and knowing still less what was to be done, got back on his horse and sat there, leaving the white men to plant the sticks.

So an hour passed, while there was quite an array of sticks and flags, and Kumalo looked on as mystified as ever. Jarvis and the magistrate stood together, and they kept on pointing at the hills, then turned and pointed down the valley. Then they talked to the chief, and the counselors stood by, listening with grave attention to the conversation. Kumalo heard Jarvis say to the magistrate, That's too long. The magistrate shrugged, saying, That's the way these things are done. Then Jarvis said, I'll go to Pretoria. Would you mind? The magistrate said, I don't mind at all. It may be the way to get it. Then Jarvis said, I don't want to lose your company, but if you want to get home dry, you'd better be starting. This'll be no ordinary storm.

But Jarvis did not start himself. He said good-by to the magistrate, and began to walk across the bare fields, measuring the distance with his strides. Kumalo heard the magistrate say to one of the white men, They say he's going queer. From what I've heard, he soon won't have any money left.

Then the magistrate said to the chief, You will see that not one of these sticks is touched or removed. He saluted the chief, and he and the other white men climbed into the car and drove away up the hill. The chief said to his counselors, You will give orders that not one of these sticks is to be touched or removed. The counselors then rode away, each to some part of the valley, and the chief rode past the church, returning Kumalo's greeting, but not stopping to tell him anything about this matter of the sticks.

Indeed it was true what Jarvis had said, that this would be no ordinary storm. For it was now dark and threatening over the valley. On the other side of the Umzimkulu the thunder was rolling without pause, and now and then the lightning would strike down among the far-off hills. But it was this for which all men were waiting, the rain at last. Women were hurrying along the paths, and with a sudden babel of sound the children poured out of the school, and the headmaster and his teachers were urging them, Hurry, hurry, do not loiter along the road.

It was something to see, a storm like this. A great bank of black and heavy cloud was moving over the Umzimkulu, and Kumalo stood for a long time and watched it. He saw Jarvis hurrying back to his horse, which stood restlessly against the fence. With a few practiced movements he stripped it of saddle and bridle, and saying a word to it, left it loose. Then he walked quickly in the direction of Kumalo, and called out to him, Umfundisi.

—Umnumzana.

—May I put these things in your porch, umfundisi, and stay in your church?

—Indeed, I shall come with you, umnumzana.

So they went into the church, and none too soon, for the thunder boomed out overhead, and they could hear the rain rushing across the fields. In a moment it was drumming on the iron roof, with a deafening noise that made all conversation impossible. Kumalo lit a lamp in the church, and Jarvis sat down on one of the benches, and remained there without moving.

But it was not long before the rain found the holes in the old rusted roof, and Jarvis had to move to avoid it.

Kumalo, nervous and wishing to make an apology, shouted at him, The roof leaks, and Jarvis shouted back at him, I have seen it.

And again the rain came down through the roof on the new place where Jarvis was sitting, so that he had to move again. He stood up and moved about in the semidarkness, testing the benches with his hand, but it was hard to find a place to sit, for where there was a dry place on a bench, there was rain coming down on the floor, and where there was a dry place on the floor, there was rain coming down on the bench.

—The roof leaks in many places, Kumalo shouted, and Jarvis shouted in reply, I have seen that also.

At last Jarvis found a place where the rain did not fall too badly, and Kumalo found himself a place also, and they sat there together in silence. But outside it was not silent, with the cracking of the thunder, and the deafening downpour on the roof.

It was a long time that they sat there, and it was not until they heard the rushing of the streams, of dead rivers come to life, that they knew that the storm was abating. Indeed the thunder sounded further away and there was a dull light in the church, and the rain made less noise.

It was nearly over when Jarvis rose and came and stood in the aisle near Kumalo. Without looking at the old man he said, Is there mercy?

Kumalo took the letter from his wallet with trembling hands; his hands trembled partly because of the sorrow, and partly because he was always so with this man. Jarvis took the letter and held it away from him so that the dull light fell on it. Then he put it back again in the envelope, and returned it to Kumalo.

—I do not understand these matters, he said, but otherwise I understand completely.

—I hear you, umnumzana.

Jarvis was silent for a while, looking towards the altar and the cross on the altar.

—When it comes to this fifteenth day, he said, I shall remember. Stay well, umfundisi.

But Kumalo did not say, Go well. He did not offer to carry the saddle and the bridle, nor did he think to thank Jarvis for the milk. And least of all did he think to ask about the matter of the sticks. And when he rose and went out, Jarvis was gone. It was still raining, but lightly, and the valley was full of sound, of streams and rivers, all red with the blood of the earth.

THE STICKS STOOD for days in the place where the men had put them, but no one came again to the valley. It was rumored that a dam was to be built here, but no one knew how it would be filled, because the small stream that ran past the church was sometimes dry, and was never a great stream at any time. Kumalo's friend told him that Jarvis had gone away to Pretoria, and his business was surely the business of the sticks, which was the business of the dam.

So the days passed. Kumalo prayed regularly for the restoration of Ndotsheni, and the sun rose and set regularly over the earth.

Kuluse's child was recovered, and Kumalo went about his pastoral duties. More and more he found himself waiting for news of Jarvis's return, so that the people might know what plans were afoot; and more and more he found himself thinking that it was Jarvis and Jarvis alone that could perform the great miracle.

The girl was happy in her new home, for she had a dependent and affectionate nature. The small boy played with the other small boys, and had asked after his mother not more than once or twice; with time he would forget her. About Absalom no one asked, and if they talked about it in their huts, they let it make no difference in their respect for the old umfundisi.

One day the small white boy came galloping up, and when Kumalo came out to greet him, he raised his cap as before, and Kumalo found himself warm with pleasure to see his small visitor again.

—I've come to talk Zulu again, said the boy. He slid down from his horse, and put the reins round the post. He walked over to the house with the assurance of a man, and dusted his feet and took off his cap before entering the house. He sat down at the table and looked round with a pleasure inside him, so that a man felt it was something bright that had come into the house.

—Are the accounts finished, umfundisi?

—Yes, they are finished, inkosana.

—Were they right?

Kumalo laughed, he could not help himself.

—Yes, they were right, he said. But not very good.

—Not very good, eh? Are you ready for the Zulu?

Kumalo laughed again, and sat down in his chair at the other side of the table, and said, Yes, I am ready for the Zulu. When is your grandfather returning?

—I don't know, said the small boy. I want him to come back. I like him, he said.

Kumalo could have laughed again at this, but he thought perhaps it was not a thing to laugh at. But the small boy laughed himself, so Kumalo laughed also. It was easy to laugh with this small boy, there seemed to be laughter inside him.

—When are you going back to Johannesburg, inkosana?

—When my grandfather comes back.

And Kumalo said to him in Zulu, When you go, something bright will go out of Ndotsheni.

The small boy laughed with pleasure. I hear you, he said in Zulu.

And Kumalo clapped his hands in astonishment, and said, Au! Au! You speak Zulu, so that the small boy laughed with still greater pleasure, and Kumalo clapped his hands again, and made many exclamations.

—Are you ready for the Zulu, umfundisi?

—Indeed I am ready.

—Tree is umuti, umfundisi.

—That is right, inkosana.

—But medicine is also umuti, umfundisi.

And the small boy said this with an air of triumph, and a kind of mock bewilderment, so that they both laughed together.

—You see, inkosana, said Kumalo seriously, our medicines come mostly from trees. That is why the word is the same.

—I see, said the small boy, pleased with this explanation. And box is ibokisi.

—That is right, inkosana. You see, we had no boxes, and so our word is from your word.

—I see. And motorbike is isitututu.

—That is right. That is from the sound that the motorbike makes, so, isi-tu-tu-tu. But, inkosana, let us make a sentence. For you are giving me all the words that you know, and so you will not learn anything that is new. Now how do you say, I see a horse?

So the lesson went on, till Kumalo said to his pupil, It is nearly twelve o'clock, and perhaps it is time you must go.

—Yes, I must go, but I'll come back for some more Zulu.

—You must come back, inkosana. Soon you will be speaking better than many Zulus. You will be able to speak in the dark, and people will not know it is not a Zulu.

The small boy was pleased, and when they went out he said,

Help me up, umfundisi. So Kumalo helped him up, and the small boy lifted his cap, and went galloping up the road. There was a car going up the road, and the small boy stopped his horse and cried, My grandfather is back. Then he struck at the horse and set out in a wild attempt to catch up with the car.

There was a young man standing outside the church, a young pleasant-faced man of some twenty-five years, and his bags were on the ground. He took off his hat and said in English, You are the umfundisi?

—I am.

—And I am the new agricultural demonstrator. I have my papers here, umfundisi.

—Come into the house, said Kumalo, excited.

They went into the house, and the young man took out his papers and showed them to Kumalo. These papers were from parsons and school inspectors and the like, and said that the bearer, Napoleon Letsitsi, was a young man of sober habits and good conduct, and another paper said that he had passed out of a school in the Transkei as an agricultural demonstrator.

—I see, said Kumalo. But you must tell me why you are here. Who sent you to me?

—Why, the white man who brought me.

—uJarvis, was that the name?

—I do not know the name, umfundisi, but it is the white man who has just gone.

—Yes, that is uJarvis. Now tell me all.

—I am come here to teach farming, umfundisi.

—To us, in Ndotsheni?

—Yes, umfundisi.

Kumalo's face lighted up, and he sat there with his eyes shining. You are an angel from God, he said. He stood up and walked about the room, hitting one hand against the other, which the young man watched in amazement. Kumalo saw him and laughed at him, and said again, You are an angel from God. He sat down again and said, Where did the white man find you?

—He came to my home in Krugersdorp. I was teaching there at

a school. He asked me if I would do a great work, and he told me about this place Ndotsheni. So I felt I would come here.

—And what about your teaching?

—I am not really a teacher, so they did not pay me well. And the white man said they would pay me ten pounds a month here, so I came. But I did not come only for the money. It was a small work there in the school.

Kumalo felt a pang of jealousy, for he had never earned ten pounds a month in all his sixty years. But he put it from him.

—The white man asked if I could speak Zulu, and I said no, but I could speak Xosa as well as I spoke my own language, for my mother was a Xosa. And he said that would do for Xosa and Zulu are almost the same.

Kumalo's wife opened the door and said, It is time for food. Kumalo said in Zulu, My wife, this is Mr. Letsitsi, who has come to teach our people farming. And he said to Letsitsi, You will eat with us. They went to eat, and Letsitsi was introduced to the girl and the small boy. After Kumalo had asked a blessing, they sat down, and Kumalo said in Zulu, When did you arrive in Pietermaritzburg?

—This morning, umfundisi. And then we came with the motor-car to this place.

—And what did you think of the white man?

—He is very silent, umfundisi. He did not speak much to me.

—That is his nature.

—We stopped there on the road, overlooking a valley. And he said, What could you do in such a valley? Those were the first words we spoke on the journey.

—And did you tell him?

—I told him, umfundisi.

—And what did he say?

—He said nothing, umfundisi. He made a noise in his throat, that was all.

—And then?

—He did not speak till we got here. He said to me, Go to the umfundisi, and ask him to find lodgings for you. Tell him I am sorry I cannot come, but I am anxious to get to my home.

Kumalo looked at his wife, and she at him.

—Our rooms are small, and this is a parson's house, said Kumalo, but you may stay here if you wish.

—My people are also of the Church, umfundisi. I should be glad to stay here.

—And what will you do in this valley?

The young demonstrator laughed. I must look at it first, he said.

—But what would you have done in that other valley?

So the young man told them all he would have done in the other valley, how the people must stop burning the dung and must put it back into the land, how they must gather the weeds together and treat them and not leave them to wither away in the sun, how they must stop ploughing up and down the hills, how they must plant trees for fuel, trees that grow quickly like wattles, in some place where they could not plough at all, on the steep sides of streams so that the water did not rush away in the storms. But these were hard things to do, because the people must learn that it is harmful for each man to wrest a living from his own little piece of ground. Some must give up their ground for trees, and some for pastures. And hardest of all would be the custom of lobola, by which a man pays for his wife in cattle, for people kept too many cattle for this purpose, and counted all their wealth in cattle, so that the grass had no chance to recover.

—And is there to be a dam? asked Kumalo.

—Yes, there is to be a dam, said the young man, so that the cattle always have water to drink. And the water from the dam can be let out through a gate, and can water this land and that, and can water the pastures that are planted.

—But where is the water to come from?

—It will come by a pipe from a river, said the young demonstrator. That is what the white man said.

—That will be his river, said Kumalo. And can all these things you have been saying, can they all be done in Ndotsheni?

—Yes, I think all these things can be done.

They all sat round the table, their faces excited and eager, for this young man could paint a picture before your eyes. Presently outside Kumalo heard the sounds of a horse, and he got up and went out, wondering if it could be the small boy again, and back so quickly. And indeed it was, but the boy did not climb down, he talked to Kumalo from his horse. He talked excitedly and earnestly, as though it were a serious matter.

—That was a close shave, he said.

—A shave, asked Kumalo. A close shave?

—That's slang, said the small boy. But he did not laugh, he was too serious. It means a narrow escape, he said. You see, if my grandfather hadn't come back so early, then perhaps it would have been too late for me to ride down here again. But because he came early, there was time.

—That means you are going tomorrow, inkosana.

—Yes, tomorrow. On the narrow-gauge train, you know, the small train.

—Au! inkosana.

—But I'm coming back for the holidays. Then we'll learn some more Zulu.

—That will be a pleasure, said Kumalo simply.

—Good-by then, umfundisi.

—Good-by, inkosana.

Then he said in Zulu, Go well, inkosana. The small boy thought for a moment, and frowned in concentration. Then he said in Zulu, Stay well, umfundisi. So Kumalo said, Au! Au! in astonishment, and the small boy laughed and raised his cap, and was gone in a great cloud of dust. He galloped up the road, but stopped and turned round and saluted, before he set out on his way. And Kumalo stood there, and the young demonstrator came and stood by him, both watching the small boy.

—And that, said Kumalo earnestly to the demonstrator, is a small angel from God.

They turned to walk back to the house, and Kumalo said, So you think many things can be done?

—There are many things that can be done, umfundisi.

—Truly?

—Umfundisi, said the young man, and his face was eager, there is no reason why this valley should not be what it was before. But it will not happen quickly. Not in a day.

—If God wills, said Kumalo humbly, before I die. For I have lived my life in destruction.

EVERYTHING WAS READY for the confirmation. The women of the church were there, in their white dresses, each with the green cloth about her neck. Those men that were not away, and who belonged to this church, were there in their Sunday clothes, which means their working clothes, patched and cleaned and brushed. The children for the confirmation were there, the girls in their white dresses and caps, the boys in their school-going clothes, patched and cleaned and brushed. Women were busy in the house, helping the wife of the umfundisi, for after the confirmation there would be a simple meal, of tea boiled till the leaves had no more tea left in them, and of heavy homely cakes made of the meal of the maize. It was simple food, but it was to be eaten together.

And over the great valley the storm clouds were gathering again in the heavy oppressive heat, so that one did not know whether to be glad or sorry. Kumalo looked at the sky anxiously, and at the road by which the Bishop would come, and while he was looking he was surprised to see his friend driving along the road, with the cart that brought the milk. For the milk never came so early.

—You are early, my friend.

—I am early, umfundisi, said his friend gravely. We work no more today. The inkosikazi is dead.

—Au! Au! said Kumalo, it cannot be.

—It is so, umfundisi. When the sun stood so—and he pointed above his head—it was then that she died.

—Au! Au! It is a sorrow.

—It is a sorrow, umfundisi.

—And the umnumzana?

—He goes about silent. You know how he is. But this time the silence is heavier. Umfundisi, I shall go and wash myself, then I can come to the confirmation.

—Go then, my friend.

Kumalo went into the house, and he told his wife, The inkosikazi is dead. And she said, Au! Au! and the women also. Some of them wept, and they spoke of the goodness of the woman that was dead. Kumalo went to his table, and sat down there, thinking what he should do. When this confirmation was over he would go up to the house at High Place, and tell Jarvis of their grief here in the valley. But there came a picture to him of the house of bereavement, of all the cars of the white people that would be there, of the black-clothed farmers that would stand about in little groups, talking gravely and quietly, for he had seen such a thing before. And he knew that he could not go, for this was not according to the custom. He would stand there by himself, and unless Jarvis himself came out, no one would ask why he was there, no one would know that he had brought a message.

He sighed, and took out some paper from the drawer. He decided it must be written in English, for although most white men of these parts spoke Zulu, there were few who could read or write it. So he wrote then. And he wrote many things, and tore them up and put them aside, but at last it was finished.

Umnumzana,

    We are grieved here at this church to hear that the mother has passed away, and we understand it and suffer with tears. We are certain also that she knew of the things you have done for us, and did something in it. We shall pray in this church for the rest of her soul, and for you also in your suffering.

Your faithful servant,
Rev. S. Kumalo.

When it was finished, he sat wondering if he should send it. For suppose this woman had died of a heart that was broken, because her son had been killed. Then was he, the father of the man who had killed him, to send such a letter? Had he not heard that she was sick and thin? He groaned as he wrestled with this difficult matter, but as he sat there uncertain, he thought of the gift of the milk, and of the young demonstrator that had come to teach farming, and above all, he remembered the voice of Jarvis saying, even as if he were speaking now in this room, Is there mercy? And he knew then that this was a man who put his feet upon a road, and that no man would turn him from it. So he sealed the letter, and went out and called a boy to him and said, My child, will you take a letter for me? And the boy said, I shall do it, umfundisi. Go to Kuluse, said Kumalo, and ask him for his horse, and take this letter to the house of uJarvis. Do not trouble the umnumzana, but give this letter to any person that you see about the place. And my child, go quietly and respectfully, and do not call to any person there, and do not laugh or talk idly, for the inkosikazi is dead. Do you understand?

—I understand completely, umfundisi.

—Go then, my child. I am sorry you cannot be here to see the confirmation.

—It does not matter, umfundisi.

Then Kumalo went to tell the people that the inkosikazi was dead. And they fell silent, and if there had been any calling or laughter or talking idly, there was no more. They stood there talking quietly and soberly till the Bishop came.

It was dark in the church for the confirmation, so that they had to light the lamps. The great heavy clouds swept over the valley, and the lightning flashed over the red desolate hills, where the earth had torn away like flesh. The thunder roared over the valleys of old men and old women, of mothers and children. The men are away, the young men and the girls are away, the soil cannot keep them any more. And some of the children are there in the church being confirmed, and after a while they too will go away, for the soil cannot keep them any more.

It was dark there in the church, and the rain came down through the roof. The pools formed on the floor, and the people moved here and there, to get away from the rain. Some of the white dresses were wet, and a girl shivered there with the cold, because this occasion was solemn for her, and she did not dare to move out of the rain. And the voice of the Bishop said, Defend, O Lord, this Thy child with Thy heavenly grace, that he may continue Thine forever, and daily increase in Thy Holy Spirit more and more, till he come unto Thy everlasting Kingdom. And this he said to each child that came, and confirmed them all.

After the confirmation they crowded into the house, for the simple food that was to be taken. Kumalo had to ask those who were not that day confirmed, or who were not parents of those confirmed, to stay in the church, for it was still raining heavily, though the lightning and the thunder had passed. Yet the house was full to overflowing.

At last the rain was over, and the Bishop and Kumalo were left alone in the room where Kumalo did his accounts. The Bishop lit his pipe and said to Kumalo, Mr. Kumalo, I should like to talk to you. And Kumalo sat down fearfully, afraid of what would be said.

—I was sorry to hear of all your troubles, my friend.

—They have been heavy, my lord.

—I did not like to worry you, Mr. Kumalo, after all you had suffered. And I thought I had better wait till this confirmation.

—Yes, my lord.

—I speak to you out of my regard for you, my friend. You must be sure of that.

—Yes, my lord.

—Then I think, Mr. Kumalo, that you should go away from Ndotsheni.

Yes, that is what would be said, it is said now. Yes, that is what I have feared. Yet take me away, and I die. I am too old to begin any more. I am old, I am frail. Yet I have tried to be a father to this people. Could you not have been here, O Bishop, the day when I came back to Ndotsheni? Would you not have seen that these people love me, although I am old? Would you not have heard a child say, We are glad the umfundisi is back? Would you take me away just when new things are beginning, when there is milk for the children, and the young demonstrator has come, and the sticks for the dam are planted in the ground? The tears fill the eyes, and the eyes shut, and the tears are forced out, and they fall on the new black suit, made for this confirmation with the money of Msimangu. The old head is bowed, and the old man sits there like a child, with not a word to be spoken.

—Mr. Kumalo, says the Bishop gently, and then again, more loudly, Mr. Kumalo.

—Sir. My lord.

—I am sorry to distress you. I am sorry to distress you. But would it not be better if you went away?

—It is what you say, my lord.

The Bishop sits forward in his chair, and rests his elbows upon his knees. Mr. Kumalo, is it not true that the father of the murdered man is your neighbor here in Ndotsheni? Mr. Jarvis?

—It is true, my lord.

—Then for that reason alone I think you should go.

Is that a reason why I should go? Why, does he not ride here to see me, and did not the small boy come into my house? Did he not send the milk for the children, and did he not get this young demonstrator to teach the people farming? And does not my heart grieve for him, now that the inkosikazi is dead? But how does one say these things to a Bishop, to a great man in the country?

—Do you understand me, Mr. Kumalo?

—I understand you, my lord.

—I would send you to Pietermaritzburg, to your old friend Ntombela. You could help him there, and it would take a load off your shoulders. He can worry about buildings and schools and money, and you can give your mind to the work of a priest.

—I understand you, my lord.

—If you stay here, Mr. Kumalo, there will be many loads on your shoulders. There is not only the fact that Mr. Jarvis is your neighbor, but sooner or later you must rebuild your church, and that will cost a great deal of money and anxiety. You saw for yourself today in what condition it is.

—Yes, my lord.

—And I understand you have brought back to live with you the wife of your son, and that she is expecting a child. Is it fair to them to stay here, Mr. Kumalo? Would it not be better to go to some place where these things are not known?

—I understand you, my lord.

There was a knock at the door, and it was the boy standing there, the boy who took the message. Kumalo took the letter, and it was addressed to the Reverend S. Kumalo, Ndotsheni. He thanked the boy and closed the door, then went and sat down in his chair, ready to listen to the Bishop.

—Read your letter, Mr. Kumalo.

So Kumalo opened the letter, and read it.

Umfundisi:

I thank you for your message of sympathy, and for the promise of the prayers of your church. You are right, my wife knew of the things that are being done, and had the greatest part in it. These things we did in memory of our beloved son. It was one of her last wishes that a new church should be built at Ndotsheni, and I shall come to discuss it with you.

Yours truly,
James Jarvis.

You should know that my wife was suffering before we went to Johannesburg.

Kumalo stood up, and he said in a voice that astonished the Bishop, This is from God, he said. It was a voice in which there was relief from anxiety, and laughter, and weeping, and he said again, looking round the walls of the room, This is from God.

—May I see your letter from God, said the Bishop dryly.

So Kumalo gave it to him eagerly, and stood impatiently while the Bishop read it. And when the Bishop had finished, he said gravely, That was a foolish jest.

He read it again, and blew his nose, and sat with the letter in his hand. What are the things that are being done? he asked.

So Kumalo told him about the milk, and the new dam that was to be built, and the young demonstrator. And the Bishop blew his nose several times, and said to Kumalo, This is an extraordinary thing. It is one of the most extraordinary things that I have ever heard.

And Kumalo explained the words, You should know that my wife was suffering before we went to Johannesburg. He explained how these words were written out of understanding and compassion. And he told the Bishop of the words, Is there mercy? and of the small boy who visited him, the small boy with the laughter inside him.

The Bishop said, Let us go into the church and pray, if there is a dry place to pray in your church. Then I must go, for I have still a long journey. But let me first say good-by to your wife, and your daughter-in-law. Tell me, what of the other matter, of your daughter-in-law, and the child she is expecting?

—We have prayed openly before the people, my lord. What more could be done than that?

—It was the way it was done in olden days, said the Bishop. In the olden days when men had faith. But I should not say that, after what I have heard today.

The Bishop said farewell to the people of the house, and he and Kumalo went to the church. At the church door he spoke to Kumalo gravely, I see it is not God's will that you leave Ndotsheni.

After the Bishop had gone, Kumalo stood outside the church in the gathering dark. It was cool, and the breeze blew gently from the great river, and the soul of the man was uplifted. And while he stood there looking out over the great valley, there was a voice that cried out of heaven, Comfort ye, comfort ye, my people, these things will I do unto you, and not forsake you.

It did not happen as men deem such things to happen, it happened otherwise, in that fashion men call illusion, or the imaginings of people overwrought, or an intimation of the divine.

When Kumalo went into the house, he found his wife and the girl, and some other women of the church, and his friend who carried the bags, busy making a wreath. They had a cypress branch, for there was a solitary cypress near the hut of his friend, the only cypress that grew in the whole valley of Ndotsheni, and how it grew there no man could remember. This branch they had made into a ring, and tied it so that it could not spring apart. Into it they had put the flowers of the veld, such as grew in the bareness of the valley.

—I do not like it, umfundisi. What is wrong with it? It does not look like a white person's wreath.

—They use white flowers, said the new teacher. I have often seen that they use white flowers there in Pietermaritzburg.

—Umfundisi, said the friend excitedly, I know where there are white flowers, arum lilies.

—They use arum lilies, said the new teacher, also excited.

—But they are far away. They grow near the railway line, on the far side of Carisbrooke, by a little stream that I know.

—That is far away, said Kumalo.

—I shall go there, said the man. It is not too far to go for such a thing as this. Can you lend me a lantern, umfundisi?

—Surely, my friend.

—And there must be a white ribbon, said the teacher.

—I have one at my house, said one of the women. I shall go and fetch it.

—Stephen, will you write a card for us? Have you such a card?

—The edges of it should be black, said the teacher.

—Yes, I can find a card, said Kumalo, and I shall put black edges on it with the ink.

He went to his room where he did the accounts, and he found such a card, and printed on it:

With sympathy from the
people of St. Mark's Church,
Ndotsheni

He was busy with the edges, careful not to spoil the card with the ink, when his wife called him to come to his food.

THERE IS PLOUGHING in Ndotsheni, and indeed on all farms around it. But the ploughing goes slowly, because the young demonstrator, and behind him the chief, tell the men they must no longer go up and down. They throw up walls of earth, and plough round the hills, so that the fields look no longer as they used to look in the old days of ploughing. Women and boys collect the dung, but it looks so little on the land that the chief has ordered a kraal to be built, where the cattle can stay and the dung be easily collected; but that is a hard thing, because there will be nothing to eat in the kraal. The young demonstrator shakes his head over the dung, but next year he says it will be better. The wattle seed is boiled, and no one has heard of such a thing before in this valley, but those that have worked for the white farmers say it is right, and so they boil it. For this seed one or two desolate places have been chosen, but the young demonstrator shakes his head over them, there is so little food in the soil. And the demonstrator has told the people they can throw away the maize they have kept for the planting, because it is inferior and he has better seed from uJarvis. But they do not throw it away, they keep it for eating.

But all this was not done by magic. There have been meetings, and much silence, and much sullenness. It was only the fear of the chief that made anything come out of these meetings. No one was more dissatisfied than those who had to give up their fields. Kuluse's brother was silent for days because the dam was to eat up his land, and he was dissatisfied with the poor piece of land they gave him. Indeed the umfundisi had to persuade him, and it was hard to refuse the umfundisi, because it was through him that had come the milk that had saved his brother's child.

The chief had hinted that there were still harder things he would ask, and indeed the young demonstrator was dissatisfied that they had not been asked at once. But it would be hard to get these people to agree to everything at once. Even this year he hoped, said the young demonstrator, that the people would see something good with their eyes, although he shook his head sadly over the poverty-stricken soil.

There was talk that the government would give a bull to the chief, and the young demonstrator explained to Kumalo that they would get rid of the cows that gave the smallest yield, but he did not talk thus in the meeting, for that was one of the hard things for a people who counted their wealth in cattle, even these miserable cattle.

But the greatest wonder of all is the great machine, that was fighting in the war they said, and pushes the earth of Kuluse's brother's land over to the line of the sticks, and leaves it there, growing ever higher and higher. And even Kuluse's brother, watching it sullenly, breaks out into unwilling laughter, but re-members again and is sullen. But there is some satisfaction for him, for next year, when the dam is full, Zuma and his brother must both give up their land that lies below the dam, for white man's grass is to be planted there, to be watered from the dam, to be cut and thrown into the kraal where the cattle will be kept. And both Zuma and his brother laughed at him, because he was sullen about the dam; so in some measure he is satisfied.

Indeed there is something new in this valley, some spirit and some life, and much to talk about in the huts. Although nothing has come yet, something is here already.

THIS WAS THE FOURTEENTH DAY. Kumalo said to his wife, I am go-ing up into the mountain. And she said, I understand you. For twice before he had done it, once when the small boy Absalom was sick unto death, and once when he had thought of giving up the min-istry to run a native store at Donnybrook for a white man named Baxter, for more money than the church could ever pay. And there was a third time, but that was without her knowledge, for she was away, and he had been sorely tempted to commit adultery with one of the teachers at Ndotsheni, who was weak and lonely.

—Would you come with me, he said, for I do not like to leave you alone.

She was touched and she said, I cannot come, for the girl is near her time, and who knows when it will be. But you must certainly go.

She made him a bottle of tea, of the kind that is made by boiling the leaves, and she wrapped up a few heavy cakes of maize. He took his coat and his stick and walked up the path that went to the place of the chief. But at the first fork you go to the side of the hand that you eat with, and you climb another hill to other huts that lie beneath the mountain itself. There you turn and walk under the mountain to the east, as though you were going to the far valley of Empayeni, which is another valley where the fields are red and bare, a valley of old men and women, and mothers and children.

But when you reach the end of the level path, where it begins to fall to this other valley, you strike upwards into the mountain itself. This mountain is called Emoyeni, which means, in the winds, and it stands high above Carisbrooke and the tops, and higher still above the valleys of Ndotsheni and Empayeni. Indeed it is a rampart of the great valley itself, the valley of the Umzimkulu, and from it you look down on one of the fairest scenes of Africa.

Now it was almost dark, and he was alone in the dusk; which was well, for one did not go publicly on a journey of this nature. But even as he started to climb the path that ran through the great stones, a man on a horse was there, and a voice said to him, It is you, umfundisi?

—It is I, umnumzana.

—Then we are well met, umfundisi. For here in my pocket I have a letter for the people of your church. He paused for a moment, and then he said, The flowers were of great beauty, umfundisi.

—I thank you, umnumzana.

—And the church, umfundisi. Do you desire a new church?

Kumalo could only smile and shake his head, there were no words in him. And though he shook his head as if it were No, Jarvis understood him.

—The plans will shortly come to you, and you must say if they are what you desire.

—I shall send them to the Bishop, umnumzana.

—You will know what to do. But I am anxious to do it quickly, for I shall be leaving this place.

Kumalo stood shocked at the frightening and desolating words. And although it was dark, Jarvis understood him, for he said swiftly, I shall be often here. You know I have a work in Ndotsheni. Tell me, how is the young man?

—He works night and day. There is no quietness in him.

The white man laughed softly. That is good, he said. Then he said gravely, I am alone in my house, so I am going to Johannesburg to live with my daughter and her children. You know the small boy?

—Indeed, umnumzana, I know him.

—Is he like him?

—He is like him, umnumzana.

And then Kumalo said, Indeed, I have never seen such a child as he is.

Jarvis turned on his horse, and in the dark the grave silent man was eager. What do you mean? he asked.

—Umnumzana, there is a brightness inside him.

—Yes, yes, that is true. The other was even so.

And then he said, like a man with hunger, Do you remember? And because this man was hungry, Kumalo, though he did not well remember, said, I remember.

They stayed there in silence till Jarvis said, Umfundisi, I must go. But he did not go. Instead he said, Where are you going at this hour?

Kumalo was embarrassed, and the words fell about on his tongue, but he answered, I am going into the mountain.

—I understand you, Jarvis said, I understand completely.

And because he spoke with compassion, the old man wept, and Jarvis sat embarrassed on his horse. Indeed he might have come down from it, but such a thing is not lightly done. But he stretched his hand over the darkening valley, and said, One thing is about to be finished, but here is something that is only begun. And while I live it will continue. Umfundisi, go well.

—Umnumzana!

—Yes.

—Do not go before I have thanked you. For the young man, and the milk. And now for the church.

—I have seen a man, said Jarvis with a grim gaiety, who was in darkness till you found him. If that is what you do, I give it willingly.

Perhaps it was something deep that was here, or perhaps the darkness gives courage, but Kumalo said, Truly, of all the white men that I have ever known—

—I am no saintly man, said Jarvis fiercely.

—Of that I cannot speak, but God put His hands on you.

And Jarvis said, That may be, that may be. He turned suddenly to Kumalo. Go well, umfundisi. Throughout this night, stay well.

And Kumalo cried after him, Go well, go well.

Indeed there were other things, deep things, that he could have cried, but such a thing is not lightly done. He waited till the sounds of the horse had died away, then started to climb heavily, holding on to the greatest stones, for he was young no longer. He was tired and panting when he reached the summit, and he sat down on a stone to rest, looking out over the great valley, to the mountains of Ingeli and East Griqualand, dark against the sky. Then recovered, he walked a short distance and found the place that he had used before on these occasions. It was an angle in the rock, sheltered from the winds, with a place for a man to sit on, his legs at ease over the edge. The first of these occasions he remembered clearly, perhaps because it was the first, perhaps because he had come to pray for the child that no prayer could save any more. The child could not write then, but here were three letters from him now, and in all of them he said, If I could come back to Ndotsheni, I would not leave it any more. And in a day or two they would receive the last he would ever write. His heart went out in a great compassion for the boy that must die, who promised now, when there was no more mercy, to sin no more. If he had got to him sooner, perhaps. He knitted his brows at the memory of that terrible and useless questioning, the terrible and useless answering, It is as my father wishes, it is as my father says. What would it have helped if he had said, My father, I do not know?

He turned aside from such fruitless remembering, and set himself to the order of his vigil. He confessed his sins, remembering them as well as he could since the last time he had been in this mountain. All this he did as fully as he could, and prayed for absolution.

Then he turned to thanksgiving, and remembered, with profound awareness, that he had great cause for thanksgiving, and that for many things. He took them one by one, giving thanks for each, and praying for each person that he remembered. There was above all the beloved Msimangu and his generous gift. There was the young man from the reformatory. There was Mrs. Lithebe, who said so often, Why else were we born? And Father Vincent, holding both his hands and saying, Anything, anything, you have only to ask, I shall do anything. And the lawyer that took the case for God, and had written to say there was no mercy in such kind and gentle words.

Then there was the return to Ndotsheni, with his wife and his friend to meet him. And the women waiting at the church. And the great joy of the return, so that pain was forgotten.

He pondered long over this, for might not another man, returning to another valley, have found none of these things? Why was it given to one man to have his pain transmuted into gladness? Why was it given to one man to have such an awareness of God? And might not another, having no such awareness, live with pain that never ended? Why was there a compulsion upon him to pray for the restoration of Ndotsheni, and why was there a white man there on the tops, to do in this valley what no other could have done? And why of all men, the father of the man who had been murdered by his son? And might not another feel also a compulsion, and pray night and day without ceasing, for the restoration of some other valley that would never be restored?

But his mind would contain it no longer. It was not for man's knowing. He put it from his mind, for it was a secret.

And then the white man Jarvis, and the inkosikazi that was dead, and the small boy with the brightness inside him. As his mind could not contain that other, neither could this be contained. But here were thanks that a man could render till the end of his days. And some of them he strove now to render.

HE WOKE WITH A START. It was cold, but not so cold. He had never slept before on these vigils, but he was old, not quite finished, but nearly finished. He thought of all those that were suffering, of Gertrude the weak and foolish one, of the people of Shanty Town and Alexandra, of his wife now at this moment. But above all of his son, Absalom. Would he be awake, would he be able to sleep, this night before the morning? He cried out, My son, my son, my son.

With his crying he was now fully awake, and he looked at his watch and saw that it was one o'clock. The sun would rise soon after five, and it was then it was done, they said. If the boy was asleep, then let him sleep, it was better. But if he was awake, then, O Christ of the abundant mercy, be with him. Over this he prayed long and earnestly.

Would his wife be awake, and thinking of it? She would have come with him, were it not for the girl. And the girl, why, he had forgotten her. But she was no doubt asleep; she was loving enough, but this husband had given her so little, no more than her others had done.

And now he prayed for all the people of Africa, the beloved country. *Nkosi Sikelel' iAfrika*, God save Africa. But he would not see that salvation. It lay afar off, because men were afraid of it. Because, to tell the truth, they were afraid of him, and his wife, and Msimangu, and the young demonstrator. And what was there evil in their desires, in their hunger? That men should walk upright in the land where they were born, and be free to use the fruits of the earth, what was there evil in it? Yet men were afraid, with a fear that was deep, deep in the heart, a fear so deep that they hid their kindness, or brought it out with fierceness and anger, and hid it behind fierce and frowning eyes. They were afraid because they were so few. And such fear could not be cast out, but by love.

It was Msimangu who had said, Msimangu who had no hate for any man, I have one great fear in my heart, that one day when they turn to loving they will find we are turned to hating.

Oh, the grave and the somber words.

WHEN HE WOKE again there was a faint change in the east, and he looked at his watch almost with panic. But it was four o'clock and he was reassured. And now it was time to be awake, for it might be they had wakened his son, and called him to make ready. He left his place and could hardly stand, for his feet were cold and numb. He found another place where he could look to the east, and if it was true what men said, when the sun came up over the rim, it would be done.

He had heard that they could eat what they wished on a morning like this. Strange that a man should ask for food at such a time.

Did the body hunger, driven by some deep dark power that did not know it must die? Is the boy quiet, and does he dress quietly, and does he think of Ndotsheni now? Do tears come into his eyes, and does he wipe them away, and stand up like a man? Does he say, I will not eat any food, I will pray? Is Msimangu there with him, or Father Vincent, or some other priest whose duty it is, to comfort and strengthen him, for he is afraid of the hanging? Does he repent him, or is there only room for his fear? Is there nothing that can be done now, is there not an angel that comes there and cries, This is for God not for man, come child, come with me?

He looked out of his clouded eyes at the faint steady lightening in the east. But he calmed himself, and took out the heavy maize cakes and the tea, and put them upon a stone. And he gave thanks, and broke the cakes and ate them, and drank of the tea. Then he gave himself over to deep and earnest prayer, and after each petition he raised his eyes and looked to the east. And the east lightened and lightened, till he knew that the time was not far off. And when he expected it, he rose to his feet and took off his hat and laid it down on the earth, and clasped his hands before him. And while he stood there the sun rose in the east.

YES, IT IS THE DAWN that has come. The titihoya wakes from sleep, and goes about its work of forlorn crying. The sun tips with light the mountains of Ingeli and East Griqualand. The great valley of the Umzimkulu is still in darkness, but the light will come there. Ndotsheni is still in darkness, but the light will come there also. For it is the dawn that has come, as it has come for a thousand centuries, never failing. But when that dawn will come, of our emancipation, from the fear of bondage and the bondage of fear, why, that is a secret.

Glossary

AFRIKÁANS
The language of the Afrikaner, a much simplified and beautiful version of the language of Holland, though it is held in contempt by some ignorant English-speaking South Africans, and indeed by some Hollanders. Afrikaans and English are the two official languages of the Union of South Africa.

INKOSÁNA
The "i" as in "pit," the "o" midway between "o" in "pot" and "o" in "born." The "a" as in "father," but the second "a" is hardly sounded. Approximate pronunciation, "inkosaan." Means little chief, or little master.

INKÓSI
As above. But the final "i" is hardly sounded. Means chief or master.

INKÓSIKAZI
As above. The second "k" is like hard "g." The final "i" is hardly sounded. Pronounced "inkosigaaz." Means mistress.

KLOOF
An Afrikaans word. Pronounced as written. Means ravine or even a valley if the sides are steep.

KRAAL
An Afrikaans word now as fully English. Pronounced in English "crawl." Means in this book an enclosure where cattle come for milking. But it may also mean a number of huts together, under the rule of the head of the family, who is subject to the chief.

TITIHÓYA
A ploverlike bird. The name is onomatopoeic.

TÍXO
I rejected the Zulu word for the Great Spirit as too long and difficult. This is the Xosa word. It may be pronounced "Teeko," the "o" being midway between the "o" in "pot" and the "o" of "born."

UMFÚNDISI
The last "i" is hardly sounded. Pronounced approximately "oomfoondees," the "oo" being as in "book," and the "ees" as "eace" in the word "peace." Means parson, but is also a title and used with respect.

UMNÚMZANA
Pronounced "oomnoomzaan." Means "sir."

VELD
An Afrikaans word now as fully English. Pronounced "felt." Means open grass country, or the grass itself.